The Oxford Book of
Travel Stories

The
Oxford Book of
Travel
Stories

Edited by
Patricia Craig

Oxford   New York
OXFORD UNIVERSITY PRESS
1996

Oxford University Press, Walton Street, Oxford OX2 6DP

Oxford New York
Athens Auckland Bangkok Bombay
Calcutta Cape Town Dar es Salaam Delhi
Florence Hong Kong Istanbul Karachi
Kuala Lumpur Madras Madrid Melbourne
Mexico City Nairobi Paris Singapore
Taipei Tokyo Toronto
and associated companies in
Berlin Ibadan

Oxford is a trade mark of Oxford University Press

British Library Cataloguing in Publication Data
Data available

Library of Congress Cataloging in Publication Data
The Oxford book of travel stories / edited by Patricia Craig.
  1. Travel—Fiction. 2. Travelers—Fiction. 3. Short stories,
English. 4. Short stories, American. I. Craig, Patricia.
PR1309.T73096 1996   823'.0108355—dc20   95–40615
ISBN 0–19–214253–4

10 9 8 7 6 5 4 3 2 1

Typeset by Graphicraft Typesetters Ltd, Hong Kong
Printed in Great Britain
on acid-free paper by
Bookcraft Ltd,
Midsomer Norton, Somerset

Contents

Introduction

> Keep moving! Steam, or Gas, or Stage,
> Hold, cabin, steerage, hencoop's cage—
> Tour, Journey, Voyage, Lounge, Ride, Walk,
> Skim, Sketch, Excursion, Travel-talk—
> For move you must! 'Tis now the rage,
> The law and fashion of the Age.

So wrote Coleridge in 1824, before tourism as an industry had come into its own, but with the idea of travel-as-exploration largely a thing of the past. Many literary and social commentators have identified the various phases of travel, and travel writing, from the Middle Ages on: first the journey-as-pilgrimage, then the 'Grand Tour' undertaken in a spirit of aloofness by the fashionable young gentleman of the seventeenth and eighteenth centuries—and, in contrast to this, the journey of exploration, breaking new ground, and with danger and outlandishness very much on the agenda. The traveller-as-student, the Casaubon figure, comes equipped with the utmost determination to fathom foreign ways, while the 'romantic traveller' is merely susceptible to the allure of abroad. Those in search of change, in one sense, are sometimes prone to resent it, in another—if it entails any diminution of the picturesque, or increase in standardization ('We can buy Harvey Sauce, and cayenne pepper, and Morison's Pills, in every city in the world', writes Thackeray in 1850, in sardonic vein). You get Henry James, for example, lamenting the sense of pioneering and discovery available to earlier travellers and settlers in Italy, such as Nathaniel Hawthorne.

Paul Fussell, in his invigorating study of British literary travel between the wars (*Abroad*, 1980), traces the beginnings of modern tourism to Thomas Cook and the mid-nineteenth century—roughly the period at which the short story was beginning to evolve into a distinct literary form (though it would take another fifty years or so before it became fully fledged). It was inevitable that the two should converge. Travel, with its association with marvels, strangeness, adventure, and so forth, has always proved an irresistible literary subject—indeed, half the point of going into foreign territory was to write an account of the whole undertaking. As it became more widely available, however, the focus of interest shifted from pioneering or anthropological travel to the more ordinary business of tourism— holiday-making. One early story, or novella, Thackeray's 'The Kickleburys on the Rhine' of 1850 (unfortunately too long and rambling for inclusion here), takes up Coleridge's tone in the lines quoted above, and pokes amiable fun at the fuss and bustle, not to mention the social manœuvring, of getting from one place to another, and taking in a fair amount of sightseeing along the way: 'her mamma calls her away to look at the ruins of Wigginstein. Everybody looks at Wigginstein. You are told in Murray to look at Wigginstein.'

Elizabeth Bowen and others have pointed out that the short story proper is really a child of the twentieth century—that before this period it wasn't sharply differentiated from the novel, in form or content: merely condensed or cut short. For this reason—since I wanted to include some examples of Victorian travelling—I have judged it legitimate to cut the first two stories in this collection even shorter. Charles Dickens's 'The Holly-Tree' was issued in three parts, and only the first part is relevant to the travel theme: this wonderfully atmospheric account of a journey by stage coach from London to Yorkshire in the snow marks a point, in the mid-century, at which the possibilities inherent in a genre of short travel fiction began to be understood. It can't be omitted, so I have simply detached Part I from the continuations. And the Dickens–Wilkie Collins piece, 'The Lazy Tour of Two Idle Apprentices', which unfolds as a series of diverting episodes, also lends itself to cutting, in a way a more compact narrative does not. The longish Trollope story in this collection, for example, needs to appear in its entirety. Not only is 'A Ride Across Palestine' the most intriguing and vivid piece in the whole two-volume *Tales of Many Countries* (1861 and 1863), but it is also the most suitable for my purposes. It moves from Jerusalem to Jericho and back again, then on to Jaffa and a steamer bound for Alexandria. 'The Dead Sea was on our right, still glittering in the distance, and behind us lay the plains of Jericho and the wretched collection of huts which still bears the name of the ancient city. Beyond that, but still seemingly within easy distance of us, were the mountains of the wilderness. . . . We wandered out at night, and drank coffee with a family of Arabs in the desert, sitting in a ring round their coffee-kettle.'

Trollope's *Tales of Many Countries* brings us to the first problem confronting an anthologist of travel stories: how is the crucial piece of writing to be defined? These *Tales*, in common with a lot of other Victorian fiction set abroad—including some by authors such as Mrs Gaskell and Mrs Oliphant—tend to get the protagonist into the foreign setting and then merely recount an episode in the life of some distinctive person encountered there: nothing to do with travel in any sense. A travel story is not, strictly speaking, a holiday story, or an expatriate story, or a story about the inhabitants of a foreign country (although these elements may come into it). It should, ideally, accord some prominence to the actual means of locomotion, whether this is by air, water, or land. It should be a work of fiction, and self-contained. However . . . it is possible to lay down certain rules and then find yourself bending or even breaking them in order to get in something which adds a new dimension, illumines the whole collection, or puts its finger on the mood of a particular era. For example—though neither exactly comes under the heading of fiction—I've included the F. Scott and Zelda Fitzgerald—what to call it? mood-piece?—about exotic hotel life in the 1920s, all palms and gilded filigree and Japanese lanterns and trips by limousine, 'Show Mr and Mrs F. to Number—'; and Jack Kerouac's 'Big Trip to Europe' of 1960, which encapsulates, if anything does, late 1950s fecklessness and the whole soft-drug-related style of indolence abroad: 'just then an old robed Bodhisattva, an old robed bearded realizer of the greatness of wisdom came walking by with a staff and a shapeless skin bag and a cotton pack and a basket on his back, with a white cloth around his hoary brown brow.—I saw him coming from miles away down the beach—the shrouded Arab by the sea.—We didn't even nod to each other—it was too much, we'd known each other too long ago—'. Both of these go in for evocation to the fullest extent.

There is a question about the exact moment at which transfigured autobiography turns into fiction. Perhaps it is possible to have it both ways: Diane Johnson, in the preface to her collection of travel stories, *Natural Opium* (1992), mentions the French neologism, translated as 'auto-fiction'—'by which the teller of true stories avails herself of some of the rights of the novelist to tidy and pace the account'. It's not a new practice, indeed; Elizabeth von Arnim was doing it in 1904, with her comic misadventures in Rügen: 'I wondered what those at home would say if they knew that on the very first day of my driving-tour I had managed to lose the carriage and had had to bear the banter of publicans.' Jump to 1980 and you get Elizabeth Hardwick looking back to 'the travels of youth, the cheapness of things, and one's intrepid poverty'. David Malouf recalls a train journey from Brisbane to Sydney in 1944, with the young protagonist already possessed of the traveller's instinct for newness, and avid for proof 'that the world was as varied as I wanted it to be'. In 'Siegfried on the Rhine' (first published in 1981 in *Scenes of Childhood and other stories*), Sylvia Townsend Warner singles out a moment from what she calls 'a dawdle through Germany' in 1908; this fragment of reminiscence comes imbued with the shimmer of fiction.

I mention these examples to show how easily the line of demarcation is blurred between fact and fiction; however, what is beyond dispute is that the travel *story* is not the same as travel *writing*. (I was surprised to pick up an anthology of 'travel stories' recently in a remainder bookshop, and to find that it consisted solely of excerpts from works of non-fiction.) Perhaps it's because there exists some confusion, in the popular mind, between these separate genres—and also, possibly, because the experiences of real-life travellers, from Lady Mary Wortley Montague to Redmond O'Hanlon, have proved so riveting to so many readers—that collections of travel stories proper seem remarkably thin on the ground. In the course of reading for this anthology I have come across no more than two, and one of those was Australian. The other— Alan Ross's *Abroad* of 1957—contains fourteen stories, all of a high quality (odd to note, though, that only half of one—the F. Scott–Zelda Fitzgerald one—has a woman author). Ross, in his foreword, makes some sensible points about the travel story and what it should encompass; it should, he says, 'be written around a journey of some kind, its point being emphasised, if not actually created by, the physical act of travelling . . . I wanted to illustrate the concept of being or going "abroad" in as diverse a manner as possible . . .'. In his opening line he mentions 'the exhilarations and consequences of a change of place', which is another way of specifying the 'natural opium' of Diane Johnson's title. The freedom and excitements of travel can go to one's head. Indeed, Brigid Brophy, in one of her essays, refers to a condition she describes as 'travellers' trauma, which is no doubt more acute in armies but may overtake even tourists'; in fact—she goes on—'it is too little appreciated how many people are slightly mad while they are abroad'.

Why do we do it? Diane Johnson offers a suggestion or two: travel is 'broadening or restorative', it provides a means of escape 'from our quotidian lives', it is simply imposed on us by some 'inner compulsion' which is not to be resisted.

> This is the fret that makes us cat-like stretch
> And then contract the fingers, gives the itch
> To open the french windows into the rain,
> Walk out and never be seen at home again . . .

So Louis MacNeice, in one of the 'Letters from Iceland' which he published jointly with W. H. Auden in 1937. Most departures, though, are not as reckless or feckless as all that. It is easy to identify a few mundane starting-points—business, family obligation, the enticement of the package tour. One or two of the stories in this collection do, it's true, contain a whiff of the supernatural or surreal—Beryl Bainbridge's playful 'The Man Who Blew Away' which might, I suppose, be said to constitute the final expression of taking off; Rachel Ingalls's 'Somewhere Else', which moves on from its uneccentric start to end by embodying a perpetual state of transit (as in Paul Muldoon's poem 'Immram', with its onward drift disorientating the senses: 'It seemed that I would forever be driving west'); Jane Gardam's 'Chinese Funeral' which (I take it) points forward to Tienanmen Square. There is an obvious sense in which travel has to do with continuation, but indeed its metaphorical possibilities are endless (we can't do anything *but* 'fare forward', as T. S. Eliot has it). Travel as *rite de passage* is a feature of the David Malouf story, and others in this collection.

The dauntless woman explorer of the eighteenth and nineteenth centuries, endowed with endless *sang froid* and apt to extol the blessings of a good thick skirt in the face of elephant traps and other hazards: this is a figure of considerable prominence in the history of travel— yet it is rare for an equivalent character to turn up in the pages of fiction (at any rate, short fiction). She was, indeed, a gift to the parodist, as Serena Livingstone-Stanley's* *Through Darkest Pondelayo* shows: 'Well even the most respectable Englishwoman cannot go on screaming for an hour on end, even when being carried upsidedown by a naked savage through the heart of a tropical forest as I can prove by experience.' You will not find many tropical forests in this collection— in fact, one of my objectives is to illustrate how a sense of danger or alienation is not necessarily tied up with putting a considerable distance between yourself and home. The journey by car, or even on foot (as in the Elizabeth Bowen story) can produce perceptions as acute, or disturbing, as those available to the most sedulous voyager.

* The pseudonym of Beckett W. Lindsay.

However, the majority of travellers are exposed to nothing more than routine annoyances: agitating hold-ups at airports without adequate lavatories (Penelope Lively), or aching legs on a trudge through the English Midlands (Elizabeth Bowen). On top of this, there are moments of exasperation or ennui: 'How dull travel really is!' (John Cheever). Henry James's hero, in the story 'Travelling Companions' (too long, again, to fit in this collection), is suddenly overtaken by 'a poignant conviction of the ludicrous folly of the idle spirit of travel' (he gets over it). George Crabbe's sardonic enquiry (in 'The Adventures of Richard'), 'Do tell me something of the miseries felt / In climes where travellers freeze, and where they melt', points up the most basic discomfort of all—one experienced to the full by the wife in Anita Desai's story, 'Scholar and Gypsy', who is completely knocked up by the heat of Bombay: 'If she stepped out of the air-conditioned hotel room, she drooped, her head hung, her eyes glazed, she felt faint.' Flagging spirits are perhaps a natural part of any trip—after the headiness of setting off—but recovery is a built-in factor too.

In most of these stories, the contretemps that occur are presented as comic—even if the comedy comes with an unsettling undertone. (This is true, I think, even of something as powerful as Flannery O'Connor's 'A Good Man is Hard to Find', which treats of a family excursion by car and its horrendous outcome.) One or two singular predicaments are devised for travellers—V. S. Pritchett's newspaper editor pursued all over the Continent by a stumpy-looking foreigner with an *idée fixe* ('The Lady from Guatemala'); septuagenarian Lady Cameron in Greece, in J. I. M. Stewart's story, 'The Bridge at Arta', getting lumbered with the ultimate in bores who is also, as it happens, her one-time husband; bemused late-night diners in Diane Johnson's 'Cuckoo Clock' who find themselves expected to toboggan down a slope in the dark. Out-and-out comedy is a feature of (for example) 'The Lazy Tour of Two Idle Apprentices', with its holiday-makers who can hardly be bothered to undergo the smallest exertion; or Evelyn Waugh's 'Cruise', which has a lot of fun at the expense of the empty-headed and incorrigible. Occasionally, however, the tone turns more sombre—with Edith Wharton, for example, whose story, 'A Journey', puts a young woman on a train with her dying husband, and fully conveys the horror of the thought that overwhelms her: is she going to be ejected, with the corpse, at some unknown station? Rebecca West, too—in 'Deliverance'—has a woman on a train brought face-to-face with death, and not greatly bothered by the prospect: 'There was nothing at the end of her journey except several sorts of pain, so if the journey had no end there was no reason for grief.' In this case, though—as the title indicates—the outcome encompasses a change of mood.

'Deliverance' is a spy story. When I first started planning this anthology I thought it might be a good idea to include examples of various distinct genres, just to get the widest possible perspective on the theme. However, I found that certain things simply would not fit the 'travel' specification—starting with Nathaniel Hawthorne's 'Celestial Railroad', which parodies Bunyan, and recounts a dream; and coming up to the present—via Kay Boyle and her story of refugees streaming along a road in France ('This They Took with Them')—with Sylvia Townsend Warner's fantasy (for example, 'The Search for an Ancestress') and T. Coraghessan Boyle's anarchy ('We are Norsemen'). One or two stories which at first seemed suitable have ultimately been omitted, with great reluctance: Saul Bellow's 'The Gonzaga Manuscripts', for instance; Sean O'Faolain's 'Something, Everything, Anything, Nothing'; and J. F. Powers's 'Tinkers', all of which (it seems to me) place insufficient emphasis on the travel aspect of the narrative. Others which I liked proved too long (Eudora Welty, Alice Munro), or endlessly available elsewhere, or both (E. M. Forster, Katherine Mansfield, Conrad, Hemingway, Somerset Maugham). Why Rebecca West, then? Well, this story, I believe, helps to extend the scope of the anthology without distorting its purpose. One distinctive feature of travel literature is the sense of constantly changing landscapes—scenes flashing past outside the train window—and here we read:

Now the train was running toward the mountains, and was passing through a valley in the foothills. There were cliffs, steel-grey where the sun caught them . . . a line of poplars . . . a broad and shallow river . . . an old man in a dark blue shirt and light blue trousers was leading a red cart . . .

Such details gain in vividness from the dramas to which they form a backdrop. Difficulties are resolved, possibilities open out, and lives are altered on trains. People take off for unknown destinations: 'He was going somewhere, he knew that. And if it was the wrong direction, sooner or later he'd find it out.' Thus Myers, in Raymond Carver's story, 'The Compartment'. The outcome of a trip is sometimes happily left to the imagination: 'it further occurred to me that travelling all

over California on the Greyhound I could meet anyone at all', thinks
Alice Adams's narrator.

Transitoriness is another motif: people going, and then gone—like
the trippers on the Scottish excursion steamer in William Sansom's
wonderfully idiosyncratic story. What else? Benedict Kiely for high
spirits, William Trevor for astringency. William Plomer, Dan Jacobson,
Paul Theroux: all of these bring their own singularity to bear on the
travel theme, and thereby enlarge it. The travel story, indeed, is more
than an account of a journey; one of my aims has been to show
how readily it accommodates itself to any number of modes or purposes. John Cheever's remarkable 'Brimmer', for example: ostensibly
about compulsive copulation on a crossing between New York and
Naples, this may be read on more than one level. And Ring Lardner's
'Travelogue': set on a train, mildly satirical in tone, concerning bragging
about travel—you could call this in many ways the last word on the
subject.

You could, but in fact I don't. I believe that the only way to compile
a travel anthology—or any anthology—is to follow one's nose, and
mine has led me to break the chronological sequence, and indeed
contradict the declaration of content, by ending with a poem, not a
story: Elizabeth Bishop's 'Questions of Travel', which seems to me to
provide a kind of intensifying gloss on everything that goes before. I
have therefore appended it as an epilogue. As for the stories themselves,
all thirty-two of them: I would hope that each illustrates, in its own
way, how travel has to do with stimulus, enrichment, a sense of
achievement that is everlasting. 'We shall certainly cease to be here',
observes the protagonist of a Henry James story, referring to Venice,
'but we shall never cease to have been here.' There's urbanity of
outlook for you.

As ever, I am indebted to Jeffrey Morgan and Gerry Keenan for the
greatest help and encouragement while I've been compiling this
anthology. Thanks are also due to Nora T. Craig, Alan Ross, Val
Warner, Brice Dickson, Judith Luna, and Araminta Whitley.

P. C.

The
Oxford Book of
Travel
Stories

The Holly-Tree

I have kept one secret in the course of my life. I am a bashful man. Nobody would suppose it, nobody ever does suppose it, nobody ever did suppose it, but I am naturally a bashful man. This is the secret which I have never breathed until now.

I might greatly move the reader by some account of the innumerable places I have not been to, the innumerable people I have not called upon or received, the innumerable social evasions I have been guilty of, solely because I am by original constitution and character a bashful man. But I will leave the reader unmoved, and proceed with the object before me.

That object is to give a plain account of my travels and discoveries in the Holly-Tree Inn; in which place of good entertainment for man and beast I was once snowed up.

It happened in the memorable year when I parted for ever from Angela Leath, whom I was shortly to have married, on making the discovery that she preferred my bosom friend. From our school-days I had freely admitted Edwin, in my own mind, to be far superior to myself; and, though I was grievously wounded at heart, I felt the preference to be natural, and tried to forgive them both. It was under these circumstances that I resolved to go to America—on my way to the Devil.

Communicating my discovery neither to Angela nor to Edwin, but resolving to write each of them an affecting letter conveying my blessing and forgiveness, which the steam-tender for shore should carry to the post when I myself should be bound for the New World, far beyond recall,—I say, locking up my grief in my own breast, and consoling myself as I could with the prospect of being generous, I quietly left all I held dear, and started on the desolate journey I have mentioned.

The dead winter-time was in full dreariness when I left my chambers for ever, at five o'clock in the morning. I had shaved by candle-light, of course, and was miserably cold, and experienced that general all-pervading sensation of getting up to be hanged which I have usually found inseparable from untimely rising under such circumstances.

How well I remember the forlorn aspect of Fleet-street when I came out of the Temple! The street-lamps flickering in the gusty north-east wind, as if the very gas were contorted with cold; the white-topped houses; the bleak, star-lighted sky; the market people and other early stragglers, trotting to circulate their almost frozen blood; the hospitable light and warmth of the few coffee-shops and public-houses that were open for such customers; the hard, dry, frosty rime with which the air was charged (the wind had already beaten it into every crevice), and which lashed my face like a steel whip.

It wanted nine days to the end of the month, and end of the year. The Post-office packet for the United States was to depart from Liverpool, weather permitting, on the first of the ensuing month, and I had the intervening time on my hands. I had taken this into consideration, and had resolved to make a visit to a certain spot (which I need not name) on the farther borders of Yorkshire. It was endeared to me by my having first seen Angela at a farmhouse in that place, and my melancholy was gratified by the idea of taking a wintry leave of it before my expatriation. I ought to explain that, to avoid being sought out before my resolution should have been rendered irrevocable by being carried into full effect, I had written to Angela overnight, in my usual manner, lamenting that urgent business, of which she should know all particulars by-and-by—took me unexpectedly away from her for a week or ten days.

There was no Northern Railway at that time, and in its place there were stage-coaches; which I occasionally find myself, in common with some other people, affecting to lament now, but which everybody dreaded as a very serious penance then. I had secured the box-seat on the fastest of these, and my business in Fleet-street was to get into a cab with my portmanteau, so to make the best of my way to the Peacock at Islington, where I was to join this coach. But when one of our Temple watchmen, who carried my portmanteau into Fleet-street for me, told me about the huge blocks of ice that had for some days past been floating in the river, having closed up in the night, and made a walk from the Temple Gardens over to the Surrey shore, I began to ask myself the question, whether the box-seat would not be likely to put a sudden and a frosty end to my unhappiness. I was heartbroken, it is true, and yet I was not quite so far gone as to wish to be frozen to death.

When I got up to the Peacock—where I found everybody drinking hot purl, in self-preservation—I asked if there were an inside seat to spare. I then discovered that, inside or out, I was the only passenger. This gave me a still livelier idea of the great inclemency of the weather, since that coach always loaded particularly well. However, I took a little purl (which I found uncommonly good), and got into the coach. When I was seated, they built me up with straw to the waist, and, conscious of making a rather ridiculous appearance, I began my journey.

It was still dark when we left the Peacock. For a little while, pale, uncertain ghosts of houses and trees appeared and vanished, and then it was hard, black, frozen day. People were lighting their fires; smoke was mounting straight up high into the rarefied air; and we were rattling for Highgate Archway over the hardest ground I have ever heard the ring of iron shoes on. As we got into the country, everything seemed to have grown old and gray. The roads, the trees, thatched roofs of cottages and homesteads, the ricks in farmers' yards. Outdoor work was abandoned, horse-troughs at roadside inns were frozen hard, no stragglers lounged about, doors were close shut, little turnpike houses had blazing fires inside, and children (even turnpike people have children, and seem to like them) rubbed the frost from the little panes of glass with their chubby arms, that their bright eyes might catch a glimpse of the solitary coach going by. I don't know when the snow began to set in; but I know that we were changing horses somewhere when I heard the guard remark, 'That the old lady up in the sky was picking her geese pretty hard today.' Then, indeed, I found the white down falling fast and thick.

The lonely day wore on, and I dozed it out, as a lonely traveller does. I was warm and valiant after eating and drinking—particularly after dinner; cold and depressed at all other times. I was always bewildered as to time and place, and always more or less out of my senses. The coach and horses seemed to execute in chorus Auld Lang Syne, without a moment's intermission. They kept the time and tune with the greatest regularity, and rose into the swell at the beginning of the Refrain, with a precision that worried me to death. While we changed horses, the guard and coachman went stumping up and down the road, printing off their shoes in the snow, and poured so much liquid consolation into themselves without being any the worse for it, that I began to confound them, as it darkened again, with two great white casks standing on end. Our horses tumbled down in solitary places, and we got them up—which was the pleasantest variety I had, for it warmed me. And it snowed and snowed, and still it snowed, and never left off snowing. All night long we went on in this manner. Thus we came round the clock, upon the Great North Road, to the performance of Auld Lang Syne all day again. And it snowed and snowed, and still it snowed, and never left off snowing.

I forget now where we were at noon on the second day, and where we ought to have been; but I know that we were scores of miles behindhand, and that our case was growing worse every hour. The drift was becoming prodigiously deep; landmarks were getting snowed out; the road and the fields were all one; instead of having fences and hedgerows to guide us, we went crunching on over an unbroken surface of ghastly white that might sink beneath us at any moment and drop us down a whole hillside. Still the coachman and guard—who kept together on the box, always in council, and looking well about them—made out the track with astonishing sagacity.

When we came in sight of a town, it looked, to my fancy, like a large drawing on a slate, with abundance of slate pencil expended on the churches and houses where the snow lay thickest. When we came within a town, and found the church clocks all stopped, the dial-faces choked with snow, and the inn-signs blotted out, it seemed as if the whole place were overgrown with white moss. As to the coach, it was a mere snowball; similarly, the men and boys who ran along beside us to the town's end, turning our clogged wheels and encouraging our horses, were men and boys of snow; and the bleak wild solitude to which they at last dismissed us was a snowy Sahara. One would have thought this enough: notwithstanding which, I pledge my word that it snowed and snowed, and still it snowed, and never left off snowing.

We performed Auld Lang Syne the whole day; seeing nothing, out of towns and villages, but the track of stoats, hares, and foxes, and sometimes of birds. At nine o'clock at night, on a Yorkshire moor, a cheerful burst from our horn, and a welcome sound of talking, with a glimmering and moving about of lanterns, roused me from my drowsy state. I found that we were going to change.

They helped me out, and I said to a waiter, whose bare head became as white as King Lear's in a single minute, 'What Inn is this?'

'The Holly-Tree, Sir,' said he.

'Upon my word, I believe,' said I, apologetically, to the guard and coachman, 'that I must stop here.'

Now the landlord, and the landlady, and the ostler, and the postboy, and all the stable authorities, had already asked the coachman, to the wide-eyed interest of all the rest of the establishment, if he meant to go on. The coachman had already replied, 'Yes, he'd take her through it'—meaning by Her the coach—'if so be as George would stand by him.' George was the guard, and he had already sworn that he *would* stand by him. So the helpers were already getting the horses out.

My declaring myself beaten, after this parley, was not an announcement without preparation. Indeed, but for the way to the announcement being smoothed by the parley, I more than doubt whether, as an innately bashful man, I should have had the confidence to make it. As it was, it received the approval even of the guard and coachman. Therefore, with many confirmations of my inclining, and many remarks from one bystander to another, that the gentleman could go for'ard by the mail tomorrow, whereas tonight he would only be froze, and where was the good of a gentleman being froze—ah, let alone buried alive (which latter clause was added by a humorous helper as a joke at my expense, and was extremely well received), I saw my portmanteau got out stiff, like a frozen body; did the handsome thing by the guard and coachman; wished them goodnight and a prosperous journey; and, a little ashamed of myself, after all, for leaving them to fight it out alone, followed the landlord, landlady, and waiter of the Holly-Tree upstairs.

I thought I had never seen such a large room as that into which they showed me. It had five windows, with dark red curtains that would have absorbed the light of a general illumination; and there were complications of drapery at the top of the curtains, that went wandering about the wall in a most extraordinary manner. I asked for a smaller room, and they told me there was no smaller room. They could screen me in, however, the landlord said. They brought a great old japanned screen, with natives (Japanese, I suppose) engaged in a variety of idiotic pursuits all over it; and left me roasting whole before an immense fire.

My bedroom was some quarter of a mile off, up a great staircase at the end of a long gallery; and nobody knows what a misery this is to a bashful man who would rather not meet people on the stairs. It was the grimmest room I have ever had the nightmare in; and all the furniture, from the four posts of the bed to the two old silver candlesticks, was tall, high-shouldered, and spindle-waisted. Below, in my sitting-room, if I looked round my screen, the wind rushed at me like a mad bull; if I stuck to my armchair, the fire scorched me to the colour of a new brick. The chimneypiece was very high, and there was a bad glass—what I may call a wavy glass—above it, which, when I stood up, just showed me my anterior phrenological developments—and these never look well, in any subject, cut short off at the eyebrow. If I stood with my back to the fire, a gloomy vault of darkness above and beyond the screen insisted on being looked at; and, in its dim remoteness, the drapery of the ten curtains of the five windows went twisting and creeping about, like a nest of gigantic worms.

I suppose that what I observe in myself must be observed by some other men of similar character in *themselves*; therefore I am emboldened to mention, that, when I travel, I never arrive at a place but I immediately want to go away from it. Before I had finished my supper of broiled fowl and mulled port, I had impressed upon the waiter in detail my arrangements for departure in the morning. Breakfast and bill at eight. Fly at nine. Two horses, or, if needful, even four.

Tired though I was, the night appeared about a week long. In oases of nightmare, I thought of Angela, and felt more depressed than ever by the reflection that I was on the shortest road to Gretna Green. What had *I* to do with Gretna Green? I was not going *that* way to the Devil, but by the American route, I remarked in my bitterness.

In the morning I found that it was snowing still, that it had snowed all night, and that I was snowed up. Nothing could get out of that spot on the moor, or could come at it, until the road had been cut out by labourers from the market-town. When they might cut their way to the Holly-Tree nobody could tell me.

It was now Christmas Eve. I should have had a dismal Christmastime of it anywhere, and consequently that did not so much matter; still, being snowed up was like dying of frost, a thing I had not bargained for. I felt very lonely. Yet I could no more have proposed to the landlord and landlady to admit me to their society (though I should have liked it very much) than I could have asked them to present me with a piece of plate. Here my great secret, the real bashfulness of my character, is to be observed. Like most bashful men, I judge of other people as if they were bashful too. Besides being far too shamefaced to make the proposal myself, I really had a delicate misgiving that it would be in the last degree disconcerting to them.

Trying to settle down, therefore, in my solitude, I first of all asked what books there were in the house. The waiter brought me a *Book of Roads*, two or three old Newspapers, a little Song-Book, terminating in a collection of Toasts and Sentiments, a little Jest-Book, an odd volume of *Peregrine Pickle*, and the *Sentimental Journey*. I knew every

word of the two last already, but I read them through again, then tried
to hum all the songs (Auld Lang Syne was among them); went entirely
through the jokes—in which I found a fund of melancholy adapted to
my state of mind; proposed all the toasts, enunciated all the sentiments,
and mastered the papers. The latter had nothing in them but stock
advertisements, a meeting about a county rate, and a highway robbery.
As I am a greedy reader, I could not make this supply hold out until
night; it was exhausted by tea-time. Being then entirely cast upon my
own resources, I got through an hour in considering what to do next.
Ultimately, it came into my head (from which I was anxious by any
means to exclude Angela and Edwin), that I would endeavour to recall
my experience of Inns, and would try how long it lasted me. I stirred
the fire, moved my chair a little to one side of the screen—not daring
to go far, for I knew the wind was waiting to make a rush at me, I
could hear it growling—and began.

My first impressions of an Inn dated from the Nursery; consequently
I went back to the Nursery for a starting-point, and found myself at
the knee of a sallow woman with a fishy eye, an aquiline nose, and a
green gown, whose specialty was a dismal narrative of a landlord by
the roadside, whose visitors unaccountably disappeared for many years,
until it was discovered that the pursuit of his life had been to convert
them into pies. For the better devotion of himself to this branch of
industry, he had constructed a secret door behind the head of the bed;
and when the visitor (oppressed with pie) had fallen asleep, this wicked
landlord would look softly in with a lamp in one hand and a knife in
the other, would cut his throat, and would make him into pies; for
which purpose he had coppers, underneath a trap-door, always boiling;
and rolled out his pastry in the dead of the night. Yet even he was not
insensible to the stings of conscience, for he never went to sleep without
being heard to mutter, 'Too much pepper!' which was eventually the
cause of his being brought to justice. I had no sooner disposed of this
criminal than there started up another of the same period, whose profession was originally housebreaking; in the pursuit of which art he
had had his right ear chopped off one night, as he was burglariously
getting in at a window, by a brave and lovely servant-maid (whom the
aquiline-nosed woman, though not at all answering the description,
always mysteriously implied to be herself). After several years, this
brave and lovely servant-maid was married to the landlord of a country
Inn; which landlord had this remarkable characteristic, that he always
wore a silk nightcap, and never would on any consideration take it off.

At last, one night, when he was fast asleep, the brave and lovely woman lifted up his silk nightcap on the right side, and found that he had no ear there; upon which she sagaciously perceived that he was the clipped housebreaker, who had married her with the intention of putting her to death. She immediately heated the poker and terminated his career, for which she was taken to King George upon his throne, and received the compliments of royalty on her great discretion and valour. This same narrator, who had a Ghoulish pleasure, I have long been persuaded, in terrifying me to the utmost confines of my reason, had another authentic anecdote within her own experience, founded, I now believe, upon *Raymond and Agnes, or the Bleeding Nun.* She said it happened to her brother-in-law, who was immensely rich—which my father was not; and immensely tall—which my father was not. It was always a point with this Ghoul to present my dearest relations and friends to my youthful mind under circumstances of disparaging contrast. The brother-in-law was riding once through a forest on a magnificent horse (we had no magnificent horse at our house), attended by a favourite and valuable Newfoundland dog (we had no dog), when he found himself benighted, and came to an Inn. A dark woman opened the door, and he asked her if he could have a bed there. She answered yes, and put his horse in the stable, and took him into a room where there were two dark men. While he was at supper, a parrot in the room began to talk, saying, 'Blood, blood! Wipe up the blood!' Upon which one of the dark men wrung the parrot's neck, and said he was fond of roasted parrots, and he meant to have this one for breakfast in the morning. After eating and drinking heartily, the immensely rich, tall brother-in-law went up to bed; but he was rather vexed, because they had shut his dog in the stable, saying that they never allowed dogs in the house. He sat very quiet for more than an hour, thinking and thinking, when, just as his candle was burning out, he heard a scratch at the door. He opened the door, and there was the Newfoundland dog! The dog came softly in, smelt about him, went straight to some straw in the corner which the dark men had said covered apples, tore the straw away, and disclosed two sheets steeped in blood. Just at that moment the candle went out, and the brother-in-law, looking through a chink in the door, saw the two dark men stealing upstairs; one armed with a dagger that long (about five feet); the other carrying a chopper, a sack, and a spade. Having no remembrance of the close of this adventure, I suppose my faculties to have been always so frozen with terror at this stage of it, that the power of listening stagnated within me for some quarter of an hour.

These barbarous stories carried me, sitting there on the Holly-Tree
hearth, to the Roadside Inn, renowned in my time in a sixpenny book
with a folding plate, representing in a central compartment of oval form
the portrait of Jonathan Bradford, and in four corner compartments
four incidents of the tragedy with which the name is associated—
coloured with a hand at once so free and economical, that the bloom
of Jonathan's complexion passed without any pause into the breeches
of the ostler, and, smearing itself off into the next division, became
rum in a bottle. Then I remembered how the landlord was found at
the murdered traveller's bedside, with his own knife at his feet, and
blood upon his hand; how he was hanged for the murder, notwithstanding his protestation that he had indeed come there to kill the
traveller for his saddle-bags, but had been stricken motionless on finding him already slain; and how the ostler, years afterwards, owned the
deed. By this time I had made myself quite uncomfortable. I stirred
the fire, and stood with my back to it as long as I could bear the heat,
looking up at the darkness beyond the screen, and at the wormy curtains
creeping in and creeping out, like the worms in the ballad of Alonzo
the Brave and the Fair Imogene.

There was an Inn in the cathedral town where I went to school,
which had pleasanter recollections about it than any of these. I took
it next. It was the Inn where friends used to put up, and where we
used to go to see parents, and to have salmon and fowls, and be
tipped. It had an ecclesiastical sign—the Mitre—and a bar that seemed
to be the next best thing to a bishopric, it was so snug. I loved the
landlord's youngest daughter to distraction—but let that pass. It was
in this Inn that I was cried over by my rosy little sister, because I had
acquired a black eye in a fight. And though she had been, that Holly-
Tree night, for many a long year where all tears are dried, the Mitre
softened me yet.

'To be continued tomorrow,' said I, when I took my candle to go
to bed. But my bed took it upon itself to continue the train of thought
that night. It carried me away, like the enchanted carpet, to a distant
place (though still in England), and there, alighting from a stage-coach
at another Inn in the snow, as I had actually done some years before,
I repeated in my sleep a curious experience I had really had here.
More than a year before I made the journey in the course of which I
put up at that Inn, I had lost a very near and dear friend by death.
Every night since, at home or away from home, I had dreamed of that
friend; sometimes as still living; sometimes as returning from the world
of shadows to comfort me; always as being beautiful, placid, and happy,

never in association with any approach to fear or distress. It was at a lonely Inn in a wide moorland place, that I halted to pass the night. When I had looked from my bedroom window over the waste of snow on which the moon was shining, I sat down by my fire to write a letter. I had always, until that hour, kept it within my own breast that I dreamed every night of the dear lost one. But in the letter that I wrote I recorded the circumstance, and added that I felt much interested in proving whether the subject of my dream would still be faithful to me, travel-tired, and in that remote place. No. I lost the beloved figure of my vision in parting with the secret. My sleep has never looked upon it since, in sixteen years, but once. I was in Italy, and awoke (or seemed to awake), the well-remembered voice distinctly in my ears, conversing with it. I entreated it, as it rose above my bed and soared up to the vaulted roof of the old room, to answer me a question I had asked touching the Future Life. My hands were still outstretched towards it as it vanished, when I heard a bell ringing by the garden wall, and a voice in the deep stillness of the night calling on all good Christians to pray for the souls of the dead; it being All Souls' Eve.

To return to the Holly-Tree. When I awoke next day, it was freezing hard, and the lowering sky threatened more snow. My breakfast cleared away, I drew my chair into its former place, and, with the fire getting so much the better of the landscape that I sat in twilight, resumed my Inn remembrances.

That was a good Inn down in Wiltshire where I put up once, in the days of the hard Wiltshire ale, and before all beer was bitterness. It was on the skirts of Salisbury Plain, and the midnight wind that rattled my lattice window came moaning at me from Stonehenge. There was a hanger-on at that establishment (a supernaturally preserved Druid I believe him to have been, and to be still), with long white hair, and a flinty blue eye always looking afar off; who claimed to have been a shepherd, and who seemed to be ever watching for the reappearance, on the verge of the horizon, of some ghostly flock of sheep that had been mutton for many ages. He was a man with a weird belief in him that no one could count the stones of Stonehenge twice, and make the same number of them; likewise, that any one who counted them three times nine times, and then stood in the centre and said, 'I dare!' would behold a tremendous apparition, and be stricken dead. He pretended to have seen a bustard (I suspect him to have been familiar with the dodo), in manner following: he was out upon the plain at the

close of a late autumn day, when he dimly discerned, going on before
him at a curious fitfully bounding pace, what he at first supposed to
be a gig-umbrella that had been blown from some conveyance, but
what he presently believed to be a lean dwarf man upon a little pony.
Having followed this object for some distance without gaining on it,
and having called to it many times without receiving any answer, he
pursued it for miles and miles, when, at length coming up with it, he
discovered it to be the last bustard in Great Britain, degenerated into
a wingless state, and running along the ground. Resolved to capture
him or perish in the attempt, he closed with the bustard; but the
bustard, who had formed a counter-resolution that he should do
neither, threw him, stunned him, and was last seen making off due
west. This weird man, at that stage of metempsychosis, may have
been a sleep-walker or an enthusiast or a robber; but I awoke one
night to find him in the dark at my bedside, repeating the Athanasian
Creed in a terrific voice. I paid my bill next day, and retired from the
county with all possible precipitation.

That was not a commonplace story which worked itself out at a
little Inn in Switzerland, while I was staying there. It was a very homely
place, in a village of one narrow zigzag street, among mountains, and
you went in at the main door through the cow-house, and among the
mules and the dogs and the fowls, before ascending a great bare staircase
to the rooms; which were all of unpainted wood, without plastering
or papering—like rough packing-cases. Outside there was nothing but
the straggling street, a little toy church with a copper-coloured steeple,
a pine forest, a torrent, mists, and mountainsides. A young man belonging to this Inn had disappeared eight weeks before (it was wintertime),
and was supposed to have had some undiscovered love affair, and to
have gone for a soldier. He had got up in the night, and dropped into
the village street from the loft in which he slept with another man;
and he had done it so quietly, that his companion and fellow-labourer
had heard no movement when he was awakened in the morning, and
they said, 'Louis, where is Henri?' They looked for him high and low,
in vain, and gave him up. Now, outside this Inn, there stood, as there
stood outside every dwelling in the village, a stack of firewood; but
the stack belonging to the Inn was higher than any of the rest, because
the Inn was the richest house, and burnt the most fuel. It began to be
noticed, while they were looking high and low, that a Bantam cock,
part of the livestock of the Inn, put himself wonderfully out of his way
to get to the top of this wood-stack; and that he would stay there for

hours and hours, crowing, until he appeared in danger of splitting himself. Five weeks went on—six weeks—and still this terrible Bantam, neglecting his domestic affairs, was always on the top of the wood-stack, crowing the very eyes out of his head. By this time it was perceived that Louis had become inspired with a violent animosity towards the terrible Bantam, and one morning he was seen by a woman, who sat nursing her goitre at a little window in a gleam of sun, to catch up a rough billet of wood, with a great oath, hurl it at the terrible Bantam crowing on the wood-stack, and bring him down dead. Hereupon the woman, with a sudden light in her mind, stole round to the back of the wood-stack, and, being a good climber, as all those women are, climbed up, and soon was seen upon the summit, screaming, looking down the hollow within, and crying, 'Seize Louis, the murderer! Ring the church bell! Here is the body!' I saw the murderer that day, and I saw him as I sat by my fire at the Holly-Tree Inn, and I see him now, lying shackled with cords on the stable litter, among the mild eyes and the smoking breath of the cows, waiting to be taken away by the police, and stared at by the fearful village. A heavy animal—the dullest animal in the stables—with a stupid head, and a lumpish face devoid of any trace of sensibility, who had been, within the knowledge of the murdered youth, an embezzler of certain small moneys belonging to his master, and who had taken this hope-ful mode of putting a possible accuser out of his way. All of which he confessed next day, like a sulky wretch who couldn't be troubled any more, now that they had got hold of him, and meant to make an end of him. I saw him once again, on the day of my departure from the Inn. In that canton the headsman still does his office with a sword; and I came upon this murderer sitting bound to a chair, with his eyes bandaged, on a scaffold in a little market-place. In that instant, a great sword (loaded with quicksilver in the thick part of the blade) swept round him like a gust of wind or fire, and there was no such creature in the world. My wonder was, not that he was so suddenly dispatched, but that any head was left unreaped, within a radius of fifty yards of that tremendous sickle.

That was a good Inn, too, with the kind, cheerful landlady and the honest landlord, where I lived in the shadow of Mont Blanc, and where one of the apartments has a zoological papering on the walls, not so accurately joined but that the elephant occasionally rejoices in a tiger's hind legs and tail, while the lion puts on a trunk and tusks, and the bear, moulting as it were, appears as to portions of himself like a leopard. I made several American friends at that Inn, who all called Mont Blanc Mount Blank,—except one good-humoured gentleman, of a very sociable nature, who became on such intimate terms with it that he spoke of it familiarly as 'Blank' observing, at breakfast, 'Blank looks pretty tall this morning'; or considerably doubting in the courtyard in the evening, whether there warn't some go-ahead naters in our country, Sir, that would make out the top of Blank in a couple of hours from first start—now!

Once I passed a fortnight at an Inn in the North of England, where I was haunted by the ghost of a tremendous pie. It was a Yorkshire pie, like a fort—an abandoned fort with nothing in it; but the waiter had a fixed idea that it was a point of ceremony at every meal to put the pie on the table. After some days I tried to hint, in several delicate ways, that I considered the pie done with; as, for example, by emptying fag-ends of glasses of wine into it; putting cheese-plates and spoons into it, as into a basket; putting wine-bottles into it, as into a cooler; but always in vain, the pie being invariably cleaned out again and brought up as before. At last, beginning to be doubtful whether I was not the victim of a spectral illusion, and whether my health and spirits might not sink under the horrors of an imaginary pie, I cut a triangle out of it, fully as large as the musical instrument of that name in a powerful orchestra. Human prevision could not have foreseen the result—but the waiter mended the pie. With some effectual species of cement, he adroitly fitted the triangle in again, and I paid my reckoning and fled.

The Holly-Tree was getting rather dismal. I made an overland expedition beyond the screen, and penetrated as far as the fourth window. Here I was driven back by stress of weather. Arrived at my winter-quarters once more, I made up the fire, and took another Inn.

It was in the remotest part of Cornwall. A great annual Miners' Feast was being holden at the Inn, when I and my travelling companions presented ourselves at night among the wild crowd that were dancing before it by torchlight. We had had a breakdown in the dark, on a stony morass some miles away; and I had the honour of leading one of the unharnessed post-horses. If any lady or gentleman, on perusal of the present lines, will take any very tall post-horse with his traces hanging about his legs, and will conduct him by the bearing-rein into the heart of a country dance of a hundred and fifty couples, that lady or gentleman will then, and only then, form an adequate idea of the extent to which that post-horse will tread on his conductor's toes.

Over and above which, the post-horse, finding three hundred people whirling about him, will probably rear, and also lash out with his hind legs, in a manner incompatible with dignity or self-respect on his conductor's part. With such little drawbacks on my usually impressive aspect, I appeared at this Cornish Inn, to the unutterable wonder of the Cornish Miners. It was full, and twenty times full, and nobody could be received but the post-horse,—though to get rid of that noble animal was something. While my fellow-travellers and I were discussing how to pass the night and so much of the next day as must intervene before the jovial blacksmith and the jovial wheelwright would be in a condition to go out on the morass and mend the coach, an honest man stepped forth from the crowd and proposed his unlet floor of two rooms, with supper of eggs and bacon, ale and punch. We joyfully accompanied him home to the strangest of clean houses, where we were well entertained to the satisfaction of all parties. But the novel feature of the entertainment was, that our host was a chairmaker, and that the chairs assigned to us were mere frames, altogether without bottoms of any sort; so that we passed the evening on perches. Nor was this the absurdest consequence; for when we unbent at supper, and any one of us gave way to laughter, he forgot the peculiarity of his position, and instantly disappeared. I myself, doubled up into an attitude from which self-extrication was impossible, was taken out of my frame, like a clown in a comic pantomime who has tumbled into a tub, five times by the taper's light during the eggs and bacon.

The Holly-Tree was fast reviving within me a sense of loneliness. I began to feel conscious that my subject would never carry on until I was dug out. I might be a week here—weeks!

There was a story with a singular idea in it, connected with an Inn I once passed a night at in a picturesque old town on the Welsh border. In a large double-bedded room of this Inn there had been a suicide committed by poison, in one bed, while a tired traveller slept unconscious in the other. After that time, the suicide bed was never used, but the other constantly was; the disused bedstead remaining in the room empty, though as to all other respects in its old state. The story ran, that whosoever slept in this room, though never so entire a stranger, from never so far off, was invariably observed to come down in the morning with an impression that he smelt Laudanum, and that his mind always turned upon the subject of suicide; to which, whatever kind of man he might be, he was certain to make some reference if he conversed with any one. This went on for years, until it at length induced the landlord to take the disused bedstead down, and bodily burn it—bed, hangings, and all. The strange influence (this was the story) now changed to a fainter one, but never changed afterwards. The occupant of that room, with occasional but very rare exceptions, would come down in the morning, trying to recall a forgotten dream he had had in the night. The landlord, on his mentioning his perplexity, would suggest various commonplace subjects, not one of which, as he very well knew, was the true subject. But the moment the landlord suggested 'Poison' the traveller started, and cried, 'Yes!' He never failed to accept that suggestion, and he never recalled any more of the dream.

This reminiscence brought the Welsh Inns in general before me; with the women in their round hats, and the harpers with their white beards (venerable, but humbugs, I am afraid), playing outside the door while I took my dinner. The transition was natural to the Highland Inns, with the oatmeal bannocks, the honey, the venison steaks, the trout from the loch, the whisky, and perhaps (having the materials so temptingly at hand) the Athol brose. Once was I coming south from the Scottish Highlands in hot haste, hoping to change quickly at the station at the bottom of a certain wild historical glen, when these eyes did with mortification see the landlord come out with a telescope and sweep the whole prospect for the horses; which horses were away picking up their own living, and did not heave in sight under four hours. Having thought of the loch-trout, I was taken by quick association to the Anglers' Inns of England (I have assisted at innumerable feats of angling by lying in the bottom of the boat, whole summer days, doing nothing with the greatest perseverance; which I have generally found to be as effectual towards the taking of fish as the finest tackle and the utmost science), and to the pleasant white, clean, flowerpot-decorated bedrooms of those inns, overlooking the river, and the ferry, and the green ait, and the church-spire, and the country bridge; and to the peerless Emma with the bright eyes and the pretty smile, who waited, bless her! with a natural grace that would have converted Blue-Beard. Casting my eyes upon my Holly-Tree fire, I next discerned among the glowing coals the pictures of a score or more of those wonderful English posting-inns which we are all so sorry to have lost, which were so large and so comfortable, and which were such monuments of British submission to rapacity and extortion. He who would see these houses pining away, let him walk from Basingstoke, or even Windsor, to London, by way of Hounslow, and moralize on their perishing remains; the stables crumbling to dust; unsettled labourers and wanderers bivouacking in the outhouses; grass growing in the yards; the rooms, where erst so many hundred beds of down were made up, let off to Irish lodgers at eighteenpence a week; a little ill-looking beer-shop shrinking in the tap of former days, burning coach-house gates for firewood, having one of its two windows bunged up, as if it had received punishment in a fight with the Railroad; a low, bandy-legged, brick-making bulldog standing in the doorway. What could I next see in my fire so naturally as the new railway-house of these times near the dismal country station; with nothing particular on draught but cold air and damp, nothing worth mentioning in the larder but new mortar, and no business doing beyond a conceited affectation of luggage in the hall? Then I came to the Inns of Paris, with the pretty apartment of four pieces up one hundred and seventy-five waxed stairs, the privilege of ringing the bell all day long without influencing anybody's mind or body but your own, and the not-too-much-for-dinner, considering the price. Next to the provincial Inns of France, with the great church-tower rising above the courtyard, the horse-bells jingling merrily up and down the street beyond, and the clocks of all descriptions in all the rooms, which are never right, unless taken at the precise minute when, by getting exactly twelve hours too fast or too slow, they unintentionally become so. Away I went, next, to the lesser roadside Inns of Italy; where all the dirty clothes in the house (not in wear) are always lying in your anteroom; where the mosquitoes make a raisin pudding of your face in summer, and the cold bites it blue in winter; where you get what you can, and forget what you can't; where I should again like to be boiling my tea in a pocket-handkerchief dumpling, for want of a teapot. So to the old palace Inns and old monastery Inns, in towns and cities of the same bright country; with their massive quadrangular staircases, whence you may look from among clustering pillars high into the blue vault of heaven; with their stately banqueting-rooms, and vast refectories; with their labyrinths of ghostly bedchambers, and their glimpses into gorgeous streets that have no appearance of reality or possibility. So to the close little inns of the Malaria districts, with their pale attendants, and their peculiar smell of never letting in the air. So to the immense fantastic Inns of Venice, with the cry of the gondolier below, as he skims the corner; the grip of the watery odours on one particular little bit of the bridge of your nose (which is never released while you stay there); and the great bell of St Mark's Cathedral tolling midnight. Next I put up for a minute at

the restless Inns upon the Rhine, where your going to bed, no matter
at what hour, appears to be the tocsin for everybody else's getting
up; and where, in the table d'hôte room at the end of the long table
(with several Towers of Babel on it at the other end, all made of white
plates), one knot of stoutish men, entirely dressed in jewels and dirt,
and having nothing else upon them, *will* remain all night, clinking
glasses, and singing about the river that flows, and the grape that
grows, and Rhine wine that beguiles, and Rhine woman that smiles
and hi drink drink my friend and ho drink drink my brother, and all
the rest of it. I departed thence, as a matter of course, to other German
Inns, where all the eatables are soddened down to the same flavour,
and where the mind is disturbed by the apparition of hot puddings,
and boiled cherries, sweet and slab, at awfully unexpected periods of
the repast. After a draught of sparkling beer from a foaming glass jug,
and a glance of recognition through the windows of the student beer-
houses at Heidelberg and elsewhere, I put out to sea for the Inns of
America, with their four hundred beds apiece, and their eight or nine
hundred ladies and gentlemen at dinner every day. Again I stood in
the bar-rooms thereof, taking my evening cobbler, julep, sling, or cocktail. Again I listened to my friend the General,—whom I had known
for five minutes, in the course of which period he had made me intimate for life with two Majors, who again had made me intimate for
life with three Colonels, who again had made me brother to twenty-
two civilians,—again, I say, I listened to my friend the General, leisurely expounding the resources of the establishment, as to gentlemen's
morning-room, Sir; ladies' morning-room, Sir; gentlemen's evening-
room, Sir; ladies' evening-room, Sir; ladies' and gentlemen's evening
reuniting-room, Sir; music-room, Sir; reading-room, Sir; over four hundred sleeping-rooms, Sir; and the entire planned and finished within
twelve calendar months from the first clearing off of the old encum-
brances on the plot, at a cost of five hundred thousand dollars, Sir.
Again I found, as to my individual way of thinking, that the greater,
the more gorgeous, and the more dollarous the establishment was,
the less desirable it was. Nevertheless, again I drank my cobbler, julep,
sling, or cocktail, in all goodwill, to my friend the General, and my
friends the Majors, Colonels, and civilians all; full well knowing that,
whatever little motes my beamy eyes may have descried in theirs,
they belong to a kind, generous, large-hearted, and great people.

I had been going on lately at a quick pace to keep my solitude out
of my mind; but here I broke down for good, and gave up the subject.

What was I to do? What was to become of me? Into what extremity was I submissively to sink? Supposing that, like Baron Trenck, I looked out for a mouse or spider, and found one, and beguiled my imprisonment by training it? Even that might be dangerous with a view to the future. I might be so far gone when the road did come to be cut through the snow, that, on my way forth, I might burst into tears, and beseech, like the prisoner who was released in his old age from the Bastille, to be taken back again to the five windows, the ten curtains, and the sinuous drapery.

The Lazy Tour of Two Idle Apprentices

In the autumn month of September, eighteen hundred and fifty-seven, wherein these presents bear date, two idle apprentices, exhausted by the long, hot summer, and the long, hot work it had brought with it, ran away from their employer. They were bound to a highly meritorious lady (named Literature), of fair credit and repute, though, it must be acknowledged, not quite so highly esteemed in the City as she might be. This is the more remarkable, as there is nothing against the respectable lady in that quarter, but quite the contrary; her family having rendered eminent service to many famous citizens of London. It may be sufficient to name Sir William Walworth, Lord Mayor under King Richard II, at the time of Wat Tyler's insurrection, and Sir Richard Whittington: which latter distinguished man and magistrate was doubtless indebted to the lady's family for the gift of his celebrated cat. There is also strong reason to suppose that they rang the Highgate bells for him with their own hands.

The misguided young men who thus shirked their duty to the mistress from whom they had received many favours, were actuated by the low idea of making a perfectly idle trip, in any direction. They had no intention of going anywhere in particular; they wanted to see nothing, they wanted to know nothing, they wanted to learn nothing, they wanted to do nothing. They wanted only to be idle. They took to themselves (after Hogarth), the names of Mr Thomas Idle and Mr Francis Goodchild; but there was not a moral pin to choose between them, and they were both idle in the last degree.

Between Francis and Thomas, however, there was this difference of character: Goodchild was laboriously idle, and would take upon himself any amount of pains and labour to assure himself that he was idle; in short, had no better idea of idleness than that it was useless industry. Thomas Idle, on the other hand, was an idler of the unmixed Irish or Neapolitan type; a passive idler, a born-and-bred idler, a consistent idler, who practised what he would have preached if he had not been too idle to preach; a one entire and perfect chrysolite of idleness.

The two idle apprentices found themselves, within a few hours of their escape, walking down into the North of England, that is to say, Thomas was lying in a meadow, looking at the railway trains as they passed over a distant viaduct—which was *his* idea of walking down into the North; while Francis was walking a mile due South against time—which was *his* idea of walking down into the North. In the meantime the day waned, and the milestones remained unconquered.

'Tom,' said Goodchild, 'the sun is getting low. Up, and let us go forward!'

'Nay,' quoth Thomas Idle, 'I have not done with Annie Laurie yet.' And he proceeded with that idle but popular ballad, to the effect that for the bonnie young person of that name he would 'lay him doon and dee'—equivalent, in prose, to lay him down and die.

'What an ass that fellow was!' cried Goodchild, with the bitter emphasis of contempt.

'Which fellow?' asked Thomas Idle.

'The fellow in your song. Lay him doon and dee! Finely he'd show off before the girl by doing *that*. A sniveller! Why couldn't he get up, and punch somebody's head!'

'Whose?' asked Thomas Idle.

'Anybody's. Everybody's would be better than nobody's! If I fell into that state of mind about a girl, do you think I'd lay me doon and dee? No, Sir,' proceeded Goodchild, with a disparaging assumption of the Scottish accent, 'I'd get me oop and peetch into somebody. Wouldn't you?'

'I wouldn't have anything to do with her,' yawned Thomas Idle. 'Why should I take the trouble?'

'It's no trouble, Tom, to fall in love,' said Goodchild, shaking his head.

'It's trouble enough to fall out of it, once you're in it,' retorted Tom. 'So I keep out of it altogether. It would be better for you, if you did the same.'

Mr Goodchild, who is always in love with somebody, and not unfrequently with several objects at once, made no reply. He heaved a sigh of the kind which is termed by the lower orders 'a bellowser', and then, heaving Mr Idle on his feet (who was not half so heavy as the sigh), urged him northward.

These two had sent their personal baggage on by train: only retaining each a knapsack. Idle now applied himself to constantly regretting the train, to tracking it through the intricacies of Bradshaw's Guide, and finding out where it is now—and where now—and where now—and to asking what was the use of walking, when you could ride at such a pace as that. Was it to see the country? If that was the object, look at it out of the carriage windows. There was a great deal more of it to be seen there than here. Besides, who wanted to see the country? Nobody. And again, whoever did walk? Nobody. Fellows set off to walk, but they never did it. They came back and said they did, but they didn't. Then why should he walk? He wouldn't walk. He swore it by this milestone!

It was the fifth from London, so far had they penetrated into the North. Submitting to the powerful chain of argument, Goodchild proposed a return to the Metropolis, and a falling back upon Euston Square Terminus. Thomas assented with alacrity, and so they walked down into the North by the next morning's express, and carried their knapsacks in the luggage-van.

It was like all other expresses, as every express is and must be. It bore through the harvest country a smell like a large washing-day, and a sharp issue of steam as from a huge brazen tea-urn. The greatest power in nature and art combined, it yet glided over dangerous heights in the sight of people looking up from fields and roads, as smoothly and unreally as a light miniature plaything. Now, the engine shrieked in hysterics of such intensity, that it seemed desirable that the men who had her in charge should hold her feet, slap her hands, and bring her to; now, burrowed into tunnels with a stubborn and undemonstrative energy so confusing that the train seemed to be flying back into leagues of darkness. Here, were station after station, swallowed up by the express without stopping; here, stations where it fired itself in like a volley of cannon-balls, swooped away four country-people with nosegays, and three men of business with portmanteaus, and fired itself off again, bang, bang, bang! At long intervals were uncomfortable refreshment-rooms, made more uncomfortable by the scorn of Beauty towards Beast, the public (but to whom she never relented, as Beauty did in the story, towards the other Beast), and where sensitive stomachs were fed, with a contemptuous sharpness occasioning indigestion. Here, again, were stations with nothing going but a bell, and wonderful wooden razors set aloft on great posts, shaving the air. In these fields, the horses, sheep, and cattle were well used to the thundering meteor, and didn't mind; in those, they were all set scampering together, and a herd of pigs scoured after them. The pastoral country darkened, became coaly, became smoky, became infernal, got better, got worse, improved again, grew rugged, turned romantic; was a wood, a stream, a chain of hills, a gorge, a moor, a cathedral town, a fortified place, a waste. Now, miserable black dwellings, a black canal, and sick black towers of chimneys; now, a trim garden, where the flowers were bright and fair; now, a wilderness of hideous altars all ablaze; now, the water meadows with their fairy rings; now, the mangy patch of unlet building ground outside the stagnant town, with the larger ring where the Circus was last week. The temperature changed, the dialect changed, the people changed, faces got sharper, manner got shorter, eyes got shrewder and harder; yet all so quickly, that the spruce guard in the London uniform and silver lace, had not yet rumpled his shirt-collar, delivered half the dispatches in his shiny little pouch, or read his newspaper.

Carlisle! Idle and Goodchild had got to Carlisle. It looked congenially and delightfully idle. Something in the way of public amusement had happened last month, and something else was going to happen before Christmas; and, in the meantime there was a lecture on India for those who liked it—which Idle and Goodchild did not. Likewise, by those who liked them, there were impressions to be bought of all the vapid prints, going and gone, and of nearly all the vapid books. For those who wanted to put anything in missionary boxes, here were the boxes. For those who wanted the Reverend Mr Podgers (artist's proofs, thirty shillings), here was Mr Podgers to any amount. Not less gracious and abundant, Mr Codgers also of the vineyard, but opposed to Mr Podgers, brotherly tooth and nail. Here, were guide-books to the neighbouring antiquities, and eke the Lake country, in several dry and husky sorts; here, many physically and morally impossible heads of both sexes, for young ladies to copy, in the exercise of the art of drawing; here, further, a large impression of Mr Spurgeon, solid as to the flesh, not to say even something gross. The working young men of Carlisle were drawn up, with their hands in their pockets, across the pavements, four and six abreast, and appeared (much to the satisfaction of Mr Idle) to have nothing else to do. The working and growing young women of Carlisle, from the age of twelve upwards, promenaded the streets in the cool of the evening, and rallied the said young men. Sometimes the young men rallied the young women, as in the case of a group gathered round an accordion-player, from among whom a young man advanced behind a young woman for whom he appeared to have a tenderness, and hinted to her that he was there and playful, by giving her (he wore clogs) a kick.

On market morning, Carlisle woke up amazingly, and became (to the two Idle Apprentices) disagreeably and reproachfully busy. There were its cattle market, its sheep market, and its pig market down by the river, with raw-boned and shock-headed Rob Roys hiding their Lowland dresses beneath heavy plaids, prowling in and out among the animals, and flavouring the air with fumes of whiskey. There was its corn market down the main street, with hum of chaffering over open sacks. There was its general market in the street too, with heather brooms on which the purple flower still flourished, and heather baskets primitive and fresh to behold. With women trying on clogs and caps at open stalls, and 'Bible stalls' adjoining. With 'Doctor Mantle's Dispensary for the cure of all Human Maladies and no charge for advice', and with Doctor Mantle's 'Laboratory of Medical, Chemical, and Botanical Science'—both healing institutions established on one pair of trestles, one board, and one sun-blind. With the renowned phrenologist from London, begging to be favoured (at sixpence each) with the company of clients of both sexes, to whom, on examination of their heads, he would make revelations 'enabling him or her to know themselves'. Through all these bargains and blessings, the recruiting-sergeant watchfully elbowed his way, a thread of War in the peaceful skein. Likewise on the walls were printed hints that the Oxford Blues might not be indisposed to hear of a few fine active young men; and that whereas the standard of that distinguished corps is full six feet, 'growing lads of five feet eleven' need not absolutely despair of being accepted.

Scenting the morning air more pleasantly than the buried majesty of Denmark did, Messrs. Idle and Goodchild rode away from Carlisle at eight o'clock one forenoon, bound for the village of Hesket, New-market, some fourteen miles distant. Goodchild (who had already begun to doubt whether he was idle: as his way always is when he has nothing to do) had read of a certain black old Cumberland hill or mountain, called Carrock, or Carrock Fell; and had arrived at the conclusion that it would be the culminating triumph of Idleness to ascend the same. Thomas Idle, dwelling on the pains inseparable from that achievement, had expressed the strongest doubts of the expediency, and even of the sanity, of the enterprise; but Goodchild had carried his point, and they rode away.

Up hill and down hill, and twisting to the right, and twisting to the left, and with old Skiddaw (who has vaunted himself a great deal more than his merits deserve; but that is rather the way of the Lake country), dodging the apprentices in a picturesque and pleasant manner. Good, weatherproof, warm, pleasant houses, well white-limed, scantily dotting the road. Clean children coming out to look, carrying other clean children as big as themselves. Harvest still lying out and much rained upon; here and there, harvest still unreaped. Well-cultivated gardens attached to the cottages, with plenty of produce forced out of their hard soil. Lonely nooks, and wild; but people can be born, and married, and buried in such nooks, and can live and love, and be loved, there as elsewhere, thank God! (Mr Goodchild's remark.) By-and-by, the village. Black, coarse-stoned, rough-windowed houses; some with outer staircases, like Swiss houses; a sinuous and stony gutter winding up hill and round the corner, by way of street. All the children running out directly. Women pausing in washing, to peep from doorways and very little windows. Such were the observations of Messrs Idle and Goodchild, as their conveyance stopped at the village shoemaker's. Old Carrock gloomed down upon it all in a very ill-tempered state; and rain was beginning.

The village shoemaker declined to have anything to do with Carrock. No visitors went up Carrock. No visitors came there at all. Aa' the world ganged awa' yon. The driver appealed to the Innkeeper. The Innkeeper had two men working in the fields, and one of them should be called in, to go up Carrock as guide. Messrs Idle and Goodchild, highly approving, entered the Innkeeper's house, to drink whiskey and eat oatcake.

The Innkeeper was not idle enough—was not idle at all, which was a great fault in him—but was a fine specimen of a north-countryman, or any kind of man. He had a ruddy cheek, a bright eye, a well-knit frame, an immense hand, a cheery outspeaking voice, and a straight, bright, broad look. He had a drawing-room, too, upstairs, which was worth a visit to the Cumberland Fells. (This was Mr Francis Goodchild's opinion, in which Mr Thomas Idle did not concur.)

The ceiling of this drawing-room was so crossed and recrossed by beams of unequal lengths, radiating from a centre, in a corner, that it looked like a broken star-fish. The room was comfortably and solidly furnished with good mahogany and horsehair. It had a snug fireside, and a couple of well-curtained windows, looking out upon the wild country behind the house. What it most developed was, an unexpected taste for little ornaments and knick-knacks, of which it contained a most surprising number. They were not very various, consisting in great part of waxen babies with their limbs more or less mutilated, appealing on one leg to the parental affections from under little cupping glasses; but Uncle Tom was there, in crockery, receiving theological instructions from Miss Eva, who grew out of his side like a wen, in an exceedingly rough state of profile propagandism. Engravings of Mr Hunt's country boy, before and after his pie, were on the wall, divided by a highly coloured nautical piece, the subject of which had all her colours (and more) flying, and was making great way through a sea of a regular pattern, like a lady's collar. A benevolent, elderly gentleman of the last century, with a powdered head, kept guard, in oil and varnish, over a most perplexing piece of furniture on a table; in appearance between a driving seat and an angular knife-box, but, when opened, a musical instrument of tinkling wires, exactly like David's harp packed for travelling. Everything became a knick-knack in this curious room. The copper tea-kettle, burnished up to the highest point of glory, took his station on a stand of his own at the greatest possible distance from the fireplace, and said: 'By your leave, not a kittle, but a bijou.' The Staffordshire-ware butter-dish with the cover on, got upon a little round occasional table in a window, with a worked top, and announced itself to the two chairs accidentally placed there, as an aid to polite conversation, a graceful trifle in china to be chatted over by callers, as they airily trifled away the visiting moments of a butter-fly existence, in that rugged old village on the Cumberland Fells. The very footstool could not keep the floor, but got upon a sofa, and therefrom proclaimed itself, in high relief of white and liver-coloured wool, a favourite spaniel coiled up for repose. Though, truly, in spite of its bright glass eyes, the spaniel was the least successful assumption in the collection: being perfectly flat, and dismally suggestive of a recent mistake in sitting down on the part of some corpulent member of the family.

There were books, too, in this room; books on the table, books on the chimneypiece, books in an open press in the corner. Fielding was there, and Smollett was there, and Steele and Addison were there, in dispersed volumes; and there were tales of those who go down to the sea in ships, for windy nights; and there was really a choice of good books for rainy days or fine. It was so very pleasant to see these things in such a lonesome by-place—so very agreeable to find these evidences of a taste, however homely, that went beyond the beautiful cleanliness and trimness of the house—so fanciful to imagine what a wonder the room must be to the little children born in the gloomy village—what grand impressions of it those of them who became wanderers over the earth would carry away; and how, at distant ends of the world, some old voyagers would die, cherishing the belief that the finest apartment known to men was once in the Hesket-Newmarket Inn, in rare old Cumberland—it was such a charmingly lazy pursuit to entertain these rambling thoughts over the choice oatcake and the genial whiskey, that Mr Idle and Mr Goodchild never asked themselves how it came to pass that the men in the fields were never heard of more, how the stalwart landlord replaced them without explanation, how his dog-cart came to be waiting at the door, and how everything was arranged without the least arrangement for climbing to old Carrock's shoulders, and standing on his head.

Without a word of enquiry, therefore, the Two Idle Apprentices drifted out resignedly into a fine, soft, close, drowsy, penetrating rain; got into the landlord's light dog-cart, and rattled off through the village for the foot of Carrock. The journey at the outset was not remarkable. The Cumberland road went up and down like all other roads; the Cumberland curs burst out from backs of cottages and barked like other curs, and the Cumberland peasantry stared after the dog-cart amazedly, as long as it was in sight, like the rest of their race. The approach to the foot of the mountain resembled the approaches to the feet of most other mountains all over the world. The cultivation gradually ceased, the trees grew gradually rarer, the road became gradually rougher, and the sides of the mountain looked gradually more and more lofty, and more and more difficult to get up. The dog-cart was left at a lonely farmhouse. The landlord borrowed a large umbrella, and, assuming in an instant the character of the most cheerful and adventurous of guides, led the way to the ascent. Mr Goodchild looked eagerly at the top of the mountain, and, feeling apparently that he was now going to be very lazy indeed, shone all over wonderfully to the eye, under the influence of the contentment within and the moisture without. Only in the bosom of Mr Thomas Idle did Despondency now hold her gloomy state. He kept it a secret; but he would have given a very handsome sum, when the ascent began, to have been back again at the inn. The sides of Carrock looked fearfully steep, and the top of Carrock was hidden in mist. The rain was falling faster and faster. The knees of Mr Idle—always weak on walking excursions—shivered and shook with fear and damp. The wet was already penetrating through the young man's outer coat to a brand new shooting-jacket, for which he had reluctantly paid the large sum of two guineas on leaving town; he had no stimulating refreshment about him but a small packet of clammy gingerbread nuts; he had nobody to give him an arm, nobody to push him gently behind, nobody to pull him up tenderly in front, nobody to speak to who really felt the difficulties of the ascent, the dampness of the rain, the denseness of the mist, and the unutterable folly of climbing, undriven, up any steep place in the world, when there is level ground within reach to walk on instead. Was it for this that Thomas had left London? London, where there are nice short walks in level public gardens, with benches of repose set up at convenient distances for weary travellers—London, where rugged stone is humanely pounded into little lumps for the road, and intelligently shaped into smooth slabs for the pavement! No! it was not for the laborious ascent of the crags of Carrock that Idle had left his native city, and travelled to Cumberland. Never did he feel more disastrously convinced that he had committed a very grave error in judgement than when he found himself standing in the rain at the bottom of a steep mountain, and knew that the responsibility rested on his weak shoulders of actually getting to the top of it.

The honest landlord went first, the beaming Goodchild followed, the mournful Idle brought up the rear. From time to time, the two foremost members of the expedition changed places in the order of march; but the rearguard never altered his position. Up the mountain or down the mountain, in the water or out of it, over the rocks, through the bogs, skirting the heather, Mr Thomas Idle was always the last, and was always the man who had to be looked after and waited for. At first the ascent was delusively easy, the sides of the mountain sloped gradually, and the material of which they were composed was a soft spongy turf, very tender and pleasant to walk upon. After a hundred yards or so, however, the verdant scene and the easy slope disappeared, and the rocks began. Not noble, massive rocks, standing upright, keeping a certain regularity in their positions, and possessing, now and then, flat tops to sit upon, but little irritating, comfortless rocks, littered about anyhow by Nature; treacherous, disheartening rocks of all sorts of small shapes and small sizes, bruisers of tender toes and trippers-up of wavering feet. When these impediments were passed, heather and slough followed. Here the steepness of the ascent was slightly mitigated; and here the exploring party of three turned round to look at the view below them. The scene of the moorland and the fields was like a feeble water-colour drawing half sponged out. The mist was darkening, the rain was thickening, the trees were dotted about like spots of faint shadow, the division-lines which mapped out the fields were all getting blurred together, and the lonely farmhouse where the dog-cart had been left, loomed spectral in the grey light like the last human dwelling at the end of the habitable world. Was this a sight worth climbing to see? Surely—surely not!

Up again—for the top of Carrock is not reached yet. The landlord, just as good-tempered and obliging as he was at the bottom of the mountain. Mr Goodchild brighter in the eyes and rosier in the face than ever; full of cheerful remarks and apt quotations; and walking with a springiness of step wonderful to behold. Mr Idle, farther and farther in the rear, with the water squeaking in the toes of his boots, with his two-guinea shooting-jacket clinging damply to his aching sides, with his overcoat so full of rain, and standing out so pyramidically stiff, in consequence, from his shoulders downwards, that he felt as if he was walking in a gigantic extinguisher—the despairing spirit within him representing but too aptly the candle that had just been put out. Up and up and up again, till a ridge is reached and the outer edge of the mist on the summit of Carrock is darkly and drizzingly near. Is this the top? No, nothing like the top. It is an aggravating peculiarity of all mountains, that, although they have only one top when they are seen (as they ought always to be seen) from below, they turn out to have a perfect eruption of false tops whenever the traveller is sufficiently ill advised to go out of his way for the purpose of ascending them. Carrock is but a trumpery little mountain of fifteen hundred feet, and it presumes to have false tops, and even precipices, as if it were Mont Blanc. No matter; Goodchild enjoys it, and will go on; and Idle, who is afraid of being left behind by himself, must follow. On entering the edge of the mist, the landlord stops, and says he hopes that it will not get any thicker. It is twenty years since he last ascended Carrock, and it is barely possible, if the mist increases, that the party may be lost on the mountain. Goodchild hears this dreadful intimation, and is not in the least impressed by it. He marches for the top that is never to be found, as if he was the Wandering Jew, bound to go on for ever, in defiance of everything. The landlord faithfully accompanies him. The two, to the dim eye of Idle, far below, look in the exaggerative mist, like a pair of friendly giants, mounting the steps of some invisible castle together. Up and up, and then down a little, and then up, and then along a strip of level ground, and then up again. The wind, a wind unknown in the happy valley, blows keen and strong; the rain-mist gets impenetrable; a dreary little cairn of stones appears. The landlord adds one to the heap, first walking all round the cairn as if he were about to perform an incantation, then dropping the stone on to the top of the heap with the gesture of a magician adding an ingredient to a cauldron in full bubble. Goodchild sits down by the cairn as if it was his study-table at home; Idle, drenched and panting, stands up with his back to the wind, ascertains distinctly that this is the top at last, looks round with all the little curiosity that is left in him, and gets, in return, a magnificent view of—Nothing!

The effect of this sublime spectacle on the minds of the exploring party is a little injured by the nature of the direct conclusion to which the sight of it points—the said conclusion being that the mountain mist has actually gathered round them, as the landlord feared it would. It now becomes imperatively necessary to settle the exact situation of the farmhouse in the valley at which the dog-cart has been left, before the travellers attempt to descend. While the landlord is endeavouring to make this discovery in his own way, Mr Goodchild plunges his hand under his wet coat, draws out a little red morocco-case, opens it, and displays to the view of his companions a neat pocket-compass. The north is found, the point at which the farmhouse is situated is settled, and the descent begins. After a little downward walking, Idle (behind as usual) sees his fellow-travellers turn aside sharply—tries to follow them—loses them in the mist—is shouted after, waited for, recovered—and then finds that a halt has been ordered, partly on his account, partly for the purpose of again consulting the compass.

The point in debate is settled as before between Goodchild and the landlord, and the expedition moves on, not down the mountain, but marching straight forward round the slope of it. The difficulty of following this new route is acutely felt by Thomas Idle. He finds the hardship of walking at all greatly increased by the fatigue of moving his feet straight forward along the side of a slope, when their natural tendency, at every step, is to turn off at a right angle, and go straight down the declivity. Let the reader imagine himself to be walking along the roof of a barn, instead of up or down it, and he will have an exact idea of the pedestrian difficulty in which the travellers had now involved themselves. In ten minutes more Idle was lost in the distance again, was shouted for, waited for, recovered as before; found Goodchild repeating his observation of the compass, and remonstrated warmly against the sideway route that his companions persisted in following.

It appeared to the uninstructed mind of Thomas that when three men want to get to the bottom of a mountain, their business is to walk down it; and he put this view of the case, not only with emphasis, but even with some irritability. He was answered from the scientific eminence of the compass on which his companions were mounted, that there was a frightful chasm somewhere near the foot of Carrock, called The Black Arches, into which the travellers were sure to march in the mist, if they risked continuing the descent from the place where they had now halted. Idle received this answer with the silent respect which was due to the commanders of the expedition, and followed along the roof of the barn, or rather the side of the mountain, reflecting upon the assurance which he received on starting again, that the object of the party was only to gain 'a certain point', and, this haven attained, to continue the descent afterwards until the foot of Carrock was reached. Though quite unexceptionable as an abstract form of expression, the phrase 'a certain point' has the disadvantage of sounding rather vaguely when it is pronounced on unknown ground, under a canopy of mist much thicker than a London fog. Nevertheless, after the compass, this phrase was all the clue the party had to hold by, and Idle clung to the extreme end of it as hopefully as he could.

More sideway walking, thicker and thicker mist, all sorts of points reached except the 'certain point'; third loss of Idle, third shouts for him, third recovery of him, third consultation of compass. Mr Goodchild draws it tenderly from his pocket, and prepares to adjust it on a stone. Something falls on the turf—it is the glass. Something else drops immediately after—it is the needle. The compass is broken, and the exploring party is lost!

It is the practice of the English portion of the human race to receive all great disasters in dead silence. Mr Goodchild restored the useless compass to his pocket without saying a word, Mr Idle looked at the landlord, and the landlord looked at Mr Idle. There was nothing for it now but to go on blindfold, and trust to the chapter of chances. Accordingly, the lost travellers moved forward, still walking round the slope of the mountain, still desperately resolved to avoid the Black Arches, and to succeed in reaching the 'certain point'.

A quarter of an hour brought them to the brink of a ravine, at the bottom of which there flowed a muddy little stream. Here another halt was called, and another consultation took place. The landlord, still clinging pertinaciously to the idea of reaching the 'point', voted for crossing the ravine, and going on round the slope of the mountain.

Mr Goodchild, to the great relief of his fellow-traveller, took another view of the case, and backed Mr Idle's proposal to descend Carrock at once, at any hazard—the rather as the running stream was a sure guide to follow from the mountain to the valley. Accordingly, the party descended to the rugged and stony banks of the stream; and here again Thomas lost ground sadly, and fell far behind his travelling companions. Not much more than six weeks had elapsed since he had sprained one of his ankles, and he began to feel this same ankle getting rather weak when he found himself among the stones that were strewn about the running water. Goodchild and the landlord were getting farther and farther ahead of him. He saw them cross the stream and disappear round a projection on its banks. He heard them shout the moment after as a signal that they had halted and were waiting for him. Answering the shout, he mended his pace, crossed the stream where they had crossed it, and was within one step of the opposite bank, when his foot slipped on a wet stone, his weak ankle gave a twist outwards, a hot, rending, tearing pain ran through it at the same moment, and down fell the idlest of the two Idle Apprentices, crippled in an instant.

The situation was now, in plain terms, one of absolute danger. There lay Mr Idle writhing with pain, there was the mist as thick as ever, there was the landlord as completely lost as the strangers whom he was conducting, and there was the compass broken in Goodchild's pocket. To leave the wretched Thomas on unknown ground was plainly impossible; and to get him to walk with a badly sprained ankle seemed equally out of the question. However, Goodchild (brought back by his cry for help) bandaged the ankle with a pocket-handkerchief, and assisted by the landlord, raised the crippled Apprentice to his legs, offered him a shoulder to lean on, and exhorted him for the sake of the whole party to try if he could walk. Thomas, assisted by the shoulder on one side, and a stick on the other, did try, with what pain and difficulty those only can imagine who have sprained an ankle and have had to tread on it afterwards. At a pace adapted to the feeble hobbling of a newly lamed man, the lost party moved on, perfectly ignorant whether they were on the right side of the mountain or the wrong, and equally uncertain how long Idle would be able to contend with the pain in his ankle, before he gave in altogether and fell down again, unable to stir another step.

Slowly and more slowly, as the clog of crippled Thomas weighed heavily and more heavily on the march of the expedition, the lost travellers followed the windings of the stream, till they came to a faintly marked cart-track, branching off nearly at right angles, to the left. After a little consultation it was resolved to follow this dim vestige of a road in the hope that it might lead to some farm or cottage, at which Idle could be left in safety. It was now getting on towards the afternoon, and it was fast becoming more than doubtful whether the party, delayed in their progress as they now were, might not be overtaken by the darkness before the right route was found, and be condemned to pass the night on the mountain, without bit or drop to comfort them, in their wet clothes.

The cart-track grew fainter and fainter, until it was washed out altogether by another little stream, dark, turbulent, and rapid. The landlord suggested, judging by the colour of the water, that it must be flowing from one of the lead mines in the neighbourhood of Carrock; and the travellers accordingly kept by the stream for a little while, in the hope of possibly wandering towards help in that way. After walking forward about two hundred yards, they came upon a mine indeed, but a mine, exhausted and abandoned; a dismal, ruinous place, with nothing but the wreck of its works and buildings left to speak for it. Here, there were a few sheep feeding. The landlord looked at them earnestly, thought he recognized the marks on them—then thought he did not— finally gave up the sheep in despair—and walked on just as ignorant of the whereabouts of the party as ever.

The march in the dark, literally as well as metaphorically in the dark, had now been continued for three-quarters of an hour from the time when the crippled Apprentice had met with his accident. Mr Idle, with all the will to conquer the pain in his ankle, and to hobble on, found the power rapidly failing him, and felt that another ten minutes at most would find him at the end of his last physical resources. He had just made up his mind on this point, and was about to communicate the dismal result of his reflections to his companions, when the mist suddenly brightened, and begun to lift straight ahead. In another minute, the landlord, who was in advance, proclaimed that he saw a tree. Before long, other trees appeared—then a cottage—then a house beyond the cottage, and a familiar line of road rising behind it. Last of all, Carrock itself loomed darkly into view, far away to the right hand. The party had not only got down the mountain without knowing how, but had wandered away from it in the mist, without knowing why—away, far down on the very moor by which they had approached the base of Carrock that morning.

The happy lifting of the mist, and the still happier discovery that the travellers had groped their way, though by a very roundabout direction, to within a mile or so of the part of the valley in which the farmhouse was situated, restored Mr Idle's sinking spirits and reanimated his failing strength. While the landlord ran off to get the dog-cart, Thomas was assisted by Goodchild to the cottage which had been the first building seen when the darkness brightened, and was propped up against the garden wall, like an artist's lay figure waiting to be forwarded, until the dog-cart should arrive from the farmhouse below. In due time—and a very long time it seemed to Mr Idle—the rattle of wheels was heard, and the crippled Apprentice was lifted into the seat. As the dog-cart was driven back to the inn, the landlord related an anecdote which he had just heard at the farmhouse, of an unhappy man who had been lost, like his two guests and himself, on Carrock; who had passed the night there alone; who had been found the next morning, 'scared and starved'; and who never went out afterwards, except on his way to the grave. Mr Idle heard this sad story, and derived at least one useful impression from it. Bad as the pain in his ankle was, he contrived to bear it patiently, for he felt grateful that a worse accident had not befallen him in the wilds of Carrock.

ANTHONY TROLLOPE

A Ride Across Palestine

Circumstances took me to the Holy Land without a companion, and compelled me to visit Bethany, the Mount of Olives, and the Church of the Sepulchre alone. I acknowledge myself to be a gregarious animal, or, perhaps, rather one of those which Nature has intended to go in pairs. At any rate I dislike solitude, and especially travelling solitude, and was, therefore, rather sad at heart as I sat one night at Z——'s hotel, in Jerusalem, thinking over my proposed wanderings for the next few days. Early on the following morning I intended to start, of course on horseback, for the Dead Sea, the banks of Jordan, Jericho, and those mountains of the wilderness through which it is supposed that Our Saviour wandered for the forty days when the Devil tempted him. I would then return to the Holy City, and remaining only long enough to refresh my horse and wipe the dust from my hands and feet, I would start again for Jaffa, and there catch a certain Austrian steamer which would take me to Egypt. Such was my programme, and I confess that I was but ill contented with it, seeing that I was to be alone during the time.

I had already made all my arrangements, and though I had no reason for any doubt as to my personal security during the trip, I did not feel altogether satisfied with them. I intended to take a French guide, or dragoman, who had been with me for some days, and to put myself under the peculiar guardianship of two Bedouin Arabs, who were to accompany me as long as I should remain east of Jerusalem. This travelling through the desert under the protection of Bedouins was, in idea, pleasant enough; and I must here declare that I did not at all begrudge the forty shillings which I was told by our British consul that I must pay them for their trouble, in accordance with the established tariff. But I did begrudge the fact of the tariff. I would rather have fallen in with my friendly Arabs, as it were, by chance, and have rewarded their fidelity at the end of our joint journeyings by a donation of piastres to be settled by myself, and which, under such circumstances, would certainly have been as agreeable to them as the stipulated sum. In the same way I dislike having waiters put down in my bill. I find that I pay them twice over, and thus lose money; and as they do not expect to be so treated, I never have the advantage of their civility. The world, I fear, is becoming too fond of tariffs.

'A tariff!' said I to the consul, feeling that the whole romance of my expedition would be dissipated by such an arrangement. 'Then I'll go alone; I'll take a revolver with me.'

'You can't do it, sir,' said the consul, in a dry and somewhat angry tone. 'You have no more right to ride through that country without paying the regular price for protection, than you have to stop in Z——'s hotel without settling the bill.'

I could not contest the point, so I ordered my Bedouins for the appointed day, exactly as I would send for a ticket-porter at home, and determined to make the best of it. The wild unlimited sands, the desolation of the Dead Sea, the rushing waters of Jordan, the outlines of the mountains of Moab—those things the consular tariff could not alter, nor deprive them of the glories of their association.

I had submitted, and the arrangements had been made. Joseph, my dragoman, was to come to me with the horses and an Arab groom at five in the morning, and we were to encounter our Bedouins outside the gate of St Stephen, down the hill, where the road turns, close to the tomb of the Virgin.

I was sitting alone in the public room at the hotel, filling my flask with brandy—for matters of primary importance I never leave to servant, dragoman, or guide—when the waiter entered, and said that a gentleman wished to speak with me. The gentleman had not sent in his card or name; but any gentleman was welcome to me in my solitude, and I requested that the gentleman might enter. In appearance the gentleman certainly was a gentleman, for I thought that I had never before seen a young man whose looks were more in his favour, or whose face and gait and outward bearing seemed to betoken better breeding. He might be some twenty or twenty-one years of age, was slight and well made, with very black hair, which he wore rather long, very dark long bright eyes, a straight nose, and teeth that were perfectly white. He was dressed throughout in grey tweed clothing, having coat, waistcoat, and trousers of the same; and in his hand he carried a very broad-brimmed straw hat.

'Mr Jones, I believe,' he said, as he bowed to me. Jones is a good travelling name, and, if the reader will allow me, I will call myself Jones on the present occasion.

'Yes,' I said, pausing with the brandy-bottle in one hand and the flask in the other. 'That's my name; I'm Jones. Can I do anything for you, sir?'

'Why, yes, you can,' said he. 'My name is Smith—John Smith.'

'Pray sit down, Mr Smith,' I said, pointing to a chair. 'Will you do anything in this way?' and I proposed to hand the bottle to him. 'As far as I can judge from a short stay, you won't find much like that in Jerusalem.'

He declined the Cognac, however, and immediately began his story. 'I hear, Mr Jones,' said he, 'that you are going to Moab tomorrow.'

'Well,' I replied; 'I don't know whether I shall cross the water. It's not very easy, I take it, at all times; but I shall certainly get as far as Jordan. Can I do anything for you in those parts?'

And then he explained to me what was the object of his visit. He was quite alone in Jerusalem, as I was myself, and was staying at H——'s hotel. He had heard that I was starting for the Dead Sea, and had called to ask if I objected to his joining me. He had found himself, he said, very lonely; and as he had heard that I also was alone, he had ventured to call and make his proposition. He seemed to be very bashful, and half ashamed of what he was doing; and when he had done speaking he declared himself conscious that he was intruding, and expressed a hope that I would not hesitate to say so if his suggestion were from any cause disagreeable to me.

As a rule I am rather shy of chance travelling English friends. It has so frequently happened to me that I have had to blush for the acquaintances whom I have selected, that I seldom indulge in any close intimacies of this kind. But, nevertheless, I was taken with John Smith, in spite of his name. There was so much about him that was pleasant, both to the eye and to the understanding! One meets constantly with men from contact with whom one revolts without knowing the cause of such dislike. The cut of their beard is displeasing, or the mode in which they walk or speak. But, on the other hand, there are men who are attractive, and I must confess that I was attracted by John Smith at first sight. I hesitated, however, for a minute; for there are sundry things of which it behoves a traveller to think before he can join a companion for such a journey as that which I was about to make. Could the young man rise early, and remain in the saddle for ten hours together? Could he live upon hard-boiled eggs and brandy-

and-water? Could he take his chance of a tent under which to sleep, and make himself happy with the bare fact of being in the desert? He saw my hesitation, and attributed it to a cause which was not present in my mind at the moment, though the subject is one of the greatest importance when strangers consent to join themselves together for a time, and agree to become no strangers on the spur of the moment.

'Of course I will take half the expense,' said he, absolutely blushing as he mentioned the matter.

'As to that there will be very little. You have your own horse, of course?'

'Oh, yes.'

'My dragoman and groom-boy will do for both. But you'll have to pay forty shillings to the Arabs! There's no getting over that. The consul won't even look after your dead body, if you get murdered, without going through that ceremony.'

Mr Smith immediately produced his purse, which he tendered to me. 'If you will manage it all,' said he, 'it will make it so much the easier, and I shall be infinitely obliged to you.' This of course I declined to do. I had no business with his purse, and explained to him that if we went together we could settle that on our return to Jerusalem. 'But could he go through really hard work?' I asked. He answered me with an assurance that he would and could do anything in that way that it was possible for man to perform. As for eating and drinking he cared nothing about it, and would undertake to be astir at any hour of the morning that might be named. As for sleeping accommodation, he did not care if he kept his clothes on for a week together. He looked slight and weak; but he spoke so well, and that without boasting, that I ultimately agreed to his proposal, and in a few minutes he took his leave of me, promising to be at Z——'s door with his horse at five o'clock on the following morning.

'I wish you'd allow me to leave my purse with you,' he said again.

'I cannot think of it. There is no possible occasion for it,' I said again. 'If there is anything to pay, I'll ask you for it when the journey is over. That forty shillings you must fork out. It's a law of the Medes and Persians.'

'I'd better give it to you at once,' he said, again offering me money. But I would not have it. It would be quite time enough for that when the Arabs were leaving us.

'Because,' he added, 'strangers, I know, are sometimes suspicious about money; and I would not, for worlds, have you think that I

would put you to expense.' I assured him that I did not think so, and
then the subject was dropped.

He was, at any rate, up to his time, for when I came down on the
following morning I found him in the narrow street, the first on
horseback. Joseph, the Frenchman, was strapping on to a rough pony
our belongings, and was staring at Mr Smith. My new friend,
unfortunately, could not speak a word of French, and therefore I had
to explain to the dragoman how it had come to pass that our party
was to be enlarged.

'But the Bedouins will expect full pay for both,' said he, alarmed.
Men in that class, and especially Orientals, always think that every
arrangement of life, let it be made in what way it will, is made with
the intention of saving some expense, or cheating somebody out of
some amount of money. They do not understand that men can have
any other object, and are ever on their guard lest the saving should be
made at their cost, or lest they should be the victims of the fraud.

'All right,' said I.

'I shall be responsible, Monsieur,' said the dragoman, piteously.

'It shall be all right,' said I, again. 'If that does not satisfy you, you
may remain behind.'

'If Monsieur says it is all right, of course it is so'; and then he
completed his strapping. We took blankets with us, of which I had to
borrow two out of the hotel for my friend Smith, a small hamper of
provisions, a sack containing forage for the horses, and a large empty
jar, so that we might supply ourselves with water when leaving the
neighbourhood of wells for any considerable time.

'I ought to have brought these things for myself,' said Smith, quite
unhappy at finding that he had thrown on me the necessity of catering
for him. But I laughed at him, saying that it was nothing; he should
do as much for me another time. I am prepared to own that I do not
willingly rush upstairs and load myself with blankets out of strange
rooms for men whom I do not know; nor, as a rule, do I make all the
Smiths of the world free of my canteen. But, with reference to this
fellow I did feel more than ordinarily good-natured and unselfish. There
was something in the tone of his voice which was satisfactory; and I
should really have felt vexed had anything occurred at the last moment
to prevent his going with me.

Let it be a rule with every man to carry an English saddle with him
when travelling in the East. Of what material is formed the nether
man of a Turk I have never been informed, but I am sure that it is not

flesh and blood. No flesh and blood—simply flesh and blood—could withstand the wear and tear of a Turkish saddle. This being the case, and the consequences being well known to me, I was grieved to find that Smith was not properly provided. He was seated in one of those hard, red, high-pointed machines, to which the shovels intended to act as stirrups are attached in such a manner, and hang at such an angle, as to be absolutely destructive to the leg of a Christian. There is no part of the Christian body with which the Turkish saddle comes in contact that does not become more or less macerated. I have sat in one for days, but I left it a flayed man; and, therefore, I was sorry for Smith.

I explained this to him, taking hold of his leg by the calf to show how the leather would chafe him; but it seemed to me that he did not quite like my interference. 'Never mind,' said he, twitching his leg away, 'I have ridden in this way before.'

'Then you must have suffered the very mischief?'

'Only a little, and I shall be used to it now. You will not hear me complain.'

'By heavens, you might have heard me complain a mile off when I came to the end of a journey I once took. I roared like a bull when I began to cool. Joseph, could you not get a European saddle for Mr Smith?' But Joseph did not seem to like Mr Smith, and declared such a thing to be impossible. No European in Jerusalem would think of lending so precious an article, except to a very dear friend. Joseph himself was on an English saddle, and I made up my mind that after the first stage, we would bribe him to make an exchange. And then we started. The Bedouins were not with us, but we were to meet them, as I have said before, outside St Stephen's gate. 'And if they are not there,' said Joseph, 'we shall be sure to come across them on the road.'

'Not there!' said I. 'How about the consul's tariff, if they don't keep their part of the engagement?' But Joseph explained to me that their part of the engagement really amounted to this—that we should ride into their country without molestation, provided that such and such payments were made.

It was the period of Easter, and Jerusalem was full of pilgrims. Even at that early hour of the morning we could hardly make our way through the narrow streets. It must be understood that there is no accommodation in the town for the fourteen or fifteen thousand strangers who flock to the Holy Sepulchre at this period of the year. Many of them sleep out in the open air, lying on low benches which run along the outside walls of the houses, or even on the ground, wrapped in their thick hoods and cloaks. Slumberers such as these are easily disturbed, nor are they detained long at their toilets. They shake themselves like dogs, and growl and stretch themselves, and then they are ready for the day.

We rode out of the town in a long file. First went the groom-boy; I forget his proper Syrian appellation, but we used to call him Mucherry, that sound being in some sort like the name. Then followed the horse with the forage and blankets, and next to him my friend Smith in the Turkish saddle. I was behind him and Joseph brought up the rear. We moved slowly down the Via Dolorosa, noting the spot at which our Saviour is said to have fallen while bearing his cross; we passed by Pilate's house, and paused at the gate of the Temple—the gate which once was beautiful—looking down into the hole of the pool in which the maimed and halt were healed whenever the waters moved. What names they are! And yet there at Jerusalem they are bandied to and fro with as little reverence as are the fanciful appellations given by guides to rocks and stones and little lakes in all countries overrun by tourists.

'For those who would still fain believe—let them stay at home,' said my friend Smith.

'For those who cannot divide the wheat from the chaff, let *them* stay at home,' I answered. And then we rode out through St Stephen's gate, having the mountain of the men of Galilee directly before us, and the Mount of Olives a little to our right, and the Valley of Jehoshaphat lying between us and it. 'Of course you know all these places now?' said Smith. I answered that I did know them well. 'And was it not better for you when you knew them only in Holy Writ?' he asked.

'No, by Jove,' said I. 'The mountains stand where they ever stood. The same valleys are still green with the morning dew, and the watercourses are unchanged. The children of Mahomet may build their tawdry temple on the threshing-floor which David bought that there might stand the Lord's house. Man may undo what man did, even though the doer was Solomon. But here we have God's handiwork and his own evidences.'

At the bottom of the steep descent from the city gate we came to the tomb of the Virgin; and by special agreement made with Joseph we left our horses here for a few moments, in order that we might descend into the subterranean chapel under the tomb, in which mass was at this moment being said. There is something awful in that chapel, when, as at the present moment, it is crowded with Eastern worshippers from the very altar up to the top of the dark steps by which the descent is made. It must be remembered that Eastern worshippers are not like the churchgoers of London, or even of Rome or Cologne. They are wild men of various nations and races—Maronites from Lebanon, Roumelians, Candiotes, Copts from Upper Egypt, Russians from the Crimea, Armenians and Abyssinians. They savour strongly of Oriental life and of Oriental dirt. They are clad in skins or hairy cloaks with huge hoods. Their heads are shaved, and their faces covered with short, grisly, fierce beards. They are silent mostly, looking out of their eyes ferociously, as though murder were in their thoughts, and rapine. But they never slouch, or cringe in their bodies, or shuffle in their gait. Dirty, fierce-looking, uncouth, repellent as they are, there is always about them a something of personal dignity which is not compatible with an Englishman's ordinary hat and pantaloons.

As we were about to descend, preparing to make our way through the crowd, Smith took hold of my arm. 'That will never do, my dear fellow,' said I, 'the job will be tough enough for a single file, but we should never cut our way two and two. I'm broad-shouldered and will go first.' So I did, and gradually we worked our way into the body of the chapel. How is it that Englishmen can push themselves anywhere? These men were fierce-looking, and had murder and rapine, as I have said, almost in their eyes. One would have supposed that they were not lambs or doves, capable of being thrust here or there without anger on their part; and they, too, were all anxious to descend and approach the altar. Yet we did win our way through them, and apparently no man was angry with us. I doubt, after all, whether a ferocious eye and a strong smell and dirt are so efficacious in creating awe and obedience in others, as an open brow and traces of soap and water. I know this, at least—that a dirty Maronite would make very little progress, if he attempted to shove his way unfairly through a crowd of Englishmen at the door of a London theatre. We did shove unfairly, and we did make progress, till we found ourselves in the centre of the dense crowd collected in the body of the chapel.

Having got so far, our next object was to get out again. The place was dark, mysterious, and full of strange odours; but darkness, mystery, and strange odours soon lose their charms when men have much work before them. Joseph had made a point of being allowed to attend mass before the altar of the Virgin, but a very few minutes sufficed for his prayers. So we again turned round and pushed our way back again, Smith still following in my wake. The men who had let us pass once let us pass again without opposition or show of anger. To them the occasion was very holy. They were stretching out their hands in every direction, with long tapers, in order that they might obtain a spark of the sacred fire which was burning on one of the altars. As we made our way out we passed many who, with dumb motions, begged us to assist them in their object. And we did assist them, getting lights for their tapers, handing them to and fro, and using the authority with which we seemed to be invested. But Smith, I observed, was much more courteous in this way to the women than to the men, as I did not forget to remind him when we were afterwards on our road together.

Remounting our horses we rode slowly up the winding ascent of the Mount of Olives, turning round at the brow of the hill to look back over Jerusalem. Sometimes I think that of all spots in the world this one should be the spot most cherished in the memory of Christians. It was there that He stood when He wept over the city. So much we do know, though we are ignorant, and ever shall be so, of the site of His cross and of the tomb. And then we descended on the eastern side of the hill, passing through Bethany, the town of Lazarus and his sisters, and turned our faces steadily towards the mountains of Moab.

Hitherto we had met no Bedouins, and I interrogated my dragoman about them more than once; but he always told me that it did not signify; we should meet them, he said, before any danger could arise. 'As for danger,' said I, 'I think more of this than I do of the Arabs,' and I put my hand on my revolver. 'But as they agreed to be here, here they ought to be. Don't you carry a revolver, Smith?'

Smith said that he never had done so, but that he would take the charge of mine if I liked. To this, however, I demurred. 'I never part with my pistol to any one,' I said, rather drily. But he explained that he only intended to signify that if there were danger to be encountered, he would be glad to encounter it; and I fully believed him. 'We shan't have much fighting,' I replied; 'but if there be any, the tool will come readiest to the hand of its master. But if you mean to remain here long I would advise you to get one. These Orientals are a people with whom appearances go a long way, and, as a rule, fear and respect mean the same thing with them. A pistol hanging over your loins is no great trouble to you, and looks as though you could bite. Many a dog goes through the world well by merely showing his teeth.'

And then my companion began to talk of himself. 'He did not,' he said, 'mean to remain in Syria very long.'

'Nor I either,' said I. 'I have done with this part of the world for the present, and shall take the next steamer from Jaffa for Alexandria. I shall only have one night in Jerusalem on my return.'

After this he remained silent for a few moments, and then declared that that also had been his intention. He was almost ashamed to say so, however, because it looked as though he had resolved to hook himself on to me. So he answered, expressing almost regret at the circumstance.

'Don't let that trouble you,' said I; 'I shall be delighted to have your company. When you know me better, as I hope you will do, you will find that if such were not the case I should tell you so as frankly. I shall remain in Cairo some little time; so that beyond our arrival in Egypt, I can answer for nothing.'

He said that he expected letters at Alexandria which would govern his future movements. I thought he seemed sad as he said so, and imagined, from his manner, that he did not expect very happy tidings. Indeed I had made up my mind that he was by no means free from care or sorrow. He had not the air of a man who could say of himself that he was 'totus teres atque rotundus'. But I had no wish to enquire, and the matter would have dropped had he not himself added—'I fear that I shall meet acquaintances in Egypt whom it will give me no pleasure to see.'

'Then,' said I, 'if I were you, I would go to Constantinople instead—indeed, anywhere rather than fall among friends who are not friendly. And the nearer the friend is, the more one feels that sort of thing. To my way of thinking, there is nothing on earth so pleasant as a pleasant wife; but then, what is there so damnable as one that is unpleasant?'

'Are you a married man?' he enquired. All his questions were put in a low tone of voice which seemed to give to them an air of special interest, and made one almost feel that they were asked with some special view to one's individual welfare. Now the fact is, that I am a married man with a family; but I am not much given to talk to strangers about my domestic concerns, and, therefore, though I had no particular object in view, I denied my obligations in this respect. 'No,' said I; 'I have not come to that promotion yet. I am too frequently on the move to write myself down as Paterfamilias.'

'Then you know nothing about that pleasantness of which you spoke just now?'

'Nor of the unpleasantness, thank God; my personal experiences are all to come—as also are yours, I presume?'

It was possible that he had hampered himself with some woman, and that she was to meet him at Alexandria. Poor fellow! thought I. But his unhappiness was not of that kind. 'No,' said he; 'I am not married; I am all alone in the world.'

'Then I certainly would not allow myself to be troubled by unpleasant acquaintances.'

It was now four hours since we had left Jerusalem, and we had arrived at the place at which it was proposed that we should breakfast. There was a large well there, and shade afforded by a rock under which the water sprung; and the Arabs had constructed a tank out of which the horses could drink, so that the place was ordinarily known as the first stage out of Jerusalem.

Smith had said not a word about his saddle, or complained in any way of discomfort, so that I had in truth forgotten the subject. Other matters had continually presented themselves, and I had never even asked him how he had fared. I now jumped from my horse, but I perceived at once that he was unable to do so. He smiled faintly, as his eye caught mine, but I knew that he wanted assistance. 'Ah,' said I, 'that confounded Turkish saddle has already galled your skin. I see how it is; I shall have to doctor you with a little brandy—externally applied, my friend.' But I lent him my shoulder, and with that assistance he got down, very gently and slowly.

We ate our breakfast with a good will; bread and cold fowl and brandy-and-water, with a hard boiled egg by way of a final delicacy; and then I began to bargain with Joseph for the loan of his English saddle. I saw that Smith could not get through the journey with that monstrous Turkish affair, and that he would go on without complaining till he fainted or came to some other signal grief. But the Frenchman, seeing the plight in which we were, was disposed to drive a very hard bargain. He wanted forty shillings, the price of a pair of live Bedouins, for the accommodation, and declared that, even then, he should make the sacrifice only out of consideration to me.

'Very well,' said I. 'I'm tolerably tough myself, and I'll change with the gentleman. The chances are, that I shall not be in a very liberal humour when I reach Jaffa with stiff limbs and a sore skin. I have a very good memory, Joseph.'

'I'll take thirty shillings, Mr Jones; though I shall have to groan all the way like a condemned devil.'

I struck a bargain with him at last for five-and-twenty, and set him to work to make the necessary change on the horses. 'It will be just the same thing to him,' I said to Smith. 'I find that he is as much used to one as to the other.'

'But how much money are you to pay him?' he asked. 'Oh, nothing,' I replied. 'Give him a few piastres when you part with him at Jaffa.' I do not know why I should have felt thus inclined to pay money out of my pocket for this Smith—a man whom I had only seen for the first time on the preceding evening, and whose temperament was so essentially different from my own; but so I did. I would have done almost anything in reason for his comfort; and yet he was a melancholy fellow, with good inward pluck as I believed, but without that outward show of dash and hardihood which I confess I love to see. 'Pray tell him that I'll pay him for it,' said he. 'We'll make that all right,' I answered; and then we remounted—not without some difficulty on his part. 'You should have let me rub in that brandy,' I said. 'You can't conceive how efficaciously I would have done it.' But he made me no answer.

At noon we met a caravan of pilgrims coming up from Jordan. There might be some three or four hundred, but the number seemed to be treble that, from the loose and straggling line in which they journeyed. It was a very singular sight, as they moved slowly along the narrow path through the sand, coming out of a defile among the hills which was perhaps a quarter of a mile in front of us, passing us as we stood still by the wayside, and then winding again out of sight on the track over which we had come. Some rode on camels—a whole family, in many cases, being perched on the same animal. I observed a very old man and a very old woman slung in panniers over a camel's back—not such panniers as might be befitting such a purpose, but square baskets, so that the heads and heels of each of the old couple hung out of the rear and front. 'Surely the journey will be their death,' I said to Joseph. 'Yes, it will,' he replied, quite coolly; 'but what matter how soon they die now that they have bathed in Jordan?' Very many rode on donkeys; two, generally, on each donkey; others, who had command of money, on horses; but the greater number walked, toiling painfully from Jerusalem to Jericho on the first day, sleeping there in tents and going to bathe in Jordan on the second day, and then returning from Jericho to Jerusalem on the third. The pilgrimage is made throughout in accordance with fixed rules, and there is a tariff for the tent accommodation at Jericho—so much per head per night, including the use of hot water.

Standing there, close by the wayside, we could see not only the garments and faces of these strange people, but we could watch their gestures and form some opinion of what was going on within their thoughts. They were much quieter—tamer, as it were—than English-men would be under such circumstances. Those who were carried seemed to sit on their beasts in passive tranquillity, neither enjoying anything nor suffering anything. Their object had been to wash in Jordan—to do that once in their lives; and they had washed in Jordan. The benefit expected was not to be immediately spiritual. No earn-est prayerfulness was considered necessary after the ceremony. To these members of the Greek Christian Church it had been handed down from father to son that washing in Jordan once during life was efficacious towards salvation. And therefore the journey had been made at terrible cost and terrible risk; for these people had come from afar, and were from their habits but little capable of long journeys. Many die under the toil; but this matters not if they do not die before they have reached Jordan. Some few there are, undoubtedly, more ecstatic in this great deed of their religion. One man I especially noticed on this day. He had bound himself to make the pilgrimage from Jerusalem to the river with one foot bare. He was of a better class, and was even nobly dressed, as though it were a part of his vow to show to all men that he did this deed, wealthy and great though he was. He was a fine man, perhaps thirty years of age, with a well-grown beard descending on his breast, and at his girdle he carried a brace of pistols. But never in my life had I seen bodily pain so plainly written in a man's face. The sweat was falling from his brow, and his eyes were strained and bloodshot with agony. He had no stick, his vow, I presume, debarring him from such assistance, and he limped along, putting to the ground the heel of the unprotected foot. I could see it, and it was a mass of blood, and sores, and broken skin. An Irish girl would walk from Jerusalem to Jericho without shoes, and be not a penny the worse for it. This poor fellow clearly suffered so much that I was almost inclined to think that in the performance of his penance he had done something to aggravate his pain. Those around him paid no attention to him, and the dragoman seemed to think nothing of the affair whatever. 'Those fools of Greeks do not understand the Christian religion,' he said, being himself a Latin or Roman Catholic.

At the tail of the line we encountered two Bedouins, who were in charge of the caravan, and Joseph at once addressed them. The men were mounted, one on a very sorry-looking jade, but the other on a good stout Arab barb. They had guns slung behind their backs, coloured handkerchiefs on their heads, and they wore the striped burnous. The parley went on for about ten minutes, during which the procession of pilgrims wound out of sight; and it ended in our being accompanied by the two Arabs, who thus left their greater charge to take care of itself back to the city. I understood afterwards that they had endeavoured to persuade Joseph that we might just as well go on alone, merely satisfying the demand of the tariff. But he had pointed out that I was a particular man, and that under such circumstances the final settlement might be doubtful. So they turned and accompanied us; but, as a matter of fact, we should have been as well without them.

The sun was beginning to fall in the heavens when we reached the actual margin of the Dead Sea. We had seen the glitter of its still waters for a long time previously, shining under the sun as though it were not real. We have often heard, and some of us have seen, how effects of light and shade together will produce so vivid an appearance of water where there is no water, as to deceive the most experienced. But the reverse was the case here. There was the lake, and there it had been before our eyes for the last two hours; and yet it looked, then and now, as though it were an image of a lake, and not real water. I had long since made up my mind to bathe in it, feeling well convinced that I could do so without harm to myself, and I had been endeavouring to persuade Smith to accompany me; but he positively refused. He would bathe, he said, neither in the Dead Sea nor in the river Jordan. He did not like bathing, and preferred to do his washing in his own room. Of course I had nothing further to say, and begged that, under these circumstances, he would take charge of my purse and pistols while I was in the water. This he agreed to do; but even in this he was strange and almost uncivil. I was to bathe from the furthest point of a little island, into which there was a rough causeway from the land made of stones and broken pieces of wood, and I exhorted him to go with me thither; but he insisted on remaining with his horse on the mainland at some little distance from the island. He did not feel inclined to go down to the water's edge, he said.

I confess that at this I almost suspected that he was going to play me foul, and I hesitated. He saw in an instant what was passing through my mind. 'You had better take your pistol and money with you; they will be quite safe on your clothes.' But to have kept the things now would have shown suspicion too plainly, and as I could not bring myself to do that, I gave them up. I have sometimes thought that I was a fool to do so.

I went away by myself to the end of the island, and then I did bathe.

It is impossible to conceive anything more desolate than the appearance of the place. The land shelves very gradually away to the water, and the whole margin, to the breadth of some twenty or thirty feet, is strewn with the debris of rushes, bits of timber, and old white withered reeds. Whence these bits of timber have come it seems difficult to say. The appearance is as though the water had receded and left them there. I have heard it said that there is no vegetation near the Dead Sea; but such is not the case, for these rushes do grow on the bank. I found it difficult enough to get into the water, for the ground shelves down very slowly, and is rough with stones and large pieces of half-rotten wood; moreover, when I was in nearly up to my hips, the water knocked me down; indeed, it did so when I had gone as far as my knees, but I recovered myself, and by perseverance did proceed somewhat further. It must not be imagined that this knocking down was effected by the movement of the water. There is no such movement. Everything is perfectly still, and the fluid seems hardly to be displaced by the entrance of the body; but the effect is that one's feet are tripped up, and that one falls prostrate on to the surface. The water is so strong and buoyant, that, when above a foot in depth has to be encountered, the strength and weight of the bather are not sufficient to keep down his feet and legs. I then essayed to swim; but I could not do this in the ordinary way, as I was unable to keep enough of my body below the surface; so that my head and face seemed to be propelled down upon it. I turned round and floated, but the glare of the sun was so powerful that I could not remain long in that position. However, I had bathed in the Dead Sea, and was so far satisfied.

Anything more abominable to the palate than this water, if it be water, I never had inside my mouth. I expected it to be extremely salt, and no doubt, if it were analysed, such would be the result; but there is a flavour in it which kills the salt. No attempt can be made at describing this taste. It may be imagined that I did not drink heartily, merely taking up a drop or two with my tongue from the palm of my hand; but it seemed to me as though I had been drenched with it. Even brandy would not relieve me from it. And then my whole body was in a mess, and I felt as though I had been rubbed with pitch. Looking at my limbs, I saw no sign on them of the fluid. They seemed to dry from this as they usually do from any other water; but still the feeling remained. However, I was to ride from hence to a spot on the banks of Jordan, which I should reach in an hour, and at which I would wash; so I clothed myself, and prepared for my departure.

Seated in my position in the island I was unable to see what was going on among the remainder of the party, and therefore could not tell whether my pistols and money were safe. I dressed, therefore, rather hurriedly, and on getting again to the shore, found that Mr John Smith had not levanted. He was seated on his horse at some distance from Joseph and the Arabs, and had no appearance of being in league with those, no doubt, worthy guides. I certainly had suspected a ruse, and now was angry with myself that I had done so; and yet, in London, one would not trust one's money to a stranger whom one had met twenty-four hours since in a coffee-room! Why, then, do it with a stranger whom one chanced to meet in a desert?

'Thanks,' I said, as he handed me my belongings. 'I wish I could have induced you to come in also. The Dead Sea is now at your elbow, and, therefore, you think nothing of it; but in ten or fifteen years' time, you would be glad to be able to tell your children that you had bathed in it.'

'I shall never have any children to care for such tidings,' he replied.

The river Jordan, for some miles above the point at which it joins the Dead Sea, runs through very steep banks—banks which are almost precipitous—and is, as it were, guarded by the thick trees and bushes which grow upon its sides. This is so much the case, that one may ride, as we did, for a considerable distance along the margin, and not be able even to approach the water. I had a fancy for bathing in some spot of my own selection, instead of going to the open shore frequented by all the pilgrims; but I was baffled in this. When I did force my way down to the river side, I found that the water ran so rapidly, and that the bushes and boughs of trees grew so far over and into the stream, as to make it impossible for me to bathe. I could not have got in without my clothes, and having got in, I could not have got out again. I was, therefore, obliged to put up with the open muddy shore to which the bathers descend, and at which we may presume that Joshua passed when he came over as one of the twelve spies to spy out the land. And even here I could not go full into the stream as I would fain have done, lest I should be carried down, and so have assisted to whiten the shores of the Dead Sea with my bones. As to getting over to the Moabitish side of the river, that was plainly impossible; and, indeed, it seemed to be the prevailing opinion that the passage of the river was not practicable without going up as far as Samaria. And yet we know that there, or thereabouts, the Israelites did cross it.

I jumped from my horse the moment I got to the place, and once more gave my purse and pistols to my friend. 'You are going to bathe again?' he said. 'Certainly,' said I; 'you don't suppose that I would come to Jordan and not wash there, even if I were not foul with the foulness of the Dead Sea!' 'You'll kill yourself, in your present state of heat;' he said, remonstrating just as one's mother or wife might do. But even had it been my mother or wife I could not have attended to such remonstrance then; and before he had done looking at me with those big eyes of his, my coat and waistcoat and cravat were on the ground, and I was at work at my braces; whereupon he turned from me slowly, and strolled away into the wood. On this occasion I had no base fears about my money.

And then I did bathe—very uncomfortably. The shore was muddy with the feet of the pilgrims, and the river so rapid that I hardly dared to get beyond the mud. I did manage to take a plunge in, head foremost, but I was forced to wade out through the dirt and slush, so that I found it difficult to make my feet and legs clean enough for my shoes and stockings; and then, moreover, the flies plagued me most unmercifully. I should have thought that the filthy flavour from the Dead Sea would have saved me from that nuisance; but the mosquitoes thereabouts are probably used to it. Finding this process of bathing to be so difficult, I enquired as to the practice of the pilgrims. I found that with them, bathing in Jordan has come to be much the same as baptism has with us. It does not mean immersion. No doubt they do take off their shoes and stockings; but they do not strip, and go bodily into the water.

As soon as I was dressed I found that Smith was again at my side with purse and pistols. We then went up a little above the wood, and sat down together on the long sandy grass. It was now quite evening, so that the short Syrian twilight had commenced, and the sun was no longer hot in the heavens. It would be night as we rode on to the tents at Jericho; but there was no difficulty as to the way, and therefore we did not hurry the horses, who were feeding on the grass. We sat down together on a spot from which we could see the stream—close together, so that when I stretched myself out in my weariness, as I did before we started, my head rested on his legs. Ah, me! one does not take such liberties with new friends in England. It was a place which led one on to some special thoughts. The mountains of Moab were before us, very plain in their outline. 'Moab is my wash-pot, and over Edom will I cast out my shoe!' There they were before us, very visible to the eye, and we began naturally to ask questions of each other. Why was Moab the wash-pot, and Edom thus cursed with indignity? Why had the right bank of the river been selected for such great purposes, whereas the left was thus condemned? Was there, at that time, any special fertility in this land of promise which has since departed from it? We are told of a bunch of grapes which took two men to carry it; but now there is not a vine in the whole countryside. Nowadays the sandy plain round Jericho is as dry and arid as are any of the valleys of Moab. The Jordan was running beneath our feet—the Jordan in which the leprous king had washed, though the bright rivers of his own Damascus were so much nearer to his hand. It was but a humble stream to which he was sent; but the spot, probably, was higher up, above the Sea of Galilee, where the river is narrow. But another also had come down to this river, perhaps to this very spot on its shores, and submitted himself to its waters; as to whom, perhaps, it will be better that I should not speak much in this light story.

The Dead Sea was on our right, still glittering in the distance, and behind us lay the plains of Jericho and the wretched collection of huts which still bears the name of the ancient city. Beyond that, but still seemingly within easy distance of us, were the mountains of the wilderness. The wilderness! In truth, the spot was one which did lead to many thoughts.

We talked of these things, as to many of which I found that my friend was much more free in his doubts and questionings than myself; and then our words came back to ourselves, the natural centre of all men's thoughts and words. 'From what you say,' I said, 'I gather that you have had enough of this land?'

'Quite enough,' he said. 'Why seek such spots as these, if they only dispel the associations and veneration of one's childhood?'

'But with me such associations and veneration are riveted the stronger by seeing the places, and putting my hand upon the spots. I do not speak of that fictitious marble slab up there; but here, among the sandhills by this river, and at the Mount of Olives over which we passed, I do believe.'

He paused a moment, and then replied: 'To me it is all nothing—absolutely nothing. But then do we not know that our thoughts are formed, and our beliefs modelled, not on the outward signs or intrinsic evidences of things—as would be the case were we always rational—but by the inner workings of the mind itself? At the present turn of my life I can believe in nothing that is gracious.'

'Ah, you mean that you are unhappy. You have come to grief in some of your doings or belongings, and therefore find that all things are bitter to the taste. I have had my palate out of order too; but the proper appreciation of flavours has come back to me. Bah—how noisome was that Dead Sea water!'

'The Dead Sea waters are noisome,' he said; 'and I have been drinking of them by long draughts.'

'Long draughts!' I answered, thinking to console him. 'Draughts have not been long which can have been swallowed in your years. Your disease may be acute, but it cannot yet have become chronic. A man always thinks at the moment of each misfortune that that special misery will last his lifetime; but God is too good for that. I do not know what ails you; but this day twelvemonth will see you again as sound as a roach.'

We then sat silent for a while, during which I was puffing at a cigar. Smith, among his accomplishments, did not reckon that of smoking—which was a grief to me; for a man enjoys the tobacco doubly when another is enjoying it with him.

'No, you do not know what ails me,' he said at last, 'and, therefore, cannot judge.'

'Perhaps not, my dear fellow. But my experience tells me that early wounds are generally capable of cure; and, therefore, I surmise that yours may be so. The heart at your time of life is not worn out, and has strength and soundness left wherewith to throw off its maladies. I hope it may be so with you.'

'God knows. I do not mean to say that there are none more to be pitied than I am; but at the present moment, I am not—not light-hearted.'

'I wish I could ease your burden, my dear fellow.'

'It is most preposterous in me thus to force myself upon you, and then trouble you with my cares. But I had been alone so long, and I was so weary of it!'

'By Jove, and so had I. Make no apology. And let me tell you this— though perhaps you will not credit me—that I would sooner laugh with a comrade than cry with him is true enough; but, if occasion demands, I can do the latter also.' He then put out his hand to me, and I pressed it in token of my friendship. My own hand was hot and rough with the heat and sand; but his was soft and cool almost as a woman's. I thoroughly hate an effeminate man; but, in spite of a certain womanly softness about this fellow, I could not hate him. 'Yes,' I continued, 'though somewhat unused to the melting mood, I also sometimes give forth my medicinal gums. I don't want to ask you any questions, and, as a rule, I hate to be told secrets, but if I can be of any service to you in any matter I will do my best. I don't say this with reference to the present moment, but think of it before we part.'

I looked round at him and saw that he was in tears. 'I know that you will think that I am a weak fool,' he said, pressing his handkerchief to his eyes.

'By no means. There are moments in a man's life when it becomes him to weep like a woman; but the older he grows the more seldom those moments come to him. As far as I can see of men, they never cry at that which disgraces them.'

'It is left for women to do that,' he answered.

'Oh, women! A woman cries for everything and for nothing. It is the sharpest arrow she has in her quiver—the best card in her hand. When a woman cries, what can you do but give her all she asks for?'

'Do you—dislike women?'

'No, by Jove! I am never really happy unless one is near me—or more than one. A man, as a rule, has an amount of energy within him which he cannot turn to profit on himself alone. It is good for him to have a woman by him that he may work for her, and thus have exercise for his limbs and faculties. I am very fond of women. But I always like those best who are most helpless.'

We were silent again for a while, and it was during this time that I found myself lying with my head in his lap. I had slept, but it could have been but for a few minutes, and when I woke I found his hand upon my brow. As I started up he said that the flies had been annoying me, and that he had not chosen to waken me as I seemed weary. 'It has been that double bathing,' I said, apologetically; for I always feel ashamed when I am detected sleeping in the day. 'In hot weather the water does make one drowsy. By Jove, it's getting dark; we had better have the horses.'

'Stay half a moment,' he said, speaking very softly, and laying his hand upon my arm, 'I will not detain you a minute.'

'There is no hurry in life,' I said.

'You promised me just now you would assist me.'

'If it be in my power, I will.'

'Before we part at Alexandria I will endeavour to tell you the story of my troubles, and then, if you can aid me—'. It struck me as he paused that I had made a rash promise, but nevertheless I must stand by it now—with one or two provisos. The chances were that the young man was short of money, or else that he had got into a scrape about a girl. In either case I might give him some slight assistance; but, then, it behoved me to make him understand that I would not consent to become a participator in mischief. I was too old to get my head willingly into a scrape, and this I must endeavour to make him understand.

'I will, if it be in my power,' I said. 'I will ask no questions now; but if your trouble be about some lady—'

'It is not,' said he.

'Well; so be it. Of all troubles those are the most troublesome. If you are short of cash—'

'No, I am not short of cash.'

'You are not. That's well too; for want of money is a sore trouble also.' And then I paused before I came to the point. 'I do not suspect anything bad of you, Smith. Had I done so, I should not have spoken as I have done. And if there be nothing bad—'

'There is nothing disgraceful,' he said.

'That is just what I mean; and in that case I will do anything for you that may be within my power. Now let us look for Joseph and the mucherry-boy, for it is time that we were at Jericho.'

I cannot describe at length the whole of our journey from thence to our tents at Jericho, nor back to Jerusalem, nor even from Jerusalem to Jaffa. At Jericho we did sleep in tents, paying so much per night, according to the tariff. We wandered out at night, and drank coffee with a family of Arabs in the desert, sitting in a ring round their coffee-kettle. And we saw a Turkish soldier punished with the bastinado— a sight which did not do me any good, and which made Smith very sick. Indeed after the first blow he walked away. Jericho is a remarkable spot in that pilgrim week, and I wish I had space to describe it. But I have not, for I must hurry on, back to Jerusalem and thence to Jaffa. I had much to tell also of those Bedouins; how they were essentially true to us, but teased us almost to frenzy by their continual begging. They begged for our food and our drink, for our cigars and our gunpowder, for the clothes off our backs, and the handkerchiefs out of our pockets. As to gunpowder I had none to give them, for my charges were all made up in cartridges; and I learned that the guns behind their backs were a mere pretence, for they had not a grain of powder among them.

We slept one night in Jerusalem, and started early on the following morning. Smith came to my hotel so that we might be ready together for the move. We still carried with us Joseph and the mucherry-boy; but for our Bedouins, who had duly received their forty shillings apiece,

we had no further use. On our road down to Jerusalem we had much
chat together, but only one adventure. Those pilgrims, of whom I
have spoken, journey to Jerusalem in the greatest number by the route
which we were now taking from it, and they come in long droves,
reaching Jaffa in crowds by the French and Austrian steamers from
Smyrna, Damascus, and Constantinople. As their number confers
security in that somewhat insecure country, many travellers from the
west of Europe make arrangements to travel with them. On our way
down we met the last of these caravans for the year, and we were
passing it for more than two hours. On this occasion I rode first, and
Smith was immediately behind me; but of a sudden I observed him to
wheel his horse round, and to clamber downwards among bushes and
stones towards a river that ran below us. 'Hallo, Smith,' I cried, 'you
will destroy your horse, and yourself too.' But he would not answer
me, and all I could do was to draw up in the path and wait. My
confusion was made the worse, as at that moment a long string of
pilgrims was passing by. 'Good morning, sir,' said an old man to me
in good English. I looked up as I answered him, and saw a grey-haired
gentleman, of very solemn and sad aspect. He might be seventy years
of age, and I could see that he was attended by three or four servants.
I shall never forget the severe and sorrowful expression of his eyes,
over which his heavy eyebrows hung low. 'Are there many English in
Jerusalem?' he asked. 'A good many,' I replied; 'there always are at
Easter.' 'Can you tell me anything of any of them?' he asked. 'Not a
word,' said I, for I knew no one; 'but our consul can.' And then we
bowed to each other and he passed on.

I got off my horse and scrambled down on foot after Smith. I found
him gathering berries and bushes as though his very soul were mad
with botany; but as I had seen nothing of this in him before, I asked
what strange freak had taken him.

'You were talking to that old man,' he said.

'Well, yes, I was.'

'That is the relation of whom I have spoken to you.'

'The d—— he is!'

'And I would avoid him, if it be possible.'

I then learned that the old gentleman was his uncle. He had no
living father or mother, and he now supposed that his relative was
going to Jerusalem in quest of him. 'If so,' said I, 'you will undoubtedly
give him leg bail, unless the Austrian boat is more than ordinarily late.
It is as much as we shall do to catch it, and you may be half over

Africa, or far gone on your way to India, before he can be on your track again.'

'I will tell you all about it at Alexandria,' he replied; and then he scrambled up again with his horse, and we went on. That night we slept at the Armenian convent at Ramlath, or Ramath. This place is supposed to stand on the site of Arimathea, and is marked as such in many of the maps. The monks at this time of the year are very busy, as the pilgrims all stay here for one night on their routes backwards and forwards, and the place on such occasions is terribly crowded. On the night of our visit it was nearly empty, as a caravan had left it that morning; and thus we were indulged with separate cells, a point on which my companion seemed to lay considerable stress.

On the following day, at about noon, we entered Jaffa, and put up at an inn there which is kept by a Pole. The boat from Beyrout, which touches at Jaffa on its way to Alexandria, was not yet in, nor even sighted; we were therefore amply in time. 'Shall we sail tonight?' I asked of the agent. 'Yes, in all probability,' he replied. 'If the signal be seen before three we shall do so. If not, then not,' and so I returned to the hotel.

Smith had involuntarily shown signs of fatigue during the journey, but yet he had borne up well against it. I had never felt called on to grant any extra indulgence as to time because the work was too much for him. But now he was a good deal knocked up, and I was a little frightened, fearing that I had over-driven him under the heat of the sun. I was alarmed lest he should have fever, and proposed to send for the Jaffa doctor. But this he utterly refused. He would shut himself for an hour or two in his room, he said, and by that time he trusted the boat would be in sight. It was clear to me that he was very anxious on the subject, fearing that his uncle would be back upon his heels before he had started.

I ordered a serious breakfast for myself, for with me, on such occasions, my appetite demands more immediate attention than my limbs. I also acknowledge that I become fatigued, and can lay myself at length during such idle days and sleep from hour to hour; but the desire to do so never comes till I have well eaten and drunken. A bottle of French wine, three or four cutlets of goats' flesh, an omelet made not of the freshest eggs, and an enormous dish of oranges, was the banquet set before me; and though I might have found fault with it in Paris or London, I thought that it did well enough in Jaffa. My poor friend could not join me, but had a cup of coffee in his room. 'At any rate take a little brandy in it,' I said to him, as I stood over his bed. 'I could not swallow it,' said he, looking at me with almost beseeching eyes. 'Beshrew the fellow,' I said to myself as I left him, carefully closing the door, so that the sound should not shake him; 'He is little better than a woman, and yet I have become as fond of him as though he were my brother.'

I went out at three, but up to that time the boat had not been signalled. 'And we shall not get out tonight?' 'No, not tonight,' said the agent. 'And at what time tomorrow?' 'If she comes in this evening, you will start by daylight. But they so manage her departure from Beyrout, that she seldom is here in the evening.' 'It will be noon tomorrow then?' 'Yes,' the man said, 'noon tomorrow.' I calculated, however, that the old gentleman could not possibly be on our track by that time. He would not have reached Jerusalem till late in the day on which we saw him, and it would take him some time to obtain tidings of his nephew. But it might be possible that messengers sent by him should reach Jaffa by four or five on the day after his arrival. That would be this very day which we were now wasting at Jaffa. Having thus made my calculations, I returned to Smith to give him such consolation as it might be in my power to afford.

He seemed to be dreadfully afflicted by all this. 'He will have traced me to Jerusalem, and then again away; and will follow me immediately.'

'That is all very well,' I said; 'but let even a young man do the best he can, and he will not get from Jerusalem to Jaffa in less than twelve hours. Your uncle is not a young man, and could not possibly do the journey under two days.'

'But he will send. He will not mind what money he spends.'

'And if he does send, take off your hat to his messengers, and bid them carry your compliments back. You are not a felon whom he can arrest.'

'No, he cannot arrest me; but, ah! you do not understand'; and then he sat up on the bed, and seemed as though he were going to wring his hands in despair.

I waited for some half hour in his room, thinking that he would tell me this story of his. If he required that I should give him my aid in the presence either of his uncle or of his uncle's myrmidons, I must at any rate know what was likely to be the dispute between them. But as he said nothing I suggested that he should stroll out with me among the orange-groves by which the town is surrounded. In answer to this he looked up piteously into my face as though begging me to be merciful to him. 'You are strong,' said he, 'and cannot understand what it is to feel fatigue as I do.' And yet he had declared on commencing his journey that he would not be found to complain! Nor had he complained by a single word till after that encounter with his uncle. Nay he had borne up well till this news had reached us of the boat being late. I felt convinced that if the boat were at this moment lying in the harbour all that appearance of excessive weakness would soon vanish. What it was that he feared I could not guess; but it was manifest to me that some great terror almost overwhelmed him.

'My idea is,' said I—and I suppose that I spoke with something less of good-nature in my tone than I had assumed for the last day or two, 'that no man should, under any circumstances, be so afraid of another man, as to tremble at his presence—either at his presence or his expected presence.'

'Ah, now you are angry with me; now you despise me!'

'Neither the one nor the other. But if I may take the liberty of a friend with you, I would advise you to combat this feeling of horror. If you do not, it will unman you. After all, what can your uncle do to you? He cannot rob you of your heart or soul. He cannot touch your inner self.'

'You do not know,' he said.

'Ah but, Smith, I do know that. Whatever may be this quarrel between you and him, you should not tremble at the thought of him; unless indeed—'

'Unless what?'

'Unless you had done aught that should make you tremble before every honest man.' I own I had begun to have my doubts of him, and to fear that he had absolutely disgraced himself. Even in such case I—I individually—did not wish to be severe on him; but I should be annoyed to find that I had opened my heart to a swindler or a practised knave.

'I will tell you all tomorrow,' said he; 'but I have been guilty of nothing of that sort.'

In the evening he did come out, and sat with me as I smoked my cigar. The boat, he was told, would almost undoubtedly come in by daybreak on the following morning, and be off at nine; whereas it was very improbable that any arrival from Jerusalem would be so early as that. 'Beside,' I reminded him, 'your uncle will hardly hurry down to Jaffa, because he will have no reason to think but what you have already started. There are no telegraphs here, you know.'

In the evening he was still very sad, though the paroxysm of his terror seemed to have passed away. I would not bother him, as he had himself chosen the following morning for the telling of his story. So I sat and smoked, and talked to him about our past journey, and by degrees the power of speech came back to him, and I again felt that I loved him. Yes, loved him! I have not taken many such fancies into my head, at so short a notice; but I did love him, as though he were a younger brother. I felt a delight in serving him, and though I was almost old enough to be his father, I ministered to him as though he had been an old man, or a woman.

On the following morning we were stirring at daybreak, and found that the vessel was in sight. She would be in the roads off the town in two hours' time, they said, and would start at eleven or twelve. And then we walked round by the gate of the town, and sauntered a quarter of a mile or so along the way that leads towards Jerusalem. I could see that his eye was anxiously turned down the road, but he said nothing. We saw no cloud of dust, and then we returned to breakfast.

'The steamer has come to anchor,' said our dirty Polish host to us in execrable English. 'And we may be off on board,' said Smith. 'Not yet,' he said; 'they must put their cargo out first.' I saw, however, that Smith was uneasy, and I made up my mind to go off to the vessel at once. When they should see an English portmanteau making an offer to come up the gangway, the Austrian sailors would not stop it. So I called for the bill, and ordered that the things should be taken down to the wretched broken heap of rotten timber which they called a quay. Smith had not told me his story, but no doubt he would as soon as he was on board.

I was in the very act of squabbling with the Pole over the last demand for piastres, when we heard a noise in the gateway of the inn, and I saw Smith's countenance become pale. It was an Englishman's voice asking if there were any strangers there; so I went into the courtyard, closing the door behind me, and turning the key upon the landlord and Smith. 'Smith,' said I to myself, 'will keep the Pole quiet if he have any wit left.'

The man who had asked the question had the air of an upper English servant, and I thought that I recognized one of those whom I had seen with the old gentleman on the road; but the matter was soon put at rest by the appearance of that gentleman himself. He walked up into the courtyard, looked hard at me from under those bushy eyebrows, just raised his hat, and then said, 'I believe I am speaking to Mr Jones.'

'Yes,' said I, 'I am Mr Jones. Can I have the honour of serving you?'

There was something peculiarly unpleasant about this man's face. At the present moment I examined it closely, and could understand the great aversion which his nephew felt towards him. He looked like a gentleman and like a man of talent, nor was there anything of meanness in his face; neither was he ill-looking, in the usual acceptation of the word; but one could see that he was solemn, austere, and overbearing; that he would be incapable of any light enjoyment, and unforgiving towards all offences. I took him to be a man who, being old himself, could never remember that he had been young, and who, therefore, hated the levities of youth. To me such a character is specially odious; for I would fain, if it be possible, be young even to my grave. Smith, if he were clever, might escape from the window of the room, which opened out upon a terrace, and still get down to the steamer. I would keep the old man in play for some time; and, even though I lost my passage, would be true to my friend. There lay our joint luggage at my feet in the yard. If Smith would venture away without his portion of it, all might yet be right.

'My name, sir, is Sir William Weston,' he began. I had heard of the name before, and knew him to be a man of wealth, and family, and note. I took off my hat, and said that I had much honour in meeting Sir William Weston.

'And I presume you know the object with which I am now here,' he continued.

'Not exactly,' said I. 'Nor do I understand how I possibly should know it, seeing that, up to this moment, I did not even know your name, and have heard nothing concerning either your movements or your affairs.'

'Sir,' said he, 'I have hitherto believed that I might at any rate expect from you the truth.'

'Sir,' said I, 'I am bold to think that you will not dare to tell me, either now, or at any other time, that you have received, or expect to receive, from me anything that is not true.'

He then stood still, looking at me for a moment or two, and I beg to assert that I looked as fully at him. There was, at any rate, no cause why I should tremble before him. I was not his nephew, nor was I responsible for his nephew's doings towards him. Two of his servants were behind him, and on my side there stood a boy and girl belonging to the inn. They, however, could not understand a word of English. I saw that he was hesitating, but at last he spoke out. I confess, now, that his words, when they were spoken, did, at the first moment, make me tremble.

'I have to charge you,' said he, 'with eloping with my niece, and I demand of you to inform me where she is. You are perfectly aware that I am her guardian by law.'

I did tremble—not that I cared much for Sir William's guardianship, but I saw before me so terrible an embarrassment! And then I felt so thoroughly abashed in that I had allowed myself to be so deceived! It all came back upon me in a moment, and covered me with a shame that even made me blush. I had travelled through the desert with a woman for days, and had not discovered her, though she had given me a thousand signs. All those signs I remembered now, and I blushed painfully. When her hand was on my forehead I still thought that she was a man! I declare that at this moment I felt a stronger disinclination to face my late companion than I did to encounter her angry uncle.

'Your niece!' I said, speaking with a sheepish bewilderment which should have convinced him at once of my innocence. She had asked me, too, whether I was a married man, and I had denied it. How was I to escape from such a mess of misfortunes? I declare that I began to forget her troubles in my own.

'Yes, my niece—Miss Julia Weston. The disgrace which you have brought upon me must be wiped out; but my first duty is to save that unfortunate young woman from further misery.'

'If it be as you say,' I exclaimed, 'by the honour of a gentleman—'

'I care nothing for the honour of a gentleman till I see it proved. Be good enough to inform me, sir, whether Miss Weston is in this house.'

For a moment I hesitated; but I saw at once that I should make myself responsible for certain mischief, of which I was at any rate hitherto in truth innocent, if I allowed myself to become a party to concealing a young lady. Up to this period I could at any rate defend myself, whether my defence were believed or not believed. I still had a hope that the charming Julia might have escaped through the window, and a feeling that if she had done so I was not responsible. When I turned the lock I turned it on Smith.

For a moment I hesitated, and then walked slowly across the yard and opened the door. 'Sir William,' I said, as I did so, 'I travelled here with a companion dressed as a man; and I believed him to be what he seemed till this minute.'

'Sir!' said Sir William, with a look of scorn in his face which gave me the lie in my teeth as plainly as any words could do. And then he entered the room. The Pole was standing in one corner, apparently amazed at what was going on, and Smith—I may as well call her Miss Weston at once, for the baronet's statement was true—was sitting on a sort of divan in the corner of the chamber, hiding her face in her hands. She had made no attempt at an escape, and a full explanation was therefore indispensable. For myself I own that I felt ashamed of my part in the play—ashamed even of my own innocency. Had I been less innocent I should certainly have contrived to appear much less guilty. Had it occurred to me on the banks of the Jordan that Smith was a lady, I should not have travelled with her in her gentleman's habiliments from Jerusalem to Jaffa. Had she consented to remain under my protection, she must have done so without a masquerade.

The uncle stood still and looked at his niece. He probably understood how thoroughly stern and disagreeable was his own face, and considered that he could punish the crime of his relative in no severer way than by looking at her. In this I think he was right. But at last there was a necessity for speaking. 'Unfortunate young woman!' he said, and then paused.

'We had better get rid of the landlord,' I said, 'before we come to any explanation.' And I motioned to the man to leave the room. This he did very unwillingly, but at last he was gone.

'I fear that it is needless to care on her account who may hear the story of her shame,' said Sir William. I looked at Miss Weston, but she still sat hiding her face. However, if she did not defend herself, it was necessary that I should defend both her and me.

'I do not know how far I may be at liberty to speak with reference to the private matters of yourself or of your—your niece, Sir William Weston. I would not willingly interfere—'

'Sir,' said he, 'your interference has already taken place. Will you have the goodness to explain to me what are your intentions with regard to that lady?'

My intentions! Heaven help me! My intentions, of course, were to leave her in her uncle's hands. Indeed, I could hardly be said to have formed any intention since I had learned that I had been honoured by a lady's presence. At this moment I deeply regretted that I had thoughtlessly stated to her that I was an unmarried man. In doing so I had had no object. But at that time 'Smith' had been quite a stranger to me, and I had not thought it necessary to declare my own private concerns. Since that I had talked so little of myself that the fact of my family at home had not been mentioned. 'Will you have the goodness to explain what are your intentions with regard to that lady?' said the baronet.

'Oh, Uncle William!' exclaimed Miss Weston, now at length raising her head from her hands.

'Hold your peace, madam,' said he. 'When called upon to speak, you will find your words with difficulty enough. Sir, I am waiting for an answer from you.'

'But, uncle, he is nothing to me—the gentleman is nothing to me!'

'By the heavens above us, he shall be something, or I will know the reason why! What! he has gone off with you; he has travelled through the country with you, hiding you from your only natural friend; he has been your companion for weeks—'

'Six days, sir,' said I.

'Sir!' said the baronet, again giving me the lie. 'And now,' he continued, addressing his niece, 'you tell me that he is nothing to you. He shall give me his promise that he will make you his wife at the consulate at Alexandria, or I will destroy him. I know who he is.'

'If you know who I am,' said I, 'you must know—'

But he would not listen to me. 'And as for you, madam, unless he makes me that promise—' And then he paused in his threat, and, turning round, looked me in the face. I saw that she also was looking at me, though not openly as he did; and some flattering devil that was at work round my heart, would have persuaded that she also would have heard a certain answer given without dismay—would even have received comfort in her agony from such answer. But the reader knows how completely that answer was out of my power.

'I have not the slightest ground for supposing,' said I, 'that the lady would accede to such an arrangement—if it were possible. My acquaintance with her has been altogether confined to—. To tell the truth, I have not been in Miss Weston's confidence, and have taken her to be only that which she has seemed to be.'

'Sir!' said the baronet, again looking at me as though he would wither me on the spot for my falsehood.

'It is true!' said Julia, getting up from her seat, and appealing with clasped hands to her uncle—'as true as Heaven.'

'Madam!' said he, 'do you both take me for a fool?'

'That you should take me for one,' said I, 'would be very natural. The facts are as we state to you. Miss Weston—as I now learn that she is—did me the honour of calling at my hotel, having heard—' And then it seemed to me as though I were attempting to screen myself by telling the story against her, so I was again silent. Never in my life had I been in a position of such extraordinary difficulty. The duty which I owed to Julia as a woman, and to Sir William as a guardian, and to myself as the father of a family, all clashed with each other. I was anxious to be generous, honest, and prudent, but it was impossible; so I made up my mind to say nothing further.

'Mr Jones,' said the baronet, 'I have explained to you the only arrangement which under the present circumstances I can permit to pass without open exposure and condign punishment. That you are a gentleman by birth, education, and position I am aware'—whereupon I raised my hat, and then he continued: 'That lady has three hundred a year of her own—'

'And attractions, personal and mental, which are worth ten times the money,' said I, and I bowed to my fair friend, who looked at me the while with sad beseeching eyes. I confess that the mistress of my bosom, had she known my thoughts at that one moment, might have had cause for anger.

'Very well,' continued he. 'Then the proposal which I name cannot, I imagine, but be satisfactory. If you will make to her and to me the only amends which it is in your power as a gentleman to afford, I will forgive all. Tell me that you will make her your wife on your arrival in Egypt.'

I would have given anything not to have looked at Miss Weston at this moment, but I could not help it. I did turn my face half round to her before I answered, and then felt that I had been cruel in doing so. 'Sir William,' said I, 'I have at home already a wife and family of my own.'

'It is not true!' said he, retreating a step, and staring at me with amazement.

'There is something, sir,' I replied, 'in the unprecedented circumstances of this meeting, and in your position with regard to that lady, which, joined to your advanced age, will enable me to regard that useless insult as unspoken. I am a married man. There is the signature of my wife's last letter,' and I handed him one which I had received as I was leaving Jerusalem.

But the coarse violent contradiction which Sir William had given me was as nothing compared with the reproach conveyed in Miss Weston's countenance. She looked at me as though all her anger were now turned against me. And yet, methought, there was more of sorrow than of resentment in her countenance. But what cause was there for either? Why should I be reproached, even by her look? She did not remember at the moment that when I answered her chance question as to my domestic affairs, I had answered it as to a man who was a stranger to me, and not as to a beautiful woman, with whom I was about to pass certain days in close and intimate society. To her, at the moment, it seemed as though I had cruelly deceived her. In truth the one person really deceived had been myself.

And here I must explain, on behalf of the lady, that when she first joined me she had no other view than that of seeing the banks of the Jordan in that guise which she had chosen to assume, in order to escape from the solemnity and austerity of a disagreeable relative. She had been very foolish, and that was all. I take it that she had first left her uncle at Constantinople, but on this point I never got certain information. Afterwards, while we were travelling together, the idea had come upon her, that she might go on as far as Alexandria with me. And then—. I know nothing further of the lady's intentions, but I am certain that her wishes were good and pure. Her uncle had been intolerable to her, and she had fled from him. Such had been her offence, and no more.

'Then, sir,' said the baronet, giving me back my letter, 'you must be a double-dyed villain.'

'And you, sir,' said I—. But here Julia Weston interrupted me.

'Uncle, you altogether wrong this gentleman,' she said. 'He has been kind to me beyond my power of words to express; but, till told by you, he knew nothing of my secret. Nor would he have known it,' she added, looking down upon the ground. As to that latter assertion, I was at liberty to believe as much as I pleased.

The Pole now came to the door, informing us that any who wished to start by the packet must go on board, and therefore, as the unreasonable old gentleman perceived, it was necessary that we should all make our arrangements. I cannot say that they were such as enable me to look back on them with satisfaction. He did seem now at last to believe that I had been an unconscious agent in his niece's stratagem, but he hardly on that account became civil to me. 'It was absolutely necessary,' he said, 'that he and that unfortunate young woman,' as he would call her, 'should depart at once—by this ship now going.' To this proposition of course I made no opposition. 'And you, Mr Jones,' he continued, 'will at once perceive that you, as a gentleman, should allow us to proceed on our journey without the honour of your company.'

This was very dreadful, but what could I say; or, indeed, what could

I do? My most earnest desire in the matter was to save Miss Weston from annoyance; and under existing circumstances my presence on board could not but be a burden to her. And then, if I went—if I did go, in opposition to the wishes of the baronet, could I trust my own prudence? It was better for all parties that I should remain.

'Sir William,' said I, after a minute's consideration, 'if you will apologize to me for the gross insults you have offered me, it shall be as you say.'

'Mr Jones,' said Sir William, 'I do apologize for the words which I used to you while I was labouring under a very natural misconception of the circumstances.' I do not know that I was much the better for the apology, but at the moment I regarded it sufficient.

Their things were then hurried down to the strand, and I accompanied them to the ruined quay. I took off my hat to Sir William as he was first let down into the boat. He descended first, so that he might receive his niece—for all Jaffa now knew that it was a lady—and then I gave her my hand for the last time. 'God bless you, Miss Weston,' I said, pressing it closely. 'God bless you, Mr Jones,' she replied. And from that day to this I have neither spoken to her nor seen her.

I waited a fortnight at Jaffa for the French boat, eating cutlets of goats' flesh, and wandering among the orange-groves. I certainly look back on that fortnight as the most miserable period of my life. I had been deceived, and had failed to discover the deceit, even though the deceiver had perhaps wished that I should do so. For that blindness I have never forgiven myself.

ELIZABETH VON ARNIM

From Miltzow to Lauterbach

Every one who has been to school and still remembers what he was taught there, knows that Rügen is the biggest island Germany possesses, and that it lies in the Baltic Sea off the coast of Pomerania.

Round this island I wished to walk this summer, but no one would walk with me. It is the perfect way of moving if you want to see into the life of things. It is the one way of freedom. If you go to a place on anything but your own feet you are taken there too fast, and miss a thousand delicate joys that were waiting for you by the wayside. If you drive you are bound by a variety of considerations, eight of the most important being the horses' legs. If you bicycle—but who that loves to get close to nature would bicycle? And as for motors, the object of a journey like mine was not the getting to a place but the going there.

Successively did I invite the most likely of my women friends, numbering at least a dozen, to walk with me. They one and all replied that it would make them tired and that it would be dull; and when I tried to remove the first objection by telling them how excellent it would be for the German nation, especially those portions of it that are still to come, if its women walked round Rügen more often, they stared and smiled; and when I tried to remove the second by explaining that by our own spirits are we deified, they stared and smiled more than ever.

Walking, then, was out of the question, for I could not walk alone. The grim monster Conventionality whose iron claws are for ever on my shoulder, for ever pulling me back from the harmless and the wholesome, put a stop to that even if I had not been afraid of tramps, which I was. So I drove, and it was round Rügen that I drove because one hot afternoon when I was idling in the library, not reading but fingering the books, taking out first one and then another, dipping into them, deciding which I would read next, I came across Marianne

North's *Recollections of a Happy Life*, and hit upon the page where she begins to talk of Rügen. Immediately interested—for is not Rügen nearer to me than any other island?—I became absorbed in her description of the bathing near a place called Putbus, of the deliciousness of it in a sandy cove where the water was always calm, and of how you floated about on its crystal surface, and beautiful jellyfish, stars of purest colours, floated with you. I threw down the book to ransack the shelves for a guide to Rügen. On the first page of the first one I found was this remarkable paragraph:

'Hearest thou the name Rügen, so doth a wondrous spell come over thee. Before thine eyes it rises as a dream of far-away, beauteous fairylands. Images and figures of long ago beckon thee across to the marvellous places where in grey prehistoric times they dwelt, and on which they have left the shadow of their presence. And in thee stirs a mighty desire to wander over the glorious, legend-surrounded island. Cord up, then, thy light bundle, take to heart Shylock's advice to put money in thy purse, and follow me without fear of the threatening sea-sickness which may overtake thee on the short crossing, for it has never yet done any one more harm than imposing on him a rapidly passing discomfort.'

This seemed to me very irresistible. Surely a place that inspired such a mingling of the lofty and the homely in its guide-books must be well worth seeing? There was a drought just then going on at home. My eyes were hot with watching a garden parch browner day by day beneath a sky of brass. I felt that it only needed a little energy, and in a few hours I too might be floating among those jellyfish, in the shadow of the cliffs of the legend-surrounded island. And even better than being surrounded by legends those breathless days would it be to have the sea all round me. Such a sea too! Did I not know it? Did I not know its singular limpidity? The divineness of its blue where it was deep, the clearness of its green where it was shallow, lying tideless along its amber shores? The very words made me thirsty—amber shores; lazy waves lapping them slowly; vast spaces for the eye to wander over; rocks, and seaweed, and cool, gorgeous jellyfish. The very map at the beginning of the guide-book made me thirsty, the land was so succulently green, the sea all round so bland a blue. And what a fascinating island it is on the map—an island of twists and curves and inland seas called Bodden; of lakes, and woods, and frequent ferries; with lesser islands dotted about its coasts; with bays innumerable stretching their arms out into the water; and with one huge forest, evidently magnificent, running nearly the whole length of the east coast, following its curves, dipping down to the sea in places, and in others climbing up chalk cliffs to crown them with the peculiar splendour of beeches.

It does not take me long to make up my mind, still less to cord up my light bundle, for somebody else does that; and I think it was only two days after I first found Marianne North and the guide-book that my maid Gertrud and I got out of a suffocating train into the freshness that blows round ryefields near the sea, and began our journey into the unknown.

It was a little wayside station on the line between Berlin and Stralsund, called Miltzow, a solitary red building on the edge of a pine-wood, that witnessed the beginning of our tour. The carriage had been sent on the day before, and round it, on our arrival, stood the station authorities in an interested group. The stationmaster, every-where in Germany an elaborate, Olympic person in white gloves, actu-ally helped the porter to cord on my holdall with his own hands, and they both lingered over it as if loath to let us go. Evidently the coach-man had told them what I was going to do, and I suppose such an enterprising woman does not get out at Miltzow every day. They packed us in with the greatest care, with so much care that I thought they would never have done. My holdall was the biggest piece of luggage, and they corded it on in an upright position at our feet. I had left the choosing of its contents to Gertrud, only exhorting her, besides my pillow, to take a sufficiency of soap and dressing-gowns. Gertrud's luggage was placed by the porter on her lap. It was almost too modest. It was one small black bag, and a great part of its inside must, I knew, be taken up by the stockings she had brought to knit and the needles she did it with; yet she looked quite as respectable the day we came home as she did the day we started, and every bit as clean. My dressing-case was put on the box, and on top of it was a brown cardboard hat-box containing the coachman's wet-weather hat. A thick coat for possible cold days made a cushion for my back, and Gertrud's waterproof did the same thing for hers. Wedged in between us was the tea-basket, rattling inharmoniously, but preventing our slipping together in sloping places. Behind us in the hood were the umbrellas, rugs, guide-books, and maps, besides one of those round shiny yellow wooden band-boxes into which every decent German woman puts her best hat. This luggage, and some mysterious bundles on the box that the coachman thought were hidden by his legs but which bulged out unhideable on either side, prevented our looking elegant; but I did not want to look elegant, and I had gathered from the remarks of those who had refused to walk that Rügen was not a place where I should meet any one who did.

Now I suppose I could talk for a week and yet give no idea whatever of the exultation that filled my soul as I gazed on these arrangements. The picnic-like simplicity of them was so full of promise. It was as though I were going back to the very morning of life, to those fresh years when shepherd boys and others shout round one for no reason except that they are out of doors and alive. Also, during the years that have come after, years that may properly be called riper, it has been a conviction of mine that there is nothing so absolutely bracing for the soul as the frequent turning of one's back on duties. This was exactly what I was doing; and oh ye rigid female martyrs on the rack of daily exemplariness, ye unquestioning patient followers of paths that have been pointed out, if only you knew the wholesome joys of sometimes being less good!

The point at which we were is the nearest from which Rügen can be reached by persons coming up from the south and going to drive. No one ever gets out there who is bound for Rügen, because no one ever drives to Rügen. The ordinary tourist, almost exclusively German, goes first to Stralsund, is taken across the narrow strip of water, train and all, on the steam ferry, and continues without changing till he reaches the open sea on the other side of the island at Sassnitz. Or he goes by train from Berlin to Stettin and then by steamer down the Oder, crosses the open sea for four hours, and arrives, probably pensive for the boats are small and the waves are often big, at Göhren, the first stopping-place on the island's east coast.

We were not ordinary tourists, and having got to Miltzow were to be independent of all such wearinesses as trains and steamers till the day we wanted to come back again. From Miltzow we were going to drive to a ferry three miles off at a place called Stahlbrode, cross the mile of water, land on the island's south shore, and go on at once that afternoon to the jellyfish of Miss North's Putbus, which were beckoning me across to the legend-surrounded island far more irresistibly than any of those grey figures the guide-book talked about.

The carriage was a light one of the victoria genus with a hood; the horses were a pair esteemed at home for their meekness; the coachman, August, was a youth who had never yet driven straight on for an indefinite period without turning round once, and he looked as though he thought he were going to enjoy himself. I was sure I was going to enjoy myself. Gertrud, I fancy, was without these illusions; but she is old, and has got out of the habit of being anything but resigned. She was the sop on this occasion thrown to the Grim One of the iron claws, for I would far rather have gone alone. But Gertrud is very silent; to go with her would be as nearly like being alone as it is possible to be when you are not. She could, I knew, be trusted to sit by my side knitting, however bumpy the road, and not opening her lips unless asked a question. Admirable virtue of silence, most precious, because most rare, jewel in the crown of female excellences, not possessed by a single one of those who had refused to walk! If either of them had occupied Gertrud's place and driven with me would she not, after the way of women, have spent the first half of the time telling me her secrets and the other half being angry with me because I knew them? And then Gertrud, after having kept quiet all day, would burst into activities at night, unpack the holdall, produce pleasant things like slippers, see that my bed was as I like it, and end by tucking me up in it and going away on tiptoe with her customary quaint benediction, bestowed on me every night at bedtime: 'The dear God protect and bless the gracious one,' says Gertrud as she blows out the candle.

'And may He also protect and bless thee,' I reply; and could as ill spare my pillow as her blessing.

It was half past two in the afternoon of the middle Friday in July when we left the station officials to go back to their dull work and trotted round the corner into the wide world. The sky was a hot blue. The road wound with gentle ups and downs between fields whitening to harvest. High over our heads the larks quivered in the light, shaking out that rapturous song that I can never hear without a throb of gratitude for being alive. There were no woods or hills, and we could see a long way on either side, see the red roofs of farms clustered wherever there was a hollow to protect them from the wild winds of winter, see the straight double line of trees where the high road to Stralsund cut across ours, see a little village a mile ahead of us with a venerable church on a mound in the middle of it gravely presiding over the surrounding wide parish of corn. I think I must have got out at least six times during the short drive between Miltzow and the ferry pretending I wanted flowers, but really to enjoy the delight of loitering. The rye was full of chickory and poppies, the ditches along the road where the spring dampness still lingered were white with the delicate loveliness of cow-parsley, that most spiritual of weeds. I picked an armful of it to hold up against the blue of the sky while we were driving; I gave Gertrud a bunch of poppies for which she thanked me without enthusiasm; I put little posies of chickory at the horses' ears; in fact I felt and behaved as if I were fifteen and out for my first summer holiday. But what did it matter? There was nobody there to see.

Stahlbrode is the most innocent-looking place—a small cluster of cottages on grass that goes down to the water. It was quite empty and silent. It has a long narrow wooden jetty running across the marshy shore to the ferry, and moored to the end of this jetty lay a big fishing-smack with furled brown sails. I got out and walked down to it to see if it were the ferry-boat, and whether the ferryman was in it. Both August and the horses had an alarmed, pricked-up expression as they saw me going out into the jaws of the sea. Even the emotionless Gertrud put away her stocking and stood by the side of the carriage watching me. The jetty was roughly put together, and so narrow that the carriage would only just fit in. A slight wooden rail was all the protection provided; but the water was not deep, and heaved limpidly over the yellow sand at the bottom. The shore we were on was flat and vividly green, the shore of Rügen opposite was flat and vividly green; the sea between was a lovely, sparkling blue; the sky was strewn across with loose clusters of pearly clouds; the breeze that had played so gently among the ears of corn round Miltzow danced along the little waves and splashed them gaily against the wooden posts of the jetty as though the freshness down there on the water had filled it with new life. I found the boat empty, a thing of steep sides and curved bottom, a thing that was surely never intended for the ferrying across of horses and carriages. No other boat was to be seen. Up the channel and down the channel there was nothing visible but the flat green shores, the dancing water, the wide sky, the bland afternoon light.

I turned back thoughtfully to the cottages. Suppose the ferry were only used for ferrying people? If so, we were in an extremely tiresome fix. A long way back against the sky I could see the line of trees bordering the road to Stralsund, and the whole dull, dusty distance would have to be driven over if the Stahlbrode ferry failed us. August took off his hat when I came up to him, and said ominously, 'Does the gracious one permit that I speak a few words?'

'Speak them, August.'

'It is very windy.'

'Not very.'

'It is far to go on water.'

'Not very.'

'Never yet have I been on the sea.'

'Well, you are going on it now.'

With an expression made up of two parts fright and one resignation he put on his hat again and relapsed into a silence that was grim. I took Gertrud with me to give me a countenance and walked across to the inn, a new red-brick house standing out boldly on a bit of rising ground, endways on to the sea. The door was open and we went in, knocking with my sunshade on the floor. We stirred up no life of any sort. Not even a dog barked at us. The passage was wide and clean with doors on each side of it and an open door at either end—the one we had come in by followed by the afternoon sun, and the other framing a picture of sky with the sea at the bottom, the jetty, the smack with folded sails, and the coast of Rügen. Seeing a door with *Gaststube* painted on it I opened it and peeped in. To my astonishment it was full of men smoking in silence, and all with their eyes fixed on the opening door. They must have heard us. They must have seen us passing the window as we came up to the house. I concluded that the custom of the district requires that strangers shall in no way be interfered with until they actually ask definite questions; that it was so became clear by the alacrity with which a yellow-bearded man jumped up on our asking how we could get across to Rügen, and told us he was the ferryman and would take us there.

'But there is a carriage—can that go too?' I inquired anxiously, thinking of the deep bottom and steep sides of the fishing-smack.

'*Alles, Alles*,' he said cheerily; and calling to a boy to come and help he led the way through the door framing the sea, down a tiny, sandy garden prickly with gooseberry bushes, to the place where August sat marvelling on his box.

'Come along!' he shouted as he ran past him.

'What, along that thing of wood?' cried August. 'With my horses? And my newly varnished carriage?'

'Come along!' shouted the ferryman, half-way down the jetty.

'Go on, August,' I commanded.

'It can never be accomplished,' said August, visibly breaking out into a perspiration.

'Go on,' I repeated sternly; but thought it on the whole more discreet to go on myself on my own feet, and so did Gertrud.

'If the gracious one insists—' faltered August, and began to drive gingerly down to the jetty with the face of one who thinks his last hour well on the way.

As I had feared, the carriage was very nearly smashed getting it over the sides of the smack. I sat up in the bows looking on in terror, expecting every instant to see the wheels wrenched off, and with their wrenching the end of our holiday. The optimistic ferryman assured us that it was going in quite easily—like a lamb, he declared, with great boldness of imagery. He sloped two ineffectual planks, one for each set of wheels, up the side of the boat, and he and August, hatless, coatless, and breathless, lifted the carriage over on to them. It was a horrid moment. The front wheels twisted right round and were as near coming off as any wheels I saw in my life. I was afraid to look at August, so right did he seem to have been when he protested that the thing could not be accomplished. Yet there was Rügen and here were we, and we had to get across to it somehow or turn round and do the dreary journey to Stralsund.

The horses, both exceedingly restive, had been unharnessed and got in first. They were held in the stern of the boat by two boys, who needed all their determination to do it. Then it was that I was thankful for the boat's steep sides, for if they had been lower those horses would certainly have kicked themselves over into the sea; and what should I have done then? And how should I have faced him who is in authority over me if I returned to him without his horses?

'We take them across daily,' the ferryman remarked, airily jerking his thumb in the direction of the carriage.

'Do so many people drive to Rügen?' I asked astonished, for the plank arrangements were staringly makeshift.

'Many people?' cried the ferryman. 'Rightly speaking, crowds.'

He was trying to make me happy. At least it reassured August to hear it; but I could not suppress a smile of deprecation at the size of the fib.

By this time we were under weigh, a fair wind sending us merrily over the water. The ferryman steered; August stood at his horses' heads talking to them soothingly; the two boys came and sat on some coiled ropes close to me, leaned their elbows on their knees and their chins on their hands, and fixing their blue fisher-boy eyes on my face kept them there with an unwinking interest during the entire crossing. Oh, it was lovely sitting up there in the sun, safe so far, in the delicious quiet of sailing. The tawny sail, darned and patched in divers shades of brown and red and orange, towered above us against the sky. The huge mast seemed to brush along across the very surface of the little white clouds. Above the rippling of the water we could hear the distant larks on either shore. August had put on his scarlet stable-jacket for the work of lifting the carriage in, and made a beautiful bit of colour among the browns of the old boat at the stern. The eyes of the ferryman lost all the alertness they had had on shore, and he stood at the rudder gazing dreamily out at the afternoon light on the Rügen meadows. How perfect it was after the train, after the clattering along the dusty road, and the heat and terror of getting on board. For one exquisite quarter of an hour we were softly lapped across in the sun, and for all that beauty we were only asked to pay three marks, which included the horses and carriage and the labour of getting us in and out. For a further small sum the ferryman became enthusiastic and begged me to be sure to come back that way. There was a single house on the Rügen shore where he lived, he said, and from which he would watch for us. A little dog came down to welcome us, but we saw no other living creature. The carriage conducted itself far more like a lamb on this side, and I drove away well pleased to have got over the chief difficulty of the tour, the soft-voiced ferryman wishing us God-speed, and the two boys unwinking to the last.

So here we were on the legend-surrounded island. 'Hail, thou isle of fairyland, filled with beckoning figures!' I murmured under my breath, careful not to appear too unaccountable in Gertrud's eyes. With eager interest I looked about me, and anything less like fairyland and more like the coast of Pomerania lately left I have seldom seen. The road, a continuation of the road on the mainland, was exactly like other roads that are dull as far as a rambling village three miles farther on called Garz . . . and after Garz I ceased to care what it was like, for reasons which I will now set forth.

There was that afternoon in the market-place of Garz, and I know not why, since it was neither a Sunday nor a holiday, a brass band playing with a singular sonorousness. The horses having never before been required to listen to music, their functions at home being solely to draw me through the solitudes of forests, did not like it. I was astonished at the vigour of the dislike they showed who were wont to be so meek. They danced through Garz, pursued by the braying of the trumpets and the delighted shouts of the crowd, who seemed to bray and shout the louder the more the horses danced, and I was considering whether the time had not come for clinging to Gertrud and shutting my eyes when we turned a corner and got away from the noise on to the familiar rattle of the hard country road. I gave a sigh of relief and stretched out my head to see whether it were as straight a bit as the last. It was quite as straight, and in the distance bearing down on us was a black speck that swelled at an awful speed into a motor car. Now the horses had not yet seen a motor car. Their nerves, already shaken by the brass band, would never stand such a horrid sight I thought, and prudence urged an immediate getting out and a rushing to their heads. 'Stop, August!' I cried. 'Jump out, Gertrud—there's a dreadful thing coming—they're sure to bolt—'

August slowed down in apparent obedience to my order, and without waiting for him to stop entirely, the motor being almost upon us, I jumped out on one side and Gertrud jumped out on the other. Before I had time to run to the horses' heads the motor whizzed past. The horses strange to say hardly cared at all, only mildly shying as August drove them slowly along without stopping.

'That's all right,' I remarked, greatly relieved, to Gertrud, who still held her stocking. 'Now we'll get in again.'

But we could not get in again because August did not stop.

'Call to him to stop,' I said to Gertrud, turning aside to pick some unusually big poppies.

She called, but he did not stop.

'Call louder, Gertrud,' I said impatiently, for we were now a good way behind.

She called louder, but he did not stop.

Then I called; then she called; then we called together, but he did not stop. On the contrary, he was driving on now at the usual pace, rattling noisily over the hard road, getting more and more out of reach.

'Shout, shout, Gertrud!' I cried in a frenzy; but how could any one so respectable as Gertrud shout? She sent a faint shriek after the ever-receding August, and when I tried to shout myself I was seized with such uncontrollable laughter that nothing whatever of the nature of a noise could be produced.

Meanwhile August was growing very small in the distance. He evidently did not know we had got out when the motor car appeared, and was under the pleasing impression that we were sitting behind him being jogged comfortably towards Putbus. He dwindled and dwindled with a rapidity distressing to witness. 'Shout, shout,' I gasped, myself contorted with dreadful laughter, half wildest mirth and half despair.

She began to trot down the road after him waving her stocking at his distant back and emitting a series of shrill shrieks, goaded by the exigencies of the situation.

The last we saw of the carriage was a yellow glint as the sun caught the shiny surface of my bandbox; immediately afterwards it vanished over the edge of a far-away dip in the road, and we were alone with nature.

Gertrud and I stared at each other in speechless dismay. Then she looked on in silence while I sank on to a milestone and laughed. There was nothing, her look said, to laugh at, and much to be earnest over in our tragic predicament, and I knew it but I could not stop. August had had no instructions as to where he was driving to or where we were going to put up that night; of Putbus and Marianne North he had never heard. With the open ordnance map on my lap I had merely called out directions, since leaving Miltzow, at crossroads. Therefore in all human probability he would drive straight on till dark, no doubt in growing private astonishment at the absence of orders and the length of the way; then when night came he would, I supposed, want to light his lamps, and getting down to do so would immediately be frozen with horror at what he saw, or rather did not see, in the carriage. What he would do after that I could not conceive. In sheerest despair I laughed till I cried, and the sight of Gertrud watching me silently from the middle of the deserted road only made me less able to leave off. Behind us in the distance, at the end of a vista of *chaussée* trees, were the houses of Garz; in front of us, a long way in front of us, rose the red spire of the church of Casnewitz, a village through which, as I still remembered from the map now driving along by itself, our road to Putbus lay. Up and down the whiteness of this road not a living creature, either in a cart or on its legs, was to be seen. The bald country, here very bald and desolate, stretched away on either side into nothingness. The wind sighed about, whisking little puffs of derisive dust into our eyes as it passed. There was a dreadful absence of anything like sounds.

'No doubt,' said Gertrud, 'August will soon return?'

'He won't,' I said, wiping my eyes; 'he'll go on for ever. He's wound up. Nothing will stop him.'

'What, then, will the gracious one do?'

'Walk after him, I suppose,' I said, getting up, 'and trust to something unexpected making him find out he hasn't got us. But I'm afraid nothing will. Come on, Gertrud,' I continued, feigning briskness while my heart was as lead, 'it's nearly six already, and the road is long and lonely.'

'*Ach*,' groaned Gertrud, who never walks.

'Perhaps a cart will pass us and give us a lift. If not we'll walk to that village with the church over there and see if we can get something on wheels to pursue August with. Come on—I hope your boots are all right.'

'*Ach*,' groaned Gertrud again, lifting up one foot, as a dog pitifully lifts up its wounded paw, and showing me a black cashmere boot of the sort that is soft and pleasant to the feet of servants who are not required to use them much.

'I'm afraid they're not much good on this hard road,' I said. 'Let us hope something will catch us up soon.'

'*Ach*,' groaned poor Gertrud, whose feet are very tender.

But nothing did catch us up, and we trudged along in grim silence, the desire to laugh all gone.

'You must, my dear Gertrud,' I said after a while, seeking to be cheerful, 'regard this in the light of healthful exercise. You and I are taking a pleasant afternoon walk together in Rügen.'

Gertrud said nothing; at all times loathing movement out of doors she felt that this walking was peculiarly hateful because it had no visible end. And what would become of us if we were forced to spend the night in some inn without our luggage? The only thing I had with me was my purse, the presence of which, containing as it did all the money I had brought, caused me to cast a careful eye at short intervals behind me, less in the hope of seeing a cart than in the fear of seeing a tramp; and the only thing Gertrud had was her half-knitted stocking. Also we had had nothing to eat but a scrappy tea-basket lunch hours before in the train, and my intention had been to have food at Putbus and then drive down to a place called Lauterbach, which being on the seashore was more convenient for the jellyfish than Putbus, and spend the night there in an hotel much recommended by the guide-book. By this time according to my plans we ought to have been sitting in Putbus eating *Kalbsschnitzel*. 'Gertrud,' I asked rather faintly, my soul drooping within me at the thought of the *Kalbsschnitzel*, 'are you hungry?'

Gertrud sighed. 'It is long since we ate,' she said.

We trudged on in silence for another five minutes.

'Gertrud,' I asked again, for during those five minutes my thoughts had dwelt with a shameful persistency on the succulent and the gross, 'are you *very* hungry?'

'The gracious one too must be in need of food,' evaded Gertrud, who for some reason never would admit she wanted feeding.

'Oh she is,' I sighed; and again we trudged on in silence.

It seemed a long while before we reached that edge over which my bandbox had disappeared flashing farewell as it went, and when we did get to it and eagerly looked along the fresh stretch of road in hopes of seeing August miraculously turned back, we gave a simultaneous groan, for it was as deserted as the one we had just come along. Something lay in the middle of it a few yards on, a dark object like a little heap of brown leaves. Thinking it was leaves I saw no reason for comment; but Gertrud, whose eyes are very sharp, exclaimed.

'What, do you see August?' I cried.

'No, no—but there in the road—the tea-basket!'

It was indeed the tea-basket, shaken out as it naturally would be on the removal of the bodies that had kept it in its place, come to us like the ravens of old to give us strength and sustenance.

'It still contains food,' said Gertrud, hurrying towards it.

'Thank heaven,' said I.

We dragged it out of the road to the grass at the side, and Gertrud lit the spirit-lamp and warmed what was left in the teapot of the tea. It was of an awful blackness. No water was to be got near, and we dared not leave the road to look for any in case August should come back. There were some sorry pieces of cake, one or two chicken sandwiches grown unaccountably horrible, and all those strawberries we had avoided at lunch because they were too small or too much squashed. Over these mournful revels the church spire of Casnewitz, now come much closer, presided; it was the silent witness of how honourably we shared, and how Gertrud got the odd sandwich because of her cashmere boots.

Then we buried the tea-basket in a ditch, in a bed of long grass and cow-parsley, for it was plain that I could not ask Gertrud, who could hardly walk as it was, to carry it, and it was equally plain that I could not carry it myself, for it was as mysteriously heavy as other tea-baskets and in size very nearly as big as I am. So we buried it, not without some natural regrets and a dim feeling that we were flying in the face of Providence, and there it is, I suppose, grown very rusty, to this day.

After that Gertrud got along a little better, and my thoughts being no longer concentrated on food I could think out what was best to be done. The result was that on reaching Casnewitz we enquired at once which of the cottages was an inn, and having found one asked a man who seemed to belong there to let us have a conveyance with as much speed as possible.

'Where have you come from?' he enquired, staring first at one and then at the other.

'Oh—from Garz.'

'From Garz? Where do you want to go to?'

'To Putbus.'

'To Putbus? Are you staying there?'

'No—yes—anyhow we wish to drive there. Kindly let us start as soon as possible.'

'Start! I have no cart.'

'Sir,' said Gertrud with much dignity, 'why did you not say so at once?'

'*Ja, ja, Fräulein*, why did I not?'

We walked out.

'This is very unpleasant, Gertrud,' I remarked, and I wondered what those at home would say if they knew that on the very first day of my driving-tour I had managed to lose the carriage and had had to bear the banter of publicans.

'There is a little shop,' said Gertrud. 'Does the gracious one permit that I make enquiries there?'

We went in and Gertrud did the talking.

'Putbus is not very far from here,' said the old man presiding, who was at least polite. 'Why do not the ladies walk? My horse has been out all day, and my son who drives him has other things now to do.'

'Oh we can't walk,' I broke in. 'We must drive because we might want to go beyond Putbus—we are not sure—it depends—'

The old man looked puzzled. 'Where is it that the ladies wish to go?' he enquired, trying to be patient.

'To Putbus, anyhow. Perhaps only to Putbus. We can't tell till we get there. But indeed, indeed you must let us have your horse.'

Still puzzled, the old man went out to consult with his son, and we waited in profound dejection among candles and coffee. Putbus was not, as he had said, far, but I remembered how on the map it seemed to be a very nest of cross roads, all radiating from a round circus sort of place in the middle. Which of them would August consider to be the straight continuation of the road from Garz? Once beyond Putbus he would be lost to us indeed.

It took about half an hour to persuade the son and to harness the horse; and while this was going on we stood at the door watching the road and listening eagerly for sounds of wheels. One cart did pass, going in the direction of Garz, and when I heard it coming I was so sure that it was August that I triumphantly called to Gertrud to run and tell the old man we did not need his son. Gertrud, wiser, waited till she saw what it was, and after the quenching of that sudden hope we both drooped more than ever.

'Where am I to drive to?' asked the son, whipping up his horse and bumping us away over the stones of Casnewitz. He sat huddled up looking exceedingly sulky, manifestly disgusted at having to go out again at the end of a day's work. As for the cart, it was a sad contrast to the cushioned comfort of the vanished victoria. It was very high, very wooden, very shaky, and we sat on a plank in the middle of so terrible a noise that when we wanted to say anything we had to shout. 'Where am I to drive to?' repeated the youth, scowling over his shoulder.

'Please drive straight on until you meet a carriage.'

'A what?'

'A carriage.'

'Whose carriage?'

'My carriage.'

He scowled round again with deepened disgust. 'If you have a carriage,' he said, looking at us as though he were afraid we were lunatics, 'why are you in my cart?'

'Oh why, why are we!' I cried wringing my hands, overcome by the wretchedness of our plight; for we were now beyond Casnewitz, and gazing anxiously ahead with the strained eyes of Sister Annes we saw the road as straight and as empty as ever.

The youth drove on in sullen silence, his very ears seeming to flap with scorn; no more good words would he waste on two mad women. The road now lay through woods, beautiful beech woods that belong to Prince Putbus, not fenced off but invitingly open to every one, with green shimmering depths and occasional flashes of deer. The tops of the great beeches shone like gold against the sky. The sea must have been quite close, for though it was not visible the smell of it was everywhere. The nearer we got to Putbus the more civilized did the road become. Seats appeared on either side at intervals that grew more frequent. Instead of the usual wooden signposts, iron ones with tarnished gilt lettering pointed down the forest lanes; and soon we met the first of the Putbus lamp-posts, also iron and elaborate, wandered out, as it seemed, beyond the natural sphere of lamp-posts, to light the innocent country road. All these signs portended what Germans call *Badegäste*—in English obviously bath-guests, or, more elegantly, visitors to a bathing resort; and presently when we were nearer Putbus we began to pass them strolling in groups and couples and sitting on the seats which were of stone and could not have been good things for warm bath-guests to sit on.

Wretched as I was I still saw the quaintness and prettiness of Putbus. There was a notice up that all vehicles must drive through it at a walking pace, so we crawled along its principal street which, whatever else it contained, contained no sign of August. This street has Prince Putbus's grounds on one side and a line of irregular houses, all white, all old-fashioned, and all charming, on the other. A double row of great trees forms a shady walk on the edge of the grounds, and it is bountifully supplied with those stone seats so fatal, I am sure, to many an honest bath-guest. The grounds, trim and shady, have neat paths winding into their recesses from the road, with no fence or wall or obstacle of any sort to be surmounted by the timid tourist; every tourist may walk in them as long and as often as he likes without the least preliminary bother of gates and lodges.

As we jolted slowly over the rough stones we were objects of the liveliest interest to the bath-guests sitting out on the pavement in front of the inns having supper. No sign whatever of August was to be seen, not even an ordnance map, as I had half expected, lying in the road. Our cart made more noise here than ever, it being characteristic of Putbus that things on wheels are heard for an amazing time before and after their passing. It is the drowsiest little town. Grass grows undisturbed between the cobbles of the street, along the gutters, and in the cracks of the pavement on the side walk. One or two shops seem sufficient for the needs of all the inhabitants, including the boys at the school here which is a sort of German Eton, and from what I saw in the windows their needs are chiefly picture-postcards and cakes. There is a white theatre with a colonnade as quaint as all the rest. The houses have many windows and balconies hung about with flowers. The place did not somehow seem real in the bright flood of evening sunlight, it looked like a place in a picture or a dream; but the bath-guests, pausing in their eating to stare at us, were enjoying themselves in a very solid and undreamlike fashion, not in the least in harmony with the quaint background. In spite of my forlorn condition I could not help reflecting on its probable charms in winter under the clear green of the cold sky, with all these people away, when the frosted branches of the trees stretch across to deserted windows, when the theatre is silent for months, when the inns only keep as much of themselves open as meets the requirements of the infrequent commercial traveller, and the cutting wind blows down the street, empty all day long. Certainly a perfect place to spend a quiet winter in, to go to when one is tired of noise and bustle and of a world choked to the point of suffocation with strenuous persons trying to do each other good. Rooms in one of those spacious old houses with the large windows facing the sun, and plenty of books—if I were that abstracted but happy form of reptile called a bookworm, which I believe I am prevented from being only by my sex, the genus, I am told, being persistently male, I would take care to spend at least one of my life's winters in Putbus. How divinely quiet it would be. What a place for him who intends to pass an examination, to write a book, or who wants the crumples got by crushing together too long with his fellows to be smoothed out of his soul. And what walks there would be, to stretch legs and spirits grown stiff, in the crisp wintry woods where the pale sunshine falls across unspoilt snow. Sitting in my cart of sorrow in summer sultriness I could feel the ineffable pure cold of winter strike my face at the mere thought, the ineffable pure cold that spurs the most languid mind into activity.

Thus far had I got in my reflections, and we had jolted slowly down about half the length of the street, when a tremendous clatter of hoofs and wheels coming towards us apparently at a gallop in starkest defiance of regulations, brought me back with a jerk to the miserable present.

'Bolted,' remarked the surly youth, hastily drawing on one side.

The bath-guests at supper flung down their knives and forks and started up to look.

'Halt! Halt!' cried some of them. 'Es ist verboten! Schritt! Schritt!'

'How can he halt?' cried others. 'His horses have bolted.'

'Then why does he beat them?' cried the first.

'It is August!' shrieked Gertrud. 'August! August! We are here! Stop! Stop!'

For with staring eyes and set mouth August was actually galloping past us. This time he did hear Gertrud's shriek, acute with anguish, and pulled the horses on to their haunches. Never have I seen unhappy coachman with so white a face. He had had, it appeared, the most stringent private instructions before leaving home to take care of me, and on the very first day to let me somehow tumble out and lose me! He was tearing back in the awful conviction that he would find Gertrud and myself in the form of corpses. 'Thank God!' he cried devoutly on seeing us, 'Thank God! Is the gracious one unhurt?'

Certainly poor August had had the worst of it.

Now it is most unlikely that the bath-guests of Putbus will ever enjoy themselves quite so much again. Their suppers all grew cold while they crowded round to see and listen. August, in his relief, was a changed creature. He was voluble and loud as I never could have believed. Jumping off his box to turn the horses round and help me out of the cart, he explained to me and to all and any who chose to listen how he had driven on and on through Putbus, straight round the circus to the continuation of the road on the north side, where signposts revealed to him that he was heading for Bergen, more and more surprised at receiving no orders, more and more struck by the extreme silence behind him. 'The gracious one,' he amplified for the benefit of the deeply interested tourists, 'exchanges occasional observations with Fräulein'—the tourists gazed at Gertrud—'and the cessation of these became by degrees noticeable. Yet it is not permissible that a well-trained coachman should turn to look, or interfere with a *Herrschaft* that chooses to be silent—'

'Let us get on, August,' I interrupted, much embarrassed by all this.

'The luggage must be seen to—the strain of the rapid driving—'

A dozen helpful hands stretched out with offers of string.

'Finally,' continued August, not to be stopped in his excited account, manipulating the string and my holdall with shaking fingers—'finally by the mercy of Providence the map used by the gracious one fell out'—I knew it would—'as a peasant was passing. He called to me, he pointed to the road, I pulled up, I turned round, and what did I see? What I then saw I shall never—no, never forget—no, not if my life should continue to a hundred.' He put his hand on his heart and gasped. The crowd waited breathless. 'I turned round,' continued August, 'and I saw nothing.'

'But you said you would never forget what you saw,' objected a dissatisfied-looking man.

'Never, never shall I forget it.'

'Yet you saw nothing at all.'

'Nothing, nothing. Never will I forget it.'

'If you saw nothing you cannot forget it,' persisted the dissatisfied man.

'I say I cannot—it is what I say.'

'That will do, August,' I said; 'I wish to drive on.'

The surly youth had been listening with his chin on his hand. He now removed his chin, stretched his hand across to me sitting safely among my cushions, and said, 'Pay me.'

'Pay him, Gertrud,' I said; and having been paid he turned his horse and drove back to Casnewitz scornful to the last.

'Go on, August,' I ordered. 'Go on. We can hold this thing on with our feet. Get on to your box and go on.'

The energy in my voice penetrated at last through his agitation. He got up on to his box, settled himself in a flustered sort of fashion, the tourists fell apart staring their last and hardest at a vision about to vanish, and we drove away.

'It is impossible to forget that which has not been,' called out the dissatisfied man as August passed him.

'It is what I say—it is what I say!' cried August, irritated.

Nothing could have kept me in Putbus after this.

Skirting the circus on the south side we turned down a hill to the right, and immediately were in the country again with cornfields on either side and the sea like a liquid sapphire beyond them. Gertrud and I put a coat between us in place of the abandoned tea-basket, and settled in with an appreciation of our comforts that we had not had before. Gertrud, indeed, looked positively happy, so thankful was she to be safely in the carriage again, and joy was written in every line of August's back. About a mile and a half off lay Lauterbach, a little straggling group of houses down by the water; and quite by itself, a mile to the left of Lauterbach, I could see the hotel we were going to, a long white building something like a Greek temple, with a portico and a flight of steps the entire length of its façade, conspicuous in its whiteness against a background of beechwoods. Woods and fields and sea and a lovely little island a short way from the shore called Vilm, were bathed in sunset splendour. Lauterbach and not Putbus, then, was the place of radiant jellyfish and crystal water and wooded coves. Probably in those distant years when Marianne North enjoyed them Lauterbach as an independent village with a name to itself did not exist. A branch railway goes down now to the very edge of the sea. We crossed the line and drove between chestnut trees and high grassy banks starry with flowers to the Greek hotel.

How delightful it looked as we got out of the deep chestnut lane into the open space in front of it before we were close enough to see that time had been unkind. The sea was within a stone's throw on the right beyond a green, marshy, rushy meadow. On the left people were mowing in a field. Across the field the spire of a little Lutheran church looked out oddly round the end of the pagan portico. Behind and on either side were beeches. Not a soul came out as we drew up at the bottom of the steps. Not a soul was to be seen except the souls with scythes in the meadow. We waited a moment, thinking to hear a bell rung and to see flying waiters, but no one came. The scythes in the meadow swished, the larks called down that it was a fine evening, some fowls came and pecked about on the sunny steps of the temple, some red sails passed between the trunks of the willows down near the water.

'Shall I go in?' enquired Gertrud.

She went up the steps and disappeared through glass doors. Grass grew between the stones of the steps, and the walls of the house were damp and green. The ceiling of the portico was divided into squares and painted sky-blue. In one corner paint and plaster had come off together, probably in wild winter nights, and this and the grass-grown steps and the silence gave the place a strangely deserted look. I would have thought it was shut up if there had not been a table in the portico with a reassuring red-check cloth on it and a coffee-pot.

Gertrud came out again followed by a waiter and a small boy. I was in no hurry, and could have sat there contentedly for any time in the pleasant evening sunshine. The waiter assured me there was just one room vacant for me, and by the luckiest of chances just one other leading out of it for the Fräulein. I followed him up the steps. The portico, open at either end, framed in delicious pictures. The waiter led me through a spacious boarded hall where a narrow table along one side told of recent supper, through intricate passages, across little inner courts with shrubs and greenery, and blue sky above, and lilac bushes in tubs looking as though they had to pretend they were orange trees and that this was Italy and that the white plaster walls, so mouldy in places, were the marble walls of some classic baths, up strange stairs that sloped alarmingly to one side, along more passages, and throwing open one of the many small white doors, said with pride, 'Here is the apartment; it is a fine, a big, a splendid apartment.'

The apartment was of the sort that produces an immediate determination in the breast of him to whom it is offered to die sooner than occupy it. Sleep in its gloomy recesses and parti-coloured bed I would not. Sooner would I brave the authorities, and taking my holdall for a pillow go out to the grasshoppers for the night. In spite of the waiter's assertion, made for the glory of the house, that this was the one room unoccupied, I saw other rooms, perhaps smaller but certainly vacant, lurking in his eye; therefore I said firmly, 'Show me something else.'

The house was nearly all at my disposal I found. It is roomy, and there were hardly a dozen people staying in it. I chose a room with windows opening into the portico, through whose white columns I would be able to see a series of peaceful country pictures as I lay in bed. The boards were bare and the bed was covered with another of those parti-coloured quilts that suggest a desire to dissemble spots rather than wash them out. The Greek temple was certainly primitive, and would hardly appeal to any but the simplest, meekest of tourists. I hope I am simple and meek. I felt as though I must be as I looked round this room and knew that of my own free will I was going to sleep in it; and not only sleep in it but be very happy in it. It was the series of pictures between the columns that had fascinated me.

While Gertrud was downstairs superintending the bringing up of the luggage, I leaned out of one of my windows and examined the delights. I was quite close to the blue and white squares of the portico's ceiling; and looking down I saw its grass-grown pavement, and the head of a pensive tourist drinking beer just beneath me. Here again big lilac bushes planted at intervals between the columns did duty for orange trees. The north end framed the sky and fields and distant church; the south end had a picture of luminous water shining through beech leaves; the pair of columns in front enclosed the chestnut-lined road we had come along and the outermost white houses of Putbus among dark trees against the sunset on high ground behind; through those on the left was the sea, hardly sea here at all the bay is so sheltered, and hardly salt at all, for grass and rushes, touched just then by the splendour of light into a transient divine brightness, lay all along the shore. 'Truly the light is sweet, and a pleasant thing it is for the eyes to behold the sun,' I thought; aloud, I suppose, for Gertrud coming in with the holdall said, 'Did the gracious one speak?'

Quite unable to repeat this rapturous conviction to Gertrud, I changed it into a modest request that she should order supper.

How often in these grey autumn days have I turned my face away from the rain on the window and the mournful mistiness of the November fields, or my mind from the talk of the person next to me, to think with a smile of the beauty of that supper. Not that I had beautiful things to eat, for lengthy consultations with the waiter led only to eggs; but they were brought down steep steps to a little nook among the beeches at the water's edge, and this little nook on that particular evening was the loveliest in the world. Enthusiastically did I eat those eggs and murmur 'Earth has not anything to show more fair'—as much, that is, of it as could be made to apply. Nobody could see me or hear me down there, screened at the sides and back and overhead by the beeches, and it is an immense comfort secretly to quote. What did it matter if the tablecloth were damp, besides having other imperfections? What if the eggs cooled down at once, and cool eggs have always been an abomination to me? What if the waiter forgot the sugar, and I dislike coffee without sugar? Sooner than go up and search for him and lose one moment of that rosy splendour on the water I felt that I would go for ever sugarless. My table was nearly on a level with the sea. A family of ducks were slowly paddling about in front of me, making little furrows in the quiet water and giving an occasional placid quack. The ducks, the water, the island of Vilm opposite, the Lauterbach jetty half a mile off across the little bay with a crowd of fisher-boats moored near it, all were on fire with the same red radiance. The sun was just down, and the sky behind the dark Putbus woods was a marvel of solemn glory. The reflections of the beech trees I was sitting under lay black along the water. I could hear the fishermen talking over at the jetty, and a child calling on the island, so absolute was the stillness. And almost before I knew how beautiful it was the rosiness faded off the island, lingered a moment longer on the masts of the fisher-boats, gathered at last only in the pools among the rushes, died away altogether; the sky paled to green, a few stars looked out faintly, a light twinkled in the solitary house on Vilm, and the waiter came down and asked if he should bring a lamp. A lamp! As though all one ever wanted was to see the tiny circle round oneself, to be able to read the evening paper, or write postcards to one's friends, or sew. I have a peculiar capacity for doing nothing and yet enjoying myself. To sit there and look out into what Whitman calls the huge and thoughtful night was a comely and sufficient occupation for the best part of me; and as for the rest, the inferior or domestic part, the fingers that might have been busy, the tongue that might have wagged, the superficial bit of brain in daily use for the planning of trivialities, how good it is that all that should often be idle.

With an impatience that surprised him I refused the waiter's lamp.

A Journey

As she lay in her berth, staring at the shadows overhead, the rush of the wheels was in her brain, driving her deeper and deeper into circles of wakeful lucidity. The sleeping car had sunk into its night silence. Through the wet windowpane she watched the sudden lights, the long stretches of hurrying blackness. Now and then she turned her head and looked through the opening in the hangings at her husband's curtains across the aisle. . . .

She wondered restlessly if he wanted anything and if she could hear him if he called. His voice had grown very weak within the last months and it irritated him when she did not hear. This irritability, this increasing childish petulance seemed to give expression to their imperceptible estrangement. Like two faces looking at one another through a sheet of glass they were close together, almost touching, but they could not hear or feel each other: the conductivity between them was broken. She, at least, had this sense of separation, and she fancied sometimes that she saw it reflected in the look with which he supplemented his failing words. Doubtless the fault was hers. She was too impenetrably healthy to be touched by the irrelevancies of disease. Her self-reproachful tenderness was tinged with the sense of his irrationality: she had a vague feeling that there was a purpose in his helpless tyrannies. The suddenness of the change had found her so unprepared. A year ago their pulses had beat to one robust measure; both had the same prodigal confidence in an exhaustless future. Now their energies no longer kept step: hers still bounded ahead of life, pre-empting unclaimed regions of hope and activity, while his lagged behind, vainly struggling to overtake her.

When they married, she had such arrears of living to make up: her days had been as bare as the whitewashed schoolroom where she forced innutritious facts upon reluctant children. His coming had broken in on the slumber of circumstance, widening the present till it became the encloser of remotest chances. But imperceptibly the horizon narrowed. Life had a grudge against her: she was never to be allowed to spread her wings.

At first the doctors had said that six weeks of mild air would set him right; but when he came back this assurance was explained as having of course included a winter in a dry climate. They gave up their pretty house, storing the wedding presents and new furniture, and went to Colorado. She had hated it there from the first. Nobody knew her or cared about her; there was no one to wonder at the good match she had made, or to envy her the new dresses and the visiting cards which were still a surprise to her. And he kept growing worse. She felt herself beset with difficulties too evasive to be fought by so direct a temperament. She still loved him, of course; but he was gradually, undefinably ceasing to be himself. The man she had married had been strong, active, gently masterful: the male whose pleasure it is to clear a way through the material obstructions of life; but now it was she who was the protector, he who must be shielded from importunities and given his drops or his beef juice though the skies were falling. The routine of the sickroom bewildered her; this punctual administering of medicine seemed as idle as some uncomprehended religious mummery.

There were moments, indeed, when warm gushes of pity swept away her instinctive resentment of his condition, when she still found his old self in his eyes as they groped for each other through the dense medium of his weakness. But these moments had grown rare. Sometimes he frightened her: his sunken expressionless face seemed that of a stranger; his voice was weak and hoarse; his thin-lipped smile a mere muscular contraction. Her hand avoided his damp soft skin, which had lost the familiar roughness of health: she caught herself furtively watching him as she might have watched a strange animal. It frightened her to feel that this was the man she loved; there were hours when to tell him what she suffered seemed the one escape from her fears. But in general she judged herself more leniently, reflecting that she had perhaps been too long alone with him, and that she would feel differently when they were at home again, surrounded by her robust and buoyant family. How she had rejoiced when the doctors at last gave their consent to his going home! She knew, of course, what the decision meant; they both knew. It meant that he was to die; but they dressed the truth in hopeful euphemisms, and at times, in the joy of preparation, she really forgot the purpose of their journey, and slipped into an eager allusion to next year's plans.

At last the day of leaving came. She had a dreadful fear that they would never get away; that somehow at the last moment he would fail her; that the doctors held one of their accustomed treacheries in reserve; but nothing happened. They drove to the station, he was installed in a seat with a rug over his knees and a cushion at his back, and she hung out of the window waving unregretful farewells to the acquaintances she had really never liked till then.

The first twenty-four hours had passed off well. He revived a little and it amused him to look out of the window and to observe the humors of the car. The second day he began to grow weary and to chafe under the dispassionate stare of the freckled child with the lump of chewing gum. She had to explain to the child's mother that her husband was too ill to be disturbed: a statement received by that lady with a resentment visibly supported by the maternal sentiment of the whole car . . .

That night he slept badly and the next morning his temperature frightened her: she was sure he was growing worse. The day passed slowly, punctuated by the small irritations of travel. Watching his tired face, she traced in its contractions every rattle and jolt of the train, till her own body vibrated with sympathetic fatigue. She felt the others observing him too, and hovered restlessly between him and the line of interrogative eyes. The freckled child hung about him like a fly; offers of candy and picture books failed to dislodge her: she twisted one leg around the other and watched him imperturbably. The porter, as he passed, lingered with vague proffers of help, probably inspired by philanthropic passengers swelling with the sense that 'something ought to be done'; and one nervous man in a skull cap was audibly concerned as to the possible effect on his wife's health.

The hours dragged on in a dreary inoccupation. Towards dusk she sat down beside him and he laid his hand on hers. The touch startled her. He seemed to be calling her from far off. She looked at him helplessly and his smile went through her like a physical pang.

'Are you very tired?' she asked.

'No, not very.'

'We'll be there soon now.'

'Yes, very soon.'

'This time tomorrow—'

He nodded and they sat silent. When she had put him to bed and crawled into her own berth she tried to cheer herself with the thought that in less than twenty-four hours they would be in New York. Her people would all be at the station to meet her—she pictured their round unanxious faces pressing through the crowd. She only hoped they would not tell him too loudly that he was looking splendidly and would be all right in no time: the subtler sympathies developed by long contact with suffering were making her aware of a certain coarseness of texture in the family sensibilities.

Suddenly she thought she heard him call. She parted the curtains and listened. No, it was only a man snoring at the other end of the car. His snores had a greasy sound, as though they passed through tallow. She lay down and tried to sleep . . . Had she not heard him move? She started up trembling . . . The silence frightened her more than any sound. He might not be able to make her hear—he might be calling her now . . . What made her think of such things? It was merely the familiar tendency of an overtired mind to fasten itself on the most intolerable chance within the range of its forebodings . . . Putting her head out, she listened: but she could not distinguish his breathing from that of the other pairs of lungs about her. She longed to get up and look at him, but she knew the impulse was a mere vent for her restlessness, and the fear of disturbing him restrained her . . . The regular movement of his curtain reassured her, she knew not why; she remembered that he had wished her a cheerful good night; and the sheer inability to endure her fears a moment longer made her put them from her with an effort of her whole sound-tired body. She turned on her side and slept.

She sat up stiffly, staring out at the dawn. The train was rushing through a region of bare hillocks huddled against a lifeless sky. It looked like the first day of creation. The air of the car was close, and she pushed up her window to let in the keen wind. Then she looked at her watch: it was seven o'clock, and soon the people about her would be stirring. She slipped into her clothes, smoothed her disheveled hair and crept to the dressing-room. When she had washed her face and adjusted her dress she felt more hopeful. It was always a struggle for her not to be cheerful in the morning. Her cheeks burned deliciously under the coarse towel and the wet hair about her temples broke into strong upward tendrils. Every inch of her was full of life and elasticity. And in ten hours they would be at home!

She stepped to her husband's berth: it was time for him to take his early glass of milk. The window shade was down, and in the dusk of the curtained enclosure she could just see that he lay sideways, with his face away from her. She leaned over him and drew up the shade. As she did so she touched one of his hands. It felt cold . . .

She bent closer, laying her hand on his arm and calling him by name. He did not move. She spoke again more loudly; she grasped his shoulder and gently shook it. He lay motionless. She caught hold of his hand again: it slipped from her limply, like a dead thing. A dead thing?

Her breath caught. She must see his face. She leaned forward, and hurriedly, shrinkingly, with a sickening reluctance of the flesh, laid her hands on his shoulders and turned him over. His head fell back; his face looked small and smooth; he gazed at her with steady eyes.

She remained motionless for a long time, holding him thus; and they looked at each other. Suddenly she shrank back: the longing to scream, to call out, to fly from him, had almost overpowered her. But a strong hand arrested her. Good God! If it were known that he was dead they would be put off the train at the next station—

In a terrifying flash of remembrance there arose before her a scene she had once witnessed in traveling, when a husband and wife, whose child had died in the train, had been thrust out at some chance station. She saw them standing on the platform with the child's body between them; she had never forgotten the dazed look with which they followed the receding train. And this was what would happen to her. Within the next hour she might find herself on the platform of some strange station, alone with her husband's body . . . Anything but that! It was too horrible—She quivered like a creature at bay.

As she cowered there, she felt the train moving more slowly. It was coming then—they were approaching a station! She saw again the husband and wife standing on the lonely platform; and with a violent gesture she drew down the shade to hide her husband's face.

Feeling dizzy, she sank down on the edge of the berth, keeping away from his outstretched body, and pulling the curtains close, so that he and she were shut into a kind of sepulchral twilight. She tried to think. At all costs she must conceal the fact that he was dead. But how? Her mind refused to act: she could not plan, combine. She could think of no way but to sit there, clutching the curtains, all day long . . .

She heard the porter making up her bed; people were beginning to move about the car; the dressing-room door was being opened and shut. She tried to rouse herself. At length with a supreme effort she rose to her feet, stepping into the aisle of the car and drawing the curtains tight behind her. She noticed that they still parted slightly with the motion of the car, and finding a pin in her dress she fastened them together. Now she was safe. She looked round and saw the porter. She fancied he was watching her.

'Ain't he awake yet?' he inquired.

'No,' she faltered.

'I got his milk all ready when he wants it. You know you told me to have it for him by seven.'

She nodded silently and crept into her seat.

At half-past eight the train reached Buffalo. By this time the other passengers were dressed and the berths had been folded back for the day. The porter, moving to and fro under his burden of sheets and pillows, glanced at her as he passed. At length he said: 'Ain't he going to get up? You know we're ordered to make up the berths as early as we can.'

She turned cold with fear. They were just entering the station.

'Oh, not yet,' she stammered. 'Not till he's had his milk. Won't you get it, please?'

'All right. Soon as we start again.'

When the train moved on he reappeared with the milk. She took it from him and sat vaguely looking at it: her brain moved slowly from one idea to another, as though they were stepping-stones set far apart across a whirling flood. At length she became aware that the porter still hovered expectantly.

'Will I give it to him?' he suggested.

'Oh, no,' she cried, rising. 'He—he's asleep yet, I think—'

She waited till the porter had passed on; then she unpinned the curtains and slipped behind them. In the semi-obscurity her husband's face stared up at her like a marble mask with agate eyes. The eyes were dreadful. She put out her hand and drew down the lids. Then she remembered the glass of milk in her other hand: what was she to do with it? She thought of raising the window and throwing it out; but to do so she would have to lean across his body and bring her face close to his. She decided to drink the milk.

She returned to her seat with the empty glass and after a while the porter came back to get it.

'When'll I fold up his bed?' he asked.

'Oh, not now—not yet; he's ill—he's very ill. Can't you let him stay as he is? The doctor wants him to lie down as much as possible.'

He scratched his head. 'Well, if he's *really* sick—'

He took the empty glass and walked away, explaining to the passengers that the party behind the curtains was too sick to get up just yet.

She found herself the center of sympathetic eyes. A motherly woman with an intimate smile sat down beside her.

'I'm real sorry to hear your husband's sick. I've had a remarkable amount of sickness in my family and maybe I could assist you. Can I take a look at him?'

'Oh, no—no please! He mustn't be disturbed.'

The lady accepted the rebuff indulgently.

'Well, it's just as you say, of course, but you don't look to me as if you'd had much experience in sickness and I'd have been glad to assist you. What do you generally do when your husband's taken this way?'

'I—I let him sleep.'

'Too much sleep ain't any too healthful either. Don't you give him any medicine?'

'Y—yes.'

'Don't you wake him to take it?'

'Yes.'

'When does he take the next dose?'

'Not for—two hours—'

The lady looked disappointed. 'Well, if I was you I'd try giving it oftener. That's what I do with my folks.'

After that many faces seemed to press upon her. The passengers were on their way to the dining car, and she was conscious that as they passed down the aisle they glanced curiously at the closed curtains. One lantern-jawed man with prominent eyes stood still and tried to shoot his projecting glance through the division between the folds. The freckled child, returning from breakfast, waylaid the passers with a buttery clutch, saying in a loud whisper, 'He's sick'; and once the conductor came by, asking for tickets. She shrank into her corner and looked out of the window at the flying trees and houses, meaningless hieroglyphs of an endlessly unrolled papyrus.

Now and then the train stopped, and the newcomers on entering the car stared in turn at the closed curtains. More and more people seemed to pass—their faces began to blend fantastically with the images surging in her brain . . .

Later in the day a fat man detached himself from the mist of faces. He had a creased stomach and soft pale lips. As he pressed himself into the seat facing her she noticed that he was dressed in black broadcloth, with a soiled white tie.

'Husband's pretty bad this morning, is he?'

'Yes.'

'Dear, dear! Now that's terribly distressing, ain't it?' An apostolic smile revealed his gold-filled teeth. 'Of course you know there's no sech thing as sickness. Ain't that a lovely thought? Death itself is but a deloosion of our grosser senses. On'y lay yourself open to the influx of the sperrit, submit yourself passively to the action of the divine force, and disease and dissolution will cease to exist for you. If you could indooce your husband to read this little pamphlet—'

The faces about her again grew indistinct. She had a vague recollection of hearing the motherly lady and the parent of the freckled child ardently disputing the relative advantages of trying several medicines at once, or of taking each in turn; the motherly lady maintaining that the competitive system saved time; the other objecting that you couldn't tell which remedy had effected the cure; their voices went on and on, like bell buoys droning through a fog . . . The porter came up now and then with questions that she did not understand, but somehow she must have answered since he went away again without repeating them; every two hours the motherly lady reminded her that her husband ought to have his drops; people left the car and others replaced them . . .

Her head was spinning and she tried to steady herself by clutching at her thoughts as they swept by, but they slipped away from her like bushes on the side of a sheer precipice down which she seemed to be falling. Suddenly her mind grew clear again and she found herself vividly picturing what would happen when the train reached New York. She shuddered as it occurred to her that he would be quite cold and that someone might perceive he had been dead since morning.

She thought hurriedly: 'If they see I am not surprised they will suspect something. They will ask questions, and if I tell them the truth they won't believe me—no one would believe me! It will be terrible'— and she kept repeating to herself—'I must pretend I don't know. I must pretend I don't know. When they open the curtains I must go up to him quite naturally—and then I must scream! She had an idea that the scream would be very hard to do.

Gradually new thoughts crowded upon her, vivid and urgent: she tried to separate and restrain them, but they beset her clamorously, like her school children at the end of a hot day, when she was too tired to silence them. Her head grew confused, and she felt a sick fear of forgetting her part, of betraying herself by some unguarded word or look.

'I must pretend I don't know,' she went on murmuring. The words had lost their significance, but she repeated them mechanically, as though they had been a magic formula, until suddenly she heard herself saying: 'I can't remember, I can't remember!'

Her voice sounded very loud, and she looked about her in terror; but no one seemed to notice that she had spoken.

As she glanced down the car her eye caught the curtains of her husband's berth, and she began to examine the monotonous arabesques woven through their heavy folds. The pattern was intricate and difficult to trace; she gazed fixedly at the curtains and as she did so the thick stuff grew transparent and through it she saw her husband's face—his dead face. She struggled to avert her look, but her eyes refused to move and her head seemed to be held in a vice. At last, with an effort that left her weak and shaking, she turned away; but it was of no use; close in front of her, small and smooth, was her husband's face. It seemed to be suspended in the air between her and the false braids of the woman who sat in front of her. With an uncontrollable gesture she stretched out her hand to push the face away, and suddenly she felt the touch of his smooth skin. She repressed a cry and half started from her seat. The woman with the false braids looked around, and feeling that she must justify her movement in some way she rose and lifted her traveling bag from the opposite seat. She unlocked the bag and looked into it; but the first object her hand met was a small flask of her husband's, thrust there at the last moment, in the haste of departure. She locked the bag and closed her eyes . . . his face was there again, hanging between her eyeballs and lids like a waxen mask against a red curtain . . .

She roused herself with a shiver. Had she fainted or slept? Hours seemed to have elapsed; but it was still broad day, and the people about her were sitting in the same attitudes as before.

A sudden sense of hunger made her aware that she had eaten nothing since morning. The thought of food filled her with disgust, but she dreaded a return of faintness, and remembering that she had some biscuits in her bag she took one out and ate it. The dry crumbs choked her, and she hastily swallowed a little brandy from her husband's flask. The burning sensation in her throat acted as a counter-irritant, momentarily relieving the dull ache of her nerves. Then she felt a gently-stealing warmth, as though a soft air fanned her, and the swarming fears relaxed their clutch, receding through the stillness that enclosed her, a stillness soothing as the spacious quietude of a summer day. She slept.

Through her sleep she felt the impetuous rush of the train. It seemed to be life itself that was sweeping her on with headlong inexorable force—sweeping her into darkness and terror, and the awe of unknown days.—Now all at once everything was still—not a sound, not a pulsation . . . She was dead in her turn, and lay beside him with smooth upstaring face. How quiet it was!—and yet she heard feet coming, the feet of the men who were to carry them away . . . She could feel too—she felt a sudden prolonged vibration, a series of hard shocks, and then another plunge into darkness: the darkness of death this time—a black whirlwind on which they were both spinning like leaves, in wild uncoiling spirals, with millions and millions of the dead . . .

She sprang up in terror. Her sleep must have lasted a long time, for the winter day had paled and the lights had been lit. The car was in confusion, and as she regained her self-possession she saw that the passengers were gathering up their wraps and bags. The woman with the false braids had brought from the dressing room a sickly ivy plant in a bottle, and the Christian Scientist was reversing his cuffs. The porter passed down the aisle with his impartial brush. An impersonal figure with a gold-banded cap asked for her husband's ticket. A voice shouted 'Baig-gage *ex*press!' and she heard the clicking of metal as the passengers handed over their checks.

Presently her window was blocked by an expanse of sooty wall, and the train passed into the Harlem tunnel. The journey was over; in a few minutes she would see her family pushing their joyous way through the throng at the station. Her heart dilated. The worst terror was past . . .

'We'd better get him up now, hadn't we?' asked the porter, touching her arm.

He had her husband's hat in his hand and was meditatively revolving it under his brush.

She looked at the hat and tried to speak; but suddenly the car grew dark. She flung up her arms, struggling to catch at something, and fell face downward, striking her head against the dead man's berth.

Human Habitation

For the twentieth time, as the wet dusk became impenetrably charged with darkness, Jefferies looked distrustfully up at Jameson and challenged him: 'I suppose you *are* sure we're going the right way?'

Jameson, the tall man, was carrying the map; he took one step to every one and a half of Jefferies, and thus their footsteps made an uneven, shuffling sound, unutterably wearisome, on the mud and shingle of the tow-path. For the last hour they had walked, save for Jefferies' interpolations, in complete silence. Now and then a pebble bounded slantwise from the impact of foot, cleared the sedgy brink of the canal, and spun with a *plonk*, vindictively, into the silent water. It was late September; not a breath of wind; the fine rain stung the air.

Jameson's thin profile had faded from against the darkening sky; his voice came from so uncannily high up that Jefferies started when it said, 'Well, my dear fellow, if you don't believe me, take the map yourself.'

'I've got no matches,' he remarked, craning up his head sullenly to give emphasis to his words. 'You said I couldn't possibly have finished my matches before we came to Middlehampton. Now I have finished them. I suppose you can lend me your matches when I want another pipe?'

Jameson stopped, stooped, fumbled, and tucking the map under his arm brought out his match-box and shook it anxiously. They both stood still to listen. 'There's not many more,' he said unnecessarily. It did not sound as though there were more than three in the box.

'We'd better not smoke for a bit,' he said aggrievedly; 'that is, if you want to see the map.'

'Oh, well, I suppose if you *know* we're making the right way. But what I can't understand is: why we don't see the lights of Middlehampton.'

'Well, the air's so dense with rain.'

'Can't be *so* dense. You said half an hour ago that Middlehampton must be three and a half miles off.'

They plodded on; collars up, caps down. 'Ow, *Lord!*' yelped little Jefferies, stumbling and skidding. 'Steady on—the canal.'

'Well, I ought to know the canal's there, oughtn't I? After walking beside it for four days.'

They had made friends towards the end of the London University session. They were reading science. Jameson knew he liked walking tours, and Jefferies thought he very likely would. Jameson's bright bird-eyes, set so near together into his long thin nose, fascinated Jefferies. He was an awfully compelling sort of chap. The way he *talked* . . . So they went on a walking tour: it was to be at the end of the summer vacation, that they might return to college fearfully fit. They chose the canals of middle England; 'There's a regular network of 'em,' said Jameson, 'and you see some awfully jolly country. One reads a lot of poetry and stuff against the Midlands, but personally I think they're fine. And from our point of view, entirely undiscovered. Now if you go down west in summer, or even into the Home Counties—and of course Wales is hopeless, besides costing such a lot to get there—you find the whole place simply crammed with rich smart people swishing about in cars. You know, the real rotten sort. Even the smaller pubs are full of them. All the year's their holiday, and yet they come blocking up the place for Us Others *now*. Of course that's all going, but it makes me awfully sick. Girls, you know, absolute butterflies, and fellows who ought to be working.'

'Sick'ning,' had said Jefferies, who also disapproved of these things.

So they walked the Midlands, following the canals from village to village, making towards the town of Middlehampton, where there were some fine old churches and Jefferies had an aunt. They stayed the nights in public houses which were not comfortable, and in the evenings they used to sit downstairs and try to talk to people in the bar. Jameson said one should get to know the English country as more than a poetic abstraction and its people as more than a political entity, and Jefferies agreed that this was very true. They did not find the people in the bars interesting, but Jameson said that that would come.

Then it had begun raining. It rained a little on the second day, nothing to speak of, and they laughed and turned their collars up. The third day was nearly all wet, though it cleared towards evening and a fine sunset crimsoned the canal. Today it had come on about lunch time, a different rain; finer, gentler, more inexorable, that made the air woolly, left a muddy taste in one's mouth and dulled everything. They trudged; the rain stung their faces to stiffness; their minds grew numb. Since four o'clock they had not passed a village; Jameson, glancing perpetually at the map, promised that there should be one, but that village hung ever back from them as they pressed on to meet it. Once, very far away, through a momentary lightening of the dimness, they had seen a church spire pricking through a blur of trees; and about four-thirty they had passed a row of brick cottages, standing uncompromis-ingly a little bit away from a bridge. Jefferies asked, 'Tea there?' and jerked his head interrogatively and wistfully towards them, but Jameson, after scanning the cottages for a moment of uncertainty, had said, 'Why, confound it all, man, we can't go bursting into English people's homes and ordering them to give us tea just because we're in a position to pay for it. Well, how'd you like . . . After all, it's not as though we were abroad.'

Jefferies had said, 'No; oh, no,' without conviction, and remembered that Jameson had eaten twice as much dinner as he had. So they went squelching on.

Since then, there had been nothing. Not even, recently, the looming blur of trees; never a house, never a light; there was not a sound to be heard of a voice calling, a dog barking, or the rattle of a cart. Only, ahead of them along the tow-path, they had the sense of just a possibil-ity that something might approach them. Yes, once two barges had come up to meet them; the horse-hoofs being wrenched after every step from the sucking mud were louder than their impact. The water swished and gurgled under the prows; the smoke trickling from the chimneys of the cabins could not rise through the rain, but hung low and sullenly diffused itself. At the first prow a bargee was visible, dusky and inhuman; another man walked at the head of the first horse. Though it seemed as if for the whole afternoon they had been imminent, the dusk so suddenly disgorged them that Jameson and Jefferies had to spring into the hedge under the very nose of the horse with a violence that sent them sprawling among the prickly branches, to escape the tow-rope that would have mown them from their legs. The steaming flanks of the horses loomed beside them, and Jameson, recovering his balance, shouted from the hedge. 'This *is* the way to Middlehampton?' For answer the man leading the horse hailed back to him tonelessly and went by, never turning his head again, as Jameson's clamoured reiteration was drowned by the clopping of the horses' hoofs, the squelching of the mud, the rushing of the water round the prows. The unlighted cavalcade faded slowly, and was swallowed up. Nothing else came to meet the two, and nothing else passed them.

As the walls of rain closed in about him and became impenetrably dark, Jefferies felt sundered by a world from the now almost invisible Jameson. There was nothing beside him but a living organism that breathed stertorously and struggled on, slanting forward a little into the rain. And beside that big, mindless body trudged another smaller body, shuffling, sometimes desperately changing step in an attempt to establish rhythm. On to these two bodies the dulling eyes of Jefferies' mind looked out. He thought dimly, 'If I lose consciousness of myself, shall I leave off being? I don't believe in Jameson, I don't believe he's even there; there's just something, if I put out my hand, to obstruct it; something against which I should fall if I fell towards the canal, sideways. Why should the fact that one of those men's legs ache bother me? I don't believe in either of them. Curse, how my legs ache! Curse my legs! There was once a man called Jameson, who asked a man called Jefferies to walk with him for years and years along a canal, and—they walked and walked till Jefferies forgot himself and forgot what he had ever been. What happened then? I can't remember . . . Curse, I'm potty. Oh, curse my legs, they're real anyhow. But are they? Perhaps somebody somewhere else feels a pain and thinks it is a pain in a man called Jefferies' legs, and so there seems to be a man called Jefferies with his legs aching, walking in the rain. But am I the person who is feeling the pain somewhere else, or am I what they imagine?' He was, he decided, something somebody else had thought; he felt utterly objective, walking, walking. Such a silence, it might have been a night in May . . . He put his hand out and brushed it along the hedge; the hedge was always there, and the rain soaked silently through it.

Jameson had stopped walking; Jefferies felt himself shoot suddenly ahead. He arrested himself and asked, 'Well?' numbly without turning round. Jameson didn't sound so sure of himself.

'Perhaps we might just look at the map again; it's reassuring—here, you're better with the matches; strike away, old man, and I'll be nippy with the map.' He rustlingly unfolded it. Jefferies took the matchbox, and before the third match, trembling out, had expired, Jameson, bending his long glistening nose over the map, had seen enough. The last glowing match-head spat as it struck the water, and Jefferies, sucking a burnt finger, looked towards Jameson with a mute and animal expectancy. The other said slowly:

'Well, I'm damned. Well, I *am* damned!'

'Why?' said Jefferies dully.

Jameson explained very quickly and with detachment that they had after all taken the wrong turning when they came to that fork. They *had* somehow; it was jolly queer. Jameson thought it really was most awfully queer. This arm of the canal only seemed to lead to a brick-field; it must be a jolly big brickfield, mustn't it, to have an arm of the canal all to itself. He laughed nervously, and they listened while his laughter died away. Jefferies was very quiet. He asked after some time, as though perfunctorily, what they were going to do.

'I saw there was a road marked from the brickfield, straight to Middlehampton. It goes without any turnings, a class B road, awfully good walking. We might pick up a bus. You see, all we shall have done is simply to have come two sides of a triangle. That is all we shall have done. It's bad luck, isn't it—we *have* had a run of bad luck.'

'Yes,' said Jefferies. 'Let's go on.' It tired him worse, just standing there. So they went on walking. They did not believe, perhaps, that they gained very much by walking; everything had slipped away from them. They just kept on for the sake of keeping on, and because they could not talk, they could not think. Jefferies felt as though an effort at coherent thought would bring about some rupture in his brain. He had begun to believe vaguely—the thing took form in his brain nebulously without any very definite mental process—that they had stepped unnoticingly over a threshold into some dead and empty hulk of a world drawn up alongside, at times dangerously accessible to the unwary. There was a canal there, but were there not canals in the moon—or was it Mars? The motionless water silently accompanied them, always just beyond Jameson, a half-tone paler than the sky—it was like a line ruled with a slate pencil, meaninglessly, across some forgotten slate that has been put away.

'Look over there,' whispered Jameson. 'I'll swear I see lights.' He spoke so softly, as though he feared to scare the lights away, that it came into Jefferies' mind that he must mean people, carrying lanterns. 'Why,' he cried, looking with narrowed eyes through the rain, 'those are house-lights. Quite square, not moving—windows.'

'Then there must be a house,' deduced Jameson. 'There'll be people, you know, and they might let us come by the fire. They'd tell us the way, but I expect they'd ask us to stay for a bit. You know,' he said, as they approached, 'those are very dull lights—muffled. It looks to me as though they'd got the blinds down.'

'Yes, I expect they have; they wouldn't want everybody looking in. There are lights upstairs, too, d'you see? It must be quite a biggish house, if it's got two storeys. I expect the people are well-to-do, and live here because they like it. It would be rather a jolly place to live.' He saw a picture of the house in summer, white-faced and somehow Continental, blistering a little in the glare from the canal, with sun-blinds, and a garden with a white fence running down to the tow-path, and crimson hollyhocks slanting lazily against the fence. He thought there might be an elm or two, a bit to the side, to give shade to the house and garden: that would be very nice, Jefferies thought. 'I expect it must be awfully nice in summer,' he said elatedly, turning to Jameson. 'Topping,' they agreed. 'Why, if the weather cleared, I expect it would look topping tomorrow.' It was extraordinary how happy they felt as they approached the lights, and how benevolent.

There *was* a little garden, and the gate swung to behind them: the latch clicked of its own accord. This brought some one to an upper window before Jameson, standing at the door with raised hand a shade portentously, had had time to knock. A blind swung sideways, displaced by a body, the window was pushed up with a rattle, and a woman's voice cried out in ecstasy and reproach, with a note in it of immeasurable relief, '*Oh Willy!*'

So certain was she, that she momentarily unconvinced Jefferies and Jameson of their own identities. They stepped back a pace or two to see her better: she leaned against the window frame, keeping the blind pushed sideways into folds with one elbow. They saw her form against the dim, dark-yellow lamplight—Woman, all the women of the world, hailing them home with relief and expectation. Something stirred warmly in both of them; it would be like this to have a wife. She was up there with her child; they could hear a burst of thin querulous wailing, at which she did not turn her head, but only peered out more closely into the darkness. The rain before the window shimmered in the outpoured lamplight.

'Well?' she cried. '*Come in*. You're late. Oh *Willy*!'

She was so blind to them down there that they were fain to stand pretending; till Jefferies, wrenching himself free of something, cried out ruefully, 'We're not.' He was so husky, it was doubtful whether she could distinguish his words, but she started back and stood rigid at the unfamiliar voice. Then she leaned forward to thrust out her head at them.

'Get on with you,' she blustered. 'Get along, will you! This isn't a public; the Green Man's beyond the brickyard. Don't come bothering here, or I'll send my husband out to you, and if you don't get along then he'll fetch his brother . . .' She listened a moment for the sound of their retreat, then added, 'and the dog.'

'But, Ma'am, I say!' expostulated Jameson in a cultured voice. This was awkward: if she were going to take it like this, how could they ask to come in to her fire? If only she could see them, if only it were not so dark! She was a kind young woman; her arm, with which she now impatiently held the blind back, was round against the light—'Just a minute, if you don't mind. We've missed our way; would you be so kind as to direct us?'

They could feel her frown with the perplexity that was in her voice as she asked: 'Who are you? What do you want?'

'We're students, walking; we've missed our way, and we've been walking hours without meeting a soul. Can we speak to your husband?'

'He's asleep,' she said quickly, 'and his brother and the dog are asleep, too, by the parlour fire. I don't want to wake them. If I stand here calling, the child won't sleep a wink all night. Will you promise you'll give no trouble? Straight? . . . Then I'll come down.'

She let the blind swing back, and they heard her footsteps recede towards the door. Then they waited, it seemed interminably. One window below, a bay on the ground floor, was lighted; the blinds were down here too, and were etched over with the symmetrical shadow of curtains. In this lighted, hidden room they heard a door open, and there was the sound of voices—statement, repetition, query, repetition, statement. Someone in there had been listening silently and noiselessly to all they said; now that someone was being deferred to and they knew that judgement on them trembled in the balance.

Though by now indifferent to rain, they had advanced instinctively into the shelter of the porch, and it was standing here that they heard the bolts creak back in their sockets and the rattle of a chain. Jameson had time to whisper, 'They're well enough barricaded!' before the woman's face looked round the door at them in a dim slit of light.

As Jameson had expected, and as Jefferies had been secretly convinced, it was not difficult to arrive at an understanding.

'You're what did you say? Students . . . oh, at college? Oh, then, you're quite young fellows.' She was easier with them now. 'Yes, you've taken the wrong turning miles away back. How did you come to? Very wet. It's a bad night; I'm sorry for any one that's out. Yes, you've still got a good bit before you. You must follow the track across the brickfield; that'll bring you out on to the Middlehampton road. Six miles, my husband reckons it, or six and a half. Yes, the buses do run on Wednesdays, but you'll have to wait now till the nine-thirty. It's about twenty minutes' walk from here to where the buses stop. No, there's no village or anything, just a cross-roads. We're in a lonely place.'

'Thanks,' said Jameson, reluctantly, 'then we'll be getting on. I dare say we shall find some shelter in the brickyard?'

She hesitated, playing with the bolt inside the door and peering urgently into their faces in the uncertain light.

'If you'd like to come in . . .' she said at last slowly, 'I know I can trust you not to make a noise and disturb the child—and my husband and his brother. You can come into the living-room, there's only Aunt in *there*.'

They followed her in.

Revealed in what then seemed to them the dazzling glory of the lamplight, the young woman showed pleasant of feature, with shy, perturbed but not unfriendly eyes. Her back was still very straight; she was quite a girl, no older than they were. It seemed strange that it should have been her child that they had heard crying upstairs. She wore a pink blouse, a string of corals round her neck; and gave the impression of having recently adorned herself, but of being now so preoccupied that she was unaware of her finery. In her eyes there was a look of the anguished evasion of some dread; she seemed to the two young men to be feverishly aware of them yet not to care whether they were there or not. The lamp stood on the waxed covering of the table; beside the lamp, a little behind the girl, sat a very stout elderly woman immobile, her hands folded under her bosom, looking dispassionately across the pool of lamplight at the two young men. They stood caps in hand, their cheeks burning in the sudden warmth, their eyes blinking in the brightness, looking from the young woman to the older one, round at the pictures, furniture and ranged china of the room with an avidity perfunctorily concealed. Here was a Wife . . . an Aunt . . . a Living-room—*home*.

'I asked the gentlemen in, Auntie.'

'Ah,' said Auntie, of whom only the eyes were mobile, summing them up. 'Yes. They're very wet—did they come far?' Though she did not directly address him, she looked enquiringly at Jameson, who replied obliquely, addressing himself to the niece, that they had been walking since two o'clock, since leaving Pidsthorpe. 'Then they can't have had no tea,' deduced the old lady with obvious pleasure. Well no, they admitted that they hadn't.

Auntie was the soul of hospitality. She now released a smile which rippled out slowly, and embedded itself in her cheeks. She invited them to sit down, and asked them if they wouldn't like to take their coats off and hang them by the fire. When they had done this, had hung their coats up on two empty, two somehow significantly empty pegs, they seated themselves opposite her and smiled politely, and Jameson blinked his bird eyes and ruffled up his hair. The great plane of Auntie's bosom was heaved up and shifted by a sigh as she said, *she* wouldn't mind a cup of tea, if anybody else were having it, as they had had to wait already more than an hour for their suppers, and it was likely that they would have to wait some hours more—Lord only knew how long. She dwelt upon them with her eyes benevolently, and said she did like a bit of company. 'I really can't think,' she said, tilting her whole bulk confidentially towards them, 'I really can't think what's become of William. He's very regular, he's never missed his tea before. Oh, I do hope nothin' hasn't happened.'

The girl had slipped out of the circle of lamplight and was standing by the window, listening intently for something outside. She turned round slowly with her eyes dilated as her aunt reiterated: 'I *should* feel bad if anything had happened.'

'Oh, *Aunt*,' she deprecated, 'how you do go on! *Happened*—what should have happened? He's just been delayed.'

'Nothing hasn't ever delayed him before,' the other mused inexorably. 'I don't remember any other occasion when he's been delayed, I'd never believe he'd been going to the public, but *really*—'

'*Ooh*,' cried the girl, writhing her shoulders, as though intolerably stung.

'But I thought—' objected Jameson eagerly, and broke off because Jefferies had kicked him under the table. They both remembered suddenly that they had seen only one window lighted on the downstairs floor. The realization that she had lied to them in fear made them both feel very large, forgiving, and protective. The old lady twinkled at them knowingly and hospitably, doing the honours of her niece's emotion as she did the honours of her niece's house. 'It's very anxious for her,' she said, inviting their appreciation with a gesture. She turned her eyes to the girl, after a few seconds' pregnant silence, and said, 'Well, Annie, let's have the supper on the table, and have a little tea and a little bit of something tasty, anyway. What I always say: expectin'' and expectin' somebody and holdin' everything over for them's not the way to make 'em come. If he's coming, he come; and all the sooner for not being waited for.'

'*If he's coming!*' echoed the girl, turning round from the dresser where she was taking some plates down off a rack. '*If* he's coming to his own home! Any one would think you thought he'd fallen into the canal,' she cried excitedly, and then caught her breath, assailed with terror by her own words as though someone else had spoken them.

'Ah,' said Auntie, like the dropping of a stone.

The plates were of white earthenware with a gilt border and a gilt flower in the middle. Jefferies, bending to study them, thought they were significant and beautiful as, having lifted the lamp for a second to wipe over the table, she ranged them round mechanically, at regular intervals, as though she were dealing out the counters for a game. It did seem to Jefferies a game that they were all playing, a game that for her life's sake she must win; and every dish and bowl and knife that she put down to glitter under the lamp seemed a concession she was making to opponents, a handicap she was accepting. She passed to and fro between the table and the dresser mechanically, yet with a faint air of deliberation, and sometimes she would pause and grope a little blindly along the dresser with her fingers. The Aunt, looking into the lamp, tucked in her lips, refolded her hands with precision, and settled down into her bosom. A clock with a big round face ticked loudly on the mantel; the dull scarlet fire rustled and twitched, and all at once the kettle began singing, so loudly and so suddenly that Jefferies started.

'Now you've only got to make the tea,' the Aunt prompted inexorably, 'and take those kippers out of the oven. Oh, those *was* good kippers; it'll be too bad if they're dried.'

Were Jefferies and Jameson to eat William's kippers? The girl knelt down before the fire, opened the little oven and half took out something the savouriness of which crept towards them. Then she slid back the dish with a clatter, and softly, deprecatingly, but very firmly shut the oven door. She remained kneeling on the hearthrug, her face to the fire, in an attitude of prayer; and said, without turning round, 'There's eggs, Auntie; I'll just do up a few eggs.'

'And yet it does seem a pity not to eat the kippers!' said Auntie thoughtfully.

This was horrible, something was being violated. 'It would be very kind,' said Jefferies, 'if you'd let us have a cup of tea and a bit of bread-

and-butter. We oughtn't to have supper till we get to where we're going to at Middlehampton; they'll be keeping supper for us there.'

'Oh?' asked Jameson, looking at him dully.

'Yes,' said Jefferies with increased conviction. 'They'll be keeping supper for us there.'

So Auntie's kipper was brought to her on a plate, and the girl came slowly to take her place at the table, carrying the enormous teapot in both hands. As she bent to place it on its saucer, she started violently, the saucer clattered, and she straightened herself, and dammed with tense face and upraised hand the flow of Auntie's conversation. Auntie had already told Jameson she had a nephew in London, and now she was telling him how nice the nephew was. They all started and hung poised: then they only heard the child upstairs faintly and fitfully crying. 'Going up?'

'Oh no, it makes him worse, it makes him cry all night,' the mother said listlessly.

The tea steamed in the cups and was fragrant. Jefferies, gazing down into the brown translucency, watched the sugar he had spooned in generously dissolve before he dimmed the clearness with a cloud of milk. He laced his fingers round his cup, and their tips, still numb, slowly thawed. The girl cut the loaf into slices very methodically, and slid the butter-dish towards him from across the table. He looked into her distraught eyes with nostalgia for something that they held.

Jameson, a creature of more easy expansions, had thawed visibly to his very depths. He beamed; his lips, slimy with excitement, glittered in the lamplight; he held the table. Aunt said 'Well, I never!' to him when she paused to take another slice of bread, or push her empty cup across to be refilled; the girl, while part of her mind (to Jefferies' understanding) still stood sentinel, leaned towards Jameson with startled eyebrows over the teapot. He painted that new Earth which was to be a new Heaven for them, which he, Jameson, and others were to be swift to bring about. He intimated that they even might participate in its creation. They gazed at it, and Jefferies gazed with them, but it was as though he had been suddenly stricken colour-blind. He could see nothing of the New Jerusalem, but the infinite criss-cross of brickwork and Jameson shouting at the corner of the empty streets. A sudden shifting of his values made him dizzy; he leaned back to think but could visualize nothing but the living-room: it expanded till its margin lay beyond the compass of his vision. After all, it all came back to this—individual outlook; the emotional factors of environment; houses that were homes; living-rooms; people going out and coming in again; people not coming in; other people waiting for them in rooms that were little guarded squares of light walled in carefully against the hungry darkness, the ultimately all-devouring darkness. After all, here was the stage of every drama. Only very faintly and thinly came the voice of Jameson crying in the wilderness.

Whatever you might deny your body, there must be always something, a somewhere, that the mind came back to.

Jameson did not refuse a third cup; he reached out across the table for it eagerly, still talking. 'Live?' he was saying: 'Why, we'll all live, live till we turn to the wall in a sleep of splendid exhaustion and never wake up again. You've seen a great perfect machine, how it roars round in an ecstasy? Well, that could be *us*—just realize it; there's nothing between our something and *that* something, cohesive, irresistible, majestic, but our *un-wills*, the feebleness of our desires. If every hand of the race were once, just once, outstretched unanimously, there would be nothing that those hands, that hand—I mean the *common* Hand—couldn't grasp; nothing too high, nothing too great. I—I always think that's an awfully solemn thought. Why, you know, there's a cry for life on the lips of every child, and we—you—people *stifle* it, because they're afraid of living. They think living's too *big*—Thanks, only half a slice, really.' He looked round vaguely for the butter-dish, and Jefferies thought that very much thus must have spoken Zarathustra.

'Well, you *do* talk!' said Aunt, with pacific enjoyment.

The girl had dropped away from Jameson; she leaned back once more, her folded hands lying listless and forgotten on the table before her, and looked up at the ring of lamplight on the ceiling. Her face was tilted back into the shadow; only her chin gleamed, and her thin throat. She didn't want what Jameson was offering her, she did not understand it. One could not feel she was a stupid girl; it was possible that she merely thought Jameson noisy. One felt that she had built up for herself an intricate and perhaps rather lonely life, monotone beneath the great shadow of William. Jameson was tapping out his points with his spoon against his cup and clamouring about cohesion, but he would be unable to understand the queer unity which had created and destroyed Annie. She might have been leaning now into the yellow circle, all one sparkle, laughing at them and flashing her eyes, a desirable and an acquirable thing.

'You know,' said Aunt archly to Jameson, 'that's Socialism you've been talking. Of course I wouldn't say I thought you meant anything of the sort by what you've been saying, but it might give some people considerable offence. It doesn't do sometimes to go talking Socialism, even for a bit of fun. But what I always say—boys will be boys, and young men too. I like a bit of fun.'

So Jameson began again: he was determined to do Auntie justice.

'Oh!' cried the girl unconsciously, beneath her breath. She turned her head and looked as though beseechingly at Jefferies, who stared back, and felt quite sick because he could do nothing for her. 'I've been listening all the time, too,' he whispered.

'Yes. You can hear steps for a long time, coming down the path.'

'Didn't you hear ours were double?'

'Yes, I did hear that. But I sort of didn't want to.'

'No. Would you like me to go out and meet him?'

'Oh no, you couldn't. He'd be angry I'd been letting on.'

'We'll have to be going now. Can't I do anything to help you?'

'Well, you can't, can you? I've just got to wait.'

'I wish I could make it be next morning,' he said violently, not quite knowing what he meant.

'What?' she asked dully. A tear trickled down her face.

'It's awful for you to be afraid.'

'Afraid? There's nothing to be afraid of; he's just—he's just late.'

'Yes, of course.' He felt there were things that could have been done to make it easier for her; he wanted to muffle Aunt's head up and wrench down the ticking clock. He could do neither of these things, so he said, 'Well, we must be getting on for that bus now,' in a loud voice, pushed back his chair and looked across at Jameson.

It was difficult to leave the living-room; they felt like candles wavering, soon to be extinguished. They hitched down their coats and struggled on with them, leaving the pegs by the fire empty and attentive for William's coat. Annie brushed her hand along Jameson's wet sleeve and sighed; then she preceded them to the door. Auntie sat amazed and plaintive at the disruption of the supper-table; after they had said goodbye she followed them with one long, hard, regretful stare, then let her eyes return to where they loved to rest. At their last glimpse of her she sat again immobile, her hands folded under her bosom, staring into the lamp.

Jefferies muttered, brushing against Annie in the doorway, 'If we pass him, is there . . . could we . . . ?'

'Oh no,' she said, with a desolate half-laugh, 'there's nothing you could say. If you pass him he'll be coming home.'

'Goodbye,' boomed Jameson abruptly holding out his big hand. 'You've been awfully good. Thank you ever so much for the tea and—and everything. You've been awfully good.'

'Oh no,' she said vaguely, and vaguely held out her hand to Jefferies. He started at the chilly contact, said 'Goodbye' gruffly, and dived past her into the cave of darkness beyond the threshold. Jameson stumbled after him and the door was abruptly shut. They heard the bolts creak forward and the chain rattle as they went, with hands before them, blindly down the path. They paused to let the fence and the canal take form again, which they did with an even greater dimness; then stepped down on to the tow-path, gently closing the gate. They went forward again, briskly, breathlessly, shuffle-shuffle; never quite in step. The air seemed colder, the rain heavier and finer. The tow-path still went on, it seemed so infinitely that, when hearing the sound of their footsteps suddenly constricted they found themselves approaching the looming masses of the brickfield, it was incredible that the path could have an end.

'Doesn't tea make one feel better?' said Jameson, speaking for the first time.

'Heaps . . . What a queer house!'

'I wonder when he'll be back?'

'Yes. We shall never know.'

They became aware half by instinct of a gap, a brief cessation in the hedge, and turned through it up a cart-track, splashing in the ruts, stumbling in the mud.

'She said the track was not long. We outstayed our time—think we'll get the bus, old fellow?'

'Don't know. Jameson, shan't we ever know if he came back?'

There was no answer.

They stumbled forward in the dark with tingling minds.

EVELYN WAUGH

Cruise

(Letters from a Young Lady of Leisure)

SS *Glory of Greece*

Darling,

Well I said I would write and so I would have only goodness it was
rough so didnt. Now everything is a bit more alright so I will tell you.
Well as you know the cruise started at Monte Carlo and when papa
and all of us went to Victoria we found that the tickets didnt include
the journey there so Goodness how furious he was and said he wouldnt
go but Mum said of course we must go and we said that too only papa
had changed all his money into Liri or Franks on account of foreigners
being so dishonest but he kept a shilling for the porter at Dover being
methodical so then he had to change it back again and that set him
wrong all the way to Monte Carlo and he wouldnt get me and Bertie
a sleeper and wouldnt sleep himself in his through being so angry
Goodness how Sad.

Then everything was much more alright the purser called him
Colonel and he likes his cabin so he took Bertie to the casino and he
lost and Bertie won and I think Bertie got a bit plastered at least he
made a noise going to bed he's in the next cabin as if he were being
sick and that was before we sailed. Bertie has got some books on
Baroque art on account of his being at Oxford.

Well the first day it was rough and I got up and felt odd in the bath
and the soap wouldnt work on account of salt water you see and came
into breakfast and there was a list of so many things including steak
and onions and there was a corking young man who said we are the
only ones down may I sit here and it was going beautifully and he had
steak and onions but it was no good I had to go back to bed just when
he was saying there was nothing he admired so much about a girl as
her being a good sailor goodness how sad.

The thing is not to have a bath and to be very slow in all movements. So next day it was Naples and we saw some Bertie churches and then that bit that got blown up in an earthquake and a poor dog killed they have a plaster cast of him goodness how sad. Papa and Bertie saw some pictures we weren't allowed to see and Bill drew them for me afterwards and Miss P. tried to look too. I havent told you about Bill and Miss P. have I? Well Bill is rather old but clean looking and I don't suppose hes very old not really I mean and he's had a very disillusionary life on account of his wife who he says I wont say a word against but she gave him the raspberry with a foreigner and that makes him hate foreigners. Miss P. is called Miss Phillips and is lousy she wears a yachting cap and is a bitch. And the way she makes up to the second officer is no ones business and its clear to the meanest intelligence he hates her but its part of the rules that all the sailors have to pretend to fancy the passengers. Who else is there? Well a lot of old ones. Papa is having a walk out with one called Lady Muriel something or other who knew uncle Ned. And there is a honeymoon couple very embarrassing. And a clergyman and a lovely pansy with a camera and white suit and lots of families from the industrial north.

So Bertie sends his love too. XXXXXXetc.

Mum bought a shawl and an animal made of lava.

Post-card

This is a picture of Taormina. Mum bought a shawl here. V. funny because Miss P. got left as shed made chums only with second officer and he wasnt allowed ashore so when it came to getting into cars Miss P. had to pack in with a family from the industrial north.

SS Glory of Greece

Darling,

Hope you got P.C. from Sicily. The moral of that was not to make chums with sailors though who I've made a chum of is the purser who's different on account he leads a very cynical life with a gramophone in his cabin and as many cocktails as he likes and welsh rabbits sometimes and I said but do you pay for all these drinks but he said no that's all right.

So we have three days at sea which the clergyman said is a good thing as it makes us all friendly but it hasn't made me friendly with

Miss P. who won't leave poor Bill alone not taking any more chances of being left alone when she goes ashore. The purser says theres always someone like her on board in fact he says that about everyone except me who he says quite rightly is different goodness how decent.

So there are deck games they are hell. And the day before we reach Haifa there is to be a fancy dress dance. Papa is very good at the deck games especially one called shuffle board and eats more than he does in London but I daresay its alright. You have to hire dresses for the ball from the barber I mean we do not you. Miss P. has brought her own. So I've thought of a v. clever thing at least the purser suggested it and that is to wear the clothes of one of the sailors I tried his on and looked a treat. Poor Miss P.

Bertie is madly unpop. he wont play any of the games and being plastered the other night too and tried to climb down a ventilator and the second officer pulled him out and the old ones at the captains table look *askance* at him. New word that. Literary yes? No?

So I think the pansy is writing a book he has a green fountain pen and green ink but I couldnt see what it was. XXXX Pretty good about writing you will say and so I am.

Post-card

This is a photograph of the Holyland and the famous sea of Gallillee. It is all v. Eastern with camels. I have a lot to tell you about the ball. *Such* goings on and will write very soon. Papa went off for the day with Lady M. and came back saying enchanting woman Knows the world.

SS *Glory of Greece*

Darling,

Well the Ball we had to come in to dinner in our clothes and everyone clapped as we came downstairs. So I was pretty late on account of not being able to make up my mind whether to wear the hat and in the end did and looked a corker. Well it was rather a faint clap for me considering so when I looked about there were about twenty girls and some women all dressed like me so how cynical the purser turns out to be. Bertie looked horribly dull as an apache. Mum and Papa were sweet. Miss P. had a ballet dress from the Russian ballet which couldnt have been more unsuitable so we had champagne for dinner and were jolly and they threw paper streamers and I threw mine before it was unrolled and hit Miss P. on the nose. Ha ha. So feeling matey I said to the steward isnt this fun and he said yes for them who hasnt got to clear it up goodness how Sad.

Well of course Bertie was plastered and went a bit far particularly in what he said to Lady M. then he sat in the cynical pursers cabin in the dark and cried so Bill and I found him and Bill gave him some drinks and what do you think he went off with Miss P. and we didnt see either of them again it only shows into what degradation the Demon Drink can drag you him I mean.

Then who should I meet but the young man who had steak and onions on the first morning and is called Robert and said I have been trying to meet you again all the voyage. Then I bitched him a bit goodness how Decent.

Poor Mum got taken up by Bill and he told her all about his wife and how she had disillusioned him with the foreigner so to-morrow we reach Port Said d.v. which is latin in case you didn't know meaning God Willing and all to go up the nile and to Cairo for a week.

Will send P.C. of Sphinx.

XXXXXX

Post-card

This is the Sphinx. Goodness how Sad.

Post-card

This is temple of someone. Darling I cant wait to tell you I'm engaged to Arthur. Arthur is the one I thought was a pansy. Bertie thinks egyptian art is v. inartistic.

Post-card

This is Tutankhamens v. famous Tomb. Bertie says it is vulgar and is engaged to Miss P. so hes not one to speak and I call her Mabel now. G how S. Bill wont speak to Bertie Robert wont speak to me Papa and Lady M. seem to have had a row there was a man with a snake in a bag also a little boy who told my fortune which was v. prosperous Mum bought a shawl.

Post-card

Saw this Mosque today. Robert is engaged to a new girl called something or other who is lousy.

SS *Glory of Greece*

Darling,

Well so we all came back from Egypt pretty excited and the cynical purser said what news and I said *news* well Im engaged to Arthur and Bertie is engaged to Miss P. and she is called Mabel now which is hardest of all to bear I said and Robert to a lousy girl and Papa has had a row with Lady M. and Bill has had a row with Bertie and Roberts lousy girl was awful to me and Arthur was sweet but the cynical purser wasnt a bit surprised on account he said people always get engaged and have quarrels on the Egyptian trip every cruise so I said I wasnt in the habit of getting engaged lightly thank you and he said I wasnt apparently in the habit of going to Egypt so I wont speak to him again nor will Arthur.

All love.

SS *Glory of Greece*

Sweet,

This is Algiers *not* very eastern in fact full of frogs. So it is all off with Arthur I was right about him at the first but who I am engaged to is Robert which is *much* better for all concerned really particularly Arthur on account of what I said originally first impressions always right. Yes? No? Robert and I drove about all day in the Botanic gardens and Goodness he was Decent. Bertie got plastered and had a row with Mabel—Miss P. again—so thats all right too and Robert's lousy girl spent all day on board with second officer. Mum bought shawl. Bill told Lady M. about his disillusionment and she told Robert who said yes we all know so Lady M. said it was very unreticent of Bill and she had very little respect for him and didn't blame his wife or the foreigner.

Love.

Post-card

I forget what I said in my last letter but if I mentioned a lousy man called Robert you can take it as unsaid. This is still Algiers and Papa ate *dubious oysters* but is all right. Bertie went to a house full of tarts when he was plastered and is pretty unreticent about it as Lady M. would say.

Post-card

So now we are back and sang old lang syne is that how you spell it and I kissed Arthur but wont speak to Robert and he cried not Robert I mean Arthur so then Bertie apologized to most of the people hed insulted but Miss P. walked away pretending not to hear. Goodness what a bitch.

Travelogue

They met for the first time at luncheon in the diner of the westbound limited that had left Chicago the night before. The girls, it turned out, were Hazel Dignan and her friend Mildred Orr. The man was Dan Chapman.

He it was who broke the ice by asking if they minded riding backwards. It was Hazel who answered. She was a seasoned traveler and knew how to talk to strangers. Mildred had been hardly anywhere and had little to say, even when she knew people.

'Not at all,' was Hazel's reply to his polite query. 'I'm so used to trains that I believe I could ride on top of them and not be uncomfortable.'

'Imagine,' put in Mildred, 'riding on top of a train!'

'Many's the time I've done it!' said their new acquaintance. 'Freight-trains, though; not passenger-trains. And it was when I was a kid.'

'I don't see how you dared,' said Mildred.

'I guess I was a kind of a reckless, wild kid,' he said. 'It's a wonder I didn't get killed, the chances I took. Some kids takes lots of chances; that is, boys.'

'Girls do, too,' said Hazel quickly. 'Girls take just as many chances as boys.'

'Oh, no, Hazel!' remonstrated her friend, and received an approving look from the male.

'Where are you headed for?' he asked.

'Frisco first and then Los Angeles,' Hazel replied.

'Listen—let me give you a tip. Don't say "Frisco" in front of them native sons. They don't like that nickname.'

'I should worry what they like and don't like!' said Hazel, rather snootily, Mildred thought.

'This your first trip out there?' Chapman inquired.

'No,' Hazel answered to Mildred's surprise, for the purpose of the journey, she had been led to believe, was to give Hazel a glimpse of one of the few parts of America that she had never visited.

'How long since you was out there last?' asked Chapman.

'Let's see,' said Hazel. 'It's been—' She was embarrassed by Mildred's wondering look. 'I don't know exactly. I've forgotten.'

'This is about my fiftieth trip,' said Chapman. 'If you haven't been—'

'I like Florida better,' interrupted Hazel. 'I generally go there in the winter.'

'Generally!' thought Mildred, who had reliable information that the previous winter had been her friend's first in the South.

'I used to go to Palm Beach every year,' said Chapman, 'but that was before it got common. It seems to be that the people that goes to Florida now, well, they're just riffraff.'

'The people that go to Tampa aren't riffraff,' said Hazel. 'I met some lovely people there last winter, especially one couple, the Babcocks. From Racine. They were perfectly lovely to me. We played Mah Jongg nearly every evening. They wanted me to come up and visit them in Racine this last summer, but something happened. Oh, yes; Sis's nurse got married. She was a Swedish girl. Just perfect. And Sis had absolute confidence in her.

'I always say that when a Swede is good, they're *good*! Now she's got a young girl about nineteen that's wild about movie actors and so absent-minded that Sis is scared to death she'll give Junior coffee and drink his milk herself. Just crazy! Jennie, her name is. So I didn't get up to Racine.'

'Ever been out to Yellowstone?'

'Oh, isn't it wonderful!' responded Hazel. 'Isn't "Old Faithful" just fascinating! You see,' she explained to Mildred, 'it's one of the geysers and they call it "Old Faithful" because it spouts every hour and ten minutes or something, just as regular as clockwork. Wonderful! And the different falls and canyons! Wonderful! And what a wonderful view from Inspiration Point!'

'Ever been to the Thousand Islands?' asked Chapman.

'Wonderful! And I was going up there again last summer with a girl friend of mine, Bess Eldridge. She was engaged to a man named Harley Bateman. A wonderful fellow when he wasn't drinking, but when he'd had a few drinks, he was just terrible. So Bess and I were in Chicago and we went to a show; Eddie Cantor. It was the first time I ever saw him when he wasn't blacked up. Well, we were walking out of the theater that night and who should we run into but Harley Bateman, terribly boiled, and a girl from Elkhart, Joan Killian. So Bess broke off her engagement and last fall she married a man named Wannop who's interested in flour-mills or something up in Minneapolis. So I didn't get to the Thousand Islands after all. That is, a second time.

'But I always think that if a person hasn't taken that trip, they haven't seen anything. And Bess would have certainly enjoyed it. She used to bite her finger-nails till she didn't have any left. But she married this man from Minneapolis.'

After luncheon the three moved to the observation-car and made a brave effort to be interested in what passes for scenery in Nebraska.

For no possible reason, it reminded Chapman of Northern Michigan.

'Have you ever been up in Northern Michigan?'

'Yes, indeed,' said Hazel. 'I visited a week once in Petoskey. Some friends of mine named Gilbert. They had their own launch. Ina Gilbert—that's Mrs Gilbert—her hair used to be the loveliest thing in the world and she had typhoid or something and lost nearly all of it. So we played Mah Jongg every afternoon and evening.'

'I mean 'way up,' said Chapman. 'Mackinac Island and the Upper Peninsula, the Copper Country.'

'Oh, wonderful!' said Hazel. 'Calumet and Houghton and Hancock! Wonderful! And the boat trip is wonderful! Though I guess I was about the only one that thought so. Everybody else was sick. The captain said it was the roughest trip he'd ever been on, and he had lived on the Great Lakes for forty years. And another time I went across from Chicago to St Joseph. But that wasn't so rough. We visited the House of David in Benton Harbor. They wear long beards. We were almost in hysterics, Marjorie Trumbull and I. But the time I went to Petoskey, I went alone.'

'You see a lot of Finns up in that Northern Peninsula,' remarked Chapman.

'Yes, and Sis had a Finnish maid once. She couldn't hardly understand a word of English. She was a Finn. Sis finally had to let her go. Now she has an Irish girl for a maid and Jennie takes care of the kiddies. Poor little Dickie, my nephew, he's nearly seven and of course he's lost all his front teeth. He looks terrible! Teeth do make such a difference! My friends always say they envy me my teeth.'

*

'Talking about teeth,' said Chapman, 'you see this?' He opened his mouth and pointed to a large, dark vacancy where once had dwelt a molar. 'I had that one pulled in Milwaukee the day before yesterday. The fella said I better take gas, but I said no. So he said, "Well, you must be pretty game." I said I faced German shell-fire for sixteen months and I guess I ain't going to be a-scared of a little forceps. Well, he said afterwards that it was one of the toughest teeth he ever pulled. The roots were the size of your little finger. And the tooth itself was full of—'

'I only had one tooth pulled in my life,' said Hazel. 'I'd been suffering from rheumatism and somebody suggested that it might be from a tooth, but I couldn't believe it at first because my teeth are so perfect. But I hadn't slept in months on account of these pains in my arms and limbs. So finally, just to make sure, I went to a dentist, old Doctor Platt, and he pulled this tooth'—she showed him where it had been— 'and my rheumatism disappeared just like that. It was terrible not to be able to sleep because I generally sleep like a log. And I do now, since I got my tooth pulled.'

'I don't sleep very good on trains,' said Chapman.

'Oh, I do. Probably on account of being so used to it. I slept just beautifully last night. Mildred here insisted on taking the upper. She said if she was where she could look out the window, she never would go to sleep. Personally, I'd just as lief have the upper. I don't mind it a bit. I like it really better. But this is Mildred's first long trip and I thought she ought to have her choice. We tried to get a compartment or drawing-room, but they were all gone. Sis and I had a compartment the time we went to New Orleans. I slept in the upper.'

Mildred wished she had gone places so she could take part in the conversation. Mr Chapman must think she was terribly dumb.

She had nothing to talk about that people would care to hear, and it was kind of hard to keep awake when you weren't talking yourself, even with such interesting, traveled people to listen to as Mr Chapman and Hazel. Mr Chapman was a dandy-looking man and it was terrible to have to appear dumb in front of him.

But after all, she *was* dumb and Hazel's erudition made her seem all the dumber. No wonder their new acquaintance had scarcely looked at her since luncheon.

'Have you ever been to San Antone?' Chapman asked his companions.

'Isn't it wonderful!' Hazel exclaimed. 'The Alamo! Wonderful! And those dirty Mexicans! And Salt Lake City is wonderful, too! That temple! And swimming in the lake itself is one of the most fascinating experiences! You know, Mildred, the water is so salt that you can't sink in it. You just lie right on top of it like it was a floor. You can't sink. And another wonderful place is Lake Placid. I was going back there last summer with Bess Eldridge, but she was engaged at the time to Harley Bateman, an awfully nice boy when he wasn't drinking, but perfectly terrible when he'd had a few drinks. He went to college with my brother, to Michigan. Harley tried for the football nine, but the coach hated him. His father was a druggist and owned the first automobile in Berrien County. So we didn't go to Placid last summer, but I'm going next summer sure. And it's wonderful in winter, too!'

'It feels funny, where that tooth was,' said Chapman.

'Outside of one experience,' said Hazel, 'I've never had any trouble with my teeth. I'd been suffering from rheumatism and somebody suggested it might be a bad tooth, but I couldn't believe it because my teeth are perfect—'

'This was all shot to pieces,' said Chapman.

'But my friends always say they envy me my teeth; my teeth and my complexion. I try to keep my mouth clean and my face clean, and I guess that's the answer. But it's hard to keep clean on a train.'

'Where are you going? Out to the coast?'

'Yes. Frisco and then Los Angeles.'

'Don't call it Frisco in front of them Californians. They don't like their city to be called Frisco. Is this your first trip out there?'

'No. I was there a good many years ago.'

She turned to Mildred.

'You didn't know that, did you?' she said. But Mildred was asleep. 'Poor Mildred! She's worn out. She isn't used to traveling. She's quite a pretty girl, don't you think so?'

'Very pretty!'

'Maybe not exactly pretty,' said her friend, 'but kind of sweet-looking, like a baby. You'd think all the men would be crazy about her, but they aren't. Lots of people don't even think she's pretty and I suppose you can't be really pretty unless you have more expression in your face than she's got. Poor Mildred hasn't had many advantages.'

'At this time of year, I'd rather be in Atlantic City than San Francisco.'

'Oh, isn't Atlantic City wonderful! There's only one Atlantic City! And I really like it better in the winter. Nobody but nice people go there in the winter. In the summer-time it's different. I'm no snob, but

I don't mind saying that I hate to mix up with some people a person has to meet at these resort places. Terrible! Two years ago I went to Atlantic City with Bess Eldridge. Like a fool I left it to her to make the reservations and she wired the Traymore, she says, but they didn't have anything for us. We tried the Ritz and the Ambassador and everywhere else, but we couldn't get in anywhere, that is, anywhere a person would want to stay. Bess was engaged to Harley Bateman at the time. Now she's married to a man named Wannop from Minneapolis. But this time I speak of, we went to Philadelphia and stayed all night with my aunt and we had scrapple and liver and bacon for breakfast. Harley was a dandy boy when he wasn't drinking. But give me Atlantic City any time of the year!'

'I've got to send a telegram at Grand Island.'

'Oh, if I sent one from there, when would it get to Elkhart?'

'Tonight or tomorrow morning.'

'I want to wire my sister.'

'Well, wire her from Grand Island.'

'I think I'll wait and wire her from Frisco.'

'But we won't be in San Francisco for over two days yet.'

'But we change time before then, don't we?'

'Yes, we change at North Platte.'

'Then I think I'll wire her from Grand Island.'

'Your sister, you say?'

'Yes. My sister Lucy. She married Jack Kingston, the Kingston tire people.'

'It certainly feels empty, where that tooth was,' said Chapman.

As the train pulled out of North Platte, later in the afternoon, Chapman rejoined the two girls in the observation-car.

'Now, girls,' he said, 'you can set your watches back an hour. We change time here. We were Central time and now we're Mountain time.'

'Mountain time,' repeated Mildred. 'I suppose that's where the expression started, "it's high time".'

Hazel and Chapman looked blank and Mildred blushed. She felt she had made a mistake saying anything at all. She opened her book, 'Carlyle on Cromwell and Others,' which Rev. N. L. Veach had given her for Christmas.

'Have you ever been to Washington?' Chapman asked Hazel.

'Oh, isn't it beautiful! "The City of Magnificent Distances". Wonderful! I was there two years ago with Bess Eldridge. We were going to meet the President, but something happened. Oh, yes; Bess got a wire from Harley Bateman that he was going to get in that afternoon. And he never came at all. He was awfully nice when he wasn't drinking, and just terrible when he drank. Bess broke off her engagement to him and married a man named Wannop, who owned some flour-mills in Minneapolis. She was a dandy girl, but bit her finger-nails just terribly. So we didn't get to see the President, but we sat through two or three sessions of the Senate and House. Do you see how they ever get anything done? And we went to Rock Creek Park and Mount Vernon and Arlington Cemetery and Keith's.

'Moran and Mack were there; you know, the black-face comedians. Moran, or maybe it's Mack, whichever is the little one, he says to the other—I've forgotten just how it went, but they were simply screaming and I thought Bess and I would be put out. We just howled. And the last night we were there we saw Thomas Meighan in "Old Home Week". Wonderful! Harley Bateman knows Thomas Meighan personally. He's got a beautiful home out on Long Island. He invited Harley out there to dinner one night, but something happened. Oh, yes; Harley lost a front tooth once and he had a false one put in and this day he ate some caramels and the tooth came out—'

'Look here,' said Chapman, opening his mouth and pointing in it. 'I got that one pulled in Milwaukee—'

'Harley was a perfect peach when he was sober, but terrible when —'

It occurred to Mildred that her presence might be embarrassing. Here were evidently kindred spirits, two people who had been everywhere and seen everything. But of course they couldn't talk anything but geography and dentistry before her.

'I think I'll go to our car and take a little nap,' she said.

'Oh, don't—' began Chapman surprisingly, but stopped there.

She was gone and the kindred spirits were alone.

'I suppose,' said Chapman, 'you've been to Lake Louise.'

'Wonderful!' Hazel responded. 'Did you ever see anything as pretty in your life? They talk about the lakes of Ireland and Scotland and Switzerland, but I don't believe they can compare with Lake Louise. I was there with Bess Eldridge just before she got engaged to Harley Bateman. He was—'

'Your friend's a mighty pretty girl.'

'I suppose some people would think her pretty. It's a matter of individual taste.'

'Very quiet, isn't she?'

'Poor Mildred hasn't much to say. You see, she's never had any advantages and there's really nothing she can talk about. But what was I saying? Oh, yes; about Harley Bateman—'

'I think that's a good idea, taking a little nap. I believe I'll try it, too.'

Hazel and Chapman lunched alone next day.

'I'm afraid Mildred is a little train sick,' said Hazel. 'She says she is all right but just isn't hungry. I guess the trip has been a little too much for her. You see, this is the first time she's ever been anywhere at all.'

The fact was that Mildred did not like to be stared at and Chapman had stared at her all through dinner the night before, stared at her, she thought, as if she were a curiosity, as if he doubted that one so dumb could be real. She liked him, too, and it would have been so nice if she had been more like Hazel, never at a loss for something to say and able to interest him in her conversation.

'We'll be in Ogden in half an hour,' said Chapman. 'We stay there twenty-five minutes. That ought to give your friend a chance to get over whatever ails her. She should get out and walk around and get some air.'

'You seem quite interested in Mildred,' Hazel said.

'She's a mighty attractive girl,' he replied. 'And besides, I feel sorry for anybody that—'

'Men don't usually find her attractive. She's pretty in a way, but it's a kind of a babyish face.'

'I don't think so at all—'

'We change time here again, don't we?'

'Yes. Another hour back. We've been on Mountain time and now we go to Pacific time. Some people say it's bad for a watch to turn it backwards, but it never seemed to hurt mine any. This watch—'

'I bought this watch of mine in New York,' said Hazel. 'It was about two years ago, the last time Bess Eldridge and I went East. Let's see; was that before or after she broke her engagement to Harley Bateman? It was before. But Harley said he knew the manager of the Belmont and he would wire him and get us a good room. Well, of course, he forgot to wire, so we finally got into the Pennsylvania, Room 1012.

No, Room 1014. It was some people from Pittsburgh, a Mr and Mrs Bradbury, in 1012. He was lame. Bess wanted to see Jeanne Eagels in "Rain" and we tried to get tickets at the newsstand, but they said fifteenth row. We finally went to the Palace that night. Ina Claire was on the bill. So the next morning we came down to breakfast and who should we run into but Dave Homan! We'd met him at French Lick in the spring. Isn't French Lick wonderful!

'Well, Dave insisted on "showing" us New York, like we didn't know it backwards. But we did have a dandy time. Dave kept us in hysterics. I remember he took us to the Aquarium and of course a lot of other people were in there and Dave gave one of the attendants a quarter to page Mr Fish. I thought they'd put us out, we screamed so! Dave asked me to marry him once, just jokingly, and I told him I wouldn't think of it because I had heard it made people fat to laugh and if I lived with him I would soon have to buy my clothes from a tent-maker. Dave said we would make a great pair as we both have such a keen sense of humor. Honestly, I wouldn't give up my sense of humor for all the money in the world. I don't see how people can live without a sense of humor. Mildred, for instance; she never sees the funny side of things unless you make her a diagram and even then she looks at you like she thought you were deranged.

'But I was telling you about Dave Homan. We were talking along about one thing and another and I happened to mention Harley Bateman and Dave said, "Harley Bateman! Do you know Harley Bateman?" and Bess and I smiled at each other and I said I guessed we did. Well, it seems that Dave and Harley had been at Atlantic City together at a Lions' convention or something and they had some drinks and Dave had a terrible time keeping a policeman from locking Harley up. He's just as different when he's drinking as day and night. Dave got him out of it all right and they met again later on, in Chicago. Or was it Duluth? So the next day was Wednesday and Dave asked Bess and I to go to the matinée of "Rain", but Bess had an engagement with a dentist—'

'Do you see this?' interrupted Chapman, opening his mouth wide.

'So Dave took me alone and he said he had been hoping for that chance right along. He said three was a crowd. I believe if I had given him any encouragement— But the man I marry must be something more than clever and witty. I like men that have been around and seen things and studied human nature and have a background. Of course they must see the funny side, too. That's the trouble with Dave

Homan—he can't be serious. Harley Bateman is twice as much of a man if he wouldn't drink. It's like two different people when he drinks. He's terrible! Bess Eldridge was engaged to him, but she broke it off after we happened to see him in Chicago one time with Joan Killian, from Elkhart. Bess is married now, to a man named Wannop, a flour man from Minneapolis. So after the matinée we met Bess. She'd been to the dentist—'

'Three days ago, in Milwaukee—' began Chapman.

'So the next afternoon we were taking the boat for Boston. I'd been to Boston before, of course, but never by boat. Harley Bateman told us it was a dandy trip, so we decided to try it. Well, we left New York at five o'clock and Bess and I were up on deck when somebody came up behind us and put their hands over my eyes and said, "Guess who it is?" Well, I couldn't have guessed in a hundred years. It was Clint Poole from South Bend. Imagine! Harley Bateman's brother-in-law!'

'Here's Ogden,' said Chapman as the train slowed down.

'Oh, and I've got to send Sis a telegram! My sister Lucy Kingston.'

'I think I'll get out and get some air,' said Chapman, but he went first to the car where Mildred sat reading.

'Miss Mildred,' he said, 'suppose you have breakfast with me early tomorrow morning. I'd like to show you the snow-sheds.'

'That would be wonderful!' said Mildred. 'I'll tell Hazel.'

'No,' said Chapman. 'Please don't tell Hazel. I'd like to show them to you alone.'

Well, even if Mildred had been used to trains, that remark would have interfered seriously with her night's sleep.

Mildred found Chapman awaiting her in the diner next morning, an hour west of Truckee.

'Are those the snow-sheds you spoke of?'

'Yes,' he replied, 'but we'll talk about them later. First I want to ask you a few questions.'

'Ask *me* questions!' said Mildred. 'Well, they'll have to be simple ones or I won't be able to answer them.'

'They're simple enough,' said Chapman. 'The first one is, do you know Harley Bateman?'

'I know *of* him, but I don't know him.'

'Do you know Bess Eldridge?'

'Just to speak to; that's all.'

'What other trips have you taken besides this?'

'None at all. This is really the first time I've ever been anywhere.'

'Has your friend ever been engaged?'

'Yes; twice. It was broken off both times.'

'I bet I know why. There was no place to take her on a honeymoon.'

'What do you mean?'

'Oh, nothing. Say, did I tell you about getting my tooth pulled in Milwaukee?'

'I don't believe so,' said Mildred.

'Well, I had a terrible toothache. It was four days ago. And I thought there was no use fooling with it, so I went to a dentist and told him to pull it. He said I'd better take gas, but I wouldn't. So he pulled it and it pretty near killed me, but I never batted an eye. He said it was one of the toughest teeth he'd ever seen; roots as big as your little finger. And the tooth itself full of poison.'

'How terrible! You must be awfully brave!'

'Look here, at the hole,' said Chapman, opening his mouth.

'Why, Mr Chapman, it must have hurt horribly!'

'Call me Dan.'

'Oh, I couldn't.'

'Well, listen—are you going to be with Miss Hazel all the time you're in San Francisco?'

'Why, no,' said Mildred. 'Hazel is going to visit her aunt in Berkeley part of the time. And I'm going to stop at the Fairmont.'

'When is she going to Berkeley?'

'Next Tuesday, I think.'

'Can I phone you next Wednesday?'

'But Hazel will be gone then.'

'Yes, I know,' said Chapman, 'but if you don't mind, I'll phone you just the same. Now about these snow-sheds—'

Show Mr and Mrs F. to Number—

We are married. The Sibylline parrots are protesting the sway of the first bobbed heads in the Biltmore panelled luxe. The hotel is trying to look older.

The faded rose corridors of the Commodore end in subways and subterranean metropolises—a man sold us a broken Marmon and a wild burst of friends spent half an hour revolving in the revolving door.

There were lilacs open to the dawn near the boarding-house in Westport where we sat up all night to finish a story. We quarrelled in the grey morning dew about morals; and made up over a red bathing-suit.

The Manhattan took us in one late night though we looked very young and gay. Ungratefully we packed the empty suitcase with spoons and the phone book and a big square pin-cushion.

The Traymore room was grey and the chaise-longue big enough for a courtesan. The sound of the sea kept us awake.

Electric fans blew the smell of peaches and hot biscuit and the cindery aroma of travelling salesmen through the New Willard halls in Washington.

But the Richmond hotel had a marble stair and long unopened rooms and marble statues of the gods lost somewhere in its echoing cells.

At the O. Henry in Greensville they thought a man and his wife ought not to be dressed alike in white knickerbockers in nineteen-twenty and we thought the water in the tubs ought not to run red mud.

Next day the summer whine of phonographs billowed out the skirts of the southern girls in Athens. There were so many smells in the drug stores and so much organdy and so many people just going somewhere.
. . . We left at dawn.

1921

They were respectful in the Cecil in London; disciplined by the long majestuous twilights on the river and we were young but we were impressed anyway by the Hindus and the Royal Processions.

At the St James and Albany in Paris we smelled up the room with an uncured Armenian goat-skin and put the unmelting 'ice-cream' outside the window, and there were dirty postcards, but we were pregnant.

The Royal Danieli in Venice had a gambling machine and the wax of centuries over the window-sill and there were fine officers on the American destroyer. We had fun in a gondola feeling like a soft Italian song.

Bamboo curtains and an asthma patient complaining of the green plush and an ebony piano were all equally embalmed in the formal parlours of the Hôtel d'Italie in Florence.

But there were fleas on the gilded filigree of the Grand Hôtel in Rome; men from the British Embassy scratched behind the palms; the clerks said it was the flea season.

Claridge's in London served strawberries in a gold dish, but the room was an inside room and grey all day, and the waiter didn't care whether we left or not, and he was our only contact.

In the fall we got to the Commodore in St Paul, and while leaves blew up the streets we waited for our child to be born.

1922–1923

The Plaza was an etched hotel, dainty and subdued, with such a handsome head waiter that he never minded lending five dollars or borrowing a Rolls Royce. We didn't travel much in those days.

1924

The Deux Mondes in Paris ended about a blue abysmal court outside our window. We bathed the daughter in the *bidet* by mistake and she drank the gin fizz thinking it was lemonade and ruined the luncheon table next day.

Goat was to eat in Grimm's Park Hotel in Hyères, and the bougainvillea was brittle as its own colour in the hot white dust. Many soldiers loitered outside the gardens and brothels listening to the nickelodeons.

The nights, smelling of honeysuckle and army leather, staggered up the mountain side and settled upon Mrs Edith Wharton's garden.

At the Ruhl in Nice we decided on a room not facing the sea, on all the dark men being princes, on not being able to afford it even out of season. During dinner on the terrace, stars fell in our plates, and we tried to identify ourselves with the place by recognizing faces from the boat. But nobody passed and we were alone with the deep blue grandeur and the *filet de sole Ruhl* and the second bottle of champagne.

The Hôtel de Paris at Monte Carlo was like a palace in a detective story. Officials got us things: tickets and permissions, maps and newly portentous identities. We waited a good while in the formalized sun while they fitted us out with all we needed to be fitting guests of the Casino. Finally, taking control of the situation, we authoritatively sent the bell-boy for a tooth-brush.

Wistaria dripped in the court of the Hôtel d'Europe at Avignon and the dawn rumbled up in market carts. A lone lady in tweeds drank Martinis in the dingy bar. We met French friends at the Taverne Riche and listened to the bells of late afternoon reverberate along the city walls. The Palace of the Popes rose chimerically through the gold end of day over the broad still Rhone, while we did nothing, assiduously, under the plane trees on the opposite bank.

Like Henri IV, a French patriot fed his babies red wine in the Continental at St Raphaël and there were no carpets because of summer, so echoes of the children's protestations fell pleasantly amidst the clatter of dishes and china. By this time we could identify a few words of French and felt ourselves part of the country.

The Hôtel du Cap at Antibes was almost deserted. The heat of day lingered in the blue and white blocks of the balcony and from the great canvas mats our friend had spread along the terrace we warmed our sunburned backs and invented new cocktails.

The Miramare in Genoa festooned the dark curve of the shore with garlands of lights, and the shape of the hills was picked out of the darkness by the blaze from the windows of high hotels. We thought of the men parading the gay arcades as undiscovered Carusos but they all assured us that Genoa was a business city and very like America and Milan.

We got to Pisa in the dark and couldn't find the leaning tower until we passed it by accident leaving the Royal Victoria on our way out. It stood stark in a field by itself. The Arno was muddy and not half as insistent as it is in the crossword puzzles.

Marion Crawford's mother died in the Quirinal Hotel at Rome. All the chamber-maids remember it and tell the visitors about how they spread the room with newspapers afterwards. The sitting-rooms are hermetically sealed and palms conceal the way to open the windows. Middle-aged English doze in the stale air and nibble stale salted peanuts with the hotel's famous coffee, which comes out of a calliope-like device for filling it full of grounds, like the glass balls that make snowstorms when shaken.

In the Hôtel des Princes at Rome we lived on Bel Paese cheese and Corvo wine and made friends with a delicate spinster who intended to stop there until she finished a three-volume history of the Borgias. The sheets were damp and the nights were perforated by the snores of the people next door, but we didn't mind because we could always come home down the stairs to the Via Sistina, and there were jonquils and beggars along that way. We were too superior at that time to use the guide-books and wanted to discover the ruins for ourselves, which we did when we had exhausted the night-life and the market places and the campagna. We liked the Castello Sant' Angelo because of its round mysterious unity and the river and the debris about its base. It was exciting being lost between centuries in the Roman dusk and taking your sense of direction from the Colosseum.

1925

At the hotel in Sorrento we saw the tarantella, but it was a *real* one and we had seen so many more imaginative adaptations . . .

A southern sun drugged the court of the Quisisana to somnolence. Strange birds protested their sleepiness beneath the overwhelming cypress while Compton Mackenzie told us why he lived in Capri: Englishmen must have an island.

The Tiberio was a high white hotel scalloped about the base by the rounded roofs of Capri, cupped to catch rain which never falls. We climbed to it through devious dark alleys that house the island's Rembrandt butcher shops and bakeries; then we climbed down again to the dark pagan hysteria of Capri's Easter, the resurrection of the spirit of the people.

When we got back to Marseilles, going north again, the streets about the waterfront were bleached by the brightness of the harbour and pedestrians gaily discussed errors of time at little cafés on the corner. We were so damn glad of the animation.

The hotel in Lyons wore an obsolete air and nobody ever heard of Lyonnaise potatoes and we became so discouraged with touring that we left the little Renault there and took the train for Paris.

The Hôtel Florida had catacornered rooms; the gilt had peeled from the curtain fixtures.

When we started out again after a few months, touring south, we slept six in a room in Dijon (Hôtel du Dump, Pens. from 2 frs. Pouring water) because there wasn't any other place. Our friends considered themselves somewhat compromised but snored towards morning.

In Salies-de-Béarn in the Pyrenees we took a cure for colitis, disease of that year, and rested in a white pine room in the Hôtel Bellevue, flush with thin sun rolled down from the Pyrenees. There was a bronze statue of Henri IV on the mantel in our room, for his mother was born there. The boarded windows of the Casino were splotched with bird droppings—along the misty streets we bought canes with spears on the end and were a little discouraged about everything. We had a play on Broadway and the movies offered $60,000, but we were china people by then and it didn't seem to matter particularly.

When that was over, a hired limousine drove us to Toulouse, careening around the grey block of Carcassonne and through the long unpopulated planes of the Côte d'Argent. The Hôtel Tivollier, though ornate, had fallen into disuse. We kept ringing for the waiter to assure ourselves that life went on somewhere in the dingy crypt. He appeared resentfully and finally we induced him to give us so much beer that it heightened the gloom.

In the Hôtel O'Connor old ladies in white lace rocked their pasts to circumspection with the lullabyic motion of the hotel chairs. But they were serving blue twilights at the cafés along the Promenade des Anglais for the price of a porto, and we danced their tangos and watched girls shiver in the appropriate clothes for the Côte d'Azur. We went to the Perroquet with friends, one of us wearing a blue hyacinth and the other in ill temper which made him buy a wagon full of roasted chestnuts and immediately scatter their warm burnt odour like largesse over the cold spring night.

In the sad August of that year we made a trip to Mentone, ordering *bouillabaisse* in an aquarium-like pavilion by the sea across from the Hôtel Victoria. The hills were silver-olive, and of the true shape of frontiers.

Leaving the Riviera after a third summer, we called on a writer friend at the Hôtel Continental at Cannes. He was proud of his independence in adopting a black mongrel dog. He had a nice house and a nice wife and we envied his comfortable installations that gave the effect of his having retired from the world when he had really taken such of it as he wanted and confined it.

When we got back to America we went to the Roosevelt Hotel in Washington and to see one of our mothers. The cardboard hotels, bought in sets, made us feel as if we committed a desecration by living in them—we left the brick pavements and the elms and the hetero-geneous qualities of Washington and went further south.

1927

It takes so long to get to California, and there were so many nickel handles, gadgets to avoid, buttons to invoke, and such a lot of newness and Fred Harvey, that when one of us thought he had appendicitis we got out at El Paso. A cluttered bridge dumps one in Mexico where the restaurants are trimmed with tissue paper and there are contraband perfumes—we admired the Texas rangers, not having seen men with guns on their hips since the war.

We reached California in time for an earthquake. It was sunny, and misty at night. White roses swung luminous in the mist from a trellis outside the Ambassador windows; a bright exaggerated parrot droned incomprehensible shouts in an aquamarine pool—of course everybody interpreted them to be obscenities; geraniums underscored the discip-line of the California flora. We paid homage to the pale aloof concision of Diana Manners's primitive beauty and dined at Pickfair to marvel at Mary Pickford's dynamic subjugation of life. A thoughtful limousine carried us for California hours to be properly moved by the fragility of Lillian Gish, too aspiring for life, clinging vine-like to occultisms.

From there we went to the DuPont in Wilmington. A friend took us to tea in the mahogany recesses of an almost feudal estate, where the sun gleamed apologetically in the silver tea-service and there were four kinds of buns and four indistinguishable daughters in riding clothes and a mistress of the house too busily preserving the charm of another era to separate out the children. We leased a very big old mansion on the Delaware river. The squareness of the rooms and the sweep of the columns were to bring us a judicious tranquillity. There were sombre horse-chestnuts in the yard and a white pine bending as graciously as a Japanese brush drawing.

We went to Princetown. There was a new colonial inn, but the campus offered the same worn grassy parade ground for the romantic spectres of Light-Horse Harry Lee and Aaron Burr. We loved the temperate shapes of Nassau Hall's old brick, and the way it seems still a tribunal of early American ideals, the elm walks and meadows, the college windows open to the spring—open, open to everything in life—for a minute.

The Negroes are in knee-breeches at the Cavalier in Virginia Beach. It is theatrically southern and its newness is a bit barren, but there is the best beach in America; at that time before the cottages were built, there were dunes and the moon tripped, fell, in the sandy ripples along the sea-front.

Next time we went, lost and driven now like the rest, it was a free trip north to Quebec. They thought maybe we'd write about it. The Château Frontenac was built of toy stone arches, a tin soldier's castle. Our voices were truncated by the heavy snow, the stalactite icicles on the low roofs turned the town to a wintry cave; we spent most of our time in an echoing room lined with skis, because the professional there gave us a good feeling about the sports at which we were so inept. He was later taken up by the DuPonts on the same basis and made a powder magnate or something.

When we decided to go back to France we spent the night at the Pennsylvania, manipulating the new radio earphones and the servidors, where a suit can be frozen to a cube by nightfall. We were still impressed by running ice-water, self-sustaining rooms that could function even if besieged with current events. We were so little in touch with the world that they gave us an impression of a crowded subway station.

The hotel in Paris was triangular shaped and faced Saint-Germain-des-Près. On Sundays we sat at the Deux Magots and watched the people, devout as an opera chorus, enter the old doors, or else watched the French read newspapers. There were long conversations about the ballet over *sauerkraut* in Lipps, and blank recuperative hours over books and prints in the dank Allée Bonaparte.

Now the trips away had begun to be less fun. The next one to Brittany broke at Le Mans. The lethargic town was crumbling away, pulverized by the heat of the white hot summer and only travelling salesmen slid their chairs pre-emptorily about the uncarpeted dining-rooms. Plane trees bordered the route to La Baule.

At the Palace in La Baule we felt raucous amidst so much chic restraint. Children bronzed on the bare blue-white beach while the tide went out so far as to leave them crabs and starfish to dig for in the sands.

1929

We went to America but didn't stay at hotels. When we got back to Europe we spent the first night at a sun-flushed hostelry, Bertolini's in Genoa. There was a green tile bath and a very attentive valet de chambre and there was ballet to practise, using the brass bedstead as a bar. It was good to see the brilliant flowers colliding in prismatic explosions over the terraced hillside and to feel ourselves foreigners again.

Reaching Nice, we went economically to the Beau Rivage, which offered many stained-glass windows to the Mediterranean glare. It was spring and was brittly cold along the Promenade des Anglais, though the crowds moved persistently in a summer tempo. We admired the painted windows of the converted palaces on the Place Gambetta. Walking at dusk, the voices fell seductively through the nebulous twilight inviting us to share the first stars, but we were busy. We went to the cheap ballets of the Casino on the jettée and rode almost to Villefranche for *Salade Niçoise* and a very special *bouillabaisse*.

In Paris we economized again in a not-yet-dried cement hotel, the name of which we've forgotten. It cost us a good deal, for we ate out every night to avoid starchy tables d'hôte. Sylvia Beach invited us to dinner and the talk was all of the people who had discovered Joyce; we called on friends in better hotels; Zoe Takins, who had sought the picturesque of the open fires at Foyot's, and Esther at the Port-Royal, who took us to see Romaine Brooks's studio, a glass-enclosed square of heaven swung high above Paris.

Then southward again, and wasting the dinner hour in an argument about which hotel: there was one in Beaune where Ernest Hemingway had liked the trout. Finally we decided to drive all night, and we ate well in a stable courtyard facing a canal—the green-white glare of Provence had already begun to dazzle us so that we didn't care whether the food was good or not. That night we stopped under the white-trunked trees to open the windshield to the moon and to the sweep of the south against our faces, and to better smell the fragrance rustling restlessly amidst the poplars.

At Fréjus Plage, they had built a new hotel, a barren structure facing the beach where the sailors bathe. We felt very superior, remembering how we had been the first travellers to like the place in summer.

After the swimming at Cannes was over and the year's octopi had grown up in the crevices of the rocks, we started back to Paris. The night of the stock-market crash we stayed at the Beau Rivage in St Raphaël in the room Ring Lardner had occupied another year. We got out as soon as we could because we had been there so many times before—it is sadder to find the past again and find it inadequate to the present than it is to have it elude you and remain for ever a harmonious conception of memory.

At the Jules César in Arles we had a room that had once been a chapel. Following the festering waters of a stagnant canal we came to the ruins of a Roman dwelling-house. There was a blacksmith's shop installed behind the proud columns and a few scattered cows ate the gold flowers off the meadow.

Then up and up; the twilit heavens expanded in the Cevennes valley, cracking the mountains apart, and there was a fearsome loneliness brooding on the flat tops. We crunched chestnut burrs on the road and aromatic smoke wound out of the mountain cottages. The Inn looked bad, the floors were covered with sawdust, but they gave us the best pheasant we ever ate and the best sausage, and the feather-beds were wonderful.

In Vichy, the leaves had covered the square about the wooden bandstand. Health advice was printed on the doors at the Hôtel du Parc and on the menu, but the salon was filled with people drinking champagne. We loved the massive trees in Vichy and the way the friendly town nestles in a hollow.

By the time we got to Tours we had begun to feel like Cardinal Balue in his cage in the little Renault. The Hôtel de l'Univers was equally stuffy but after dinner we found a café crowded with people playing checkers and singing choruses and we felt we could go on to Paris after all.

Our cheap hotel in Paris had been turned into a girls' school—we went to a nameless one in the Rue du Bac, where potted palms withered in the exhausted air. Through the thin partitions we witnessed the private lives and natural functions of our neighbours. We walked at night past the moulded columns of the Odéon and identified the gangrenous statue behind the Luxembourg fence as Catherine de Medici.

It was a trying winter and to forget bad times we went to Algiers. The Hôtel de l'Oasis was laced together by Moorish grills; and the bar was an outpost of civilization with people accentuating their eccentricities. Beggars in white sheets were propped against the walls, and the dash of colonial uniforms gave the cafés a desperate swashbuckling air. Berbers have plaintive trusting eyes but it's really Fate they trust.

In Bou Saada, the scent of amber was swept along the streets by wide desert cloaks. We watched the moon stumble over the sand hillocks in a dead white glow and believed the guide as he told us of a priest he knew who could wreck railroad trains by wishing. The Ouled Nails were very brown and clean-cut girls, impersonal as they turned themselves into fitting instruments for sex by the ritual of their dance, jangling their gold to the tune of savage fidelities hid in the distant hills.

The world crumbled to pieces in Biskra; the streets crept through the town like streams of hot white lava. Arabs sold nougat, the cakes of poisonous pink, under the flare of open gas jets. Since *The Garden of Allah* and *The Sheik* the town has been filled with frustrate women. In the steep cobbled alleys we flinched at the brightness of mutton carcasses swung from the butchers' booths.

We stopped in El Kantara at a rambling inn whiskered with wistaria. Purple dusk steamed up from the depths of a gorge and we walked to a painter's house, where, in the remoteness of those mountains, he worked at imitations of Meissonier.

Then Switzerland and another life. Spring bloomed in the gardens of the Grand Hotel in Glion, and a panorama world scintillated in the mountain air. The sun steamed delicate blossoms loose from the rocks while far below glinted the lake of Geneva.

Beyond the balustrade of the Lausanne Palace, sail-boats plume themselves in the breeze like birds. Willow trees weave lacy patterns on the gravel terrace. The people are chic fugitives from life and death, rattling their teacups in querulous emotion on the deep protective balcony. They spell the names of hotels and cities with flower-beds and laburnum in Switzerland and even the street lights wore crowns of verbena.

1931

Leisurely men played checkers in the restaurant of the Hôtel de la Paix in Lausanne. The depression had become frank in the American papers so we wanted to get back home.

But we went to Annecy for two weeks in summer, and said at the end that we'd never go there again because those weeks had been perfect, and no other time could match them. First we lived at the

Beau-Rivage, a rambler rose-covered hotel, with a diving platform wedged beneath our window between the sky and the lake, but there were enormous flies on the raft so we moved across the lake to Menthone. The water was greener there and the shadows long and cool and the scraggly gardens staggered up the shelved precipice to the Hôtel Palace. We played tennis on the baked clay courts and fished tentatively from a low brick wall. The heat of summer seethed in the resin of the white pine bath-houses. We walked at night towards a café blooming with Japanese lanterns, white shoes gleaming like radium in the damp darkness. It was like the good gone times when we still believed in summer hotels and the philosophies of popular songs. Another night we danced a Wiener waltz, and just simply swept around.

At the Caux Palace, a thousand yards in the air, we tea-danced on the uneven boards of a pavilion and sopped our toast in mountain honey.

When we passed through Munich the Regina-Palast was empty; they gave us a suite where the princes stayed in the days when royalty travelled. The young Germans stalking the ill-lit streets wore a sinister air—the talk that underscored the beer-garden waltzes was of war and hard times. Thornton Wilder took us to a famous restaurant where the beer deserved the silver mugs it was served in. We went to see the cherished witnesses to a lost cause; our voices echoed through the planetarium and we lost our orientation in the deep blue cosmic presentation of how things are.

In Vienna, the Bristol was the best hotel and they were glad to have us because it, too, was empty. Our windows looked out on the mouldy baroque of the Opera over the tops of sorrowing elms. We dined at the widow Sacher's—over the oak panelling hung a print of Franz Joseph going some happier place many years ago in a coach; one of the Rothschilds dined behind a leather screen. The city was poor already, or still, and the faces about us were harassed and defensive.

We stayed a few days at the Vevey Palace on Lake Geneva. The trees in the hotel gardens were the tallest we had ever seen and gigantic lonely birds fluttered over the surface of the lake. Farther along there was a gay little beach with a modern bar where we sat on the sands and discussed stomachs.

We motored back to Paris: that is, we sat nervously in our six-horse-power Renault. At the famous Hôtel de la Cloche in Dijon we had a nice room with a very complicated mechanical inferno of a bath, which the valet proudly referred to as American plumbing.

In Paris for the last time, we installed ourselves amidst the faded grandeurs of the Hôtel Majestic. We went to the Exposition and yielded up our imaginations to gold-lit facsimiles of Bali. Lonely flooded rice fields of lonely far-off islands told us an immutable story of work and death. The juxtaposition of so many replicas of so many civilizations was confusing, and depressing.

Back in America we stayed at the New Yorker because the advertisements said it was cheap. Everywhere quietude was sacrificed to haste and, momentarily, it seemed an impossible world, even though lustrous from the roof in the blue dusk.

· In Alabama, the streets were sleepy and remote and a calliope on parade gasped out the tunes of our youth. There was sickness in the family and the house was full of nurses so we stayed at the big new elaborate Jefferson Davis. The old houses near the business section were falling to pieces at last. New bungalows lined the cedar drives on the outskirts; four o'clocks bloomed beneath the old iron deer and arborvitae boxed the prim brick walks while vigorous weeds uprooted the pavements. Nothing had happened there since the Civil War. Everybody had forgotten why the hotel had been erected, and the clerk gave us three rooms and four baths for nine dollars a day. We used one as a sitting-room so the bell-boys would have some place to sleep when we rang for them.

1932

At the biggest hotel in Biloxi we read *Genesis* and watched the sea pave the deserted shore with a mosaic of black twigs.

We went to Florida. The bleak marshes were punctuated by biblical admonitions to a better life; abandoned fishing-boats disintegrated in the sun. The Don Ce-sar Hotel in Pass-A-Grille stretched lazily over the stubbed wilderness, surrendering its shape to the blinding brightness of the gulf. Opalescent shells cupped the twilight on the beach and a stray dog's footprints in the wet sand staked out his claim to a free path round the ocean. We walked at night and discussed the Pythagorean theory of numbers, and we fished by day. We were sorry for the deep-sea bass and the amberjacks—they seemed such easy game and no sport at all. Reading the *Seven Against Thebes*, we browned on a lonely beach. The hotel was almost empty and there were so many waiters waiting to be off that we could hardly eat our meals.

1933

The room in the Algonquin was high up amidst the gilded domes of New York. Bells chimed hours that had yet to penetrate the shadowy streets of the canyon. It was too hot in the room, but the carpets were soft and the room was isolated by dark corridors outside the door and bright façades outside the window. We spent much time getting ready for theatres. We saw Georgia O'Keefe's pictures and it was a deep emotional experience to abandon oneself to that majestic aspiration so adequately fitted into eloquent abstract forms.

For years we had wanted to go to Bermuda. We went. The Elbow Beach Hotel was full of honeymooners, who scintillated so persistently in each other's eyes that we cynically moved. The Hotel St George was nice. Bougainvillea cascaded down the tree trunks and long stairs passed by deep mysteries taking place behind native windows. Cats slept along the balustrade and lovely children grew. We rode bicycles along the windswept causeways and stared in a dreamy daze at such phenomena as roosters scratching amidst the sweet alyssum. We drank sherry on a verandah above the bony backs of horses tethered in the public square. We had travelled a lot, we thought. Maybe this would be the last trip for a long while. We thought Bermuda was a nice place to be the last one of so many years of travelling.

WILLIAM PLOMER

Local Colour

Upon certain kinds of Nordics the effect of living in Mediterranean countries is the reverse of bracing. The freedom, warmth and glamour of their surroundings begin to sap their intellectual or artistic activity and ambition. They drift into idleness and weaken in will. While constantly talking about what they are going to do and accomplish, they do nothing and make nothing, and at last discover that in gaining liberty and sunshine they have lost purpose and vigour. It is a matter of taste and temperament. You can't have everything.

But when the Nordic, young, enterprising and healthy, first finds himself enjoying freedom, warmth and glamour, the effect upon him is indescribably delightful. He is without responsibilities, he has a susceptible body and an impressionable mind; the sun warms his skin and the blood sings in his veins. Life is full of promise, he is ready for anything, and if anybody asks him if he doesn't feel the heat he says, 'No, I love it.'

Two people in this happy condition were sitting in basket chairs on the veranda of the best hotel in Athens. They were English undergraduates who had come to spend the long vacation in Greece. They were not sitting there alone. They had a guest—nobody less than Madame Hélène Strouthokámelos.

'Don't you feel the heat?' she said, looking from one to the other.

'Not a bit,' said Grant.

'We love it,' said Spencer.

It *was* extremely hot, all the same. The glare was dazzling. It was just that hour when nothing seems likely ever to cast a shadow again, and the air itself buzzes like a cicada. The young men, neatly dressed in light summer clothing, sat in easy attitudes, but there was much more assurance in their voices than in their feelings. They had brought a letter of introduction to Madame Strouthokámelos and in delivering it had added an invitation to lunch. And here she was in the flesh, and they felt rather shy. Spencer, the English one, was uneasy because he was wearing rather too pretty a tie, which he had bought in Paris, and Madame Strouthokámelos kept glancing at it every now and again as if it offered a clue to his soul. Grant, the Scotch one, had begun looking at the toes of his shoes, and that was always a bad sign with him. Just then an important looking man in a straw hat came up the steps, and catching sight of Madame Strouthokámelos made her an obsequious bow, to which she replied with a cool nod. *Cool*, that was it. It was her coolness that was so disconcerting.

She was neither young nor middle-aged. She had dignity without stiffness, she was handsome, healthy, powerful. There was no powder on her face, she wore no jewellery, and her clothes were simple. She had taken off her little soft hat, just as a girl might have done, with a single gesture and laid it on the table at her side, and now she sat there with her head, most appropriately, against a white marble background. Spencer was facing her, Grant saw her in profile, and if they had been in the presence of Juno herself they could scarcely have been more impressed.

Before meeting her they had tried to imagine what she would be like, and they had invented a perspiring Levantine matron in black which the sun had faded, with a bluish moustache, bad teeth, and voluble French. And here was Juno at forty, or the Venus of Milo come to life, a woman of noble proportions, with naturally wavy hair, black, becomingly streaked with grey, and drawn back from a smooth forehead, from a face with regular features supported grandly on a firm neck like a cylinder of honey-coloured marble. Her skin was clear and honey-coloured too, and it made the white of her eyes and her fine teeth seem to be ever so slightly tinged with very pale blue. Her strong arms were bare, and her cool dress hung loosely over her firm breasts and clung against her hips and thighs. So much for her appearance. She had a manner to match it.

She had once had a baby—but rather a small one. It often happens with amazonian, mammoth, or merely muscular women that their offspring comes into the world as an embodied protest against size and strength—in fact, the little Strouthokámelos weighed at birth no more than four pounds. It was, however, her husband rather than her child who had mainly disappointed her. Had he been dutiful, she would no doubt have worn him out, but he was casual, and she lost him. Strouthokámelos had been a little too Greek in his nature for her taste—she had been 'finished' in Paris and Vienna, but they hadn't prepared her for what happened. And when it *did* happen she took pains to inform herself about aspects of life, of Greek life, to which she had hitherto paid little attention. And having been informed, she was resentful. What she could no longer ignore she blamed, frowned upon, or affected not to notice, according to circumstances. And whenever any reflection happened to be cast by foreigners upon the Greeks in general she hastened to proclaim her countrymen's conformity with Christian morality, with the finishing-school view of human nature, failing altogether to remind herself that they are scarcely a European people.

Madame Strouthokámelos was not a fool. She was very much the reverse. Like so many citizens of the lesser European countries she was an excellent linguist, equally at home in English, French, German and Italian. She had read a great deal and was still reading. She was a capable housewife, a born organizer and to some extent a woman of the world. She could stride through thistles in Thessaly, hold her own at the bridge table, make a speech or sack a maid, was a personal friend of the prime minister, and of course was fully equal to the present occasion. She glanced in the direction of the dining-room, and then said:

'Do you specially want us to have lunch here?'

'No,' said Spencer.

'Not if you know of anywhere better,' said Grant.

'Ah, I see you're the practical one,' she said, displaying her classical, milk-blue teeth. 'I don't know about *better*, but hotels are all the same everywhere. I think while you are in Greece you ought to do as the Greeks do. I know a little place down by the sea, towards Vouliagméni, where we could get a nice *Greek* lunch. Do you think you would like that?'

'We should love it,' said Spencer.

'I'm all for local colour,' said Grant.

'Ah, that's just it,' she said. 'If we go there, it will be *Greek*, whereas *this* . . .' She shrugged her shoulders, but there was a delicious smell of food wafted from the dining-room. 'Then we may as well go at once?' she said, rising to her feet.

Her hosts got up obediently. She was used to obedience.

'You've left your book behind,' she said to Spencer. 'What is it? May I see? Ah, Proust.'

'Do you like Proust?' said Spencer.

'He's very clever, of course, but I don't much care for the atmosphere.'

Spencer popped *Sodome et Gomorrhe* into his pocket.

'And now,' she said, leading the way, 'we'd better get into a taxi.'

The taxis, open touring cars, were lined up under some pepper trees on the opposite side of the road. Madame Strouthokámelos waved away the svelte hotel porter as if he was an insect, led the way, chose a taxi, instructed the driver brusquely, and climbed in. Spencer and Grant exchanged glances and followed. She made them sit one on each side of her, and the taxi drove off, rushing down the Amalia Boulevard towards the sea.

'She doesn't like men,' thought Spencer.

'She despises us,' thought Grant.

'It isn't many miles,' said Madame Strouthokámelos, and began asking them the usual questions about how long they were going to stay, where they were going, and so on.

'I'm afraid we Greeks are rather misunderstood or misrepresented,' she said. 'But there is a wonderful new spirit in the people. The refugees from Asia Minor have increased the population enormously, and have helped to consolidate the national feeling. The younger generation, the Greeks of your age, are manly and patriotic. I think there is great hope for the future.'

'*Manly*,' thought Spencer. 'She's thinking of my tie.'

'What is she getting at?' Grant wondered. 'Is this propaganda?'

It was propaganda.

'So I hope,' she went on, 'that although you'll be here such a short time you'll really be able to get in touch with the people a little and get an idea of what they're really like. That's one reason why I'm taking you to this place for lunch. I don't suppose any foreigner's ever been there before.'

'That's much more interesting than the hotel,' said Grant.

'Much,' said Spencer a little half-heartedly, remembering the smell of the hotel lunch.

'Hotels are *so* much the same everywhere,' she repeated.

They had passed Phaleron, and the conversation turned to Byron. They sped towards Glyphada, along what was then one of the only two decent roads in Greece, and the asphalt was like burnished steel. There was almost no traffic at this time of day. The sea was like a fiery glass and Byron had given place to the Greek language. The road was about to be very bad, when Madame Strouthokámelos, employing that language with great determination, brought the car to a standstill. They all got out, and she waited for her hosts to pay the fare. Then she led the way across a piece of waste land to a little white house by the sea.

There was no path. The way was through loose, burning sand which filled one's shoes. There were some prickly bushes about. They passed a pine tree, sighing to itself. The rays of the sun seemed to be vertical. Presently there was a crazy noticeboard decorated with broken fairy-lamps and the inscription PANTHEON.

'Here we are,' said Madame Strouthokámelos as if she owned the place.

And immediately a man came out to welcome them. He treated his visitor with deference—she was known to have influence in important circles; her bearing would have demanded respect in any case; and she had brought two young foreigners with her. Well, three lunches meant three profits. He led the trio round to the seaward side of the Pantheon.

'Now, surely this is better than the hotel!' cried Madame Strouthokámelos.

And indeed it was.

A veranda thatched with myrtle branches, and floored with the earth itself, on which stood three round tables covered with coarse but clean tablecloths, and chairs; and only a few yards away, the Aegean sparkling like a million diamonds. There was even a suggestion of a breeze.

The table at the far end was occupied. Four men, workmen or peasants apparently, were seated there, eating a cheerful meal. Beyond them were some rocks and bushes. At the corner of the house a single plant of maize had grown to a great height. It looked very green and was in flower. Beneath it some fowls were enjoying a dust-bath, and tied to one of the veranda-posts was a goat, recumbent in the shade. With clear yellow eyes which looked as though they missed nothing and saw through everything it watched what was going on. It looked so independent that one could not tell whether it was enjoying what it saw, enjoying a cynical attitude to what it saw, or simply indulging in sheer observation for its own sake.

The proprietor approached Madame Strouthokámelos for orders. She took off her little soft hat again, with the characteristic sweeping gesture, and then, with a clean, capable hand on which the nails were cut short like a man's, she patted her hair, though its wiry waves had not lost their shape.

'There's not much to choose from,' she remarked. 'Of course they weren't expecting us.'

'We leave the choosing to you,' said Grant.

She ordered red mullets, black olives, white bread, a tomato salad, with yoghourt and coffee to follow.

'It sounds marvellous,' said Spencer.

'You'd better taste it first,' she said. 'At least everything here will be fresh.'

The fact that she never wore gloves aided the general impression that she was 'classical' in appearance.

'And what are we going to drink?' she said.

Spencer stole a glance at the other table.

'What are *they* drinking?' he said.

'*Retsina*, probably,' said Madame Strouthokámelos. 'Do you know what that is? White wine with resin in it. It's very nice. Would you like to try some?'

Spencer and Grant said they would, though somebody had told them that it was perfectly revolting.

'I adore the goat,' said Spencer.

'Isn't *adore* rather a strong word?' said Madame Strouthokámelos. 'It seems to me it stinks slightly.' She laughed.

'Exactly what are those people?' said Grant, looking at the other table.

'Oh, just country boys. It's a pity you can't talk to them. Very cheerful, aren't they? And they're really typical.'

They were, indeed, very cheerful, and had just ordered some more wine.

'Would you like to offer them some cigarettes?' said Madame Strouthokámelos. 'They would be very pleased.'

'Would they?' said Grant, and crossed rather shyly to the other table with an open cigarette-case. The 'country boys', even more shyly, helped themselves. And Madame Strouthokámelos, leaning forward graciously, addressed them in Greek.

'These are two young Englishmen,' she said, 'visiting Greece for the first time.'

The country boys expressed interest.

'So I've brought them down here to lunch, so that they can see a bit of the *real* Greece.'

The country boys registered approval and pleasure.

'I see you've got a guitar there,' said Madame Strouthokámelos. 'Won't you sing for these foreigners?'

The country boys laughed and looked at one another and then addressed themselves to one of their number who wore a lilac shirt, urging him to play. He took up the guitar just as the food arrived for the foreigners.

In spite of the heat Spencer and Grant were hungry, and the pleasant atmosphere and the pretty song that was now being sung to the guitar combined to whet their appetites.

'What a delicious lunch,' said Spencer.

'Perfect,' said Grant.

'I'm so glad you're enjoying it,' said Madame Strouthokámelos, and then, turning to the country boys, she suggested another tune for them to play. Her manner was gracious and patronizing and did not go down with them very well. However, the tune she suggested happened to be a favourite with Lilac Shirt, so he soon struck up with it. Drink had made him confident, and vanity made him self-conscious, so he became rather noisy, laughed, and now and then flashed a glance at Spencer and Grant. Madame Strouthokámelos wore an indulgent smile and nodded a gracious acknowledgement.

Conversation turned to the *retsina*. Grant thought it even more disgusting than he had anticipated—it tasted to him like pure turpentine, and he did his best not to make a wry face as he swallowed it. Spencer, who was rather romantic, pretended to himself and to the others that he liked it.

'It has such a nice *piny* sort of taste,' he said. 'But I don't think I could put away quite as much as *they* do—not in the middle of the day, at any rate.'

As he spoke he indicated the country boys, who had opened a fresh lot of wine and were getting very merry.

'Is that what they do every day?' said Grant.

'No, I think they must be celebrating rather a special occasion.'

The proprietor appeared in the doorway, looking genial above his apron. Somebody else had taken the guitar now and was playing a rapid syncopated tune. Lilac Shirt was looking rather flushed. His shirt had come unbuttoned, revealing a lean brown chest, very hairy. He was supporting the head of one of his companions in his lap, and making remarks which surely *must* be ribald. Spencer stole a glance at Madame Strouthokámelos. Yes, sure enough, she was looking at her plate, and a faint frown now marred her rather too regular features. Then Spencer looked at Grant, and Grant looked at Spencer and kicked him under the table, then they both looked at the other table, on which somebody was beating with a spoon just to add to the noise of the guitar and the laughing and the singing.

'They *are* getting gay,' said Spencer, in an affectedly innocent tone of voice.

'They have been drinking a little too much,' said Madame Strouthokámelos with an expression of something like distaste. 'Have you had enough to eat, or shall I order some cheese?'

'Aha,' thought Grant, 'she's trying to hurry us away just when it's beginning to get interesting.' And he said, 'Yes, please. I should like to try the cheese. I expect it's very good here.'

With obvious reluctance Madame Strouthokámelos ordered cheese. The proprietor made a laughing comment on his other visitors, but she did not reply.

At this moment one of the country boys rose to his feet. He was very slender, with lank black hair and rather sleepy-looking eyes. He was going to dance. The others clapped and uttered cries of delight, encouragement and facetiousness. The dancer raised his arms and spread out his hands and began to dance to the guitar. He was skilful and kept excellent time and for a moment it seemed as if Madame Strouthokámelos' slightly disdainful expression might vanish.

'The cheese is excellent,' said Grant.

Spencer lighted a cigarette.

Just then Lilac Shirt rose to his feet, approached the other dancer and clasping one hand round his partner's waist and the other round his loins he called for a tune. Shouts of laughter, and one of the remaining two began again on the guitar. Madame Strouthokámelos frowned once more. The frown was deeper this time.

The tune was a tango. Lilac Shirt proceeded to sway his partner into a caricature of a tango. With absurdly languorous movements they danced, still keeping excellent time with the music. Lilac Shirt's white trousers were, however, a little too tight for really free movement.

'How well they dance,' said Spencer, smiling. 'I think we ought to join in.'

He got another kick under the table.

He then saw that Lilac Shirt's way of holding his partner was perhaps a little too daring, a little too intimate, for the open air, at midday, in public. As the dance continued the goat rose to its feet—as if to get a better view. It stared with its pale amber eyes at the dancers, then turned to look at Madame Strouthokámelos—it was a look that spoke volumes, but banned volumes—and then again fastened its keen, glassy, unblinking stare on the dancers.

The guitar-player paused. Lilac Shirt, leaning against his partner who was leaning against one of the veranda posts, embraced him and kissed him on the mouth. This brought loud cheers from the other two. All four of them had forgotten the two foreigners and Madame Strouthokámelos—a fact which made her next words rather wide of the mark.

'They have forgotten themselves,' she said in a tone of disgust. 'They have drunk too much.'

Lilac Shirt's kiss was so prolonged that she averted her eyes and rose abruptly to her feet.

'We had better go,' she said in a quiet and furious voice, and picking up her hat she went round to the landward side of the Pantheon to demand the bill. Spencer and Grant followed to pay it. Glancing back, they saw Lilac Shirt and his partner disappear behind some rocks a few yards away.

As for the goat, it had settled down again, and was quietly chewing the cud. Its yellow eyes were shut for the siesta.

Gliding Gulls and Going People

Two girls in high shorts, thin plump thighs redly raw in the blue cold; a blood-filled man in black broadcloth, his big stomach carrying him like a sail along; a queer-eyed girl in a transparent white mackintosh; an old gentleman and an old lady eyeing each other, strangers yet; a young man, curly-haired and hard-fleshed, whose frank grey eyes bristled with sneaking contempt; two wives in soldier-peaked hats, navy and nigger, cheery and cake-loving; a small lean man in blue serge and a woolly chequered cap whose friends and family, at his expense, flowed round him only to exclaim and demand.

Such were some of the six hundred lined up raggedly along the quay-side waiting for several strolling ample officers to give them permission to embark. Already the gulls, thick and dark as snowflakes above, gliding and hovering and always crying, had showered them over with confetti and streamers of white—so that in all their darkish throng they looked like wedding guests come to a white funeral.

The driven smell of kippering smoke blew in gusts from sheds about. Red lead of funnels shone orange against the metal-grey water, corrugated-tin sheds stepped like large mauve flamingos on their thin pile-legs, tarred black sheds nudged blue-washed weather-boards of a chandler's, barrels and buckets and drums and feeding-carts spent oil and oil, everywhere oil—these salt things with a huddled rigging of masts made up the quay of Mallaig, mainland port on the Sound of Sleat opposite Skye. A place of high rubber boots, of seaman's wool, of oilskins against the fresh wind and the white bright light. And all those people walked straight off the train and from the hotels along the quay to board this excursion steamer to the sea-loch Scavaig and the dark monstrous Cuillins.

Although their greatest wish was for a refreshing cup of tea, the navy and the nigger hats remained for some minutes in dumb confabulation on the departing glories of those weird mountains above the Kyle of Lochalsh. Leaning over the rail, while the ship throbbed below and the gulls questioned the air about, their ample bodies almost touched. In speechless approbation they regarded those mountains, some black, some lizard-green as shafts of sun spotlighted them from the indigo anger of clouds above. A wild improbable mass, sun-green and rock-black abstraction, nothing here of the human world, across the metal water huge and towering as a threat from old Norse gods—for even here in Scotland there was the feeling of being on top of the world, on a barren place uncongenial to man.

Little of Scotland, much of cold Viking ferocity. Yet—those two in their dear pleasure saw Scottish hills, they saw what on a hundred calendars had been dreamed and painted for them. Though none were to be seen—stags stood about in cosy might, and there was heather for these two, everywhere surely a purple mass of heather—'a veritable blaze of colour', warm paintbox purple. And where now the sun shone sickly green, was there not a golden glow? Gold touching russet? Winking on crofter's cottage, neat-thatched, washed clean white? Of course one had to admit it was very wild, had one not? But then one expected wildness from these dear Scottish hills, homely hills so glenny and good.

So despite the fresh wind the two ladies stood and surveyed their calendar imposition. A smile for each other, a knowing nod, and once more they turned to the scene and their eyes became distant—pleased, pleased that they had come and that what they expected was there, most content and kindly in the dream picture made by their eyes upon the real scene. Then, as if enough was as good as a feast, they turned to each other and sighed—and one, simply and from the generosity of her heart, said the first thing that came to her: 'How I wish Ellen were here, she *would* have enjoyed it so.'

The other sighed 'Yes'; and then together they turned to the companion-way and a cup of good warming tea, eager now to discuss the interesting topic of Ellen.

But they were not the only two on deck—as they staggered along, as laughing they clutched each other and in their thick coats clutched the companion-way, they passed in between that hard-eyed young man and on the other side of the doorway the girl in the pale mackintosh: and further on stood those two girls in such high cold shorts.

The young man saw nothing of the great receding mountains, nor did he see Mallaig grown small like a doll's town under its confetti of gulls—he saw nothing but the girls. And those eyes under their short lids, bitter and ambitious, lustful, swivelled warily between the two grouped and the one sitting. Where was the better chance? Those two with their legs bare nearly to their bottoms—they looked something. Two out together on the spree, hikers probably, they had wool caps and oilskin jackets and bloody great boots with spikes. Their legs looked funny all bare from boot to bum—still they were legs, young legs and soft if indeed cold. Fine place to choose for a spree though, and there was your youth movements for you, giving girls outlandish ideas like coming to this iceberg, and outlandish was the word. Still, two together was always something, two chances in one, and each would vie with the other for his attentions, they would smile the larger and give great willing looks. Till he chose one, and then the other would mope, and that was always the worst of two—it became three's no company. Still. And yet—that other in the natty mack sitting alone, she might want company on any account, and he'd be well in nice and easy. A bit snooty! But the snooty ones turned out often enough the best, they knew what they wanted. And there she was settled, not reading, nothing but looking out at that bloody cold sea. She looked lonely enough. Still. He knew better than to go straight up. Might get a back-hander, the old one-two. Perhaps a gentle enquiry: 'Excuse me, miss—I see you have a map there, would I be right in thinking those the Cuillins? They aren't? Why, it must be a pleasure to know as much as you, it's difficult being a stranger in these parts.' And all that. Or drop his gloves at her feet? Or simply lurch across her, as if the ship had done it—that often brought a laugh.

He put a match between his teeth, and ground those small ingrowers viciously into the wood. Pretending to look at none of them he walked stiff-legged over to the rail and placed himself exactly between them. He wrinkled up his short forehead into deep horizontal furrows— those that looked casual, as though he were emptying a full mind the better to perceive new things—and gazed blindly out to sea. So he stood for minutes, and the gulls glided and swooped around. Sometimes these hung on the air at the speed of the ship, and turned their faces inwards, curious, looking him in the eye. The bare girls in oilskins were throwing them bread-chunks from a screw of coloured comic. They laughed and their screams came down on the wind, and though they were so near those screams sounded like an echo. The gulls adroitly caught the pieces in mid-air—at which always the girls burst into fresh screams. So it was very easy for the young man first to smile amiably and then fully to burst out laughing with them as one particular gull missed its piece.

But the girls acted strangely. Together, with no sign between them, motivated like twin puppets, they stared straight at him: their eyes blanked up: they were looking through him: then as if they had never seen him they both turned to gaze slowly out to sea. Their two faces plainly said: 'There is no one on the ship but us, but her and me.' And oh bored, bored the young man too looked out to sea—the match snapped in his teeth, snapped at this trick he knew so well, snapped that two such oilskinned bums should prink themselves into such importance. He said softly to himself, spitting out the match: 'Sod that then.'

A minute later he turned casually the other way, taking a quick squint at the girl sitting still there along in her white gummy mackintosh. Taking a breath he moved away from the rail, walked across to the companion-way door just by her side, seemed there to trip, to stagger, to drop his gloves and all he had and lurch all over her.

Meanwhile that fat man in black was nowhere to be seen. But on the way from their warming cup of tea the two matrons passed very near where he was, they glimpsed through a glass porthole into a small wooden room and saw there a mass of black already it seemed asleep. They saw his bulged black waistcoat jutted into the little wood flap-table, they saw the empty beer-bottles and the little wicked whisky glasses like chessmen on that board, they saw his hands pouched with blood resting sideways and almost on their backs palms upward in sleep. 'Is he ill, then?' they thought. Then worried by this they agreed he must be all right—though what he came on such a trip for just to sit inside and drink it was difficult for their lives to think. There he sat, his red chin lurched deeply down on his black waistcoat top, his large black hat overshadowing like poet or priest. And there, after they had passed on their way to the ladies' lounge, he continued to sit; a figure framed by the inquisitive porthole, more of a round picture hung on the wall than a person inside who at some time, impossibly, might move.

The lean-faced little father from Liverpool remained on deck. He and all his family sat huddled in chairs behind the funnel, all nestled and rugged like wealthy emigrants. Father tough and lean-faced beneath his checked cap nodded a superior approbation of the air—he had blown

some money on this trip, he was going to enjoy it, he was in command—and he smoked his cigarette from an arm held bent with muscle,
holding it between finger and thumb and with little finger curled out
in showful ease. He turned to Mother and pointed sternly with this
superior hand:

'See, Ma? Muck there, the Isle o' Muck.'

Mother turned to the horizon, where she saw far away a shapeless
piece of rock. She nodded, pleased and satisfied:

'Muck is it? Well.'

Father peered at her from beneath his great peak, together their
eyes gravely conspired. They both nodded, satisfied. They had experienced the Isle of Muck, Muck could be crossed off, it was there still,
nobody had been tricked. And instantly was forgotten—Father was
back at the sports page and Mother began at her brood:

'Alfie, stop touching, it's the Captain's. Clarie, make Alfie leave the
bleedin' funnel be.'

The ship churned on into the sullen sea, great bullying iron pushing
into cold waters of mineral green. To starboard now was a corner of
Skye, to port there came slowly harsh Eigg and thunderous Rum. But
that cold-eyed young man saw nothing of those coming islands he
might have come to see, he sat to starboard with his plastic girl. He
had succeeded. Whether or not she knew it was a dodge scarcely
mattered. If she had known, then at least it acted like an excuse. She
was simply willing to speak and sit with him. And from then on there
began the fearful old tragedy—innocence enchanted by vice.

His tight face unscrewed into a hung-open sham of courtesy, his
forehead creased up in horizontal humble enquiry, he asked:

'Excuse me, Miss—I see you have a map there, would I be right in
thinking those the Cuillins?'

Her face brightened, she became alive not in pleasure at expressing
what she knew but simply in talking to that man:

'No, not here, they're further up. See right up there where we're
going. But you can't see the tops, the tops are in cloud.'

'Indeed? Why, it must be a real pleasure to know as much as you,
it's difficult being a stranger in these parts.'

'Oh, I'm not a stranger. I've lived here all my life. Over in Mallaig.'

'Now that's interesting, that's interesting. Lived in these parts all
your life, have you? *Have* you, now.'

'Well I *think* all my life. You see—'

'What's that, *think*? *Think*?'

'You see—'

'Come off it, you're pulling my leg, you can't tell *me* you don't know where you've been all your life, a smart girl like you. Telling me you don't know who you are next.'

'That's it, I don't really.'

'Uh.'

'Of course I know I'm me, But who me is I couldn't ever be sure.'

'Ho?'

'I'm a changeling.'

'Wassat? *Wassat*?'

'They say I'm a changeling.'

She stared at him waiting, her deep dark eyes moist between the collars of her plastic mack, against her halo hood of water white. In those eyes there lay a slight cast. But that young man saw no eyes, he was looking at her lips, hoping like hell nothing more like what he had heard would come. Somehow the boot had got on the wrong foot, he should have been doing the talking and now she had gummed up the works with this fancy stuff. What the hell was a changeling, anyway? He furrowed up his brow in perplexed sympathy, coughed, then remembered—it was the old doorstep dodge. He cooed:

'Orphan, eh? Poor kid, no mum nor dad. Doesn't seem to've done you a packet of harm though. Not by the look of you. Foundling, eh?'

'No. Changeling.'

'Ah, you mean foundling. Foundling's what you mean.'

'No, *changeling*. They say when you're a baby someone comes and changes you with another baby. I've been sort of queer all my life. That's why mum and my sisters say I was changed. The fairies come and changed me, I'm like a fairy, see?'

'Fairies? Come off it.'

'I am, I really am.'

'Oho.'

She's nuts, he thought. A nice balls-up—fairies. He edged a bit away from her. Then a slow, rich, gluey smile stretched his mouth. His eyes stared still hard scheming. This wasn't so bad after all? If she was nuts, she might be that much easier? You sometimes got round a soft-head easier.

He got towards her:

'I get you. That's interesting what you say, real interesting. Tell you what, you and me's going to have one. Drop of nice port wine, eh?'

'Well . . .'
'Come on, do you handsome a parky day like this.'
'Well, I'd not say no to a cup of tea now . . .'
'Cupper tea? That what fairies drink?'
'Now you mustn't laugh . . .'
'Whatever you say, princess. Lead the way.'

Now chuckling together, he falsely and she in real delight, they rose and staggered off against the wind to the companion-way. For one moment, before going down, they paused—she pointed to where a gull stood high and solitary on the summit of the after flag-pole. It stood with the careful genius birds have for showing up statues. Other gulls wheeled and swooped round, but that one stood stiffly still and careful. The girl tittered:

'I wonder what he's thinking up there.'

He looked quickly up, then shrugged—eyes already on the companion-way and action:

'Ask me. Just ask *me*.'

That man in black in the wooden bar with a grunt woke up. He looked startled, turned to the empty bench beside him and said:

'What's time? We there?'

Receiving no answer he looked with suspicion round the rest of that bare wooden cabin, saw his empty whisky glasses in front and again grunted. It was a final grunt. Stretching his huge stomach more, he put both hands in pockets at the same time, drew out with one hand a red silk handkerchief and with the other a small black book, blew his nose and commenced to read at the same time. Once a dark shape flashed winging by the porthole. He brushed it away from his page like a fly, but never looked up. The engine throbbed with his silence.

The engine throbbed, the boat shuddered, and now that Liverpool father was up and standing by the rail with a pink-faced scrubbed old gentleman. Perhaps his silk white hair made this old man look so clean—or perhaps it was the little old lady who fitted so neatly near his arm. She wore a straggled tippet round her throat, from this her live little face came like a small round vegetable. From time to time, as the three talked, these two looked at each other with twinkling affection. The Liverpool man was saying:

'Turbines, steam turbines, that's what they are. And I'm *telling* you.

I'm telling *you*—it won't be long before *you'll* be seeing diesels along this line. Diesels, you'll see.'

He was looking with small fury at the old man. His checked peak thrust forward, the lines deep in his cheeks dragging his mouth down in scorn. But it was the scorn of approval; scorning all other times, astonished by this world of plenty that rained diesels. The old man nodded:

'Times are changing. It's a turn of speed they're after.'

The old lady smiled up at him:

'That's it.'

The checked cap nodded emphasis. Then the old gentleman went on:

'But us'll have in mind the old paddlers, won't us, madam? Foof foof foofle foof—that's the stuff to give 'em!'

He churned wide with his hands, turning them round like paddle-wheels. The old lady pressed her small face backwards with laughter. The man with the cap relaxed, and again in approval nodded:

'Ay, they did their turn rightly and no one's goin' to say a word agin' 'em.'

Creeping up nearer on the starboard came Eigg and Rum, queer masses of rock and mountain presiding over the sea aloof and insolent as battleships. Unique shapes—Eigg low like half a huge whale of grey stone cut open and exposing its great scar of ribbed blubber: Rum lowering behind, mountainous and jagged, black against the silver sunlight like a giant tooth extracted and roots upmost planted in the sea. People looked, and looked away consumed with their own affairs. The gulls flew round and round, pacing the ship, swooping up and down, planing no one knew how or where or why, on a voyage instinctive but unaware. Their piping over the cold green sea came and then was lost on the wind.

Those militant fanciers of cake, the navy and the nigger, had already confessed to an empty feeling in their tum-tums, and now stood at the head of a small queue forming far down in the ship outside the glass-doored dining-saloon. Inside the doors stewards stood, themselves a scattered queue, also waiting. No one moved. The clock only slowly wound the minutes forward across its marine and brass-bound face.

Since no teas were then served, the young man had thankfully been able to guide his changeling to a port and lemon. They sat in the small bar, as far away as possible from the man in black. That was not far.

The fat man, deep in Johnson's tour of the Hebrides, with these in fact passing unseen through the dark bulwarks, had no wish to speak to them. But being there he spoiled the young man's hopes of privacy, and so this one kept the steward behind the bar in conversation. Talk to impress his changeling, talk of two men together. On he talked. The steward only nodded.

'Wouldn't suit me, this job. I like to get going. How much do you pull in a week? Chicken-feed. Me, I'm the best man on the road. Give me a good line and I'll sell it to anybody. Mind you it's got to be a good line, you can't sell a dud. Not even me, I can't.'

He paused and looked round with wonder at himself to the steward. The steward gave him back a grim look. He went on quickly, now thumping the bar:

'Know what I do? I take night trains. So I get there early. None of your nine o'clocks. Seven, that's me. Like this I can go to my hotel and then I have a bath and then I change and then I'm there for my first call at *ten minutes past nine*. On the dot. *And* fresh. What's that?'

Somewhere distantly in the ship a gong droned, approached and retreated and was lost. The steward sighed taciturn, seamanly relief. Looking hard at the young man he said:

'*That's* your dinner.'

As the young man and the pleased girl rose, as the fat man reminded drew from his pocket still reading a bag of sandwiches, as those two motherly ones at the head of their queue victorious and satisfied swept through the glass door into the dining-saloon, as all over the ship others—the check-cap and his brood, the old gentleman and his new old lady, the healthy cold girls purpling in their short pants and everyone else aboard who had paid eighteen shillings for this most enjoyable round trip—as everybody turned from their places to the companion-way and the blind bowels of the dining-saloon, so Eigg and Rum came magnificently at last into full view.

And the ship, naked of sightseers, ploughed past them.

Empty decks as empty as the great rock-mass of near Eigg, empty as the mineral cold sea, empty as the wide northern sky whistling forlorn over this part where life showed no warm profusion and few things chose to live. On the long scarred face of grey Eigg a little grass grew. The wind-dried salt emptiness of those seas was not changed since the dragon-headed longboats ran through, since that desolate day when the raiding Macleods of Skye came in their fierce craft to board the island and light at the cave-mouth a suffocating fire that smothered to death all the women, children and men of Eigg driven there to shelter. Similar winds must have driven across in those days, similarly the mountains to either side must have loomed. And the far-away white sun must have shone its pale light on similar clouds scudding like wet canvas. All around, mountains and misted horizon and metal-green sea would have lain as empty in those days as now, as when that lonely steamship, the only moving thing in view, dogged its midget course past drama into greater drama. Gigantic mountainous Rum came to port—and at last the Cuillins topped in vertiginous cloud towered terribly to starboard.

Yet no one saw. Even the gulls, questing open-eyed round, had swooped to the sea and were pecking the first plate-emptyings thrown out in the ship's wake.

The ship turned in past shark-curing Soay and entered more sheltered water, the sea-loch Scavaig. Dinner was finished and most of the passengers had come on deck again. A sharp new wind had risen that brought sudden whirls of spray spiralling like furious little waterspouts: these, coming from nowhere, bidden it seemed by an unseen presence, heightened the uneasy feeling of that strange precipitous place. They had entered into the first reaches of the dark Cuillins.

So that now—whether from a certain uneasiness that hung in that place, or from a sense of satiety and arrival, or from a bewildering wonder as to what should happen next—now all those different ones stood about the decks and stared at the grey rock that surrounded them. The ship's engines stopped. Then they started again: but churning backwards. One did not know quite what was happening. Yet all the time the ship slewed nearer the rock. And they had reached the end of the loch, they drifted dangerously in the small cove-like end which was no bigger in radius than some five lengths of the ship. Could one then control a ship so unwieldy in such short space? But the captain must know. And one saw that though not exactly a harbour, there was some sort of a stone jetty built out from low-lying rock. Could one then land here?

Really, in all that sharp rock? But it was on the schedule to land.

Already a motor launch had put off from the jetty and was spitting over the hundred yards or so to the ship. Yet how was one to get into that boat? So low down? There must be some difficult seamanship here—would not each passenger be involved? That father in the checked cap thought for a terrible moment: 'Breeches' Buoy?' And thought:

'Women and children.' And thought of his wife swinging helpless and fat out in the cradle over horrible water.

The iron sides of the ship invited sharp rock. One felt that a sound would echo for years round and round that hard place. If one shouted. Nobody shouted.

And above, as though the cold and friendless near cliffs were not menacing enough, a great dark jagged Cuillin blasphemed black against the highest sky. So they stood not knowing. And then perceptibly, having come up, there began a movement down. Soon all the passengers had sheeped onto the inside stairs and were standing queued and pressed on those steep steps inside. Brass-bound and embellished with the framed monochromes of life-belts and statistics of draught, those stairs led to where a door had been opened miraculously in the ship's very side just above the waterline. Pressed together, not knowing what was coming but herded and willing, they waited.

Somewhere up above, from the upper deck perhaps to that extraordinary door below, sailors were shouting to one another. There came a shuffling at the front of the queue—an oilskinned man from the launch had stepped up into the ship, he was making his way along to where a short fat bluff double-breasted officer stood. Together these two, talking closely, disappeared through a door into some most watertight-looking part. The people waited. They grew silent. There was no more to be said.

Waited and waited. The ship rolled slightly. Nobody knew quite how near those rocks they were now.

Then up above, quite suddenly, and for some reason that will never be known, one of the circling seagulls swooped into a wild ellipse and headed off. Low on the water it flew straight as a line back across the lonely miles to Mallaig.

After waiting minutes, those who formed the last half of the queue gradually dispersed. Having no valuable precedence, being far up the staircase by the deck, they thinned and straggled up for air and to see.

It had been promised in the itinerary that a landing would be made here at the end of the loch. For with a short walk inland one could really see the Cuillins, feel the Cuillins—and lying just out of sight was the inland Loch Coruisk, a still water closed in forever by frowning cliffs. This was reputed to be the most desolate and terrifying place in the British Isles. Something one should see. And now—to their surprise—those who climbed again on deck saw that in fact the launch was putting off again, empty but for one passenger, a rough-looking man in broadcloth. The ship still lay safely in the centre of that cold claustrophobic cup of water. But now there was more commotion on the stairs, the people parted and climbing up came that great figure in black. Impassively he passed, gripping his book, and his stomach carried him off the staircase and straight back to the bar. The cold-eyed young man, letting him pass, thought: 'Well, that's that.' For the whole twenty minutes he had been trying to persuade his changeling to stay behind in the empty ship. He had described in detail the trivial nature of a Loch Coruisk he had never seen. But the changeling allowed nothing to alter her mind. She liked nature. Especially in her new white mack.

But a further commotion followed the fat man up the stairs. The whole queue had turned and now were slowly remounting the stairs, grumbling with surprise, laughing with surprise, unsurprised and silent. There was to be no landing—the water was too low from the level of the jetty. Last of all came those who had made certain to be first, the nigger and the navy caps—now for the moment undone.

'And all this way too!'

'They ought to know. Telling us and then not.'

'I was never so surprised.'

'What I mean is they ought to know. The captain ought, really. What I mean is it's his job. It's his job, isn't it, Cora?'

'I was never so surprised.'

But not for long. A few stairs higher, and it was all over. The future had to be looked to. Already the boat was moving homeward.

'There, we're moving! It won't be long now.'

Already visions of home presented themselves. After the first dismay, all minds had turned to thoughts of home. Watches were consulted. Ideas of the length of the homeward trip were exchanged. The father with the checked cap, eagerly always pacing the deck and admiring the mechanical prowess of the ship, had found again that old lady and gentleman:

'We'll be ashore by four o'clock! She's making a pretty turn. Twelve knots, I'm reckoning. We've the wind behind us and all.'

The old gentleman made no reply. This was unfair, such a statement called for argument. So the checked cap repeated, intruding his chin:

'Twelve knots, I said.'

The old gentleman nodded:

'I expect you're right. Yes. Twelve knots.'

So the other said:

'Well. Well then could you tell me the time, the time it is now, the right time?'

'I'm afraid I haven't a watch.'

'What about the missus?'

The old man turned and smiled. His eyes twinkled. The old lady pressed her chin into her fur, blushing, though her pale cheeks showed no colour.

'She's not my missus.'

He looked down twinkling at her small beaming face:

'In fact—my dear—I don't even know your name, do I?'

He turned back to the checked-cap man and said slowly, emphatically and softly, as though telling a story from a long time ago:

'You see—this has been my lucky day.'

So the ship went churning back past Soay and Rum and Eigg and distant Muck. The sun paled low, silvering the western waters, giving to all those islands lying Atlanticwards a romance of lost lands. Islands reaching out towards some place irrevocable, a place that only might have been, and now in a visionary moment at end of day shown somehow as a real possibility. Perhaps for the first time many of those people began to look at what was passing with moved hearts, with curious regret.

They stood about the decks in groups, or sat sheltered on the long wooden seats to leeward by the funnel. They had fallen silent and their eyes were on the sea. The homeward journey rests the soul, nothing to be done but to arrive. A shorter journey—no danger of surprise, no new climates to assail.

And in this very relaxation the senses may at last blossom. For the first time the journey is seen as it is, for the first time it is felt to be sliding away forever from grasp. Never again, nevermore. Evanescent as the water at the ship's keel, the white ephemeral wake, water that marks the passage, white and wide, that melts and vanishes in personless flat green. A journey made, no more. Soon forgotten. Thus the deep iron sides of the ship sailed on relentless homewards—leaving behind the magic of the westering sun, flying on what felt a following wind, sailing ever faster home.

Even that cold-eyed young man seemed to feel some of this melancholy beauty of a journey ending. He stood by the ship's rail half hidden by the curved white prow of a lifeboat, his changeling tucked in his arm. He never tried to kiss her. His eyes rested, a shade softer, on the horizon and the last of those great receding island shapes. He had planned, complacently, to make no kiss until they were ashore. He had told himself that by holding off he would impress her with trust of himself—and provoke her at the same time with a wish to entice him. This decided, he could relax the better, he could give himself to the scene.

But the man in black still sat in the bar. He read on with comfort and seclusion of the Doctor's journey two centuries before: within the square of his book it was warmer, more defined too, than the great and gusty outside.

Gulls circled and swooped high round the wind-proud mast, swooped low to kiss the water—but among these too there were thoughts of home, some suddenly took off ahead of the ship and flew swiftly arcing to where now Mallaig began to show its colour and indeed its own white smoke of gulls.

They drew in, the *Pride of the Isles* and her wool-wrapped passengers. Steam of gulls and smoke from the curing-sheds greeted them. The black iron touched the hard stone quay, great ropes flung out to the bollards and winches, small dock machines began to grind, the first burnt smell of kippering blew over all. So stationary things looked! Here the hotels and the houses and the long-legged sheds had stood all that while waiting, not moving up and down but settled and dry and, most of all, stationary. Suddenly it came over many how dull all these things were. Homely and welcoming—but dull, dull, dull.

Yet as soon as they had set foot on the quay this feeling vanished. The solidity of the land claimed them, here it was safe and sound, one could relax here as—with on the calmest seas always some gentle motion—one can never relax on a boat.

First ashore were those two matrons. Only pausing to rebutton once more their coats, to set homewards their scarves and the peaks of those two hat-caps, they set off at once along the quay. Their direction had been planned long before.

'It was a lovely, lovely day.'

'It was worth every shilling we paid. But I shall be glad to be home.'

'A nice sit-down, Cora. A nice cup of tea.'

Soon after the mother and her brood came stumbling down the gangway, clotted together like one large animal disturbed in the unloading process. Behind, with the nonchalance of a drover, came the father.

He kept a wary eye on the mechanism of landing—on hawsers, bollards, gangway and all practical arrangements. That eye never questioned 'why' a thing was—but always 'how is it done?' Then he too took a last look up at the ship and was gone.

The man in black, staggering a little from weight or alcohol, hurried at speed down the gangway, carried as always by his own great momentum. He took no last backward glance. He carried it in his hand, in the little black book.

The old gentleman and the lady were among the last to leave, they had lingered as long as possible. Now they too came slowly, unsurely down that difficult slope. At the bottom the old gentleman turned, and with courtesy handed his new lady off. His eyes were watering in the cold, his shoulders bent, he breathed harder from even this slight effort: together they turned and passed along the quay.

Suddenly the changeling, who still stood at the deck-rail, started to wave. The young man by her side started. He had been waiting casually, feeling he had so much time, pleasurably possessive. But now that plastic white arm was pumping up and down, that face was smiling excited! She was looking somewhere down along the quay. He said quickly, eyes hard, lips thin:

'Hello what's this? What's up?'

'It's him! I thought he'd never come!'

'Him? Oo?'

'My boy.'

'Wassat you said?'

'My boy that I'm engaged with.'

'Christ.'

'I *beg* your pardon.'

'Nothing, oh nothing. Oh nuts. So long.'

'But I wanted you to meet . . . ?'

He was already at the gangway, dancing down with long stiff strides, his mackintosh belted tight and hard round him.

Those two girls with the high shorts had their oilcloth capes on, and these capes reaching just to the bottom of the shorts at the tops of their blue legs gave them a look of naked pixies. Together they stooped by the door of a kippering hut. Inside, the little dark kippers hung above a fire of cinders spread over the floor. Each kipper looked like a small ebony god in a temple full of incense braziers. The girls giggled: then turned away. The young man eyed them, considering. But they simply turned, hands in pockets. And with heads bent trudged off down the quay. Heads bent, two together walking intent only on themselves, talking, walled-in and unassailable as young and pretty girls can surely be.

Soon, when the sun set, the gulls themselves stopped circling. The white-streaked quays grew quiet. The gliding gulls had gone to roost, the people going . . . gone.

Deliverance

One autumn evening a woman in her early forties walked along the platform of the Terminal Station in Rome and boarded a wagon-lit in the Paris Express. She sat down on the made-up bed in her compartment, took off her small, perfect, inconspicuous hat, and looked about her with an air of annoyance. It was a long time since she had travelled by rail, and she had been pushed to it against her will, because there had not been a seat free on any of the planes leaving Rome that day or the next. But this was the least of her worries, and she wasted no time on it, but set about arranging her passport and her tickets in order to have them ready when the wagon-lit attendant arrived. This required close scrutiny, for although she was a Frenchwoman named Madame Rémy, another impression was conveyed by her passport, her tickets and the labels on her luggage, and she had to remind herself what that impression was, for only a few hours before she had been yet a third person.

Such inconsistencies, however, never made her nervous. They were unlikely to be noticed because she herself was so unnoticeable. She was neither tall nor short, dark nor fair, handsome nor ugly. She left a pleasant impression on those she met in her quiet passage through the world, and then these people forgot her. She had no remarkable attributes except some which were without outward sign, such as a command of six languages and an unusually good memory.

When the door opened, Madame Rémy had not quite finished getting her papers out of a handbag which had more than the usual number of pockets and flaps in it, and some very intricate fastenings. Without raising her head, she asked the attendant to wait a moment, in her excellent Italian, which, just for verisimilitude, had a slight Florentine accent. Then, as he did not answer, she looked up sharply. She had only time to remark that he was wearing not the uniform of a wagon-lit attendant but a dark grey suit with a checked blue muffler, and that his pale face was shining with sweat. Then the door banged between them. She did not follow him, because she was as highly disciplined as any soldier, and she knew that her first concern must be with the tiny ball of paper which he had dropped in her lap.

When she had unrolled it she read a typewritten message: 'A man is travelling on this train under orders to kill you.' She rolled it up again and went into the corridor and stood there, looking out at the crowds on the ill-lit platform. It would have been unwise to leave the train. A clever man with a knife, she calculated, could do his work among the shadows and get away quite easily. Several times she had to step back into her compartment, to get out of the way of passengers who were coming aboard, and at these, if they were male, she looked with some interest. She was standing thus, looking up with a noncommittal glance, neither too blank nor too keenly interested, at a tall man in a tweed overcoat and wondering if he were so tall as to be specially memorable, and therefore ineligible as an assassin, when she heard shouts from the platform.

The tall man came to a halt, and she crushed past him and stood beside him, looking out through the wide corridor window at a scene still as a painted picture. Everybody was motionless, even the porters with their luggage barrows, while four men made their way back to the platform gates, at a quiet and steady pace, two in front, and two behind who were walking backwards. Their faces were darkened by masks, and all held revolvers which they pointed at the crowd. The man beside Madame Rémy made a scandalized and bluff noise which told her that he was not an assassin, and at that moment the train began to move. He went on his way to his compartment and left Madame Rémy standing alone at the window, waiting to see what had happened at the end of the platform. But she saw nothing unusual till the train was leaving the station behind it and sliding out into the open evening. Then her eye was caught by the last iron pillar that held up the platform roof. A man was embracing it as if it were a beloved woman to whom he was bidding farewell. His suit was dark grey; and as he slid to the ground and toppled over and fell face upward, it could be seen that he was wearing a checked blue muffler.

Madame Rémy went back to her compartment and said a prayer for his soul. She looked at her hands with some distaste, because they were shaking, and took the little ball of paper out of her bag and read the message again. This was not because she feared she had forgotten it, or thought she had overlooked any of its implications, but because it interested her as a technician to see if there were any distinguishing marks in the typefaces which recalled any typed letters that she had received before. Then she thought of all the things it would be sensible to do, such as ringing for the attendant and showing him the message, out in the corridor, in front of some open door, in the hearing of some other passenger, preferably a woman, and she decided to do none of them.

She said aloud, 'I am a lucky woman.' Leaning back her head against the cushions, she repeated, 'How very lucky I am.'

There had seemed no way out of the wretchedness that was all around her. She was under no illusion as to the reason why the doctor she had consulted in Rome concerning a slight but persistent symptom had begged her to go into hospital for an X-ray examination the next day, and had urged her, when he found she was resolved to go back to Paris, not to let one day pass after she got there without seeking a surgeon. The thing was in her father's family, and she was familiar with its method of approach.

She was, moreover, in financial difficulties to which there could be no end. She had loved her dead husband very much, so much that she felt that she could deny nothing to the child of his first marriage. But Madeleine was sullen and unaffectionate, had early insisted on marrying a worthless young man and had three children already and might have more; and her only remarkable characteristic was a capacity for getting into debt without having anything to show for it in purchased goods. Madame Rémy really did not see how she could meet this last crop of bills without selling either the few jewels remaining to her, which were those she wore so constantly, except when she was on duty, that they seemed part of her body, or her little house in Passy, where she had spent all her married life. In either case it would be a joyless sacrifice, for Madeleine had nothing of her father in her.

Also, it was evident to Madame Rémy that her long-standing friendship with Claude was over. Just before she left Paris she had heard again the rumour that he was going to marry the Armenian heiress, and his denial had left her in no doubt that they were going to part before very long, perhaps even without tenderness. That would take from the last five years of her life the value which she had believed made them remarkable. She had always thought that she had taken up her peculiar work because she and a distinguished member of the French Foreign Office had fallen in love with each other, and that had made it a romantic adventure. But now she suspected that a member of the French Foreign Office had had a love affair with her because she had an aptitude for a certain peculiar kind of work; and though she recognized that even if this were so, Claude had formed some real affection for her, and that she owed him gratitude for much charming companionship, she knew that she would never be able to look back on their relations without a sense of humiliation. Even her work, in which she had hoped to find her main interest as her life went on, would now be darkened in her mind by association with a long pretence, and her own gullibility. There was nothing at the end of her journey except several sorts of pain, so if the journey had no end there was no reason for grief.

When she had worked it out to her final satisfaction she found that the wagon-lit attendant was standing in front of her, asking for her tickets and passport. She gave them to him slowly, feeling a certain sense of luxury, because his presence meant her last hope of life, and she was not taking it. They wished each other good night, and then she called him back, because it had occurred to her that it would be hardly fair if he had to go without his tip in the morning just because she was dead. Agents were trained never to make themselves memorable by giving more or less than the standard tip, and she acted according to habit, but regretted it, for surely the occasion called for a little lavishness. As she explained to him that she was giving him the tip in case they were rushed at the other end she noted his casual air. He was evidently to be the second-last man she was to see, not the last.

Once she was alone, she burned the message in her washbasin, and pulled up the window blind so that she could look at the bright villages and the dark countryside that raced by. She thought of the smell of anaesthetics that hangs about the vestibules of clinics, and she thought of the last time she had met Madame Couthier in the Champs Elysées and how Madame Couthier had looked through her as if they had never been at school together, and how it had turned out that Madeleine had run up a huge bill with young Couthier, who was finding it hard to make his way as an interior decorator. She thought of an evening, just before she had heard the rumour about the Armenian heiress, when Claude had driven her back from dinner at Ville-d'Avray, and she had rested her head against his shoulder for a minute when the road was dark, and had kissed his sleeve. Claude and she were the same age, yet she felt hot with shame when she remembered this, as if she had been an old woman doting on a boy.

She pulled down the blind, and began to make very careful preparations for the night. Her large case was on the rack, and she did not care to ring for the attendant and ask him to move it for her, lest somebody else should come in his stead and the attack be precipitated before she was ready for it. But she was obliged to get it down, because she had packed in it her best nightgown, which was made of pleated white chiffon. For a reason she had never understood she had always liked to carry it with her when she went on a specially dangerous enterprise; and now she saw that it had been a sensible thing to do. It was very pleasant to put it on after she had undressed and washed very carefully, rubbing herself down with toilet water, as she could not have a bath. After she had made up her face again and recoiffed her hair, she lay down between the sheets. Then it occurred to her that she had not unpacked her bedroom slippers, and she made a move to get out of bed before she realized that she need not take the trouble.

She turned out the big light in the compartment ceiling, and left on only the little reading lamp at the head of her bed. She had not locked the door. Her careful toilette had made her tired: and indeed she had been working very hard for some days, preparing all the papers that were now safe in her embassy. She thought of Madeleine and Claude, and bleakly realized that she had no desire to see either of them ever again. She tried to remember something pleasant, and found that for that she had to go back to the days when her husband was alive. It had been delightful when he came back in the evenings from his office, particularly at this very time of year, in the autumn, when he brought her sweet-smelling bouquets of bronze and gold chrysanthemums, and after tea they did not light the lamps, and sat with the firelight playing on the Japanese gilt wallpaper. It had been delightful, too, when they went for holidays in Switzerland and skied in winter and climbed in summer, and he always was astounded and pleased by her courage. But dear Louis was not at the end of her journey. There was nothing waiting for her there but Madeleine and Claude, and the smell that hangs about the vestibules of clinics.

The train slowed down at a station. There were cries, lurchings and trampings in the corridors, long periods of silence and immobility, a thin blast on a trumpet; and the train jerked forward again. That happened a second time, and a third. But still the man who was travelling under orders did not come to carry them out.

Madame Rémy turned out the reading lamp and prayed to the darkness that he might hurry; and then for a little, retreating again from the thought of Madeleine and Claude to the memory of her husband, she passed into something nearly a dream. But she was fully awake as soon as someone tried the lock of the door with a wire. It was as if a bucket had been emptied over her, a bucket filled, not with water, but with fear. There was not a part of her which was not drenched with terror. She disliked this emotion, which she had never felt before except in a slight degree, just as much as added to the zest of an enterprise. To escape from this shuddering abasement she reminded herself that she wanted to die, she had chosen to die, and she sat up and cried, '*Entrez! Entrate!*'

The door swung open, and softly closed again. There followed a silence, and, feeling fear coming on her again, she switched on the light. It was a relief to her that the man who was standing with his back to the door did not wear the uniform of a wagon-lit attendant, and that he was the sort of person who would be selected for such a mission. He was young and lean and spectacled, and wore a soft hat crushed down over his brows and a loose greatcoat with the collar turned up, in a way that she tenderly noted as amateurish. It would be very hard for him to get away from the scene of a crime without arousing suspicion. There was also a sign that he was the man for whom she was waiting, in the woodenness of his features and his posture. He knew quite well that what he was doing was wrong, and to persuade himself that it was right, he had had to stop the natural flow of not only his thoughts and feelings but his muscles.

Yet he made no move to commit the violent act for which this rigidity had been a preparation. Simply he stood there, staring at her. She thought 'Poor child, he is very young' and remained quite still, fearing to do anything which might turn him from his resolution. But he went on staring at her. 'Is he never going to do it?' she asked herself, wondering at the same time whether it was a cord or a knife that he was fingering in the pocket of his greatcoat. It occurred to her that with such a slow-moving assailant she had still a very good chance of making a fight for her life and saving it. But then there came to her the look of surgical instruments on a tray, the whine that came into Madeleine's voice when she spoke of the inevitability of debt, and the fluency, which now recalled to her a conjurer's patter, of Claude's love-making; and she was conscious of the immense distance that divided her from the only real happiness she had ever known. She flung open her arms in invitation to the assassin, smiling at him to assure him that she felt no ill will against him, that all she asked of him was to do his work quickly.

Suddenly he stepped backwards, and she found herself looking at the door with a stare as fixed as his own. She had made an absurd mistake. This was simply a fellow passenger who had mistaken the number of his compartment, and all the signs she had read in his appearance were fictions of her own mind, excited by the typewritten message. It was a disappointment, but she did not allow it to depress her. When she thought of the man in the dark grey suit with the checked blue muffler, sliding down the pillar and turning over as he reached the ground, it was as a child might think of an adult who had made it a promise. She contemplated in sorrow and wonder the fact that a stranger had given up his life because he wished her well, and switched out the light and again said a prayer for him into the darkness. Then, although she had no reason to suppose that the man who was travelling under orders would come sooner or later to carry them out, she grew drowsy.

'What, not stay awake even to be assassinated?' she muttered to her pillow, and laughed, and was swallowed up by sleep, deep sleep, such as had often come on her at the end of a long day on the mountains.

The next morning a spectacled young man, wearing a soft hat and a loose greatcoat, who had made his way back to Rome while the sun came up, stood in a hotel room and gave a disappointing report to his superior.

He said, 'Madame Rémy was not on the train. It was all a mistake. There was one woman who answered to the description, and I went into her compartment, but I found she was quite a different sort of person. She was not at all haggard and worn; indeed, she looked much younger than the age you gave me, and she was very animated. And though we know that if Ferrero found Madame Rémy on the train he must have warned her, this woman was not at all frightened. She had left her door unlocked, and when she saw me she showed no fear at all. Indeed,' he said gloomily, 'she was evidently a loose woman. Though she was in bed her face was painted, and her hair was done up as if she were going to a ball, and it was really quite extraordinary— she even stretched out her arms and smiled at me. I think', he asserted, blushing faintly, 'that if I had cared to stay in her compartment I would have received quite a warm welcome.'

His superior expressed an unfavourable opinion regarding the morals of all bourgeois women, but had his doubts, and made certain enquiries.

As a result the spectacled young man was doomed not to realize what was at that time his dearest ambition, for he was never given another chance to commit a political assassination. He regretted this much less than he would have owned. Even then, standing in the golden sunshine of a Roman morning, he was not really disturbed because the night had been so innocent.

At that moment Madame Rémy was sitting in the restaurant car of the Paris Express, eating breakfast. She could have had it brought to her in her compartment, but she had felt a desire to have it where the windows were wider and she could see more of the countryside. Her first pot of coffee had been so good that she had ordered a second, and she was spreading the butter on a roll, smiling a little, because it seemed so absurd that after such a night she should have awakened to find herself suddenly freed from the wretchedness that had hung about her for so long. Certainly she had lost none of her troubles; but they no longer appalled her. There came to mind the names of several among her friends who had survived serious operations. As for Madeleine's debts, if nobody paid them it might help the poor silly child to grow up; and the wisest thing, even the loyallest thing, for her stepmother to do was to keep the jewels and the house that Louis Rémy had given her and leave them intact to Madeleine's children. It might well be true that she could no longer support the desperate nature of her present work, but there was no need for her days to be idle, for the great dressmaker, Mariol, had always had a liking for her and had more than once offered her a post in his business. And there was no need for her to think of Claude. If she wanted to think of someone who was not there any more, she could remember Louis.

Some other names occurred to her: the names of people who had not survived operations. But they cast no darkness on her mind; she was conscious only of a certain grandeur, and they went from her. For all her interest was given to looking out of the window at what she was seeing again only because of some inexplicable carelessness on the part of those who were usually careful.

Now the train was running toward the mountains, and was passing through a valley in the foothills. There were cliffs, steel-grey where the sun caught them, dark blue in the shadow, rising to heights patterned with the first snows, glistening sugar-white under the sharp blue sky. At the foot of the cliffs a line of poplars, golden with autumn, marked the course of a broad and shallow river racing over grey shingle; and between the river and the railway track was a field where a few corn shocks, like dried, gesticulating men, were still standing among some trailing morning mists. Across this field, through the mists, an old man in a dark blue shirt and light blue trousers was leading a red cart, drawn by two oxen the colour of the coffee and milk in her cup. Deliberately the two beasts trod, so slowly that they seemed to sleep between paces, so dutifully that if they were dreaming it must be of industry. There was nothing very beautiful in the scene, yet it was wonderful, and it existed, it would go on being there when she was far away.

As the train met the mountains and passed into a tunnel, she closed her eyes so that she could go on seeing the cliffs and the snow and the poplars, the man and his cart and his oxen. Amazed by what the world looked like when one had thought it lost and had found it again, she sat quite still, in a trance of contentment, while the train carried her on to the end of her journey.

A Good Man is Hard to Find

The grandmother didn't want to go to Florida. She wanted to visit some of her connections in east Tennessee and she was seizing at every chance to change Bailey's mind. Bailey was the son she lived with, her only boy. He was sitting on the edge of his chair at the table, bent over the orange sports section of the *Journal*. 'Now look here, Bailey,' she said, 'see here, read this', and she stood with one hand on her thin hip and the other rattling the newspaper at his bald head. 'Here this fellow that calls himself The Misfit is aloose from the Federal Pen and headed toward Florida and you read here what it says he did to these people. Just you read it. I wouldn't take my children in any direction with a criminal like that aloose in it. I couldn't answer to my conscience if I did.'

Bailey didn't look up from his reading so she wheeled around then and faced the children's mother, a young woman in slacks, whose face was as broad and innocent as a cabbage and was tied around with a green head-kerchief that had two points on the top like rabbit's ears. She was sitting on the sofa, feeding the baby his apricots out of a jar. 'The children have been to Florida before,' the old lady said. 'You all ought to take them somewhere else for a change so they would see different parts of the world and be broad. They never have been to east Tennessee.'

The children's mother didn't seem to hear her but the eight-year-old boy, John Wesley, a stocky child with glasses, said, 'If you don't want to go to Florida, why dontcha stay at home?' He and the little girl, June Star, were reading the funny papers on the floor.

'She wouldn't stay at home to be queen for a day,' June Star said without raising her yellow head.

'Yes and what would you do if this fellow, The Misfit, caught you?' the grandmother asked.

'I'd smack his face,' John Wesley said.

'She wouldn't stay at home for a million bucks,' June Star said. 'Afraid she'd miss something. She has to go everywhere we go.'

'All right, Miss,' the grandmother said. 'Just remember that the next time you want me to curl your hair.'

June Star said her hair was naturally curly.

The next morning the grandmother was the first one in the car, ready to go. She had her big black valise that looked like the head of a hippopotamus in one corner, and underneath it she was hiding a basket with Pitty Sing, the cat, in it. She didn't intend for the cat to be left alone in the house for three days because he would miss her too much and she was afraid he might brush against one of the gas burners and accidentally asphyxiate himself. Her son, Bailey, didn't like to arrive at a motel with a cat.

She sat in the middle of the back seat with John Wesley and June Star on either side of her. Bailey and the children's mother and the baby sat in front and they left Atlanta at eight forty-five with the mileage on the car at 55890. The grandmother wrote this down because she thought it would be interesting to say how many miles they had been when they got back. It took them twenty minutes to reach the outskirts of the city.

The old lady settled herself comfortably, removing her white cotton gloves and putting them up with her purse on the shelf in front of the back window. The children's mother still had on slacks and still had her head tied up in a green kerchief, but the grandmother had on a navy blue straw sailor hat with a bunch of white violets on the brim and a navy blue dress with a small white dot in the print. Her collars and cuffs were white organdy trimmed with lace and at her neckline she had pinned a purple spray of cloth violets containing a sachet. In case of an accident, anyone seeing her dead on the highway would know at once that she was a lady.

She said she thought it was going to be a good day for driving, neither too hot nor too cold, and she cautioned Bailey that the speed limit was fifty-five miles an hour and that the patrolmen hid themselves behind billboards and small clumps of trees and sped out after you before you had a chance to slow down. She pointed out interesting details of the scenery: Stone Mountain; the blue granite that in some places came up to both sides of the highway; the brilliant red clay banks slightly streaked with purple; and the various crops that made rows of green lace-work on the ground. The trees were full of silver-white sunlight and the meanest of them sparkled. The children were reading comic magazines and their mother had gone back to sleep.

'Let's go through Georgia fast so we won't have to look at it much,' John Wesley said.

'If I were a little boy,' said the grandmother, 'I wouldn't talk about my native state that way. Tennessee has the mountains and Georgia has the hills.'

'Tennessee is just a hillbilly dumping ground,' John Wesley said, 'and Georgia is a lousy state too.'

'You said it,' June Star said.

'In my time,' said the grandmother, folding her thin veined fingers, 'children were more respectful of their native states and their parents and everything else. People did right then. Oh look at the cute little piccaninny!' she said and pointed to a Negro child standing in the door of a shack. 'Wouldn't that make a picture, now?' she asked and they all turned and looked at the little Negro out of the back window. He waved.

'He didn't have any britches on,' June Star said.

'He probably didn't have any,' the grandmother explained. 'Little niggers in the country don't have things like we do. If I could paint, I'd paint that picture,' she said.

The children exchanged comic books.

The grandmother offered to hold the baby and the children's mother passed him over the front seat to her. She set him on her knee and bounced him and told him about the things they were passing. She rolled her eyes and screwed up her mouth and stuck her leathery thin face into his smooth bland one. Occasionally he gave her a far-away smile. They passed a large cotton field with five or six graves fenced in the middle of it, like a small island. 'Look at the graveyard!' the grandmother said, pointing it out. 'That was the old family burying ground. That belonged to the plantation.'

'Where's the plantation?' John Wesley asked.

'Gone With the Wind,' said the grandmother. 'Ha. Ha.'

When the children finished all the comic books they had brought, they opened the lunch and ate it. The grandmother ate a peanut butter sandwich and an olive and would not let the children throw the box and the paper napkins out the window. When there was nothing else to do they played a game by choosing a cloud and making the other two guess what shape it suggested. John Wesley took one the shape of a cow and June Star guessed a cow and John Wesley said, no, an automobile, and June Star said he didn't play fair, and they began to slap each other over the grandmother.

The grandmother said she would tell them a story if they would keep quiet. When she told a story, she rolled her eyes and waved her head and was very dramatic. She said once when she was a maiden lady she had been courted by a Mr Edgar Atkins Teagarden from Jasper, Georgia. She said he was a very good-looking man and a gentleman and that he brought her a watermelon every Saturday afternoon with his initials cut in it, E. A. T. Well, one Saturday, she said, Mr Teagarden brought the watermelon and there was nobody at home and he left it on the front porch and returned in his buggy to Jasper, but she never got the watermelon, she said, because a nigger boy ate it when he saw the initials, E. A. T! This story tickled John Wesley's funny bone and he giggled and giggled but June Star didn't think it was any good. She said she wouldn't marry a man that just brought her a watermelon on Saturday. The grandmother said she would have done well to marry Mr Teagarden because he was a gentleman and had bought Coca-Cola stock when it first came out and that he had died only a few years ago, a very wealthy man.

They stopped at The Tower for barbecued sandwiches. The Tower was a part stucco and part wood filling station and dance hall set in a clearing outside of Timothy. A fat man named Red Sammy Butts ran it and there were signs stuck here and there on the building and for miles up and down the highway saying, TRY RED SAMMY'S FAMOUS BARBECUE. NONE LIKE FAMOUS RED SAMMY'S! RED SAM! THE FAT BOY WITH THE HAPPY LAUGH. A VETERAN! RED SAMMY'S YOUR MAN!

Red Sammy was lying on the bare ground outside the Tower with his head under a truck while a gray monkey about a foot high, chained to a small chinaberry tree, chattered nearby. The monkey sprang back into the tree and got on the highest limb as soon as he saw the children jump out of the car and run toward him.

Inside, The Tower was a long dark room with a counter at one end and tables at the other and dancing space in the middle. They all sat down at a board table next to the nickelodeon and Red Sam's wife, a tall burnt-brown woman with hair and eyes lighter than her skin, came and took their order. The children's mother put a dime in the machine and played 'The Tennessee Waltz', and the grandmother said that tune always made her want to dance. She asked Bailey if he would like to dance but he only glared at her. He didn't have a naturally sunny disposition like she did and trips made him nervous. The grand-mother's brown eyes were very bright. She swayed her head from side to side and pretended she was dancing in her chair. June Star said play something she could tap to so the children's mother put in another dime and played a fast number and June Star stepped out onto the dance floor and did her tap routine.

'Ain't she cute?' Red Sam's wife said, leaning over the counter. 'Would you like to come be my little girl?'

'No I certainly wouldn't,' June Star said. 'I wouldn't live in a broken-down place like this for a million bucks!' and she ran back to the table.

'Ain't she cute?' the woman repeated, stretching her mouth politely.

'Arn't you ashamed?' hissed the grandmother.

Red Sam came in and told his wife to quit lounging on the counter and hurry up with these people's order. His khaki trousers reached just to his hip bones and his stomach hung over them like a sack of meal swaying under his shirt. He came over and sat down at a table nearby and let out a combination sigh and yodel. 'You can't win,' he said. 'You can't win,' and he wiped his sweating red face off with a gray handkerchief. 'These days you don't know who to trust,' he said. 'Ain't that the truth?'

'People are certainly not nice like they used to be,' said the grandmother.

'Two fellers come in here last week,' Red Sammy said, 'driving a Chrysler. It was a old beat-up car but it was a good one and these boys looked all right to me. Said they worked at the mill and you know I let them fellers charge the gas they bought? Now why did I do that?'

'Because you're a good man!' the grandmother said at once.

'Yes'm, I suppose so,' Red Sam said as if he were struck with this answer.

His wife brought the orders, carrying the five plates all at once without a tray, two in each hand and one balanced on her arm. 'It isn't a soul in this green world of God's that you can trust,' she said. 'And I don't count nobody out of that, not nobody,' she repeated, looking at Red Sammy.

'Did you read about that criminal, The Misfit, that's escaped?' asked the grandmother.

'I wouldn't be a bit surprised if he didn't attack this place right here,' said the woman. 'If he hears about it being here, I wouldn't be none surprised to see him. If he hears it's two cent in the cash register, I wouldn't be a tall surprised if he . . .'

'That'll do,' Red Sam said. 'Go bring these people their Co'-Colas,' and the woman went off to get the rest of the order.

'A good man is hard to find,' Red Sammy said. 'Everything is getting terrible. I remember the day you could go off and leave your screen door unlatched. Not no more.'

He and the grandmother discussed better times. The old lady said that in her opinion Europe was entirely to blame for the way things were now. She said the way Europe acted you would think we were made of money and Red Sam said it was no use talking about it, she was exactly right. The children ran outside into the white sunlight and looked at the monkey in the lacy chinaberry tree. He was busy catching fleas on himself and biting each one carefully between his teeth as if it were a delicacy.

They drove off again into the hot afternoon. The grandmother took cat naps and woke up every few minutes with her own snoring. Outside of Toombsboro she woke up and recalled an old plantation that she had visited in this neighborhood once when she was a young lady. She said the house had six white columns across the front and that there was an avenue of oaks leading up to it and two little wooden trellis arbors on either side in front where you sat down with your suitor after a stroll in the garden. She recalled exactly which road to turn off to get to it. She knew that Bailey would not be willing to lose any time looking at an old house, but the more she talked about it, the more she wanted to see it once again and find out if the little twin arbors were still standing. 'There was a secret panel in this house,' she said craftily, not telling the truth but wishing that she were, 'and the story went that all the family silver was hidden in it when Sherman came through but it was never found . . .'

'Hey!' John Wesley said. 'Let's go see it! We'll find it! We'll poke all the woodwork and find it! Who lives there? Where do you turn off at? Hey Pop, can't we turn off there?'

'We never have seen a house with a secret panel!' June Star shrieked. 'Let's go to the house with the secret panel! Hey Pop, can't we go see the house with the secret panel!'

'It's not far from here, I know,' the grandmother said. 'It wouldn't take over twenty minutes.'

Bailey was looking straight ahead. His jaw was as rigid as a horseshoe. 'No,' he said.

The children began to yell and scream that they wanted to see the house with the secret panel. John Wesley kicked the back of the front

seat and June Star hung over her mother's shoulder and whined desperately into her ear that they never had any fun even on their vacation,
that they could never do what THEY wanted to do. The baby began to
scream and John Wesley kicked the back of the seat so hard that his
father could feel the blows in his kidney.

'All right!' he shouted and drew the car to a stop at the side of the
road. 'Will you all shut up? Will you all just shut up for one second?
If you don't shut up, we won't go anywhere.'

'It would be very educational for them,' the grandmother murmured.

'All right,' Bailey said, 'but get this: this is the only time we're going
to stop for anything like this. This is the one and only time.'

'The dirt road that you have to turn down is about a mile back,' the
grandmother directed. 'I marked it when we passed.'

'A dirt road,' Bailey groaned.

After they had turned around and were headed toward the dirt road,
the grandmother recalled other points about the house, the beautiful
glass over the front doorway and the candle-lamp in the hall. John
Wesley said that the secret panel was probably in the fireplace.

'You can't go inside this house,' Bailey said. 'You don't know who
lives there.'

'While you all talk to the people in front, I'll run around behind and
get in a window,' John Wesley suggested.

'We'll all stay in the car,' his mother said.

They turned onto the dirt road and the car raced roughly along in
a swirl of pink dust. The grandmother recalled the times when there
were no paved roads and thirty miles was a day's journey. The dirt
road was hilly and there were sudden washes in it and sharp curves
on dangerous embankments. All at once they would be on a hill, looking down over the blue tops of trees for miles around, then the next
minute, they would be in a red depression with the dust-coated trees
looking down on them.

'This place had better turn up in a minute,' Bailey said, 'or I'm
going to turn around.'

The road looked as if no one had traveled on it in months.

'It's not much farther,' the grandmother said and just as she said it,
a horrible thought came to her. The thought was so embarrassing that
she turned red in the face and her eyes dilated and her feet jumped up,
upsetting her valise in the corner. The instant the valise moved, the
newspaper top she had over the basket under it rose with a snarl and
Pitty Sing, the cat, sprang onto Bailey's shoulder.

The children were thrown to the floor and their mother, clutching the baby, was thrown out the door onto the ground; the old lady was thrown into the front seat. The car turned over once and landed right-side-up in a gulch off the side of the road. Bailey remained in the driver's seat with the cat—gray-striped with a broad white face and an orange nose—clinging to his neck like a caterpillar.

As soon as the children saw they could move their arms and legs, they scrambled out of the car, shouting, 'We've had an ACCIDENT!' The grandmother was curled up under the dashboard, hoping she was injured so that Bailey's wrath would not come down on her all at once. The horrible thought she had had before the accident was that the house she had remembered so vividly was not in Georgia but in Tennessee.

Bailey removed the cat from his neck with both hands and flung it out the window against the side of a pine tree. Then he got out of the car and started looking for the children's mother. She was sitting against the side of the red gutted ditch, holding the screaming baby, but she only had a cut down her face and a broken shoulder. 'We've had an ACCIDENT!' the children screamed in a frenzy of delight.

'But nobody's killed,' June Star said with disappointment as the grandmother limped out of the car, her hat still pinned to her head but the broken front brim standing up at a jaunty angle and the violet spray hanging off the side. They all sat down in the ditch, except the children, to recover from the shock. They were all shaking.

'Maybe a car will come along,' said the children's mother hoarsely.

'I believe I have injured an organ,' said the grandmother, pressing her side, but no one answered her. Bailey's teeth were clattering. He had on a yellow sport shirt with bright blue parrots designed in it and his face was as yellow as the shirt. The grandmother decided that she would not mention that the house was in Tennessee.

The road was about ten feet above and they could see only the tops of the trees on the other side of it. Behind the ditch they were sitting in there were more woods, tall and dark and deep. In a few minutes they saw a car some distance away on top of a hill, coming slowly as if the occupants were watching them. The grandmother stood up and waved both arms dramatically to attract their attention. The car continued to come on slowly, disappeared around a bend and appeared again, moving even slower, on top of the hill they had gone over. It was a big black battered hearse-like automobile. There were three men in it.

It came to a stop just over them and for some minutes, the driver looked down with a steady expressionless gaze to where they were sitting, and didn't speak. Then he turned his head and muttered something to the other two and they got out. One was a fat boy in black trousers and a red sweat shirt with a silver stallion embossed on the front of it. He moved around on the right side of them and stood staring, his mouth partly open in a kind of loose grin. The other had on khaki pants and a blue striped coat and a gray hat pulled down very low, hiding most of his face. He came around slowly on the left side. Neither spoke.

The driver got out of the car and stood by the side of it, looking down at them. He was an older man than the other two. His hair was just beginning to gray and he wore silver-rimmed spectacles that gave him a scholarly look. He had a long creased face and didn't have on any shirt or undershirt. He had on blue jeans that were too tight for him and was holding a black hat and a gun. The two boys also had guns.

'We've had an ACCIDENT!' the children screamed.

The grandmother had the peculiar feeling that the bespectacled man was someone she knew. His face was as familiar to her as if she had known him all her life but she could not recall who he was. He moved away from the car and began to come down the embankment, placing his feet carefully so that he wouldn't slip. He had on tan and white shoes and no socks, and his ankles were red and thin. 'Good afternoon,' he said. 'I see you all had you a little spill.'

'We turned over twice!' said the grandmother.

'Oncet,' he corrected. 'We seen it happen. Try their car and see will it run, Hiram,' he said quietly to the boy with the gray hat.

'What you got that gun for?' John Wesley asked. 'Whatcha gonna do with that gun?'

'Lady,' the man said to the children's mother, 'would you mind calling them children to sit down by you? Children make me nervous. I want all you all to sit down right together there where you're at.'

'What are you telling US what to do for?' June Star asked.

Behind them the line of woods gaped like a dark open mouth. 'Come here,' said their mother.

'Look here now,' Bailey began suddenly, 'we're in a predicament! We're in . . .'

The grandmother shrieked. She scrambled to her feet and stood staring. 'You're The Misfit!' she said. 'I recognized you at once!'

'Yes'm,' the man said, smiling slightly as if he were pleased in spite of himself to be known, 'but it would have been better for all of you, lady, if you hadn't of reckernized me.'

Bailey turned his head sharply and said something to his mother that shocked even the children. The old lady began to cry and the Misfit reddened.

'Lady,' he said, 'don't you get upset. Sometimes a man says things he don't mean. I don't reckon he meant to talk to you thataway.'

'You wouldn't shoot a lady, would you?' the grandmother said and removed a clean handkerchief from her cuff and began to slap at her eyes with it.

The Misfit pointed the toe of his shoe into the ground and made a little hole and then covered it up again. 'I would hate to have to,' he said.

'Listen,' the grandmother almost screamed, 'I know you're a good man. You don't look a bit like you have common blood. I know you must come from nice people!'

'Yes mam,' he said, 'finest people in the world.' When he smiled he showed a row of strong white teeth. 'God never made a finer woman than my mother and my daddy's heart was pure gold,' he said. The boy with the red sweat shirt had come around behind them and was standing with his gun at his hip. The Misfit squatted down on the ground. 'Watch them children, Bobby Lee,' he said. 'You know they make me nervous.' He looked at the six of them huddled together in front of him and he seemed to be embarrassed as if he couldn't think of anything to say. 'Ain't a cloud in the sky,' he remarked, looking up at it. 'Don't see no sun but don't see no cloud neither.'

'Yes, it's a beautiful day,' said the grandmother. 'Listen,' she said, 'you shouldn't call yourself The Misfit because I know you're a good man at heart. I can just look at you and tell.'

'Hush!' Bailey yelled. 'Hush! Everybody shut up and let me handle this!' He was squatting in the position of a runner about to sprint forward but he didn't move.

'I pre-chate that, lady,' The Misfit said and drew a little circle in the ground with the butt of his gun.

'It'll take a half a hour to fix this here car,' Hiram called, looking over the raised hood of it.

'Well, first you and Bobby Lee get him and that little boy to step over yonder with you,' The Misfit said, pointing to Bailey and John Wesley. 'The boys want to ast you something,' he said to Bailey. 'Would you mind stepping back in them woods there with them?'

'Listen,' Bailey began, 'we're in a terrible predicament! Nobody realizes what this is,' and his voice cracked. His eyes were as blue and intense as the parrots in his shirt and he remained perfectly still.

The grandmother reached up to adjust her hat brim as if she were going to the woods with him but it came off in her hand. She stood staring at it and after a second she let it fall on the ground. Hiram pulled Bailey up by the arm as if he were assisting an old man. John Wesley caught hold of his father's hand and Bobby Lee followed. They went off toward the woods and just as they reached the dark edge, Bailey turned and supporting himself against a gray naked pine trunk, he shouted, 'I'll be back in a minute, Mamma, wait on me!'

'Come back this instant!' his mother shrilled but they all disappeared into the woods.

'Bailey Boy!' the grandmother called in a tragic voice but she found she was looking at The Misfit squatting on the ground in front of her. 'I just know you're a good man,' she said desperately. 'You're not a bit common!'

'Nome, I ain't a good man,' The Misfit said after a second as if he had considered her statement carefully, 'but I ain't the worst in the world neither. My daddy said I was a different breed of dog from my brothers and sisters. "You know," Daddy said, "it's some that can live their whole life out without asking about it and it's others has to know why it is, and this boy is one of the latters. He's going to be into everything!"' He put on his black hat and looked up suddenly and then away deep into the woods as if he were embarrassed again. 'I'm sorry I don't have on a shirt before you ladies,' he said, hunching his shoulders slightly. 'We buried our clothes that we had on when we escaped and we're just making do until we can get better. We borrowed these from some folks we met,' he explained.

'That's perfectly all right,' the grandmother said. 'Maybe Bailey has an extra shirt in his suitcase.'

'I'll look and see terrectly,' The Misfit said.

'Where are they taking him?' the children's mother screamed.

'Daddy was a card himself,' The Misfit said. 'You couldn't put anything over on him. He never got in trouble with the Authorities though. Just had the knack of handling them.'

'You could be honest too if you'd only try,' said the grandmother. 'Think how wonderful it would be to settle down and live a comfortable life and not have to think about somebody chasing you all the time.'

The Misfit kept scratching in the ground with the butt of his gun as if he were thinking about it. 'Yes'm, somebody is always after you,' he murmured.

The grandmother noticed how thin his shoulder blades were just behind his hat because she was standing up looking down on him. 'Do you ever pray?' she asked.

He shook his head. All she saw was the black hat wiggle between his shoulder blades. 'Nome,' he said.

There was a pistol shot from the woods, followed closely by another. Then silence. The old lady's head jerked around. She could hear the wind move through the tree tops like a long satisfied insuck of breath. 'Bailey Boy!' she called.

'I was a gospel singer for a while,' The Misfit said. 'I been most everything. Been in the arm service, both land and sea, at home and abroad, been twict married, been an undertaker, been with the railroads, plowed Mother Earth, been in a tornado, seen a man burnt alive oncet,' and he looked up at the children's mother and the little girl who were sitting close together, their faces white and their eyes glassy; 'I even seen a woman flogged,' he said.

'Pray, pray,' the grandmother began, 'pray, pray . . .'

'I never was a bad boy that I remember of,' The Misfit said in an almost dreamy voice, 'but somewheres along the line I done something wrong and got sent to the penitentiary. I was buried alive,' and he looked up and held her attention to him by a steady stare.

'That's when you should have started to pray,' she said. 'What did you do to get sent to the penitentiary that first time?'

'Turn to the right, it was a wall,' The Misfit said, looking up again at the cloudless sky. 'Turn to the left, it was a wall. Look up it was a ceiling, look down it was a floor. I forget what I done, lady. I set there and set there, trying to remember what it was I done and I ain't recalled it to this day. Oncet in a while, I would think it was coming to me, but it never come.'

'Maybe they put you in by mistake,' the old lady said vaguely.

'Nome,' he said. 'It wasn't no mistake. They had the papers on me.'

'You must have stolen something,' she said.

The Misfit sneered slightly. 'Nobody had nothing I wanted,' he said. 'It was a head-doctor at the penitentiary said what I had done was kill my daddy but I known that for a lie. My daddy died in nineteen ought nineteen of the epidemic flu and I never had a thing to do with it. He was buried in the Mount Hopewell Baptist churchyard and you can go there and see for yourself.'

'If you would pray,' the old lady said, 'Jesus would help you.'

'That's right,' The Misfit said.

'Well then, why don't you pray?' she asked trembling with delight suddenly.

'I don't want no hep,' he said. 'I'm doing all right by myself.'

Bobby Lee and Hiram came ambling back from the woods. Bobby Lee was dragging a yellow shirt with bright blue parrots in it.

'Thow me that shirt, Bobby Lee,' The Misfit said. The shirt came flying at him and landed on his shoulder and he put it on. The grandmother couldn't name what the shirt reminded her of. 'No, lady,' The Misfit said while he was buttoning it up, 'I found out the crime don't matter. You can do one thing or you can do another, kill a man or take a tire off his car, because sooner or later you're going to forget what it was you done and just be punished for it.'

The children's mother had begun to make heaving noises as if she couldn't get her breath. 'Lady,' he asked, 'would you and that little girl like to step off yonder with Bobby Lee and Hiram and join your husband?'

'Yes, thank you,' the mother said faintly. Her left arm dangled helplessly and she was holding the baby, who had gone to sleep, in the other. 'Help that lady up, Hiram,' The Misfit said as she struggled to climb out of the ditch, 'and Bobby Lee, you hold onto that little girl's hand.'

'I don't want to hold hands with him,' June Star said. 'He reminds me of a pig.'

The fat boy blushed and laughed and caught her by the arm and pulled her off into the woods after Hiram and her mother.

Alone with The Misfit, the grandmother found that she had lost her voice. There was not a cloud in the sky nor any sun. There was nothing around her but woods. She wanted to tell him that he must pray. She opened and closed her mouth several times before anything came out. Finally she found herself saying, 'Jesus. Jesus,' meaning, Jesus will help you, but the way she was saying it, it sounded as if she might be cursing.

'Yes'm,' The Misfit said as if he agreed. 'Jesus thown everything off balance. It was the same case with Him as with me except He hadn't committed any crime and they could prove I had committed one because they had the papers on me. Of course,' he said, 'they never shown me my papers. That's why I sign myself now. I said long ago, you get you a signature and sign everything you do and keep a copy of it. Then you'll know what you done and you can hold up the crime to the punishment and see do they match and in the end you'll have something to prove you ain't been treated right. I call myself The Misfit,' he said, 'because I can't make what all I done wrong fit what all I gone through in punishment.'

There was a piercing scream from the woods, followed closely by a pistol report. 'Does it seem right to you, lady, that one is punished a heap and another ain't punished at all?'

'Jesus!' the old lady cried. 'You've got good blood! I know you wouldn't shoot a lady! I know you come from nice people! Pray! Jesus, you ought not to shoot a lady. I'll give you all the money I've got!'

'Lady,' The Misfit said, looking beyond her far into the woods, 'there never was a body that give the undertaker a tip.'

There were two more pistol reports and the grandmother raised her head like a parched old turkey hen crying for water and called, 'Bailey Boy, Bailey Boy!' as if her heart would break.

'Jesus was the only One that ever raised the dead,' The Misfit continued, 'and He shouldn't have done it. He thown everything off balance. If He did what He said, then it's nothing for you to do but throw away everything and follow Him, and if He didn't, then it's nothing for you to do but enjoy the few minutes you got left the best way you can—by killing somebody or burning down his house or doing some other meanness to him. No pleasure but meanness,' he said and his voice had become almost a snarl.

'Maybe He didn't raise the dead,' the old lady mumbled, not knowing what she was saying and feeling so dizzy that she sank down in the ditch with her legs twisted under her.

'I wasn't there so I can't say He didn't,' The Misfit said. 'I wisht I had of been there,' he said, hitting the ground with his fist. 'It ain't right I wasn't there because if I had of been there I would of known. Listen lady,' he said in a high voice, 'if I had of been there I would of known and I wouldn't be like I am now.' His voice seemed about to crack and the grandmother's head cleared for an instant. She saw the man's face twisted close to her own as if he were going to cry and she murmured, 'Why you're one of my babies. You're one of my own children!' She reached out and touched him on the shoulder. The Misfit sprang back as if a snake had bitten him and shot her three times through the chest. Then he put his gun down on the ground and took off his glasses and began to clean them.

Hiram and Bobby Lee returned from the woods and stood over the ditch, looking down at the grandmother who half sat and half lay in a puddle of blood with her legs crossed under her like a child's and her face smiling up at the cloudless sky.

Without his glasses, The Misfit's eyes were red-rimmed and pale and defenseless-looking. 'Take her off and thow her where you thown the others,' he said, picking up the cat that was rubbing itself against his leg.

'She was a talker, wasn't she?' Bobby Lee said, sliding down the ditch with a yodel.

'She would of been a good woman,' The Misfit said, 'if it had been somebody there to shoot her every minute of her life.'

'Some fun!' Bobby Lee said.

'Shut up, Bobby Lee,' The Misfit said. 'It's no real pleasure in life.'

DAN JACOBSON

Request Stop

The door of the aeroplane opened, and the hostess's voice rang in the dazed silence: 'All passengers out, please.' There was a pause, then a stir among the passengers. Slowly they stood up, stretched themselves, felt the stillness of the plane swaying beneath them like the sea. Then they began filing out, stepping carefully down the ladder that an African had wheeled to receive them. At the door another African squirted them with some sort of insecticide. They gasped a little at this, and smiled shakily. Then they stepped out on the runway and looked around them. There was only the bush to be seen, just bush, and one road leading from the airport, disappearing very shortly in the bush. The airport itself was long and clean and almost entirely deserted. A small two-seater plane, bright red, was parked near a corrugated iron hangar. Heat hung over the airport, as heavy as water; the air was quite still, it almost seemed to sag within the heat-bound, bush-bound space that had been cleared to receive the silver planes dropping out of the sky.

The passengers moved in a bedraggled little group across the runway towards the refreshment room. An African sat at a table and took their passports. He was very neatly dressed, and very cool, paging through each passport, and then putting it aside in a little heap with the others. Another African, perhaps an apprentice, sat to the side and watched him. A white South African passenger stared for a long time at the two Africans: he had not yet recovered from being squirted by a black man. He looked around for someone to talk to, but the few fellow South Africans on the plane seemed too sunken under the heat to take any notice of who took their passports or who squirted them with insecticide. He did approach one, and gestured towards the trim black man looking through the passports: 'Wouldn't have that sort of thing in our country, would we?'

'No,' the other replied, staring listlessly at the black man. 'It's their funeral, not ours.' But whether it was a funeral for the whites or for the blacks in the country they were flying over, he did not say. Carrying his jacket slung over his shoulders, and with his shirt hanging out of his trousers, he walked into the refreshment room. The other South African was still staring at the African, then his gaze shifted to the passengers straggling across the runway, a ragged troupe in bright colours, but all walking wearily. Then across the bare length of the airport, then to the bush, and then to the great exhausted sky, where high up, two birds circled against the yellowish frame, two small lazy specks gyrating meaninglessly and frighteningly in the desert of air.

The African was querying a passport possessed by a small hairy Greek who could only speak Greek. He was flying back to Greece. No one among the passengers or anyone on the airport could speak Greek. So they all stared accusingly at him, and he stared back at them deprecatingly. He wore black steel spectacles, and his false teeth moved uneasily within his closed mouth. The African went on with the other passports, only leaving the Greek's out of the little pile, and keeping the Greek waiting in the shade. The other passengers filed past him, going into the refreshment room. They stared at him without pity, without any emotion at all. It was too hot, and in any case, he did seem to be impossible, in his neat black suit that spoke of poverty among the coloured rags of the other passengers. Yet he did not seem to ask for pity: he was quite blank. The gauze door clattered behind the last of the passengers, and then the crew, consciously casual, like all air-crews, sauntered across the tarmac. One remained behind, to watch the Africans disinfecting the plane, standing with his hands in his pockets and his cap on the back of his head. Another, also with his hands in his pockets, was walking to the control tower. The door of the refreshment room clattered again, and now only the Greek was still outside, with the two Africans.

Inside the refreshment room it was very crowded. The passengers drooped on the wooden benches, too fatigued even to get the cool drinks that an African was offering behind a counter. Another African stood behind the counter too, behind a little collection of wood-carvings: little elephants, lions, queer drooping faces. There was another room behind the main one, separated from it by a bead curtain. The women passengers looked at it enquiringly; one of the bolder approached the flight engineer who was nursing a bottle of green cool drink in his hand. 'Is that the ladies' lavatory?'

'No, that's where they make tea.'

'Where—then?' She gestured questioningly.

'Outside I suppose.'

'Oh.' The woman hesitated. 'Well, I'll go and ask outside,' she said. Uncertainly she moved to the door. With a great heaving, another woman got up to follow her, and then another. The flight engineer put the bottle to his forehead, to get the coolness from the glass, and rested like that.

Then the bead curtain rustled aside and a tall Englishman came into the room. All the passengers looked up at him. He stood with the beads swaying slightly behind him, and a small smile flickered for a moment across his face. He said in a strained, rather tired voice: 'Is everybody being attended to all right?'

'Yes,' they said. He was tall and thin, dressed in khaki, with khaki hose pulled up neatly just below his knees, and he had a long thin face, with a drooping brown moustache beneath his prominent nose. His skin was sallow, quite washed out by the heat, and the hair on the back of his thin, bony hands was burned to yellow. He looked around the room, his eyes jerking from point to point, from passenger to passenger. At last he walked behind the counter and stood next to the African there. His smile still flickered now and again. He did not seek to open a conversation, but stood still and upright.

With a few guffaws, some of the male passengers got up to go to the lavatory outside. The men seemed to recover from their flight more quickly than the women still remaining in the refreshment room, who were drooping and haggard, clutching lace handkerchiefs in the palms of their sweating hands, their blouses and tailored linen suits in disorder.

But one woman was negotiating with the African selling the wooden curios. 'Will he take my money?' she asked the white man behind the counter.

The Englishman's smile flickered again on his face. 'He'll take any sort of money,' he said.

Automatically, the woman smiled back at him. She flirted without thought, as a cat arches its back. Even there, lost in the bush and dependent on the aeroplane alone on the runway, she lifted an eyebrow, leaned slightly forward and smiled, running through her repertory of tricks as water runs when released down a gulley. And the man responded to it: his hand came forward on the counter and beat a couple of raps on the flattened zinc sheet. He said suddenly: 'I wouldn't buy them, you know.'

'Oh—why not?'

'They're not the real thing,' he said a little jerkily. 'It's tourist stuff.' He made an indecisive gesture with his hand. He smiled at the woman. She was hovering, with her handbag open, wondering whether to buy or not. She took out her purse, and cast an appealing glance towards him. She came to her decision.

'They're cheap enough.' And she took out some silver.

He said in a disinterested voice, 'Yes, they're cheap enough.' And he did not look again while the woman made her purchase. Once she had done so, others among the passengers came forward and toyed with the carvings. But few of them bought one. Nothing seemed important but the heat and the continuation of the flight, awaiting them. It was impossible to take a tourist's interest in what was around them. No one snapped anything, though one or two carried cameras, and those who were outside were looking only for a lavatory, and were not aware at all of the bush and the heat and the banana trees, except as an oppression. So they bought practically nothing, and soon drifted away from the counter.

The passengers talked quietly to one another, and a fly that had managed to get in despite the gauze buzzed loudly above the opened but unused cool drinks. The African waved his hand at it and it flew off. 'Don't send it to me!' a man said and got up waving his hands. A few people smiled. The fly buzzed against the gauze, until the door opened with a bang, and the air hostess stood there: 'All aboard for Entebbe,' she cried.

A general moan went up from the passengers, complaining, humorous.

'Goodness me!' the hostess said. 'You wouldn't like to stay here, would you?'

'Christ, no,' somebody said fervently, and they all began filing out. The gauze door swung open, leaving behind the cool drinks and the Africans and the tall and lonely Englishman. The glare struck at the passengers; they flinched before it, and then went on towards the plane shining like a mirror on the whitish tarmac. The last of the crew was entering the plane. Nearer, the Greek still stood in the shade.

'The hostess will return your passports on the plane,' one of the officials enunciated. He still held one passport in his hand, waving it as he spoke. He looked at it, looked at the Greek, who now had clear drops of sweat on his forehead, and sliding slowly down his cheeks. The official turned and said something to the younger man next to him, and then at last, very slowly, pushed the passport away from him. The Greek stepped forward and took it and began walking to the plane. The two men watched him walk away. One smiled with all his white teeth.

But the passengers had halted, and were pointing in surprise. Someone was staying there. Look, he was in a jeep, with all his baggage, and two people had come to meet him. The traveller was easily recognizable, he was wearing long trousers, while the others who had come to meet him were in khaki shirts and shorts. One or two of the airport officials in peaked caps were also standing around. The jeep was pointed towards the road that led to the bush, and the passengers stared in wonder at the man who had come with them, but was now to be left behind. A gear grated in, and with a whine, the jeep was off. As it turned into the impenetrable-seeming bush, the passenger half-turned and waved, but whether at the airport officials whom he knew, or just farewell to his former fellow-passengers, no one could say. The jeep was out of sight, but through the sluggard air they still heard its noise as they dragged slowly towards the plane. One man had his hand on the back of his neck, shielding it from the sun. A passenger came from behind a banana tree near the refreshment hut, and hurried after the others. They had all climbed into the plane, except for one woman passenger. She stood hesitating for a moment before the flight of steps, and then went to the side of it, looking up at the plane. She turned her head and was violently sick. The hostess stood bored at her elbow, then helped the gasping woman into the plane. The bright silver door swung closed, and now the plane was sealed, ready to travel, with all the passengers sealed inside it.

The plane taxied to a far corner of the field, and then tested its engines, each of them rising to a great roar, and slackening off again. Dust and bits of grass blew wildly, brown and white, in a funnel of wind, towards the bush. The last engine slackened off, and from the control tower strange sounds came loud across the runway. Then slowly, moving slowly at first, but gaining speed quickly, moving on black round legs, the plane roared across the airport, and lifted, and swung up towards the sky. The sky, that yellow daze of space, roared with the noise of its engines, until it was far away, far above the bush, and the refreshment room where the Englishman stood in the doorway and watched it go, far above the control tower and the limp windsock, above the white tarmac, far away from the streak of vomit that had been left, a human mark on the ground.

Vibrating in their padded shell, the passengers undid their safety-belts and stared at their *Readers' Digests*. The airport was a white strip in the bush beneath them, but soon that disappeared, and then there was only the bush, meaninglessly scarred, and later some cloud near to hand.

JACK KEROUAC

Big Trip to Europe

I saved every cent and then suddenly I blew it all on a big glorious trip to Europe or anyplace, and I felt light and gay, too.

It took a few months but I finally bought a ticket on a Yugoslavian freighter bound from Brooklyn Busch Terminal for Tangier, Morocco.

A February morning in 1957 we sailed. I had a whole double state-room to myself, all my books, peace, quiet and study. For once I was going to be a writer who didnt have to do other people's work.

Gastank cities of America fading beyond the waves here we go across the Atlantic now on a run that takes twelve days to Tangier that sleepy Arabic port on the other side—and after the west waved land had receded beneath the cap lick, bang, we hit a bit of a tem-pest that builds up till Wednesday morning the waves are two stories high coming in over our bow and crashing over and frothing in my cabin window enough to make any old seadog duck and those poor Yugoslavian buggers out there sent to lash loose trucks and fiddle with halyards and punchy whistling lines in that salt boorapoosh gale, blam, and twasnt until later I learned these hardy Slavs had two little kittykats stashed away belowdecks and after the storm had abated (and I had seen the glowing white vision of God in my tremors of thought to think we'd might have to lower the boats away in the hopeless mess of mountainous seas—pow pow pow the waves coming in harder and harder, higher and higher, till Wednesday morning when I looked out of my porthole from a restless try-sleep on my belly with pillows on each side of me to prevent me from pitching, I look and see a wave so immense and Jonahlike coming at me from starboard I just cant believe it, just cant believe I got on that Yugoslav freighter for my big trip to Europe at just the wrong time, just the boat that would carry me indeed to the other shore, to go join coral Hart Crane in those undersea gardens)—the poor little kitty cats tho when the storm's abated and moon come out and looked like a dark olive prophesying

Africa (O the history of the world is full of olives) here are the two
little swickle jaws sitting facing each other on a calm eight o'clock
hatch in the calm Popeye moonlight of the Sea Hag and finally I got
them to come in my stateroom and purr on my lap as we thereafter
gently swayed to the other shore, the Afric shore and not the one
death'll take us to.—But in the moment of the storm I wasnt so cocky
as I am now writing about it, I was certain it was the end and I did see
that everything is God, that nothing ever happened except God, the
raging sea, the poor groomus lonesome boat sailing beyond every
horizon with big long tortured body and with no arbitrary conception
of any awakened worlds or any myriads of angel flower bearing Devas
honoring the place where the Diamond was studied, pitching like a
bottle in that howling void, but soon enough the fairy hills and honey
thighs of the sweethearts of Africa, the dogs, cats, chickens, Berbers,
fish heads and curlylock singing keeners of the sea with its Mary star
and the white house lighthouse mysterioso supine—'What was that
storm anyway?' I manage to ask by means of signs and pig English of
my blond cabinboy (go up on mast be blond Pip) and he says to me
only 'BOORAPOOSH! BOORAPOOSHE!' with pig poosh of his lips, which
later from English-speaking passenger I learn means only 'North Wind',
the name given for North Wind in the Adriatic.—
Only passenger on the ship beside myself is a middleaged ugly
woman with glasses a Yugoslavian iron curtain Russian spy for sure
sailed with me so she could study my passport in secret in the captain's
cabin at night and then forge it and then finally I never gets to Tangier
but am hid belowsides and taken to Yugoslavia forever nobody hears
from me ever again and the only thing I dont suspect the crew of the
Red ship (with her Red Star of the blood of the Russias on the stack)
is of starting the tempest that almost done us in and folded us over the
olive of the sea, that was how bad it was in fact then I began to have
reverse paranoiac reveries that they themselves were holding con-
claves in the sea sway lantern foc'sle saying 'That capitalist scum
American on board is a Jonah, the storm has come because of him,
throw him over' so I lie there on my bunk rolling violently from side
to side dreaming of how it will be with me thrun in that ocean out
there (with her 80 mile an hour sprays coming off the top of waves
high enough to swamp the Bank of America) how the whale if it can
get to me before I drown upsidedown will indeed swallow me and
leave me in its groomus dick interior to go salt me off its tip tongue
on some (O God amighty) on some cross shore in the last curlylock

forbidden unknown sea shore, I'll be laying on the beach Jonah with my vision of the ribs—in real life tho all it is, the sailors werent particularly worried by the immense seas, to them just another boorapoosh, to them just only what they call 'Veoory bod weather' and in the diningroom there I am every evening alone at a long white table cloth with the Russian spy woman, facing her dead center, a Continental seating arrangement that prevents me from relaxing in my chair and staring into space as I eat or wait for the next course, it's tuna fish and olive oil and olives for breakfast, it's salted fish for breakfast, what I wouldnt have given for some peanut butter and milkshakes I cant say.—I canna say the Scotch neer invented seas like that to put the mouse scare in the hem haw roll plan—but the pearl of the water, the swiggin whirl, the very glisten-remembered white cap flick in high winds, the Vision of God I had as being all and the same myself, the ship, the others, the dreary kitchen, the dreary slob kitchen of the sea with her swaying pots in the gray gloom as tho the pots know they're about to contain fish stew in the serious kitchen below the kitchen of the serious sea, the swaying and clank clank, O that old ship tho with all her long hull which at first in Brooklyn dock I'd secretly thought 'My God it is too long', now is not long enough to stay still in the immense playfulnesses of God, plowing on, plowing on and shuddering all iron—and too after I'd thought 'Why do they have to spend a whole day here in gastank majoun town' (in New Jersey, what's the name, Perth Amboy) with a big black sinister I must say hose bent in over from the gas dock pumping in and pumping in quietly all that whole Sunday, with lowering winter skies all orange flare crazy and nobody on the long empty pier when I go out to walk after the olive oil supper but one guy, my last American, walking by looking at me a little fishy thinking I'm a member of the Red crew, pumping in all day filling those immense fuel tanks of the old *Slovenia* but once we're at sea in that God storm I'm so glad and groan to think we did spend all day loading fuel, how awful it would have been to run out of fuel in the middle of that storm and just bob there helpless turning this way and that.—To escape the storm on that Wednesday morning for instance the captain simply turned his back to it, he could never take it from the side, only front or back, the roll-in biggies, and when he did make his turn about 8 A.M. I thought we were going to founder for sure, the whole ship with that unmistakable wrack snap went swiftly to the one side, with elastic bounce you could feel she was coming back the other way all the way, the waves from boorapoosh helped, hanging on to my porthole and looking out (not cold but spray in my face) here we go pitching over again into an upcoming sea rise and I'm looking face to face with a vertical wall of sea, the ship jerks, the keel holds, the long keel underneath that's now a little fish flapper after in the dock I'd thought 'How deep these pier slips have to be hold in those long keels so they wont scrape bottom.'—Over we go, the waves wash onto the deck, my porthole and face is splashed completely, the water spills into my bed (O my bed the sea) and over again the other way, then a steady as she goes as the captain gets the *Slovenia* around with her back to the storm and we flee south.—Soon enough I thought we'd be deep with inward stare in an endless womb bliss, drowned—in the grinning sea that restores impossibly.—O snowy arms of God, I saw His arms there on the side of the Jacob's Ladder place where, if we had to disembark and go over (as tho lifeboats would do anything but crash like splinter against the shipside in that madness) the white personal Face of God telling me 'Ti Jean, dont worry, if I take you today, and all the other poor devils on this tub, it's because nothing ever happened except Me, everything is Me—' or as Lankavatara Scripture says, 'There's nothing in the world but Mind itself' ('There's nothing in the world but the Golden Eternity of God's mind', I say)—I saw the words EVERYTHING IS GOD, NOTHING EVER HAPPENED EXCEPT GOD writ in milk on that sea dip—bless you, an endless train into an endless graveyard is all this life is, but it was never anything but God, nothing else but that—so the higher the monstrous sinker comes fooling and calling me down names the more I shall joy old Rembrandt with my bear cup and wrassle all the Tolstoy kidders in this side of fingertwick, pluck as you will, and Afric we'll reach, and did reach anyway, and if I learned a lesson it was lesson in WHITE— radiate all you will sweet darkness and bring ghosts and angels and so we'll put-put right along to the tree shore, the rocky shore, the final swan salt, O Ezekiel for came that afternoon so sweet and calm and Mediterranean-like when we began to see land, twasnt till I saw the keen little grin on the captain's face as he gazed through his binoculars I really believed it, but finally I could see it myself, Africa, I could see the cuts in the mountains, the dry arroyo rills before I could see the mountains themselves and finally did see them, pale green gold, not knowing till about 5 they were really the mountains of Spain, old Hercules was somewhere up there ahead holding up the world on his shoulders thus the hush and glassy silence of these entry waters to Hesperid.—Sweet Mary star ahead, and all the rest, and further on too

I could see Paris, my big kleig light vision Paris where I'd go get off a train at outside town Peuples du Pais, and walk 5 miles deeper and deeper as in a dream into the city of Paris itself arriving finally at some golden center of it I envisioned then, which was silly, as it turned out, as tho Paris had a center.—Faint little white dots at the foot of the long green Africa mountain and yessiree that was the sleepy little Arab city of Tangier waiting for me to explore it that night so I go down into my stateroom and keep checking my rucksack to see it's well packed and ready for me to swing down the gangplank with and get my passport stamped with Arabic figures 'Oieieh eiieh ekkei'.— Meanwhile a lot of trade going by, boats, several beat Spanish freighters you couldnt believe so beat, bleak, small, that have to face boorapooshes with nothing but half our length and half our girth and over there the long stretches of sand on the shore of Spain indicative of dryer Cadizes that I had dreamed yet I still insisted on dreaming of the Spanish cape, the Spanish star, the Spanish gutter song.—And finally one amazing little Moroccan fishingboat putting out to sea with a small crew of about five, in sloppy Catch-Mohammed pants some of them (balloony pantaloons they wear in case they give birth to Mohammed) and some with red fezzes but red fezzes like you never thought they'd be real fezzes with wow grease and creases and dust on them, real red fezzes of real life in real Africa the wind blowing and the little fishing sloop with its incredible high poop made of Lebanon wood—putting out to the curlylock song of the sea, the stars all night, the nets, the twang of Ramadan . . .

Of course world travel isn't as good as it seems, it's only after you've come back from all the heat and horror that you forget to get bugged and remember the weird scenes you saw.—In Morocco I went for a walk one beautiful cool sunny afternoon (with breeze from Gibraltar) and my friend and I walked to the outskirts of the weird Arab town commenting on the architecture, the furniture, the people, the sky which he said would look green at nightfall and the quality of the food in the various restaurants around town, adding, he did, 'Besides I'm just a hidden agent from another planet and the trouble is I dont know why they sent me, I've forgotten the goddam message dearies' so I says 'I'm a messenger from heaven too' and suddenly we saw a herd of goats coming down the road and behind it an Arab shepherd boy of ten who held a little baby lamb in his arms and behind him came the mother lamb bleating and baa haa ing for him to take real good extryspecial care of the babe, which the boy said 'Egraya fa y kapata katapatafataya' and spat it out of his throat in the way Semites speak.— I said 'Look, a real shepherd boy carrying a baby lamb!' and Bill said: 'O well, the little prigs are always rushing around carrying lambs.' Then we walked down the hill to a place where a holy man or that is, a devout Mohammedan, kneeled praying to the setting sun towards Mecca and Bill turned to me and said: 'Wouldnt it be wonderful if we were real American tourists and I suddenly rushed up with a camera to snap his picture?' . . . then added: 'By the way, how do we walk around him?'

'Around his right,' I said anyway.

We wended our way homeward to the chatty outdoor cafe where all the people gathered at nightfall beneath screaming trees of birds, near the Zoco Grande, and decided to follow the railroad track. It was hot but the breeze was cool from the Mediterranean. We came to an old Arab hobo sitting on the rail of the track recounting the Koran to a bunch of raggedy children listening attentively or at least obediently. Behind them was their mother's house, a tin hut, there she was in white hanging white and blue and pink wash in front of a pale blue tin hovel in the bright African sun.—I didnt know what the holy man was doing, I said 'He's an idiot of some kind?'—'No,' says Bill, 'he's a wandering Sherifian pilgrim preaching the gospel of Allah to the children—he's a *hombre que rison*, a man who prays, they got some *hombres que rison* in town that wear white robes and go around barefoot in the alleys and dont let no bluejeaned hoodlums start a fight on the street, he just walks up and stares at them and they scat. Besides, the people of Tangiers aint like the people of West Side New York, when there's a fight starts in the street among the Arab hoods all the men rush up out of mint tea shops and beat the shit out of them. They aint got men in America any more, they just sit there and eat pizzas before the late show, my dear.' This man was William Seward Burroughs, the writer, and we were heading now down the narrow alleys of the Medina (the 'Casbah' is only the Fort part of town) to a little bar and restaurant where all the Americans and exiles went. I wanted to tell somebody about the shepherd boy, the holy man and the man on the tracks but no one was interested. The big fat Dutch owner of the bar said 'I cant find a good poy in this town' (saying 'poy,' not boy, but meaning boy).—Burroughs doubled up in laughter.

We went from there to the late afternoon cafe where sat all the decayed aristocrats of America and Europe and a few eager enlightened healthy Arabs or near-Arabs or diplomats or whatever they were.—I said to Bill: 'Where do I get a woman in this town?'

He said: 'There's a few whores that hang around, you have to know a cabdriver or something, or better than that there's a cat here in town, from Frisco, Jim, he'll show you what corner and what to do' so that night me and Jim the painter go out and stand on the corner and sure enough here come two veiled women, with delicate cotton veil over their mouths and halfway up their noses, just their dark eyes you see, and wearing long flowing robes and you see their shoes cuttin through the robes and Jim hailed a cab which was waiting there and off we went to the pad which was a patio affair (mine) with tile patio overlooking the sea and a Sherifian beacon that turned on and turned on, around and around, flashing in my window every now and again, as, alone with one of the mysterious shrouds, I watched her flip off the shroud and veil and saw standing there a perfect little Mexican (or that is to say Arab) beauty perfect and brown as ye old October grapes and maybe like the wood of Ebon and turned to me with her lips parted in curious 'Well what are you doing standing there?' so I lighted a candle on my desk. When she left she went downstairs with me where some of my connections from England and Morocco and USA were all blasting home made pipes of Opium and singing Cab Calloway's old tune, 'I'm gonna kick the gong around'.—On the street she was very polite when she got into the cab.

From there I went to Paris later, where nothing much happened except the most beautiful girl in the world who didnt like my rucksack on my back and had a date anyway with a guy with a small mustache who stands hand in sidepocket with a sneer in the nightclub movies of Paris.

Wow—and in London what do I see but a beautiful, a heavenly beautiful blonde standing against a wall in Soho calling out to well-dressed men. Lots of makeup, with blue eye shadow, the most beautiful women in the world are definitely English . . . unless like me you like em dark.

But there was more to Morocco than walks with Burroughs and whores in my room, I took long hikes by myself, sipped Cinzano at sidewalk cafes *solitaire*, sat on the beach . . .

There was a railroad track on the beach that brought the train from Casablanca—I used to sit in the sand watching the weird Arab brakemen

and their funny little CFM Railroad (Central Ferrocarril Morocco).—
The cars had thin spoked wheels, just bumpers instead of couplings,
double cylindrical bumpers each side, and the cars were tied on by
means of a simple chain.—The tagman signalled with ordinary stop-
hand and go-ahead goose and had a thin piercing whistle and screamed
in Arabic spitting-from-the-throat to the rear man.—The cars had no
handbrakes and no rung ladders.—Weird Arab bums sat in coal hoppers
being switched up and down the sandy seashore, expecting to go to
Tetuan . . .

One brakeman wore a fez and balloon pantaloons—I could just picture the dispatcher in a full Jalaba robe sitting with his pipe of hasheesh
by the phone.—But they had a good Diesel switch engine with a fezzed
hoghead inside at the throttle and a sign on the side of the engine that
said DANGER A MORT (danger unto death).—Instead of handbrakes they
ran rushing in flowing robes and released a horizontal bar that braked
the wheels with brake shoes—it was insane—they were miraculous railroad men.—The tagman ran yelling 'Thea! Thea! Mohammed! Thea!'—
Mohammed was the head man, he stood up at the far end of the sand
gazing sadly.—Meanwhile veiled Arab women in long Jesus robes
walked around picking up bits of coal by the tracks—for the night's
fish, the night's heat.—But the sand, the rails, the grass, was as universal
as old Southern Pacific. . . . White robes by the blue sea railroad bird
sand . . .

I had a very nice room as I say on the roof, with a patio, the stars at
night, the sea, the silence, the French landlady, the Chinese house-
keeper—the six foot seven Hollander pederast who lived next door
and brought Arab boys up every night.—Nobody bothered me.

The ferry boat from Tangier to Algeciras was very sad because it
was all lit up so gayly for the terrible business of going to the other
shore.—

In the Medina I found a hidden Spanish restaurant serving the following menu for 35 cents: one glass red wine, shrimp soup with little
noodles, pork with red tomato sauce, bread, one egg fried, one orange
on a saucer and one black espresso coffee: I swear on my arm.—

For the business of writing and sleeping and thinking I went to
the local cool drugstore and bought Sympatina for excitement, Diosan
for the codeine dream, and Soneryl for sleep.—Meanwhile Burroughs
and I also got some opium from a guy in a red fez in the Zoco Chico
and made some home made pipes with old olive oil cans and smoked

singing 'Willie the Moocher' and the next day mixed hash and kif with honey and spices and made big 'Majoun' cakes and ate them, chewing, with hot tea, and went on long prophetic walks to the fields of little white flowers.—One afternoon high on hasheesh I meditated on my sun roof thinking 'All things that move are God, and all things that dont move are God' and at this re-utterance of the ancient secret all things that moved and made noise in the Tangier afternoon seemed to suddenly rejoice, and all things that didnt move seemed pleased . . .

Tangier is a charming, cool, nice city, full of marvelous Continental restaurants like *El Paname* and *L'Escargot* with mouth-watering cuisine, sweet sleeps, sunshine, and galleries of holy Catholic priests near where I lived who prayed to the seaward every evening.—Let there be orisons everywhere!—

Meanwhile mad genius Burroughs sat typing wild-haired in his garden apartment the following words:—'Motel Motel Motel loneliness moans across the continent like fog over still oily water tidal rivers . . .' (meaning America.) (America's always rememberable in exile.)

On Moroccan Independence Day my big 59-year-old sexy Arab Negress maid cleaned my room and folded my filthy unwashed T-shirt neatly on a chair . . .

And yet sometimes Tangier was unutterably dull, no vibrations, so I'd walk two miles along the beach among the ancient rhythmic fishermen who hauled nets in singing gangs with some ancient song along the surf, leaving the fish slopping in sea-eye sand, and sometimes I'd watch the terrific soccer games being played by mad Arab boys in the sand some of them throwing in scores with backward tosses of their heads to applause of galleries of children.—

And I'd walk the Maghreb Land of huts which is as lovely as the land of old Mexico with all those green hills, burros, old trees, gardens.—

One afternoon I sat in a riverbottom that fed into the sea and watched the high tide swelling in higher than my head and a sudden rainstorm got me to running back along the beach to town like a trotting track star, soaked, then suddenly on the boulevard of cafes and hotels the sun came out and illuminated the wet palm trees and it gave me an old feeling—I had that old feeling—I thought of everybody.

Weird town. I sat in the Zoco Chico at a cafe table watching the types go by: a weird Sunday in Fellaheen Arabland with you'd expect mystery white windows and ladies throwing daggers and do see but by God the woman up there I saw in a white veil sitting and peering by a Red Cross above a little sign that said:—'Practicantes, Sanio Permanente, TF No. ✠ 9766' the cross being red—right over a tobacco shop with luggage and pictures, where a little barelegged boy leaned on a counter with a family of wristwatched Spaniards.—Meanwhile English sailors from the submarines passed trying to get drunker and drunker on Malaga yet quiet and lost in home regret.—Two little Arab hepcats had a brief musical confab (boys of ten) and then parted with a push of arms and wheeling of arms, one boy had a yellow skull-cap and a blue zoot suit.—The black and white tiles of the outdoor cafe where I sat were soiled by lonely Tangier time—a little baldcropped boy walked by, went to a man at a table near me, said 'Yo' and the waiter rushed up and scatted him off shouting 'Yig'.—A brown ragged robe priest sat with me at a table (an *hombre que rison*) but looked off with hands on lap at brilliant red fez and red girl sweater and red boy shirt green scene . . . Dreaming of Sufi . . .

Oh the poems that a Catholic will get in an Islam Land:—'Holy Sherifian Mother blinking by the black sea . . . did you save the Phoenecians drowning three thousand years ago? . . . O soft queen of the midnight horses . . . bless the Marocaine rough lands!' . . .

For they were suren hell rough lands and I found out one day by climbing way up into the back hills.—First I went down the coast, in the sand, where the seagulls all together in a group by the sea were like having a refection at table, a shiny table—at first I thought they were praying—the head gull said grace.—Sitting in the sea side sand I wondered if the microscopic red bugs in it ever met and mated.—I tried to count a pinch of sand knowing there are as many worlds as the sands in all the oceans.—O honored of the worlds! for just then an old robed Bodhisattva, an old robed bearded realizer of the greatness of wisdom came walking by with a staff and a shapeless skin bag and a cotton pack and a basket on his back, with white cloth around his hoary brown brow.—I saw him coming from miles away down the beach—the shrouded Arab by the sea.—We didnt even nod to each other—it was too much, we'd known each other too long ago—

After that I climbed inland and reached a mountain overlooking all Tangier Bay and came to a quiet shepherd slope, ah the honk of asses and maaaa of sheep up there rejoicing in Vales, and the silly happy trills of crazybirds goofing in the solitude of rocks and brush swept by sun heat swept by sea wind, and all the warm ululations shimmering. —Quiet brush-and-twig huts looking like Upper Nepal.—Fierce looking Arab shepherds went by scowling at me, dark, bearded, robed, bare knee'd.—To the south were the distant African mountains.—Below

me on the steep slope where I sat were quiet powder blue villages.—
Crickets, sea roar.—Peaceful mountain Berber villages or farm settlements, women with huge bundles of twigs on their backs going down
the hill—little girls among browsing bulls.—Dry arroyos in the fat
green meadowland.—And the Carthaginians have disappeared?

When I went down back to the beach in front of Tangier White
City it was night and I looked at the hill where I lived all be-sparkled,
and thought, 'And I live up there full of imaginary conceptions?'

The Arabs were having their Saturday night parade with bagpipes,
drums and trumpets: it put me in the mind of a Haiku:—

> Walking along the night beach
> —Military music
> On the boulevard.

Suddenly one night in Tangier where as I say I'd been somewhat
bored, a lovely flute began to blow around three o'clock in the morning,
and muffled drums beat somewhere in the depths of the Medina.—I
could hear the sounds from my sea-facing room in the Spanish quarter,
but when I went out on my tiled terrace there was nothing there but
a sleeping Spanish dog.—The sounds came from blocks away, toward
the markets, under the Mohammedan stars.—It was the beginning of
Ramadan, the month-long fast. How sad: because Mohammed had
fasted from sunrise to sundown, a whole world would too because of
belief under these stars.—Out on the other crook of the bay the beacon
turned and sent its shaft into my terrace (twenty dollars a month),
swung around and swept the Berber hills where weirder flutes and
stranger deeper drums were blowing, and out into the mouth of the
Hesperides in the softing dark that leads to the dawn off the coast of
Africa.—I suddenly felt sorry that I had already bought my boat ticket
to Marseille and was leaving Tangier.

If you ever take the packet from Tangier to Marseille never go
fourth-class.—I thought I was such a clever world-weary traveler and
saving five dollars, but when I got on the packet the following morning at 7 A.M. (a great blue shapeless hulk that had looked so romantic
to me steaming around the little Tangier jetty from down-the-coast
Casablanca) I was instantly told to wait with a gang of Arabs and then
after a half hour herded down into the fo'c'sle—a French Army barracks. All the bunks were occupied so I had to sit on the deck and wait
another hour. After a few desultory explorations among the stewards

I was told that I had not been assigned a bunk and that no arrangements had been made to feed me or anything. I was practically a stowaway. Finally I saw a bunk no one seemed to be using and appropriated it, angrily asking the soldier nearby, '*Ill y a quelqu'un ici?*' He didnt even bother to answer, just gave me a shrug, not necessarily a Gallic shrug but a great world-weary life-weary shrug of Europe in general. I was suddenly sorry I was leaving the rather listless but earnest sincerity of the Arab world.

The silly tub took off across the Strait of Gibraltar and immediately began to pitch furiously in the long ground swells, probably the worst in the world, that take place off the rock bottom of Spain.—It was almost noon by now.—After a short meditation on the burlap-covered bunk I went out to the deck where the soldiers were scheduled to line up with their ration plates, and already half the French Army had regurgitated on the deck and it was impossible to walk across it without slipping.—Meanwhile I noticed that even the third-class passengers had dinner set out for them in their dining room and that they had rooms and service.—I went back to my bunk and pulled out my old camp pack equipment, an aluminum pot and cup and spoon from my rucksack, and waited.—The Arabs were still sitting on the floor.—The big fat German chief steward, looking like a Prussian bodyguard, came in and announced to the French troops fresh from duty on the hot borders of Algeria to snap to it and do a cleaning job.—They stared at him silently and he went away with his retinue of ratty stewards.

At noon everybody began to stir about and even sing.—I saw the soldiers straggling forward with their pans and spoons and followed them, then advanced with the line to a dirty kitchen pot full of plain boiled beans which were slopped into my pot after a desultory glance from the scullion who wondered why my pot looked a little different.—But to make the meal a success I went to the bakery in the bow and gave the fat baker, a Frenchman with a mustache, a tip, and he gave me a beautiful oven-fresh little loaf of bread and with this I sat on a coil of rope on the bow hatch and ate in the clean winds and actually enjoyed the meal.—Off to the portside Gibraltar rock was already receding, the waters were getting calmer, and soon it would be lazy afternoon with the ship well into the route toward Sardinia and southern France.—And suddenly (as I had had such long daydreams about this trip, all ruined now, of a beautiful glittering voyage on a magnificent 'packet' with red wine in thin-stemmed glasses and jolly Frenchmen and blondes) a little hint of what I was looking for in France (to which

I'd never been) came over the public-address system: a song called *Mademoiselle de Paris* and all the French soldiers on the bow with me sitting protected against the wind behind bulkheads and housings suddenly got romantic-looking and began to talk heatedly about their girls at home and everything suddenly seemed to point to Paris at last.

I resolved to walk from Marseille up on Route N8 toward Aix-en-Provence and then start hitchhiking. I never dreamed that Marseille was such a big town. After getting my passport stamped I strode across the rail yards, pack on back. The first European I greeted on his home soil was an old handlebar-mustached Frenchman who crossed the tracks with me, but he did not return my happy greeting, *'Allo l'Père!'*—But that was all right, the very cobbles and trolley tracks were paradise for me, the ungraspable springtime France at last. I walked along, among those 18th-century smokepot tenements spouting coal smoke, passing a huge garbage wagon with a great work horse and the driver in a beret and striped polo shirt.—An old 1929 Ford suddenly rattled by toward the water front containing four bereted toughs with butts in mouth like characters in some forgotten French movie of my mind.—I went to a kind of bar that was open early Sunday morning where I sat at a table and drank hot coffee served by a dame in her bathrobe, though no pastries—but I got them across the street in the *boulangerie* smelling of crisp fresh Napoleons and *croissants*, and ate heartily while reading *Paris Soir* and with the music on the radio already announcing news of my eagered-for Paris—sitting there with inexplicable tugging memories as though I'd been born before and lived before in this town, been brothers with someone, and bare trees fuzzing green for spring as I looked out of the window.—How old my old life in France, my long old Frenchness, seemed—all those names of the shops, *épicerie*, *boucherie*, the early-morning little stores like those of my French Canadian home, like Lowell Massachusetts on a Sunday.—*Quel différence?* I was very happy suddenly.

My plan, seeing the largeness of the city, was to take a bus to Aix and the road north to Avignon and Lyon and Dijon and Sens and Paris, and I figured that tonight I would sleep in the grass of Provence in my sleeping bag, but it turned out different.—The bus was marvelous, it was just a local bus and went climbing out of Marseille through tiny communities where you'd see little French fathers puttering in neat gardens as their children came in the front door with long loaves of bread for breakfast, and the characters that got on and off the bus were so familiar I wished my folks had been there to see them, hear them say, '*Bonjour, Madame Dubois. Vous avez été à la Messe?*' It didnt take long to get to Aix-en-Provence where I sat at a sidewalk café over a couple of vermouths and watched Cézanne's trees and the gay French Sunday: a man going by with pastries and two-yard-long breads and sprinkled around the horizon the dull-red rooftops and distant blue-haze hills attesting to Cézanne's perfect reproduction of the Provençal color, a red he used even in still-life apples, a brown red, and backgrounds of dark smokeblue.—I thought 'The gaiety, the sensibleness of France is so good after the moroseness of the Arabs.'

After the vermouths I went to the Cathedral of St Sauveur, which was just a shortcut to the highway, and there passing an old man with white hair and beret (and all around on the horizon Cézanne's springtime 'green' which I had forgotten went with his smoky-blue hills and rust-red roof) I cried.—I cried in the Cathedral of the Savior to hear the choir boys sing a gorgeous old thing, while angels seemed to be hovering around—I couldnt help myself—I hid behind a pillar from the occasional inquiring eyes of French families on my huge rucksack (eighty pounds) and wiped my eyes, crying even at the sight of the 6th-century Baptistery—all old Romanesque stones with the hole in the ground still, where so many other infants had been baptized all with eyes of lucid liquid diamond understanding.

I left the church and headed for the road, walked about a mile, disdaining to hitchhike at first, and finally sat by the side of the road on a grassy hill overlooking a pure Cézanne landscape—little farm roofs and trees and distant blue hills with the suggestions of the type of cliff that is more predominant northward toward Van Gogh's country at Arles.—The highway was full of small cars with no room or cyclists with their hair blowing.—I trudged and thumbed hopelessly for five miles, then gave it up at Eguilles, the first bus stop on the highway, there was no hitchhiking in France I could see.—At a rather expensive café in Eguilles, with French families dining in the open patio, I had coffee and then knowing the bus would come in about an hour, went strolling down a country dirt road to examine the inner view of Cézanne's country and found a mauve-tan farmhouse in a quiet fertile rich valley—rustic, with weathered pink-powder roof tiles, a gray-green mild warmness, voices of girls, gray stacks of baled hay, a fertilized chalky garden, a cherry tree in white bloom, a rooster crowing at mid-day mildly, tall 'Cézanne' trees in back, apple trees, pussywillows in the meadow in the clover, an orchard, an old blue wagon under the barn port, a pile of wood, a dry white-twig fence near the kitchen.

Then the bus came and we went through the Arles country and now I saw the restless afternoon trees of Van Gogh in the high mistral wind, the cypress rows tossing, yellow tulips in window boxes, a vast outdoor café with huge awning, and the gold sunlight.—I saw, understood, Van Gogh, the bleak cliffs beyond. . . . At Avignon I got off to transfer to the Paris Express. I bought my ticket to Paris but had hours to wait and wandered down in late afternoon along the main drag—thousands of people in Sunday best on their dreary interminable provincial stroll.

I strolled into a museum full of stone carvings from the days of Pope Benedict XIII, including one splendid woodcarving showing the Last Supper with bunched Apostles grieving head-to-head, Christ in the middle, hand up, and suddenly one of the bunched heads in deeper-in relief is staring right at you and it is Judas!—Farther down the aisle one pre-Roman, apparently Celtic monster, all old carved stone.—And then out in the cobblestoned back-alley of Avignon (city of dust), alleys dirtier than Mexico slums (like New England streets near the dump in the thirties), with women's shoes in gutters running with medieval slop water, and all along the stone wall raggedy children playing in forlorn swirls of mistral dust, enough to make Van Gogh weep.—

And the famous much-sung bridge of Avignon, stone, half-gone now in the spring-rushing Rhône, with medieval-walled castles on the horizon hills (for tourists now, once the baronial castle-supporter of the town).—Sort of juvenile delinquents lurking in the Sunday afternoon dust by the Avignon wall smoking forbidden butts, girls of thirteen smirking in high heels, and down the street a little child playing in the watery gutter with the skeleton of a doll, bonging on his upturned tub for a beat.—And old cathedrals in the alleys of town, old churches now just crumbling relics.

Nowhere in the world is as dismal as Sunday afternoon with the mistral wind blowing in the cobbled back streets of poor old Avignon. When I sat in a café in the main street reading the papers, I understood the complaint of French poets about provincialism, the dreary provincialism that drove Flaubert and Rimbaud mad and made Balzac muse.

Not one beautiful girl to be seen in Avignon except in that café, and she a sensational slender rose in dark glasses confiding love affairs to her girl friend at the table next to mine, and outside the multitudes roamed up and down, up and down, back and forth, nowhere to go, nothing to do—Madame Bovary is wringing her hands in despair behind lace curtains, Genêt's heroes are waiting for the night, the De Musset youth is buying a ticket for the train to Paris.—What can you do in Avignon on a Sunday afternoon? Sit in a café and read about the comeback of a local clown, sip your vermouth, and meditate the carved stone in the museum.

But I did have one of the best five-course meals in all Europe in what appeared to be a 'cheap' side-street restaurant: good vegetable soup, an exquisite omelet, broiled hare, wonderful mashed potatoes (mashed through a strainer with lots of butter), a half bottle of red wine and bread and then a delicious flan with syrup, all for supposedly ninety-five cents, but the waitress raised the price from 380 francs to 575 as I ate and I didn't bother to contest the bill.

In the railroad station I stuck fifty francs into the gum machine, which didnt give, and all the officials most flagrantly passed the buck ('*Demandez au contrôleur!*') and ('*Le contrôleur ne s'occupe pas de çà!*') and I became somewhat discouraged by the dishonesty of France, which I'd noticed at once on that hellship packet especially after the honest religiousness of the Moslems.—Now a train stopped, southbound to Marseille, and an old woman in black lace stepped out and walked along and soon dropped one of her black leather gloves and a well-dressed Frenchman rushed up and picked up the glove and dutifully laid it on a post so that I had to grab the glove and run after her and give it to her.—I knew then why it is the French who perfected the guillotine—not the English, not the Germans, not the Danes, not the Italians and not the Indians, but the French my own people.

To cap it all, when the train came there were absolutely no seats and I had to ride all night in the cold vestibule.—When I got sleepy I had to flatten my rucksack on the cold-iron vestibule doors and I lay there curled, legs up, as we rushed through the unseen Provences and Burgundys of the gnashing French map.—Six thousand francs for this great privilege.

Ah but in the morning, the suburbs of Paris, the dawn spreading over the moody Seine (like a little canal), the boats on the river, the outer industrial smokes of the city, then the Gare de Lyon and when I stepped out on Boulevard Diderot I thought seeing one glimpse of long boule-vards leading every direction with great eight-story ornate apartments with monarchial façades, 'Yes, they made themselves a *city!*'—Then crossing Boulevard Diderot to have coffee, good *espresso* coffee and *croissants* in a big city place full of workingmen, and through the glass I could see women in full long dresses rushing to work on motorbikes, and men with silly crash helmets (*La Sporting France*), taxis, broad old cobblestoned streets, and that nameless city smell of coffee, antiseptics and wine.

Walking, thence, in a cold brisk-red morning, over the Austerlitz Bridge, past the Zoo on the Quai St-Bernard where one little old deer stood in the morning dew, then past the Sorbonne, and my first sight of Notre Dame strange as a lost dream.—And when I saw a big rimed woman statue on Boulevard St-Germain I remembered my dream that I was once a French schoolboy in Paris.—I stopped at a café, ordered Cinzano, and realized the racket of going-to-work was the same here as in Houston or in Boston and no better—but I felt a vast promise, endless streets, streets, girls, places, meanings, and I could understand why Americans stayed here, some for lifetimes.— And the first man in Paris I had looked at in the Gare de Lyon was a dignified Negro in a Homburg.

What endless human types passed my café table: old French ladies, Malay girls, schoolboys, blond boys going to college, tall young brunettes headed for the law classes, hippy pimply secretaries, bereted goggled clerks, bereted scarved carriers of milk bottles, dikes in long blue laboratory coats, frowning older students striding in trench coats like in Boston, seedy little cops (in blue caps) fishing through their pockets, cute pony-tailed blondes in high heels with zip notebooks, goggled bicyclists with motors attached to the rear of their cycles, bespectacled Homburgs walking around reading *Le Parisien* and breathing mist, bushyheaded mulattoes with long cigarettes in their mouths, old ladies carrying milk cans and shopping bags, rummy W. C. Fieldses spitting in the gutter and with hands-a-pockets going to their shops for another day, a young Chinese-looking French girl of twelve with separated teeth almost in tears (frowning, and with a bruise on her shin, schoolbooks in hand, cute and serious like Negro girls in Greenwich Village), porkpie executive running and catching his bus sensationally and vanishing with it, mustachioed longhaired Italian youths coming in the bar for their morning shot of wine, huge bumbling bankers of the Bourse in expensive suits fishing for newspaper pennies in their palms (bumping into women at the bus stop), serious thinkers with pipes and packages, a lovely redhead with dark glasses trotting pip pip on her heels to the bus, and a waitress slopping mop water in the gutter.—

Ravishing brunettes with tight-fitting skirts. Schoolgirlies with long boyish bobs plirping lips over books and memorizing lessons fidgetly (waiting to meet young Marcel Proust in the park after school), lovely young girls of seventeen walking with low-heeled sure strides in long red coats to downtown Paris.—An apparent East Indian, whistling, leading a dog on a leash.—Serious young lovers, boy arming girl's shoulders.—Statue of Danton pointing nowhere, Paris hepcat in dark glasses faintly mustached waiting there.—Little suited boy in black beret, with well-off father going to morning joys.

The next day I strolled down Boulevard St-Germain in a spring wind, turned in at the church of St-Thomas-d'Aquin and saw a huge gloomy painting on the wall showing a warrior, fallen off his horse, being stabbed in the heart by an enemy, at whom he looked directly with sad understanding Gallic eyes and one hand outheld as if to say, 'It's my life' (it had that Delacroix horror). I meditated on this painting in the bright colorful Champs-Élysées and watched the multitudes go by. Glum I walked past a movie house advertising *War and Peace*, where two Russian-sabered sablecaped grenadiers chatted amiably and in French come-on with two American women tourists.

Long walks down the boulevards with a flask of cognac.—Each night a different room, each day four hours to find a room, on foot with full pack.—In the skid-row sections of Paris numerous frowsy dames said '*complet*' coldly when I asked for unheated cockroach rooms in the gray Paris gloom.—I walked and hurried angrily bumping people along the Seine.—In little cafés I had compensatory steaks and wine, chewing slowly.

Noon, a café near Les Halles, onion soup, *pâté de maison* and bread, for a quarter.—Afternoon, the girls in fur coats along Boulevard St-Denis, perfumed.—'*Monsieur?*'

'Sure. . . .'

Finally I found a room I could keep for all of three days, a dismal dirty cold hovel hotel run by two Turkish pimps but the kindest fellows I'd met yet in Paris. Here, window open to dreary rains of April, I slept my best sleeps and gathered strength for daily twenty-mile hikes around the Queen of Cities.

But the next day I was suddenly unaccountably happy as I sat in the park in front of Trinité Church near Gare St-Lazare among children and then went inside and saw a mother praying with a devotion that startled her son.—A moment later I saw a tiny mother with a barelegged little son already as tall as she.

I walked around, it started to sleet on Pigalle, suddenly the sun broke out on Rochechouart and I discovered Montmartre.—Now I knew where I would live if I ever came back to Paris.—Carousels for children, marvelous markets, *hors d'œuvres* stalls, wine-barrel stores, cafés at the foot of the magnificent white Sacré-Cœur basilica, lines of women and children waiting for hot German crullers, new Norman cider inside.—Beautiful girls coming home from parochial school.—A place to get married and raise a family, narrow happy streets full of children carrying long loaves of bread.—For a quarter I bought a huge chunk of Gruyère cheese from a stall, then a huge chunk of jellied meat delicious as crime, then in a bar a quiet glass of port, and then I went to see the church high on the cliff looking down on the rain-wet roofs of Paris.—

La Basilique du Sacré-Cœur de Jésus is beauteous, maybe in its way one of the most beautiful of all churches (if you have a rococo soul as I have): blood-red crosses in the stainedglass windows with a westerly sun sending golden shafts against opposite bizarre Byzantine blues representing other sacristies—regular blood baths in the blue sea—and all the poor sad plaques commemorating the building of the church after the sack by Bismarck.

Down the hill in the rain, I went to a magnificent restaurant on Rue de Clignancourt and had that unbeatable French puréed soup and a whole meal with a basket of French bread and my wine and the thin-stemmed glasses I had dreamed about.—Looking across the restaurant at the shy thighs of a newlywed girl having her big honeymoon supper with her young farmer husband, neither of them saying anything.— Fifty years of this they'd do now in some provincial kitchen or dining room.—The sun breaking through again, and with full belly I wandered among the shooting galleries and carousels of Montmartre and I saw a young mother hugging her little girlie with a doll, bouncing her and laughing and hugging her because they had had so much fun on the hobbyhorse and I saw Dostoevsky's divine love in her eyes (and above on the hill over Montmartre, He held out His arms).

Feeling wonderful now, I strolled about and cashed a traveler's check at the Gare du Nord and walked all the way, gay and fine, down Boulevard de Magenta to the huge Place de la République and on down, cutting sometimes into side streets.—Night now, down Boulevard du Temple and Avenue Voltaire (peeking into windows of obscure Breton restaurants) to Boulevard Beaumarchais where I thought I'd see the gloomy Bastille prison but I didn't even know it was torn down in 1789 and asked a guy, '*Où est la vieille prison de la Révolution?*' and he laughed and told me there were a few remnant stones in the subway station.— Then down in the subway: amazing clean artistic ads, imagine an ad for wine in America showing a naked ten-year-old girl with a party hat coiled around a bottle of wine.—And the amazing map that lights up and shows your route in colored buttons when you press the destination button.—Imagine the New York IRT. And the clean trains, a bum on a bench in a clean surrealistic atmosphere (not to be compared with the 14th Street stop on the Canarsie line).

Paris paddywagons flew by singing *dee* da, *dee* da.—

The next day I strolled examining bookstores and went into the Benjamin Franklin Library, the site of the old Café Voltaire (facing the Comédie Française) where everybody from Voltaire to Gauguin to Scott Fitzgerald drank and now the scene of prim American librarians with no expression.—Then I strolled to the Pantheon and had delicious pea soup and a small steak in a fine crowded restaurant full of students and vegetarian law professors.—Then I sat in a little park in Place Paul-Painlevé and dreamily watched a curving row of beautiful rosy tulips rigid and swaying fat shaggy sparrows, beautiful short-haired *mademoiselles* strolling by. It's not that French girls are beautiful, it's their cute mouths and the sweet way they talk French (their mouths pout rosily), the way they've perfected the short haircut and the way they amble slowly when they walk, with great sophistication, and of course their chic way of dressing and undressing.

Paris, a stab in the heart finally.

The Louvre—miles and miles of hiking before great canvases.

In David's immense canvas of Napoleon I and Pius VII I could see little altar boys far in the back fondling a *maréchal*'s sword hilt (the scene in Nôtre-Dame-de-Paris, with the Empress Josephine kneeling pretty as a boulevard girl). Fragonard, so delicate next to Van Dyck, and a big smoky Rubens (*La Mort de Dido*).—But the Rubens got better as I looked, the muscle tones in cream and pink, the rimshot luminous eyes, the dull purple velvet robe on the bed. Rubens was happy because nobody was posing for him for a fee and his gay *Kermesse* showed an old drunk about to be sick.—Goya's *Marquesa de la Solana* could hardly have been more modern, her silver fat shoes pointed like fish criss-crossed, the immense diaphanous pink ribbons over a sisterly pink face.—A typical French woman (not educated) suddenly said, '*Ah, c'est trop beau!*' 'It's too beautiful!'

But Brueghel, wow! His *Battle of Arbelles* had at least 600 faces clearly defined in an impossibly confused mad battle leading nowhere.—No wonder Céline loved him.—A complete understanding of world madness, thousands of clearly defined figures with swords and above them the calm mountains, trees on a hill, clouds, and everyone laughed when they saw that insane masterpiece that afternoon, they knew what it meant.

And Rembrandt.—The dim trees in the darkness of crépuscule château with its hints of a Transylvanian vampire castle.—Set side by side with this his *Hanging Beef* was completely modern with its splash of blood paint. Rembrandt's brushstroke swirled in the face of the *Christ at Emmaus*, and the floor in *Sainte Famille* was completely detailed in the color of planks and nails.—Why should anyone paint after Rembrandt, unless Van Gogh? The *Philosopher in Meditation* was my favorite for its Beethoven shadows and light, I liked also *Hermit Reading* with his soft old brow, and *St Matthew Being Inspired by the Angel* was a miracle—the rough strokes, and the drip of red paint in the angel's lower lip and the saint's own rough hands ready to write the Gospel . . . ah miraculous too the veil of mistaken angel smoke on Tobias' departing angel's left arm.—What can you do?

Suddenly I walked into the 19th-century room and there was an explosion of light—of bright gold and daylight. Van Gogh, his crazy blue Chinese church with the hurrying woman, the secret of it the Japanese spontaneous brushstroke that, for instance, made the woman's back show, her back all white unpainted canvas except for a few black thick script strokes.—Then the madness of blue running in the roof where Van Gogh had a ball—I could see the joy red mad gladness he rioted in in that church heart.—His maddest picture was gardens with insane trees whirling in the blue swirl sky, one tree finally exploding into just black lines, almost silly but divine—the thick curls and butter burls of color, beautiful oil rusts, glubs, creams, greens.

I studied Dégas' ballet pictures—how serious the perfect faces in the orchestra, then suddenly the explosion on the stage—the pink film rose of the ballerina gowns, the puffs of color.—And Cézanne, who painted exactly as he saw, more accurate and less divine than holy Van Gogh—his green apples, his crazy blue lake with acrostics in it, his trick of hiding perspective (one jetty in the lake can do it, and one mountain line). Gauguin—seeing him beside these masters, he seemed to me almost like a clever cartoonist.—Compared to Renoir, too, whose painting of a French afternoon was so gorgeously colored with the Sunday afternoon of all our childhood dreams—pinks, purples, reds, swings, dancers, tables, rosy cheeks and bubble laughter.

On the way out of the bright room, Frans Hals, the gayest of all painters who ever lived. Then one last look at Rembrandt's St Matthew's angel—its smeared red mouth *moved* when I looked.

April in Paris, sleet in Pigalle, and last moments.—In my skidrow hotel it was cold and still sleeting so I put on my old blue jeans, old muffcap, railroad gloves and zip-up rain jacket, the same clothes I'd worn as a brakeman in the mountains of California and as a forester in the Northwest, and hurried across the Seine to Les Halles for a last supper of fresh bread and onion soup and *pâté*.—Now for delights, walking in the cold dusk of Paris amid vast flower markets, then succumbing to thin crisp *frites* with rich sausage hot dog from a stall on the windswept corner, then into a mobbed mad restaurant full of gay workers and bourgeois where I was temporarily peeved because they forgot to bring me wine too, so gay and red in a clean stemmed glass.—After eating, sauntering on home to pack for London tomorrow, then deciding to buy one final Parisian pastry, intending a Napoleon as usual, but because the girl thought I'd said 'Milanais' I accepted her offer and took a bite of my Milanais as I crossed the bridge and bang! the absolutely final greatest of all pastries in the world, for the first time in my life I felt overpowered by a taste sensation, a rich brown mocha cream covered with slivered almonds and just a touch of cake but so pungent that it stole through my nose and taste buds like bourbon or rum with coffee and cream.—I hurried back, bought another and had the second one with a little hot *espresso* in a café across the street from the Sarah Bernhardt Theater—my last delight in Paris savoring the taste and watching Proustian showgoers coming out of the theater to hail cabs.

In the morning, at six, I rose and washed at the sink and the water running in my faucet talked in a kind of Cockney accent.—I hurried out with full pack on back, and in the park a bird I never heard, a Paris warbler by the smoky morning Seine.

I took the train to Dieppe and off we went, through smoky suburbs, through Normandy, through gloomy fields of pure green, little stone cottages, some red brick, some half-timbered, some stone, in a drizzle along the canal-like Seine, colder and colder, through Vernon and little places with names like Vauvay and Something-sur-Cie, to gloomy

Rouen, which is a horrible rainy dreary place to have been burned at the stake.—All the time my mind excited with the thought of England by nightfall, London, the fog of real old London.—As usual I was standing in the cold vestibule, no room inside the train, sitting occasionally on my pack crowded in with a gang of shouting Welsh schoolboys and their quiet coach who loaned me the *Daily Mail* to read.—After Rouen the ever-more-gloomy Normandy hedgerows and meadows, then Dieppe with its red rooftops and old quais and cobblestoned streets with bicyclists, the chimney pots smoking, gloom rain, bitter cold in April and I sick of France at last.

The channel boat crowded to the hilt, hundreds of students and scores of beautiful French and English girls with pony tails and short haircuts.—Swiftly we left the French shore and after a spate of blank water we began to see green carpets and meadows stopped abruptly as with a pencil line at chalk cliffs, and it was that sceptered isle, England, springtime in England.

All the students sang in gay gangs and went through to their chartered London coach car but I was made to sit (I was a take-a-seater) because I had been silly enough to admit that I had only fifteen shillings equivalent in my pocket.—I sat next to a West Indies Negro who had no passport at all and was carrying piles of strange old coats and pants—he answered strangely the questions of the officers, looked extremely vague and in fact I remembered he had bumped into me absentmindedly in the boat on the way over.—Two tall English bobbies in blue were watching him (and myself) suspiciously, with sinister Scotland Yard smiles and strange long-nosed brooding attentiveness like in old Sherlock Holmes movies.—The Negro looked at them terrified. One of his coats dropped on the floor but he didn't bother to pick it up.—A mad gleam had come into the eyes of the immigration officer (young intellectual fop) and now another mad gleam in some detective's eye and suddenly I realized the Negro and I were surrounded.—Out came a huge jolly red-headed customs man to interrogate us.

I told them my story—I was going to London to pick up a royalty check from an English publisher and then on to New York on the *Île de France*.—They didn't believe my story—I wasn't shaved, I had a pack on my back, I looked like a bum.

'What do you *think* I am!' I said and the red-headed man said 'That's just it, we don't quite know in the least what you were doing in Morocco, or in France, or arriving in England with fifteen bob.' I told them to call my publishers or my agent in London. They called and got no answer—it was Saturday. The bobbies were watching me, stroking their chins.—The Negro had been taken into the back by now—suddenly I heard a horrible moaning, as of a psychopath in a mental hospital, and I said 'What's that?'

'That's your Negro friend.'

'What's the matter with him?'

'He has no passport, no money, and is apparently escaped from a mental institution in France. Now do you have any way to verify this story of yours, otherwise we'll have to detain you.'

'In custody?'

'Quite. My dear fellow, you can't come into England with fifteen bob.'

'My dear fellow, you can't put an American in jail.'

'Oh yes we can, if we have grounds for suspicion.'

'Dont you believe I'm a writer?'

'We have no way of knowing this.'

'But I'm going to miss my train. It's due to leave any minute.'

'My dear fellow . . .' I rifled through my bag and suddenly found a note in a magazine about me and Henry Miller as writers and showed it to the customs man. He beamed:

'Henry Miller? That's most unusual. We stopped *him* several years ago, he wrote quite a bit about Newhaven.' (This was a grimmer New Haven than the one in Connecticut with its dawn coalsmokes.) But the customs man was immensely pleased, checked my name again, in the article and on my papers, and said, 'Well, I'm afraid it's going to be all smiles and handshakes now. I'm awfully sorry. I think we can let you through—with the provision that you leave England inside a month.'

'Don't worry.' As the Negro screamed and banged somewhere inside and I felt a horrible sorrow because he had not made it to the other shore, I ran to the train and made it barely in time.—The gay students were all in the front somewhere and I had a whole car to myself, and off we went silently and fast in a fine English train across the countryside of olden Blake lambs.—And I was safe.

English countryside—quiet farms, cows, meads, moors, narrow roads and bicycling farmers waiting at crossings, and ahead, Saturday night in London.

Outskirts of the city in late afternoon like the old dream of sun rays through afternoon trees.—Out at Victoria Station, where some of the students were met by limousines.—Pack on back, excited, I started walking in the gathering dusk down Buckingham Palace Road seeing for the first time long deserted streets. (Paris is a woman but London is an independent man puffing his pipe in a pub.)—Past the Palace, down the Mall through St James's Park, to the Strand, traffic and fumes and shabby English crowds going out to movies, Trafalgar Square, on to Fleet Street where there was less traffic and dimmer pubs and sad side alleys, almost clear to St Paul's Cathedral where it got too John-soniany sad.—So I turned back, tired, and went into the King Lud pub for a sixpenny Welsh rarebit and a stout.

I called my London agent on the phone, telling him my plight. 'My dear fellow it's awfully unfortunate I wasnt in this afternoon. We were visiting mother in Yorkshire. Would a fiver help you?'

'Yes!' So I took a bus to his smart flat at Buckingham Gate (I had walked right past it after getting off the train) and went up to meet the dignified old couple.—He with goatee and fireplace and Scotch to offer me, telling me about his one-hundred-year-old mother reading all of Trevelyan's *English Social History*.—Homburg, gloves, umbrella, all on the table, attesting to his way of living, and myself feeling like an American hero in an old movie.—Far cry from the little kid under a river bridge dreaming of England.—They fed me sandwiches, gave me money, and then I walked around London savoring the fog in Chelsea, the bobbies wandering in the milky mist, thinking, 'Who will strangle the bobby in the fog?' The dim lights, the English soldier strolling with one arm around his girl and with the other hand eating fish and chips, the honk of cabs and buses, Piccadilly at midnight and a bunch of Teddy Boys asking me if I knew Gerry Mulligan.—Finally I got a fifteen-bob room in the Mapleton Hotel (in the attic) and had a long divine sleep with the window open, in the morning the carillons blowing all of an hour round eleven and the maid bringing in a tray of toast, butter, marmalade, hot milk and a pot of coffee as I lay there amazed.

And on Good Friday afternoon a heavenly performance of the *St Matthew Passion* by the St Paul's choir, with full orchestra and a special service choir.—I cried most of the time and saw a vision of an angel in my mother's kitchen and longed to go home to sweet America again.— And realized that it didn't matter that we sin, that my father died only of impatience, that all my own petty gripes didnt matter either.—Holy Bach spoke to me and in front of me was a magnificent marble bas-relief showing Christ and three Roman soldiers listening: 'And he spake unto them do violence to no man, nor accuse any falsely, and be content with thy wages.' Outside as I walked in the dusk around Christopher Wren's great masterpiece and saw the gloomy overgrown ruins of Hitler's blitz around the cathedral, I saw my own mission.

In the British Museum I looked up my family in *Rivista Araldica*, IV, page 240, 'Lebris de Keroack. Canada, originally from Brittany. Blue on a stripe of gold with three silver nails. Motto: Love, work and suffer.'

I could have known.

At the last moment I discovered the Old Vic while waiting for my boat train to Southampton.—The performance was *Antony and Cleopatra*.—It was a marvelously smooth and beautiful performance, Cleopatra's words and sobbings more beautiful than music, Enobarbus noble and strong, Lepidus wry and funny at the drunken rout on Pompey's boat, Pompey warlike and harsh, Antony virile, Caesar sinister, and though the cultured voices criticized the Cleopatra in the lobby at intermission, I knew that I had seen Shakespeare as it should be played.

On the train en route to Southampton, brain trees growing out of Shakespeare's fields, and the dreaming meadows full of lamb dots.

JOHN CHEEVER

Brimmer

No one is interested in a character like Brimmer because the facts are indecent and obscene; but come then out of the museums, gardens, and ruins where obscene facts are as numerous as daisies in Nantucket. In the dense population of statuary around the Mediterranean shores there are more satyrs than there are gods and heroes. Their general undesirability in organized society only seems to have whetted their aggressiveness and they are everywhere; they are in Paestum and Syracuse and in the rainy courts and porches north of Florence. They are even in the gardens of the American Embassy. I don't mean those pretty boys with long ears—although Brimmer may have been one of those in the beginning. I mean the older satyrs with lined faces and conspicuous tails. They always carry grapes or pipes, and the heads are up and back in attitudes of glee. Aside from the long ears, the faces are never animal—these are the faces of men, sometimes comely and youthful, but advanced age does not change in any way the lively cant of the head and the look of lewd glee.

I speak of a friend, an acquaintance anyhow—a shipboard acquaintance on a rough crossing from New York to Naples. These were his attitudes in the bar where I mostly saw him. His eyes had a pale, horizontal pupil like a goat's eye. Laughing eyes, you might have said, although they were sometimes very glassy. As for the pipes, he played, so far as I know, no musical instrument; but the grapes could be accounted for by the fact that he almost always had a glass in his hand. Many of the satyrs stand on one leg with the other crossed over in front—toe down, heel up—and that's the way he stood at the bar, his legs crossed, his head up in that look of permanent glee, and the grapes, so to speak, in his right hand. He was lively—witty and courteous and shrewd—but had he been much less I would have been forced to drink and talk with him anyhow. Excepting Mme Troyan, there was no one else on board I would talk with.

How dull travel really is! How, at noon, when the whistle sounds and the band plays and the confetti has been thrown, we seem to have been deceived into joining something that subsists upon the patronage of the lonely and the lost—the emotionally second-rate of all kinds. The whistle blows again. The gangways and the lines are cleared and the ship begins to move. We see the faces of our dearly beloved friends and relations rubbed out by distance, and going over to the port deck to make a profoundly emotional farewell to the New York skyline we find the buildings hidden in rain. Then the chimes sound and we go below to eat a heavy lunch. Obsolescence might explain that chilling unease we experience when we observe the elegance of the lounges and the wilderness of the sea. What will we do between now and tea? Between tea and dinner? Between dinner and the horse races? What will we do between here and landfall?

She was the oldest ship of the line and was making that April her last Atlantic crossing. Many seasoned travelers came down to say goodbye to her famous interiors and to filch an ashtray or two, but they were sentimentalists to a man, and when the go-ashore was sounded they all went ashore, leaving the rest of us, so to speak, alone. It was a cheerless, rainy midday with a swell in the channel and, beyond the channel, gale winds and high seas. Her obsolescence you could see at once was more than a matter of marble fireplaces and grand pianos. She was a tub. It was not possible to sleep on the first night out, and going up on deck in the morning I saw that one of the lifeboats had been damaged in the gale. Below me, in second class, some undiscourageable travelers were trying to play Ping-Pong in the rain. It was a bleak scene to look at and a hopeless prospect for the players and they finally gave up. A few minutes later a miscalculation of the helmsman sent a wall of water up the side of the ship and filled the stern deck with a boiling sea. Up swam the Ping-Pong table and, as I watched, it glided overboard and could be seen bobbing astern in the wake, a reminder of how mysterious the world must seem to a man lost overboard.

Below, all the portable furniture had been corralled and roped together as if this place were for sale. Ropes were strung along all the passageways, and all the potted palm trees had been put into some kind of brig. It was hot—terribly hot and humid—and the elegant lounges, literally abandoned and very much abandoned in their atmosphere, seemed to be made, if possible, even more forlorn by the continuous music of the ship's orchestra. They began to play that morning and they played for the rest of the voyage and they played for no one.

They played day and night to those empty rooms where the chairs were screwed to the floor. They played opera. They played old dance music. They played selections from *Show Boat*. Above the crashing of the mountainous seas there was always this wild, tiresome music in the air. And there was really nothing to do. You couldn't write letters, everything tipped so; and if you sat in a chair to read, it would withdraw itself from you and then rush up to press itself against you like some apple-tree swing. You couldn't play cards, you couldn't play chess, you couldn't even play Scrabble. The grayness, the thinly jubilant and continuous music, and the roped-up furniture all made it seem like an unhappy dream, and I wandered around like a dreamer until twelve-thirty, when I went into the bar. The regulars in the bar then were a Southern family—Mother, Father, Sister, and Brother. They were going abroad for a year. Father had retired and this was their first trip. There were also a couple of women whom the bartender identified as a 'Roman businesswoman' and her secretary. And there was Brimmer, myself, and presently Mme Troyan. I had drinks with Brimmer on the second day out. He was a man of about my age, I should say, slender, with well-kept hands that were, for some reason, noticeable, and a light but never monotonous voice and a charming sense of urgency—liveliness—that seemed to have nothing to do with nervousness. We had lunch and dinner together and drank in the bar after dinner. We knew the same places, but none of the same people, and yet he seemed to be an excellent companion. When we went below—he had the cabin next to mine—I was contented to have found someone I could talk with for the next ten days.

Brimmer was in the bar the next day at noon, and while we were there Mme Troyan looked in. Brimmer invited her to join us and she did. At my ripe age, Mme Troyan's age meant nothing. A younger man might have placed her in her middle thirties and might have noticed that the lines around her eyes were ineradicable. For me these lines meant only a proven capacity for wit and passion. She was a charming woman who did not mean to be described. Her dark hair, her pallor, her fine arms, her vivacity, her sadness when the bartender told us about his sick son in Genoa, her impersonations of the captain—the impression of a lovely and a brilliant woman who was accustomed to seeming delightful was not the listed sum of her charms.

We three had lunch and dinner together and danced in the ballroom after dinner—we were the only dancers—but when the music stopped and Brimmer and Mme Troyan started back to the bar I excused myself and went down to bed. I was pleased with the evening and when I closed my cabin door I thought how pleasant it would have been to have Mme Troyan's company. This was, of course, impossible, but the memory of her dark hair and her white arms was still strong and cheering when I turned out the light and got into bed. While I waited patiently for sleep it was revealed to me that Mme Troyan was in Brimmer's cabin.

I was indignant. She had told me that she had a husband and three children in Paris—and what, I thought, about them? She and Brimmer had only met by chance that morning and what carnal anarchy would crack the world if all such chance meetings were consummated! If they had waited a day or two—long enough to give at least the appearance of founding their affair on some romantic or sentimental basis —I think I would have found it more acceptable. To act so quickly seemed to me skeptical and depraved. Listening to the noise of the ship's motors and the faint sounds of tenderness next door, I realized that I had left my way of life a thousand knots astern and that there is no inclination to internationalism in my disposition. They were both, in a sense, Europeans.

But the sounds next door served as a kind of trip wire: I seemed to stumble and fall on my face, skinning and bruising myself here and there and scattering my emotional and intellectual possessions. There was no point in pretending that I had not fallen, for when we are stretched out in the dirt we must pick ourselves up and brush off our clothes. This then, in a sense, is what I did, reviewing my considered opinions on marriage, constancy, man's nature, and the importance of love. When I had picked up my possessions and repaired my appearance, I fell asleep.

It was dark and rainy in the morning—now the wind was cold—and I walked around the upper deck, four laps to the mile, and saw no one. The immorality next door would have changed my relationship to Brimmer and Mme Troyan, but I had no choice but to look forward to meeting them in the bar at noon. I had no resources to enliven a deserted ship and a stormy sea. My depraved acquaintances were in the bar when I went there at half past twelve, and they had ordered a drink for me. I was content to be with them and thought perhaps they regretted what they had done. We lunched together, amiably, but when I suggested that we find a fourth and play some bridge Brimmer said that he had to send some cables and Mme Troyan wanted to rest.

There was no one in the lounges or on the decks after lunch, and when the orchestra began, dismally, to tune up for their afternoon concert, I went down to my cabin, where I discovered that Brimmer's cables and Mme Troyan's rest were both fabrications, meant, I suppose, to deceive me. She was in his cabin again. I went up and took a long walk around the deck with an Episcopalian clergyman. I found him to be a most interesting man, but he did not change the subject, since he was taking a vacation from a parish where alcoholism and morbid promiscuity were commonplace. I later had a drink with the clergyman in the bar, but Brimmer and Mme Troyan didn't show up for dinner.

They came into the bar for cocktails before lunch on the next day. I thought they both looked tired. They must have had sandwiches in the bar or made some other arrangement because I didn't see them in the dining room. That evening the sky cleared briefly—it was the first clearing of the voyage—and I watched this from the stern deck with my friend the minister. How much more light we see from an old ship than we see from the summit of a mountain! The cuts in the overcast, filled with colored light, the heights and reaches all reminded me of my dear wife and children and our farm in New Hampshire and the modest pyrotechnics of a sunset there. I found Mme Troyan and Brimmer in the bar when I went down before dinner, but they didn't know the sky had cleared.

They didn't see the Azores, nor were they around two days later when we sighted Portugal. It was half past four or five in the afternoon. First, there was some slacking off in the ship's roll. She was still rolling, but you could go from one place to another without ending up on your face, and the stewards had begun to take down the ropes and rearrange the furniture. Then on our port side we could see some cliffs and, above them, round hills rising to form a mountain, and on the summit some ruined fort or bastion—low-lying, but beautiful—and behind this a bank of cloud so dense that it was not until we approached the shore that you could distinguish which was cloud and which was mountain. A few gulls picked us up, and then villas could be seen, and there was the immemorial smell of inshore water like my grandfather's bathing shoes. Here was a different sea—catboats and villas and fish nets and sand castles flying flags and people calling in their children off the beach for supper. This was the landfall, and as I went up toward the bow I heard the Sanctus bell in the ballroom, where the priest was saying prayers of thanksgiving over water that has seen, I suppose, a million, million times the bells and candles of the Mass. Everyone was at the bow, as pleased as children to see Portugal. Everyone stayed late to watch the villas take shape, the lights go on, and to smell the shallows. Everyone but Brimmer and Mme Troyan, who were still in Brimmer's cabin when I went down, and who couldn't have seen anything.

Mme Troyan left the ship at Gibraltar the next morning, when her husband was to meet her. We got there at dawn—very cold for April—cold and bleak with snow on the African mountains and the smell of snow in the air. I didn't see Brimmer around, although he may have been on another deck. I watched a deckhand put the bags aboard the cutter, and then Mme Troyan walked swiftly onto the cutter herself, wearing a coat over her shoulders and carrying a scarf. She went to the stern and began to wave her scarf to Brimmer or to me or to the ship's musicians—since we were the only people she had spoken to on the crossing. But the boat moved more swiftly than my emotions and, in the few minutes it took for my stray feelings of tenderness to accumulate, the cutter had moved away from the ship, and the shape, the color of her face was lost.

When we left Gibraltar, the potted palms were retired again, the lines were put up, and the ship's orchestra began to play. It remained rough and dreary. Brimmer was in the bar at half past twelve looking very absent-minded, and I suppose he missed Mme Troyan. I didn't see him again until after dinner, when he joined me in the bar. Something, sorrow I suppose, was on his mind, and when I began to talk about Nantucket (where we had both spent some summers) his immense reservoirs of courtesy seemed taxed. He excused himself and left; half an hour later I saw that he was drinking in the lounge with the mysterious businesswoman and her secretary.

It was the bartender who had first identified this couple as a 'Roman businesswoman' and her secretary. Then, when it appeared that she spoke a crude mixture of Spanish and Italian, the bartender decided that she was a Brazilian—although the purser told me that she was traveling on a Greek passport. The secretary was a hard-faced blonde, and the businesswoman was herself a figure of such astonishing unsavoriness—you might say evil—that no one spoke to her, not even the waiters. Her hair was dyed black, her eyes were made up to look like the eyes of a viper, her voice was guttural, and whatever her business was, it had stripped her of any appeal as a human being. These two were in the bar every night, drinking gin and speaking a jumble of languages. They were never with anyone else until Brimmer joined them that evening.

This new arrangement excited my deepest and my most natural disapproval. I was talking with the Southern family when, perhaps an hour later, the secretary strayed into the bar alone and ordered whiskey. She seemed so distraught that rather than entertain any obscene suspicions about Brimmer, I lit up the whole scene with an artificial optimism and talked intently with the Southerners about real estate. But when I went below I could tell that the businesswoman was in Brimmer's cabin. They made quite a lot of noise, and at one point they seemed to fall out of bed. There was a loud thump. I could have knocked on the door—like Carrie Nation—ordering them to desist, but who would have seemed the most ridiculous?

But I could not sleep. It has been my experience, my observation, that the kind of personality that emerges from this sort of promiscuity embodies an especial degree of human failure. I say observation and experience because I would not want to accept the tenets of any other authority—any preconception that would diminish the feeling of life as a perilous moral adventure. It is difficult to be a man, I think; but the difficulties are not insuperable. Yet if we relax our vigilance for a moment we pay an exorbitant price. I have never seen such a relationship as that between Brimmer and the businesswoman that was not based on bitterness, irresolution, and cowardice—the very opposites of love—and any such indulgence on my part would, I was sure, turn my hair white in a moment, destroy the pigmentation in my eyes, incline me to simper, and leave a hairy tail coiled in my pants. I knew no one who had hit on such a way of life except as an expression of inadequacy—a shocking and repugnant unwillingness to cope with the generous forces of life. Brimmer was my friend and consequently enough of a man to make him deeply ashamed of what he was doing. And with this as my consolation I went to sleep.

He was in the bar at twelve-thirty the next day, but I did not speak to him. I drank my gin with a German businessman who had boarded the ship at Lisbon. It may have been because my German friend was dull that I kept scrutinizing Brimmer for some telling fault—insipidity or bitterness in his voice. But even the full weight of my prejudice, which was immense, could not project, as I would have liked, traces of his human failure. He was just the same. The businesswoman and her secretary rejoined one another after dinner, and Brimmer joined the Southern family, who were either so obtuse or so naïve that they had seen nothing and had no objection to letting Brimmer dance with Sister and walk her around in the rain.

*

I did not speak to him for the rest of the voyage. We docked at Naples at seven o'clock on a rainy morning, and when I had cleared customs and was leaving the port with my bags, Brimmer called to me. He was with a good-looking, leggy blonde who must have been twenty years younger than he, and he asked if they could drive me up to Rome. Why I accepted, why I arose with such agility over my massive disapproval, seems to have been, in retrospect, a dislike of loneliness. I did not want to take the train alone to Rome. I accepted their offer and drove with them to Rome, stopping in Terracina for lunch. They were driving up to Florence in the morning, and since this was my destination, I went on with them.

Considering Brimmer's winning ways with animals and small children—they were all captivated—and his partiality (as I was to discover later) to the Franciscan forms of prayer, it might be worth recounting what happened that day when we turned off the road and drove up into Assisi for lunch. Portents mean nothing, but the truth is that when we begin a journey in Italy to a clap of thunder and a sky nearly black with swallows we pay more emotional attention to this spectacle than we would at home. The weather had been fair all that morning, but as we turned off toward Assisi a wind began to blow, and even before we reached the gates of the town the sky was dark. We had lunch at an inn near the duomo with a view of the valley and a good view of the storm as it came up the road and struck the holy city. It was darkness, wind, and rain of an unusual suddenness and density. There was an awning over the window where we sat and a palm tree in a garden below us, and while we ate our lunch we saw both the awning and the palm tree picked to pieces by the wind. When we finished lunch it was like night in the streets. A young brother let us into the duomo, but it was too dark to see the Cimabues. Then the brother took us to the sacristy and unlocked the door. The moment Brimmer entered that holy place the windows exploded under the force of the wind, and it was only by some kind of luck that we were not all cut to pieces by the glass that flew against the chest where the relics are stored. For the moment or two that the door was opened, the wind ranged through the church, extinguishing every candle in the place, and it took Brimmer and me and the brother, all pulling, to get the door shut again. Then the brother hurried off for help, and we climbed to the upper church. As we drove out of Assisi the wind fell, and looking back I saw the clouds pass over the town and the place fill up and shine with the light of day.

*

We said goodbye in Florence and I did not see Brimmer again. It was
the leggy blonde who wrote to me in July or August, when I had
returned to the United States and our farm in New Hampshire. She
wrote from a hospital in Zurich, and the letter had been forwarded
from my address in Florence. 'Poor Brimmer is dying,' she wrote.
'And if you could get up here to see him I know it would make him
very happy. He often speaks of you, and I know you were one of
his best friends. I am enclosing some papers that might interest you
since you are a writer. The doctors do not think he can live another
week. . . .' To refer to me as a friend exposed what must have been
the immensity of his loneliness; and it seemed all along that I had
known he was going to die, that his promiscuity was a relationship not
to life but to death. That was in the afternoon—it was four or five—
the light glancing, and that gratifying stillness in the air that falls over
the back country with the earliest signs of night. I didn't tell my wife.
Why should I? She never knew Brimmer and why introduce death
into such a tranquil scene? What I remember feeling was gladness.
The letter was six weeks old. He would be dead.

I don't suppose she could have read the papers she sent on. They
must have represented a time of life when he had suffered some kind
of breakdown. The first was a facetious essay, attacking the modern
toilet seat and claiming that the crouched position it enforced was dis-
advantageous to those muscles and organs that were called into use.
This was followed by a passionate prayer for cleanliness of heart. The
prayer seemed to have gone unanswered, because the next piece was
a very dirty essay on sexual control, followed by a long ballad called
The Ups and Downs of Jeremy Funicular. This was a disgusting account
of Jeremy's erotic adventures, describing many married and unmarried ladies and also one garage mechanic, one wrestler, and one lighthouse keeper. The ballad was long, and each stanza ended with a
reprise lamenting the fact that Jeremy had never experienced remorse
—excepting when he was mean to children, foolish with money, or
overate of bread and meat at table. The last manuscript was the remains
or fragments of a journal. '*Gratissimo Signore,*' he wrote, 'for the creaking
shutter, the love of Mrs Pigott, the smells of rain, the candor of friends,
the fish in the sea, and especially for the smell of bread and coffee,
since they mean mornings and newness of life.' It went on, pious and
lewd, but I read no more.

My wife is lovely, lovely were my children, and lovely that scene,
and how dead he and his dirty words seemed in the summer light. I
was glad of the news, and his death seemed to have removed the

perplexity that he had represented. I could remember with some sadness that he had been able to convey a feeling that the exuberance and the pain of life was a glass against which his nose was pressed: that he seemed able to dramatize the sense of its urgency and its deadly seriousness. I remembered the fineness of his hands, the light voice, and the cast in his eye that made the pupil seem like a goat's; but I wondered why he had failed, and by my lights he had failed horribly. Which one of us is not suspended by a thread above carnal anarchy, and what is that thread but the light of day? The difference between life and death seemed no more than the difference between going up to see the landfall at Lisbon and remaining in bed with Mme Troyan. I could remember the landfall—the pleasant, brackish smell of inshore water like my grandfather's bathing shoes—distant voices on a beach, villas, sea bells, and Sanctus bells, and the singing of the priest and the faces of the passengers all raised, all smiling in wonder at the sight of land as if nothing like it had ever been seen before.

But I was wrong, and set the discovery of my mistake in any place where you can find an old copy of *Europa* or *Epoca*. It is a Monday and I am spearfishing with my son off the rocks near Porto San Stefano. My son and I are not good friends, and it is at our best that we seem to be in disagreement with one another. We seem to want the same place in the sun. But we are great friends under water. I am delighted to see him there like a figure in a movie, head down, feet up, armed with a fishing spear, air streaming from his snorkel—and the rilled sand, where he stirs it, turning up like smoke. Here, in the deep water among the rocks, we seem to escape the tensions that make our relationships in other places vexatious. It is lovely here. With a little chop on the surface, the sun falls to the bottom of the sea in a great net of light. There are starfish in the colors of lipstick, and all the rocks are covered with white flowers. And after a *festa*, a Sunday when the beaches have been crowded, there are other things so many fathoms down—bits of sandwich paper, the crossword-puzzle page from *Il Messaggero*, and water-logged copies of *Epoca*. It is out of the back pages of one of these that Brimmer looks up to me from the bottom of the sea. He is not dead. He has just married an Italian movie actress. He has his left arm around her slender waist, his right foot crossed in front of his left and in his right hand the full glass. He looks no better and no worse, and I don't know if he has sold his lights and vitals to the devil or only discovered himself. I go up to the surface, shake the water out of my hair, and think that I am worlds away from home.

A Journey to the Seven Streams

My father, the heavens be his bed, was a terrible man for telling you about the places he had been and for bringing you there if he could and displaying them to you with a mild and gentle air of proprietorship. He couldn't do the showmanship so well in the case of Spion Kop where he and the fortunate ones who hadn't been ordered up the hill in the ignorant night had spent a sad morning crouching on African earth and listening to the deadly Boer guns that, high above the plain, slaughtered their hapless comrades. Nor yet in the case of Halifax nor the Barbadoes where he had heard words of Gaelic from coloured girls who were, he claimed, descended from the Irish transported into slavery in the days of Cromwell. The great glen of Aherlow, too, which he had helped to chain for His Majesty's Ordnance Survey, was placed inconveniently far to the south in the mystic land of Tipperary, and Cratloe Wood, where the fourth Earl of Leitrim was assassinated, was sixty miles away on the winding Donegal fjord called Mulroy Bay. But townlands like Corraheskin, Drumlish, Cornavara, Dooish, the Minnieburns and Claramore, and small towns like Drumquin and Dromore were all within a ten-mile radius of our town and something of moment or something amusing had happened in every one of them.

The reiterated music of their names worked on him like a charm. They would, he said, take faery tunes out of the stone fiddle of Castle Caldwell; and indeed it was the night he told us the story of the stone fiddle and the drowned fiddler, and recited for us the inscription carved on a fiddle in memory of the fiddler, that he decided to hire a hackney car, a rare and daring thing to do in those days, and bring us out to see in one round trip those most adjacent places of his memories and dreams.

—In the year 1770 it happened, he said. The landlord at the time was Sir James Caldwell, Baronet. He was also called the Count of Milan, why, I never found anybody to tell me. The fiddler's name was

Dennis McCabe and by tradition the McCabes were always musicians and jesters to the Caldwells. There was festivity at the Big House by Lough Erne Shore and gentry there from near and far, and out they went to drink and dance on a raft on the lake, and wasn't the poor fiddler so drunk he fiddled himself into the water and drowned.

—Couldn't somebody have pulled him out, Da?

—They were all as drunk as he was. The story was that he was still sawing away with the bow when he came up for the third time. The party cheered him until every island in Lough Erne echoed and it was only when they sobered up they realized they had lost the fiddler. So the baronet and Count of Milan had a stone fiddle taller than a man made to stand at the estate gate as a monument to Dennis McCabe and as a warning for ever to fiddlers either to stay sober or to stay on dry land.

—Ye fiddlers beware, ye fiddler's fate, my father recited. Don't attempt the deep lest ye repent too late. Keep to the land when wind and storm blow, but scorn the deep if it with whisky flow. On firm land only exercise your skill; there you may play and safely drink your fill.

Travelling by train from our town to the seaside you went for miles along the green and glistening Erne shore but the train didn't stop by the stone fiddle nor yet at the Boa island for the cross-roads' dances. Always when my father told us about those dances, his right foot rhythmically tapped and took music out of the polished steel fireside fender that had Home Sweet Home lettered out on an oval central panel. Only the magic motor, bound to no tracks, compelled to no fixed stopping places, could bring us to the fiddle or the crowded cross-roads.

—Next Sunday then, he said, as certain as the sun sets and rises, we'll hire Hookey and Peter and the machine and head for Lough Erne.

—Will it hold us all, said my mother. Seven of us and Peter's big feet and the length of the driver's legs.

—That machine, he said, would hold the twelve apostles, the Connaught Rangers and the man who broke the bank at Monte Carlo. It's the size of a hearse.

—Which is just what it looks like, said the youngest of my three sisters who had a name for the tartness of her tongue.

She was a thin dark girl.

—Regardless of appearance, he said, it'll carry us to the stone fiddle and on the way we'll circumnavigate the globe: Clanabogan, and Cav-anacaw, Pigeon Top Mountain and Corraduine, where the barefooted priest said Mass at the Rock in the penal days and Corraheskin where the Muldoons live . . .

—Them, said the third sister.

She had had little time for the Muldoons since the day their lack of savoir faire cost her a box of chocolates. A male member, flaxen-haired, pink-cheeked, aged sixteen, of those multitudinous Muldoons had come by horse and cart on a market day from his rural fastnesses to pay us a visit. Pitying his gaucherie, his shy animal-in-a-thicket appear-ance, his outback ways and gestures, she had grandly reached him a box of chocolates so as to sweeten his bitter lot with one honeyed morsel or two, or, at the outside three; but unaccustomed to towny ways and the mores of built-up areas the rural swain had appropriated the whole box.

—He thought, she said, I was a paleface offering gifts to a Comanche.

—But by their own hearth, said my father, they're simple hospitable people.

—And Cornavara, he said, and Dooish and Carrick Valley and your uncle Owen, and the two McCannys the pipers, and Claramore where there are so many Gormleys every family has to have its own nickname, and Drumquin where I met your mother, and Dromore where you (pointing to me) were born and where the mail train was held up by the IRA and where the three poor lads were murdered by the Specials when you (again indicating me) were a year old, and the Minnieburns where the seven streams meet to make the head waters of the big river. Hookey and Peter and the machine will take us to all those places.

—Like a magic carpet, said my mother—with just a little dusting of the iron filings of doubt in her voice.

Those were the days, and not so long ago, when cars were rare and every car, not just every make of car, had a personality of its own. In our town with its population of five thousand, not counting the soldiers in the barracks, there were only three cars for hire and one of them was the love-child of the pioneer passion of Hookey Baxter for the machine. He was a long hangle of a young fellow, two-thirds of him made up of legs, and night and day he was whistling. He was as forward-looking as Lindbergh and he dressed like Lindbergh, for the air, in goggles, leather jacket and helmet; an appropriate costume, possibly, considering

Hookey's own height and the altitude of the driver's seat in his machine. The one real love of his young heart was the love of the born tinkerer, the instinctive mechanic, for that hybrid car: the child of his frenzy, the fruit of days spent deep in grease giving new life and shape to a wreck he had bought at a sale in Belfast. The original manufacturers, who-ever they had been, would have been hard put to it to recognize their altered offspring.

—She's chuman, Peter Keown would say as he patted the sensitive quivering bonnet.

Peter meant human. In years to come his sole recorded comment on the antics of Adolf Hitler was that the man wasn't chuman.

—She's as nervous, he would say, as a thoroughbred.

The truth was that Peter, Hookey's stoker, grease-monkey and errand boy, was somewhat in awe of the tall rangy metal animal yet wherever the car went, with the tall goggled pilot at the wheel, there the pilot's diminutive mate was also sure to go. What living Peter earned he earned by digging holes in the street as a labouring man for the town council's official plumber so that, except on Sundays and when he motored with Hookey, nobody in the town ever saw much of him but the top of his cloth cap or his upturned face when he'd look up from the hole in the ground to ask a passer-by the time of day. Regularly once a year he spent a corrective month in Derry Jail, because his opportunities as a municipal employee and his weakness as a kleptomaniac meant that good boards, lengths of piping, coils of electric wire, monkey wrenches, spades, and other movable properties faded too frequently into thin air.

—A wonderful man, poor Peter, my father would say. That cloth cap with the turned up peak. And the thick-lensed, thin-rimmed spectacles—he's half-blind—and the old tweed jacket too tight for him, and the old Oxford-bag trousers too big for him, and his shrill voice and his waddle of a walk that makes him look always like a duck about to apologize for laying a hen-egg. How he survives is a miracle of God's grace. He can resist the appeal of nothing that's portable.

—He's a dream, said the third sister. And the feet are the biggest part of him.

—The last time he went to Derry, said my brother, all the old women from Brook Street and the lanes were at the top of the Courthouse Hill to cheer him as he passed.

—And why not, said my mother. They're fond of him and they say he's well-liked in the jail. His heart's as big as his feet. Everything he steals he gives away.

—Robin Hood, said the third sister. Robbing the town council to pay Brook Street.

—The Council wouldn't sack him, said my eldest sister, if he stole the town.

—At the ready, roared my father. Prepare to receive cavalry.

In the street below the house there was a clanking, puffing, grinding tumult.

—God bless us look at Peter, said my father. Aloft with Hookey like a crown prince beside a king. Are we all ready? Annie, Ita, May, George, yourself ma'am, and you the youngest of us all. Have we the sandwiches and the flasks of tea and the lemonade? Forward.

A lovelier Sunday morning never shone. With the hood down and the high body glistening after its Saturday wash and polish, the radiator gently steaming, the car stood at the foot of the seven steps that led down from our door. The stragglers coming home from early mass, and the devout setting off early for late mass had gathered in groups to witness our embarkation. Led by my father and in single file, we descended the steps and ascended nearly as high again to take our lofty places in the machine.

There was something of the Citroen in the quivering mongrel, in the yellow canvas hood now reclining in voluminous ballooning folds, in the broad back-seat that could hold five fair-sized people. But to judge by the radiator, the absence of gears, and the high fragile-spoked wheels, Citroen blood had been crossed with that of the Model T. After that, any efforts to spot family traits would have brought confusion on the thought of the greatest living authorities. The thick slanting glass windscreen could have been wrenched from a limousine designed to divert bullets from Balkan princelings. The general colour-scheme, considerably chipped and cracked, was canary yellow. And there was Hookey at the wheel, then my brother and father, and Peter on the outside left where he could leap in and out to perform the menial duties of assistant engineer; and in the wide and windy acres of the back seat, my mother, myself and my three sisters.

High above the town the church bell rang. It was the bell to warn the worshippers still on their way that in ten minutes the vested priest would be on the altar but, as it coincided with our setting out, it could have been a quayside bell ringing farewell to a ship nosing out across the water towards the rim of vision.

Peter leaped to the ground, removed the two stones that, blocked before the front wheels, acted as auxiliaries for the hand brake. Hookey released the brake. The car was gathering speed when Peter scrambled aboard, settled himself and slammed the yellow door behind him. Sparing fuel, we glided down the slope, backfired twice loudly enough to drown the sound of the church bell, swung left along John Street and cleared the town without incident. Hands waved from watching groups of people but because this was no trivial event there were no laughs, no wanton cheers. The sound of the bell died away behind us. My mother expressed the hope that the priest would remember us at the offertory. Peter assured her that we were all as safe as if we were at home in bed. God's good green Sunday countryside was softly all around us.

Squat to the earth and travelling at seventy you see nothing from cars nowadays, but to go with Hookey was to be above all but the highest walls and hedges, to be among the morning birds.

—Twenty-seven em pee haitch, said Hookey.

—Four miles covered already, said Peter.

—The Gortin Mountains over there, said my father. And the two mountains to the north are Bessy Bell and Mary Grey, so named by the Hamiltons of Baronscourt, the Duke of Abercorn's people, after fancied resemblance to two hills in Stirlingshire, Scotland. The two hills in Stirlingshire are so called after two ladies of the Scottish court who fled the plague and built their hut in the wild wood and thatched it o'er with rushes. They are mentioned by Thomas Carlyle in his book on the French Revolution. The dark green on the hills by Gortin Gap is the new government forestry. And in Gortin village Paddy Ford the contractor hasn't gone to mass since, fifteen years ago, the parish priest gave another man the job of painting the inside of the sacristy.

—No paint no prayers, said the third sister.

—They're strange people in Gortin, my mother said.

—It's proverbial, said my father, that they're to be distinguished anywhere by the bigness of their backsides.

—Five miles, said Peter. They're spinning past.

—Running sweet as honey, said Hookey.

He adjusted his goggles and whistled back to the Sunday birds.

—Jamie Magee's of the Flush, said my father.

He pointed to a long white house on a hill slope and close to a waterfalling stream.

—Rich as Rockefeller and too damned mean to marry.

—Who in heaven would have him, said the third sister.

—Six miles, said Peter.

Then, with a blast of backfiring that rose my mother a foot in the air, the wobbling yellow conveyance came to a coughing miserable halt. The air was suddenly grey and poisoned with fumes.

—It's her big end Hookey, said Peter.

—She's from Gortin so, said the third sister.

The other two sisters, tall and long-haired and normally quiet girls, went off at the deep end into the giggles.

—Isn't it providential, said my mother, that the cowslips are a glory this year. We'll have something to do, Henry, while you're fixing it.

Hookey had been christened Henry, and my mother would never descend to nicknames. She felt that to make use of a nickname was to remind a deformed person of his deformity. Nor would she say even of the town's chief inebriate that he was ever drunk: he was either under the influence or he had a drop too many taken. She was, my mother, the last great Victorian euphemizer.

—We won't be a jiffy, ma'am, said Hookey. It's nothing so serious as a big end.

The three sisters were convulsed.

The fields and the roadside margins were bright yellow with blossom.

—Gather ye cowslips while you may, said my father.

He handed the ladies down from the dizzy heights. Peter had already disembarked. Submitting to an impulse that had gnawed at me since we set sail I dived forwards, my head under Hookey's left elbow, and butted with both fists the black rubber punch-ball horn; and out over the fields to startle birds and grazing cattle went the dying groan of a pained diseased ox.

—Mother of God, said my father, that's a noise and no mistake. Here boy, go off and pick flowers.

He lifted me down to the ground.

—Screw off the radiator cap, Peter, said Hookey.

—It's scalding hot, Hookey.

—Take these gauntlet gloves, manalive. And stand clear when you screw it off.

A geyser of steam and dirty hot water went heavenwards as Peter and my brother, who was always curious about engines, leaped to safety.

—Wonderful, said my father to my brother, the age we live in. They say that over in England they're queued up steaming by the roadsides, like Iceland or the Yellowstone Park.

—Just a bit overheated, said Hookey. We won't be a jiffy.

—Does it happen often? said my father.

Ignoring the question, descending and opening the bonnet to peer and poke and tinker, Hookey said: Do you know a funny thing about this car?

—She's chuman, said Peter.

—You know the cross-roads at Clanabogan churchyard gate, Hookey said. The story about it.

—It's haunted, said my father.

—Only at midnight, said Peter.

As was his right and custom, my father stepped into the role of raconteur: Do you know that no horse ever passed there at midnight that didn't stop—shivering with fear. The fact is well attested. Something comes down that side road out of the heart of the wood.

Hookey closed over the bonnet, screwed back the radiator cap and climbed again to the throne. He wiped his hands on a bunch of grass pulled for him and handed to him by Peter. Slowly he drew on again his gauntlet gloves. Bedecked with cowslips and dragging me along with them the ladies rejoined the gentlemen.

—Well, would you credit this now, Hookey said. Peter and myself were coming from Dromore one wet night last week.

—Pouring rain from the heavens, said Peter, and the hood was leaking.

—A temporary defect, said Hookey. I mended it. Jack up the back axle, Peter, and give her a swing. And would you credit it, exactly at twelve o'clock midnight she stopped dead at the gate of Clanabogan churchyard?

With an irony that was lost on Hookey, my mother said: I could well believe it.

—She's chuman, said Peter.

—One good push now and we're away, said Hookey. The slight gradient is in our favour.

—Maybe, he said to my father and brother, you'd lend Peter a hand.

Twenty yards ahead he waited for the dusty pushers to climb aboard, the engine chug-chugging, little puffs of steam escaping like baby genii from the right-hand side of the bonnet. My father was thoughtful. He could have been considering the responsibilities of the machine age particularly because when it came to team pushing Peter was more of a cheer leader, an exhorter, a counter of one two three, than an actual motive force.

—Contact, said Hookey.

—Dawn patrol away, said Peter. Squadron Leader Baxter at the joystick.

He mimicked what he supposed to be the noises of an aeroplane engine and, with every evidence of jubilation, we were once again under way; and a day it was, made by the good God for jubilation. The fields, all the colours of all the crops, danced towards us and away from us and around us; and the lambs on the green hills, my father sang, were gazing at me and many a strawberry grows by the salt sea, and many a ship sails the ocean. The roadside trees bowed down and then gracefully swung their arms up and made music over our heads and there were more birds and white cottages and fuchsia hedges in the world than you would readily imagine.

—The bride and bride's party, sang my father, to church they did go. The bride she goes foremost, she bears the best show . . .

—They're having sports today at Tattysallagh, said Hookey.

—But I followed after my heart full of woe, for to see my love wed to another.

We swept by a cross-roads where people and horses and traps were congregated after the last mass. In a field beside the road a few tall ash plants bore fluttering pennants in token of the sports to be.

—Proceed to Banteer, sang my father, to the athletic sporting and hand in your name to the club comm-i-tee.

—That was a favourite song of Pat O'Leary the Corkman, he said, who was killed at Spion Kop.

Small country boys in big boots, knickerbockers, stiff celluloid collars that could be cleaned for Sunday by a rub of a wet cloth, and close-cropped heads with fringes like scalping locks above the foreheads, scattered before us to the hedges and the grass margins, then closed again like water divided and rejoining, and pursued us, cheering, for a hundred yards. One of them, frantic with enthusiasm, sent sailing after us a half-grown turnip, which bounced along the road for a bit, then sought rest in a roadside drain. Looking backwards I pulled my best or worst faces at the rustic throng of runners.

—In Tattysallagh, said my father, they were always an uncivilized crowd of gulpins.

He had three terms of contempt: Gulpin, Yob and, when things became very bad he became Swiftian, and described all offenders as Yahoos.

—Cavanacaw, he said, and that lovely trout stream, the Greevan Burn. It joins the big river at Blacksessiagh. That there's the road up to Pigeon Top Mountain and the mass rock at Corraduine, but we'll come back that way when we've circumnavigated Dooish and Cornavara.

We came to Clanabogan.

—Clanabogan planting, he said.

The tall trees came around us and sunlight and shadow flickered so that you could feel them across eyes and hands and face.

—Martin Murphy the postman, he said, who was in the survey with me in Virginia, County Cavan, by Lough Ramor, and in the Glen of Aherlow, worked for a while at the building of Clanabogan Church. One day the vicar said to him: 'What height do you think the steeple should be?' 'The height of nonsense like your sermons', said Martin, and got the sack for his wit. In frosty weather he used to seal the cracks in his boots with butter and although he was an abrupt man he seldom used an impolite word. Once when he was aggravated by the bad play of his wife who was partnering him at whist he said: 'Maria, dearly as I love you there are yet moments when you'd incline a man to kick his own posterior.'

—There's the church, my father said, and the churchyard and the haunted gate and the cross-roads.

We held our breath but, with honeyed summer all around us and bees in the tender limes, it was no day for ghosts, and in glory we sailed by.

—She didn't hesitate, said Peter.

—Wonderful, said the third sister.

It was more wonderful than she imagined for, as the Lord would have it, the haunted gate and the cross-roads of Clanabogan was one of the few places that day that Hookey's motor machine did not honour with at least some brief delay.

—I'd love to drive, said my brother. How did you learn to drive, Hookey?

—I never did. I just sat in and drove. I learned the basic principles on the county council steamroller in Watson's quarries. Forward and reverse.

—You have to have the natural knack, Peter explained.

—What's the cut potato for, Hookey? asked my brother.

—For the rainy day. Rub it on the windscreen and the water runs off the glass.

—It's oily you see, said Peter.

—Like a duck's back, said the third sister.

—Where, said my father—sniffing, do you keep the petrol?

—Reserve in the tins clipped on the running board. Current supply, six gallons. You're sitting on it. In a tank under the front seat.

—Twenty miles to the gallon, said Peter. We're good for more than a hundred miles.

—Godalmighty, said my father. Provided it isn't a hundred miles straight up. 'Twould be sad to survive a war that was the end of better men and to be blown up between Clanabogan and Cornavara. On a quiet Sunday morning.

—Never worry, said Hookey. It's outside the bounds of possibility.

—You reassure me, said my father. Twenty miles to the gallon in any direction. What care we? At least we'll all go up together. No survivors to mourn in misery.

—And turn right here, he said, for Cornavara. You'll soon see the hills and the high waterfalls.

We left the tarred road. White dust rose around us like smoke. We advanced half a mile on the flat, attempted the first steep hill and gently, wearily, without angry fumes or backfiring protests, the tremulous chuman car, lying down like a tired child, came to rest.

—We'll hold what we have, said Hookey. Peter . . . pronto. Get the stones behind the back wheels.

—Think of a new pastime, said the third sister. We have enough cowslips to decorate the town for a procession. With the sweet face of girlish simplicity she asked, Do you buy the stones with the car?

—We'd be worse off without them, Hookey muttered.

Disguised as he was in helmet and goggles it was impossible to tell exactly if his creative soul was or was not wounded by her hint of mockery, but my mother must have considered that his voice betrayed pain for she looked reprovingly at the third sister and at the other two who were again impaled by giggles, and withdrew them out of sight down a boreen towards the sound of a small stream, to—as she put it—freshen up.

—Without these stones, Peter panted, we could be as badly off as John MacKenna and look what happened to him.

—They're necessary precautions, said Hookey. Poor John would never use stones. He said the brakes on his car would hold a Zeppelin.

The bonnet was open again and the radiator cap unscrewed but there was no steam and no geyser, only a cold sad silence, and Hookey bending and peering and probing with pincers.

—She's a bit exhausted, Peter said.

—It's simple, Hookey said. She'll be right as rain in a jiffy. Going at the hill with a full load overstrained her.

—We should walk the bad hills, Peter explained.

—Poor John MacKenna, Hookey said, was making four fortunes drawing crowds to the Passionist monastery at Enniskillen to see the monk that cures the people. But he would never use the stones, and the only parking place at the monastery is on a sharp slope. And one evening when they were all at devotions doesn't she run backways and ruin all the flowerbeds in the place and knock down a statue of Our Lord.

—One of the monks attacked him, said Peter, as a heathen that would knock the Lord down.

—Ruined the trade for all, said Hookey. The monks now won't let a car within a mile of the place.

—Can't say as I blame them, said my father.

—Poor John took it bad, said Hookey. The lecture he got and all. He was always a religious man. They say he raises his hat now every time he passes any statue: even the Boer War one in front of the courthouse.

—So well he might, said my father.

Suddenly, mysteriously responding to Hookey's probing pincers, the very soul of the machine was again chug-chugging. But with or without cargo she could not or, being weary and chuman, would not assault even the first bastion of Cornavara.

—She won't take off, said Hookey. That run to Belfast and back took the wind out of her.

—You never made Belfast, said my father, in this.

—We did Tommy, said Peter apologetically.

—Seventy miles there and seventy miles back, said my father incredulously.

—Bringing a greyhound bitch to running trials for Tommy Mullan the postman, said Hookey.

—The man who fishes for pearls in the Drumragh river, said Peter.

They were talking hard to cover their humiliation.

—If she won't go at the hills, my father said, go back to the main road and we'll go on and picnic at the seven streams at the Minnieburns. It's mostly on the flat.

So we reversed slowly the dusty half-mile to the main road.

—One night in John Street, Peter said, she started going backways and wouldn't go forwards.

—A simple defect, Hookey said. I remedied it.

—Did you turn the other way? asked the third sister.

Artlessly, Peter confessed: She stopped when she knocked down the schoolchildren-crossing sign at the bottom of Church Hill. Nipped it off an inch from the ground, as neat as you ever saw. We hid it up a laneway and it was gone in the morning.

My father looked doubtfully at Peter. He said: One of those nice shiny enamelled pictures of two children crossing the road would go well as an overmantel. And the wood of the post would always make firewood.

Peter agreed: You can trust nobody.

Hurriedly trying to cut in on Peter's eloquence, Hookey said: In fact the name of Tommy Mullan's bitch was Drumragh Pearl. Not that that did her any good at the trials.

—She came a bad last, burst out the irrepressible Peter.

—And to make it worse we lost her on the way back from Belfast.

—You what? said my father.

—Lost her in the dark where the road twists around Ballymacilroy Mountain.

My mother was awed: You lost the man's greyhound. You're a right pair of boys to send on an errand.

—'Twas the way we stepped out of the car to take the air, said Hookey.

By the husky note in his voice you could guess how his soul suffered at Peter's shameless confessions.

—And Peter looked at the animal, ma'am, and said maybe she'd like a turn in the air too. So we took her out and tied her lead to the left front wheel. And while we were standing there talking didn't the biggest brute of a hare you ever saw set out as cool as sixpence in the light of the car. Off like a shot with the bitch.

—If the lead hadn't snapped, Peter said, she'd have taken the wheel off the car or the car off the road.

—That would have been no great exertion, said my father. We should have brought a greyhound along with us to pull.

—We whistled and called for hours but all in vain, said Peter.

—The hare ate her, said the third sister.

—Left up the slope there, said my father, is the belt of trees I planted in my spare time to act as a wind-breaker for Drumlish school-house.

Paddy Hamish, the labouring man, gave me a hand. He died last year in Canada.

—You'd have pitied the children on a winter's day, my mother said, standing in the playground at lunchtime taking the fresh air in a hilltop wind that would sift and clean corn. Eating soda bread and washing it down with buttermilk. On a rough day the wind from Lough Erne would break the panes of the windows.

—As a matter of curiosity, my father said, what did Tommy Mullan say?

—At two in the morning in Bridge Lane, said Peter, he was waiting for us. We weren't too happy about it. But when we told him she was last in the trials he said the bloody bitch could stay in Ballymacilroy.

—Hasn't he always the pearls in the river, my mother said.

So we came to have tea and sandwiches and lemonade in a meadow by the cross-roads in the exact centre of the wide saucer of land where seven streams from the surrounding hills came down to meet. The grass was polished with sunshine. The perfume of the meadowsweet is with me still. That plain seemed to me then as vast as the prairies, or Siberia. White cottages far away on the lower slopes of Dooish could have been in another country. The chief stream came for a long way through soft deep meadowland. It was slow, quiet, unobtrusive, perturbed only by the movements of water fowl or trout. Two streams met, wonder of wonders, under the arch of a bridge and you could go out under the bridge along a sandy promontory to paddle in clear water on a bottom as smooth as Bundoran strand. Three streams came together in a magic hazel wood where the tiny green unripe nuts were already clustered on the branches. Then the seven made into one, went away from us with a shout and a song towards Shaneragh, Blacksessiagh, Drumragh and Crevenagh, under the humpy crooked King's Bridge where James Stuart had passed on his way from Derry to the fatal brackish Boyne, and on through the town we came from.

—All the things we could see, said my father, if this spavined brute of a so-called automobile could only be persuaded to climb the high hills. The deep lakes of Claramore. The far view of Mount Errigal, the Cock of the North, by the Donegal sea. If you were up on the top of Errigal you could damn' near see, on a clear day, the skyscrapers of New York.

In his poetic imagination the towers of Atlantis rose glimmering from the deep.

—What matter, said my mother. The peace of heaven is here.

*

For that day that was the last peace we were to experience. The energy the machine didn't have or wouldn't use to climb hills or to keep in motion for more than two miles at a stretch, she expended in thunderous staccato bursts of backfiring. In slanting evening sunlight people at the doors of distant farmhouses shaded their eyes to look towards the travelling commotion, or ran up whinny hills for a better view, and horses and cattle raced madly around pastures, and my mother said the country would never be the same again, that the shock of the noise would turn the milk in the udders of the cows. When we came again to the crossroads of Tattysallagh the majority of the spectators, standing on the road to look over the hedge and thus save the admission fee, lost all interest in the sports, such as they were, and came around us. To oblige them the right rear tyre went flat.

—Peter, said Hookey, jack it up and change it on.

We mingled unobtrusively with the gulpins.

—A neat round hole, said Peter.

—Paste a patch on it.

The patch was deftly pasted on.

—Take the foot pump and blow her up, said Hookey.

There was a long silence while Peter, lines of worry on his little puckered face, inspected the tube. Then he said: I can't find the valve.

—Show it to me, said Hookey.

He ungoggled himself, descended and surveyed the ailing member.

—Peter, he said, you're a prize. The valve's gone and you put a patch on the hole it left behind it.

The crowd around us was increasing and highly appreciative.

—Borrow a bicycle Peter, said Hookey, cycle to the town and ask John MacKenna for the loan of a tube.

—To pass the time, said my mother, we'll look at the sports.

So we left Hookey to mind his car and, being practically gentry as compared with the rustic throng around us, we walked to the gateway that led into the sportsfield where my mother civilly enquired of two men, who stood behind a wooden table, the price of admission.

—Five shillings a skull missus, barring the cub, said the younger of the two. And half a crown for the cub.

—For the what? said my mother.

—For the little boy ma'am, said the elder of the two.

—It seems expensive, said my mother.

—I'd see them all in hell first—let alone in Tattysallagh, my father said. One pound, twelve shillings and sixpence to look at six sally rods stuck in a field and four yahoos running round in rings in their sock soles.

We took our places on the roadside with the few who, faithful to athletics and undistracted by the novelty of the machine, were still looking over the hedge. Four lean youths and one stout one in Sunday shirts and long trousers with the ends tucked into their socks were pushing high framed bicycles round and round the field. My father recalled the occasion in Virginia, County Cavan, when Martin Murphy was to run at sports and his wife Maria stiffened his shirt so much with starch it wouldn't go inside his trousers, and when he protested she said: Martin, leave it outside and you will be able to fly.

We saw two bicycle races and a tug-of-war.

—Hallions and clifts, he said.

Those were two words he seldom used.

—Yobs and sons of yobs, he said.

He led us back to the car. Peter soaked in perspiration had the new tube on and the wheel ready.

—Leave the jack in and swing her, Hookey said. She's cold by now.

There was a series of explosions that sent gulpins, yobs and yahoos reeling backwards in alarm. Peter screwed out the jack. We scrambled aboard, a few of the braver among the decent people rushing into the line of fire to lend a hand to the ladies. Exploding, we departed, and when we were a safe distance away the watchers raised a dubious cheer.

—In God's name, Henry, said my father, get close to the town before you blow us all up. I wouldn't want our neighbours to have to travel as far as Tattysallagh to pick up the bits. And the yobs and yahoos here don't know us well enough to be able to piece us together.

Three miles further on Peter blushingly confessed that in the frantic haste of embarkation he had left the jack on the road.

—I'll buy you a new one, Henry, my father said. Or perhaps Peter here could procure one on the side. By now at any rate, they're shoeing jackasses with it in Tattysallagh.

—A pity in a way, he said, we didn't make as far as the stone fiddle. We might have heard good music. It's a curious thing that in the townlands around that place the people have always been famed for music and singing. The Tunneys of Castle Caldwell now are noted. It could be that the magic of the stone fiddle has something to do with it.

—Some day, he said, we'll head for Donegal. When the cars, Henry, are a bit improved.

He told us about the long windings of Mulroy Bay. He explained exactly how and why and in what year the fourth Earl of Leitrim had been assassinated in Cratloe Wood. He spoke as rapidly and distinctly as he could in the lulls of the backfiring.

Then our town was below us in the hollow and the Gortin mountains, deep purple with evening, away behind it.

—Here we'll part company, Henry boy, said my father. 'Tisn't that I doubt the ability of Peter and yourself to navigate the iron horse down the hill. But I won't have the town blaming me and my family for having hand, act or part in the waking of the dead in Drumragh graveyard.

Sedately we walked down the slope into the town and talked with the neighbours we met and asked them had they heard Hookey and Peter passing and told them of the sports and of the heavenly day it had been out at the seven streams.

My father died in a seaside town in the County Donegal—forty miles from the town I was reared in. The road his funeral followed back to the home places led along the Erne shore by the stone fiddle and the glistening water, across the Boa Island where there are no longer cross-roads' dances. Every roadside house has a television aerial. It led by the meadowland saucer of the Minnieburns where the river still springs from seven magic sources. That brooding place is still much as it was but no longer did it seem to me to be as vast as Siberia. To the left was the low sullen outline of Cornavara and Pigeon Top, the hurdle that our Bucephalus refused to take. To the right was Drumlish. The old schoolhouse was gone and in its place a white building, ten times as large, with drying rooms for wet coats, fine warm lunches for children and even a gymnasium. But the belt of trees that he and Paddy Hamish planted to break the wind and shelter the children is still there.

Somebody tells me, too, that the engine of Hookey Baxter's car is still with us, turning a circular saw for a farmer in the vicinity of Clanabogan.

As the Irish proverb says: It's a little thing doesn't last longer than a man.

Scholar and Gypsy

Her first day in Bombay wilted her. If she stepped out of the air-conditioned hotel room, she drooped, her head hung, her eyes glazed, she felt faint. Once she was back in it, she fell across her bed as though she had been struck by calamity, was extinguished, and could barely bring herself to believe that she had, after all, survived. Sweating, it seemed to her that life, energy, hope were all seeping out of her, flowing down a drain, gurgling ironically.

'But you knew it would be hot,' David said, not being able to help a sense of disappointment in her. He had bought himself crisp bush-shirts of madras cotton and open Kolhapur sandals. He was drinking more than was his habit, it was true, but it did not seem to redden and coarsen him as it did her. He looked so right, so fitting on the Bombay streets, striding over the coconut shells and betel-stained papers and the fish scales and lepers' stumps. 'You could hardly come to India and expect it to be cool, Pat.'

'Hot, yes,' she moaned, 'but not—not *killing*. Not so like death. I feel half-dead, David, sometimes *quite* dead.'

'Shall we go and have a gin-and-lime in the bar?'

She tried that since it seemed to do him so much good. But the bar in the hotel was so crowded, the people there were so large and vital and forceful in their brilliant clothes and with their metallic voices and their eyes that flashed over her like barbers' shears, cutting and exposing, that she felt crushed rather than revived.

David attracted people like a magnet—with his charm, his nonchalance, his grace, he did it so well, so smoothly, his qualities worked more efficiently than any visiting card system—and they started going to parties. It began to seem to her that this was the chief occupation of people in Bombay—going to parties. She was always on the point of collapse when she arrived at one: the taxi invariably stank, the driver's hair dripped oil, and then the sights and scenes they passed on the streets, the congestion and racket of the varied traffic, the virulent cinema posters, the blazing colours of women's clothing, the profusion of toys and decorations of coloured paper and tinsel, the radios and loudspeakers never tuned to less than top volume, and amongst them flower sellers, pilgrims, dancing monkeys and performing bears . . . that there should be such poverty, such disease, such filth, and that out of it boiled so much vitality, such irrepressible life, seemed to her unnatural and sinister—it was as if chaos and evil triumphed over reason and order. Then the parties they went to were all very large ones. The guests all wore brilliant clothes and jewellery, and their eyes and teeth flashed with such primitive lust as they eyed her slim, white-sheathed blonde self, that the sensation of being caught up and crushed, crowded in and choked sent her into corners where their knees pushed into her, their hands slid over her back, their voices bored into her, so that when she got back to the hotel, on David's arm, she was more like a corpse than an American globe-trotter.

Folding her arms about her, she muttered at the window, 'I never expected them to be so primitive. I thought it would all be modern, up-to-date. Not this—this wild jungle stuff.'

He was pouring himself a night-cap and splashed it in genuine surprise. 'What do you mean? We've only been seeing the modern and up-to-date. These people would be at home at any New York cocktail party—'

'No,' she burst out, hugging herself tightly. 'No, they would *not*. They haven't the polish, the smoothness, the softness. David, they're *not* civilized. They're still a primitive people. When I see their eyes I see how primitive they are. When they touch me, I feel frightened— I feel I'm in danger.'

He looked at her with apprehension. They had drunk till it was too late to eat and now he was hungry, tired. He found her exhausting. He would have liked to sit back comfortably in that air-conditioned cool, to go over the party, to discuss the people they had met, to share his views with her. But she seemed launched in some other direction, she was going alone and he did not want to be drawn into her deep wake. 'You're very imaginative tonight,' he said lightly, playing with the bottle-opener and not looking at her. 'Here was I, disappointed at finding them so westernized. I would have liked them a bit more primitive—at least for the sake of my thesis. Now look at the Gidwanis. Did you ever think an Indian wife would be anything like Gidwani's wife—what was her name?'

'Oh, she was terrible, terrible,' Pat whispered, shuddering, as she thought of the vermilion sari tied below the navel, of the uneven chocolate-smooth expanse of belly and the belt of little silver bells around it. She didn't care to remember the dance she had danced with David on the floor of the night-club. She had never even looked at the woman's face, she had kept her eyes lowered and not been able to go any further than that black navel. If that was not primitive, what could David, a sociology student, mean by the word?

It was at the Gidwanis' dinner later that week that she collapsed. She had begun to feel threatened, menaced, the moment they entered that flat. Leaving behind them the betel-stained walls of the elevator shaft, the servant boys asleep on mats in the passage, the cluster of watchmen and chauffeurs playing cards under the unshaded bulb in the lobby, they had stepped onto a black marble floor that glittered like a mirror and reflected the priceless statuary that sailed on its surface like ships of stone. Scarlet and vermilion ixora in pots. Menservants in stiffly starched uniform. Jewels, enamel, brocade and gold. Gidwani with a face like an amiable baboon's, immediately sliding a soft hand across her back. His wife's chocolate pudding belly with the sari slipping suggestively about her hips. Pat shrank and shrank. Her lips felt very dry and she licked and licked them, nervously. She lost David's arm. Her feet in their sandals seemed to swell grotesquely. She sat at the table, her head slanting. She saw David looking at her concernedly. The manservant's stomach pushed against her shoulder as he lowered the dishes for her. The dishes smelt, she wondered of what—oil, was it, or goat's meat? It was not conducive to appetite. Her fork slipped. The table slipped. She had fainted. They were all crying, shoving, crowding. She pushed at them with her hands in panic.

'David, get me out, get me out,' she blubbered, trying to free herself of them.

Later, sitting at the foot of her bed, 'We'd better leave,' he said sadly. Was it Gidwani's wife's belly that saddened him, she wondered. It was not a sight that one could forget, or discard, or deny. 'Delhi's said to be drier,' he said, 'not so humid. It'll be better for you.'

'But your thesis, David?' she wept, repentantly. 'Will you be able to work on it there?'

'I suppose so,' he said gloomily, looking down at her, shrunk into something small on the bed, paler and fainter each day that she spent in the wild jungles of the city of Bombay.

*

Delhi was drier. It was dry as a skeleton. Yellow sand seethed and
stormed, then settled on wood, stone, flesh and skin, brittle and gritty
as powdered bone. Trees stood leafless. Red flowers blazed on their
black branches, golden and purple ones burgeoned. Beggars drowsed
in their shade, stretched unrecognizable limbs at her. I will pull myself
together, Pat said, walking determinedly through the piled yellow dust,
I must pull myself together. Her body no longer melted, it did not
ooze and seep out of her grasp any more. It was dry, she would hold
herself upright, she would look into people's eyes when they spoke to
her and smile pleasantly—like David, she thought. But the dust inside
her sandals made her feet drag. If she no longer melted, she burnt. She
felt the heat strike through to her bones. Even her eyes, protected by
giant glare glasses, seemed on fire. She thought she would shrivel up
like a piece of paper under a magnifying glass held to reflect the sun.
Rubbing her fingers together, she made a scraping, papery sound. Her
hair was full of sand.

'But you can't let climate get you down, dear,' David said softly, in
order to express tenderness that he hardly felt any longer, seeing her
suffer so unbeautifully, her feet dusty, her hair stringy, her face thin
and appalled. 'Climate isn't *important*, Pat—rise above it, there's so
much *else*. Try to concentrate on *that*.' He wanted to help her. It made
things so difficult for him if she wouldn't come along but kept drifting
off loosely in some other direction, obliging him to drop things and go
after her since she seemed so uncontrolled, dangerously so. He couldn't
meet people, work on his thesis, do anything. He had never imagined
she could be a burden—not the companion and fellow gypsy she had
so fairly promised to be. She came of plain, strong farmer stock—she
ought to have some of that blood in her, strong, simple and capable.
Why wasn't she capable? He held his hand to her temple—it throbbed
hard. They sat sipping iced coffee in a very small, very dark restaurant
that smelt, somehow, of railway soot.

'I must try,' she said, flatly and without conviction.

That afternoon she went round the antique shops of New Delhi,
determined to take an interest in Indian art and culture. She left the
shopping arcade after an hour, horror rising in her throat like vomit.
She felt pursued by the primitive, the elemental and barbaric, and kept
rubbing her fingers together nervously, recalling those great heavy
bosoms of bronze and stone, the hips rounded and full as water-pots,
the flirtatious little bells on ankles and bellies, the long, sly eyes that
curved out of the voluptuous stone faces, not unlike those of the

shopkeepers themselves with their sibilant, inviting voices. Then the gods they showed her, named for her, with their flurry of arms, their stamping feet, their blazing, angered eyes and flying locks, all thunder and lightning, revenge and menace. Scraping the papery tips of her fingers together, she hurried through the dust back to the hotel. Back on her bed, she wept into her pillow for the lost home, for apple trees and cows, for red barns and swallows, for icecream sodas and drive-in movies, all that was innocent and sweet and lost, lost, lost.

'I'm just not sophisticated enough for you,' she gulped over the iced lemon tea David brought her. It was the first time she mentioned the disparity in their backgrounds—it had never seemed to matter before. Laying it bare now was like digging the first rift between them, the first division of raw, red clay. It frightened them both. 'I expect you knew about such things—you must have learnt them in college. You know I only went to high school and stayed home after that—'

'Darling,' he said, with genuine pain and tenderness, and could not go on. His tastes would not allow him to, or his scruples: the vulgarity appalled him as much as the pain. 'Do take a shower and have a shampoo, Pat. We're going out—'

'No, no, no,' she moaned in anguish, putting away the iced tea and falling onto her pillow.

'But to quite different people this time, Pat. To see a social worker—I mean, Sharma's wife is a social worker. She'll show you something quite different. I know it'll interest you.'

'I couldn't bear it,' she wept, playing with the buttons of her dress like a child.

But they did prove different. The Delhi intellectual was poorer than the Bombay intellectual, for one thing. He lived in a small, airless flat with whitewashed walls and a divan and bits of folk art. He served dinner in cheap, bright ceramic ware. Of course there was the inevitable long-haired intellectual—either journalist or professor—who sat cross-legged on the floor and held forth, abusively, on the crassness of the Americans, to David's delight and Pat's embarrassment. But Sharma's wife was actually a new type, to Pat. She was a genuine social worker, trained, and next morning, having neatly tucked the night before under the divan, she took Pat out to see a milk centre, a crèche, a nursery school, clinics and dispensaries, some housed in cow sheds, others in ruined tombs. Pat saw workers' babies asleep like cocoons in hammocks slung from tin sheds on building sites; she saw children with kohl-rimmed eyes solemnly eating their free lunches out of brass containers, and schools where children wrote painstakingly on wooden boards with reed pens and the teacher sneezed brown snuff sneezes at her. It was different in content. It was the same in effect. Her feet dragged, dustier by the hour. Her hair was like string on her shoulders. When she met David in the evening, at the hotel, he was red from the sun, like a well-ripened tomato, longing to talk, to tell, to ask and question, while she drooped tired, dusty, stringy, dry, trying to revive herself, for his sake, with little sips of some iced drink but feeling quite surely that life was shrivelling up inside her. She never spoke of apple trees or barns, of popcorn or drug stores, but he saw them in her eyes, more remote and faint every day. Her eyes had been so blue, now they were fading, as if the memory, the feel of apple trees and apples were fading from her. He panicked.

'We'd better go to the hills for a while,' he said: he did not want murder on his hands. 'Sharma said June is bad, very bad, in Delhi. He says everyone who can goes to the hills. Well, we can. Let's go, Pat.'

She looked at him dumbly with her fading eyes, and tried to smile. She thought of the way the child at the hospital had smiled after the doctor had finished painting her burns with gentian violet and given her a plastic doll. It had been a cheap, cracked pink plastic doll and the child had smiled at it through the gentian violet, its smile stamped in, or cut out, in that face still taut with pain, as by a machine. Pat had known that face would always be in pain, and the smile would always be cut out as by the machine of charity, mechanically. The plastic doll and the gentian violet had been incidental.

At the airlines office, the man could only find them seats on the plane to Manali, in the Kulu Valley. To Manali they went.

Not, however, by plane, for there were such fierce sandstorms sweeping through Delhi that day that no planes took off, and they went the three hundred miles by bus instead. The sandstorm did not spare the highway or the bus—it tore through the cracked windows and buried passengers and seats under the yellow sand of the Rajasthan desert. The sun burnt up the tin body of the bus till it was a great deal hotter inside than out in the sun. Pat sat stone-still, as though she had been beaten unconscious, groping with her eyes only for a glimpse of a mango grove or an avenue of banyans, instinctively believing she would survive only if she could find and drink in their dark, damp shade. David kept his eyes tightly shut behind his glare glasses. Perspiration poured from under his hair down his face, cutting rivers through the map of dust. The woman in the seat behind his was sick all the way up the low hills to Bilaspur. In front of him a small child wailed without stop while its mother ate peanuts and jovially threw the shells over her shoulder into his lap. The bus crackled with sand, peanut shells and explosive sounds from the protesting engine. There was a stench of diesel oil, of vomit, of perspiration and stale food such as he had never believed could exist—it was so thick. The bus was long past its prime but rattled, roared, shook and vibrated all the way through the desert, the plains, the hills, to Mandi where it stopped for a tea-break in a rest house under some eucalyptus trees in which cicadas trilled hoarsely. Then it plunged, bent on suicide, into the Beas river gorge.

After one look down the vertical cliff-side of slipping, crumbling slate ending in the wild river tearing through the narrow gorge in a torrent of ice-green and white spray, David's head fell back against the seat, lolled there loosely, and he muttered 'This is the end, Pat, my girl, I'm afraid it's the end.'

'But it's cooler,' fluted a youthful voice in a rising inflection, and David's head jerked with foolish surprise. Who had spoken? He turned to his wife and found her leaning out of the window, her strings of hair flying back at him in the breeze. She turned to him her excited face—dust-grimed and wan but with its eyes alive and observant. 'I can feel the spray—*cold* spray, David. It's better than a shower or air-conditioning or even a drink. Do just feel it.'

But he was too baffled and stunned and slain to feel anything at all. He sat slumped, not daring to watch the bus take the curves of that precarious path hewn through cliffs of slate, poised above the river that hurtled and roared over the black rocks and dashed itself against the mountainside. He was not certain what exactly would happen— whether the overhanging slate would come crashing down upon them, burying them alive, or if they would lurch headlong into the Beas and be dashed to bits on the rocks—but he had no doubt that it would be one or the other. In the face of this certainty, Pat's untimely revival seemed no more than a pathetic footnote.

To Pat, being fanned to life by that spray-spotted breeze, no such possibility occurred. She was watching the white spray rise and spin over the ice-green river and break upon the gleaming rocks, looking out for small sandy coves where pink oleanders bloomed and banana trees hung their limp green flags, exclaiming with delight at the small birds that skimmed the river like foam—feeling curiosity, pleasure and amusement stir in her for the first time since she had landed in India.

She no longer heard the retching of the woman behind them or the faint mewing of the exhausted child in front. Peanut shells slipped into her shoes and out of them. The stench of fifty perspiring passengers was lost in the freshness of the mountains. Up on the ridge, if she craned her neck, she could see the bunched needles of pine trees flashing.

When they emerged from the gorge into the sunlight, apricot-warm and mild, of the Kulu valley, she sat back with a contented sigh and let the bus carry them alongside the now calm and wide river Beas, through orchards in which little apples knobbed the trees, past flocks of royal mountain goats and their blanketed shepherds striding ahead with the mountaineer's swing, up into the hills of Manali, its deodar forests indigo in the evening air and the snow-streaked rocks of the Rohtang Pass hovering above them, an incredible distance away.

Then they were disgorged, broken sandals, shells, hair, rags, children and food containers, into the Manali bazaar, and the bus conductor swung himself onto the roof of the bus and hurled down their bags and boxes. David was on his knees, picking up the pieces of his broken suitcase and holding them together. The crying child was fed hot fritters his father had fetched from a wayside food stall. The vomiting woman squatted, holding her head in her hands, and a *pai* dog sniffed at her in curiosity and consolation. A big handsome man with a pigtail and a long turquoise ear-ring came up to Pat with an armful of red puppies, his teeth flashing in a cajoling smile. 'Fifty *rupees*,' he murmured, and raised it to 'Eighty' as soon as Pat reached out to fondle the smallest of them. Touts and pimps, ubiquitously small and greasy, piped around David 'Moonlight Hotel, plumbing and flush toilet,' and 'Hotel Paradise, non-vegetarian and best view, sir.'

David, holding his suitcase in his arms, looked over the top of their heads and at the mountain peaks, as if for succour. Then his face tilted down at them palely and he shook his head, his eyes quite empty. 'Let's go, Pat,' he sighed, and she followed him up through the bazaar for he had, of course, made bookings and they had rooms at what had been described to them as an 'English boarding house'.

It was on the hillside, set in a sea of apple trees, and they had to walk through the bazaar to it, nudging past puppy-sellers, women who had spread amber and coral and bronze prayer bells on the pavement, stalls in which huge pans of milk boiled and steamed and fritters jumped up and hissed, and holiday crowds that stood about eating, talking and eyeing the newcomers.

'Jesus,' David said in alarm, 'the place is full of hippies.'

Pat looked at the faces they passed then and saw that the crowd outside the baker's was indeed one of fair men and women, even if they seemed to be beggars. Some were dressed like Indian gurus, in loincloths or saffron robes, with beads around their necks, others as gypsies in pantaloons or spangled skirts, some in plain rags and tatters. All were barefoot and had packs on their backs, and one or two had silent, stupefied babies astride their hips. 'Why,' she said, watching one woman with a child approach an Indian couple with her empty hand outstretched, 'they might be Americans!' David shuddered and turned up a dusty path that went between the deodar trees to the red-roofed building of the boarding house. But several hippies were climbing the same path, not to the boarding house but vanishing into the forest, or crossing the wooden bridge over the river into the meadows beyond. Americans, Europeans, here in Manali, at the end of the world—what were they doing? she wondered. Well, what was *she* doing? Ah, she'd come to try and live again. She threw back her shoulders and took in lungfuls of the clear, cold air and it washed through her like water, cleansing and pure. Someone in a red cap was sawing wood outside the boarding house, she saw, and blue smoke curled out of its chimney as in a Grandma Moses painting. There was a sound of a rushing stream below. A cuckoo called. Above the tips of the immense deodars the sky was a clear turquoise, an evening colour, without heat although still distilled with sunlight. Dog roses bloomed open and white on the hillside. She tried to clasp David's arm with joy but he was holding onto the suitcase which had broken its locks and burst open and he could not spare her a finger.

'But David,' she coaxed, 'it's going to be lovely.'

'I'm glad,' he said, white-lipped, and pitched the suitcase onto the wooden veranda at the feet of the proprietor who sat benignly as a Buddha on a wooden upright chair, in a white pullover and string cap, gazing down at them with an expression of pity under his bland welcome.

The room was clean, although bare but for two white iron bedsteads and a dressing table with a small yellow mirror. Its window overlooked a yard in which brown hens pecked and climbed onto overturned buckets and wood piles, and wild daisies bloomed, as white and yellow as fresh bread and butter, around a water pump. The bathroom had no tub but a very well polished brass bucket, a green plastic mug and, holy of holies, a flush toilet that worked, however reluctantly and complainingly. The proprietor, apple-cheeked and woolly—was he an Anglo-Indian, European or Indian? Pat could not tell—sent them tea and Glaxo biscuits on a tin tray. They sat on the bed and drank the black, bitter tea, sighing 'Well, it's *hot*.'

But Pat could not stay still. Once she had examined the drawers of the dressing table and read scraps from the old newspaper with which they were lined, turned on the taps in the bathroom and washed, changed into her Delhi slippers and drunk her tea, she wanted to go out and 'Explore!' David looked longingly at the clean white, although thin and darned, sheets stretched on the beds and the hairy brown blanket so competently tucked in, but she was adamant.

'We can't waste a minute,' she said urgently, for some unknown reason. 'We mustn't waste this lovely evening.'

He did not see how it would be wasted if they were to lie down on their clean beds, wait for hot water to be brought for their baths and then sleep, but realized it would be somehow craven and feeble for him to say so when she stood at the window with something strong and active in the swing of her hips and a fervour in her newly pink and washed face that he had almost forgotten was once her natural expression—in a different era, a different land.

'We're surrounded by apple trees,' she enticed him, 'and I think, I *think* I heard a cuckoo.'

'Why not?' he grumbled, and followed her out onto the wooden veranda where the proprietor continued to look comfortable on that upright chair, and down the garden path to the road that took them into the forest.

It was a deodar forest. The trees were so immensely old and tall that while the lower boughs already dipped their feet into the evening, the tops still brushed the late sunlight, and woolly yellow beams slanted through the black trunks as through the pillars of a shadowy cathedral. The turf was soft and uneven under their feet, wild iris bloomed in clumps and ferns surrounded rocks that were conspicuously stranded here and there. Pat fell upon the wild strawberries that grew with a careless luxuriance—small, seed-ridden ones she found sweet. The few people they passed, village men and women wrapped in white Kulu blankets with handsome stripes, had faces that were brown and russet, calm and pleasant, although they neither smiled nor greeted Pat and David, merely observed them in passing. Pat liked them for that—for not whining or wheedling or begging or sneering as the crowds in Bombay and Delhi had done—but simply conferring on them a status not unlike their own. 'Such independence,' she glowed, 'so self-contained. True mountain people, you know.'

David looked at her a little fearfully, not having noted such a surge of Vermont pride in his country wife before. 'Do you feel one of them yourself?' he asked, a little tentatively.

He was startled by the positive quality of the laugh that rang out of her, by the way she threw out her arms in an open embrace. 'Why, *sure*,' she cried, explosively, and sprang over a small stream that ran over the moss like a trickle of mercury. 'Look, here's dear old Jack in the pulpit,' she cried, darting at some ferns from which protruded that rather sinister gentleman, striped and hooded, David thought, like a silent cobra. She plucked it and strode on, her hair no longer like string but like drawn toffee, now catching fire in the sunbeams, now darkening in the shade. After a while, she remarked 'It isn't much like the friendly Vermont woods, really. It's more like a grand medieval cathedral, isn't it?'

'An observation several before you have made on forests,' he remarked, a trifle drily. 'Is one permitted to sit in your cathedral or can one only kneel?' he asked, lowering himself onto a rock. 'Jesus, is my bottom sore from that bus ride.'

She laughed, threw the Jack in the pulpit into his lap and flung herself on the grass at his feet. And so they might have stopped and talked and laughed a bit before going back to an English supper and their fresh, clean beds but, swinging homewards hand-in-hand, they came suddenly upon a strange edifice on a slope in the forest, like a great pagoda built of wood, heavy and dark timber, rough-hewn and sculpted as a stone temple might be, with trees rearing about it in the twilight, shaggy and dark, like Himalayan bears.

'Could it be a temple?' Pat wondered, for the temples she had so far seen had been bursting at the seams with loud pilgrims and busy beggars and priests, affairs of garish paint and plaster, clatter of bells and malodorous marigolds. A still temple in a silent forest—she had quite lost hope of finding such a thing in this overpopulated land.

'We might go in,' David said since she was straining at his hand and, after hovering at the threshold for a bit, they slipped off their sandals and crossed its high wooden plinth.

It was very much darker inside, like a cave scooped out of a tree trunk. The floor, however, was of clay, hard-packed and silky. A shelf of rock projected from the dark wall and a lamp hung from it with a few flowers bright around its wick. It had that minute been blown out by a tall woman with an appropriately wooden face who wore her hair in a tight plait around her head. She lifted her hand, swung only once but vigorously a large bell, and left with a quick stride, barely glancing at them as she went. They bent to study the stone slab beneath the gently smoking lamp and could only just make out the outline of a giant footprint on it. That was all by way of an image and there were neither offerings nor money-box, neither priest nor pilgrim around.

They came out in silence and walked away slowly, as though afraid something would jump out at them from it, or from the forest—they were so much a part of each other, that forest and its temple.

Finally they emerged from the trees and were within sight of the red roof and chimney pot of the English boarding house amongst its apple trees, far below the snow-streaked black ridges of the mountain pass, still pale and luminous against the darkening sky, at once threatening and protective in its attitude, like an Indian god.

'I'm sure I've never seen anything like that before,' Pat murmured then.

'What, not even in Vermont?' he teased, but received no answer.

They ate their dinner in silence, Pat hugely although reflectively, while David sipped a cup of soup and felt as peevish as a neglected invalid.

Perhaps it was only the smallness of Manali—barely a town, merely an overgrown village, a place for shepherds to halt on their way up to the Pass and over it to Lahaul, and apple growers to load their fruit onto lorries bound for the plains, suddenly struck and swollen by a seasonal avalanche of tourists and their vehicles—that led Pat so quickly to know it and feel it as home. It presented no difficulty, as other Indian towns of her acquaintance had, it was innocent and open and if it did not clamorously and cravenly invite, it did not shut its doors either— it had none to shut. It lay in the cup of the valley, the river and forest to one side, bright paddy fields and apple orchards to the other, open and sunlit, small and easy.

She bought herself a cloth bag to sling over her shoulder and with it strode down the single street of Manali in her friendlily squeaking sandals. She stopped at the baker's for ginger biscuits and to smile, somewhat tentatively, at the hippies who stood barefoot at the door, begging for loaves of bread from Indian tourists who seemed as embarrassed as stupefied to discover that it was not only Indians who could beg, and always gave them far more than they did to poorer

Indian beggars. She eyed the vegetable stalls and the baskets of ripe fruit on the pavements with envy, wishing she could set up house and do her own marketing. This walk through the bazaar invariably took her to the Tibetan quarter, a smelly lane that took off to one side. Pat could not explain why she had to visit it daily. David refused to accompany her after one visit. He could not face the open drain that one had to jump over in order to enter one of its shops. He could not face the yellow *pai* dogs and the abjectly filthy children one had to pass, nor the extraordinary odour of the shops in which sweaty cast-away woollens discarded by returning mountaineers and impecunious hippies made soft furry mountains along with Tibetan rugs, exquisitely chased silver candlesticks and bronze icons that democratically lived together with tawdry plastic and glass jewellery, all presided over by stolid women with faces carved intricately out of hard wood. So David thought them. To Pat they were wise and inscrutable old ladies who parted with objects of great value at pathetically low prices. Pushing through old dresses and woollen pullovers that hung from the rafters, she knelt on worn rugs and shuffled through the baubles and beads in order to pick out a lama carved in wood with the elegance of extreme simplicity, bits of turquoise, a ball of amber like solidified honey, a string of prayer beads as cool as river pebbles between her fingers . . .

'Junk, junk, junk,' David groaned as she spread them out on the bed for him to see. 'Couldn't you walk in some other direction? Must it be that bloody bazaar every day?'

'It isn't,' she protested. 'I walk all over. Just come with me and I'll show you,' she offered, but rather indifferently, and he saw that she did not care at all if he came with her or not, while in Bombay or Delhi she would have cared passionately. This needled him into closing his typewriter, laying his papers in the dressing table drawer and coming with her for once, stepping gingerly over the goat droppings and puddles in the yard, out onto the dusty road.

He found she did know, as she had claimed to, every path and stream and orchard in the place for miles, and was determined to prove it to him. To his horror, she even waved and beamed at the drug-struck, meditative hippies as they swung past the Happy Café where they invariably gathered to eat, talk, play on flutes and gaze into space in that dim, dusty interior where a chart hung on the wall offering the table d'hôte: daily it was Brown Rice, Beans and Custard. What hippy had carried his macroculture to Manali, David wondered, pinning it to the wall above the counter where flies circled plates of yellow sweetmeats and Britannia Biscuit packets? The faces of the pale Europeans who gathered there seemed to him distressingly vacant, their postures defeated and vague, but when he mentioned this to Pat, she was scornful.

'You're just making up your mind about them without really looking,' she claimed. 'Now look at that man in white robes—doesn't he look like Christ? And it isn't just the bone structure. And see that young man who's always laughing? That's his pet loris on his shoulder. There's another I see in that bazaar sometimes, who has a pet eagle, but he lives way off in the mountains. It's true they don't talk much— but you often see them laugh. Or else they just sit and think. Isn't that beautiful, to be able to do that? I think it's beautiful.'

'I think they're stoned,' he said, happy to leave the Happy Café to its shadowy, macrocultural bliss and climb the steep hill into the deodar forest. 'Lord, must we go to the temple *again?*' he moaned, as she led him forward, having already seen it till he could no longer keep his yawns from cracking his jaws apart while he had again to sit outside, on some excruciating roots, and wait for his wife to pay it a ritual visit. He was not really sure what she did in there, nor did he wish to know. Surely she didn't pray? No, she came out looking much too jolly for that.

But no, today she was taking him for a walk and for a walk she would take him, she said, with that new positivism in her jawline and swing of her arms that he rather feared. She led him along a stream in which a man and a woman in gypsy dress—and bald patch, and red curls, respectively—were scrubbing some incredibly blackened pots and pans, like children at play—'Aren't they charming?' Pat enquired, as if of a painted landscape tastefully peopled with just a few rural figures, and David retorted 'Damn vagabonds'—and down lanes that wound through orchards overhung with apricot trees from which fruit dropped ripe and soft onto the stones under their feet, past farm houses screened by daisies and day lilies from which issued bursts, sometimes of tubercular coughing and sometimes of abstract, atonal music, both curiously foreign, and then uphill, beside a stream that leaped over the rocks like a startled hare, white and flashing between ferns and boulders, to a village of large, square stone and wood houses—the ground floors smaller, built solidly of square blocks of stone, the upper floors larger, their elaborately carved wooden balconies overhanging the courtyards in which cows ate the apricots swept up in hills for them, and children climbed crackling haystacks. Apricot trees festooned with unhealthy-

looking mistletoe shaded that village and Pat stopped to ask an old
man in a blue cap if he had some to sell. They waited in his courtyard,
amongst dung pats and milk pails, standing close to the stone wall to
let a herd of mountain goats go by, silk-shawled, tip-tapping and bleat-
voiced as a party of tipsy ladies, while the man climbed his tree and
plucked them a capful. Eating them out of their pockets—they proved
not quite ripe and not as sweet as those sold in the bazaar, but Pat
wouldn't say so and David did—they continued uphill, out of the village (David glimpsed a lissome brunette in purple robes and biblical
sandals climbing down to the stream but averted his eyes) into the
deodar forest again. David was so grateful for its blue shade, and so
overfull with bucolic scenes and apricots, that he was ready to sprawl.
His wife sprang on ahead, calling, and then he saw her destination.
Another temple. He might have known.

Catching up with her, he found Pat fondling the ears of a big tawny
dog that had come barking out of the temple courtyard, with familiar-
ity and a wag of its royal tail. 'We can't go in, it's shut,' she reassured
him, 'but do see,' she coaxed, and led him through the courtyard and
eventually he had to admit that even as Kulu temples went, this one
in Nasogi was a pearl. It was no larger than Hansel and Gretel's hut,
its roof sloping steeply to the ground, edged with carved icicles of
wood. Its doors and beams were massive, but every bit was elegantly
carved and fitted. There was a paved courtyard opening into others,
all open and inviting, possibly for pilgrims, and around it a grandeur
of trees. David lowered himself onto a root, put his arms around his
knees, tilted his head to one side and said 'Well yes, you have something
here, Pat, I'll give that to you.'

She glowed. 'I think it's the most magical spot on earth, if you'd like
to know.'

'Aren't you funny?' he commented. 'I take you the length and breadth
of India, I show you palaces and museums, jewels and tiger skins—and
all the time you were hankering after a forest and an orchard and a
village. Little Gretchen you, little Martha, hmm?'

'Do you think that's all I see in it?' she enquired, and he did not
quite like, quite trust her sudden gravity that had something too set
about it, too extreme, like that of a fanatic. But what was she being so
fanatical about—the country life? A mountain idyll? Surely that was
obtainable and possible without fanaticism.

She gave only a hint—it was obvious she had thought nothing out
yet, however much she had felt. 'This isn't like the rest of India, Dave.

It's come to me as a relief, as an escape from India. You know, down in those horrible cities, I'd gotten to think of India as one horrible temple, bursting, *crawling* with people—people on their knees, *hopeless* people—and those horrible idols towering over them with their hundred legs and hundred heads—all *horrible* . . .' (David, tiring of that one adjective, clicked his tongue like an impatient pedagogue, making her veer, only slightly, then return to her track, sifting dry deodar needles through nervous brown fingers) . . . 'and then, to walk through the forest and come upon this—this little shrine—it's like escaping from all those Hindu horrors—it's like coming out into the open and breathing naturally again, without fear. That's what I feel here, you know,' she said with a renewed burst of confidence, '—without *fear*. And you can see that's something I share with, or perhaps have just learnt from, the mountain people here. That's what I admire so in them, in the Tibetans. I don't mean the ones down in the bazaar—those are just like the greasy Indian masses, whining and cajoling and sneering—oh, *horrible*—but the ones one sees on the mountain roads. They're upright, they're honest, independent. They have such a strong swing and a stride to their walk—they walk like gods amongst those crawling, cringing masses. And they haven't those furtive Indian faces either—eyes sliding this way and that, expressions showing and then closing up—*their* faces are all open, and they laugh and sing. All they have is a black old kettle and a pack of wood on their backs, rope sandals and a few sheep, but they laugh and sing and go striding up the mountains like—like lords. I watch them all the time, I admire them, you know, and I got to thinking what makes them so different? I wondered if it was their religion. I feel, being Buddhists, they're different from the Hindus, and it must be something in their belief that gives them this—this fearlessness. When I come to this shrine and sit and think things out quietly, I can see where they get their strength from, and their joy . . .'

But here he could stand it no longer. 'Pat, Pat,' he cried, jumping up and striking his sides. 'You're all confused, Pat, you're so muddled, so hopelessly muddled! My dear, addled wife, Pat!'

She frowned and squinted, her fist closed on a handful of needles, ceased to sift them. 'What do you mean?' she asked, in a tight, closed voice.

'What do I mean? Don't you know? You're sitting outside a *Hindu* shrine, this is a *Hindu* temple, and you're making it out to be a source of Buddhist strength and serenity! Don't you even know that the Kulu

Valley has a Hindu population, and the shrines you see here are Hindu shrines?' He whooped with laughter, he pulled her to her feet and dragged her homeward, laughing so much that every time she opened her mouth to protest, he drowned her out with his roars of derision. In the end, that laughter gave him a headache.

He tired of his thesis—the notes he had collected while in Bombay and Delhi and the typescript he was now preparing—long before it was done. The whole job had begun to seem totally irrelevant. Ramming the cover onto the little flat Olivetti, he pushed his legs out so that the waste-paper basket went sprawling, and yawned angrily. The cock on the woodpile at the window caught his eye and gave a wicked wink, but David looked away almost without registering it. Where was Pat?

That was the perennial question these days. Pat was never there. What was more, he no longer asker her where she had been when she appeared for meals or to throw herself down on the bed for the night, her feet raw and dirty from walking in sandals, her cloth bag flung onto the floor. (Once he saw a ragged copy of the Dhammapada slip out of it and hastily looked away: the idea of his poor, addled wife poring over ancient Buddhist texts embarrassed him acutely.) He merely eyed her with accusation and with distaste: she was playing a role he had not engaged her to play, she was making a fool of herself, she was embarrassing him, she was absolutely outrageous. As she grew browner from the outdoor life and her limbs sturdier from the exercise, it seemed to him she was losing the fragility, the gentleness that he had loved in her, that she was growing into some tough, sharp countrywoman who might very well carry loads, chop wood, haul water and harvest, but was scarcely fit to be his wife—his, David's, the charming and soci-ally graceful young David of Long Island upbringing—and her move-ments were marked by rough angles that jarred on him, her voice, when she bothered at all to reply to his vague questions, was brusque and abrupt. It was clear there was no meeting-point between them any more—he would have considered it lowering in status to make a move towards her and she clearly had no interest in meeting him half-way, or anywhere.

He had not cared for the answers she had given him when he had first, mistakenly, asked. On coming upon her one morning, while slouching through the bazaar to post a packet of letters, in, of all places, the Happy Café, round-shouldered on a bench, drinking something

cloudy out of a thick glass, in the company of those ragged pilgrims
with the incongruously fair heads, he had questioned her with some
heat.

'Yes, they're friends of mine,' she shrugged, standing with her
new stolidity in the centre of the room to which he had insisted on
taking her back. 'I could have told you about them earlier if you'd
asked. There's no need for you to spy.'

'Don't be ridiculous,' he snapped. 'Spy on *you*? What for? Why
should it interest me what you do with yourself while I'm slogging
away in here—'

'Then why ask?' she snapped back.

His curiosity was larger than his distaste in the beginning. Over
dinner he asked her the questions he had earlier resolved not to ask
and, pleased with the big plateful of food before her, she had talked
pleasantly about the Californian couple she had taken up with, and
told him the story of their erratic and precipitous voyage from the
forests of Big Sur to those of the Kulu Valley, via Afghanistan and
Nepal, in search of a guru they had indeed found but now discarded
in favour of communal life, vegetarianism and *bhang* which seemed
to them a smooth and gentle path to earthly nirvana.

'Nirvana on earth!' he snorted. 'That's a contradiction in terms,
don't you know?' Then, seeing her nostrils flare dangerously, went on
hastily, but no more wisely, 'Is that what you were drinking down
there in that joint, Pat?'

She gave a whoop of delight on seeing the pudding—caramel
custard—and buried her nose in a plateful with greed. 'Gee, all this
walking makes me hungry,' she apologized, 'and sleepy. Jesus, *how*
sleepy.' She went straight to bed.

On another and even more uncomfortable occasion, he had found
her while out taking the air after a particularly dull and boring day at
the typewriter, in the park in front of the Moonlight Hotel and Rama's
Bakery where the hippies were wont to gather, some even to sleep at
night, rolled in their blankets on the grass. One of the Indian gurus
who held court there was seated, lotus style, under a sun-dressed lime
tree, with an admiring crowd of fair and tattered hippies about him,
his wife Pat as cross-legged, as smiling and as tattered as the rest. He
was too far away to hear what they were saying but it seemed more as
if they were bandying jokes—what jokes could East and West possibly
share?—than meditating or discoursing on theology. What particularly
anguished him was the sight of the Indian tourists who had made an

outer circle around this central core of seekers of nirvana and bliss-through-*bhang*, as if this were one of the sights of the Kulu Valley that they had paid to see. They stood about with incredulous faces, smiling uneasily, exchanging whispered asides with one another, exactly as if they were watching some disquieting although amusing play. There was condescension and, in some cases, pity in their expressions and attitudes that he could not bear to see directed at his fellow fair-heads, much less at his own wife. He turned and almost raced back to the boarding house.

That evening he had tried to question her again but she was tired, vague, merely brushed the hair from her face and murmured 'Yes, that's Guru Dina Nath. He's so sweet—so gay—so—' and went up to bed. He sniffed the air in the room suspiciously. Was it *bhang*? But he wouldn't know what it smelt like if it were. He imagined it would be sweetish and the air in their room was sour, acid. He wrenched the window open, with violence, hoping to wake her. It did not.

The day he gave up questioning her or pursuing her was when she came in, almost prancing, he thought, like some silly mare, burbling, 'Do you remember Nasogi, David? That darling village where we ate apricots? You remember its temple like a little dolls' house? Well, I met some folks who live in a commune right next to it—a big attic over a cow shed actually, but it overlooks the temple and has an orchard all around it, so it's real nice. Edith—she's from Harlem—took me across, and I had coffee with some of them—'

'Sure it was coffee?' he snarled and, turning his back, hurled himself at the typewriter with such frenzy that she could not make herself heard. She sat on her bed, chewing her lip for a while, then got up and went out again. What she had planned to say to him was put away, like an unsuccessful gift.

She kept out of his way after that, and made no further attempts to take him along with her on the way to nirvana. When, at breakfast, he told her, 'It's time I got back to Delhi. I've got more material to research down there and I can't sit here in your valley and contemplate the mountains any more. I plan to book some seats on that plane for Delhi.'

She was shocked, although she made a stout attempt to disguise it, and he was gratified to see this. 'When d'you want to leave?' she asked, spitting a plum seed into her fist.

'Next Monday, I think,' he said.

She said nothing and disappeared for the rest of the day. She was out again before he'd emerged from his bath next morning, and he had to go down to the bus depot by himself, hating every squalid step of the way: the rag market where Tibetans sold stained and soiled imported clothes to avid Indian tourists and played dice in the dust while waiting for customers, the street where snot-gobbed urchins raced and made puppies scream, only just managing to escape from under roaring lorries and stinking buses. He directed looks of fury at the old beggar without a nose or fingers who solicited him for alms and at the pig-tailed Tibetan with one turquoise ear-ring who tried to sell him a mangy pup. 'We're going to get out of here,' he ground out at them through his teeth, and they smiled at him with every encouragement. The booking office was, however, not yet open for business and he was obliged to wait outside the bus depot which was the filthiest spot in the whole bazaar. He stood slouching against a wooden pillar, watching a half-empty bus push through a herd of worriedly bleating sheep and then come up, boiling and steaming, its green-painted, rose-wreathed sides almost falling apart with the effort. It groaned the last few yards of the way and expired at his feet, with a hiss of steam that made its bonnet rise inches into the air.

The driver, a wiry young Sikh who had hung his turban on a peg by the seat and wore only a purple handkerchief over his top-knot, leaped out and raced around to fling open the bonnet before the contraption exploded. His assistant, who had jumped down from the back door and vanished into the nearest shop, a grocer's, now came running out with an enamel jug of water which the driver grabbed from his hands and, before David's incredulous eyes, threw onto the radiator.

The next thing that David knew was that an explosion of steam and boiling water had hit him, hit the driver, the assistant and he didn't know how many bystanders—he couldn't see, he flung his hands to his face, but too late, he was on fire, he was howling—everyone was howling. Someone grabbed his shoulders, someone shouted 'Sir, sir, are you blind? Are you blind?' and he roared 'Yes, damn you, I'm blind, *blind*.' And where was Pat, his bloody useless wife, where was *she*? Here was he, blinded, scalded, being dragged through the streets by strangers, madmen, all trying to carry him, all babbling as at a universal holocaust.

'There, try opening your eyes now. I think you can, son, just try it,' a blessedly American voice spoke, and prised away his hands from his face. In his desperation to see the owner of this blessed voice, David allowed his hands to be loosed from his face and actually opened his eyes—an act he had never thought to perform again—and gazed upon the American doctor with the auburn sideburns and the shirt of blue and brown checked wool as at a vision of St Michael at the golden gates. 'That's wonderful, just wonderful,' beamed the gorgeous man, solid and middle-aged and wondrously square. 'You haven't lost your eyes, see. Now let me just paint those burns for you and you'll leave here as fit as a fiddle, see if you don't . . .' So he burbled on, in that rich, heavy voice from the Middle West, and David sat back as helpless as a baby, and felt those large dry hands with their strong growth of ginger hair gently dab at his face, bringing peace and blessing in their wake. He was the American mission hospital doctor but to David he was God himself on an inspection visit mercifully timed to coincide with David's accident.

It was David's accident. He quite forgot to ask about the driver or his brainless help or the hapless bystanders who had been standing too close to the boiling radiator. He merely sat there, limp and helpless, feeling the doctor's voice flow over him like a stream of American milk. And then he was actually handed a glass of milk—Horlicks, the doctor called it, sweet and hot, and he sipped it with bowed head like a child, afraid he would cry now that the agony was over and the convalescence so sweetly begun.

'It's the shock,' the doctor was saying kindly. 'Your eyes are quite safe, son, and the burns are superficial—luckily—it's just the shock,' and he patted David on the back with those ginger-tufted hands that were so square and sure. 'We see all kinds of accidents up here, you know. Yesterday it was one of those crazy hippies who had to be brought in on a stretcher. He'd fallen off a mountain. Now can you credit that? A grown man just going and falling off a mountain like he was a kid? He'd broken both legs, see. I had to send my assistant with him to Delhi. They'll have quite a time getting him on his feet again but the Holy Family Hospital tries its best. Still,' he added, in the considerate manner of one who knows how to deal with a patient, 'yours sure is the most *unnecessary* accident we've had, I'll say that,' he declared, filling David with sweet pride. Bowing his head, he sipped his milk and drank in the doctor's kindly gossip. He tried to say 'Yeah, those hippies—they shouldn't be allowed—I don't see how they're allowed—' but his voice died away and the doctor shrugged tolerantly and laughed. 'It takes all kinds, you know, but they really are kids, they shouldn't be allowed out of their mamma's sight. How about another

drink of Horlicks? You think you can walk home now? Feel okay, son?'
David would have given a great deal to say he was not okay at all, that
he couldn't possibly walk home, that he wanted to stay and tell the
doctor all about Pat, how she had practically deserted him, and about
the unsavoury friends she had made here. He wanted to ask him to
speak to Pat, reason with her, return his wife to him, return his former
life to him. It made him weep, almost, to think that he was expected
to get up and walk out. He threw a look of anguish at the doctor as
he was seen down the rickety stairs to the bus depot, and did not
realize that no one could make out his expression through that coating
of gentian violet that coloured his entire face, neck and ears with an
extraordinary neon glow.

'My God, what's up with *you*?' screamed Pat when she came in, hours
later, and was struck still by shock.

He glared at her, exulting at having elicited such a response from
her. But a minute later he saw that she had collapsed against the door
frame, not with shock, but with laughter.

'What have you *done*, Dave?' she squealed. 'What made you do *that*?'

Harsh words were exchanged then. David, having lost his tight-
lipped control (that morning's sweet Horlicks had washed it away)
demanded roughly where she had been when he was standing in the
sun to buy tickets and getting scalded and very nearly blinded in the
process. Didn't she care about him, he wanted to know, and what *did*
she care about at all now? And she, revolted, she said, by his egoism
and conceit that didn't allow him to see beyond the tip of his nose—
what was wrong with him that he couldn't move out of the way of
a bus, for Christ's sake, didn't it just show that he saw nothing, noticed
nothing outside himself?—told him what she cared about. She had
found a place for herself in the commune at Nasogi. It was what she
was meant for, she realized—not going to parties with David, but to
live with other men and women who shared her beliefs. They were
going to live the simple life, wash themselves and their dishes in a
stream, cook brown rice and lentils, pray and meditate in the forest
and, at the end, perhaps, become Buddhists—'A Buddhist, you crack-
pot? In a Hindu temple?' he spluttered—but she continued calmly that
she was sure to find, in the end, something that could not be found
on the cocktail rounds of Delhi, Bombay or even, for that matter,
Long Island, but that she was positive existed here, in the forest, on
the mountains.

'What cocktail rounds? Are you trying to imply I'm a social gadabout, not a serious student of sociology, working on a thesis on which my entire career is based?'

'Working on a thesis?' she screeched derisively. 'Sociology? The idea of you, Dave, when you've never so much as looked, I mean really looked, into the soul, the *prana*, of the next man—is just too—' she spluttered to a stop, wildly threw her hair about her face and burst out 'You, you don't even know it's possible to find Buddha in a Hindu temple. Why, you can find him in a church, a forest, anywhere. Do you think he's as narrow-minded as *you*?' she flung at him, and the explosiveness with which this burst from her showed how his derision had cut into her, how it had festered in her.

The English boarding house was treated to much more hurling of American abuse that night, to throwing around of suitcases, to sounds of packing and dramatic partings and exits, and many heads leant out of the windows into the chalky moonlight to see Pat set off, striding through the daisy-spattered yard in her newly acquired hippy rags that whipped against her legs as she marched off, bag and prayer beads in hand, with never a backward look. There was no one, however, but the proprietor, bland and inscrutable as ever, to see David off next morning making a quieter, neater and sadder departure for Delhi, unconventional only on account of the brilliant purple hue of his face.

If the truth were to be told, he felt greater regret at having to arrive in Delhi with a face like a painted baboon's than to arrive without his wife.

The Lady from Guatemala

Friday afternoon about four o'clock, the week's work done, time to kill; the editor disliked this characterless hour when everyone except his secretary had left the building. Into his briefcase he had slipped some notes for a short talk he was going to give in a cheap London hall, worn by two generations of protest against this injustice or that, before he left by the night plane for Copenhagen. There his real lecture tour would begin and turn into a short holiday. Like a bored card player he sat shuffling his papers and resented that there was no one except his rude, hard-working secretary to give him a game.

The only company he had in his room—and it was a moody friend—was his portrait hanging behind him on the wall. He liked cunningly to draw people to say something reassuring about the picture. It was 'terribly good', as the saying is; he wanted to hear them say it lived up to him. There was a strange air of rivalry in it. It rather overdid the handsome mixture of sunburned satyrlike pagan and shady jealous Christian saint under the happy storm of white hair. His hair had been grey at thirty; at forty-seven, by a stroke of luck, it was silken white. His face was an actor's, the nose carved for dramatic occasions, the lips for the public platform. It was a face both elated and ravaged by the highest beliefs and doubts. He was energized by meeting this image in the morning and, enviously, he said goodbye to it at night. Its nights would be less tormented than his own. Now he was leaving it to run the paper in his absence.

'Here are your tickets,' his secretary breezed into the room. 'Copenhagen, Stockholm, Oslo, Berlin, Hamburg, Munich—the lot,' she said. She was mannerless to the point of being a curiosity.

She stepped away and wobbled her tongue in her cheek. She understood his restless state. She adored him; he drove her mad and she longed for him to go.

'Would you like to know what I've got outside?' she said. She had a malicious streak. 'A lady. A lady from Guatemala. Miss Mendoza. She has got a present for you. She worships you. I said you were busy. Shall I tell her to buzz off?'

The editor was proud of his tolerance in employing a girl so sportive and so familiar; her fair hair was thin and looked harassed, her spotty face set off the knowledge of his own handsomeness in face and behaviour.

'Guatemala! Of course I must see her!' he exclaimed. 'What *are* you thinking about? We ran three articles on Guatemala. Show her in.'

'It's your funeral,' said the girl and gave a vulgar click with her tongue. The editor was, in her words, 'a sucker for foreigners'; she was reminding him that the world was packed with native girls like herself as well.

All kinds of men and women came to see Julian Drood; politicians who spoke to him as if he were a meeting, quarrelling writers, people with causes, cranks and accusers, even criminals and the mad. They were opinions to him and he did not often notice what they were like. He knew they studied him and that they would go away boasting: 'I saw Julian Drood today and he said . . .' Still he had never seen any person quite like the one who now walked in. At first, because of her tweed hat, he thought she was a man and would have said she had a moustache. She was a stump, as square as a box, with tarry chopped off hair, heavy eyebrows and yellow eyes set in her sallow skin like cut glass. She looked like some unsexed and obdurate statement about the future—or was it the beginning?—of the human race, long in the body, short in the legs and made of wood. She was wearing on this hot day a thick, bottle-green velvet dress. Indian blood obviously; he had seen such women in Mexico. She put out a wide hand to him; it could have held a shovel; in fact she was carrying a crumpled brown-paper bag.

'Please sit down,' he said. A pair of heavy feet moved her with a surprisingly light skip to a chair. She sat down stiffly and stared without expression, like geography.

'I know you are a very busy man,' she said. 'Thank you for sparing a minute for an unknown person.' She looked formidably unknown.

The words were nothing; but the voice! He had expected Spanish or broken English of some grating kind, but instead he heard the small, whispering, birdlike monotone of a shy English child.

'Yes, I *am* very busy,' he said. 'I've got to give a talk in an hour and then I'm off to lecture in Copenhagen . . . What can I do for you?'

'Copenhagen,' she said, noting it.

'Yes, yes, yes,' said the editor. 'I'm lecturing on apartheid.'

There are people who listen; there are people upon whom anything said seems not to be heard but, rather, to be stamped or printed. She was also receiving the impress of the walls, the books, the desk, the carpet, the windows of the room, memorizing every object. At last, like a breathless child, she said: 'In Guatemala I have dreamed of this for years. I'm saying to myself, "Even if I could just see the *building* where it all happens!" I didn't dare think I would be able to *speak* to Julian Drood. It is like a dream to me. "If I see him I will tell him," I said, "what this building and what his articles have done for my country."'

'It's a bad building. Too small,' he said. 'We're thinking of selling it.'

'Oh no,' she said. 'I have flown across the ocean to see it. And to thank you.'

The word thank came out like a kiss.

'From Guatemala? To thank me?' The editor smiled.

'To thank you from the bottom of our hearts for those articles.' The little voice seemed to sing.

'So people read the paper in Guatemala,' said the editor, congratulating that country and moving a manuscript on to another pile on his desk.

'Only a few,' she said. 'The important few. You are keeping us alive in all these dark years. You are holding the torch of freedom burning. You are a beacon of civilization in our darkness.'

The editor sat taller in his chair. Certainly he was vain, but he was a good man. Virtue is not often rewarded. A nationalist? Or not? he wondered. He looked at the ceiling, where, as usual—for he knew everything—he found the main items of the Guatemalan situation. He ran over them like a tune on the piano. 'Financial colonialism,' he said, 'foreign monopoly, uprooted peasants, rise of nationalism, the dilemma of the mountain people, the problem of the coast. Bananas.'

'It is years since I've eaten a banana,' he said.

The woman's yellow eyes were not looking at him directly yet. She was still memorizing the room and her gaze now moved to his portrait. He was dabbling in the figures of the single-crop problem when she interrupted him.

'The women of Guatemala,' she said, addressing the portrait, 'will never be able to repay their debt to you.'

'The women?'

He could not remember; was there anything about women in those articles?

'It gives us hope. "Now", I am saying, "the world will listen",' she said. 'We are slaves. Man-made laws, the priests, bad traditions hold us down. *We* are the victims of apartheid, too.'

And now she looked directly at him.

'Ah,' said the editor, for interruptions bored him. 'Tell me about that.'

'I know from experience,' said the woman. 'My father was Mexican, my mother was an English governess. I know what she suffered.'

'And what do you *do?*' said the editor. 'I gather you are not married?'

At this sentence, the editor saw that something like a coat of varnish glistened on the woman's wooden face.

'Not after what I saw of my mother's life. There were ten of us. When my father had to go away on business, he locked her and all of us in the house. She used to shout for help from the window, but no one did anything. People just came down the street and stood outside and stared and then walked away. She brought us up. She was worn out. When I was fifteen, he came home drunk and beat her terribly. She was used to that, but this time she died.'

'What a terrible story. Why didn't she go to the Consul? Why—'

'He beat her because she had dyed her hair. She had fair hair and she thought if she dyed her hair black like the other women he went with, he would love her again,' said the childish voice.

'Because she dyed her hair?' said the editor.

The editor never really listened to astonishing stories of private life. They seemed frivolous to him. What happened publicly in the modern world was far more extravagant. So he only half listened to this tale. Quickly, whatever he heard turned into paragraphs about something else and moved on to general questions. He was wondering if Miss Mendoza had the vote and which party she voted for. Was there an Indian bloc? He looked at his watch. He knew how to appear to listen, to charm, ask a jolly question and then lead his visitors to the door before they knew the interview was over.

'It was a murder,' said the woman complacently.

The editor suddenly woke up to what she was saying.

'But you are telling me she was *murdered!*' he exclaimed.

She nodded. The fact seemed of no further interest to her. She was pleased she had made an impression. She picked up her paper bag and out of it she pulled a tin of biscuits and put it on his desk.

'I have brought you a present,' she said, 'with the gratitude of the women of Guatemala. It is Scottish shortbread. From Guatemala.' She smiled proudly at the oddity of this fact. 'Open it.'

'Shall I open it? Yes, I will. Let me offer you one,' he humoured her.

'No,' she said. 'They are for you.'

Murder. Biscuits, he thought. She *is* mad.

The editor opened the tin and took out a biscuit and began to nibble. She watched his teeth as he bit; once more, she was memorizing what she saw. She was keeping watch. Just as he was going to get up and make a last speech to her, she put out a short arm and pointed to his portrait.

'That is not you,' she pronounced. Having made him eat, she was now in command of him.

'But it is,' he said. 'I think it is very good. Don't you?'

'It is wrong,' she said.

'Oh.' He was offended and that brought out his saintly look.

'There is something missing,' she said. 'Now I am seeing you I know what it is.'

She got up.

'Don't go,' said the editor. 'Tell me what you miss. It was in the academy, you know.'

He was beginning to think she was a fortune teller.

'I am a poet,' she said. 'I see vision in you. I see a leader. That picture is the picture of two people, not one. But you are one man. You are a god to us. You understand that apartheid exists for women too.'

She held out her prophetic hand. The editor switched to his wise, pagan look and his sunny hand held hers.

'May I come to your lecture this evening?' she said. 'I asked your secretary about it.'

'Of course, of course, of course. Yes, yes, yes,' he said and walked with her to the outer door of the office. There they said goodbye. He watched her march away slowly, on her thick legs, like troops.

The editor went into his secretary's room. The girl was putting the cover on her typewriter.

'Do you know,' he said, 'that woman's father killed her mother because she dyed her hair?'

'She told me. You copped something there, didn't you? What d'you bet me she doesn't turn up in Copenhagen tomorrow, two rows from the front?' the rude girl said.

She was wrong. Miss Mendoza was in the fifth row at Copenhagen.
He had not noticed her at the London talk and he certainly had not
seen her on the plane; but there she was, looking squat, simple and
tarry among the tall fair Danes. The editor had been puzzled to know
who she was for he had a poor visual memory. For him, people's faces
merged into the general plain lineaments of the convinced. But he did
become aware of her when he got down from the platform and when
she stood, well planted, on the edge of the small circle where his white
head was bobbing to people who were asking him questions. She listened, turning her head possessively and critically to each questioner
and then to him, expectantly. She nodded with reproof at the questioner
when he replied. She owned him. Closer and closer she came, into the
inner circle. He was aware of a smell like nutmeg. She was beside him.
She had a long envelope in her hand. The chairman was saying to him:

'I think we should take you to the party now.' Then people went
off in three cars. There she was at the party.

'We have arranged for your friend . . .' said the host. 'We have
arranged for you to sit next to your friend.'

'Which friend?' the editor began. Then he saw her, sitting beside
him. The Dane lit a candle before them. Her skin took on, to the
editor's surprised eye, the gleam of an idol. He was bored; he liked
new women to be beautiful when he was abroad.

'Haven't we met somewhere?' he said. 'Oh yes. I remember. You
came to see me. Are you on holiday here?'

'No,' she said. 'I drink at the fount.'

He imagined she was taking the waters.

'Fount?' said the editor, turning to others at the table. 'Are there
many spas here?' He was no good at metaphors.

He forgot her and was talking to the company. She said no more
during the evening until she left with the other guests, but he could
hear her deep breath beside him.

'I have a present for you,' she said before she went, giving him the
envelope.

'More biscuits?' he said waggishly.

'It is the opening canto of my poem,' she said.

'I'm afraid,' said the editor, 'we rarely publish poetry.'

'It is not for publication. It is dedicated to you.'

And she went off.

'Extraordinary,' said the editor, watching her go; and, appealing to
his hosts, 'That woman gave me a poem.'

He was put out by their polite, knowing laughter. It often puzzled him when people laughed.

The poem went into his pocket and he forgot it until he got to Stockholm. She was standing at the door of the lecture hall there as he left. He said: 'We seem to be following each other around.'

And to a minister who was wearing a white tie: 'Do you know Miss Mendoza from Guatemala? She is a poet,' and escaped while they were bowing.

Two days later, she was at his lecture in Oslo. She had moved to the front row. He saw her after he had been speaking for a quarter of an hour. He was so irritated that he stumbled over his words. A rogue phrase had jumped into his mind—'murdered his wife'—and his voice, always high, went up one more semitone and he very nearly told the story. Some ladies in the audience were propping a cheek on their forefinger as they leaned their heads to regard his profile. He made a scornful gesture at his audience. He had remembered what was wrong. It had nothing to do with murder; he had simply forgotten to read her poem.

Poets, the editor knew, were remorseless. The one sure way of getting rid of them was to read their poems at once. They stared at you with pity and contempt as you read and argued with offence when you told them which lines you admired. He decided to face her. After the lecture he went up to her.

'How lucky,' he said. 'I thought you said you were going to Hamburg. Where are you staying? Your poem is on my conscience.'

'Yes?' the small girl's voice said. 'When will you come and see me?'

'I'll ring you up,' he said, drawing back.

'I'm going to hear you in Berlin,' she said with meaning.

The editor considered her. There was a look of magnetized inhuman committal in her eyes. They were not so much looking at him as reading him. She knew his future.

Back in the hotel, he read the poem. The message was plain. It began:

> I have seen the liberator
> The foe of servitude
> The godhead.

He read on, skipping two pages and put out his hand for the telephone. First he heard a childish intake of breath, and then the small determined voice. He smiled at the instrument; he told her in a forgiving voice how good the poem was. The breathing became heavy, like the sound of the ocean. She was steaming or flying to him across the Caribbean, across the Atlantic.

'You have understood my theme,' she said. 'Women are being history. I am the history of my country.'

She went on and boredom settled on him. His cultivated face turned to stone.

'Yes, yes, I see. Isn't there an old Indian belief that a white god will come from the East to liberate the people? Extraordinary, quite extraordinary. When you get back to Guatemala you must go on with your poem.'

'I am doing it now. In my room,' she said. 'You are my inspiration. I am working every night since I saw you.'

'Shall I post this copy to your hotel in Berlin?' he said.

'No, give it to me when we meet there.'

'Berlin!' the editor exclaimed. Without thinking, without realizing what he was saying, the editor said: 'But I'm *not* going to Berlin. I'm going back to London at once.'

'When?' said the woman's voice. 'Could I come and talk to you now?'

'I'm afraid not. I'm leaving in half an hour,' said the editor. Only when he put the telephone receiver back did the editor realize that he was sweating and that he had told a lie. He had lost his head. Worse, in Berlin, if she were there, he would have to invent another lie.

It *was* worse than that. When he got to Berlin she was not there. It was perverse of him—but he was alarmed. He was ashamed. The shadiness of the saint replaced the pagan on his handsome face; indeed, on the race question after his lecture, a man in the audience said he was evasive.

But in Hamburg at the end of the week, her voice spoke up from the back of the hall: 'I would like to ask the great man who is filling all our hearts this evening whether he is thinking that the worst racists are the oppressors and deceivers of women.'

She delivered her blow and sat down, disappearing behind the shoulders of bulky German men.

The editor's clever smiles went; he jerked back his heroic head as if he had been shot; he balanced himself by touching the table with the tips of his fingers. He lowered his head and drank a glass of water, splashing it on his tie. He looked for help.

'My friends,' he wanted to say, 'that woman is following me. She has followed me all over Scandinavia and Germany. I had to tell a lie to escape from her in Berlin. She is pursuing me. She is writing a poem. She is trying to force me to read it. She murdered her father—I mean, her father murdered her mother. She is mad. Someone must get me out of this.'

But he pulled himself together and sank to that point of desperation to which the mere amateurs and hams of public speaking sink.

'A good question,' he said. Two irreverent laughs came from the audience, probably from the American or English colony. He had made a fool of himself again. Floundering, he at last fell back on one of those drifting historical generalizations that so often rescued him. He heard his voice sailing into the eighteenth century, throwing in Rousseau, gliding on to Tom Paine and *The Rights of Man*.

'Is there a way out of the back of this hall?' he said to the chairman afterwards. 'Could someone keep an eye on that woman? She is following me.'

They got him out by a back door.

At his hotel, a poem was slipped under his door.

> Suckled on Rousseau
> Strong in the divine message of
> Nature
> Clasp Guatemala in your arms.

'Room 363' was written at the end. She was staying in the same hotel! He rang down to the desk, said he would receive no calls and demanded to be put on the lowest floor, close to the main stairs and near the exit. Safe in his new room he changed the time of his flight to Munich.

There was a note for him at the desk.

'Miss Mendoza left this for you,' said the clerk, 'when she left for Munich this morning.'

Attached to the note was a poem. It began:

> Ravenous in the long night of the centuries
> I waited for my liberator
> He shall not escape me.

His hand was shaking as he tore up the note and the poem and made for the door. The page boy came running after him with the receipt for his bill which he had left on the desk.

The editor was a well-known man. Reporters visited him. He was often recognized in hotels. People spoke his name aloud when they saw it on passenger lists. Cartoonists were apt to lengthen his neck when they drew him, for they had caught his habit of stretching it at parties or meetings, hoping to see and be seen.

But not on the flight to Munich. He kept his hat on and lowered his chin. He longed for anonymity. He had a sensation he had not had for years, not, indeed, since the pre-thaw days in Russia; that he was being followed not simply by one person but by dozens. Who were all those passengers on the plane? Had those two men in raincoats been at his hotel?

He made for the first cab he saw at the airport. At the hotel he went to the desk.

'Mr and Mrs Julian Drood,' the clerk said. 'Yes. Four-fifteen. Your wife has arrived.'

'My wife!' In any small group the actor in him woke up. He turned from the clerk to a stranger standing at the desk beside him and gave a yelp of hilarity. 'But I am not married!' The stranger drew away. The editor turned to a couple also standing there. 'I'm saying I am not married,' he said. He turned about to see if he could gather more listeners.

'This is ludicrous,' he said. No one was interested and loudly to the clerk he said: 'Let me see the register. There is no Mrs Drood.'

The clerk put on a worldly look to soothe any concern about the respectability of the hotel in the people who were waiting. But there, on the card, in her writing, were the words: Mr and Mrs J. Drood—London.

The editor turned dramatically to the group.

'A forgery,' he cried. He laughed, inviting all to join the comedy. 'A woman travelling under my name.'

The clerk and the strangers turned away. In travel one can rely on there being one mad Englishman everywhere.

The editor's face darkened when he saw he had exhausted human interest.

'Four-fifteen. Baggage,' called the clerk.

A young porter came up quick as a lizard and picked up the editor's bags.

'Wait. Wait,' said the editor. Before a young man so smoothly uniformed he had the sudden sensation of standing there with most of his clothes off. When you arrived at the Day of Judgement there would be some worldly youth, humming a tune you didn't know the name of, carrying not only your sins but your virtues indifferently in a couple of bags and gleaming with concealed knowledge.

'I have to telephone,' the editor said.

'Over there,' said the young man as he put the bags down. The editor did not walk to the telephone but to the main door of the hotel. He considered the freedom of the street. The sensible thing to do was to leave the hotel at once, but he knew that the woman would be at his lecture that night. He would have to settle the matter once and for all now. So he turned back to the telephone box. It stood there empty, like a trap. He walked past it. He hated the glazed, whorish, hypocritically impersonal look of telephone boxes. They were always unpleasantly warmed by random emotions left behind in them. He turned back: the thing was still empty. 'Surely,' he wanted to address the people coming and going in the foyer, 'someone among you wants to telephone?' It was wounding that not one person there was interested in his case. It was as if he had written an article that no one had read. Even the porter had gone. His two bags rested against the desk. He and they had ceased to be news.

He began to walk up and down quickly but this stirred no one. He stopped in every observable position, not quite ignored now, because his handsome hair always made people turn.

The editor silently addressed them again. 'You've entirely missed the point of my position. Everyone knows who has read what I have written, that I am opposed on principle to the whole idea of marriage. That is what makes this woman's behaviour so ridiculous. To think of getting *married* in a world that is in one of the most ghastly phases of its history is puerile.'

He gave a short sarcastic laugh. The audience was indifferent.

The editor went into the telephone box and, leaving the door open for all to hear, he rang her room.

'Julian Drood,' he said brusquely. 'It is important that I should see you at once, privately, in your room.'

He heard her breathing. The way the human race thought it was enough if they breathed! Ask an important question and what happens? Breath. Then he heard the small voice: it made a splashing, confusing sound.

'Oh,' it said. And more breath: 'Yes.'

The two words were the top of a wave that is about to topple and come thumping over on to the sand and then draws back with a long, insidious hiss.

'Please,' she added. And the word was the long, thirsty hiss.

The editor was surprised that his brusque manner was so wistfully treated.

'Good heavens,' he thought, 'she *is* in that room!' And because she was invisible and because of the distance of the wire between them, he felt she was pouring down it, head first, mouth open, swamping him. When he put the telephone down, he scratched his ear; a piece of her seemed to be coiled there. The editor's ear had heard passion. And passion at its climax.

He had often heard of passion. He had often been told of it. He had seen it in opera. He had friends—who usually came to him for advice—who were entangled in it. He had never felt it and he did not feel it now; but when he walked from the telephone box to the lift, he saw his role had changed. The woman was not a mere nuisance—she was something like Tosca. The pagan became doggish, the saint furtive as he entered the lift.

'Ah,' the editor burst out aloud to the liftman. '*Les femmes.*' The German did not understand French.

The editor got out of the lift and, passing one watchful white door after another, came to 415. He knocked twice. When there was no answer, he opened the door.

He seemed to blunder into an invisible wall of spice and scent and stepped back, thinking he had made a mistake. A long-legged rag doll with big blue eyes looked at him from the bed, a half-unpacked suitcase was on the floor with curious clothes hanging out of it. A woman's shoes were tipped out on the sofa.

And then, with her back to a small desk where she had been writing, stood Miss Mendoza. Or, rather, the bottle-green dress, the boxlike figure were Miss Mendoza's; the head was not. Her hair was no longer black; it was golden. The idol's head had been chopped off and was replaced by a woman's. There was no expression on the face until the shock on the editor's face passed across to hers; then a searching look of horror seized her, the look of one caught in an outrage. She lowered her head, suddenly cowed and frightened. She quickly grabbed a stocking she had left on the bed and held it behind her back.

'You are angry with me,' she said, holding her head down like an obstinate child.

'You are in *my* room. You have no right to be here. I *am* very angry with you. What do you mean by registering in my name—apart from anything else it is illegal. You know that, don't you? I must ask you to go or I shall have to take steps . . .'

Her head was still lowered. Perhaps he ought not to have said the last sentence. The blonde hair made her look pathetic.

'Why did you do this?'

'Because you would not see me,' she said. 'You have been cruel to me.'

'But don't you realize, Miss Mendoza, what you are doing? I hardly know you. You have followed me all over Europe; you have badgered me. You take my room. You pretend to be my wife . . .'

'Do you hate me?' she muttered.

Damn, thought the editor. I ought to have changed my hotel at once.

'I know nothing about you,' he said.

'Don't you want to know about me? What I am like? I know everything about you,' she said, raising her head.

The editor was confused by the rebuke. His fit of acting passed. He looked at his watch.

'A reporter is coming to see me in half an hour,' he said.

'I shall not be in the way,' she said. 'I will go out.'

'*You* will go out!' said the editor.

Then he understood where he was wrong. He had—perhaps being abroad addressing meetings, speaking to audiences with only one mass face had done this—forgotten how he dealt with difficult people.

He pushed the shoes to one end of the sofa to find himself a place. One shoe fell to the floor, but after all it was his room, he had a right to sit down.

'Miss Mendoza, you are ill,' he said.

She looked down quickly at the carpet.

'I am not,' she said.

'You are ill and, I think, very unhappy.' He put on his wise voice.

'No,' she said in a low voice. 'Happy. You are talking to me.'

'You are a very intelligent woman,' he said. 'And you will understand what I am going to say. Gifted people like yourself are very vulnerable. You live in the imagination, and that exposes one. I know that.'

'Yes,' she said. 'You see all the injustices of the world. You bleed from them.'

'I? Yes,' said the editor with his saint's smile. But he recovered from the flattery. 'I am saying something else. Your imagination is part of your gift as a poet, but in real life it has deluded you.'

'It hasn't done that. I see you as you are.'

'Please sit down,' said the editor. He could not bear her standing over him. 'Close the window, there is too much noise.'

She obeyed. The editor was alarmed to see the zipper of her dress was half undone and he could see the top of some garment with ominous lace on it. He could not bear untidy women. He saw his case was urgent. He made a greater effort to be kind.

'It was very kind of you to come to my lectures. I hope you found them interesting. I think they went down all right—good questions. One never knows, of course. One arrives in a strange place and one sees a hall full of people one doesn't know—and you won't believe me perhaps because I've done it scores of times—but one likes to see a face that one recognizes. One feels lost, at first . . .'

She looked hopeful.

This was untrue. The editor never felt lost. Once on his feet he had the impression that he was talking to the human race. He suffered with it. It was the general human suffering that had ravaged his face.

'But, you know,' he said sternly, 'our feelings deceive us. Especially at certain times of life. I was worried about you. I saw that something was wrong. These things happen very suddenly. God knows why. You see someone whom you admire perhaps—it seems to happen to women more than men—and you project some forgotten love on him. You think you love him, but it is really some forgotten image. In your case, I would say, probably some image of your father whom you have hated all these years for what he did when you were a child. And so, as people say, one becomes obsessed or infatuated. I don't like the word. What we mean is that one is not in love with a real man or woman but a vision sent out by oneself. One can think of many examples . . .'

The editor was sweating. He wished he hadn't asked her to close the window. He knew his mind was drifting toward historic instances. He wondered if he would tell her the story of Jane Carlyle, the wife of the historian, who had gone to hear the famous Father Matthew speak at a temperance meeting and how, hysterical and exalted, she had rushed to the platform to kiss his boots. Or there were other instances. For the moment he couldn't remember them. He decided on Mrs Carlyle. It was a mistake.

'Who is Mrs Carlyle?' said Miss Mendoza suspiciously. 'I would never kiss any man's feet.'

'Boots,' said the editor. 'It was on a public platform.'

'Or boots,' Miss Mendoza burst out. 'Why are you torturing me? You are saying I am mad.'

The editor was surprised by the turn of the conversation. It had seemed to be going well.

'Of course you're not mad,' he said. 'A madwoman could not have written that great poem. I am just saying that I value your feeling, but you must understand I, unfortunately, do not love you. You *are* ill. You have exhausted yourself.'

Miss Mendoza's yellow eyes became brilliant as she listened to him.

'So,' she said grandly, 'I am a mere nuisance.'

She got up from her chair and he saw she was trembling.

'If that is so, why don't you leave this room at once?' she said.

'But,' said the editor with a laugh, 'if I may mention it, it is mine.'

'I signed the register,' said Miss Mendoza.

'Well,' said the editor smiling, 'that is not the point, is it?'

The boredom, the sense of the sheer waste of time (when one thought of the massacres, the bombings, the imprisonments in the world) in personal questions, overcame him. It amazed him, at some awful crisis—the Cuban, for example—how many people left their husbands, wives or lovers, in a general post; the extraordinary, irresponsible persistence of outbreaks of love. A kind of guerrilla war in another context. Here he was in the midst of it. What could he do? He looked around the room for help. The noise of the traffic outside in the street, the dim sight of people moving behind office windows opposite, an advertisement for beer were no help. Humanity had deserted him. The nearest thing to the human—now it took his eye—was the doll on the bed, an absurd marionette from the cabaret, the raffle or the nursery. It had a mop of red hair, silly red cheeks and popping blue eyes with long cotton lashes. It wore a short skirt and had long insane legs in checked stockings. How childish women were. Of course (it now occurred to him), Miss Mendoza was as childish as her voice. The editor said playfully: 'I see you have a little friend. Very pretty. Does she come from Guatemala?' And frivolously, because he disliked the thing, he took a step or two towards it. Miss Mendoza pushed past him at once and grabbed it.

'Don't touch it,' she said with tiny fierceness.

She picked up the doll and, hugging it with fear, she looked for somewhere to put it out of his reach. She went to the door, then changed her mind and rushed to the window with it. She opened the window; as the curtains blew, she looked as if a desperate idea had occurred to her—to throw herself and the doll out of the window. She turned to fight him off. He was too bewildered to move and when

she saw that he stood still, her frightened face changed. Suddenly, she
threw the doll on the floor and, half falling on to a chair near it, her
shoulders rounded, she covered her face with her hands and sobbed,
shaking her head from side to side. Tears crawled through her fingers
down the backs of her hands. Then she took her hands away and, soft
and shapeless, she rushed to the editor and clawed at his jacket.

'Go away. Go away,' she cried. 'Forgive me. Forgive. I'm sorry.'
She began to laugh and cry at once. 'As you said—ill. Oh, please forgive. I don't understand why I did this. For a week I haven't eaten
anything. I must have been out of my mind to do this to you. Why?
I can't think. You've been so kind. You could have been cruel. You
were right. You had the courage to tell me the truth. I feel so ashamed,
so ashamed. What can I do?'

She was holding on to his jacket. Her tears were on his hands. She
was pleading. She looked up.

'I've been such a fool,' she said.

'Come and sit here,' said the editor, trying to move her to the sofa.
'You are not a fool. You have done nothing. There is nothing to be
ashamed of.'

'I can't bear it.'

'Come and sit here,' he said putting his arm on her shoulder. 'I was
very proud when I read your poem. Look,' he said, 'you are a very
gifted and attractive woman.'

He was surprised that such a heavy woman was not like iron to the
touch but light and soft. He could feel her skin, hot through her dress.
Her breath was hot. Agony was hot. Grief was hot. Above all, her
clothes were hot. It was perhaps because of the heat of her clothes
that for the first time in years he had the sensation of holding a human
being. He had never felt this when, on a few occasions, he had held
a woman naked in her bed. He did something then that was incredible
to himself. He gently kissed the top of her head on the blonde hair he
did not like. It was like kissing a heated mat and it smelled of burning.

At his kiss she clawed no longer and her tears stopped. She moved
away from him in awe.

'Thank you,' she said gravely and he found himself being studied,
even memorized, as she had done when she had first come to his
office. The look of the idol was set on her again. Then she uttered a
revelation. 'You do not love anyone but yourself.' And, worse, she
smiled. He had thought, with dread, that she was waiting to be kissed
again, but now he couldn't bear what she said. It was a loss.

'We must meet,' he said recklessly. 'We *shall* meet at the lecture tonight.'

The shadow of her future passed over her face.

'Oh no,' she said. She was free. She was warning him not to hope to exploit her pain.

'This afternoon?' he said trying to catch her hand, but she drew it away. And then, to his bewilderment, she was dodging round him. She was packing. She began stuffing her few clothes into her suitcase. She went to the bathroom and while she was there, the porter came in with his two bags.

'Wait,' said the editor.

She came out of the bathroom looking very pale and put the remaining things into her suitcase.

'I asked him to wait,' the editor said.

The kiss, the golden hair, the heat of her head, seemed to be flying round in the editor's head.

'I don't want you to leave like this,' the editor said.

'I heard what you said to the man,' she said hurriedly shutting the suitcase. 'Goodbye. And thank you. You are saving me from something dreadful.'

The editor could not move when he saw her go. He could not believe she had gone. He could feel the stir of her scent in the air and he sat down exhausted but arguing with his conscience. Why had she said that about loving only himself? What else could he have done? He wished there were people there to whom he could explain, whom he could ask. He was feeling loneliness for one of the few times in his life. He went to the window to look down at the people. Then, looking back to the bed, he was astounded by a thought, 'I have never had an adventure in my life.' And with that, he left the room and went down to the desk. Was she still in the hotel?

'No,' said the desk clerk. 'Mrs Drood went off in a taxi.'

'I am asking for Miss Mendoza.'

'No one of that name.'

'Extraordinary,' lied the editor. 'She was to meet me here.'

'Perhaps she is at the Hofgarten, it's the same management.'

For the next hour he was on the telephone, trying all the hotels. He got a cab to the station; he tried the airlines and then, in the afternoon, went out to the airport. He knew it was hopeless. 'I must be mad too,' he thought. He looked at every golden-haired woman he could see: the city was full of golden-haired women. As the noisy city afternoon moved by, he gave up. He liked to talk about himself but here was a day he could never describe to anyone. He could not return to his room but sat in the lounge trying to read a paper, wrangling with himself and looking up at every woman who passed. He could not eat nor even drink and when he went out to his lecture he walked all the way to the hall on the chance of seeing her. He had the fancy once or twice, which he laughed at bitterly, that she had just passed and had left two or three of her footprints on the pavement. The extraordinary thing was that she was exactly the kind of woman he could not bear: squat, ugly. How awful she must look without clothes on. He tried to exorcize her by obscene images. They vanished and some transformed idealized vision of her came back. He began to see her tall and dark or young and fair; her eyes changing colour, her body voluptuously rounded, athletically slim. As he sat on the lecture platform, listening to the introduction, he made faces that astonished the audience with a mechanical display of eagerness followed by scorn, as his gaze went systematically from row to row, looking for her. He got up to speak. 'Ladies and gentlemen,' he began. He knew it would be the best lecture he had ever given. It was. Urging, appealing, agonizing, eloquent. It was an appeal to her to come back.

And then, after a lot of discussion which he hardly heard, he returned to the hotel. He had now to face the mockery of the room. He let himself in and it did mock. The maid had turned the bed back and on it lay the doll, its legs tidied, its big ridiculous eyes staring at him. They seemed to him to blink. She had forgotten it. She had left her childhood behind.

Loser Wins

The insects warbled at the windows, and on the wall a pale gecko chattered and flicked its tail. It was one of those intimate late-night pauses—we had been drinking for two hours and had passed the point of drunken chit-chat. Then, to break the silence, I said, 'I've lost my spare pair of glasses.'

'I hadn't noticed,' said Strang. A surveyor, he had the abrupt manner of one who works alone. He was mapping this part of the state and he had made Ayer Hitam his base. His wife, Milly, was devoted to him, people said; it seemed an unusual piece of praise. Strang picked up his drink. 'You won't find them.'

'It's an excuse to go down to Singapore for a new pair.'

Strang looked thoughtful. I expected him to say something about Singapore. We were alone. Stanley Chee had slammed the door for the last time and had left a tray of drinks on the bar that we could sign for on the chit-pad.

Still Strang didn't reply. The ensuing silence made my sentence about Singapore a frivolous echo. He walked over and poured himself a large gin, emptied a bottle of tonic into the tall glass and pinched a new slice of lemon into it.

'I ever tell you about the Parrishes?'

A rhetorical question: he was still talking.

'Married couple I met up in Kota Bahru. Jungle bashers. Milly and I lived there our first year—looked like paradise to us, if you could stand the sand-flies. Didn't see much of the Parrishes. They quarrelled an awful lot, so we stayed as far away as possible from their arguments. Seemed unlucky. We'd only been married a few months.' He smiled. 'Old Parrish took quite a shine to Milly.'

'What did the Parrishes argue about?' Was this what he wanted me to ask? I hoped he was not expecting me to drag the story out of him. I wanted him to keep talking and let it flow over me. But even at the best of times Strang was no spellbinder; tonight he seemed agitated.

'See, that shows you've never been spliced,' he said. 'Married people argue about everything—anything. A tone of voice, saying please, the colour of the wallpaper, something you forgot, the speed of the fan, food, friends, the weather. That tie of yours—if you had a wife she'd hate you for it. A bone of contention,' said Strang slowly, 'is just a bone.'

'Perhaps I have that in store for me.' I filled my own drink and signed for that and Strang's.

'Take my advice,' he said. 'No—it was something you said a minute ago. Oh, you lost your specs. That's what I was going to say. The Parrishes argued about everything, but most of all they argued about things they lost. I mean, things *she* lost. She was incredible. At first he barely noticed it. She lost small things, lipstick, her cigarettes, her comb. She didn't bother to look for them. She was very county—her parents had money, and she had a kind of contempt for it. Usually she didn't even try to replace the things she lost. The funny thing is, she seemed to do it on purpose—to lose things she hated.

'He was the local magistrate. An Outward Bound type. After a week in court he was dead keen to go camping. Old Parrish—he looked like a goat, little pointed beard and those sort of hairy ears. They went on these camping trips and invariably she lost something en route—the house keys, her watch, the matches, you name it. But she was a terrific map-reader and he was appalling, so he really depended on her. I think he had some love for her. He was a lot older than she was—he'd married her on a Long Leave.

'Once, he showed how much he loved her. She lost fifty dollars. Not a hard thing to do—it was a fifty-dollar note, the one with the mosque on it. I would have cried, myself, but she just shrugged, and knowing how she was continually losing things he was sympathetic. "Poor thing," he says, "you must feel a right charlie." But not a bit of it. She had always had money. She didn't take a blind bit of notice, and she was annoyed that he pitied her for losing the fifty sheets. Hated him for noticing it.

'They went off on their camping trips—expeditions was more like it—and always to the same general area. Old Parrish had told me one or two things about it. There was one of these up-country lakes, with a strange island in the middle of it. They couldn't find it on the map, but they knew roughly where it was supposed to be—there's never been a detailed survey done of the Malaysian interior. But that's where the Parrishes were headed every weekend during that dry season. The attraction was the monkeys. Apparently, the local *sakais*—they might have been Laruts—had deported some wild monkeys there. The monkeys got too stroppy around the village, so being peace-loving buggers the *sakais* just caught them and tied them up and brought them to the island where they wouldn't bother anyone. There were about a dozen of these beasts, surrounded by water. An island of wild monkeys—imagine landing there on a dark night!

'In the meantime, we saw the Parrishes occasionally in the compound during the week and that's where I kept up to date with the story. As I say, his first reaction when she lost things was to be sympathetic. But afterwards, it irritated him. She lost her handbag and he shouted at her. She lost her watch—it was one he had given her—and he wouldn't speak to her for days. She mislaid the bathplug, lost some jewellery, his passport disappeared. And that's the way it went—bloody annoying. I don't know what effect this had on her. I suppose she thought she deserved his anger. People who lose things get all knotted up about it, and the fear of losing things makes them do it all the more. That's what I thought then.

'And the things she lost were never found. It was uncanny, as if she just wished them away. He said she didn't miss them.

'Then, on one of these expeditions she lost the paraffin. Doesn't seem like much, but the place was full of leeches and a splash of paraffin was the only thing that'd shake them loose from your arms or legs. They both suffered that weekend and didn't find the island either. Then, the next weekend, she lost the compass, and that's when the real trouble started. Instead of pitying her, or getting angry, or ignoring it, old Parrish laughed. He saw how losing the compass inconvenienced her in her map-reading, and she was so shaken by that horrible laugh of his she was all the more determined to do without it. She succeeded, too. She used a topographical map and somehow found the right landmarks and led them back the way they'd come.

'But Parrish still laughed. I remember the day she lost the car-keys—*his* car-keys, mind you, because she'd lost practically everything she owned and now it was his stuff up the spout. You could hear old Parrish half-way to Malacca. Then it was the malaria tablets. Parrish laughed even harder—he said he'd been in the Federation so long he was immune to it, but being young and new to the place she'd get a fever, and he found that screamingly funny. This was too much for

her, and when his wedding ring just went missing—God only knows
how *that* happened—and Parrish just laughed, that was the last straw.
I suppose it didn't help matters when Parrish set off for the courthouse
in the morning saying, "What are you going to lose today, my darling?"

'Oh, there was much more. He talked about it at parties, laughing
his head off, while she sulked in a corner, and we expected to find him
dead the next morning with a knitting-needle jammed through his
wig.

'But, to make a long story short, they went off on one of their usual
expeditions. No compass, no paludrine, no torch—she'd lost practically everything. By this time, they knew their way, and they spent all
that Saturday bush-whacking through the *ulu*. They were still headed
in that deliberate way of theirs for the monkey island, and now I remember that a lot of people called him "Monkey" Parrish. She claimed
it was mythical, didn't exist, except in the crazy fantasies of a lot of
sakais; but Monkey said, "I know what you've done with it, my
darling—you've lost that island!" And naturally he laughed.

'They were making camp that night in a grove of bamboos when
it happened. It was dusk, and looking up they saw one of those
enormous clouds of flying foxes in the sky. Ever see them? They're
really fruit-bats, four feet from tip to tip, and they beat the air slowly.
You get them in the *ulu* near the coast. Eerie, they are—scare the wits
out of you the way they fly, and they're ugly as old boots. You can tell
the old ones by the way they move, sort of dropping behind and
losing altitude while the younger ones push their noses on ahead. It's
one of the weirdest sights in this country, those flying foxes setting off
in the twilight, looking so fat and fearsome in the sky. Like a bad
dream, a kind of monster film—they come out of nowhere.

'She said, "Look they're heading for the island."

'He said, "Don't be silly—they're flying east, to the coast."

' "There's the light," she said, "that's west." She claimed the bats
preferred islands and would be homing in on one where there was
fruit—monkey food. The wild monkeys slept at night, so they wouldn't
bother the bats. She said, "I'm going to have a look."

' "There's no torch," he says, and he laughs like hell.

' "There's a moon," she says. And without another word she's
crashing through the bamboos in the direction the foxes are flying.
Parrish—Monkey Parrish—just laughed and sat down by the fire to
have a pipe before bed. Can you see him there, chuckling to himself
about this wife of his who loses everything, how he suddenly realizes

that she's lost herself and he has a fit of laughter? Great hoots echoing through the jungle as old Parrish sees he's rid of her at last!

'Maybe. But look at it another way. The next morning he wakes up and sees she's not there. She never came back. At first he slaps his thigh and laughs and shouts, "She's lost!" Then he looks around. No map, no compass, no torch—only that low dense jungle that stretches for hundreds of miles across the top of the country, dropping leeches on anyone who's silly enough to walk through it. And the more he thinks about it the more it becomes plain to him that *he's* the one who's lost—she's wished him away, like the wedding ring and the torch and the fifty-dollar bill. Suddenly, he's not laughing any more.

'I'm only guessing. I don't really know what he was thinking. I had the story from her, just before she left the country. She said there were only two monkeys on the island, a male and a female, bickering the whole time, like her and her late husband. Yes, *late* husband. No one ever found him—certainly not her, but she wouldn't would she?'

WILLIAM TREVOR

Death in Jerusalem

'Till then,' Father Paul said, leaning out of the train window. 'Till Jerusalem, Francis.'

'Please God, Paul.' As he spoke the Dublin train began to move and his brother waved from the window and he waved back, a modest figure on the platform. Everyone said Francis might have been a priest as well, meaning that Francis's quietness and meditative disposition had an air of the cloister about them. But Francis contented himself with the running of Daly's hardware business, which his mother had run until she was too old for it. 'Are we game for the Holy Land next year?' Father Paul had asked that July. 'Will we go together, Francis?' He had brushed aside all Francis's protestations, all attempts to explain that the shop could not be left, that their mother would be confused by the absence of Francis from the house. Rumbustiously he'd pointed out that there was their sister Kitty, who was in charge of the household of which Francis and their mother were part and whose husband, Myles, could surely be trusted to look after the shop for a single fortnight. For thirty years, ever since he was seven, Francis had wanted to go to the Holy Land. He had savings which he'd never spent a penny of: you couldn't take them with you, Father Paul had more than once stated that July.

On the platform Francis watched until the train could no longer be seen, his thoughts still with his brother. The priest's ruddy countenance smiled again behind cigarette smoke; his bulk remained impressive in his clerical clothes, the collar pinching the flesh of his neck, his black shoes scrupulously polished. There were freckles on the backs of his large, strong hands; he had a fine head of hair, grey and crinkly. In an hour and a half's time the train would creep into Dublin, and he'd take a taxi. He'd spend a night in the Gresham Hotel, probably falling in with another priest, having a drink or two, maybe playing a game of bridge after his meal. That was his brother's way and always had been —an extravagant, easy kind of way, full of smiles and good humour.

It was what had taken him to America and made him successful there. In order to raise money for the church that he and Father Steigmuller intended to build before 1980 he took parties of the well-to-do from San Francisco to Rome and Florence, to Chartres and Seville and the Holy Land. He was good at raising money, not just for the church but for the boys' home of which he was president, and for the Hospital of Our Saviour, and for St Mary's Old People's Home on the west side of the city. But every July he flew back to Ireland, to the town in Co. Tipperary where his mother and brother and sister still lived. He stayed in the house above the shop which he might have inherited himself on the death of his father, which he'd rejected in favour of the religious life. Mrs Daly was eighty now. In the shop she sat silently behind the counter, in a corner by the chicken-wire, wearing only clothes that were black. In the evenings she sat with Francis in the lace-curtained sitting-room, while the rest of the family occupied the kitchen. It was for her sake most of all that Father Paul made the journey every summer, considering it his duty.

Walking back to the town from the station, Francis was aware that he was missing his brother. Father Paul was fourteen years older and in childhood had often taken the place of their father, who had died when Francis was five. His brother had possessed an envied strength and knowledge; he'd been a hero, quite often worshipped, an example of success. In later life he had become an example of generosity as well: ten years ago he'd taken their mother to Rome, and their sister Kitty and her husband two years later; he'd paid the expenses when their sister Edna had gone to Canada; he'd assisted two nephews to make a start in America. In childhood Francis hadn't possessed his brother's healthy freckled face, just as in middle age he didn't have his ruddy complexion and his stoutness and his easiness with people. Francis was slight, his sandy hair receding, his face rather pale. His breathing was sometimes laboured because of wheeziness in the chest. In the ironmonger's shop he wore a brown cotton coat.

'Hullo, Mr Daly,' a woman said to him in the main street of the town. 'Father Paul's gone off, has he?'

'Yes, he's gone again.'

'I'll pray for his journey so,' the woman promised, and Francis thanked her.

A year went by. In San Francisco another wing of the boys' home was completed, another target was reached in Father Paul and Father Steigmuller's fund for the church they planned to have built by 1980.

In the town in Co. Tipperary there were baptisms and burial services and First Communions. Old Loughlin, a farmer from Bansha, died in Flynn's grocery and bar, having gone there to celebrate a good price he'd got for a heifer. Clancy, from behind the counter in Doran's drapery, married Maureen Talbot; Mr Nolan's plasterer married Miss Driscoll; Johneen Lynch married Seamus in the chip shop, under pressure from her family to do so. A local horse, from the stables on the Limerick road, was said to be an entry for the Fairyhouse Grand National, but it turned out not to be true. Every evening of that year Francis sat with his mother in the lace-curtained sitting-room above the shop. Every weekday she sat in her corner by the chicken-wire, watching while he counted out screws and weighed staples, or advised about yard brushes or tap-washers. Occasionally, on a Saturday, he visited the three Christian Brothers who lodged with Mrs Shea and afterwards he'd tell his mother about how the authority was slipping these days from the nuns and the Christian Brothers, and how Mrs Shea's elderly maid, Agnes, couldn't see to cook the food any more. His mother would nod and hardly ever speak. When he told a joke— what young Hogan had said when he'd found a nail in his egg or how Agnes had put mint sauce into a jug with milk in it—she never laughed and looked at him in surprise when he laughed himself. But Dr Grady said it was best to keep her cheered up.

All during that year Francis talked to her about his forthcoming visit to the Holy Land, endeavouring to make her understand that for a fortnight next spring he would be away from the house and the shop. He'd been away before for odd days, but that was when she'd been younger. He used to visit an aunt in Tralee, but three years ago the aunt had died and he hadn't left the town since.

Francis and his mother had always been close. Before his birth two daughters had died in infancy, and his very survival had often struck Mrs Daly as a gift. He had always been her favourite, the one among her children whom she often considered least able to stand on his own two feet. It was just like Paul to have gone blustering off to San Francisco instead of remaining in Co. Tipperary. It was just like Kitty to have married a useless man. 'There's not a girl in the town who'd touch him,' she'd said to her daughter at the time, but Kitty had been headstrong and adamant, and there was Myles now, doing nothing whatsoever except cleaning other people's windows for a pittance and placing bets in Donovan's the turf accountant's. It was the shop and the arrangement Kitty had with Francis and her mother that kept her and the children going, three of whom had already left the town, which in Mrs Daly's opinion they mightn't have done if they'd had a better type of father. Mrs Daly often wondered what her own two babies who'd died might have grown up into, and imagined they might have been like Francis, about whom she'd never had a moment's worry. Not in a million years would he give you the feeling that he was too big for his boots, like Paul sometimes did with his lavishness and his big talk of America. He wasn't silly like Kitty, or so sinful you couldn't forgive him, like you couldn't forgive Edna, even though she was dead and buried in Toronto.

Francis understood how his mother felt about the family. She'd had a hard life, left a widow early on, trying to do the best she could for everyone. In turn he did his best to compensate for the struggles and disappointments she'd suffered, cheering her in the evenings while Kitty and Myles and the youngest of their children watched the television in the kitchen. His mother had ignored the existence of Myles for ten years, ever since the day he'd taken money out of the till to pick up the odds on Gusty Spirit at Phoenix Park. And although Francis got on well enough with Myles he quite understood that there should be a long aftermath to that day. There'd been a terrible row in the kitchen, Kitty screaming at Myles and Myles telling lies and Francis trying to keep them calm, saying they'd give the old woman a heart attack.

She didn't like upsets of any kind, so all during the year before he was to visit the Holy Land Francis read the New Testament to her in order to prepare her. He talked to her about Bethlehem and Nazareth and the miracle of the loaves and fishes and all the other miracles. She kept nodding, but he often wondered if she didn't assume he was just casually referring to episodes in the Bible. As a child he had listened to such talk himself, with awe and fascination, imagining the walking on the water and the temptation in the wilderness. He had imagined the cross carried to Calvary, and the rock rolled back from the tomb, and the rising from the dead on the third day. That he was now to walk in such places seemed extraordinary to him, and he wished his mother was younger so that she could appreciate his good fortune and share it with him when she received the postcards he intended, every day, to send her. But her eyes seemed always to tell him that he was making a mistake, that somehow he was making a fool of himself by doing such a showy thing as going to the Holy Land. *I have the entire itinerary mapped out*, his brother wrote from San Francisco. *There's nothing we'll miss.*

*

It was the first time Francis had been in an aeroplane. He flew by Aer Lingus from Dublin to London and then changed to an El Al flight to Tel Aviv. He was nervous and he found it exhausting. All the time he seemed to be eating, and it was strange being among so many people he didn't know. 'You will taste honey such as never before,' an Israeli businessman in the seat next to his assured him. 'And Galilean figs. Make certain to taste Galilean figs.' Make certain too, the businessman went on, to experience Jerusalem by night and in the early dawn. He urged Francis to see places he had never heard of, the Yad Va-Shem, the treasures of the Shrine of the Book. He urged him to honour the martyrs of Masada and to learn a few words of Hebrew as a token of respect. He told him of a shop where he could buy mementoes and warned him against Arab street traders.

'The hard man, how are you?' Father Paul said at Tel Aviv airport, having flown in from San Francisco the day before. Father Paul had had a drink or two and he suggested another when they arrived at the Plaza Hotel in Jerusalem. It was half-past nine in the evening. 'A quick little nightcap,' Father Paul insisted, 'and then hop into bed with you, Francis.' They sat in an enormous open lounge with low, round tables and square modern armchairs. Father Paul said it was the bar.

They had said what had to be said in the car from Tel Aviv to Jerusalem. Father Paul had asked about their mother, and Kitty and Myles. He'd asked about other people in the town, old Canon Mahon and Sergeant Malone. He and Father Steigmuller had had a great year of it, he reported: as well as everything else, the boys' home had turned out two tip-top footballers. 'We'll start on a tour at half-nine in the morning,' he said. 'I'll be sitting having breakfast at eight.'

Francis went to bed and Father Paul ordered another whisky, with ice. To his great disappointment there was no Irish whisky in the hotel so he'd had to content himself with Haig. He fell into conversation with an American couple, making them promise that if they were ever in Ireland they wouldn't miss out Co. Tipperary. At eleven o'clock the barman said he was wanted at the reception desk and when Father Paul went there and announced himself he was given a message in an envelope. It was a telegram that had come, the girl said in poor English. Then she shook her head, saying it was a telex. He opened the envelope and learnt that Mrs Daly had died.

Francis fell asleep immediately and dreamed that he was a boy again, out fishing with a friend whom he couldn't now identify.

On the telephone Father Paul ordered whisky and ice to be brought to his room. Before drinking it he took his jacket off and knelt by his bed to pray for his mother's salvation. When he'd completed the prayers he walked slowly up and down the length of the room, occasionally sipping at his whisky. He argued with himself and finally arrived at a decision.

For breakfast they had scrambled eggs that looked like yellow ice-cream, and orange juice that was delicious. Francis wondered about bacon, but Father Paul explained that bacon was not readily available in Israel.

'Did you sleep all right?' Father Paul enquired. 'Did you have the jet-lag?'

'Jet-lag?'

'A tiredness you get after jet flights. It'd knock you out for days.'

'Ah, I slept great, Paul.'

'Good man.'

They lingered over breakfast. Father Paul reported a little more of what had happened in his parish during the year, in particular about the two young footballers from the boys' home. Francis told about the decline in the cooking at Mrs Shea's boarding-house, as related to him by the three Christian Brothers. 'I have a car laid on,' Father Paul said, and twenty minutes later they walked out into the Jerusalem sunshine.

The hired car stopped on the way to the walls of the old city. It drew into a lay-by at Father Paul's request and the two men got out and looked across a wide valley dotted with houses and olive trees. A road curled along the distant slope opposite. 'The Mount of Olives,' Father Paul said. 'And that's the road to Jericho.' He pointed more particularly. 'You see that group of eight big olives? Just off the road, where the church is?'

Francis thought he did, but was not sure. There were so many olive trees, and more than one church. He glanced at his brother's pointing finger and followed its direction with his glance.

'The Garden of Gethsemane,' Father Paul said.

Francis did not say anything. He continued to gaze at the distant church with the clump of olive trees beside it. Wild flowers were profuse on the slopes of the valley, smears of orange and blue on land that looked poor. Two Arab women herded goats.

'Could we see it closer?' he asked, and his brother said that definitely they would. They returned to the waiting car and Father Paul ordered it to the Gate of St Stephen.

Tourists heavy with cameras thronged the Via Dolorosa. Brown, barefoot children asked for alms. Stall-keepers pressed their different wares, cotton dresses, metal-ware, mementoes, sacred goods. 'Get out of the way,' Father Paul kept saying to them, genially laughing to show he wasn't being abrupt. Francis wanted to stand still and close his eyes, to visualize for a moment the carrying of the Cross. But the ceremony of the Stations, familiar to him for as long as he could remember, was unreal. Try as he would, Christ's journey refused to enter his imagination, and his own plain church seemed closer to the heart of the matter than the noisy lane he was now being jostled on. 'God damn it, of course it's genuine,' an angry American voice proclaimed, in reply to a shriller voice which insisted that cheating had taken place. The voices argued about a piece of wood, neat beneath plastic in a little box, a sample or not of the cross that had been carried.

They arrived at the Church of the Holy Sepulchre, and at the Chapel of the Nailing to the Cross, where they prayed. They passed through the Chapel of the Angel, to the tomb of Christ. Nobody spoke in the marble cell, but when they left the church Francis overheard a quiet man with spectacles saying it was unlikely that a body would have been buried within the walls of the city. They walked to Hezekiah's Pool and out of the old city at the Jaffa Gate, where their hired car was waiting for them. 'Are you peckish?' Father Paul asked, and although Francis said he wasn't they returned to the hotel.

Delay funeral till Monday was the telegram Father Paul had sent. There was an early flight on Sunday, in time for an afternoon one from London to Dublin. With luck there'd be a late train on Sunday evening and if there wasn't they'd have to fix a car. Today was Tuesday. It would give them four and a half days. *Funeral eleven Monday* the telegram at the reception desk now confirmed. 'Ah, isn't that great?' he said to himself, bundling the telegram up.

'Will we have a small one?' he suggested in the open area that was the bar. 'Or better still a big one.' He laughed. He was in good spirits in spite of the death that had taken place. He gestured at the barman, wagging his head and smiling jovially.

His face had reddened in the morning sun; there were specks of sweat on his forehead and his nose. 'Bethlehem this afternoon,' he laid down. 'Unless the jet-lag . . . ?'

'I haven't got the jet-lag.'

In the Nativity Boutique Francis bought for his mother a small metal plate with a fish on it. He had stood for a moment, scarcely able to believe it, on the spot where the manger had been, in the church of the Nativity. As in the Via Dolorosa it had been difficult to rid the imagination of the surroundings that now were present, of the exotic Greek Orthodox trappings, the foreign-looking priests, the oriental smell. Gold, frankincense and myrrh, he'd kept thinking, for somehow the church seemed more the church of the kings than of Joseph and Mary and their child. Afterwards they returned to Jerusalem, to the Tomb of the Virgin and the Garden of Gethsemane. 'It could have been anywhere,' he heard the quiet, bespectacled sceptic remarking in Gethsemane. 'They're only guessing.'

Father Paul rested in the late afternoon, lying down on his bed with his jacket off. He slept from half-past five until a quarter-past seven and awoke refreshed. He picked up the telephone and asked for whisky and ice to be brought up and when it arrived he undressed and had a bath, relaxing in the warm water with the drink on a ledge in the tiled wall beside him. There would be time to take in Nazareth and Galilee. He was particularly keen that his brother should see Galilee because Galilee had atmosphere and was beautiful. There wasn't, in his own opinion, very much to Nazareth but it would be a pity to miss it all the same. It was at the Sea of Galilee that he intended to tell his brother of their mother's death.

We've had a great day, Francis wrote on a postcard that showed an aerial view of Jerusalem. *The Church of the Holy Sepulchre, where Our Lord's tomb is, and Gethsemane and Bethlehem. Paul's in great form.* He addressed it to his mother, and then wrote other cards, to Kitty and Myles and to the three Christian Brothers in Mrs Shea's, and to Canon Mahon. He gave thanks that he was privileged to be in Jerusalem. He read St Mark and some of St Matthew. He said his rosary.

'Will we chance the wine?' Father Paul said at dinner, not that wine was something he went in for, but a waiter had come up and put a large padded wine-list into his hand.

'Ah, no, no,' Francis protested, but already Father Paul was running his eye down the listed bottles.

'Have you local wine?' he enquired of the waiter. 'A nice red one?'

The waiter nodded and hurried away, and Francis hoped he wouldn't get drunk, the red wine on top of the whisky he'd had in the bar

before the meal. He'd only had the one whisky, not being much used
to it, making it last through his brother's three.

'I heard some gurriers in the bar,' Father Paul said, 'making a great
song and dance about the local red wine.'

Wine made Francis think of the Holy Communion, but he didn't
say so. He said the soup was delicious and he drew his brother's attention to the custom there was in the hotel of a porter ringing a bell and
walking about with a person's name chalked on a little blackboard on
the end of a rod.

'It's a way of paging you,' Father Paul explained. 'Isn't it nicer than
bellowing out some fellow's name?' He smiled his easy smile, his
eyes beginning to water as a result of the few drinks he'd had. He
was beginning to feel the strain: he kept thinking of their mother
lying there, of what she'd say if she knew what he'd done, how she'd
savagely upbraid him for keeping the fact from Francis. Out of duty
and humanity he had returned each year to see her because, after all,
you only had the one mother. But he had never cared for her.

Francis went for a walk after dinner. There were young soldiers
with what seemed to be toy guns on the streets, but he knew the
guns were real. In the shop windows there were television sets for
sale, and furniture and clothes, just like anywhere else. There were
advertisements for some film or other, two writhing women without
a stitch on them, the kind of thing you wouldn't see in Co. Tipperary.
'You want something, sir?' a girl said, smiling at him with broken front
teeth. The siren of a police car or an ambulance shrilled urgently near
by. He shook his head at the girl. 'No, I don't want anything,' he said,
and then realized what she had meant. She was small and very dark,
no more than a child. He hurried on, praying for her.

When he returned to the hotel, he found his brother in the lounge
with other people, two men and two women. Father Paul was ordering
a round of drinks and called out to the barman to bring another whisky.
'Ah, no, no,' Francis protested, anxious to go to his room and to think
about the day, to read the New Testament and perhaps to write a few
more postcards. Music was playing, coming from speakers that could
not be seen.

'My brother Francis,' Father Paul said to the people he was with,
and the people all gave their names, adding that they came from New
York. 'I was telling them about Tipp,' Father Paul said to his brother,
offering his packet of cigarettes around.

'You like Jerusalem, Francis?' one of the American women asked him and he replied that he hadn't been able to take it in yet. Then, feeling that that didn't sound enthusiastic enough, he added that being there was the experience of a lifetime.

Father Paul went on talking about Co. Tipperary and then spoke of his parish in San Francisco, the boys' home and the two promising footballers, the plans for the new church. The Americans listened and in a moment the conversation drifted on to the subject of their travels in England, their visit to Istanbul and Athens, an argument they'd had with the Customs at Tel Aviv. 'Well, I'm for the hay-pile,' one of the men announced eventually, standing up.

The others stood up too and so did Francis. Father Paul remained where he was, gesturing in the direction of the barman. 'Sit down for a nightcap,' he urged his brother.

'Ah, no, no—' Francis began.

'Bring us two more of those,' the priest ordered with a sudden abruptness, and the barman hurried away. 'Listen,' said Father Paul. 'I've something to tell you.'

After dinner, while Francis had been out on his walk, before he'd dropped into conversation with the Americans, Father Paul had said to himself that he couldn't stand the strain. It was the old woman stretched out above the hardware shop, as stiff as a board already, with the little lights burning in her room: he kept seeing all that, as if she wanted him to, as if she was trying to haunt him. Nice as the idea was, he didn't think he could continue with what he'd planned, with waiting until they got up to Galilee.

Francis didn't want to drink any more. He hadn't wanted the whisky his brother had ordered him earlier, nor the one the Americans had ordered for him. He didn't want the one that the barman now brought. He thought he'd just leave it there, hoping his brother wouldn't see it. He lifted the glass to his lips, but he managed not to drink any.

'A bad thing has happened,' Father Paul said.

'Bad? How d'you mean, Paul?'

'Are you ready for it?' He paused. Then he said, 'She died.'

Francis didn't know what he was talking about. He didn't know who was meant to be dead, or why his brother was behaving in an odd manner. He didn't like to think it but he had to: his brother wasn't fully sober.

'Our mother died,' Father Paul said. 'I'm after getting a telegram.'

The huge area that was the lounge of the Plaza Hotel, the endless tables and people sitting at them, the swiftly moving waiters and bar-men, seemed suddenly a dream. Francis had a feeling that he was not where he appeared to be, that he wasn't sitting with his brother, who was wiping his lips with a handkerchief. For a moment he appeared in his confusion to be struggling his way up the Via Dolorosa again and then in the Nativity Boutique.

'Take it easy, boy,' his brother was saying. 'Take a mouthful of whisky.'

Francis didn't obey that injunction. He asked his brother to repeat what he had said, and Father Paul repeated that their mother had died.

Francis closed his eyes and tried as well to shut away the sounds around them. He prayed for the salvation of his mother's soul. 'Blessed Virgin, intercede,' his own voice said in his mind. 'Dear Mary, let her few small sins be forgiven.'

Having rid himself of his secret, Father Paul felt instant relief. With the best of intentions in the world it had been a foolish idea to think he could maintain the secret until they arrived in a place that was perhaps the most suitable in the world to hear about the death of a person who'd been close to you. He took a gulp of his whisky and wiped his mouth with his handkerchief again. He watched his brother, waiting for his eyes to open.

'When did it happen?' Francis asked eventually.

'Yesterday.'

'And the telegram only came—'

'It came last night, Francis. I wanted to save you the pain.'

'Save me? How could you save me? I sent her a postcard, Paul.'

'Listen to me, Francis—'

'How could you save me the pain?'

'I wanted to tell you when we got up to Galilee.'

Again Francis felt he was caught in the middle of a dream. He couldn't understand his brother: he couldn't understand what he meant by saying a telegram had come last night, why at a moment like this he was talking about Galilee. He didn't know why he was sitting in this noisy place when he should be back in Ireland.

'I fixed the funeral for Monday,' Father Paul said.

Francis nodded, not grasping the significance of this arrangement. 'We'll be back there this time tomorrow,' he said.

'No need for that, Francis. Sunday morning's time enough.'

'But she's dead—'

'We'll be there in time for the funeral.'

'We can't stay here if she's dead.'

It was this, Father Paul realized, he'd been afraid of when he'd argued with himself and made his plan. If he'd have knocked on Francis's door the night before, Francis would have wanted to return immediately without seeing a single stone of the land he had come so far to be moved by.

'We could go straight up to Galilee in the morning,' Father Paul said quietly. 'You'll find comfort in Galilee, Francis.'

But Francis shook his head. 'I want to be with her,' he said.

Father Paul lit another cigarette. He nodded at a hovering waiter, indicating his need of another drink. He said to himself that he must keep his cool, an expression he was fond of.

'Take it easy, Francis,' he said.

'Is there a plane out in the morning? Can we make arrangements now?' He looked about him as if for a member of the hotel staff who might be helpful.

'No good'll be done by tearing off home, Francis. What's wrong with Sunday?'

'I want to be with her.'

Anger swelled within Father Paul. If he began to argue his words would become slurred: he knew that from experience. He must keep his cool and speak slowly and clearly, making a few simple points. It was typical of her, he thought, to die inconveniently.

'You've come all this way,' he said as slowly as he could without sounding peculiar. 'Why cut it any shorter than we need? We'll be losing a week anyway. She wouldn't want us to go back.'

'I think she would.'

He was right in that. Her possessiveness in her lifetime would have reached out across a dozen continents for Francis. She'd known what she was doing by dying when she had.

'I shouldn't have come,' Francis said. 'She didn't want me to come.'

'You're thirty-seven years of age, Francis.'

'I did wrong to come.'

'You did no such thing.'

The time he'd taken her to Rome she'd been difficult for the whole week, complaining about the food, saying everywhere was dirty. Whenever he'd spent anything she'd disapproved. All his life, Father Paul felt, he'd done his best for her. He had told her before anyone else when he'd decided to enter the priesthood, certain that she'd be pleased. 'I thought you'd take over the shop,' she'd said instead.

'What difference could it make to wait, Francis?'

'There's nothing to wait for.'

As long as he lived Francis knew he would never forgive himself. As long as he lived he would say to himself that he hadn't been able to wait a few years, until she'd passed quietly on. He might even have been in the room with her when it happened.

'It was a terrible thing not to tell me,' he said. 'I sat down and wrote her a postcard, Paul. I bought her a plate.'

'So you said.'

'You're drinking too much of that whisky.'

'Now, Francis, don't be silly.'

'You're half drunk and she's lying there.'

'She can't be brought back no matter what we do.'

'She never hurt anyone,' Francis said.

Father Paul didn't deny that, although it wasn't true. She had hurt their sister Kitty, constantly reproaching her for marrying the man she had, long after Kitty was aware she'd made a mistake. She'd driven Edna to Canada after Edna, still unmarried, had had a miscarriage that only the family knew about. She had made a shadow out of Francis although Francis didn't know it. Failing to hold on to her other children, she had grasped her last-born to her, as if she had borne him to destroy him.

'It'll be you'll say a mass for her?' Francis said.

'Yes, of course it will.'

'You should have told me.'

Francis realized why, all day, he'd been disappointed. From the moment when the hired car had pulled into the lay-by and his brother had pointed across the valley at the Garden of Gethsemane he'd been disappointed and had not admitted it. He'd been disappointed in the Via Dolorosa and in the Church of the Holy Sepulchre and in Bethlehem. He remembered the bespectacled man who'd kept saying that you couldn't be sure about anything. All the people with cameras made it impossible to think, all the jostling and pushing was distracting. When he'd said there'd been too much to take in he'd meant something different.

'Her death got in the way,' he said.

'What d'you mean, Francis?'

'It didn't feel like Jerusalem, it didn't feel like Bethlehem.'

'But it is, Francis, it is.'

'There are soldiers with guns all over the place. And a girl came up to me on the street. There was that man with a bit of the Cross. There's you, drinking and smoking in this place—'

'Now, listen to me, Francis—'

'Nazareth would be a disappointment. And the Sea of Galilee. And the Church of the Loaves and Fishes.' His voice had risen. He lowered it again. 'I couldn't believe in the Stations this morning. I couldn't see it happening the way I do at home.'

'That's nothing to do with her death, Francis. You've got a bit of jet-lag, you'll settle yourself up in Galilee. There's an atmosphere in Galilee that nobody misses.'

'I'm not going near Galilee.' He struck the surface of the table, and Father Paul told him to contain himself. People turned their heads, aware that anger had erupted in the pale-faced man with the priest.

'Quieten up,' Father Paul commanded sharply, but Francis didn't.

'She knew I'd be better at home,' he shouted, his voice shrill and reedy. 'She knew I was making a fool of myself, a man out of a shop trying to be big—'

'Will you keep your voice down? Of course you're not making a fool of yourself.'

'Will you find out about planes tomorrow morning?'

Father Paul sat for a moment longer, not saying anything, hoping his brother would say he was sorry. Naturally it was a shock, naturally he'd be emotional and feel guilty, in a moment it would be better. But it wasn't and Francis didn't say he was sorry. Instead he began to weep.

'Let's go up to your room,' Father Paul said, 'and I'll fix about the plane.'

Francis nodded but did not move. His sobbing ceased, and then he said, 'I'll always hate the Holy Land now.'

'No need for that, Francis.'

But Francis felt there was and he felt he would hate, as well, the brother he had admired for as long as he could remember. In the lounge of the Plaza Hotel he felt mockery surfacing everywhere. His brother's deceit, and the endless whisky in his brother's glass, and his casualness after a death seemed like the scorning of a Church which honoured so steadfastly the mother of its founder. Vivid in his mind, his own mother's eyes reminded him that they'd told him he was making a mistake, and upbraided him for not heeding her. Of course there was mockery everywhere, in the splinter of wood beneath plastic, and in the soldiers with guns that were not toys, and the writhing nakedness in the Holy City. He'd become part of it himself, sending postcards to the dead. Not speaking again to his brother, he went to his room to pray.

'Eight a.m., sir,' the girl at the reception desk said, and Father Paul asked that arrangements should be made to book two seats on the plane, explaining that it was an emergency, that a death had occurred. 'It will be all right, sir,' the girl promised.

He went slowly downstairs to the bar. He sat in a corner and lit a cigarette and ordered two whiskies and ice, as if expecting a companion. He drank them both himself and ordered more. Francis would return to Co. Tipperary and after the funeral he would take up again the life she had ordained for him. In his brown cotton coat he would serve customers with nails and hinges and wire. He would regularly go to Mass and to Confession and to Men's Confraternity. He would sit alone in the lace-curtained sitting-room, lonely for the woman who had made him what he was, married forever to her memory.

Father Paul lit a fresh cigarette from the butt of the last one. He continued to order whisky in two glasses. Already he could sense the hatred that Francis had earlier felt taking root in himself. He wondered if he would ever again return in July to Co. Tipperary, and imagined he would not.

At midnight he rose to make the journey to bed and found himself unsteady on his feet. People looked at him, thinking it disgraceful for a priest to be drunk in Jerusalem, with cigarette ash all over his clerical clothes.

Siegfried on the Rhine

My grandmother, knowing her own mind as usual, had gone to Cortina d'Ampezzo as fast as trains could carry her, to await us in civilized surroundings, she said, while we dawdled our way through Germany. My mother had never seen Germany, whereas she had frequently seen her mother-in-law, and to please my mother we began our dawdle through Germany with a journey up the Rhine. That is how we came to be sitting in the public gardens of Coblenz on a Sunday in July in the year 1908.

The town band was playing. All around the bandstand were ranks of little metal tables each with three or four metal chairs, and though the band was playing with great volume and amplitude, and though the listeners were engaged in loud and happy conversations, the noise of band and listeners combined was quite often swamped by the noise of the metal chairs grating on the gravel as the family parties at the little tables got up to greet their friends or to call on waiters. Over our heads was a reef of plane tree boughs, quite notably silent, for there was not a breath of air.

And so we sat at our little table while the band played its way through a succession of massive potpourris, and my mother fanned herself in time with the band, since there was nothing else for her idle hands to do. Most of the ladies of Coblenz had brought their Sunday needlework with them. My father and I were feeling less conspicuous, as we were drinking beer; a matter of deep satisfaction to us both, for it signified a victory over my mother's determination to boil all the child's drinking water in case of typhoid. It was my third day as an infant alcoholic. I was quite accustomed to my state, and had even left off feeling belittled at the sight of children demonstrably younger than myself also drinking beer. My mother fanned herself, my father sat draped around his metal chair looking like a black puma in an hour of ease, the potpourri oscillated ponderously between dominant and tonic and came to a close.

There was a pause. The players spruced themselves, the horns emptied their instruments with particular attention, the drummer interrogated his drums. The conductor rose with a stern expression, gathered his instrumentalists, loosened his shoulders, and launched into the Funeral March from *The Twilight of the Gods*.

With a roar of gravel as when an Atlantic wave hits the beach, metal chairs were thrust back and all the men present rose to their feet and stood bareheaded at attention. So did my father. So would my mother and I have done, but he waved us down, to sit in conformity with the indigenous women and children.

For the puma was an ardent Wagnerian. Sachs could not muse too thoroughly for him, nor Wotan appear too often or stay too long. He loved Wagner as much as he disliked Germans. It was a matter of personal resentment to him that a nation that otherwise afforded Europe no manifestations of being much troubled by having music in its soul should have been allowed by some miscarrying providence to produce *Tristan* and *The Ring*. But now, while the players clashed and swam through the résumé of Siegfried's heroic career, he began to eat his words and make an amend. These exasperating Germans must be better than they seemed. Somewhere under that bellicose and pettifogging exterior there lay a genuine sensibility. For here they were, rising unprompted from their Sunday repose to honour a noble piece of music.

The Funeral March came to an end, the males of Coblenz sat down again, the band had a drink and set off on a polka, the waiters brought more mugs and more mats, the ladies embroidered on. But my father looked at all this with new eyes. After all, and little as the rest of the afternoon bore it out, there was music in their souls. Presently he began to talk to a gentleman at a neighbouring table, saying that it was a fine performance of the Funeral March.

'Yes, indeed,' said the gentleman warmly. 'Very fine. It was played as a tribute to our town clerk, who died last week, the unfortunate man! But how strange that you should know this music. The English are not a musical people.'

Pumas, after a momentary loss of balance, go walking along the bough with increased blandness, more impenetrable suavity. Just as did my father, talking with his new acquaintance, display a courteous interest in the life and death of an exemplary functionary.

The Faithful

The travels of youth, the cheapness of things, and one's intrepid poverty. 'All ye who love the Prince of Orange take heart and follow me.' So it was Holland that year, 1951. Descartes, more than three hundred years before, had spoken of himself as the only foreigner in Amsterdam not on business.

Everywhere we went in Europe that year, everywhere except for Amsterdam, there were Americans just like ourselves: those who had not been married long or were not married at all, most of us with fellowships and a little savings. We were to be seen now in December wearing winter coats pleated with the wrinkles of a long summer's rest in torn suitcases. Holland: led there by Motley's *The Rise of the Dutch Republic* and Fromentin's *The Masters of Past Time* in its neat little Phaidon edition.

An unfashionable *gracht* in the center of Amsterdam—the Nicolaas Witsenkade. A busy, bourgeois street bordering on sloppy waters, and the towers of the Rijksmuseum in view toward the west. Houses with stone steps and made of yellow or red brick were lined up in a business-like, practical, nineteen-twenties decency and dullness. Autumnal tile decorations on the façades, and here and there fans of purple and amber glass over the doorways.

Housewives of centuries had created the pleasantly stuffy little rooms with their dark paneling, had hung round lamps, with shades of old tasseled silk, over the carpeted dining tables. The house was not handsome, and the landlady worried about the apartment because it had been her own and everything in it was dear to her. Anyway, he and I said as we met her anxious glance: What a triumph every country is.

We observed that the coziness of small countries could not always be expropriated by an invader. Yes, a squat, round, shiny black stove that had worked for years with the solemn obedience of an old donkey tormented our days and nights with its balky resentment of a new and ignorant hand. Perplexing dying of the embers so soon after they had been coaxed to blaze. We crept into the cold sheets under the ancient thick coverlets and were held at head and foot by the heavy frame of the bed, pierced by the sharp metal of carved leaves and fruits, acute reminders of spring. Daylight came in a rush and the whole town came alive at dawn. The baker and coal seller arrived with such swiftness they might have been dressed and waiting throughout the night. Greedy travelers, Americans, hail the dawn of a new experience!

In the winter, sleet blew through the beautiful town, graying the waters of the Amstel. In the spring, in daylight and in the early evening, we used to watch on the porch that faced us the life of the unemployed Indonesians. Their ancestors had been exiles, once flung out from the swamps of the Zuiderzee to the humid airs of Djakarta. Now their children were returned colons, geographical curiosities, back once more to the sluices and polders of home, the unfamiliar homeland that received them with the chagrin proper to what they were: a delayed bill, finally arriving.

The Indonesians gathered on their porch, sitting there as a depressed late testament to the great energy of the Dutch, to old mapmakers, shipbuilders, moneylenders, diamond cutters, receivers of Jews, Huguenots, Puritans. The unions we were staring at had taken place on unimaginable sugar plantations, in the deranging heat of exhausting empires. Beautiful, liquid-brown women—silky petite mother-in-law, dust-colored child—their little wrists and ankles delicate as chicken bones. And the heavy, dry, freckled, tufted Dutchmen, homely and reassuring.

The disasters of the war still lay over the country, and yet all of our Dutch friends were reading Valéry Larbaud's A. O. Barnabooth: His Diary, enjoying the sly chic of the fabulously rich hero and his addiction to 'boutiqueism'.

The crowds of Amsterdam, and even the countryside filled with people in their houses, each one a sort of declassed nobleman sharing the space as a tree would patiently accept the nightly roosting of flocks and flocks of starlings. All the knowledge of Europe seemed to be nesting there, too. And a certain sadness, a gasping for breath: No, no, the strain is nothing; take no notice of it; I have just had a wish for the mountains.

In Amsterdam we knew many people, and not a single one has slipped from memory. Just now, dreaming, I am drawn back to a woman painter named Simone and to her fervent romancer, the eternal husband, Dr Z.

Dr Z had the moderate, well-nourished egotism suitable to his small, learned group of colleagues and friends and proper to the educated professional world of Amsterdam. He had his success, some of it medical, as a specialist in blood diseases, and some of it amorous. Because of the time he devoted to women, he might be surprised to find himself remembered as a *husband*.

In Holland, the coziness of life is so complete it cannot even be disturbed by the violent emotional ruptures that tear couples and friends forever apart in other places. Instead, their first husbands and first wives are always at the same dinner parties and birthday celebrations with their second husbands and wives. Divorces and fractured loves mingle together as if the past were a sort of vinegar blending with the oil of the present. Where can one flee to? New alliances among this restless people are like the rearrangement of familiar furniture. Houses and lives are thus transformed—up to a point. My dear, look, there is the man who plays his violin in the street and there is his son with the saxophone. Coins are falling from the windows. The shadow has passed and everything is in order once more. She moves into his place.

The *Herengracht*, a great improvement. His wife settles someplace else, taking along her volumes of the existentialist philosophers. What a pleasure to be recombining and yet not going anyplace. The old map of the central city, with its faded tintings, catches the sunlight.

Dr Z, all day in his white coat and in the evenings wearing a tie of bright red and blue stripes, was born in Amsterdam. But the blood of the East ran in his veins. There was something sheikish about him, and although there were more flamboyant men around, handsomer and younger, he occupied his space with a kindly, intense assurance. His personal life was rich in variety and yet thoughtful. His originality was that he did not shift so much as acquire.

Fidelity, consideration, sweet-natured uxoriousness were the marks of this faithless husband. In a way, he was like a cripple who yearly enters the hundred-yard dash. Bravo, everyone cried out when he scored. Of course, his exploits were not large in number and he was a busy, serious man who was often called to the platforms of universities and academies to receive honors. Still, he had his entanglements, rather plain and serious like himself, but worthy, intense, absorbing. Without ever leaving his only wife, he turned each of the women in his life into a wife. Have you paid your taxes? he would say; have you called your mother this week? Oh, dearest, I do not like the sound of that cough.

Many times, he was seized by the impulse to flee and thought himself ready or forced by love to 'make a new life'. But this was impossible for one who could not throw anything away. What a commitment intimacy always is, he would sigh. The sacred flow between men and women, in bed, conversing in a café, talking on the telephone, passing time. What didn't he know about the treacherous, beautiful, golden yoke of time?

Does one still enjoy his old schoolmates, his first cousins? That is not the point. They are one's schoolmates, one's cousins, and there is always something there, like the enduring presence of one's big toe.

Mevrouw Z: She had been there forever. They had been separated by the war, but managed to get back together in their same old house. Mevrouw Z liked to be called Madame Z, because she was French. Small, she must have become in her first youth one of those petite, compact persons who never change, who find a certain exterior style and accept it, as one accepts a piece of architecture for purchase. When her young black hair began to turn gray, she dyed it back to the old color and wore it in the short bob of her youth. The moment she got out of bed in the morning, she recolored her eyelashes with black mascara. She wore velvet berets and held firmly to her *look*, which announced like a trumpet that she was not Dutch, she was French. Otherwise, she did not conform to any of the notions of a French-woman. She did not cook well, she was not interested in attracting men, she did not have a shrewd hand with household accounts. She let an old Dutchwoman from the country look after the house. Madame Z was idle except for the enormous amount of reading she did and except for her passion for the French theater. She read about the theater in French papers every day and went to Paris often, taking in a performance every night.

After you had seen her a few times, you found that she was vain but not argumentative. Little appeared to her as new in life, little came as a surprise. It was appealing. She had the idea that a gross, uncomplicated self-interest was the old truth that a new force or person was trying to disguise.

Dr Z, who found the events of his own life flushed with the glow of the unique, the unexpected, the inexplicable, sometimes chewed his lip in annoyance when she expressed her belief in the principle of repetition. They lived in a profound intimacy nevertheless.

*

From Holland I wrote many complaining letters. Dear M: How cold the house is. How we fight after too much gin, etc., etc.

Complaining letters—and this one of the happiest periods of my life: With what gratitude I look back on Europe for the first time. So, that wraps up Verona. We take in the cracked windows and the brilliant dishevelment of Istanbul. And the long time in Holland: time to take trains, one to Haarlem to see the old almshouse governors painted in their unforgiving black-and-white misery by Frans Hals in his last days. The laughing cavaliers perhaps had eaten too many oysters, drunk too much beer, and died a replete, unwilling death, leaving the poor and their guardians, freed by a bitter life from the killing pleasures, to shrivel on charity, live on with their strong, blackening faces.

Antwerp and Ghent: what wonderful names, hard as the heavy cobbles in the square. Amsterdam, a city of readers. All night long, you seemed to hear the turning of pages: pages of French, Italian, English, and the despised German. Those fair heads remembered Ovid, Yeats, Baudelaire—and remembered suffering, hiding, freezing. The weight of books and wars.

Dr Z had acquired the nurse in his office. A fresh-looking woman who had never married and who lived frugally outside the center—a long trip on her bicycle. She had her occasional afternoons with Dr Z, afternoons now grown, according to gossip, as perfunctory and health-giving as a checkup. Oh, the burdens.

Dr Z acquired Simone, the painter, after her husband left her. He nudged the other two to make room. Simone was often spoken of as the most independent woman in Amsterdam. She was also the only female painter anyone talked about, and it was from her long, anxious struggle to establish herself that the independence had arrived. If indeed it had. She did not display any special happiness or confidence from 'doing something well'.

Why should painting pictures make you happy? she said. It is not a diversion. Her nerves were frazzled and she had a strong leaning toward melancholy and exhaustion. Yet, worn down by life as she saw herself to be, she was always in movement, and always running up and down the stairs to her studio on the fifth floor. In her agitated fatigue, Simone was a striking figure in tattered, mysterious clothes that she apparently bought in junk shops on her travels. Skirts and blouses and jackets of satin or flowered cloth, Balkan decorations, old beads, capes, shawls, earrings. The effect was sometimes that of a deranged frugality, and other times she brought it off, like the church dignitaries in Florence when they go in their worn velvets and shredded furs to release the dove from the altar of the Duomo.

Perhaps if she had been a man she would have become a cardinal. She had been born a Catholic, and although this had been set aside in the libertarian Amsterdam intellectual world, which was a sort of archive of Trotskyist, Socialist, and anarchist learning, Simone was sometimes seen slipping into church, wearing several large shawls in pitiful disguise. It was whispered that perhaps she was praying for the soul of her brother, who had collaborated with the Nazis.

Simone's husband looked like an Alpine skier and was, instead, a professor of history. He actually went off alone on a long skiing holiday in Austria, and in about six months a new woman arrived in Amsterdam, an American. I've always wanted an American, the husband said.

Dr Z was sympathetic to Simone and outraged by the husband's complacency, and more by his ridiculous happiness with the pretty American. The doctor would have managed differently somehow, in some way, man of binding memories that he was. He took to quoting the Russian folk song mentioned in Pushkin's story 'The Captain's Daughter':

> *If you find one better than*
> *me—you'll forget me,*
> *If one who is worse—you'll*
> *remember.*

Worse? How does he know now, and if it turns out that way it will be too late, Madame Z insisted.

Slowly, or not so slowly, Dr Z's duet became a trio. He and his wife had known Simone for years. Was that not favorable? Wasn't the ex-husband living with his American in the apartment below Simone's?

Dr Z was a passive man *by nature*; that is, he was often led to actions and moods quite the contrary. Certainly at the beginning of his affairs, this natural passivity took flight. He began in a frenzy of passionate feeling. He fell in love; he drank too much; he rushed through his work as quickly as possible and got home very late for dinner and sometimes not until midnight. His nest was shaken by the new windstorm, and the squawking of birds began. His wife said that this was exactly what she had expected and that it did not interest her. Simone hesitated, but there was the infatuated Dr Z with theater tickets. There he was holding fast to her arm as they passed her husband and the American girl at the door of the house. Soon she said with a disheartened sigh that she, too, was in love.

The nurse cried all day, even in front of the patients. When Simone sometimes called the office, the nurse abused and threatened her.

It is very poor medicine to have nurses in such a state, Simone said. Perhaps another position could be found for her.

Dr Z was taken aback but quickly resumed his ground. It's all over with her, he insisted, but I cannot turn away someone I have known and worked with for seven years.

Dr Z was jealous of Simone, and her silences filled him with terrible alarm. He pushed his love back a few years. Yes, he remembered being overcome with feeling years ago just at the sight of her buying a book in the square, and at a New Year's party when she was wearing green velvet shoes.

I don't remember anything of that sort. Right now is soon enough for me, she said.

At times, the doctor did not want to go home at night and announced that he was prepared to give his house to his wife or to set her up in France. For weeks, some new plan would seem to be working itself out. Yes, I am working it out, he said to everyone. But then the time came when his mood turned crestfallen and sad. He said Madame Z hated change.

No one likes change, Simone said. Dr Z wept. But it has been more than twenty years. Think of that.

In Amsterdam, there were no celebrated expatriates living in the hills or set up in flowery villas near the sea. One week, a lot of snow. Where are we? we wondered. In Iowa City? Northern Europe—many times, it was as if all of the trams were leading back to America. At night, feeling uprooted because so much was familiar, we would tell each other the stories of our lives. The downy, musty embrace of the bed set us afloat, not as travelers but as ones somehow borne backward to the bricks and stuffs of home.

We went to the flower market. A thousand still lifes. People, rushing about on the Leidseplein, revealed ghostly similarities to those we had left behind. The stove died, the snow clung to the panes, the outline of our fringed lamps caught the light of the street. In the shadows, listening to the bells ringing the hours, we would lie smoking and talking. The hills of home in the flatness of Holland. Think of it, he would say, our parents were born in the last century. The czar was out chopping wood for exercise.

History assaults you, and if you live you are restored to the world of gossip. That is what it had been for Dr Z. He was half Jewish and had spent time in a labor camp in Germany. This well-established Neder-lands lover, with his nervous alliances and peculiar fidelities, had looked death in the eye, had lived through the extermination of his younger brother. This life, his *aura*, remained in his proud, olive-tinted eyes, in his researches on the devastations flowing in the blood stream, in his death-defying lovemaking. He was a small, shrewd European country, moving about carefully in peacetime, driven on by the force of ghastly memories.

So, life after death is to fall in love once more, to set up a little business, to learn to drive a car, take airplane trips, go to the sun for vacations.

It began to appear that Simone was not suited to the role of mistress. She said: This thing has brought a coarsening of my nature. I hate Madame Z. What is she—a general? She seems to be giving a great many orders to those of us behind the lines.

Hate? Dr Z said. That's quite extreme. She has her qualities.

When Simone saw the wife on the street, she rushed off in the opposite direction. So fearful was she of a meeting that she would not go to her friends' houses without making careful inquiries.

The whole of their circle in Amsterdam was involved in the affair. This wish to oust Madame Z and the nurse is Simone's cardinal side, people decided. Yes, the little girl who held the hand of so many nuns cannot accept the purgatory of Dr Z's confusing nature and intentions.

One time, Madame Z went to Paris for several weeks. With a round-trip ticket of course, Simone observed bitterly. But in the freedom she and the doctor went for a weekend to London to look at pictures. It was not a happy time. Dr Z was always calling Paris to speak to his wife or calling his office to speak to the nurse. Telling them tremendous lies about a 'conference'. Simone spent most of her time in London saying: It will soon be over and we will be back where we started.

Dearest darling, do not rush to suffer future pain, the doctor said. But all went as she had predicted. Back once more, Simone could be seen several evenings a week at the window of her top floor, looking down on the street, waiting for the hurried approach of her lover. And late in the night, when he was returning to his wife, Simone would open the shutters and wave a long goodbye to the swarthy, badly dressed, vivacious man, now turning a corner and fading from sight.

Dr Z was happy in his love pains. He adored to spend the evening in Simone's studio, smoking a cigarette, drinking coffee, eating little chocolate cakes, and sipping gin. He was honestly more and more in love, and the genuineness of his feelings often caused Simone to burst into tears of anger.

Dr Z had studied the body and its workings and liked to say: We human beings are, *au fond*, put together quite simply. Yes, quite simply. The part that is complicated, even we as scientists are ignorant of that.

In matters of love he seemed to feel the same. His distressing trio caused him to be often fretful, sleepless, anxious, jealous, even drunken. But he also knew well the dejection of resignation and the torture of absence. So, tormented, accused, even guilty, there was still happiness to be found in reassuring the weeping nurse at the end of the day, in bringing home a pâté and cheese to his wife, in going down a dark canal on the arm of Simone and singing 'In questa tomba oscura'. Somehow he could lend to the noble composition a heartfelt flirtatiousness.

During our year in Holland, there was at last a movement of reclamation on the part of Simone. She broke off with the doctor and stayed in the house for weeks, for fear of meeting him and once more surrendering to his passion for her. He whistled below the window; potted tulips arrived. Look at the colors! A late Mondrian, no? his note would say.

He called upon the help of European poetry:

Alas for me, where shall I get the flowers when it is winter and where the sunshine and shadow of earth? The walls stand speechless and cold, the weather vanes rattle in the wind.

Simone was assisted by an attack of depression and did not turn back. She hurt the doctor's feelings by saying: I do not seem to care for anyone just now. Least of all myself.

The doctor's wife and the nurse were affronted by Simone's revolt. They accused her of triviality and shallowness, of heartlessness. The doctor's suffering fell alike upon them, as if it were a contagion. His alarm, his loss, his humiliation were an insult to themselves. And perhaps the two women, so accustomed to his ways, sensed that the singularity of endings may slowly gather into a plural.

*

Love affairs, with their energy and hope, do not arrive again and again forever. So you no longer play tennis, no longer move from place to place in the summer, no longer understand what use you can make of the sight of the Andes or the columns of Luxor. It gradually became clear that Simone would not be replaced. Poor Dr Z, with his infidelities and agreeable lies, his new acquisitions and engaging disruptions: they vanished suddenly but so quietly and naturally he was the last to know.

As Ralegh said about Queen Elizabeth: old age took her by surprise, like a frost.

In a few years, the nurse went home to retire, to look after her old mother in the country. Simone died. It turned out that she had done more than a dozen portraits of Dr Z, and one was sold to an American museum for a fair price. In it Dr Z is seen in a white jacket, and there are instruments of his profession about him. On the wall not one but three stylized skeletons are dangling from hooks.

Nineteen seventy-three. The doctor and his wife were in New York for a conference. I went to meet them at a shabby, depressing hotel in the West Seventies where Europeans who are not rich often stay. They were like two woolen dolls, and I could not decide whether the Frenchwoman had grown to the size of the Dutchman or whether he had, with a courteous condescension, simply inclined downward to the size of his little French wife. She was still wearing her black berets, and her fingernails shone with a wine-colored polish. She spoke in tongues: Dutch, German, French, and English, as if choosing cakes from a tray.

Dr Z met a mild New York winter day clothed in Siberian layers. He was wearing a heavy black overcoat, a woolen vest, a dark-gray sweater, and when he sat down in the waiting room off the lobby, gray winter underwear appeared above his socks.

He talked: he told the Amsterdam gossip, he spoke of his work, of the fearful cost of things, of hippies in Vondel Park.

Madame Z smoked cigarettes and coughed. They were studying the map of the city, looking for subway and bus lines. The outstanding difficulties of thrift in New York bewildered them, and they sat there as if pulled down into the mud of a dismaying displacement, the confusion that afflicts unfashionable, elderly foreigners when they visit America. They who had been everywhere, from Djakarta to Tokyo to India and every country in Europe.

Dr Z smiled and bowed and dashed about looking for chairs and a quiet corner. In fact, he seemed to be groping in the New York air for the supports of his life in Amsterdam, for his weathered little house on the Amstel, with his office on the first floor and the rooms above with the old patterned carpets, the comfort of the hideous abstract paintings given by patients, abstractions that covered the walls next to the stairs like so many colored water spots left over from an old leak.

Where is my life? he seemed to be saying. My plates of pickled mussels, the slices of cheese, the tumblers of lemon gin?

Still, importance flickered in his eyes—his olive eyes still shining with the oil of remembered vanity and threatening to water with the tears of all he had learned and forgotten in his long life.

We in Holland were the first to do certain important blood studies, he said. I no longer have my laboratory at the hospital, but I keep up with the developments in my field. How can one not? A life's work.

We in Holland kept appearing in his conversation. The vastness of the skies they had flown over and the large abyss into which they had fallen on the ground made him call forth his country—like an ambassador, one who stands for the whole.

You remember that he was well known there, his wife said without any special inflection. Oh, I know, I know. I remember well the well-known Dr Z.

Enough of that, he said. Edam cheese is better known than any Dutchman. That it is well to recall also.

As it got to be near six o'clock, I asked if they wanted to go to a nearby Irish saloon for a drink. The doctor drew back with a frightened look, but his wife took up the suggestion vehemently. Indeed, yes, she would like a drink, she said with a peculiar insistence and defiance.

We sat in a dark booth, and Madame Z ordered a martini. An American martini, she said twice. The doctor crumpled and sagged over a beer—Heineken's.

Supporting home industries, his wife said.

Suddenly in the gloom, Madame Z began her lilting harangue, all of it pouring forth with an appalling energy. She did not use to talk very much, the doctor said, attempting a smile. See the unbeckoned, unpredicted changes of age, the sky full of falling stars!

It was clear that the recitation was not new and that in the midst of it she could pause only to order another drink.

I have always hated Holland. I am not Dutch. I am French, born in Paris.

There are many Frenchmen, the doctor interrupted. It is not what I would call a special distinction in itself.

She went on. There are many Dutchmen, too, and all alike. The men and the women. The provincialism. Can you imagine a country proud of skinny Indonesians, dark and slow and surly primitives, serving in red coats? *Rijsttafel*—a joke. Nuts and raisins and bananas. I would rather have herring, if the choice must be made . . . And it must be made or starve . . . But the worst thing is the ugliness of the people. Who can tell the men and the women apart in their rotten mackintoshes, their rubber-soled shoes . . . Look at the queen—a joke. And old Wilhelmina in her tweeds, like a buffalo . . . And the weather, steaming like hell in the summer and drizzling sleet the rest of the year . . . *Drizzling*, is that English? . . . What is going on in Amsterdam, tell me? Someone playing the organ in a church. They think they are masters of culture when they speak French, but if you want to write something you write it in Dutch, which no one reads. And why should they? Even the Poles are better off. Warsaw is a real city, not a puppet-show setting like Amsterdam.

Her black, black hair, her tiny little black feet, her wine-colored fingers heavy with red and green semiprecious stones set in gold. She was like an old glazed vessel, veined and cracked, that nevertheless held water.

The doctor trembled. This is not what you would call a discussion, he said.

And, turning aside, he made an effort to change the awful flow. I am not a patriot, he said; still, couldn't I claim that the Dutch are a civilized people? A bit tiresome about the loss of Indonesia and all that, perhaps, but . . .

Indonesia! she shrieked, and the bartender shrugged. How all of you used to complain when you had to go out there to lecture—to advise, as you called it. To visit the rich men on their plantations. Little cries all night about the bugs and the humidity. The suffering sweat of the lordly Dutchman. Imagine Holland with colonies. Have you ever seen the so-called city of Paramaribo? It's a scandal, a joke.

Madame Z tottered to her feet, exhausted. The doctor took her arm and gave a sigh as deep as death itself. Out on the street, in the cold wind, he supported his little wife, who could not stand alone. She dangled on his arm like a black shopping bag. For the moment, she was quiet, and he attempted a lighthearted manner, a whispered addition.

As you can see, she has taken to drink in a disastrous fashion. A sigh, and then he bowed with something of his old sheikishness, drawing me into his memories.

It's all those love affairs—especially the darling Simone. They don't forgive you, after all. They have their revenge.

It seemed to soothe the doctor to try to take the blame, as if even the revenge brought him back to his younger days. It was not clear whether he believed what he was saying. The ruefulness of his smile.

As we neared the hotel, he said bitterly: It is only eight o'clock. But what can we do except go to bed without dinner? She will sleep it off and not remember a thing, the way they do. So mysterious. Yes, she must go to bed.

Bed! Madame Z cried out, calling upon her last breath. They are all terrible lovers. Frauds, every one of them. Fiascos!

They passed into the brown-and-gray lobby, old companions, sad but not quite miserable. They were waving goodbye. He was bowing and she was now winking and smiling.

She had hit the doctor like the Spanish Fury, but fortunately he was accustomed to the wind from the North Sea. Her hat askew and a strand of hair slanted down her cheek, Madame Z of Paris had at last become Dutch, needing only a few strewn oyster shells and a ragged dog to bring to mind those tippling, pipe-smoking women in the paintings of the seventeenth century, creatures of the common life the Dutch bourgeoisie were pleased to admire and purchase.

J. I. M. STEWART

The Bridge at Arta

Lady Cameron had recognized Charles Hornett at once.

It was in the departure lounge of Number Two Terminal at Heathrow. She had shown her passport, briefly resigned her hand-bag for rummaging, and walked through the contraption that rings a bell or flashes a light should one happen to be secreting any substantial metallic object about one's person. There was something slightly ignominious about this last manœuvre. Perhaps it suggested to cultivated persons (and on this trip, incidentally, they would all be that) the symbolic driving beneath a yoke which in the ancient world had transformed a free man into a slave. Lady Cameron had once, in a sense, been a slave, and she hadn't liked it at all.

Yes, there was Charles—instantly known, although unglimpsed for fifty years. He was among a group of people not themselves labelled (as happens on packaged tours within the simpler reaches of society) but with the distinctive yellow and red tags supplied by Messrs Pipkin and Pipkin dutifully attached to their hand-baggage. So here was another instantaneous discovery. She and Charles were together going to do 'Sites and Flowers of Thessaly and Epirus' under the guidance of Professor and Mrs Boss-Baker.

Lady Cameron had never gone out of her way to avoid a meeting with Charles, and she had from time to time envisaged—with amusement rather than discomposure—various circumstances under which a casual encounter might take place. It hadn't, indeed, been like that at the beginning; for a long period after their divorce she would have regarded anything of the sort as quite horrible. But after fifty years! It was almost something that *ought* to take place when each had survived their disaster so long. It would not be a touching occasion, or sentimental in any way. Essentially it would be curious. They would both comport themselves properly, and that would be that.

Lady Cameron saw a number of familiar faces in the little group.

There was a pronounced element of reunion in the occasion for many of them. Like Lady Cameron herself, they had 'been with' the Boss-Bakers before. Indeed, if you hadn't 'been with' the Boss-Bakers before, you were apt to feel, at least at the start, a bit of an outsider in the party. So what about Charles? He was already talking fluently to two elderly women a little wedged into a corner of the lounge. But as a conversationalist he had always been quick off the mark, and it was quite possible that he was a new boy in the Pipkin and Pipkin fold.

Mrs Boss-Baker bore down on Lady Cameron with enthusiastic acclaim. This wasn't because Lady Cameron, being a baronet's widow, was likely to be the person of most formal consequence in the group. Mrs Boss-Baker was always enthusiastic, although it didn't prevent her from also being wary and alert. She had a genius for smoothing things over almost before they were ruffled. If you had been promised that your 'facilities' would include a proper bath and you found yourself fobbed off with a shower, Mrs Boss-Baker would know in advance precisely how cross you were likely to be, and proceed to action in the light of this knowledge. And nobody could call her shy. Professor Boss-Baker *was* shy. He was invariably voted, indeed, wholly delightful; he was a marvellous lecturer; and although he claimed competence only over the flowers he was a classical man by training and knew quite as much about the sites as did the young Greek archaeologists commonly turned on to expatiate about them. Only Professor Boss-Baker did have an odd propensity for simply slipping away. At one moment he would be talking charmingly and instructively to the ladies of his party on this wild flower and that, and the next moment he would have disappeared, mysteriously and unaccountably, into a landscape that ought not to have afforded cover for a mouse. His wife, however, was always to hand.

Mrs Boss-Baker recalled former trips, and Lady Cameron made suitable replies. It gave her time to think about Charles, and also to assess as a whole the party as so far constituted. It was an elderly crowd; indeed it was possible to suppose that she and Charles, both in their mid-seventies, were going to consort with several people a good deal older than themselves. Some of them, it occurred to her, might go in for remembering insignificant social events remote in time. But the small history of Charles Hornett and herself had been very insignificant indeed, and it was only her second marriage that had made her known beyond the bounds of a single parish. So although she had met some of these elderly people on previous trips it was unlikely that any of them would have a story to tell the others about Charles and herself. Which was just as well—trivial although the whole thing was. A divorced couple finding themselves fortuitously on the same tour would come under a good deal of covert scrutiny were their relationship—or former relationship—discovered and bruited abroad.

There was, of course, Mrs Boss-Baker. It was quite clear that she never set out on one of these expeditions without doing vigorous homework on the pedigree of her flock. This enabled her never to put a foot wrong. She and her husband, she would cheerfully confide to you, had to hold down the job year after year if their two sons were to continue at their public school. It was only a commendable love of Greece on the part of a small section of the English prosperous classes that stood between these youths and the horrors of comprehensive education. So Mrs Boss-Baker, although she might well know the truth, would be discretion itself.

'Charles, this is after more years than one cares to remember . . .' Lady Cameron had decided to begin—and for the moment pretty well to end—with that. Later on, she and Charles would work it out that there had formerly been some slight acquaintanceship between them. It would be deception—but deception of a civilized sort, designed to obviate any occasion of embarrassment to other people. And perhaps she had better not turn to Charles at once. For one thing, it didn't look as if he had yet noticed her; for another, the Peppers were now in evidence, and had. The Peppers frequented the enterprises of Messrs Pipkin and Pipkin with an assiduity suggesting both uncommon physical vitality and enormous wealth. Yet they were a weedy couple, and it was demonstrably not to the 'higher' clergy that the Reverend Mr Pepper belonged. So there was something enigmatical about the Peppers, although a modicum of light was perhaps cast on it by Mrs Boss-Baker's occasional discreet reference to Mrs Pepper as coming of 'people very well known in the City'. Lady Cameron conversed for a few minutes with the Peppers. Mr Pepper, as usual on these occasions, retained his somewhat shabby clerical attire. But this effect he had a little lightened—as again was his custom—by superimposing upon it a new and therefore immaculate panama hat. Such objects, Lady Cameron vaguely believed, nowadays cost about as much as an air ticket to Athens.

And now for Charles, Lady Cameron resolved. He was still talking to the two women in a corner. But no: that was incorrect. It was the same corner, but a different brace of women. And as Lady Cameron approached they moved away. It had been a shade oddly, she thought. Could they conceivably have been aware of an awkward moment as in prospect? Or was it simply that Charles *still* . . . ? But there was no time for speculation, and Lady Cameron's prepared words were on her lips. They died there. Charles, planted squarely in front of her, was looking at her absolutely blankly. For a moment she supposed that this was what used to be called the cut direct; that Charles was simply going to refuse to know her. Then the truth came to her. He hadn't recognized her. He was totally failing to recognize her now. It was rather a bewildering situation. Curiously, too, it was an intensely humiliating one.

Mrs Boss-Baker was at their side. The admirable woman had sensed some *contretemps* from afar and on the instant, and now she was performing an introduction.

'Lady Cameron,' she said, 'may I introduce Mr Hornett? Mr Hornett has not been with us before, but has travelled extensively in the Far East. Mr Hornett, this is Lady Cameron, who has been President of the Alpine Flower Society.' Having thus provided two little spring-boards towards acquaintanceship, Mrs Boss-Baker departed on some further diplomatic mission. She would keep it up untiringly until their flight was called and they had all been settled in their seats.

'How do you do?' Charles said with the perfunctory air (which Lady Cameron well remembered) of one getting through a useless preliminary. 'I'm afraid I know nothing about alpine flowers. But I can tell you something I remember about my tactics when I decided I had as much information as I needed about the plans I had been working on when I was in Persia.'

'In Persia?' It was in a tone of well-bred interest that Lady Cameron contrived to respond to this prolix remark. Inwardly, she was overwhelmed. Charles *was* just as he had been. And how could it be otherwise? Leopards don't change their spots, nor bores their blotches. Her former husband's egotism, so mysteriously masked during their brief courtship, had calamitously revealed itself in the earliest days of their marriage. And now (if the thing were possible) he was even more of a monomaniac than he had proved to be fifty years ago.

'Of course I hadn't believed a word they told me,' Charles was saying. 'I'm not a fool, and it was as simple as that. I didn't believe a word of it.' Charles's tone had now become aggressive, resentful, aggrieved —although what he was embarking upon was plainly an anecdote designed to show how he had triumphed over enemies. 'I rather fancy

I always know just where I stand when I find that it's with cattle of that sort that I have to deal.'

Charles continued in this vein without any sign of stopping. It was all hideously of the past, and yet present here and now. She had been buried under this, stifled by it, crushed by it as by a cartload of stone, when she had been no more than a young bride. But now there was a bizarre superaddition to the burden. He still hadn't a clue about her. He still believed her to be a stranger—an empty pot, a blank sheet or *tabula rasa*, for the reception, for the remorseless inscribing or incising, of all this compulsive self-absorption.

Lily Cameron had been a beauty. She liked to believe that people still spoke of her as a handsome woman. Was she in brutal truth an unrecognizable ruin? Charles wasn't. Age had not withered him nor custom staled his infinite monotony. And again she had that dreadful sense of humiliation. Feebly, she told herself that his eyesight might have become defective—and his hearing, surely, as well. But that was a wholly unnecessary conjecture. As a young man his self-regard had been a literal thing. Even on their bridal night he probably hadn't really *seen* her. So why should he be seeing her now?

Nor, presumably, had he ever thought of her after they had parted, or acquainted himself with her subsequent fortune in any regard. Her second married name would mean nothing to him. Hence this strange situation. There seemed no reason why it should not continue through the fortnight that lay ahead. That, certainly, would be the most comfortable thing: that when they parted here at Heathrow he should be in the same state of ignorance as held him now. But would playing it that way be quite—well, spirited? Ought there not to be, at some time during their trip, a denouement to this small absurd episode? Lady Cameron, who owned a sense of style, was not at all sure that it oughtn't to be so.

The flight to Athens was called, and the Pipkin and Pipkin party—individually scurrying or at leisure according to their degree of experience as pilgrims—made their way down the long sloping corridor leading to their plane. Lady Cameron, it need scarcely be related, secured herself a seat comfortably remote from Charles Hornett.

'Sites and Flowers' didn't, as it happened, begin too well. Athens duly appeared below them, and the Acropolis was glimpsed. Both disappeared; a little later both turned up again; and a little later still they were plainly over nowhere in particular. Then the captain's voice announced with careful indifference that there was trouble at Alexandria, and that Athens was in a bit of a fuss as a result. For the time being, in fact, Athens would have nothing to do with them. So they were now on their way to Salonika, which it was to be hoped would prove more hospitable, as their endurance was running out. This last was an ambiguous expression, since it might refer either to human patience or to aviation fuel. Mr Pepper, who had a map, announced that Salonika appeared to be about two hundred miles away.

In circumstances such as these the English are not, indeed, tight-lipped, since anything of the kind may indicate nervous strain. Rather they are low-keyed. The Pipkin and Pipkin party, although their ears were alert to catch the first spluttering of an engine which would draw upon them an Icarian fate in the Aegean now so unexpectedly expansed beneath them, conversed quietly from time to time on indifferent topics. Or they all did this except Charles Hornett—who conversed, or rather monologized, unintermittedly and in a penetrating voice to the two unfortunate ladies of his first acquaintance. His subject, being that of a battle fought with a recalcitrant Inspector of Taxes in the previous year, could have been only of a somewhat confined interest to his hearers, but this didn't prevent Charles from according it a saga-like breadth of treatment. Mrs Boss-Baker (who had just been constrained to announce to her charges that tea and biscuits had run out on the plane, but that drinking-water was still in moderate supply) must already have been aware that in Mr Hornett (widely travelled in the Far East though he might be) she had a first-class problem on her hands.

Salonika made no bones about receiving them, and after half an hour even permitted them to disembark—although it then immediately incarcerated them in an enormous glass box. The acoustics of this were notable as combining great resonance with the qualities of an echo-chamber of the kind favoured by the BBC when in quest of eerie effects. It was just right for Charles, who lived up to its opportunities for something under three hours. The party was then embarked again, flown back to Athens, given a meal in a restaurant distinguishably over-taxed and appalled by their arrival, and then driven for three hours in a coach through magnificent scenery which was unfortunately invis-ible. Finally, at two o'clock in the morning, they tumbled into bed in a hotel which the less bemused or better informed understood to be in the neighbourhood of Delphi. For a few quite appreciable periods during this Odyssey Charles was out of action. He owned the enviable faculty of being able to fall asleep at will, and to wake up fifteen min-utes later, restored and alert for new exertions. During this nocturnal journey, too, he made the happy discovery that the coach in which the succeeding twelve days were to be largely spent was half as big again as the Pipkin and Pipkin crowd required. This meant that he could move round the vacant seats in turn—'chatting' (as he would have outrageously expressed it) to a succession of small captive audiences.

On the following morning the party, to a man (or woman) heroically declaring itself refreshed and fit for anything, paid a visit to Hosios Loukas. Professor Boss-Baker, declaring himself wholly uninstructed on early Byzantine art, in fact knew at once which were the most approved mosaics, and was charmingly perceptive, if also a little whimsical, in front of them.

'He means business, you know,' Professor Boss-Baker said of the Christ of *The Harrowing of Hell.* 'You can see he won't let go of Adam easily. Eve is expected to look after herself. And as for David and Solomon—I'm told it's David and Solomon there on the left—they're quite clearly just you and me. So you can see how amazement and gratification are expected of us—and quite right, too, of course.'

There was a murmur of appreciation among the Pipkins—evoked partly by this important artistic object itself and partly by the Professor's lightness of touch in hinting the propriety of mild reverence before such strange old things. Mrs Pepper ventured to explain with agreeable diffidence why the sun and moon were simultaneously present at the Crucifixion, and her husband translated the inscriptions on several of the mosaics. It was in the middle of this that Charles's voice was again heard, addressing an unwary individual who had strayed from the company.

'And he had the damned cheek,' Charles's voice was heard by all to declare, 'to propose raising an assessment under Schedule D.'

Lady Cameron slipped out of the *catholicon* into the warm sun. Here in mid-April there was already the scent of lemon blossom in the air, and across the groves and orchards the eye travelled to the foothills of Helicon. '"Where Helicon breaks down in cliffs to the sea",' she murmured to herself. But she wasn't feeling poetical. She was feeling ashamed. She knew—although she was now almost certain that none of her present companions were aware of her as having been Charles's wife—that she was going to feel her heart sink every time she heard him speak. It would be her impulse always to edge away from him, as one used to edge away from a rashly chosen schoolfriend when she proved liable to talk shaming nonsense.

On the following day the party 'did' Delphi, but Lady Cameron cried off. She had been to Delphi before, and could recall being properly awed by the undeniable numinousness of the site. She had been told, however, that it was now much commercialized. ('"Not here, O Apollo, are haunts fit for thee",' she pronounced, returning to Matthew Arnold's poem.) And of this she made an excuse to herself for a get-away plan. She ordered sandwiches and summoned a taxi—for she was a capable woman—and proposed to spend the day in solitude on the plateau of Mount Parnassus. But quite this was not to be. Mrs Boss-Baker appeared as she was about to drive off—a Mrs Boss-Baker all conspiratorial fun.

'Please, can I come too?' Mrs Boss-Baker asked childishly. 'Oh, I am wicked! Here's only the second day, and I'm dying for a little time off.'

Lady Cameron produced the necessary cordial acquiescence, although inwardly she was inclined to be annoyed. Just because she was seventy-four this interfering woman was judging her unfit to go off for a day's ramble by herself. It was totally insufferable! But then Lady Cameron remembered those two boys at Rugby—paid for year by year at the cost of this sort of eternal vigilance on their parents' part. If the Boss-Bakers lost a baronet's doddering old widow over a precipice it was quite certain that Messrs Pipkin and Pipkin wouldn't be too pleased. So Lady Cameron's heart warmed towards Mrs Boss-Baker, and they got on excellently together throughout the day.

There was a lake and there was a deserted village. ('Goldsmith in Phocis', Lady Cameron said—to the bewilderment of Mrs Boss-Baker, who was not literary.) They walked through irises and tiny forget-me-nots and sheets of blue veronica; chats and pipits and buntings enlivened the immediate scene; falcons and vultures hovered; in the distance the Muses' haunt lay under brilliant sunlit snow. It was a perfect day, and ought to have been totally absorbing. Yet for Lady Cameron it wasn't quite that. Ought she to have stuck it out? She asked herself the question again and again as it returned to her from its hiding-place half-a-century back. Had she hung on, could she have broken through the dreadful prison of self-absorption that Charles had constructed for himself? Its walls had thickened over the years, and were certainly impregnable now. Even at the time of her first horrified realization of his malady— for it was certainly that—she had judged it to be already so. But she had been very young—and might she not have been wrong? And to have stood before an altar with a man, taking tremendous vows—and then to have divorced him merely because he was a bore! And that had been it. Not, of course, in law. Only in queer places in America could you at that time have parted with a husband for such a reason.

She had detected poor Charles in sporadic low amours—and had hardly blamed him in the least. It would have been unfair to do so, since her own going to bed with him had proved mutually unrewarding. But it was something upon which she was entitled to seize, and she *had* seized upon it—unscrupulously, she now told herself. It had, naturally, all been very uncomfortable. In those days any sort of airing adultery in court had been very uncomfortable indeed.

Thus did Lady Cameron, sharing her sandwiches with Mrs Boss-Baker on the slopes of Mount Parnassus, meditate a distant past. She knew that it wasn't a very effective meditation, in the sense of being one that might lead to a changed course of conduct. She knew that she couldn't have done other than she had done, and that if it could all happen again she would do it again. And she *had* stuck it out—for quite long enough to *know*. Why, for two whole years it was almost literally true that she had been reduced to silence—since from dawn to dusk there had scarcely been an opportunity of getting a word in edgewise! And how different it had been with her second husband. She and Donald had been endlessly interested each in the other. They had chattered together like happy children through a long married life.

Mrs Boss-Baker did not intrude upon these periods of abstraction on the part of her companion. From time to time their conversation strayed from the birds and flowers to one or another member of their party—sometimes not without amusement, but predominantly on the proper note of cordial regard. Mrs Boss-Baker said nothing about Mr Hornett. Was this because he was fast becoming such a pain in the neck (Lady Cameron had a brother who would have used this phrase) that any reference to him had tacitly been voted taboo? Or was it because Mrs Boss-Baker had indeed done her homework only too well? Lady Cameron didn't much mind. Only she was coming to feel a little sorry for Charles. Surely through the terrible bars he had forged for himself he sometimes peered out and was aware of the figure he cut? Yes—she told herself again—she might have done something about it once, but it was too late now. The weird fact of his continued failure to identify her surely spoke of a pathological condition of a formidable sort, not to be resolved by amateurs.

The taxi reappeared, and in half an hour restored the two wanderers to their companions. Mrs Pepper, it seemed, had taken a photograph of the Castalian Spring, but was apprehensive that she had superimposed it upon one of the Sanctuary of Athena Pronaea. Another lady was triumphing in the discovery of an unfamiliar bee-orchid, pronounced by Professor Boss-Baker to be quite a surprise in this habitat. A third had stolen some bay leaves, and was enquiring whether it would be a further misdemeanour to smuggle them into England. Lady Cameron joined the group she judged likeliest to suggest a preliminary glass of *ouzo* before changing for dinner. Fortified by this, she ventured to speculate anew to herself on what would happen were she to confront Charles with the revelation that she was his former wife. She decided that it would be merely wounding and bewildering, and therefore a wicked and silly thing to do.

It was the agreeable custom of Professor Boss-Baker to spend half an hour or so after dinner talking about the following day's prospects to any members of his party who cared to gather around. He did this with the most casual air, but in fact was contriving to keep a cunning balance of interest between one sort of activity and another. Everybody was going to get a fair share of their sort of thing. The botanical ladies (who were in a majority) would be afforded ample scampering grounds for hunting down the rarer flora of the region. But the archaeologically minded, and those who (like the Peppers) were deeply versed in the Glory that was Greece, and again those more modish persons who were becoming well seen in Byzantine art: all would be catered for in the most accommodating fashion. Professor Boss-Baker performed this task in a slightly throwaway manner which—as has been recorded—was judged very delightful in an overpoweringly learned man.

He mounted such an occasion on the evening before their arrival at Arta. Arta, it seemed, was stuffed with history—mainly of the ecclesiastical order. There were little churches all over the place, acting as a kind of supporting chorus to one big one. The Panagia Parigoritissa—which somebody had told him meant the Virgin of Consolation—was a very rum thirteenth-century effort indeed: so rum that they mustn't mistake it for a bank and try to cash their travellers' cheques in it. Once inside the unlikely cube they would be in the presence of a naked architecture which was quite breathtakingly strange. There would be a guide who would have a great deal to say about it. In fact what with cyclopean walls, and the palace of the Greek metropolitan, and mosques and synagogues thrown in, they would be hurried round for the whole day after their arrival if they cared to be. So it had occurred to him that it might be a good idea to drive straight to the bridge before going to their hotel.

'Is it an *important* bridge?' one of the botanical ladies asked. Bridges were not her thing, but she had been brought up to respect objects adequately starred in Baedeker or Michelin.

'It has a certain historical interest,' Professor Boss-Baker said mildly. 'The river, you know, is the ancient Arachthos. Not long ago—or not long ago as one reckons time in these parts—it marked the frontier between Greece and Turkey. It's a Turkish bridge, although that fact is probably ignored locally. But it was treated as neutral ground, and what happened when it required repair, I don't know. It's a handsome and picturesque structure—on nine semi-circular arches, if I remember aright.'

'But isn't there a legend?' Mrs Pepper asked. 'I'm sure I've read somewhere about the legend of the bridge at Arta.'

'There's certainly a legend, and it's even older than this particular bridge is. Like the trade-winds, such things move with the sun from country to country, changing a little as they go.'

'Like ballads,' one of the botanical ladies said with a flash of erudition in an unexpected field.

'Just so. And it's in a Greek folk ballad—not, I believe, a particularly ancient one—that the legend hitches on to the bridge at Arta. But it's a slightly macabre affair, I'm afraid.' Professor Boss-Baker glanced round his auditory—which was, of course, predominantly female—in a hesitant way. But this was a merely teasing manœuvre, since he had every intention of telling his story. 'The bridge-builder got into trouble every time his work neared completion. At the final and critical moment, when the principal keystone was just about to be slipped into place, the whole affair fell down. It kept on happening until one night along came a raven and had a word with him. The raven was some sort of tutelary spirit, I imagine, and it told him just what to do. He must immure in the foundations—alive, needless to say—the first living creature that came in sight. This might have been a goat or a donkey, I suppose, but as things turned out it was the builder's wife. So there was no help for it. Professional success and duty were paramount, and in she went.'

'How extremely horrible!' one of the botanical ladies said.

'Well, yes.' Professor Boss-Baker was delighted at having elicited this reaction. 'And it wasn't, if the ballad is to be believed, any sort of sharp and short occasion. There is some difficulty in lowering the unfortunate woman into position, and she makes a long and lugubrious speech while the job is going on. One gets the impression of a somewhat insistently talkative person. She enters, in fact, on a good deal of family history. Two of her sisters, it seems, were married to bridge-builders, and precisely this fate overtook them. It seems improbable, one must admit. But that sort of thing is constantly happening in ballads the world over, is it not? I believe it's known as the technique of incremental repetition. However, the bridge got completed; it's there to this day; and we're all going to stand on it and meditate the tale. I don't know whether it can be said to have a moral.'

'I rather think it has,' Mr Pepper said. He had perhaps observed that some of the ladies were really shocked by Professor Boss-Baker's recital, and aimed at offering some droll comment upon it. 'Prudent wives will keep clear of their husbands' work. For my part, I deprecate the suggestion. Long may my own wife continue to find time and inclination to cast a critical eye over my sermons.'

From Mr Pepper, this was quite a sally, and it was strongly approved of. Lady Cameron, however, was among those not much amused by the story—or rather by the slightly morbid notion of a kind of tourist attraction having been manufactured out of it. She would have been glad enough not herself to have to visit the bridge at Arta. But this, she saw, could not be, since the coach was going to take the whole party straight there at the end of their next day's run. She glanced across at Charles, whom as usual on these after-dinner occasions she had contrived a little to distance. He had actually listened in silence to Professor Boss-Baker's narrative. He even appeared to have been much struck by it.

Perhaps because of the build-up it had received, the bridge at Arta proved rather a flop. Unlike Delphi, or Dodona, or even the charming island where Ali Pasha had lived so unspeakably scandalous a life (and which is still in the charge, most improperly, of half-a-dozen extremely personable young men), the bridge and its environs were by no means heavy with the spirit of place, whether numinous or otherwise. The Arachthos flowed in a rapid but well-conducted way beneath its arches; on its banks there were a few old men fishing and a few young couples making not particularly passionate love; at one end there were some broken-down farm buildings and a low pot-house of the most unpromising sort. But the parapet was of a height convenient for leaning upon and its stone was warm from the sun. People lit cigarettes, or took photographs, or talked about English gardens. The more elderly exchanged information about ailments or grandchildren. Nobody much thought about the bridge-builder's wife. There was perhaps a slight impatience to board the coach again, be driven on to their hotel and discover whether in Arta bathrooms had baths or not.

Lady Cameron did again think of the ballad. Professor Boss-Baker had told her that, although there was almost certainly no woman's skeleton imprisoned beneath her feet, it was likely enough that some member of the brute creation had been unkindly done by at an appropriate stage in the bridge's fashioning. She disliked the idea of such a ritual, and as a consequence walked the full length of the structure and got on innocent earth again. It was possible to follow the farther bank for some way downstream to a point from which the bridge would appear at least pleasingly picturesque. In this interest she strolled on, not much regarding the time, or reflecting that she had injudiciously sundered herself from her fellow-travellers. But this she suddenly found was not entirely so. Immediately in front of her the figure of a man had emerged abruptly from behind a tree—perhaps having withdrawn there for some trivial private purpose. And this last circumstance absurdly lent a small additional edge of unease to the disconcerting fact that the man was Charles.

'Oh, Lady Cunningham!' Charles said in his perfunctory way. He hadn't bothered to acquire more than random approximations to the names of any members of the party. 'I wonder whether I left my camera on my seat when I got out of the bus. And I happened to have an eye on the driver and I don't think I saw him lock the doors as he ought to have done. I can tell you something about how I came by that camera in a way I'm rather proud of.' Charles didn't sound proud; he sounded, as he always did, immensely aggrieved about something that he would communicate to you in due course. And *that*—Lady Cameron suddenly remembered—had really been it. It had been the constant note of discontent and self-commiseration accompanying Charles's solipsistic maunderings that had put the final lid on things. And this had continued, like the drone on a bagpipe, through all the varied exigencies, whatever they had been, of the past fifty years of his life! It was a horrible thought: much more horrible, even, than the thought of a woman buried in a bridge.

Lady Cameron tried to think of something to say. So far, she had been very successful in avoiding Charles, and this sudden encounter with him in near solitude almost frightened her. Tête-à-tête like this, it was surely impossible that he shouldn't recognize her at last. She felt, too, as she had not felt before, that on her own part it was demeaning to continue concealing her identity as if she were ashamed of it. She even wondered how she had conceivably justified the deception to herself in the first place. Yet she knew that this was only a matter of a momentary failure of nerve. Why should she take any step that involved having more to do with Charles than the odd coincidence of their both being on this Pipkin and Pipkin affair made necessary?

'I think we had better go back to the coach,' Lady Cameron said.

But in the very moment that she uttered these words, Lady Cameron realized that they proposed something no longer possible of fulfilment. Beyond the bridge the roof of the coach was visible above the small tumble-down farm building. And it was evident that the vehicle was in motion.

'I suppose the fellow's just turning round,' Charles said, having himself become aware of what was happening. But he spoke without conviction, and it quite clearly wouldn't do. The coach was gathering speed. The coach disappeared in the direction of Arta.

'I've known Mrs Boss-Baker do it before,' Lady Cameron said, with a casualness she didn't actually feel. 'She's extremely careful, but she does occasionally count the heads incorrectly. It must be very easy to do.'

'But I can't believe she'd fail to see I wasn't yet on board the damned thing!' Charles exclaimed indignantly. 'It's impossible! It's an outrage! I'll have the woman sacked.'

'I don't think we ought to take it too seriously, Mr Hornett. And we had better return over the bridge at once. It's probable they'll turn back in a few minutes. They mayn't miss me, but they're certain to miss your voice.'

'I bloody well hope so.' Charles had been conscious of no barb in his companion's words. 'But if they don't miss me until it comes to allocating the rooms in the hotel, they mayn't come back to pick me up for more than an hour.' Charles paused, broodingly. 'Or you,' he added as an unexpected afterthought.

'Let us hope it won't be as long as that.' Lady Cameron now felt that it quite probably would be. Her former husband did, after all, take those fifteen-minute naps on board the coach. So her small witticism hadn't meant much. 'For I rather think,' she said, 'that it's going to turn chilly.' This was undeniable. As they reached the apex of the bridge a cold wind caught them. She regretted that she had left her overcoat in the coach. For that matter she had left her handbag as well, which wasn't at all her habit. This meant that she was penniless. It wasn't important, but it was a shade vexatious. The town of Arta was invisible, and might be several miles away. The anglers and the courting couples had departed, and the surroundings now registered a back-of-beyond effect which was far from pleasing. There was nothing but the pot-house they were now approaching, and it was no more than a low hovel with a couple of dirty benches outside. Lady Cameron disliked the effect of dependence on Charles which all this engendered.

'I'd say it was a pub of sorts,' Charles announced. 'I dare say I can get a drink. I'll ask them for an *ouzo*.' He glanced absently at Lady Cameron, and it was as if a vague memory of the usages of civilization stirred in his head. 'What about you, Lady Cunningham?'

'A *café grecque*, perhaps.' Lady Cameron had been so surprised that she sat down abruptly on one of the grubby benches, although it was something she had just decided not to do.

'Ten drachmas.'

It was not the habit of Messrs Pipkin and Pipkin's pilgrims to be perpetually standing one another drinks, but in the present circumstances this demand was decidedly peculiar.

'My purse is in the coach,' Lady Cameron said briefly.

'Ah, yes.' Charles spoke as if this settled the matter, and departed. When he emerged again from the hovel he was carrying a single glass. It wasn't a matter, his former wife told herself, of brutish bad manners. Charles wasn't exactly like that. It was much more that the very existence of other people in the universe was a fact continually slipping from him even between one second and the next. Strictly regarded, much of his monologue was really pure soliloquy. And now, when he had sat down with his drink in front of him, he was actually silent for some time. Any attention that he did pay to the external world appeared to be directed towards the bridge, close to which they were still sitting. Lady Cameron was silent too; she felt rather like one of those bespangled females whose function is to disappear opportunely on the stage of an illusionist. Once or twice she detected Charles as producing a sound which she had very little memory of associating with him: a kind of semi-internalized laughter. He seemed to be tickled by the bridge.

Then something very disturbing happened. Charles ceased gazing at the bridge and gazed at her instead. He was actually gazing at her with genuine, if fleeting, curiosity. And he was looking puzzled, as well.

'I'll tell you an odd thing about myself,' Charles said abruptly. 'It has come into my head that you remind me of somebody.'

'Indeed, Mr Hornett?'

Lady Cameron had offered this convention of mild encouragement automatically. She still didn't in the least want to encourage or coax her former husband's pathologically defective memory. But clearly the thing now had to come. There was no point in attempting diversion or delay.

'Only I can't remember who it is. Perhaps it will come back to me later. Of course it can't be of any importance to me, can it?'

'Almost certainly not, I should imagine.' Lady Cameron produced this reply with some relief, and at the same time she looked anxiously in the direction of what she supposed to be the road from Arta. There was always the possibility that a relief expedition would heave into view. And now for the moment the crisis had passed. Charles's attention had wandered again. It was once more engaged with the bridge.

'I call that a damned good yarn,' he said. 'Sensible chap, eh? And resourceful, too. I'll bet he made up that raven.'

'Perhaps the whole story is made up. It's not a particularly agreeable one.'

'Depends on how you look at it. And I'll tell you another interesting thing about myself, Lady Cunningham. I had a wife just like that myself. Never stopped chattering at me. I tell you I just could not shut her up. But this chap managed that in the simplest and most literal manner. Piled up the rubble on her, eh? Stout fellow! I drink to him.'

Charles Hornett raised his glass and drained it. He showed no awareness that the woman vaguely known to him as Lady Cunningham was staring at him in naked horror. And even when she had a little recovered herself she didn't attempt to speak. The strangeness of this neat and convinced reversal of historical fact was too much for her. For the present, at least, she simply wanted to get away, to be released from a nightmare at once absurd and insupportable.

And release was at hand. Suddenly as if by magic, the coach had appeared and was drawing to a halt beside them. It contained only the driver and Mrs Boss-Baker—who was already lavishly signalling rescue and apology.

'Well, thank goodness for that,' Charles said. 'I was getting damned bored, sitting outside this God-forsaken pub and talking about nothing at all. At least I shan't be late for my dinner.' He stood up, glancing blankly at Lady Cameron as he did so. Or glancing, so to speak, at where she was. For it was reassuringly evident—she somehow knew this—that her former husband wouldn't give her another thought during the remaining course of 'Sites and Flowers of Thessaly and Epirus'.

ALICE ADAMS

Greyhound People

As soon as I got on the bus, in the Greyhound station, in Sacramento, I had a frightened sense of being in the wrong place. I had asked several people in the line at Gate 6 if this was the express to San Francisco, and they all said yes, but later, reviewing those assenting faces, I saw that in truth they all wore a look of people answering a question they have not entirely understood. Because of my anxiety and fear, I took a seat at the very front of the bus, across from and slightly behind the driver. There nothing very bad could happen to me, I thought.

What did happen, immediately, was that a tall black man, with a big mustache, angry and very handsome, stepped up into the bus and looked at me and said, 'That's my seat. You in my seat. I got to have that seat.' He was staring me straight in the eye, his flashing black into my scared pale blue.

There was nothing of his on the seat, no way I could have known that it belonged to him, and so that is what I said: 'I didn't know it was your seat.' But even as I was saying that, muttering, having ceased to meet his eye, I was also getting up and moving backward, to a seat two rows behind him.

Seated, apprehensively watching as the bus filled up, I saw that across the aisle from the black man were two women who seemed to be friends of his. No longer angry, he was sitting in the aisle seat so as to be near them; they were all talking and having a good time, glad to be together.

No one sat beside me, probably because I had put my large briefcase in that seat; it is stiff and forbidding-looking.

I thought again that I must be on the wrong bus, but just as I had that thought the driver got on, a big black man; he looked down the aisle for a second and then swung the door shut. He started up the engine as I wondered, What about tickets? Will they be collected in

San Francisco? I had something called a commuter ticket, a book of ten coupons, and that morning, leaving San Francisco, I'd thought the driver took too much of my ticket, two coupons; maybe this was some mysterious repayment? We lurched out of the station and were on our way to San Francisco—or wherever.

Behind me, a child began to shout loud but not quite coherent questions: 'Mom is that a river we're crossing? Mom do you see that tree? Mom is this a bus we're riding on?' He was making so much noise and his questions were all so crazy—senseless, really—that I did not see how I could stand it, all the hour and forty minutes to San Francisco, assuming that I was on the right bus, the express.

One of the women in the front seat, the friends of the man who had displaced me, also seemed unable to stand the child, and she began to shout back at him. 'You the noisiest traveler I ever heard, in fact you ain't a traveler, you an observer.'

'Mom does she mean me? Mom who is that?'

'Yeah I means you. You the one that's talking.'

'Mom who is that lady?' The child sounded more and more excited, and the black woman angrier. It was a terrible dialogue to hear.

And then I saw a very large white woman struggling up the aisle of the bus, toward the black women in the front, whom she at last reached and addressed: 'Listen, my son's retarded and that's how he tests reality, asking questions. You mustn't make fun of him like that.' She turned and headed back toward her seat, to her noisy retarded son.

The black women muttered to each other, and the boy began to renew his questions. 'Mom see that cow?'

And then I heard one of the black women say, very loudly, having the last word: 'And I got a daughter wears a hearing aid.'

I smiled to myself, although I suppose it wasn't funny, but something about the black defiant voice was so appealing. And, as I dared for a moment to look around the bus, I saw that most of the passengers were black: a puzzle.

The scenery, on which I tried to concentrate, was very beautiful: smooth blond hills, gently rising, and here and there crevasses of shadow; and sometimes a valley with a bright white farmhouse, white fences, green space. And everywhere the dark shapes of live oaks, a black drift of lace against the hills or darkly clustered in the valleys, near the farms.

All this was on our left, the east, as we headed south toward San Francisco (I hoped). To our right, westward, the view was even more glorious: flat green pasturelands stretching out to the glittering bay, bright gold water and blue fingers of land, in the late May afternoon sunshine.

The retarded boy seemed to have taken up a friendly conversation with some people across the aisle from him, although his voice was still very loud. 'My grandfather lives in Vallejo,' he was saying. 'Mom is that the sun over there?'

Just then, the bus turned right, turned off the freeway, and the driver announced, 'We're just coming into Vallejo, folks. Next stop is Oakland, and then San Francisco.'

I was on the wrong bus. Not on the express. Although this bus, thank God, did go on to San Francisco. But it would be at least half an hour late getting in. My heart sank, as I thought, Oh, how angry Hortense will be.

The bus swung through what must have been the back streets of Vallejo. (A question: Why are bus stations always in the worst parts of town, or is it that those worst parts grow up around the station?) As our bus ground to a halt, pushed into its slot in a line of other Greyhounds, before anyone else had moved, one of the women in the front seat stood up; she was thin, sharply angular, in a purple dress. She looked wonderful, I thought. 'And you, you just shut up!' she said to the boy in the back.

That was her exit line; she flounced off the bus ahead of everyone else, soon followed by her friend and the handsome man who had dislodged me from my seat.

A few people applauded. I did not, although I would have liked to, really.

This was my situation: I was working in San Francisco as a statistician in a government office having to do with unemployment, and that office assigned me to an office in Sacramento for ten weeks. There was very little difference between the offices; they were interchangeable, even to the pale-green coloring of the walls. But that is why I was commuting back and forth to Sacramento.

I was living with Hortense (temporarily, I hoped, although of course it was nice of her to take me in) because my husband had just divorced me and he wanted our apartment—or he wanted it more than I did, and I am not good at arguing.

Hortense is older than I am, with grown-up children, now gone. She seems to like to cook and take care; and when I started commuting she told me she'd meet me at the bus station every night, because she worried about the neighborhood, Seventh Street near Market, where the bus station is. I suppose some people must have assumed that we were a lesbian couple, even that I had left my husband for Hortense, but that was not true; my husband left me for a beautiful young Japanese nurse (he is in advertising), and it was not sex or love that kept me and Hortense together but sheer dependency (mine).

A lot of people got off the bus at Vallejo, including the pale fat lady and her poor son; as they passed me I saw that he was clinging closely to his mother, and that the way he held his neck was odd, not right. I felt bad that in a way I had sided against him, with the fierce black lady in purple. But I had to admit that of the two of them it was her I would rather travel with again.

A lot of new people began to get on the bus, and again they were mostly black; I guessed that they were going to Oakland. With so many people it seemed inconsiderate to take up two seats, even if I could have got away with it, so I put my briefcase on the floor, at my feet.

And I looked up to find the biggest woman I had ever seen, heading right for me. Enormous—she must have weighed three times what I did—and black and very young.

She needed two seats to herself, she really did, and of course she knew that; she looked around, but almost all the seats were taken, and so she chose me, because I am relatively thin, I guess. With a sweet apologetic smile, she squeezed in beside me—or, rather, she squeezed me in.

'Ooooh, I am so *big*,' she said, in a surprisingly soft small voice. 'I must be crushing you almost to death.'

'Oh no, I'm fine,' I assured her, and we smiled at each other.

'And you so thin,' she observed.

As though being thin required an apology, I explained that I was not that way naturally, I was living with an overweight friend who kept me on fish and salads, mostly.

She laughed. 'Well, maybe I should move in with your friend, but it probably wouldn't do me no good.'

I laughed, too, and I wondered what she did, what job took her from Oakland to Vallejo.

We talked, and after a while she told me that she worked in Oakland, as well as lived there, not saying at what, but that she was taking a course in Vallejo in the care of special children, which is what she really wanted to do. ' "Special" mean the retards and the crazies,' she said, but she laughed in a kindly way, and I thought how good she probably would be with kids.

I told her about the retarded boy who got off the bus at Vallejo, after all those noisy questions.

'No reason you can't tell a retard to quiet down,' she said. 'They got no call to disturb folks, it don't help them none.'

Right away then I felt better; it was OK for me not to have liked all that noise and to have sided with the black woman who told the boy to shut up.

I did like that big young woman, and when we got to Oakland I was sorry to see her go. We both said that we had enjoyed talking to each other; we said we hoped that we would run into each other again, although that seemed very unlikely.

In San Francisco, Hortense was pacing the station—very worried, she said, and visibly angry.

I explained to her that it was confusing, three buses leaving Sacramento for San Francisco at just the same time, five-thirty. It was very easy to get on the wrong one.

'Well, I suppose you'll catch on after a couple of weeks,' she said, clearly without much faith that I ever would.

She was right about one thing, though: the San Francisco bus station, especially at night, is a cold and scary place. People seem to be just hanging out there—frightened-looking young kids, maybe runaways, belligerent-looking drunks, and large black men, with swaggering hats, all of whom look mysteriously enraged. The lighting is a terrible white glare, harsh on the dirty floors, illuminating the wrinkles and grime and pouches of fatigue on all the human faces. A cold wind rushes in through the swinging entrance doors. Outside, there are more dangerous-looking loiterers, whom Hortense and I hurried past that night, going along Seventh Street to Market, where she had parked in a yellow zone but had not (thank God) been ticketed.

For dinner we had a big chef's salad, so nutritious and slenderizing, but also so cold that it felt like a punishment. What I really would have liked was a big hot fattening baked potato.

I wondered, How would I look if I put on twenty pounds?

Early mornings at the Greyhound station are not so bad, with only a few drunks and lurching loiterers on the street outside, and it is easy to walk past them very fast, swinging a briefcase. Inside, there are healthy-looking, resolute kids with enormous backpacks, off to conquer the wilderness. And it is easy, of course, to find the right bus, the express to Sacramento; there is only one, leaving every hour on the hour. I almost always got to sit by myself. But somehow the same scenery that you see coming down to San Francisco is very boring viewed from the other direction. Maybe this is an effect of the leveling morning light—I don't know.

One day, though, the bus was more crowded than usual and a young girl asked if she could sit next to me. I said OK, and we started up one of those guarded and desultory conversations that travel dictates. What most struck me about her was her accent; I could tell exactly where she was from—upstate New York. I am from there, too, from Binghamton, although I have taken on some other accents along the way, mainly my husband's—Philadelphia. (I hope I do not get to sound like Hortense, who is from Florida.) Of course I did not ask the girl where she was from—too personal, and I didn't have to—but she told me, unasked, that she worked in an office in Sacramento, which turned out to be in the building next to mine. That seemed ominous to me: a girl coming from exactly where I am from, and heading in my same direction. I did not want her to tell me any more about her life, and she did not.

Near Sacramento, the concrete road dividers have been planted with oleander, overflowing pink and white blossoms that quite conceal oncoming traffic in the other lanes. It is hard to believe that the highway commissioners envisioned such a wild profusion, and somehow it makes me uneasy to see all that bloom, maybe because I read somewhere that oleander is poisonous. Certainly it is unnaturally hardy.

The Sacramento station is more than a little weird, being the jumping-off place for Reno, so to speak. Every morning there are lines for the Reno buses, lines of gamblers, all kinds: big women in bright synthetic fabrics, and seedy old men, drunks, with their tired blue eyes and white indoor skin, smoking cigarillos. Gamblers seem to smoke a lot, I noticed. I also noticed that none of them are black.

A large elevated sign lists the departures for South Lake Tahoe and Reno: the Nugget express, which leaves at 3.40 a.m.; the dailies to Harrah's, starting at 9.05 a.m.; and on weekends you can leave for Reno any time between 2.35 a.m. and 11.15 p.m. I find it very hard to imagine going to Reno at any of those times, but then I am not a gambler.

*

Unfortunately, I again saw that same girl, Miss Upstate New York, the next few times that I took the correct bus, the express at 5.30 to San Francisco. She began to tell me some very boring things about her office—she did not like her boss, he drank—and her boyfriend, who wanted to invest in some condominiums at South Lake Tahoe.

I knew that Hortense would never believe that it was a mistake, and just possibly it was not, but a few nights later I took another wrong bus, really wrong: the local that stops everywhere, at Davis and Dixon and Fairfield, all down the line. Hortense was going to be furious. I began to work on some plausible lies: I got to the station late, this wrong bus left from the gate that the right bus usually leaves from. But then I thought, How ridiculous; and the very fact of Hortense's being there waiting for me began to seem a little silly, both of us being grown up.

Again most of the passengers were black, and I sensed a sort of camaraderie among them. It occurred to me that they were like people who have recently won a war, although I knew that to be not the case, not at all, in terms of their present lives. But with all the stops and starts the trip was very interesting; I would have been having a very good time if it were not for two things: one, I was worried about Hortense, and, two, I did not see again any of those people who were on my first wrong trip—not the very fat black woman or the skinny one in purple, or the handsome man who displaced me from my seat.

Just in front of me were an elderly man and woman, both black, who seemed to be old friends accidentally encountered on this bus. They exchanged information about how they both were, their families, and then the woman said, 'Well, the weekend's coming up.' 'Yep, jes one more day.' 'Then you can rest.' 'Say, you ever see a poor man rest?'

Recently I read an interview with a distinguished lady of letters, in which she was asked why she wrote so obsessively about the very poor, the tiredest and saddest poorest people, and that lady, a Southerner, answered, 'But I myself am poor people.'

That touched me to the quick, somehow. I am too. Hortense is not, I think.

Across the aisle from me I suddenly noticed the most beautiful young man I had ever seen, sound asleep. A golden boy: gold hair and tawny skin, large beautiful hands spread loosely on his knees, long careless legs in soft pale washed-out jeans. I hardly dared look at him;

some intensity in my regard might have wakened him, and then on my face he would have seen—not lust, it wasn't that, just a vast and objectless regard for his perfection, as though he were sculptured in bronze, or gold.

I haven't thought much about men, or noticed male beauty, actually, since my husband left, opted out of our marriage—and when I say that he left it sounds sudden, whereas it took a long and painful year.

Looking back, I now see that it began with some tiny wistful remarks, made by him, when he would come across articles in the paper about swingers, swapping, singles bars. 'Well, maybe we should try some of that stuff,' he would say, with a laugh intended to prove nonseriousness. 'A pretty girl like you, you'd do OK,' he would add, by which he really meant that he thought he would do OK, as indeed he has—did, does. Then came some more serious remarks to the effect that if I wanted an occasional afternoon with someone else, well, I didn't have to tell him about it, but if I did, well, he would understand. Which was a little silly, since when I was not at my office working I was either doing some household errand or I was at home, available only to him.

The next phase included a lot of half-explained or occasionally over-explained latenesses, and a seemingly chronic at-home fatigue. By then even I had caught on, without thinking too specifically about what he must have been doing, which I could not have stood. Still, I was surprised, and worse than surprised, when he told me that he was 'serious' about another woman. The beautiful Japanese nurse.

The golden boy got off at Vallejo, without our exchanging any look. Someone else I won't see again, but who will stay in my mind, probably.

Hortense was furious, her poor fat face red, her voice almost out of control. 'One hour—one hour I've been waiting here. Can you imagine my thoughts, in all that time?'

Well, I pretty much could. I felt terrible. I put my hand on her arm in a gesture that I meant as calming, affectionate, but she thrust it off, violently.

That was foolish, I thought, and I hoped no one had seen her. I said, 'Hortense, I'm really very sorry. But it's getting obvious that I have a problem with buses. I mix them up, so maybe you shouldn't come and meet me anymore.'

I hadn't known I was going to say that, but, once said, those words made sense, and I went on. 'I'll take a taxi. There're always a couple out front.'

And just then, as we passed hurriedly through the front doors, out onto the street, there were indeed four taxis stationed, a record number, as though to prove my point. Hortense made a strangled, snorting sound.

We drove home in silence; silently, in her dining room, we ate another chef's salad. It occurred to me to say that since our dinners were almost always cold my being late did not exactly spoil them, but I forbore. We were getting to be like some bad sitcom joke: Hortense and me, the odd couple.

The next morning, as I got in line to buy a new commuter ticket, there was the New York State girl. We exchanged mild greetings, and then she looked at the old ticket which for no reason I was clutching, and she said, 'But you've got one ticket left.'

And she explained what turned out to be one more system that I had not quite caught on to: the driver takes the whole first page, which is why, that first day, I thought he had taken two coupons. And the back page, although another color, pink, is a coupon, too. So my first ride on the wrong bus to Vallejo and Oakland was free; I had come out ahead, in that way.

Then the girl asked, 'Have you thought about a California Pass? They're neat.' And she explained that with a California Pass, for just a few dollars more than a commuter ticket, you can go *anywhere in California*. You can't travel on weekends, but who would want to, and you can go anywhere at all—Eureka, La Jolla, Santa Barbara, San Diego; you can spend the weekend there and come back on an early Monday bus. I was fascinated, enthralled by these possibilities. I bought a California Pass.

The Sacramento express was almost empty, so I told the girl that I had some work to do, which was true enough. We sat down in our separate seats and concentrated on our briefcases. I was thinking, of course, in a practical way about moving out from Hortense's. That had to be next—and more generally I was considering the possibilities of California, which just then seemed limitless, enormous.

Actually, the Greyhound system of departure gates for buses to San Francisco is very simple; I had really been aware all along of how it worked. Gate 5 is the express, Gate 6 goes to Vallejo and Oakland before San Francisco, and Gate 8 is the all-stop local, Davis, Dixon, everywhere. On my way home, I started to line up at Gate 6, my true favorite route, Vallejo and Oakland, when I realized that it was still very early, only just five, and also that I was extremely hungry. What I would really have liked was what we used to call a frappe in Binghamton, something cold and rich and thick and chocolate. Out here called a milkshake. And then I thought, Well, why not? Is there some law that says I can't weigh more than one-ten?

I went into the station restaurant, and at the counter I ordered a double-scoop milkshake. I took it to a booth, and then, as I was sitting there, savoring my delicious drink, something remarkable happened, which was: the handsome black man who so angrily displaced me on that first trip came up to me and greeted me with a friendly smile. 'Say, how you, how're you doing this evening?'

I smiled back and said that I was fine, and he went on past with his cup of coffee, leaving me a little out of breath. And as I continued to sip and swallow (it tasted marvelous) I wondered: Is it possible that he remembers me from that incident and this is his way of apologizing? Somehow that seemed very unlikely, but it seemed even more unlikely that he was just a friendly sort who went around greeting people. He was not at all like that, I was sure. Even smiling he had a proud, fierce look.

Was it possible that something about me had struck him in just the right way, making him want to say hello?

In any case, I had to read his greeting as a very good sign. Maybe the fat young woman would get on the bus at Vallejo again. Maybe the thin one in purple. And it further occurred to me that traveling all over California on the Greyhound I could meet anyone at all.

The Compartment

Myers was traveling through France in a first-class rail car on his way to visit his son in Strasbourg, who was a student at the university there. He hadn't seen the boy in eight years. There had been no phone calls between them during this time, not even a postcard since Myers and the boy's mother had gone their separate ways—the boy staying with her. The final break-up was hastened along, Myers always believed, by the boy's malign interference in their personal affairs.

The last time Myers had seen his son, the boy had lunged for him during a violent quarrel. Myers's wife had been standing by the side-board, dropping one dish of china after the other onto the dining-room floor. Then she'd gone on to the cups. 'That's enough,' Myers had said, and at that instant the boy charged him. Myers sidestepped and got him in a headlock while the boy wept and pummeled Myers on the back and kidneys. Myers had him, and while he had him, he made the most of it. He slammed him into the wall and threatened to kill him. He meant it. 'I gave you life,' Myers remembered himself shouting, 'and I can take it back!'

Thinking about that horrible scene now, Myers shook his head as if it had happened to someone else. And it had. He was simply not that same person. These days he lived alone and had little to do with anybody outside of his work. At night, he listened to classical music and read books on waterfowl decoys.

He lit a cigarette and continued to gaze out the train window, ignoring the man who sat in the seat next to the door and who slept with a hat pulled over his eyes. It was early in the morning and mist hung over the green fields that passed by outside. Now and then Myers saw a farmhouse and its outbuildings, everything surrounded by a wall. He thought this might be a good way to live—in an old house surrounded by a wall.

It was just past six o'clock. Myers hadn't slept since he'd boarded the train in Milan at eleven the night before. When the train had left Milan, he'd considered himself lucky to have the compartment to himself. He kept the light on and looked at guidebooks. He read things he wished he'd read before he'd been to the place they were about. He discovered much that he should have seen and done. In a way, he was sorry to be finding out certain things about the country now, just as he was leaving Italy behind after his first and, no doubt, last visit.

He put the guidebooks away in his suitcase, put the suitcase in the overhead rack, and took off his coat so he could use it for a blanket. He switched off the light and sat there in the darkened compartment with his eyes closed, hoping sleep would come.

After what seemed a long time, and just when he thought he was going to drop off, the train began to slow. It came to a stop at a little station outside of Basel. There, a middle-aged man in a dark suit, and wearing a hat, entered the compartment. The man said something to Myers in a language Myers didn't understand, and then the man put his leather bag up into the rack. He sat down on the other side of the compartment and straightened his shoulders. Then he pulled his hat over his eyes. By the time the train was moving again, the man was asleep and snoring quietly. Myers envied him. In a few minutes, a Swiss official opened the door of the compartment and turned on the light. In English, and in some other language—German, Myers assumed—the official asked to see their passports. The man in the compartment with Myers pushed the hat back on his head, blinked his eyes, and reached into his coat pocket. The official studied the passport, looked at the man closely, and gave him back the document. Myers handed over his own passport. The official read the data, examined the photograph, and then looked at Myers before nodding and giving it back. He turned off the light as he went out. The man across from Myers pulled the hat over his eyes and put out his legs. Myers supposed he'd go right back to sleep, and once again he felt envy.

He stayed awake after that and began to think of the meeting with his son, which was now only a few hours away. How would he act when he saw the boy at the station? Should he embrace him? He felt uncomfortable with that prospect. Or should he merely offer his hand, smile as if these eight years had never occurred, and then pat the boy on the shoulder? Maybe the boy would say a few words—*I'm glad to see you—how was your trip?* And Myers would say—something. He really didn't know what he was going to say.

The French *contrôleur* walked by the compartment. He looked in on Myers and at the man sleeping across from Myers. This same *contrôleur* had already punched their tickets, so Myers turned his head and went back to looking out the window. More houses began to appear. But now there were no walls, and the houses were smaller and set closer together. Soon, Myers was sure, he'd see a French village. The haze was lifting. The train blew its whistle and sped past a crossing over which a barrier had been lowered. He saw a young woman with her hair pinned up and wearing a sweater, standing with her bicycle as she watched the cars whip past.

How's your mother? he might say to the boy after they had walked a little way from the station. *What do you hear from your mother?* For a wild instant, it occurred to Myers she could be dead. But then he understood that it couldn't be so, he'd have heard something—one way or the other, he'd have heard. He knew if he let himself go on thinking about these things, his heart could break. He closed the top button of his shirt and fixed his tie. He laid his coat across the seat next to him. He laced his shoes, got up, and stepped over the legs of the sleeping man. He let himself out of the compartment.

Myers had to put his hand against the windows along the corridor to steady himself as he moved toward the end of the car. He closed the door to the little toilet and locked it. Then he ran water and splashed his face. The train moved into a curve, still at the same high speed, and Myers had to hold on to the sink for balance.

The boy's letter had come to him a couple of months ago. The letter had been brief. He wrote that he'd been living in France and studying for the past year at the university in Strasbourg. There was no other information about what had possessed him to go to France, or what he'd been doing with himself during those years before France. Appropriately enough, Myers thought, no mention was made in the letter of the boy's mother—not a clue to her condition or whereabouts. But, inexplicably, the boy had closed the letter with the word *Love*, and Myers had pondered this for a long while. Finally, he'd answered the letter. After some deliberation, Myers wrote to say he had been thinking for some time of making a little trip to Europe. Would the boy like to meet him at the station in Strasbourg? He signed his letter, 'Love, Dad'. He'd heard back from the boy and then he made his arrangements. It struck him that there was really no one, besides his secretary and a few business associates, that he felt it was necessary to tell he was going away. He had accumulated six weeks of vacation at the engineering firm where he worked, and he decided he would take all of the time coming to him for this trip. He was glad he'd done this, even though he now had no intention of spending all that time in Europe.

He'd gone first to Rome. But after the first few hours, walking around by himself on the streets, he was sorry he hadn't arranged to be with a group. He was lonely. He went to Venice, a city he and his wife had always talked of visiting. But Venice was a disappointment. He saw a man with one arm eating fried squid, and there were grimy, water-stained buildings everywhere he looked. He took a train to Milan, where he checked into a four-star hotel and spent the night watching a soccer match on a Sony color TV until the station went off the air. He got up the next morning and wandered around the city until it was time to go to the station. He'd planned the stopover in Strasbourg as the culmination of his trip. After a day or two, or three days—he'd see how it went—he would travel to Paris and fly home. He was tired of trying to make himself understood to strangers and would be glad to get back.

Someone tried the door to the WC. Myers finished tucking his shirt. He fastened his belt. Then he unlocked the door and, swaying with the movement of the train, walked back to his compartment. As he opened the door, he saw at once that his coat had been moved. It lay across a different seat from the one where he'd left it. He felt he had entered into a ludicrous but potentially serious situation. His heart began to race as he picked up the coat. He put his hand into the inside pocket and took out his passport. He carried his wallet in his hip pocket. So he still had his wallet and the passport. He went through the other coat pockets. What was missing was the gift he'd bought for the boy—an expensive Japanese wrist-watch purchased at a shop in Rome. He had carried the watch in his inside coat pocket for safe-keeping. Now the watch was gone.

'Pardon,' he said to the man who slumped in the seat, legs out, the hat over his eyes. 'Pardon.' The man pushed the hat back and opened his eyes. He pulled himself up and looked at Myers. His eyes were large. He might have been dreaming. But he might not.

Myers said, 'Did you see somebody come in here?'

But it was clear the man didn't know what Myers was saying. He continued to stare at him with what Myers took to be a look of total incomprehension. But maybe it was something else, Myers thought. Maybe the look masked slyness and deceit. Myers shook his coat to

focus the man's attention. Then he put his hand into the pocket and
rummaged. He pulled his sleeve back and showed the man his own
wristwatch. The man looked at Myers and then at Myers's watch. He
seemed mystified. Myers tapped the face of his watch. He put his
other hand back into his coat pocket and made a gesture as if he were
fishing for something. Myers pointed at the watch once more and
waggled his fingers, hoping to signify the wristwatch taking flight out
the door.

The man shrugged and shook his head.

'Goddamn it,' Myers said in frustration. He put his coat on and went
out into the corridor. He couldn't stay in the compartment another
minute. He was afraid he might strike the man. He looked up and
down the corridor, as if hoping he could see and recognize the thief.
But there was no one around. Maybe the man who shared his compartment hadn't taken the watch. Maybe someone else, the person
who tried the door to the WC, had walked past the compartment,
spotted the coat and the sleeping man, and simply opened the door,
gone through the pockets, closed the door, and gone away again.

Myers walked slowly to the end of the car, peering into the other
compartments. It was not crowded in this first-class car, but there
were one or two people in each compartment. Most of them were
asleep, or seemed to be. Their eyes were closed, and their heads were
thrown back against the seats. In one compartment, a man about his
own age sat by the window looking out at the countryside. When
Myers stopped at the glass and looked in at him, the man turned and
regarded him fiercely.

Myers crossed into the second-class car. The compartments in this
car were crowded—sometimes five or six passengers in each, and the
people, he could tell at a glance, were more desperate. Many of them
were awake—it was too uncomfortable to sleep—and they turned
their eyes on him as he passed. Foreigners, he thought. It was clear to
him that if the man in his compartment hadn't taken the watch, then
the thief was from one of these compartments. But what could he do?
It was hopeless. The watch was gone. It was in someone else's pocket
now. He couldn't hope to make the *contrôleur* understand what had
happened. And even if he could, then what? He made his way back to
his own compartment. He looked in and saw that the man had stretched
out again with his hat over his eyes.

Myers stepped over the man's legs and sat down in his seat by the
window. He felt dazed with anger. They were on the outskirts of the

city now. Farms and grazing land had given over to industrial plants with unpronounceable names on the fronts of the buildings. The train began slowing. Myers could see automobiles on city streets, and others waiting in line at the crossings for the train to pass. He got up and took his suitcase down. He held it on his lap while he looked out the window at this hateful place.

It came to him that he didn't want to see the boy after all. He was shocked by this realization and for a moment felt diminished by the meanness of it. He shook his head. In a lifetime of foolish actions, this trip was possibly the most foolish thing he'd ever done. But the fact was, he really had no desire to see this boy whose behavior had long ago isolated him from Myers's affections. He suddenly, and with great clarity, recalled the boy's face when he had lunged that time, and a wave of bitterness passed over Myers. This boy had devoured Myers's youth, had turned the young girl he had courted and wed into a nervous, alcoholic woman whom the boy alternately pitied and bullied. Why on earth, Myers asked himself, would he come all this way to see someone he disliked? He didn't want to shake the boy's hand, the hand of his enemy, nor have to clap him on the shoulder and make small talk. He didn't want to have to ask him about his mother.

He sat forward in the seat as the train pulled into the station. An announcement was called out in French over the train's intercom. The man across from Myers began to stir. He adjusted his hat and sat up in the seat as something else in French came over the speaker. Myers didn't understand anything that was said. He grew more agitated as the train slowed and then came to a stop. He decided he wasn't going to leave the compartment. He was going to sit where he was until the train pulled away. When it did, he'd be on it, going on with the train to Paris, and that would be that. He looked out the window cautiously, afraid he'd see the boy's face at the glass. He didn't know what he'd do if that happened. He was afraid he might shake his fist. He saw a few people on the platform wearing coats and scarves who stood next to their suitcases, waiting to board the train. A few other people waited, without luggage, hands in their pockets, obviously expecting to meet someone. His son was not one of those waiting, but, of course, that didn't mean he wasn't out there somewhere. Myers moved the suitcase off his lap onto the floor and inched down in his seat.

The man across from him was yawning and looking out the window. Now he turned his gaze on Myers. He took off his hat and ran his hand through his hair. Then he put the hat back on, got to his feet, and pulled his bag down from the rack. He opened the compartment door. But before he went out, he turned around and gestured in the direction of the station.

'Strasbourg,' the man said.

Myers turned away.

The man waited an instant longer, and then went out into the corridor with his bag and, Myers felt certain, with the wristwatch. But that was the least of his concerns now. He looked out the train window once again. He saw a man in an apron standing in the door of the station, smoking a cigarette. The man was watching two trainmen explaining something to a woman in a long skirt who held a baby in her arms. The woman listened and then nodded and listened some more. She moved the baby from one arm to the other. The men kept talking. She listened. One of the men chucked the baby under its chin. The woman looked down and smiled. She moved the baby again and listened some more. Myers saw a young couple embracing on the platform a little distance from his car. Then the young man let go of the young woman. He said something, picked up his valise, and moved to board the train. The woman watched him go. She brought a hand up to her face, touched one eye and then the other with the heel of her hand. In a minute, Myers saw her moving down the platform, her eyes fixed on his car, as if following someone. He glanced away from the woman and looked at the big clock over the station's waiting room. He looked up and down the platform. The boy was nowhere in sight. It was possible he had overslept or it might be that he, too, had changed his mind. In any case, Myers felt relieved. He looked at the clock again, then at the young woman who was hurrying up to the window where he sat. Myers drew back as if she were going to strike the glass.

The door to the compartment opened. The young man he'd seen outside closed the door behind him and said, 'Bonjour.' Without waiting for a reply, he threw his valise into the overhead rack and stepped over to the window. 'Pardonnez-moi.' He pulled the window down. 'Marie,' he said. The young woman began to smile and cry at the same time. The young man brought her hands up and began kissing her fingers.

Myers looked away and clamped his teeth. He heard the final shouts of the trainmen. Someone blew a whistle. Presently, the train began to move away from the platform. The young man had let go of the woman's hands, but he continued to wave at her as the train rolled forward.

But the train went only a short distance, into the open air of the railyard, and then Myers felt it come to an abrupt stop. The young man closed the window and moved over to the seat by the door. He took a newspaper from his coat and began to read. Myers got up and opened the door. He went to the end of the corridor, where the cars were coupled together. He didn't know why they had stopped. Maybe something was wrong. He moved to the window. But all he could see was an intricate system of tracks where trains were being made up, cars taken off or switched from one train to another. He stepped back from the window. The sign on the door to the next car said, POUSSEZ. Myers struck the sign with his fist, and the door slid open. He was in the second-class car again. He passed along a row of compartments filled with people settling down, as if making ready for a long trip. He needed to find out from someone where this train was going. He had understood, at the time he purchased the ticket, that the train to Strasbourg went on to Paris. But he felt it would be humiliating to put his head into one of the compartments and say, 'Paree?' or however they said it—as if asking if they'd arrived at a destination. He heard a loud clanking, and the train backed up a little. He could see the station again, and once more he thought of his son. Maybe he was standing back there, breathless from having rushed to get to the station, wondering what had happened to his father. Myers shook his head.

The car he was in creaked and groaned under him, then something caught and fell heavily into place. Myers looked out at the maze of tracks and realized that the train had begun to move again. He turned and hurried back to the end of the car and crossed back into the car he'd been traveling in. He walked down the corridor to his compartment. But the young man with the newspaper was gone. And Myers's suitcase was gone. It was not his compartment after all. He realized with a start they must have uncoupled his car while the train was in the yard and attached another second-class car to the train. The compartment he stood in front of was nearly filled with small, dark-skinned men who spoke rapidly in a language Myers had never heard before. One of the men signaled him to come inside. Myers moved into the compartment, and the men made room for him. There seemed to be a jovial air in the compartment. The man who'd signaled him laughed and patted the space next to him. Myers sat down with his back to the front of the train. The countryside out the window began to pass faster and faster. For a moment, Myers had the impression of the landscape shooting away from him. He was going somewhere, he knew that. And if it was the wrong direction, sooner or later he'd find it out.

He leaned against the seat and closed his eyes. The men went on talking and laughing. Their voices came to him as if from a distance. Soon the voices became part of the train's movements—and gradually Myers felt himself being carried, then pulled back, into sleep.

A Long Night at Abu Simbel

In Cairo they had complained about the traffic and at Saqqara Mrs Marriott-Smith and Lady Hacking had wanted a lavatory and blamed her when eventually they had to retire, bleating, behind a sand-dune. She had lost two of them at Luxor airport and the rest had sat in the coach in a state of gathering mutiny. Some of them were given to exclaiming, within her hearing, 'Where's that wretched girl got to?' At Karnak the guide hadn't shown up when he should and she had had to mollify them for half an hour with the shade temperature at 94°. On the boat, a contingent had complained about having cabins on the lower deck and old Mr Appleton, apparently, was on a milk pudding diet, a detail not passed on to the chef by the London office. She knew now that not only did she not like foreign travel or tour leading but she didn't much care for people either. She continued to smile and repeat that they would be able to cash cheques between five and six and that no, she didn't think there was a chiropodist in Assuan. When several of them succumbed vociferously to stomach upsets she refrained from saying that so had she. They sought her out with their protests and their demands when she was skulking in a far corner of the sun deck and throughout every meal. In the privacy of her cabin she drafted her letter of application to the estate agent in Richmond where there was a nice secretarial job going.

At Edfu the woman magistrate from Knutsford was short-changed by a carpet-seller, to the quiet satisfaction of some of the others. At Esna Miss Crawley lost her travellers' cheques and Julie had to go all the way back to the temple and search, amid the pi-dogs and the vendors of basalt heads and the American party from Minnesota Institute of Art (biddable and co-operative, joshing their ebullient blue-rinsed tour leader). They all called her Julie now, but on a note of querulous requirement, except for the retired bank manager, who had tried to grope her bottom behind a pillar at Kom Ombo, and followed her around suggesting a drink later on when his wife was taking a nap.

None of them had read the itinerary properly. When they discovered that they had an hour and a half to wait at Assuan for the flight to Abu Simbel they rounded on her with their objections. They wanted another plane laid on and they wanted to be assured that they wouldn't be with the French and the Japanese tours and Lady Hacking said over and over again that at least one took it, for goodness sake, that there would be adequate restaurant facilities. She got them, eventually, into the plane and off the plane on to the coach, where the guide, Fuad, promised by the Assuan agency, most conspicuously was not. She went back to the airport building and telephoned; the Assuan office was closed. The man at the EgyptAir desk knew of no Fuad. She returned to the coach and broke the news in her most sprightly manner. The American coach and the French coach and the Japanese coach, smoothly united with their Fuad or their Ashraf, were already descending the long road to the temples in three clouds of dust.

They said their say. The coach driver spat out of the window and closed the door. They bumped across the desert. Lake Nasser lay to their right, bright blue fringed with buff-coloured hills. Those who had sufficiently recovered from their irritation at the non-appearance of Fuad exclaimed. Those who had not continued loudly to reiterate their complaints. The coach driver pulled up at the top of the track down to the temple site. They disembarked. Miss Crawley said she hadn't realized there was going to be even more walking. They straggled off in twos and threes and stood, at last, in front of the blindly gazing immensities of the god–king. Mrs Marriott-Smith said it made you think, despite everything, and Miss Crawley found she had blistered both feet and the chartered surveyor's wife was sorry to tell everyone she couldn't, frankly, see a sign of anywhere to eat. They stood around and took photographs and trailed in the wake of the guided and instructed French and Japanese into the sombre depths of the temple and when they were all out of sight Julie left them.

She walked briskly up the hill to where the American coach, its party already aboard, was revving its engine. She got on and went with them back to the airport, where, with a smile, she deposited an envelope containing twenty-two return halves of Assuan–Abu Simbel–Assuan air tickets with the fellow at the EgyptAir desk. She then boarded the plane, along with the American party. They were shortly joined by the Japanese and the French. The plane left on time; it always did, the stewardess said, truculently, glancing out of the window at the solitary airport building tipping away beneath.

The Magitours party continued to devote themselves to the site. They gathered in front of the stone plaque unveiled by Gamal Abdul Nasser as a memorial of international collaboration for preserving a human heritage. The other tours were now wending their way up the track to the coaches. 'Peace at last!' said Lady Hacking. 'I don't know which drive me dottier—those American women screaming at each other or the French pushing and shoving.' Mr Campion, the senior police inspector, being in possession of an adequate guide-book, assumed the role of the absent Fuad and briefed them on Rameses the Second and on the engineering feat involved in hoisting the temples to their present position. The party, appropriately humbled by the magnitude of both concepts, moved in awe around the towering pillars of the temple and the equally inhuman twentieth-century shoring-up process within the artificial hillside. They all agreed that it was frightfully impressive and well worth coming for. Those still suffering from internal disorders were becoming a little fidgety, and Mrs Marriott-Smith was longing for her dinner, but on the whole the mood was genial. They emerged from the temple and sat around admiring the lake, tinged now with rose-coloured streaks as the late-afternoon sun sank towards the desert. Some of the women put their woollies on; it was extraordinary how quickly it got chilly in the evenings. Mr Campion read out more from the guide-book. None of them paid any attention to the distant hootings of the coach driver, at the top of the hill. Someone said, 'That damn girl's vanished again.'

The coach driver, hired for so long and no longer, hooted for five minutes. Then, in the absence of any instructions, he threw his cigarette out of the window and drove his empty coach back to the depot.

The sun had almost completely set when the first of them reached the airport building. The stragglers, including the grimly stoical Miss Crawley, now hideously blistered, continued to arrive in dribs and drabs for another quarter of an hour. It had been a good two miles. It was Mr Campion who discovered the envelope with the flight tickets, shoved carelessly to one side of the EgyptAir desk. And it was another ten minutes or so, as the party slowly gathered around him, subdued now and in a state of mingled fury and apprehension, before the penny dropped. 'I simply do not believe it,' said the chartered surveyor's wife, over and over again. The EgyptAir official, subjected to a barrage of queries, shrugged, impassive. Those on the edges of the group, who could not quite catch what was going on, pushed closer, and as the enormity of their plight was conveyed from one to another, the murmurs grew louder. Mr Campion, determinedly keeping his cool, concentrated on the EgyptAir fellow. 'When is the next plane, then?' There was not another plane; the last plane left each evening at five-thirty.

'Then,' said Mr Campion with restraint, 'you'll have to call Assuan, won't you, and have them send up another plane.' The EgyptAir official smiled.

'Oh, rubbish,' said Mrs Marriott-Smith. 'Of course they can send another plane. Tell him not to be so silly.' The EgyptAir official shrugged again and made a phone call with the air of a man prepared, up to a point, to placate lunatics. The outcome of the call was clear to all before he put the receiver down.

'All right, then,' said Lady Hacking. 'We shall just have to endure. Ask him where the local hotel is.'

The police inspector, a man accustomed to matters of life and death, did not bother to reply. The woman's manner had been getting on his nerves for days anyway. He simply pointed towards the long windows of the airport building, overlooking a vista of desert enlivened here and there with a scrubby tree or a skulking pi-dog and sliced by the single runway. The sand, now, was lilac, pink and ochre in the sunset. The rest of the group also followed Mr Campion's pointing finger.

'Heavenly colours,' said the Knutsford magistrate. She had tended to display artistic sensibilities since the first morning in Cairo Museum.

The dismay, now, was universal. 'I don't *believe* it,' said the chartered surveyor's wife. 'You'll damn well have to,' snapped her husband. The group, with appalled mutterings, surveyed the uncompromising reality of the airport hall. There were half a dozen rows of solid plastic bucket seats in bright orange, welded to a stone floor with a thick covering of dust, two or three plastic tables, and a soft-drinks counter attended by a young boy who, like the EgyptAir official and the several cleaners or porters, watched them now with mild interest. There was also the EgyptAir desk, on which the official had placed a grubby sign saying CLOSED, some tattered posters on the walls of the Taj Mahal and Sri Lanka, and a great many overflowing rubbish bins. Those who had already sped into the ladies' lavatory had found it awash at one end with urine and attended by a woman who handed each client a dirt-spattered towel and stood expectantly at their sides. Lady Hacking pointed accusingly at the swilling floor; the woman nodded and indicated one of the cubicles from which fumed a trail of sodden toilet paper: 'Is no good.' 'Then *do* something,' said Lady Hacking sternly.

It was now six-thirty. The group, with gathering urgency, had converged on the soft-drinks counter. It was Miss Crawley, a latecomer, who revealed that all that was left were half a dozen cans of 7-Up and four packets of crisps. Those in possession of the only three packets of sandwiches and the single carton of biscuits sat watching, in defiance or guilt according to temperament. 'There are thirteen of us,' announced Miss Crawley loudly, 'without anything at all,' The principle of first come first served was in direct collision now with some reluctant flickerings of community spirit. The two retired librarians offered a sandwich to Mrs Marriott-Smith, who accepted it graciously; they did not offer, it was noted, to anyone else. The temperature had now fallen quite remarkably. The few who had coats put them on; most people shivered in shirt-sleeves and light dresses. The architect who had served in Libya in 1942 reminisced, as he had done before—too often—about the desert campaign. The chartered surveyor's wife told everyone that bloody girl would be bound to get the sack, if that was any comfort. Miss Crawley, with a sigh, took a book from her bag and began ostentatiously to read. A clip-eared white cat lay on one of the plastic tables, luxuriantly squirming. The Knutsford magistrate reached out to stroke it; the cat flexed its claws and opened a red mouth in a soundless mew; Miss Crawley observed without comment.

Outside, it became dark. The EgyptAir official was no longer there. Those sufficiently interested—and resentful—pin-pointed a bungalow at a far corner of the airfield in which lights cosily glimmered. The soft-drinks boy continued to slump at his counter and the ladies' lavatory attendant emerged and squatted on the floor outside. The one remaining porter or watchman came to squat beside her, smoking and exchanging the occasional desultory remark. They ignored the Magitours party, who were now dispersed all over the hall in morose clumps, sitting on the upright bucket seats or leaning against the EgyptAir counter. The architect tried, unsuccessfully, to get together a foursome for whist. Those who were unwell sat near the lavatories, grim-faced. The Knutsford magistrate offered the cat a crumpled ball of newspaper; it lashed out a paw and she withdrew her hand with a squeak.

'I hope it's not rabid,' said Miss Crawley with interest. 'You have to expect that, in places like this.' The magistrate examined her hand, on which beads of blood had appeared. 'Oh *dear . . .*' said Miss Crawley. 'I wonder if it's worth putting on some antiseptic.' The magistrate, glaring, applied Kleenex.

It was at around nine-thirty that the feelings of those without provisions of any kind became insupportable. The mutiny was provoked by the revelation that the surveyor's wife was in possession of a cache of oranges, Ryvita and Garibaldi biscuits which she now attempted furtively to distribute among those of her choice. The murmurings of those excluded became impossible to ignore; Mr Campion, eventually, rose to his feet, crossed the hall and had a brief and gruff word with the surveyor's wife, who bridled angrily. He then cleared his throat and announced that given the circumstances some kind of a kitty situation as regards food might be a good idea. This produced a small assorted pile which Mrs Campion, with evident embarrassment, divided up and carried round on a tray borrowed from the soft-drinks counter. The several sick said they didn't want anything, prompting further complex and minute division. These comings and goings caused a considerable diversion, so that it was some while before anyone— including his wife—noticed that there was something wrong with old Mr Appleton. He sat slumped down in his seat, intently muttering and emitting, from time to time, a sort of bark that was neither laughter nor a cry of distress. His wife, with as much embarrassment as concern, leaned over him, murmuring exhortations. Presently one of the librarians bustled across with a bottle of mineral water. Aspirins were also produced, and a variety of throat lozenges.

'Poor old chap,' said the Knutsford magistrate. 'Mind, I've been thinking all week he was ever so slightly gaga. What a shame.' Others declared that they weren't surprised—this was enough to unbalance anyone. 'You know what it makes me think of?' said the Knutsford magistrate. 'That place in Orkney—Maeshowe. Anyone been there?' No one had; those for whom she had already overdone the widely travelled bit returned emphatically to their books or their magazines. 'Oh, it's quite extraordinary—you really should go. BC three thousand or something but the fascinating thing is these Viking inscriptions by some sailors who spent the night there in a storm and one of them went barmy.' There was a silence. The cat, writhing seductively, wrapped itself round the magistrate's calf; she pushed it away with her bag.

'How does your hand feel?' enquired Miss Crawley.

'Perfectly all right,' said the magistrate with irritation. She watched the cat, which sat lashing its tail. Miss Crawley lowered her book and eyed it. 'Of course all the animals out here look unhealthy. What *is* that on its mouth?'

At eleven o'clock the only functioning ladies' lavatory packed up, a circumstance causing a frail-looking and hitherto silent woman to burst into ill-concealed sobs. Someone else's husband admitted some amateur plumbing proficiency, rolled up his sleeves and braved the now softly rippling floor. 'Good chap,' said the police inspector loudly.

The attendant at the soft-drinks counter wrapped himself up in a tartan rug, lay down and was seen to fall instantly into deep and tranquil sleep. 'Lucky sod,' said the architect. 'Mind, we used to be able to do that, back on the Halfaya Ridge.'

'Oh, do shut up about the Halfaya Ridge,' said Mrs Marriott-Smith, her voice inadequately lowered. The architect, a more sensitive man than was superficially apparent, and who had shared a genial lunch-table with her and Lady Hacking only yesterday, sat in bristling silence. 'Ssh, dear,' said Lady Hacking. 'Of course, these people aren't made like us physically. It's something to do with their pelvises. Haven't you noticed how they can squat for hours?'

'What absolute nonsense,' muttered the police inspector's wife. Lady Hacking swung round, but was unable to identify the speaker.

The party, by now, had divided into those determinedly enduring in as much isolation as possible and those seeking—tacitly—the faint comfort of collective suffering. One or two had tried to clean up a section of the floor and lie down upon it, inadequately cushioned by newspapers and the contents of handbags, but soon gave up. A few people, drawn to authority, had settled themselves around Mr Campion, as though in wistful belief that he might yet effect some miracle. Old Mr Appleton continued to mumble and bark; his wife, now a little wild-eyed, plied him with mineral water.

Mrs Marriott-Smith said, 'Oh my goodness, it *can't* only be half past midnight . . .'

'Tell you what,' said the chartered surveyor's wife. 'We should do community singing. Like people stuck on Scottish mountains.' She giggled self-consciously. 'Don't be so damn silly,' muttered her husband. Miss Crawley, lowering her book, stared with contempt: 'A peculiarly inappropriate analogy, if I may say so.' No one else spoke. The chartered surveyor's wife got out a powder compact and dabbed angrily at her nose.

A detached observer, arriving now at Abu Simbel airport, could not have failed to detect something awry. The complex lines of hostility and aversion linking the members of the Magitours group were like some invisible spider-web, grimly pulsing. Apart from the small group of acolytes around Mr and Mrs Campion, the bucket seats, in their uncompromising welded lines, were occupied in as scattered a manner as possible. Married couples were divided from other married couples by an empty seat or two. Solo travellers like Miss Crawley and the Knutsford magistrate sat in isolation. The two retired librarians had fenced themselves off, pointedly, with a barrier of possessions spread over two unoccupied seats. Old Mr Appleton's barking and muttering had cleared a substantial area around him; he appeared, now, to be asleep, his jaw sagging. From time to time someone would cough, shuffle, murmur to spouse or companion. An uneasy peace reigned, its fragility manifest when someone grated a table against the floor. 'Some of us,' said Lady Hacking loudly, 'are trying to get what rest we can.'

It was at one forty-five that Mr Appleton, apparently, died. He sagged forward and then toppled to the ground with a startling thud, like a mattress dropped from a considerable height. His wife, for a moment or two, did nothing whatsoever; then she began, piercingly, to shriek.

Everyone stood up. Some, like the Campions, the Knutsford magistrate and the librarians, hurried over. Others hovered uncertainly. Miss Crawley, moving to a position where she could see what was going on, said loudly that one must assume a stroke, so there probably wasn't a lot to be done but in any case there was no point in crowding round. Those trying to offer assistance had split into two groups, one devoted to Mr Appleton, the other admonishing his wife, who continued, with quite extraordinary vigour, to scream. 'Hysterics,' said Mrs Marriott-Smith. 'Something I know all about. We had a girl for the children who used to do it, years ago. Someone should slap her face—it's the only thing.'

Mrs Campion, her arm round Mrs Appleton's shoulders, was imploring her to be quiet. 'It's all *right*. Everyone's doing what they can. Do please stop making that noise. *Please*.' Mrs Appleton paused for a moment to draw breath, glanced down at the prone body of her husband, and began again. 'Be quiet!' ordered the inspector. 'Stop that noise!' The librarians and the magistrate were arguing about whether or not to turn Mr Appleton over. 'I tell you, I *know* about this sort of thing—he shouldn't be moved.' 'Excuse me but you're wrong, I know what I'm doing. Is he breathing?' 'I don't think so,' said the magistrate, her words unfortunately falling into a momentary respite in Mrs Appleton's screams, and serving to set her off again nicely.

The soft-drinks attendant had unfurled himself from the tartan rug and, along with the lavatory attendant and the porter, stood watching with interest. 'Tell them to get a doctor,' said Lady Hacking. 'I should think that's the best thing to do.'

'Shut up, for Christ's sake, you stupid woman,' said the police inspector. There was a startled silence; even Mrs Appleton, briefly, was distracted. Lady Hacking went brick red and turned her back. The chartered surveyor's wife burst into frenzied laughter. The Knutsford magistrate, kneeling over Mr Appleton, looked up and snapped that she didn't frankly see what there was to laugh about just at the moment. Mrs Appleton had been led to a seat somewhat apart and was being damped down, with some success, by Mrs Campion. Mr Campion, having picked up the receiver of the phone on the EgyptAir desk and listened for a moment, was trying to convey to the porter that the EgyptAir official must be summoned. 'Is sleeping,' said the porter. 'Office closed.' 'Give him some baksheesh,' advised the architect. The police inspector, a big man, ignored this; he leaned forward, seized the porter's jacket in either hand, and violently shook him. The lavatory attendant uttered a shrill cry of outrage.

'Frightfully unwise,' said Mrs Marriott-Smith loudly. 'That simply isn't how to deal with these people.' Interest, now, was diverted from the Appletons to the EgyptAir counter.

The porter, muttering angrily, picked up the phone, and, presently, was heard to speak into it. 'Tell him to bloody well get over here at once,' said Mr Campion, 'and bloody well get on to Assuan for us.'

'The man doesn't understand English,' said Miss Crawley.

'At least some of us are trying to *do* something,' hissed the magistrate. 'Which is more than can be said for others.'

Miss Crawley stared, icily: 'There's no need to be offensive.'

Lady Hacking, tight-lipped, was sitting stiffly while Mrs Marriott-Smith spoke in a mollifying undertone. 'I have no intention,' said Lady Hacking loudly, 'of getting involved. One simply ignores such behaviour, is what one does.' The chartered surveyor's wife gazed at her, beady-eyed.

The porter had put down the phone and was loudly reiterating his grievances. 'All right, all right, old chap,' said the engineer. 'We've got the message. Calm down.' Mrs Appleton continued keening; Mrs

Campion, still in attendance, was becoming visibly impatient. The woman who had been reduced to tears by the collapse of the surviving ladies' lavatory was again quietly weeping. 'I just want to be at home,' she kept saying. 'That's all. I want to go home.'

At this point Mr Appleton twitched convulsively and made an attempt to roll on to his back. 'He's coming round,' announced the magistrate. 'Good grief! I thought he'd croaked, between you and me.' The librarians, with cries of encouragement, heaved him into a sitting position.

The porter, shrugging, looked meaningfully at Mr Campion: 'Is OK now.' 'Go to hell,' said the police inspector, advancing towards Mr Appleton, who was heard to ask where he was. 'Don't tell him,' advised the engineer. 'It'll be enough to knock the poor fellow out again.'

Mrs Appleton, supported by Mrs Campion, was led across to her husband and began attempting to brush the dust off his trousers and jacket while reproaching him for giving everyone such a nasty shock. The old man, ignoring her, allowed himself to be helped up into a seat; he stared round, wheezing. 'That's the ticket,' said the police inspector, patting him on the shoulder.

The EgyptAir official arrived, tie-less and with one shirt-tail untucked. The porter fell on him in noisy complaint. The police inspector, cutting in, took him aside. 'Spot of baksheesh might save the situation,' said the architect. Mr Campion continued, in quiet but authoritative tones, to explain that a member of the party had been taken ill, and was undoubtedly in need of medical attention, but that fortunately the immediate crisis seemed to have passed. 'Man not dead,' stated the EgyptAir official, aggrievedly. 'No, I'm happy to say,' said Mr Campion.

And when, presently, dawn broke over the desert and a grey light crept into the airport building the scene there was one of, if not peace, at least an exhausted truce. A few of the Magitours party, done for, were in restless sleep; the others, raw-eyed, sat staring out of the windows at the reddening desert or braved the lavatories to attempt whatever might be done by way of physical repairs. The librarians graciously offered cologne-soaked tissues. A few people ventured outside for a breath of air and even wandered a little way along the road to the temples, at the far end of which those stone immensities, in their solitude, were contemplating yet another sunrise.

And when, three hours later, the first flight from Assuan decanted its passengers the arrivals found the place occupied by a party of people grim-faced but composed. Members of a Cook's tour bore down on

them: 'I say, is it true you've been here all night? It must have been
ghastly!' Those who saw fit to respond were deprecating. 'The odd
little contretemps,' said Lady Hacking graciously. 'But on the whole
we muddled through quite nicely.' Miss Crawley, in sepulchral tones,
warned of the condition of the lavatories. The librarians, gaily, said it
had been a bit like an air-raid in the war, if you were old enough to
remember. Mrs Appleton, supporting her husband, who was demand-
ing a morning paper, valiantly smiled. The wan appearance of the
party was defied by an air of determined solidarity, even perhaps of
reticence. 'The thing was,' said the Knutsford magistrate, 'we were all
in the same boat, so there was nothing for it but grin and bear it.' The
exclamations and queries of the Cook's tour members were parried
with understated evasions. Mrs Marriott-Smith assured the new arrivals
that the temples were absolutely amazing, unforgettable, no question
about that. 'Absolutely,' said the police inspector heartily. 'Extraordinary
place.' There was a murmur of agreement and, as the Cook's tour
filed towards their coach, the Magitours party, rather closely clumped
together, made their way across the sand-strewn tarmac to the waiting
plane.

BERYL BAINBRIDGE

The Man Who Blew Away

From the moment he arrived at Gatwick, Pinkerton began to be bothered by God, or rather by signs and portents of a religious nature. It was unexpected, and quite out of character, and he imagined it had something to do with suppressed guilt.

For instance, he was standing in the queue at the bookstall, waiting to pay for a newspaper, when the man in front of him turned abruptly round and uttered the words 'Go back'. The man wore a chain round his neck from which dangled a crucifix; it was easy to spot because his shirt was unbuttoned to the waist. And then, later, standing in line ready to check in his baggage, Pinkerton realized that he was encircled by nuns. They were not those counterfeit sisters in short modern skirts but proper nuns clad in black from head to foot, moon faces caught in starched wimples. Pinkerton was not a Catholic—if anything, he was a quarter Jewish, though he often kept that to himself—but he immediately felt unworthy at being in such sanctified company and stood aside, losing his place in the queue. It was then that one of the nuns distinctly said, 'It's too late, you have been chosen', and Pinkerton replied, 'You're right, you're absolutely right.' Then he shivered, because she had spoken in a foreign language and he had answered in one, though he had always been hopeless as a linguist and until that moment had never been vouchsafed the gift of tongues. At least, that is how it struck him at the time.

Thinking it over on the aeroplane, he wondered if there wasn't a simple explanation. The man with the crucifix had obviously not been urging him to return to Crawley but merely requesting that he should step back a few paces. Perhaps his heels had been trodden on. As for the nun, far from alluding either to life in general or to *his* life in particular, she had referred only to the passing of the hour. Possibly she had meant that there was no time to go to the Duty Free and buy *crème de menthe* for the Mother Superior. The business of his sudden comprehension of Dutch or German, or whatever guttural language it had been, was a little more tricky to explain. But then, hadn't he muddled it up a little and got the words in the wrong order? What she must have said, to a nun behind him, was *You were chosen* and then added the bit about it being too late, not the other way round. It made far more sense.

He had just decided that he had been the victim of one of those flashes of intuition which women seemed to be afflicted with most of the time, when he happened to glance out of the window. In the fraction of the second before he blinked, he saw a dazzling monster swimming through the blue sky, half fish, half bird, with scales of gold and wings of silver. He turned his head away instantly, and ordered a Scotch and soda. Afterwards he fell asleep and dreamed he was having a liaison, of a dangerous kind, with a woman who had been convent-educated.

At Athens there was some hitch in the operational schedule and he learnt that his flight to Corfu would be delayed for several hours. There was nowhere for him to sit down and the place was crowded. After two hours he gave in and, spreading his newspaper on the floor, sat hunched against a concrete ash-tray. Miserably hot, he was afraid to remove his sports jacket in case his passport was stolen. It would be all up with him if he had to turn to the British Consulate for help. They would very probably telex home and ask Gloria to describe him, and she, believing him to be elsewhere, would almost certainly say that it couldn't be him; disowned, he would be flung into jail. He had heard about foreign jails. A youngster in the office had been involved in some minor infringement of the traffic regulations in Spain and it had cost his widowed mother three hundred pounds to have him released. It was obviously a racket. To add insult to injury, he had been stabbed in the ankle by a demented Swiss who happened to be sharing his cell.

When at last Pinkerton's flight was called it was fearfully late. He arrived on Corfu in the middle of the night and was persuaded to share a cab with a large woman who wore white trousers and an immense quantity of costume jewellery. She was booked into the Chandros Hotel, which, she assured him, was in the general direction of Nisaki, and it would be a saving for both of them. It was pitch dark inside the car save for a red bulb above the dashboard illuminating a small cardboard grotto containing a plastic saint with horribly black eyebrows. The woman sat excessively close to Pinkerton, though in

all fairness he thought that at the pace they were travelling, and bearing in mind the villainous turns in the road, she had little choice.
He himself clung to the side of the window and tried not to think of
death. Now and then, in response to something he said, his companion slapped him playfully on the knee.

At first, when she enquired his name and what part of London he
hailed from, he answered cagily; after all, he was supposed to be in
Ireland, coarse-fishing with Pitt Rivers. But then, well-nigh drunk with
fatigue, and dreadfully anxious as to what he was doing driving through
foreign parts in the small hours, he found himself confiding in her.
Talking to a stranger, he told himself, as long as it was in darkness,
was almost as private as praying and hardly counted. With any luck
he would never set eyes on his confessor again. 'I'm meeting a lady
friend,' he said. 'She gave me a sort of ultimatum. I'm married, of
course, though I'm not proud of it.'

'Of course you're not,' the woman said.

'Either I came out and joined her for a few days, or it was all off
between us.'

'Oh, dear,' said the woman.

'Half of me rather wants it to be all off.'

'But not your other half,' said the woman. 'Your worst half', and
they both laughed.

'I shouldn't be here,' he said. 'I should be sitting in the damp grass
at the side of a river.'

'Of course you should,' she said. 'You've been chosen.' And she
slapped him again, and he heard her bracelets tinkling as they slid on
her wrist.

She was quite inventive. When he admitted that he was worried
about being out in the sun—it always rained in Ireland in July—she
said why didn't he come up with some allergy. One that brought him
out in bumps.

He agreed it was a jolly good idea. 'I tan very easily,' he explained.
'On account of Spanish blood some way back.'

'You'd be best under an umbrella,' advised the woman. 'You can
hire them by the day for a couple of roubles. Failing that, if you want
to economize you can always hide in your room.'

They both laughed louder than ever because it was very droll, her
confusing the currency like that. He would have told her about the
allegorical creature outside the aeroplane window but he didn't want
her to find him too memorable.

Upon arrival at the hotel it became evident that the woman was a bit of an expert on economy. She kept her handbag firmly tucked under her arm and appeared to have altogether forgotten her suggestion that she should contribute to the cost of the journey. He carried her luggage into the lobby, hoping that the sight of his perspiring face would remind her, but it didn't. She merely thanked him for his gallantry and urged him to get in touch should he and his lady friend fall out before the end of the week.

Pinkerton didn't think much of the hotel. The fellow behind the reception desk had a mouth full of gold teeth, and there was a display of dying geraniums in a concrete tub set in front of the lifts. If he had not been so exhausted he would have insisted on their being watered immediately.

'I really must be off,' he said, and he and the woman pecked each other on the cheek. It was natural, he felt, seeing they were abroad.

'Don't forget,' she said. 'You know where I am. We don't want you coming up in bumps all on your own, do we?' And winked, and this time, his knee being out of reach, slapped his hand.

All the same, he was sorry to lose her. The moment he was again seated behind the silent driver his worries returned. What if there was an emergency at home and Gloria was compelled to telephone Ireland? Supposing one of the children had an accident and he was required at a moment's notice to donate a kidney? And what if Pitt Rivers' wife ran into Gloria in town and was asked a direct question? Pitt Rivers had boasted that though he himself, if called upon, would lie until hell froze over, he couldn't possibly speak for his wife, not with her Methodist background. How absurd in this day and age, thought Pinkerton, to be troubled with religious scruples, and he peered anxiously out of the window into the impenetrable blackness and watched, in his mind's eye, the roof of his half-timbered house outside Crawley engulfed in forty-foot flames. In the squeal of the tyres on the road he heard the cracking of glass in his new greenhouse as the structure buckled in the heat and his pampered tomatoes bubbled on their stems. It was so warm in the car that he struggled out of his jacket and rolled up his shirt-sleeves.

He had fallen into a doze when the car stopped outside a taverna set in a clearing of olive trees at the side of the road. For the moment he feared that he had arrived at the hotel, and was shocked at its dilapidated appearance. Not even Agnes, who was capable of much deception, would have described it as three-star accommodation.

A young woman sat at a rickety table, holding an infant on her lap. The driver left the car and approached her; Pinkerton imagined that she was his wife and that he was explaining why he was so late home.

In any event the young woman was dissatisfied. An argument ensued.

Pinkerton grimaced and smiled through the window, conveying what he hoped was the right mixture of apologetic sympathy. 'The plane was delayed,' he called. 'It was quite beyond our control.'

The young woman rose to her feet and she and the driver, both shouting equally violently, began to stalk one another round the tables.

'Look here,' called Pinkerton. 'I'm terribly tired.'

They took no notice of him.

Presently, he got out of the car and joined them under the canopy of tattered plastic. Yawning exaggeratedly, pointing first at his watch and then at the road, he attempted to communicate with the driver. For all the notice that was taken of him he might not have been there. Wandering away, he inspected with disgust various petrol tins planted with withered begonias.

He was just thinking that it bordered on the criminal, this wanton and widespread neglect of anything that grew, when the young woman broke off her perambulation of the tables and darting towards him thrust the child into his arms.

Taken by surprise he held it awkwardly against his shoulder and felt its tiny fingers plucking at the skin of his arm. 'Look here,' he said again, and clumsily jogged up and down, for the child had begun a thin wailing. 'There, there,' he crooned, and guided by some memory in the past he tucked its head under his chin, as though he held a violin, and swayed on his feet.

He was looking up, ready to receive smiles of approbation from the parents—after all, he was coping frightfully well considering he had been on the go for almost a day and a half—when to his consternation he saw that the man was walking back to the car. As gently as was possible in the circumstances he dumped the child on the ground, propping it against a petrol drum, and ran in pursuit.

The driver handled the car as if it had done him a personal injury. He beat at the driving wheel with his fists and drove erratically, continuing to shout for several miles. At last his voice fell to an irritated muttering, and then, just as Pinkerton had leant back in his seat and settled into a more relaxed position, the car veered sickeningly to the right, almost jerking him to the floor, and stopped.

Pinkerton tried to reason with the driver, but it was no use. The domestic crisis had evidently unsettled him; he refused adamantly to go any further. Jumping out of the car he opened the side door and dragged Pinkerton on to the road.

'I'll pay you anything you want,' cried Pinkerton, foolishly.

Three thousand drachmas were extorted from him before his suitcase was flung out into the darkness, and the driver, taking advantage of his stumbling search for it on the stony verge, leapt back into the car, reversed, swung round and drove off at speed in the direction from which they had just come. Pinkerton was left alone, stranded in the middle of nowhere.

It was another hour, perhaps two, before he reached his destination. If he had understood the driver correctly, the track leading to the hotel was unsuitable for vehicles and dangerous for pedestrians to walk down at night, being nothing more substantial than a treacherous path between two chasms cut by the Ionian Sea. Remembering his days as a Boy Scout he had sat for a while on his suitcase, which he had retrieved from a clump of bushes so densely studded with thorns as to resemble a bundle of barbed wire, and waited for his eyes to adjust to the darkness. In time he saw the sky threaded with stars, but the earth remained hidden. He had wasted precious matches lighting his pipe and, puffing on it furiously, held the bowl out in front of him like a torch; to no avail. He had jumped to his feet and bellowed unashamedly, 'Help, help, I am Inglesi', and fallen over a boulder, bruising his shin. Finally he had sat on his bottom and dragging his suitcase behind him, begun laboriously to descend. Now and then, as the breeze shifted the branches of the olive trees below him, he caught a glimpse of a glittering ship on the horizon, and heard a roll of thunder as an unseen plane approached the airstrip of the distant town.

He was perhaps half way down the mountain when a curious light appeared above his left shoulder, illuminating the path ahead. Startled, he looked round and saw nothing. As he later tried to explain to a sceptical Agnes, it was as though someone was following him, someone rather tall, carrying a lantern. He was too relieved to have found what he took to be the means of his salvation to be frightened at such a phenomenon.

Soon the darkness melted altogether and he stood bathed in the electric lights of the car park of the Nisaki Beach Hotel. He climbed the shallow steps up to the reception area and only then did he look back. In the instant before the hotel was plunged into darkness he thought he saw a man dressed all in white, whose shadowy brow was flecked with blood.

The woman at the reception desk mercifully spoke English. She assured Pinkerton that the power cut was temporary and that it was not an unusual occurrence. She also said that it wasn't allowed for him to enter Mrs Lowther's room. It had nothing to do with the hour. Mrs Lowther was a package holiday and he wasn't included. She would rent him a room on the same floor, with twin beds, shower and use of cot. The latter convenience would be two thousand drachmas extra. Too tired to argue, and aware that the seat of his trousers was threadbare and his jacket torn at the elbow, he paid what was asked and, the lifts being out of order, borrowed a torch and toiled up the eight flights of stairs to his room on the fourth floor.

He was awakened during the night by a severe tingling in his arm. Finding that he was still in his clothes, he sat wearily on the edge of the bed and began to undress. The sensation in his arm had now become one of irritation; he scratched himself vigorously, imagining that he had been attacked on the mountainside by mosquitoes. Looking down, he was astonished to see a patch of skin on his forearm fan-shaped and topped by a pattern of dots so pale in contrast to the rest of his skin as to appear luminous. He tried to find the light switch so that he could examine his arm more closely. It was not inconceivable that he had been bitten by a snake, or even by a series of snakes, for he counted six puncture marks, though his flesh was perfectly smooth to the touch. Unable to locate the bedside lamp and not suffering from either pain or nausea, he fell back on to the pillow and slept.

Agnes telephoned his room the next morning. 'So you've turned up,' she said. She made it sound like an accusation, as if he was pestering her rather than that he was here at her insistence.

'I've had a terrible time,' he told her. 'You wouldn't believe it. First of all there was the plane journey, travelling all that way alone.'

'You mean you flew in an empty aeroplane?' she asked.

'You know perfectly well what I mean,' he said crossly. 'And there was a five-hour delay at Athens.'

'Stop moaning,' she said. 'I'll see you at breakfast.'

He shaved and showered and put on a clean shirt and the only other pair of trousers he had brought with him. He hid the woollen socks and jumpers, packed by his wife, inside the wardrobe and bundled his wellington boots under the bed. He hoped Agnes wouldn't spot them.

In spite of his experiences of the night before he felt amazingly fit, almost a new man. True, his hands were covered in cuts and scratches and his shin somewhat grazed and tender, but in every other respect he had never felt so healthy, so carefree. The view from his balcony— the green lawns, the flowering shrubs, the gravel paths leading to bowers roofed with straw and overhung with bougainvillaea, the glimpse of swimming pool—delighted him. Beyond the pool he could see striped umbrellas on a pebbled beach beside a stretch of water that sparkled to an horizon edged with purple mountains. It was all so pretty, so picturesque. The whole world was drenched in sunshine. A tiny figure, suspended beneath a scarlet parachute, drifted between the blue heavens and the bright blue sea.

Even Agnes sensed the change in him. 'I thought you said you'd had an awful time.'

'I did,' he replied cheerfully. 'Absolutely dreadful.' And he helped himself to yoghurt and slices of peach and didn't once grumble at the absence of bacon and eggs.

He wasn't quite sure how much he dare tell her: and yet he longed to confide in someone. Agnes could be very cruel on occasions. Omitting only the words *You've been chosen*, he told her about the nun at the airport at Gatwick.

Agnes listened earnestly, and when he had finished remarked that she herself had often understood foreign languages, even when she didn't know any of the words. She'd met a Russian once at a party and she'd known, really known, exactly what he was saying. She thought it had probably something to do with telepathy. 'Mind you,' she admitted, 'the vodka was coming out of my ears.'

'Yes,' he said doubtfully, 'but I answered her. In Dutch as far as I know.'

Agnes agreed that it was odd; she looked at him with interest. She was frowning and he was pleased because he recognized her expression of intense concentration as one of sexual arousal. As far as he remembered she had never been excited by nuns before. Encouraged, he recounted the episode on the mountainside and his terrible descent.

There's a perfectly good road higher up,' she said. 'It's signposted. It's only a hundred yards further along from that track.'

'How was I to know,' he said. 'It seems to me that I had no choice.' He described the guide dressed in white.

'No,' said Agnes. 'I can't buy that. It's almost blasphemous.'

'I'm only telling you what I saw,' he protested.

'But a crown of thorns,' she cried. 'How can you say such a thing? It's far more likely that you saw a fisherman in his nightshirt and one of those straw hats they all wear.'

'I know a hat when I see one,' he argued. 'I'm not blind.'

'It had probably been chewed by a goat,' she said. 'Or a donkey. You just saw the chewed bits, damn it.'

He attempted to change the subject and tell her about the baby at the taverna. Agnes was still aroused, though no longer in a way that would be beneficial to him. If he didn't watch his step she would lock him out of her room for days. 'It was a dear little soul,' he said. 'Quite enchanting, if a little pale.'

'Why the hell,' interrupted Agnes, 'would Jesus want to guide *you* to the Nisaki Beach Hotel? You're an adulterer.'

'An unwilling one,' he snapped, and fell into an offended silence.

He apologized to her that afternoon. She forgave him and consented to come to his room. When he closed the shutters the bars of the cot lay in striped shadows across her thighs. Her body was so dark after a week in the sun that it was like making advances to a stranger. He wasn't sure that the experience was enjoyable.

'Why have you kept your shirt on?' she asked him later, and he explained that he was perspiring so copiously with the heat that he was afraid she'd find him unpleasant.

'You are a bit sweaty,' she said, and wrapped the sheet round her like a shroud.

After three days he decided that he ought to go home. Agnes was behaving badly. He had run out of excuses for keeping out of reach of the sun and was tired of being insulted. When he lay in the shade of the olive trees Agnes snatched the newspaper from his face and complained that he could be mistaken for an old dosser. 'For God's sake,' she ordered, 'take off those woollen socks', and for his own sake he fought her off as she clawed at the laces of his shoes. All the same, he couldn't make up his mind when to leave, and lingered, dozing in his room or in one of those fragrant bowers in the pleasant garden. He still felt well, he still felt that absence of care which he now realized he had last known as a child. At night he put his pillow at the foot of the bed and fell asleep with his hand clutching the bars of the cot.

Towards the end of the week they went on an excursion into Corfu Town. Pinkerton said he wanted to buy Agnes a piece of jewellery. They both knew that it was his farewell gift to her. She pretended that it was kind of him. When she returned to England he would telephone her once or twice to ask how she was, perhaps even take her out to lunch, and then the relationship would be over. Something had changed in him; he no longer needed her to berate him, and she was too old to change her ways. He could tell that she was uneasy with him, and wondered if his wife would feel the same.

Agnes chose an inexpensive bracelet and stuffed it carelessly into her handbag. She said she was off to buy postcards. He offered to go with her but she wouldn't hear of it. 'You hate shopping,' she said.

He arranged to wait for her at a café in the square. She didn't look back, which was a bad sign. He wasn't at all sure that she hadn't gone straight off to hire a cab to take her back to the hotel.

Half an hour passed. He was sitting at a table at the edge of the cricket pitch, smoking his pipe, when a woman in a red dress sat down opposite him and slapped his wrist.

'Good heavens,' he cried, recognizing the gesture if not the face.

'I owe you some money,' she said. 'My share of the cab fare', and though he protested, she insisted. She had also bought him a little present, because she had known she would bump into him sooner or later. She took an envelope from her handbag and gave it to him. Inside was a cardboard bookmark with a picture on it.

'How very kind of you,' Pinkerton said, and began to tremble.

'It's St John of Hiding,' said the woman. 'The saint of all those who carry a secret burden of hidden sin.'

Before they parted she asked him how he was getting on with his lady friend. He admitted that it was pretty well all over between them.

'I'm glad to hear it,' the woman said. 'I'm sure you're destined for higher things.'

Agnes saw the bookmark by mistake. When they got back to the hotel and Pinkerton was looking for money to pay the cab fare, he inadvertently pulled it out of his pocket. 'Why did you buy that?' she asked.

'It's a picture of a saint,' he said. 'A Greek one.'

'It's not very well drawn,' she said. 'One of the hands has got six fingers.'

Alone in his room he took off his jacket and laid it on the bed beside the bookmark. Rubbing his arm he went out onto the balcony and watched the scarlet parachute blow across the sky.

The next morning he told Agnes that he was leaving. He thought she looked relieved. He said that before he went he was determined to have one of those parachute rides.

'Good God,' she said. 'I mustn't miss this.'

She went to the jetty with him and watched, grinning, while he was strapped into his harness. 'Wonders will never cease,' she called out, as he took off his shirt.

He was instructed to hold on to the bar and break into a run when he felt the tug of the rope. When he was in the air he must hold on to the bar even though the harness would support him. He said he understood.

The speedboat chugged in a half circle beyond the jetty, waiting for the signal to be given; then, accelerating, it roared out to sea. Pinkerton was jerked forward, and gasping he ran and jumped and was swung upwards, his mouth wide open and his heart thudding fit to burst. Then he was riding through the air, not floating as he had hoped, for he was still tethered to the boat. He felt cheated.

The sudden and furious gust of wind that seized the rope in its giant fist and tore it, steel hook and all from the funnel of the boat, was spent in an instant. Then Pinkerton, free as a bird, soared into the blue under the red umbrella of his parachute.

Everything else that had happened to him, he thought, had a logical explanation; the nuns, the man who had come to his aid on the dark mountain, the woman and her choice of bookmark. Even the creature outside the aeroplane window had been nothing more than a reflection of the sunlight on the fuselage. Everything but that—

And before he blew away he looked up at that luminous imprint of a six-fingered hand which was stamped on the flesh of his arm.

Chinese Funeral

'I could do without the coffin,' said the Englishwoman. 'Going to China with a coffin.'

'It won't be here for long,' said her husband. 'They're taking it off at Lamma Island. We call in there. He's going to be buried at home. We're dropping him off. He died in Hong Kong.'

'How do you know it all?'

'Oh. I do. What's the matter with you? Coffins go all over the place. Aeroplanes. Ships. Cruise ships are full of them—empties for emergencies. I saw three in a stack once in Victoria Station. In Spain they arrange them round the undertakers' offices. On shelves. I've seen them. Wrapped in plastic, like long chocolates.'

'Oh, for heaven's sake,' she said. 'Anyway those aren't full ones. This is a full one.'

'They were full,' he said. 'In Spain. No two ways.'

'Glib. Silly,' she said.

'Anyway,' said the husband, 'this one's out of sight. Below deck. You wouldn't know it was there if you hadn't seen it coming on board.'

'I can see the awful people,' she said.

Near the stern of the boat noisy men with excited eyes pushed each other about like lads on a treat. They wore sacking robes and their heads and hands were covered by slap-happy bloodstained bandages, loose and trailing. The blood was not blood but vermilion paint. One man held a long trumpet. All had bare feet.

The husband said, 'I wonder if they're the professional mourners?'

She said, 'It's awful. They're enjoying it.'

'Yes,' he said. 'A bit wild. The afterlife for them is horrible, you know. The sleep of oblivion. Desolate. Frightening.'

'They're *enjoying* being frightened,' she said. 'They're getting a kick.'

'Yes and no,' said the husband. 'Yes and no. Don't forget they're surrounded by spirits.'

'Brandy.'

'No. Evil spirits. The trumpet is to frighten them away. Hong Kong isn't all computerspeak and banking. Well, Lamma Island isn't anyway. Superstition goes deep, deep.'

'It does with me too,' she said. 'There's something about travelling with a coffin.'

'I'm surprised at you, Ann.'

'Not bad luck exactly,' she said. 'I don't know. Inopportune. Time rolling on. And back.'

'Well so it does,' he said.

When the boat came alongside the sunny island he watched the waiting crowd of mourners on the quay and the bandaged people shouldering the coffin and bearing it away to the sound of the trumpet. The woman stayed in her seat reading the guide-book, her hands over her ears.

Fourteen were going on the day trip to China from Hong Kong. One was a Nigerian, the rest British, all unknown to each other. They had met on the Star Ferry waterfront, Kowloon side, before dawn. They were all middle-aged to old, a rather heavy, thoughtful lot, too early awake. As the sun rose and they headed north to the southern tip of China, threading the islands that lay in strings like the humps of sea monsters ('It's where they got the idea of dragons,' said the husband), the Nigerian began to read a copy of *Time* magazine and the others clicked about with cameras. One big old Englishman as they stepped from the boat on to true Chinese soil straightened his shoulders and tightly blinked his eyes. His wife took his hand and they interlaced their fingers. They stood not looking at anything in particular.

At the Customs, a woman in khaki, watching a screen, stretched for Ann's handbag and removed from it two apples that must have shown up on the X-ray. 'I suppose they looked like hand grenades,' said Ann. The unpainted mask-face did not smile but the eyes of soldiers standing by looked sharp. 'I didn't know we couldn't bring them in,' she said. 'Here—we'll eat them. It's a shame to waste them.'

But there was a sudden great flustering and the apples were seized back from her hand and thrown in a bucket with other wicked things— Cadbury's chocolate, sandwiches in foil and a bottle of something. 'I hope they get a pain,' said Ann. 'I suppose they'll eat them the minute we're out of sight.'

'That we do not enquire,' said a voice. Standing by the minibus that was to be their home till nightfall was the Chinese guide, brilliant-eyed, happy, young. He ran about laughing and shaking hands with the English group. 'Here you leave Hong Kong behind and give yourselves to me and to our driver here. He is a wonderful driver though he speaks and understands no English. He is my friend. I am a student of a Chinese university and he is uneducated, but he is my friend. For several years now, together in vacations, we have guided western tourists. We ask you to be patient with us. I ask you to ask me any questions you wish. I will answer everything. *Everything*. But we have much to do and far to go and when I say, "Come, hurry up please, no longer", you must obey. Thank you and get in.'

The driver had a long, unsmiling face. A precise and perfect line ran from eye-socket to the point of the jaw. A leaf. A Picasso. His white hands lay for the moment loose on the wheel. The hands of Moiseiwitsch. The guide was jolly, square-faced, amiable, with shaggy fetching hair. Side by side the two heads turned to the road, giving it all attention. Ann suddenly saw the driver's hands running with blood and the guide with upflung arms, facing the dark. She cried out.

'What's the matter?' said the husband. '*What* did you say? You're shivering. Put your sweater on.'

'It's—.'

'Whatever is it? You look awful. Oh lord, are you car-sick? The road's going to get much worse than this.'

'No. I saw something. I don't know what—. Something—.'

'Will you forget that coffin?'

'No. Not the coffin. Something coming. Rolling like a sea.'

'They'll give us some tea soon,' he said. 'When we stop to see the kindergarten show and the market.'

'We got up too soon,' he said in a moment, and put an arm round her shoulders.

At the kindergarten show the human marionettes danced and sang and tipped their perfect little heads from side to side. Afterwards they ran across to the audience to shake every hand, fixed smile on every blank-eyed face. 'Come now,' called the guide with his different smile. 'We have much to see and a hundred miles before lunch.'

'I'll find some tea,' said Ann's husband. 'There's always tea,' and she stood waiting, watching the children being marshalled together for the next performance as a new load of tourists came streaming in. 'Could I see some of the ordinary children?' she asked, but the guide said 'No, no, no—come.'

She sat in the bus, drank tea, felt better. And soon began to watch the endless fields on either side of the road. Endless, endless. Grey. The thin crops, the frail, earth-coloured houses, here and there a pencilled, fine-leaved tree and a matchstick-figure in a round hat scratching and chopping at the dun earth with a hoe. Chop and drag. Chop and drag. For hours they drove under a rainy sky. 'Time is over,' she said.

'Better?'

'Yes. I don't know what it was. It must have been a dream. It was a sort of—day-mare.'

'It was a short night,' he said. 'You're tired.'

As the country faded by she began to see beauty in the timelessness and silence and hugeness of the land, the people scarcely touched down on it like specks. At a lay-by worn by other tourists' feet they all got out to take photographs of peasants sowing seed on the plain. One ancient leather face looked up into Ann's camera. Looked away.

'Come now, come,' laughed the young guide. 'The road soon changes. It will become bad. After lunch it may be slow. We are going to a beautiful place for lunch. Well, it is the only place. Here it comes. It is perfectly hygienic. Do not judge by its surroundings.'

They picked their way through filth to the one new building in a sad town. Driver and guide disappeared and the party spinning a turntable of food at two round dining tables loosened up a little. The old Englishman ate sparingly, expert with chopsticks, the rest hungrily with spoons. The Nigerian ate hardly at all. All the food was fawn. 'Not exactly Hong Kong,' said Ann's husband.

'It is *amazingly* good. Amazing,' said the old Englishman. 'Amazing that they can do this. You have no idea.'

'You know China?'

'Oh yes. For twenty years. And we left twenty years ago.' He looked at his wife who had no need to look back at him.

'*And*,' he said, 'we are unlikely to be here again.'

'Oh—don't say that,' said Ann.

'Not because of our age,' he said. 'None of us may come back again.'

'And now we shall hurry on,' said the guide. They noticed under the high electric bulbs of the echoing restaurant that he was rather older than they had thought and that some of the earlier insouciance was gone. Some of the acting. 'I shall warn you,' he said, 'we come soon to a point where it is not impossible that we must turn back. Before we get to the city there is often a huge traffic condition and we stand still a long time. It is known as the Rush Hour. A misnomer. I ask you to be patient if this happens and perhaps read books or sleep. Ask me questions or we perhaps might sing? May I ask you now at this moment, not to look out to the left of the bus please? Look only straight ahead, please, or to the *right*.'

Everyone at once looked out to the left, where a bedraggled and very long string of people dressed in white was moving at an urgent jog-trot over the fields towards the main road. Some wore tall white dunces' caps. All had fluttering streamers and dabs of vermilion paint. Four shouldered a skimpy coffin.

'To the right. To the right,' called the guide, 'the *right*. It is a Chinese funeral. Funerals are very important in China. It is not polite to watch them. In East or West it is considered ill-mannered to watch people's grief. It is not civilized to watch a Chinese funeral.'

'It is bad luck to watch a Chinese funeral,' said the big old Englishman in Ann's ear—he sat behind her. 'He is being kind to us.'

'It is our second today,' said Ann.

The driver slammed his foot down and they sped on, over a road full of holes and lakes of rain, past a sugar-beet factory red with rust. 'The Russians flogged to us that factory,' the guide announced over his microphone—his lunch and the funeral had excited him. 'The Russians made mugs of us. As usual. Nothing works.'

On they sped, past stagnant black water, ditches crammed with lotus leaves. A village. A temple. A snowstorm of white ducks waiting to be cooked. In a dirty town, pavement-artists gathered round the bus in front of a defunct red-lacquered palace, calling and laughing. 'These are all students,' said the guide. 'These are my tribe. Though they do not speak such good English as I do. I am very good.' He laughed at himself and the bus laughed with him and said he was telling the truth. Someone began to clap. The Nigerian looked loftily out of the window. They flew on, rounded a bend and hit the traffic.

It stood ahead of them as far as they could see. 'And this,' said the guide, 'is where we must put to the test the capacity for patience. At first I suggest we take some sleep.'

Guide and driver, expert as grasshoppers, folded themselves in their seats and a little of the black cap of hair on each head, one polished, one shaggy, showed above the ramshackle head-rests. The heads leaned together, like babes-in-the-wood. Ann felt her hands ache to stretch and caress.

She felt again, darkness round the two young men and turning quickly, frightened, said to the old English woman, 'This can't be much fun for you. This new China. Having lived here before. We thought it was all supposed to be so much better now. Is it just that we've been in Hong Kong for a week? Cloud cuckoo?'

She said, 'Oh no. It is wonderful to be back.'

'Ha,' said the guide, bobbing up, arranging himself on a perch by the dashboard, taking up the mike. 'This it seems is a good opportunity. The driver does not speak English and is in any case asleep. None of you will stay in China for more than a day. I tell you then this. China now looks forward with hope and joy. There is to be a great and glorious transformation. Blood will flow, but we stand to overthrow evil men and we shall win liberty. I ask you to think of me soon. At the time when the world will be watching us. You will remember me and what I say.'

Tottering as the bus jerked forward again, he fell aslant back in to his seat and turned away from them. For perhaps a mile they bowled easily along.

But then—round the next bend—the traffic again before them, ramshackle, dead still, solid, and more came swinging up behind them, hemming them tight.

'We shall now miss our train to Hong Kong from the city,' said the Nigerian, speaking for the first time.

'There is nothing to be done,' said the old Englishman, and settled back comfortably. His wife smiled.

Ann's husband said, 'Better sleep, Ann. We don't know what the end of this is going to be.'

'No.'

'Don't look so *doom-laden*,' he said. 'It's all education. After all, it's not our country.'

He hoped that she had not seen that the funeral party of an hour ago had caught up with them and was jogging along the side of the bus between it and the oily ditch of lotuses. The mourners' feet were black with dust, faces were hidden by white hoods. The crazed tall hats bobbed up and down as they passed by, and out of sight.

DAVID MALOUF

The Kyogle Line

In July 1944, when train travel was still romantic, and hourly flights
had not yet telescoped the distance between Brisbane and Sydney to
a fifty-five-minute interval of air-conditioned vistas across a tumble
of slow-motion foam, we set out, my parents, my sister and I, on the
first trip of my life—that is how I thought of it—that would take me
over a border. We left from Kyogle Station, just a hundred yards
from where we lived, on a line that was foreign from the moment
you embarked on it, since it ran only south out of the state and had
a gauge of four-foot-eight. Our own Queensland lines were three-foot-
six and started from Roma Street Station on the other side of the river.

I was familiar with all this business of gauges and lines from school,
where our complicated railway system, and its origins in the jealously
guarded sovereignty of our separate states, was part of our lessons and
of local lore, but also because, for all the years of my later childhood,
I had seen transports pass our house ferrying troops across the city
from one station to the other, on their way to Townsville and the far
north. We lived in a strip of no-man's-land between lines; or, so far as
the thousands of Allied troops were concerned, between safe, cosmopolitan Sydney and the beginning, at Roma Street, of their passage to
the war.

Our own journey was for a two weeks' stay at the Balfour Hotel
at the corner of King and Elizabeth Streets, Sydney. The owner was
an old mate of my father's, which is why, in wartime, with all hotel
rooms occupied, we had this rare chance of accommodation. Train
bookings too were hard to come by. We would sit up for sixteen hours
straight—maybe more, since the line was used for troop movements.
I was delighted. It meant I could stay up all night. Staying awake past
midnight was also, in its way, a border to be crossed.

I had been many times to see people off on the 'First Division',
and loved the old-fashioned railway compartments with their foliated

iron racks for luggage, their polished woodwork, the spotty black-and-white pictures of Nambucca Heads or the Warrumbungles, and the heavy brocade that covered the seats and was hooked in swags at the windows. When we arrived to claim our seats, people were already crammed into the corridor, some of them preparing to stand all the way. There were soldiers in winter uniform going on leave with long khaki packs, pairs of gum-chewing girls with bangles and pompadours, women with small kids already snotty or smelly with wet pants, serious men in felt hats and double-breasted suits. The afternoon as we left was dry and windy, but hot in the compartment. It was still officially winter. When the sun went down it would be cold.

My mother would spend the journey knitting. She was, at that time, engaged in making dressing-gowns, always of the same pattern and in the same mulberry-coloured nine-ply, for almost everyone she knew. There was rationing, but no coupons were needed for wool. I had been taught to knit at school and my mother let me do the belts—I had already made nine or ten of them—but was waiting because I didn't want to miss the border and the view.

What I was hungry for was some proof that the world was as varied as I wanted it to be; that somewhere, on the far side of what I knew, difference began, and that the point could be clearly recognized.

The view did change, and frequently, but not suddenly or sharply enough. It was a matter of geological forms I couldn't read, new variants of eucalypt and pine. The journey from this point of view was a failure, though I wouldn't admit it. I stayed excited and let my own vivid expectations colour the scene. Besides, it wasn't a fair test. We had barely passed the border when it was dark. It did get perceptibly colder. But was that a crossing into a new climate zone or just the ordinary change from day to night? The train rocked and sped, then jolted and stopped for interminable periods in a ring-barked nowhere; then jerked and clashed and started up again. We saw lights away in the darkness, isolated farmhouses or settlements suggesting that some of the space we were passing through was inhabited. We got grimy with smuts.

My mother knitted, even after the lights were lowered and other people had curled up under blankets. I too kept wide awake. I was afraid, as always, of missing something—the one thing that might happen or appear, that was the thing I was intended not to miss. If I did, a whole area of my life would be closed to me for ever.

So I was still awake, not long after midnight, when we pulled into

Coff's Harbour and the train stopped to let people get off and walk for a bit, or buy tea at the refreshment room.

'Can *we*?' I pleaded. 'Wouldn't you like a nice cup of tea, Mummy? I could get it.'

My mother looked doubtful.

'It wouldn't do any harm,' my father said, 'to have a bit of a stretch.'

'I need to go to the lav,' I threw in, just to clinch the thing. It had been difficult to make your way through standing bodies and over sleeping ones to the cubicles at either end of the carriage. The last time we went we had had to step over a couple, one of them a soldier, who were doing something under a blanket. My father, who was modest, had been shocked.

'Come on then.' We climbed down.

It was a clear cold night and felt excitingly different, fresher than I had ever known, with a clean smell of dark bushland sweeping away under stars to the escarpments of the Great Divide. People, some of them in dressing-gowns and carrying thermos flasks, were bustling along the platform. The train hissed and clanged. It was noisy; but the noise rose straight up into the starry night as if the air here were thinner, offered no resistance. It felt sharp in your lungs.

We passed a smoky waiting-room where soldiers were sprawled in their greatcoats, some on benches, others on the floor, their rifles in stacks against the wall; then the refreshment room with its crowded bar. It was a long walk to the Men's, all the length of the platform. I had never been out after midnight, and I expected it to be stranger. It *was* strange but not strange enough. In some ways the most different thing of all was to be taking a walk like this with my father.

We were shy of one another. He had always worked long hours, and like most children in those days I spent my time on the edge of my mother's world, always half-excluded but half-involved as well. My father's world was foreign to me. He disappeared into it at six o'clock, before my sister and I were up, and came back again at tea-time, not long before we were packed off to bed. If we went down under-the-house on Saturdays to watch him work, with a stub of indelible pencil behind his ear, as some men wear cigarettes, it was to enter a world of silence there that belonged to his deep communication with measurements, and tools, and dove-tail joints that cast us back on our own capacity for invention.

He was not much of a talker, our father. He seldom told us things unless we asked. Then he would answer our questions too carefully, as if he feared, with his own lack of schooling, that he might lead us wrong. And he never told stories, as our mother did, of his family and youth. His family were there to be seen, and however strange they might be in fact, did not lend themselves to fairytale. My father had gone out to work at twelve. If he never spoke of his youth it was, perhaps, because he had never had one, or because its joys and sorrows were of a kind we could not be expected to understand. There was no grand house to remember, as my mother remembered New Cross; no favourite maids; no vision of parents sweeping into the nursery to say goodnight in all the ballroom finery of leg o'mutton sleeves and pearl combs and shirt-fronts stiff as boards. His people were utterly ordinary. The fact that they were also *not* Australian, that they ate garlic and oil, smelled different, and spoke no English, was less important than that they had always been there and had to be taken as they were. Our father himself was as Australian as anyone could be—except for the name. He had made himself so. He had played football for the State, and was one of the toughest welterweights of his day, greatly admired for his fairness and skill by an entire generation.

But all this seemed accidental in him. A teetotaller and non-smoker, very quiet in manner, fastidiously modest, he had an inner life that was not declared. He had educated himself in the things that most interested him, but his way of going about them was his own; he had worked the rules out for himself. He suffered from never having been properly schooled, and must, I see now, have hidden deep hurts and humiliations under his studied calm. The best he could do with me was to make me elaborate playthings—box-kites, a three-foot yacht—and, for our backyard, a magnificent set of swings. My extravagance, high-strung fantasies, which my mother tended to encourage, intimidated him. He would have preferred me to become, as he had, a more conventional type. He felt excluded by my attachment to books.

So this walk together was in all ways unusual, not just because we were taking it at midnight in New South Wales.

We walked in silence, but with a strong sense, on my part at least, of our being together and at one. I liked my father. I wished he would talk to me and tell me things. I didn't know him. He puzzled me, as it puzzled me too that my mother, who was so down on our speaking or acting 'Australian', should be so fond of these things as they appeared, in their gentler form, in him. She had made, in his case, a unique dispensation.

On our way back from the Men's we found ourselves approaching a place where the crowd, which was generally very mobile, had stilled, forming a bunch round one of the goods wagons.

'What is it?' I wanted to know.

'What is it?' my father asked another fellow when we got close. We couldn't see anything.

'Nips,' the man told us. 'Bloody Nips. They got three Jap POWs in there.'

I expected my father to move away then, to move me on. If he does, I thought, I'll get lost. I wanted to see them.

But my father stood, and we worked our way into the centre of the crowd; and as people stepped away out of it we were drawn to the front, till we stood staring in through the door of a truck.

It was too big to be thought of as a cage, but was a cage, just the same. I thought of the circus wagons that sometimes came and camped in the little park beside South Brisbane Station, or on the waste ground under Grey Street Bridge.

There was no straw, no animal smell. The three Japs, in a group, if not actually chained then at least huddled, were difficult to make out in the half-dark. But looking in at them was like looking in from our own minds, our own lives, on another species. The vision imposed silence on the crowd. Only when they broke the spell by moving away did they mutter formulas, 'Bloody Japs,' or 'The bastards', that were meant to express what was inexpressible, the vast gap of darkness they felt existed here—a distance between people that had nothing to do with actual space, or the fact that you were breathing, out here in the still night of Australia, the same air. The experience was an isolating one. The moment you stepped out of the crowd and the shared sense of being part of it, you were alone.

My father felt it. As we walked away he was deeply silent. Our moment together was over. What was it that touched him? Was he thinking of a night, three years before, when the Commonwealth Police had arrested his father as an enemy alien?

My grandfather came to Brisbane from Lebanon in the 1880s; though in those days of course, when Australia was still unfederated, a parcel of rival states, Lebanon had no existence except in the mind of a few patriots. It was part of greater Syria; itself then a province of the great, sick Empire of the Turks. My grandfather had fled his homeland in the wake of a decade of massacres. Like other Lebanese Christians, he had sorrowfully turned his back on the Old Country and started life all over again in the New World.

His choice of Australia was an arbitrary one. No one knows why he made it. He might equally have gone to Boston or to São Paulo in Brazil. But the choice, once made, was binding. My father and the rest of us were Australians now. That was that. After Federation, in the purely notional view of these things that was practised by the immigration authorities, greater Syria (as opposed to Egypt and Turkey proper) was declared white—but only the Christian inhabitants of it, a set of official decisions, in the matter of boundary and distinction, that it was better not to question. My father's right to be an Australian, like any Scotsman's for example, was guaranteed by this purely notional view—that is, officially. The rest he had to establish for himself; most often with his fists. But my grandfather, by failing to get himself naturalized, remained an alien. At first a Syrian, later a Lebanese. And when Lebanon, as a dependency of France, declared for Vichy rather than the Free French, he became an enemy as well.

He was too old, at more than eighty, to be much concerned by any of this, and did not understand perhaps how a political decision made on the other side of the world had changed his status, after so long, on this one. He took the bag my aunts packed for him and went. It was my father who was, in his quiet way—what?—shaken, angered, disillusioned?

The authorities—that is, the decent local representatives—soon recognized the absurdity of the thing and my grandfather was released: on personal grounds. My father never told us how he had managed it, or what happened, what he *felt*, when he went to fetch his father home. If it changed anything for him, the colour of his own history for example, he did not reveal it. It was just another of the things he kept to himself and buried. Like the language. He must, I understood later, have grown up speaking Arabic as well as he spoke Australian; his parents spoke little else. But I never heard him utter a word of it or give any indication that he understood. It went on as a whole layer of his experience, of his understanding and feeling for things, of alternative being, that could never be expressed. It too was part of the shyness between us.

We got my mother her nice cup of tea, and five minutes later, in a great bustle of latecomers and shouts and whistles, the train started up again and moved deeper into New South Wales. But I thought of it now as changed. Included in its string of lighted carriages, along with the sleeping soldiers and their packs and slouch-hats with sunbursts on the turn-up, the girls with their smeared lipstick and a wad of gum hardening now under a rim of the carriage-work, the kids blowing snotty bubbles, the men in business suits, was that darker wagon with the Japs.

Their presence imposed silence. That had been the first reaction. But what it provoked immediately after was some sort of inner argument or dialogue that was in a language I couldn't catch. It had the rhythm of the train wheels over those foreign four-foot-eight-inch rails—a different sound from the one our own trains made—and it went on even when the train stalled and waited, and long after we had come to Sydney and the end of our trip. It was, to me, as if I had all the time been on a different train from the one I thought. Which would take more than the sixteen hours the timetable announced and bring me at last to a different, unnameable destination.

Cuckoo Clock

The ice on the roads, which had melted slightly during the day, had refrozen after dark into sheets of perilous glass, slippery as if they had been oiled, and the tail end of the bus as it took the curves was skidding badly. We were afraid the whole thing would overturn. It didn't help that the driver wouldn't slow at any point, except once or twice to pick up people who shouted at him out of the blackness by the snow-banked roadside and climbed on, talking in German, laughing, seeming drunk. The driver, who might have been drunk too, chattered in a loud, slurred voice and laughed—it seemed to us inappropriately—at the lashing and swaying of his bus. The members of the party, doctors and their wives or husbands, many of them from warm climates, clung terrified to each other or to the seats. The person sitting next to me, Penny Deckhorne, clung with one hand to the thin chrome rim of the bus window, spreading her fingers along it as if to stay the lurching vehicle. J. and Sir Randy Deckhorne were sitting in front with the organizer, Dr Schneider, to talk about some program matter. I wished one of them would walk back down the aisle to say something reassuring to the passengers.

'When we signed up for it, I thought the dinner would be at the hotel,' Penny said through her teeth.

I agreed. Penny's large and heavily overcoated body fell across me with each whiplash. 'Sorry,' she said each time, and I said, 'Sorry,' when we went the other way. I withdrew my knee from the enforced lurch of Penny against me as we swerved again.

'I'm just going to get Randy to speak to the man,' said Penny, climbing over me and proceeding up the aisle, clinging to the seats as she made her way. The International Infectious Disease Council was giving a course, under the auspices of its parent, the World Health Organization, in epidemiological methods to be used in studying developing countries. Perhaps two hundred professors of medicine or chiefs of hospitals, and their spouses, had come for it to Grindelwald, Switzerland. The hours of the lectures had been arranged for those who wanted to take advantage of the pistes and alpine walks, so that the time was free from nine-thirty to four. Now we were on our way to the dinner gala and toboggan ride.

Penny's intercession made no noticeable difference. The bus continued to climb along the dark road, more slowly as it grew steeper, but still slipping and swerving. The lights of the village appeared below us like the tiny lights of Christmas trees peeking through the dark branches of the forest on either side of the road. Through the window, I could see here and there an isolated chalet, lights behind closed shutters suggesting the inhabitants cozy at their dinners. As the bus toiled at the incline, I could hear the continued little exclamations of fear and distress, and murmured conversations among the passengers, many of them Asians from warm climates, bundled unfamiliarly into winter clothes. An odor of wet wool and boots, and a faint mothball smell, permeated the bus. Penny came back and sat down.

We had thought that dinner and a toboggan ride would be a pleasant thing to do, especially for the Asians, to experience the wintry night, the frosty beauty, the preposterous fairy-tale drifts of snow. But logistically it was turning out to be more complicated than we had expected—two busloads of doctors, and miles to go. Apart from the Japanese, who skied with enthusiasm, the Asians had not seemed comfortable on the slippery streets of Grindelwald, but most had signed up for this more restful and festive-sounding dinner.

'It's much farther than I thought,' I said.

'It's bloody miles,' hissed Penny. 'Randy says he doesn't know how far it is.' I noticed that Mrs Kora, across the aisle from us, had buried her face in her hands.

From the first, I had not felt quite at ease in this German part of Switzerland; despite the vaunted comfort of their hotels, the appearance concealed an essentially puritanical edge of discomfort; the pool in our hotel, advertised as 'indoor', was nonetheless kept two degrees below a temperature that human beings could find tolerable; and the skis I had rented had proved at the top of a glacier to be completely without edges, obliging me to sideslip fearfully down more than a mile of ice field as a crevasse above us emitted frightening, strange creaks of moving snow and the menace of avalanche. In the shop windows, which I scrutinized for amusing artifacts for presents, I found only figures of unpleasant-looking little dwarves and witches, and people with twisted Brueghel faces, or displays of gleaming cutlery and sinister steel dental implements. There seemed to be nothing pink, light, luxurious, no concept of decor, the food an endless succession of veal cutlets of a midwestern plainness. Yet my children were delighted with their respective activities—ski school for the younger ones, and for the older skiing with us and dinners in the hotel restaurant, like world travelers.

Then there had been the strange events of yesterday. While J. was at his meeting in the morning, I had set out with the children toward the bottom of the lifts, our skis on our shoulders. Around, above, the mountains were shrouded in mists rising from the warmer floor of the valley, and on every side, muffled in the cottony soft clouds, came the tinny chimes and clunks of tuneless bells. It was a sound I had heard before in summer, in the Alps, bells borne by the grazing cows on the upper slopes, their sound amplified by the strange acoustics of rock and crevasse into a sort of charming bucolic orchestra. But at this season all the cows were still snugly in their winter barns, warming the human inhabitants above their heads, if such was still the practice, insulated from the tempests by bales of hay and mounds of redolent dung.

'Listen, listen,' I told the children. We stood in the street, wondering as sounds seemed to be advancing on us, like elfin marauders. Gradually we could see through the mist that people were creeping down the slopes, human beings carrying cowbells converging on the town from the peaks above. Crouching, creeping, like the conspirators in an opera, holding their cowbells aloft, clinking, ringing, sneaking down the hills, hundreds of bells. As we watched, a pair of old men darted behind a Mercedes-Benz parked at the curb, crouched low behind a Citroën, and sneaked into the narrow strip between two chalets. It was as if this prosperous Swiss village, with its sumptuous fondue restaurants and giant sheds housing the enormous gears of the aerial tramways, had been taken over by bell-ringing mountain gnomes.

It was charming. I could think of nothing like this in America, people sneaking through the streets carrying bells—though Hallowe'en might strike foreigners as odd. The richness of the world in irrational customs was not to be deplored. Merely to contemplate it was a kind of happiness: the strangeness even of old, sober Europe. One thought of the blood of Charlemagne's empire, the rich legacy of popes and janissaries and followers of Hannibal, and on the other hand our American blood thinned by a diet of turkey and all that puritan Sunday reading and the practical problems of getting the wagons from here to there, leaving no time for all the elves and mountain sprites left behind us in the Old Country. The strangeness of the world. We had a pleasant day skiing and dinner *en famille* in the village, and I was ready to forgive Switzerland its attitude to untuned ski equipment and the cold swimming pool.

When the children were in bed, J. and I went out to walk in the moonlit streets. As we strolled along, we became slowly aware that people were following us. Their footsteps on ice gave curious squeaks, synchronized with the speed of our own walking. Without speaking we slowed, quickened, slowed our steps again, to see whether it could be true that we were being followed, and in each case heard other steps behind us that stopped when we did.

But, at first, this didn't seem frightening, just odd. We were after all not in America, and so did not fear robbery or mugging; the streets of a little Swiss town are safe to walk. Yet we were Americans, and by habit looked behind us, puzzled not to see what it was that produced the echo of our own steps.

'I thought there was somebody,' I said.

J. said, 'Look—there is somebody.' Two people stood in the shadow of a porch across from us, almost invisible. Relieved at having found an explanation, we continued. Those people had nothing to do with us. We lost sight of them, and no longer heard the steps.

Then at the corner three people leapt out from behind a hedge to block our way. I cried out in surprise, J. grabbed my arm. One person was dressed in green clothes and wore a Ronald Reagan mask, one was dressed in an Uncle Sam costume, and one was dressed and masked like Mickey Mouse. In a sliver of frosty moonlight we could see that two of the figures were pointing guns at us.

J. shoved me behind him and bravely advanced; I screamed for him to hold still. As we watched, Uncle Sam extended his gun and pointed it at J.'s head. With chilling, excruciating deliberation he made ready to shoot. We heard the first click—perhaps the gun had misfired—then another, then a third click, a pantomime of shooting J. Then, as suddenly as they had appeared, the three figures danced away into the shadows.

Only seconds had passed, it was the briefest of encounters, yet the fear, the surge of adrenaline, the sweat now chilled us and left us limp. 'Jesus,' J. said. Weak-legged, we staggered into the nearest haven, a bar at the end of the street, and crumpled into a booth. I put my face in my hands and tried to quell my heart by taking deep breaths. Later I thought of Dostoevsky and the firing squad.

For minutes I felt my hands shake. I felt sick to my stomach, felt the drained, shocked feeling people have after they have been robbed or injured, the interminable seconds when you believe you are about to die, and then the absence of this powerful stimulus. J., too, I could see, had the pallor of the drowned. 'They spared us when they saw we were in ski clothes, they could tell we didn't have money,' we said.

'They weren't muggers,' J. said. 'They were assassins. It's just that we weren't the people they were looking for.'

Inside the little bar, fresh geraniums, a wooden clock, loden-clad drinkers in booths. From where we sat we could see the door, which now opened, and the three assassins came in carrying their guns. We stiffened like wolves, but the other patrons seemed unconcerned. They paid no attention to the curious fact that Mickey Mouse was having a drink next to them. A man at the bar moved over onto another stool so that the three could sit together. J. and I stared. The three did not seem to notice us seated in the booth at the rear, or didn't care that we were here.

The bartender was speaking to the three, but they were ostentatiously silent. Instead they mimed, pointing silently to beer and whiskey. Soon we understood that the people were in costume, and seemed to be under some oath of silence, and that the whole thing was sufficiently ordinary as to bring no comment at all from the other Swiss people. Mickey Mouse sipped his whiskey through a straw fitted into the tiny mouth aperture of his mask, and Uncle Sam hoisted his giant beer stein for a refill. Their guns, recognizably plastic, lay on the bar.

'What I really thought was terrorists, and they were going to kill us because we were Americans,' I said at last.

'Yes, I did too,' J. admitted. 'American paranoia. But, well, the costumes, for one thing. The costumes were American. If they'd been dressed like Heidi or William Tell, we wouldn't have been so scared. Mickey Mouse was scary. Besides, where we come from, all the guns are real.'

'Doesn't every Swiss have a gun? That's something the gun nuts at home always bring up.'

'They never shoot each other, though. We ought to have remembered that. But how did we know they were Swiss? They could be anything—drug-running Colombians, Syrian terrorists,' J. said.

'Let's face it, we were scared because we thought they were Americans,' he said.

'And because *we* were Americans. I thought they knew we were Americans,' I said. Basically we're used to thinking that everyone hates us and wants to kill us. Americans. It's an idea we have without thinking about it. We automatically expect to be the target.

We sat talking about the oddness of being an American, something you couldn't help but carry around like a brand on your forehead, attracting emotions like a lightning rod, different emotions in different places, but most of them hostile. Where might you go to be loved, where did they love Americans? When, presently, J. said, 'I suppose we ought to go,' his voice was still a little thinned by relief. We felt a sense of the fragility of existence, but also of the oddness of feeling for two times in mortal danger in a safe country like Switzerland, the old soul of Europe. What did this mean?

And now to feel in mortal danger again, on this demented bus. At last we slowed and stopped in front of a charming, small chalet, built in the cuckoo-clock style typical of the region, with gingerbread balconies and window boxes, steeply pitched roofs, and a barn on the ground floor where in former days the cows would spend the winter.

The prospect of warmth and dinner lifted everybody's spirits, and we trooped out of the bus with merry voices in a confusion of languages. Inside were long tables covered with checkered cloths, a forest of wineglasses glittering like the icicles that dripped from the pine trees during the day, chafing dishes positioned at each few places, and a long fondue fork by every plate. This cheering sight dispelled the last notes of criticism and discontent about the ride. I found my place at one end of the head table, with another Swiss host, Dr Wurfel, and my French friend Huguette Cosset. J. was sitting at the other end with Narcisse Cosset and Frau Freddi Wurfel. Through the lane of candles down the center, he appeared far away and flushed, like a character in a painting by La Tour. The flame reflecting on his glasses made his countenance as distant and unreadable as his mood of late.

'Fondue is a fabulous, delicious dish,' I raved to Dr Wurfel.

'Yah, you see, we have more than the cuckoo clock,' he said. So that I would understand this reference, he added, ' "After three hundred years of democracy and peace, what do they have? The cuckoo clock." That's Orson Welles in *The Third Man*, you know, talking of Switzerland. Don't drop your bread into the fondue, you know what that means.'

'Bad luck?' asked I.

Dr Wurfel seemed reluctant to explain.

'It means you are *au monde*,' whispered Huguette. Available to the world.'

As the dessert was being served, a group of Swiss at the end of the second table burst into a song whose words sounded like *Oleoyolle-yoleyyolee*, followed by actual yodels—this peculiar and inimitable sound coming out of the mouths of people who before dinner had seemed rather prim and plainly dressed. Tears ran down their cheeks. I strained for the words, and now heard something like '*le Roi des Vaches*'.

'Not a French song, German Swiss. They are forever singing,' Huguette remarked. I nodded. Sometimes packs of young German tourists broke into songs while marching up my street in San Francisco.

'This is a song,' said Dr Wurfel, 'that the Swiss guards of Louis Quatorze, in France, were forbidden to sing, for when they sang, they wept, transported by nostalgic emotion, and while weeping they would be ineffective at protecting the king.'

'I don't think Americans have any equivalent songs,' I said, 'except maybe "Old Black Joe", which is probably politically incorrect, or "The Battle Hymn of the Republic". Nobody ever cries at "The Star-Spangled Banner".'

Fondue, salad, some sort of torte, wine—lots of wine, gratefully enjoyed by the guests for its soothing effect after the fright of the ride. Even Mrs Prangithornbupu drank, I observed, quite a large glass of wine. Bottles disappeared, were replaced, were drunk—the delicious Riesling of the area. Next, after the schnapps and coffee, the flushed and merry revelers were interrupted by Dr Wurfel, who rapped his glass and got up. 'Ladies and gentlemen, our host for this fine feast will announce some things about the toboggan ride, which is scheduled for after dinner.'

The merry, pink-cheeked proprietor, in his turtleneck with little medals pinned to it, came to stand next to Wurfel. In his hand he carried a child's sled. 'The toboggans are outside,' he said. 'This is just to show you how they steer and how they operate. They can be used by one or two people each. The person in front steers, by moving this crossbar, while the person behind controls the speed by means of his feet, or the driver can do this. It's really very easy to control." He raised the sled over his head for all to see. It looked like what I remembered as a Flexible Flyer. It began to dawn on me that he was saying that we would now be going out into the icy night to slide downhill on sleds, and moreover that this was our means of returning to our hotels, many miles below. It seemed that our host and instructor did not immediately perceive that his silent guests were struck with horror. I at least had thought of toboggans as large, comfortable sleighs towed by horses or tractors that would drive us festively through the country lanes around the town. I tried to read J.'s expression at the other end of the table, but could not. I could see that my nearer neighbors were staring with shocked eyes at the flimsy apparatus with which this man was suggesting they would have to regain the village of Grindelwald. 'The bus will be waiting for you at the end of the course, and we would appreciate it if you would assemble there, for though it is only a short walk from there to the hotel, still we want to be sure everyone is accounted for.' Now a murmur of dismay went up. Someone came to the table to speak to Dr Wurfel. People turned to each other, gasping.

Dr Wurfel stood up beside the host and rapped with his spoon. He spoke more loudly, as if to override the surge of tense complaint. 'Of course, for those of you who may not wish to take the toboggan ride, the bus will return,' he said. 'Ladies and gentlemen, the bus will be coming back if there are those who do not wish the toboggan ride.'

I knew immediately that I did not wish the toboggan ride. We were in an unknown Swiss forest, temperature below zero, at eleven at night. We had dined well, had drunk wine and kirschwasser. It was perhaps not too much to say that we were some of us slightly drunk. I could hardly bring myself to believe that the organizers intended that this group of doctors, many stout and elderly, or delicate island people, should go outside and hurtle into the night on these dangerous contraptions, especially all the way down to Grindelwald, many miles below us. 'I don't think I'm going to do it, are you?' I asked Huguette.

'Mais oui! It will be very agreeable,' said Huguette with a bright smile. 'I adore winter sport, do not you?'

'But it must be miles down to Grindelwald, is there some sort of path? It's pitch black.'

'The distance is four and one-half kilometers,' the host was explaining. I thought of Bataan, of the Long March, of a photo I had seen of a woman who had died on Everest, her corpse lying unburied, beyond reach on the open snowfield, forever preserved in the icy air.

The aghast revelers were prodded outside. Those who in their relief at having survived the bus ride had drunk incautiously at the dinner now tottered slightly, their voices loud. I felt this to be my case. I wished my head clearer. Many lapsed out of English and spoke in panicky whispers in the unfamiliar languages of Asia and eastern Europe. The moon was full, which did something to illumine the dark path that led from the chalet down the mountain into the black night-time forest, but path was perhaps not the word, for the moon was bright enough to reveal it as a rutted track, glinting icily, rising at its edge in a slight embankment that might impede the pilot of a sled from running off into the ravine or crevasse that yawned invisibly on the downhill side. From the depth of the ruts, carved by skis or the runners of sleds, the apprehensive could reassure themselves that it would be difficult for the tiny sleds to jump the track, but it would be hard to steer too. While this diminished the possibility of falling into the abyss, it also eliminated the possibility of discretionary turns for the purpose of slowing down. The rider would be as committed as on a roller coaster, with no turning back. And it was more than just an unpleasant, scary descent down steep slopes; the rider would risk running into trees or over the embankment into one of the mountain ravines that had seemed in the daylight on the pistes so dangerously deep and rocky. Despair sealed my ears.

One would also risk running into any of the other fifty or so sedentary, tipsy, maladroit, and terrified passengers—dignified international doctors transformed unwillingly into feckless adventurers defying death with their portly bodies and bejeweled wives. Various males approached the track, studying it with deliberation, but most of the wives shrank back, drawn to the comforting light that shone through the windows of the chalet, where the waitresses could be seen clearing the remains of the feast. This differentiation of sex roles was cross-cultural, common to the Japanese and American and Thai and African and German and English wives alike, leaving only one or two Swiss women, the American woman doctors, and the sportive Huguette Cosset; these, intending to pilot their own sleds, stood along with the men gazing downhill into the perilous obscurity. National differences too were apparent. Prudent Filipinos withdrew to the bus, angrily denouncing the whole folly. I caught the eye of the Thai Dr Prangithornbupu, who seemed to be giving me a glance of sympathy as he escorted Mrs Prangithornbupu toward the bus. Several elderly English couples also announced in tones of indignation that they would ride down.

'Mind you, that will probably be just as dangerous,' said one.

I walked over to where J. was extracting a sled from the stack.

'I think we ought to go on the bus,' I said. 'This is stupid.'

'Stupid and perilous,' he agreed somewhat grimly. An Englishman, Dr Knight, whom I guessed to be about seventy, was also selecting a sled.

'J.,' I went on, surprising myself to hear my wail, 'I don't see the point of this. This is a cold, long, dangerous, dumb idea. I'd rather keep my limbs intact to ski tomorrow.'

'Honey, I absolutely agree, go ahead on the bus,' J. said. 'I almost have to go along with the others, as one of the responsibles, and all that.'

'I don't want to go on the bus! I don't want to go on the sled!' I cried, my panic intensifying as I saw I was now doomed to this freakish adventure, clinging behind J., perhaps to be thrown into a chasm. For I also recognized that I would have been ashamed of myself if I went on the bus with the feeble elderly or inept young. Some deeply internalized sense of competition, or sport, or shame was prompting me, some invisible pressure of the group controlling me. I was going to go against my will on this sled ride, J. too. How could he go back on the bus if the other men slid down? How was Dr Prangithornbupu so blithely free from these imperatives? We were going to do something perilous and stupid because others were doing it. I shivered. I was already cold, the night was icy, and I shivered too from fear and compulsion. Why had I not inherited some of the intrepid genes of my woman cousin who drove the Indy 500?

The organizers had now begun to notice, it seemed for the first time, that many of their guests were underdressed, in dinner shoes, gloveless, with no idea of how to direct a sled, let alone in the dark on a long-distance track, and they began to suggest that perhaps after all many would be more comfortable in the bus. At this, a certain perverse determination required the guests to persist. All hope abandoned, their wills stiffened with the courage of the desperate. Many people were, I knew, attracted to danger and to proving themselves, and even the most ordinary journey gives the traveler the satisfying sense of dangers overcome and outlasted. It is one of the charms of travel that mere cultural differences can present themselves as dangers in order to provide this gratifying sense of having survived them—I have survived, the traveler can say: strange food, for example. I thought of eating bats in Canton. All Chinese public toilets. Indian trains. Swiss midnight downhill toboggan runs. I have survived, therefore I will survive. Perhaps this was the whole point of travel. But, even as this idea came to me, it came with the conviction that I didn't need to prove myself doing this. 'Of course we're going to do it; besides, we paid for it,' I heard someone remark in English.

'Honest, J., this isn't funny, people are going to get hurt,' I said, hoping it would all be called off.

'That's why I need to go.' I could see that he was angry. J. was brave but never foolhardy. 'D., please go down on the bus.'

'Deenee, eet weel be fun!' cried Huguette Cosset. 'Come weeth me. I have done this toboggan, no, not here, but many times and I know well how to do it. You will sit behind me and be the brakes.'

I had forgotten the insouciant attitude of the French toward danger. To go or not to go, and with J. or with Huguette? I eyed the tiny sled. J., large and long legged, would fill up his sled all by himself. I envisioned myself, ass dragging, bouncing off my pillory and over the cliff. Would J. mind, feel wounded, insulted, if I chose to go with Huguette? Did Huguette really want me? My ambivalence, already painful, now increased. Was Huguette really experienced, or was she —like other French people I had met—simply indifferent to danger and mad for sporty fun, or compelled by some cultural imperative of which Americans were unaware to feel that mentioning danger and seeming scared were to be scorned? I thought of another time I had been scared like this, skiing *hors piste* in France, in the spring, when the whole snowfield above us could be heard to groan with its need to break loose and slide down on us, and my French companions had laughed. It had seemed to me that their laughter was enough to bring the whole thing down with the vibrations of their merriment. As they led us deeper and deeper into the steep valley, I had wondered whether I was just a cowardly, stiff American or they were mad. But then, like now, I had been unwilling to go back, and fear had made me twist my knee, so that I greatly increased my chances of not being able to outski the expected avalanche.

To my horror, I now noticed that Dr Kora had pulled down a sled and was gazing intently at it with the beatified, dreamy expression of the Japanese kamikaze pilots depicted in American World War II movies. He was buttoning up his purple and white ski parka in a purposeful way, clearly intending to make the run. I worried; there was something fragile about little Dr Kora, though I reassured myself that in Japan they had snow, that Dr Kora skied well, and that he was probably less likely than tall J. to break his neck. Now Dr Kora was smiling at Penny Deckhorne, and waving with bravado and laughing. The

Deckhornes were taking separate sleds. The younger American doctors, professional as astronauts, were making short practice runs on a gentle hill to the left. The collective mind was now focused on survival.

The first to start out were gleeful, experienced Swiss, who whooped and called as they pushed off, their cries becoming fainter with chilling rapidity, which, according to Huguette, meant the track was fast. A perception of danger seemed to animate the Western Europeans generally into a special sort of gaiety; perhaps it was all those wars. I had often noticed the British attitude. When it came to the British, even the automobile seemed to inspire them, as if driving were a sport. I thought of those mad little cars with straps around the hoods. I wished now that I could bring myself to say to Huguette, 'Perhaps J. would like me to go with him,' though that was manifestly untrue.

I did not really expect to die—I did and I didn't. It was more the discomfort and possible broken bones that I minded. Probably this was really less dangerous than skiing, which I do with reckless happiness. I drew breath and settled myself on the sled behind Huguette. I snuggled up as close as I could, but even so could feel that my bottom was quite near the back edge of the wooden seat.

'Get set. When I call to you, drag your feet, you are the brakes,' Huguette reminded me.

'I'm ready,' I said. As soon as I had wrapped my arms around Huguette, I was sorry not to be going with J. I could see him behind us, with his sled under his arm. J. could be reckless. I felt a stab of protective concern. Men felt obliged to be reckless, while women were safe. On this principle I had chosen to ride with Huguette. Yet I knew there was a flaw—the inbred recklessness of French people. The innate prudence of Americans ought to have directed me to choose differently. Did my defection mean I did not actually trust J.? When faced with a choice I had chosen life over loyalty, had preferred to take my chances on survival with Huguette rather than go down to disaster with J. But if we were to crash in a gully, wouldn't I have been better off with doctor J.? I despised myself for this selfish attitude of *sauve qui peut*. I was ashamed of the thoughts that flashed through my mind with a rush, like all the frames of a film superimposed on one another, producing a deep, jumbled shadow forest of images of destruction— all of them were of the impending snowy, icy, dark destruction that awaited us—if not myself, then J., or some elderly doctor gamely boarding his sled, or perhaps all of us, dashed like lemmings into the bottom of an icy crevasse.

Mind on death, I had not been prepared for the abruptness with which we went from a standing start to reckless speed, the icy night air filling my ears and lifting my hair, and billowing my coat with the wind that rushed down my neck. Our runners made the noise of an underground stream, or of someone walking on an icy pond, dangerously crunching and cutting the ice. We were in utter darkness, careening through blackest space, with the saving mound of snow to the downhill side broken in places—perhaps places where others had crashed through it into the mountain chasms. 'Brake, brake,' Huguette called. Minutes of icy, rushing misery passed as we careered downward, my heels digging in as fiercely as I could make them, and seeming not to impede our speed.

It happened as my foreknowledge told me it would. With a lurch of the sled, a sharp banking of its angle, my arms loosened dreamlike from around Huguette, and I slipped from off the back, or the sled slipped from under me, so that in an instant I felt myself hit the rutted ice, and then bounce toward the mound of soft snow at the edge of the track. This gave way under me, and I tumbled, flailing, down a steep slope, the ice and rocks skinning the backs of my legs and the palms of my hands, and landed headfirst against the bare branches of a small tree ten feet below the embankment. I felt the crack of my forehead on the trunk.

In a minute I could tell that I was all right, though I thought I had hit my head quite badly. It all happened so fast that Huguette could not have realized I was gone, and could not anyway have stopped. Now I thought I heard her faint call. Only seconds had passed, but in the dream-sequence way that peril has of extending a moment, I already felt all the hazards of my situation, bruised, cold, and lost.

But I was not hurt, I soon decided, except for the sting of my palms. Snow had crowded into my boots and inside my underpants as I slid and now melted icily against my skin. Tears of chagrin filled my eyes at my own stupidity to have done this. Now I would have to wander down the track in the freezing dark, hoping to avoid being run down by others on their sleds, could maybe be picked up by someone coming with prudent slowness, digging his heels into the ice. I tried to find a handhold of shrubbery to help me scramble up the bank again. I should be glad, I knew, not to have fallen farther into the ravine.

It seemed for hours that I lurched and slipped on foot down the infinitely long mountain, shame and chagrin making me hide my face in my coat as people came by on their sleds. Snow trickled into my shoes, and my feet had begun to feel dangerously solid, as if they had frozen. It seemed to me the longest and most disagreeable experience of my life. Once, in Iran, I had been in peril of my life and been afraid, but those events had had a kind of interest, a stimulating effect. Now I understood why people lost in snowstorms simply stopped and froze in their tracks. The cold bores them, life comes to bore them as they stumble along, oppressed by the ennui of cold. If I stopped, I supposed, someone would find me, they would miss me at the bottom, Huguette would remark my absence. Yet I stumbled along. It must have been more than an hour, was perhaps hours before I saw the lights of a bus pulled into a clearing below me and heard the babble of languages that was probably my group.

J., surprisingly, was frightened. I saw the angry pinch of his nostrils, knew what his rough grasp of my arm meant. 'You're freezing,' he said, and, seeing my scratched forehead, 'Did you hit your head?'

'No. Maybe,' I said. 'It hurts.' I realized that my head hurt.

'Did you lose consciousness?'

'No. No, I'm fine.'

J. peered at me. 'How can I tell if it's concussion or hypothermia?' he snapped. 'Go get in the bus.'

Others were not accounted for—two Swiss men, news that the rest of the party received with a certain satisfaction. But Dr Kora had not appeared either. Search parties began to climb upward along the toboggan run. It was another two hours before everyone was found, the Swiss doctor with a head injury that was possibly serious. Dr Kora refused medical attention and did not thank the others for finding him. I had heard many stories like that, of lives saved, and the saved not thanking their saviors. I had heard it too often not to think there must be an inner reason people cannot thank others for their lives. Fearing to be bound to the saviors, perhaps, as the Chinese believe, or else moved beyond expression, unable to speak. That was my mood too, silent, going back to the hotel on the bus, in the Swiss night.

Somewhere Else

Beth was still working on the crossword puzzle when Alan finished his section of the paper. He reached for the pile of letters that looked like bills and throwaways. There was a time when the mailman delivered letters from living people, not just from organizations and offices. Of course nowadays practically everyone picked up the phone instead of a pen. Beth, and Alan too, preferred the telephone. Unless they had to send a contract somewhere, nearly all their business was done over the phone and by fax. They had answering machines at the office and in the house. The telephone dominated their lives. It was a blessing; and it was a nuisance.

He lifted the heap of catalogues and magazines and dumped them at the right of her coffee cup. 'Clothes, handbags, shoes,' he said. 'Save the environment. One for jigsaws, one for music boxes, one that sells replicas of prehistoric animals. Two book clubs you can join.'

'I don't have time to read anything.'

'Except the catalogues, and that's a real waste of time.' He shuffled through some more bills. She went back to her puzzle.

'Hey,' he said. 'I think I've won a prize.'

'What for?'

'Being good, of course.'

'Oh, ha-ha.'

He held the paper up to her, but she didn't bother to look. She was trying to think of a six-letter word meaning stop. 'Listen to this,' he told her. 'Two thousand dollars if I apply within forty-eight hours of receiving the enclosed. It's got a date and a time-stamp on it. We've got a day more than they say.'

'Desist,' she said. 'Those urgent things are never important. Alan Q. Beasley, you could win a million dollars: remember?'

'This looks okay. No pictures of Colonel Kentucky. No free stamps.'

'Another bonanza from the black-diamond mine,' she said.

The black diamond episode had been about three years before; they'd been carrying on a smoldering quarrel for a couple of months. She'd begun to think that they weren't going to pull out of it—that this time their marriage would end: and she wouldn't have cared a bit if it had. One morning, another of those prize envelopes arrived for Alan. He'd actually sent for it. How dumb could you be, she said. He told her huffily that he'd written back to them just to see if they were crooked. 'And,' he announced, 'I've won a black diamond.' He opened the envelope and took out a little transparent plastic packet, in one corner of which rested a tiny brown ball of something that might possibly have been a piece of low-grade coal. He held it up. They stared at it. Then, both of them burst into laughter. They laughed so hard that they had to hold their heads in their hands. 'A putative diamond,' he shouted. 'An alleged diamond,' she gasped. They stopped for breath and started each other off again. They laughed, uncontrollably, until they ached. And somehow the quarrel had ended.

'Two thousand bucks,' he said, 'if I apply within the time-limit.'

'What's the hitch?'

'You'll never guess. It's got to be used on travel.'

'That's a joke.'

They ran a travel agency. They'd been in the business for six years. It took all their energy and thought. It was the reason why they didn't have children: they kept figuring that next year they'd find time to plan their own lives. But they couldn't even squeeze in the hours to work on future holiday schemes. They only just managed to keep up. Their range of vacation trips was still the same as when they'd started. If your standards were high, you had to spend money. Alan saw it as his job to make the past—from which we ought to be able to learn— usable and habitable in modern terms. There was no point in going to a quaint English village or a picturesque Greek temple if you were going to have to sleep in a place with no running water. That would be ridiculous. Even Beth, who tended to get worked up over authentic atmosphere, agreed with him about that.

'We do need to do some research,' he said. 'Find a couple of new places.'

'We can't spare the time. We'd need lots of . . . we'd need weeks. Can you see Rosa in charge for that long?'

'The Stones might help out for a while.'

'And you know what they'd expect in return. They want our list. If they got their hands on that, we could say goodbye to the business. I don't just mean what they got out of Mr Pettifer.'

'I'm going to put in for it anyway. It can't hurt.'

'That's right. We might win a fun-filled holiday in Butte, Montana.'

'With two thousand extra, you could come, too.'

'Too?'

'Two thousand. That's what it says. What we should really do is go over our itinerary. I wish people would let us know how things went.'

'It's like everything else,' she said. 'Who's going to spend the time on it? People don't like writing letters. Except cranks.'

'If they send the money, would you come along?'

'We can't both leave the office at the same time.'

'For a week, we could. Just.'

'What could we do in a week?'

'We could go over the part of the British tour we never got to. Wouldn't you like that?'

'Well, sure. I guess.'

'Fine,' he said. 'That's settled.'

Beth still wasn't certain, but since she thought nothing was ever going to come of the idea, she didn't say anything.

It was her day to have lunch with Faye. Faye worked in the magazine office a few doors away. Ella, Beth's other lunchtime crony, was at the opposite end of the shopping mall. Beth had once tried to introduce them to each other; everything had seemed to go well, but the next time she suggested a meeting, Ella and Faye complained so much about the distance, the dates, the pressure of work, that she knew it hadn't been a success. So, she saw them separately, which took twice as much time. That was another thing, she realized: she'd been trying to get her two friends together in order to save herself an hour or two.

For three years, until the crisis in Ella's life, Beth used to see her for a coffee break in the afternoons. Ella now needed that time for what she called 'contemplation' and what Alan described as 'goofing off'. Ella's life had been irreversibly altered on the day she'd lost her Filofax. She'd had a breakdown. Her doctor had referred her to a psychiatrist and a time-management consultant, but neither one had been able to help her. Someone—an aunt, or some other relative—had advised her to pray. Ella did better than that; she went on a pilgrimage. She got on a plane to Venice, took the train to Padua and joined the crowd of people waiting to beg St Anthony to find things, or people, they had lost. She moved with the others to the left of the silver altar, filed past the stone carvings that illustrated the miracles worked by the saint in his lifetime, and at last reached out, put her hand on the casket and asked him to get her Filofax back.

When Beth told the story, Alan said, 'I can see it coming: she got home and there it was, right where she'd left it.'

'No, she really had lost it. But when she got home, there was a package waiting for her. Somebody'd found it and mailed it back.'

'St Anthony, no doubt,' he said. He thought Ella was crazed and affected. To Beth, the story seemed a little zany but it made perfect sense. If there were such things as saints, no task could be too enormous for them, no request so silly that it was unimportant: they could do anything.

He said, 'Why would a saint bother about something so trivial?'

'Why not? For a saint, a big favor would be easy. So, a little one wouldn't be any trouble at all. I think you could also count on his tolerance of human folly and petty-mindedness. It wouldn't be any skin off his back to grant something really idiotic. If you accept the basic principle—'

'Well, if you accept that, you're beyond hope to begin with.'

'Maybe,' she said, meaning that she didn't agree. It wasn't surprising to her that ever since Ella had had her Filofax restored to her, she'd been preoccupied by questions of religion; she hadn't gone so far as to take instruction, but she'd begun to spend a lot of time reading, meditating and trying to pray, which—she told Beth—wasn't so easy as you might think. It took discipline. It was hard work. The afternoon break was no good any more. Ella became another lunchtime friend, like Faye.

On three days of the week, Beth would usually stay in the office through the lunch break. Rosa, their secretary, would run around the corner to buy her a sandwich from the delicatessen. Occasionally Beth would say to Rosa that this was going to be a diet day. She never made it past two-thirty. Rosa didn't mind the extra trip; she was on good terms with one of the boys behind the counter.

Their office was in an arcade, one of four that radiated from a central area where trees in tubs surrounded a large fountain. Between the trees there were benches. It was a pleasant spot for people to sit in after they'd done some shopping and were wondering where to go next. It was also a meeting place. The planners of the mall had originally called the center a piazza; when most shoppers were making an effort to get the name right, they'd come up with the word 'pizza', although normally everybody just said, 'By the fountain.'

You were doing all right to have an office in one of the arcades near the fountain. The only trouble with the location was that a customer who tried to find you for the first time could get mixed up between the four arcades, which looked alike: they had been given the names of the four main points of the compass, but who knew one direction from another? Left and right were fairly easy for most people to remember, but you couldn't expect everyone to race outside in order to check where the sun was; and anyway, that depended on something else, too. A mapmaker or a navigator would know about directions. Ordinary shoppers didn't. They got lost. That was how Beth had met Ella, who had ended up at the office after her first morning in the mall. 'Where am I?' she'd said, like someone coming out of a faint.

The great advantages of the mall were for those who worked there. Almost all the people Beth thought of as her friends were her neighbors at work. In fact, it seemed to her that the mall was really the neighborhood where she lived. The house that she and Alan owned was just for sleeping in and for giving parties.

She wouldn't mind getting away from the house for a while. She wouldn't mind leaving everything for a week.

As she picked up her tunafish sandwich, she asked Faye, 'Have you and Hutch had one of those prize envelopes offering you two thousand dollars to travel with?'

'No. Wish we had. What is it—something to do with a rival firm?'

'I don't think so.' She bit in and munched, thinking that she'd have to ask Alan about that: it hadn't occurred to her. 'As far as I know, it's just another one of those win-a-million things.'

'But if you got the money, you'd go, wouldn't you?'

'You bet. I wasn't so sure this morning at breakfast, but I am now. We both need a break. And I need some time to think about things. We just keep going and going.'

'You love it.'

'In a way.'

'In every way. You thrive on it.'

'But it's taken over. I'm beginning to suspect that it's done something bad to me. I think maybe Alan would like to get out, too. At least— well. I don't know. We don't have time to talk about anything at all any more.'

'That sounds like a good time to take a vacation. You two should read some of your little leaflets.'

'Aren't they brilliant?'

'You'll have a great time.'

'We haven't won it yet.'

'Don't wait to win anything. Just go.'

'That's the trouble with you, Faye. You encourage my weaknesses. Act now, think later.'

'It's a good idea, isn't it? You could afford a week off.'

'Afford, sure. It isn't a question of the money. Not really. It's the time, as usual. The thing is—I have the feeling that if I went, I might not come back. I've been feeling that way for a long while.'

'Something wrong at work?'

'Nothing's ever wrong at work. That's the point. The work is always just great. It's a substitute for everything else. I'm beginning to think it's my excuse for not living my life.'

'Oh wow, Elizabeth. Let me write that one down.'

'You know what I mean. It's everything; not just that we don't have kids. Well, that's the main thing. I realized a few months ago, last year: I kind of feel I've left it too late.'

'What are you talking about? You're still in your twenties, aren't you?'

'Well, not quite.' She wasn't prepared to say anything more exact, unless Faye spoke first. From the beginning of their acquaintance it had been obvious that Faye didn't want any questions asked about her age; or, for that matter, about her first husband, her daughter's experience at the boarding school they'd sent her to, or about anything at all connected with Trenton, New Jersey. 'You know what I mean,' Beth told her. 'I've sort of run out of steam. I've put it all into the agency. Now I couldn't start a family unless I gave up work. But that's the one thing that keeps me going. It's fun.'

'It's fun, but it's killing you. I see.'

'I guess I'm what they call a workaholic. Alan's the same.'

'Does he want to go on this trip?'

'He was the one who suggested it. He's sending in the form.'

'Good.'

'You could be right, you know. Maybe some other travel company's doing a promotion. I'd better ask around.'

They said goodbye at the fountain. Beth turned off into her arcade. The clock in the jeweler's window caught her eye. She began to hurry.

As she opened the agency door, Alan came out, saying, 'Where were you? I've got to get over to Meyerson's.' He ran off, not looking back.

She sat down at her desk and reached for the telephone. She didn't stop working until four o'clock, when she asked Rosa to go across the

arcade for some coffee. She stretched in her chair and yawned. It had
been a good afternoon.

The pleasure she took in describing places was founded on her
need to communicate enthusiasm. You couldn't call her exaggeration
falsehood; it was a slight emphasis in the process of persuading and con-
vincing someone about the fictions she already believed in. It wouldn't
be right to say that her work required her to engage in deliberate acts
of dishonesty. She simply tried to get prospective clients into the right
mood: to create an atmosphere. If people took off on their holidays
with a few skilfully devised impressions in mind, they were pretty well
certain to find them justified. That wasn't doing anything wrong. It
was smart salesmanship backing a worthwhile product—that was what
Alan said.

She picked up the receiver again and punched the buttons for the
Stones' number. The Stones were their friends but it was a business
friendship, not personal. A personal friendship might be like marriage,
whereas this particular business friendship was like having a lover
who lied and cheated and was unfaithful with friends and enemies, yet
who managed to remain so attractive and charming in other ways, so
desirable, that one didn't want to break off the affair. They liked the
Stones and they didn't trust them an inch. Several times Pete and
Marcie Stone had tried to poach customers away from them. They
were, Beth believed, the kind of people her grandmother had once
described to her: they'd come to dinner and try to hire your cook out
from under you. Once or twice Alan had done things back to them,
just to show that he and Beth weren't pushovers. There was no point
in ending the friendship, as long as the others kept within bounds;
Marcie and Pete had shown that they could be useful people to know.
On the other hand, one more outrageous stunt like the one with Mr
Pettifer, and Alan and Beth would cut them adrift.

She got Marcie at the other end of the line. They talked about the
new airline prices and Beth asked about the two-thousand-dollar offer.

Marcie said, 'It's news to me. But I'll ask around.'

'I was thinking: it might be nice to get away for a week anyhow.
We could check out the places they never bother to tell us about.'

'Hey, I got news about that. I had a customer drop in. Two of
them—husband and wife.'

'I don't believe it.'

'Honest to God. Five years in the travel business and these are the
first people that ever came back to tell us what the trip was like. When

you see them again, they never stop to talk—they just ask how much it's going to cost to go somewhere else. Nobody's ever got a spare minute. God, they were so nice. I nearly cried. They said they just wanted to thank us, because they'd had such a good time.'

'I hope you asked them a lot of questions.'

'I certainly did. And there were a few changes I thought I'd pass on to you: opening times at a couple of country houses, restaurant hours—that kind of thing. It was the south of England, including London, and over to Paris and Rome.'

'We'd love any information,' Beth said. She thought Marcie must be feeling guilty about wangling Mr Pettifer's little list away from him.

'Okay. I'll send you a copy of what we've got. And if you're taking a trip, let us know what you find out, hm?'

'Sure,' Beth promised. 'Unless we have such a good time that we just never come back.'

After she'd hung up, she thought, *I've said something like that before: today, at lunch. When I was talking to Faye.*

Rosa brought some hazelnut cookies with the coffee. The delicatessen was giving them away as a special, introductory offer. She had a big bag of them and she was chewing on one as she came in. Beth said, 'Don't let them near me.' Rosa tried to break her down, but she wouldn't be tempted. She concentrated on work until closing time.

She sat in the rush-hour traffic with Alan and blanked out a little, while he complained about Meyerson's. They were always having trouble with the brochure, but they never did anything about it. There weren't any other printers around who could do a good job. It was specialized work. Their only consolation was that half of the other agencies in the vicinity used Meyerson's, so they were all in the same boat.

When he'd talked everything out of his system and then done the paraphrase, Beth told him about her afternoon phone call.

He'd been thinking all day about a trip, he said. 'I think we should go anyway. Cassie could take over for a while. She's always said she'd be happy to.'

'But it might not be a good time for her.'

'I don't want Pete and Marcie in there, not for a hundred peace-offerings.'

'Why don't we just close for a week? We could send out a leaflet to everybody.'

Alan thought the idea was impossible. Cassie was related to his brother-in-law and was trustworthy. She and Rosa could keep things running: he thought so until they got through the traffic, reached home and sat down to cocktails. He thought so until well into the first bourbon; but by the end of his second drink, he'd changed his mind. 'We'll wait a week,' he suggested, 'to find out if we've won the prize.'

'Nobody wins those prizes.'

'We'll see.'

He made the airline reservations for two on the transatlantic flight; it left in the evening and arrived in England early in the morning, London time, which would still be night for them. He bought himself a new suitcase. She tapped out a letter on the computer, printed out stacks of copies and gave them to Rosa. Then she had a quick word with the people next door, before running in to town to buy a new raincoat. While she was hanging the coat up in the front hall closet, she saw Alan's suitcase and decided that it was just the kind of thing she needed. The next morning she went out and bought one, to find on her return that he—having admired her new raincoat on its hanger—had gone shopping again and had found a coat just like it for himself. 'We ought to have done everything together,' she told him. 'We'd have saved a lot of time.'

He said, 'I'm looking forward to this. We should have taken a trip a long time ago. I think I was in a rut.'

'And I was in something worse. I didn't realize until a few days back. I'd lost hope.'

'About what?'

'I'll tell you when we're away from everything.'

'Let me take you away from all this,' he said, throwing an arm around her.

The day before they were set to fly out, a check came through from the prize people. There were no stipulations, no strings attached.

'See?' he said. 'I was right.'

The check was issued by an organization called *United Holdings and Travel Co.* They'd never heard of it. Beth picked up the brochure that came with the letter of congratulation. She flipped through the pages, saying, 'I'd like to know who their printers are. Look at the quality of the pictures. Isn't that incredible—color reproduction like that? This is as good as one of those art magazines.' She reached the section where, at last, they found the catch. She read out the passage: *Prizewinners who apply for the Finborg weekend will automatically receive a further one thousand dollars.*

'It's in the letter, too,' Alan said. 'You agree to go there, all the expenses are paid, they give you the round-trip ticket from whatever city you name, and you've got a luxury weekend in this top-notch castle full of swimming pools and gourmet cooking. It's a promotional gimmick. I guess they've just converted it.'

'Our clients aren't in that league. I suppose we wouldn't have to tell anyone that. Just turn up and have a ball.'

'We aren't going to have the time, unless I change the plane tickets. We have to tell these United people right now.'

'For an extra thousand?' she said. 'And it might be interesting. If all the other people they wrote to are travel agents, we could learn a lot.'

'That's a point,' he said. 'Okay.'

They stayed up all night, writing memos and leaving messages, taking things out of their suitcases and putting them back again. When, the next evening, they were finally on the plane, they both felt slugged. He wanted to order some drinks, to relax.

'You can't be serious,' she told him. 'That dehydrates you. It'll make you feel terrible. And they say jet-lag hits you a lot worse if you drink. That's what I read in that body book.'

'Well, my body book says a little drink never hurt anyone.' He ordered a double for himself. She stuck to water. They came out nearly equal, because she'd been tired to begin with and she always fretted more than he did.

They landed in the morning, had an hour's sleep, made themselves get up and go sightseeing, and ate their evening meal early. Already they were glad they had come. Beth kept saying, 'Isn't it wonderful? Isn't everything beautiful?' He said yes; he was more interested in seeing what was happening to her than in looking at the sights. He'd been worried about her for a long time. Her friend, Faye, was all right but the other one, Ella, was certifiable: she had a bad influence on Beth. Ella had turned into some sort of religious or ESP fanatic. She'd tried to make Beth believe totally crazy things, such as that it was possible to go through walls by concentrating on an imaginary black dot in front of your eyes. She'd told Beth to meditate and to sing certain notes and melodic phrases and to go on diets. Luckily Beth couldn't prevent herself from nibbling potato chips, wasn't able to carry a tune for long and fell asleep as soon as she relaxed; she hadn't needed all that. One look at her now would have convinced anyone: what she'd needed was a break. She'd even become flirtatious.

'It's like our honeymoon,' she said.

'Without the mosquitoes,' he reminded her.

'But, darling, that was the best part.' She made a face at him. The phrase was from a family joke—something to do with the part of a lobster you weren't supposed to eat because it could kill you.

'The second-best,' he said, leaning over from the other side of the table to catch hold of her hand.

They spent the weekend in London, then they visited the two Devon hotels on their list, looked in at the Stratford guesthouse and did the Stonehenge trip. On the fifth day they felt tired, but that was simply the reaction they called 'traveler's dip': everyone had at least one day of it. After that, you straightened out.

The temperature dropped as they boarded the plane. Beth wondered if she should have brought an extra sweater with her; she'd had her shopping-spree clothes sent back home.

'Cold,' Alan said, lifting his head. 'Scandinavia, here we come.' He settled down to read, while Beth shut her eyes and tried to doze. She didn't like flying. What she used to tell her clients was that it was exactly like a bus ride, only safer; but, naturally, that wasn't quite true: even if you could adjust the air-conditioning nozzles so that they didn't shoot jets of air straight on to your head, the pressure made a differ- ence. It did something to the fluid in all the sinus passages. It gave you a headache. That was funny, she thought: the travel agent who didn't like to travel.

She went right under for a few minutes. Alan had to touch her shoulder to wake her up. They were beginning the descent.

She got her handbag from under the seat in front of her, redid her lipstick and combed her hair. She pulled her seat belt tighter. At the same instant the plane braked suddenly, unnaturally; everyone was tossed forward. A steward's voice, omitting the usual, 'Ladies and gen- tlemen', spoke loudly over the address system, saying, 'Fasten your safety belts, please. We're experiencing some turbulence.' Although there was no indication of what it could be, everyone knew: something had gone seriously wrong. This wasn't a small or incidental disturbance. There were murmurs of distress among the passengers. Several people had been thrown against the seats and had hurt their heads or broken the glasses they were wearing. And they were frightened.

The engines of the plane began to roar. Beth wanted to reach for Alan's hand, but she knew he wouldn't like it. She was relieved and pleased when, without saying anything, he placed his hand lightly over hers.

The noise stopped, but they seemed to be falling fast. All at once they were plunging, rushing. A man's voice, abruptly, announced, 'Attention, all passengers. Prepare for an emergency landing.' The rest of the message was cut off as the plane screamed. Many of the passengers too were shrieking, crying, moaning. Beth and Alan looked at each other. His hand gripped hers. Her lips moved. She said, into the uproar, that she loved him. He said something back, which she couldn't lip-read; it might have been *Thanks for everything, Happy landings*, or *We should have drunk our duty-free bottle*. The plane crashed.

She was still trying to undo her belt while he was up from his seat and out into the aisle, pushing a space clear for both of them. The air was bitter with smoke. Everyone was yelling and fighting. Fire fanned towards them from the rear of the aircraft. She kicked herself free of the seat in front of her. She scrambled to her feet. Alan had gone. The thrashing crowd had carried him away from her. She could just see him, a long way off. He turned back. He was shouting. She tried to get into the aisle, but it was no use. She held her arms out to him. There was an explosion. High flames shot up from the seats near the front exits. Across a wave of fire she saw him, looking back at her. A fierce heat blasted the left side of her face, her shoulder and hand. She jumped back. She couldn't protect herself: the flames were everywhere. She knew it was too late.

She woke up. Alan was standing in the aisle. He was getting the coats down from the overhead locker. They had landed. The other passengers were collecting their belongings.

'Okay?' he said. She nodded, unbuckling her seat belt. She was too shaken to speak. She never wanted to talk about the dream. She didn't even want to go over it in her mind. It had made her feel sick in a way that was worse than anything she could remember, even the nightmares of childhood. She kept herself busy with her flight bag and shoulder bag until everyone began to move down the aisle. Alan said, 'All we have to do now is find that other plane.'

They put their carry-on luggage on a trolley they found in the airport building. Beth stayed with it while Alan went to investigate. Now that she felt calmer, she would have liked to tell him something about the dream—only a hint, to get rid of it herself by sharing it; but she had the feeling that to mention it at all would bring bad luck. It might turn something into a reality that, so far, was only thought.

It would be nice, she thought, to have a long, cool drink; better yet, to wade into a pool of refreshing water. She imagined doing it—stepping in slowly. She could picture the water, pure and effervescent as a drink of bottled mineral water. She thought of the fountain back at the mall, in the center of the meeting place by the arcades, near their office, at home.

Alan was at her side again. He said, 'I've found it. We'll have to walk a long way, but there's plenty of time.'

'Good. I'd love a nice, big drink of spring water.'

'Oh, Beth. Can't it wait?'

'I guess so. I thought we had so much time.'

He started to push the trolley forward. 'We've got time to catch the plane,' he said. 'No customs. They'll look at our passports and cards at the gate.'

She followed him. She wondered if her thirst had been brought on by dreaming of fire; or, it might have been the other way around—that her mind had produced a fire-dream to account for a thirst she'd already felt in her sleep.

They reached a smooth passageway, slightly ramped. Alan raced along it with the trolley. She trotted to keep up. 'I had a terrible dream,' she said.

'So did I.'

'About the plane.'

'Uh-huh. Don't tell me.'

She didn't think he'd had any dream. He simply hoped to stop her talking. There were times when he didn't enjoy keeping up a conversation: when she'd be rattling away on some topic and all at once would notice that he was taking part reluctantly. In the early days of their marriage she'd been hurt by that kind of thing. Now it didn't bother her. People were different not just in temperament but in their sense of pace. There was no reason why they should be in perfect symmetry every moment of the day and night; it was probably just those incongruities that kept them attached to each other for so long.

They had to wait for two officials to look at their airline tickets and passports, then they were motioned towards another hallway; it led to a waiting room where their bags were taken from them, to be loaded on to the plane.

They studied the other people in the room—four couples, one man on his own and a single woman. The couples seemed to be much like themselves; one of the women was pretty, one had red hair, one was fat. The redhead's husband had a mustache, slicked-back hair and a sharp-featured face. He looked like a bandleader from the thirties. Another husband, standing up, was tall and beefy and was dressed in a frontiersman's outfit: fringed deerskin jacket, stetson and western boots. 'Myron,' his wife called to him. Myron returned to his seat. He put his hands on his knees. His wife—definitely a city type—had on a dark business suit and black patent-leather shoes with very high heels. She handed him a map, which he accepted without interest.

'Look at that woman's shoes,' Beth said to Alan. 'I thought we were all supposed to be travel agents. One of the first things I tell a female client is not to wear exaggerated heels on a plane. She must be incredibly uncomfortable.'

'Maybe they came here by car. It's a short flight, anyway.'

'Well, just the same.'

The single man—tidy, bespectacled and wearing tweeds—resembled a math teacher at the school Alan had gone to the year before high-school. The man reminded him all at once of the whole year: of the street corner where he'd waited for the bus; and the drive out to the school through the suburbs and into what looked almost like real country. There were several nice houses they passed; a park, and streets with big trees on either side. There was one particular part of the ride he'd never forget—a stretch of road lined by tall maple trees that arched over and formed a tunnel: in the fall it was like driving through a land of jewelry, the leaves scarlet and gold. Every morning for about two weeks he was made happy by the sight of that gorgeous avenue. He would have liked to see it going in the other direction too, but in the afternoon the busdriver took a different route. He'd thought then: some places made an impression on you that you never recovered from. They were special. Some of them used to be hard to reach, yet now that air travel was so easy, it was possible to get to countries and landscapes that—only as far back as the last century—couldn't have been visited by anyone but explorers and pilgrims. That was one way in which the world had improved; the convenience of modern travel was wonderful.

At that age, when he was young, he'd wanted to go everywhere, anywhere: after Europe, to Asia, the South Seas, Africa and South America. He'd wanted to get to the Arctic. He'd yearned for places where no one else had ever been. And later, he'd hoped to open up the world to other people; to allow them to be in marvelous places and to see fascinating things. He'd never quite outgrown his adolescent longing, never completely achieved his dream, which was to find himself suddenly, and as if magically, somewhere else. And, as it had turned out, the one place that was the most beautiful for him had been at home: on that ride through the maple trees. They had remained his vision of beauty on earth, of the best from all the world outside the school bus. He hadn't realized it before. He'd forgotten, for years.

'That woman looks like your Aunt Nora,' Beth said.

He looked. The woman was the one he'd decided was unattached. When he'd first noticed her, she'd had her head down and was reading a booklet. Now that she was talking with the tweedy man, he could see what Beth meant, although he didn't agree. 'Sort of,' he told her, 'but not much.'

Two airline officials, a man and a woman, came through the entrance. Their uniforms were immaculate, their smiles toothy. They looked a little like mannikins from a store window—perfectly regular and bland. The woman stood at the microphone and made an announcement: they could board the plane. Everything was ready. The passengers stood. Beth and Alan joined the group.

They had to duck to get into the small plane, and to crouch as they moved to their seats. The aircraft had fourteen seats, seven on each side.

It was a bumpy ride. The engines made so much noise that conversation was out of the question. Beth tried to sleep. She closed her eyes, but couldn't drift off. She felt as if they'd been traveling for years. It was impossible to imagine going back home. London had vanished from her mind, together with America. The house, work, the office in the mall, were like memories from as long ago as early childhood.

Alan looked across the aisle at her. They were near enough to hold hands without stretching, if they wanted to. He would have liked to reach out to her, but he saw that she was trying to sleep. He had no wish to sleep. He'd had his fill of nightmares. The one he'd had on the plane from London was enough to last him a lifetime; he'd dreamt that they'd crash-landed in flames, that he'd jumped out of his seat to get a place for both of them in the aisle; and as soon as he'd turned around to help pull Beth clear, the other passengers had swept him away. The dream ended as she was holding her hands out after him, the fire roaring towards her, and he was being carried ever farther away.

It was only a cliché, of course—one of the basic dreams; one of the earliest myths: Lot's wife, Orpheus and Euridice. You turned around and she was gone, or dying, or transformed. Or, maybe, just divorced. It was possible that that was his real fear. Years before, for a long time, he'd wanted to leave her. He'd waited for the right moment to talk about it. But time passed, the moment never came and suddenly everything was all right again. Now he was afraid that perhaps what had happened to him could happen to her. One day she might feel that she'd just had enough, and she'd want to get out.

Their landing this time was easy. All the passengers had to stoop, almost to crawl, out of the cramped cabin. It was like emerging from a cocoon or coming up from a tunnel.

The plane sat in the middle of an enormous clearing surrounded by pinewoods. A road ran across one end. Near the road stood a shed with a corrugated metal roof. Boxes were stacked against two of the walls and piled up next to a neighboring shack. A mound of fuel drums had been set some distance away from the buildings and also from the trees. There were no other planes in sight.

Their transportation was waiting. As Alan and Beth stepped down from the narrow ladder, people were already pointing at two old-fashioned, horse-drawn carriages that were heading towards them from the shelter of the woods.

'Not bad,' Beth said. 'Right on time.'

'They probably pulled up back in the trees there,' he told her. 'Otherwise the horses might have been spooked by the plane.' He knew nothing about horses. He was guessing. In the early days of their marriage she'd been in the habit of asking him all kinds of questions, as though he were an authority on everything; and he'd taken to acting like one: if he thought or suspected a thing, he'd say it was true, certain. It gave him confidence in his abilities. His speculation became fact. The odd thing was that so often he turned out to be right. Sometimes he even felt that he had insights of a kind that could be called psychic; he'd know things almost before they happened—not that he really believed in such powers, but belief was part of the phenomenon: her faith in him had made him capable. It might also be true that his unwillingness to concede an equal capacity in her had kept her in a state where she didn't feel that her life was important, or that she had anything special to contribute. He'd taught her to assert herself when she was at the office. Outside business hours, she was unchanged. What she needed, he thought, was just one or two friends who weren't crazy. A woman should have a few women friends, so that they could all get together every week and complain about their husbands and families, not bring everything home to the dinner table.

The robotlike steward and stewardess unloaded suitcases. The carriages stood one beside the other, facing the same way; every so often one of the horses on the inside would swing its head over and try to nip the nearby horse of the other pair.

They joined the rest of their group, who were already getting into the high seats. Alan chose the carriage that had their bags on it. He climbed up and held out a hand to pull Beth after him. They were sitting next to the redhead, Gina, and her bandleader husband, who was called Sonny. Like Beth, Gina worked in her husband's business. 'We met,' she told Beth, 'when we were both operating one-man outfits.'

'She kept cutting my sales down to nothing,' Sonny said. 'I got to thinking: Who is this broad? I figured I'd better go straighten her out, make some kind of a deal with her. So, one day I drop in at the address, I open the door, and—wham, it's just like the songs: there she is sitting there, and Love came and tapped me on the shoulder. That's how we amalgamated.'

Gina said, 'We sure did. We amalgamated in under twenty-four hours.'

The single woman, who had taken her seat in front of them, turned around and smiled. She introduced herself. Her name was Myrtle. She'd been talking to the tweedy man, Horace, who was worried about whether the coachman had packed his bag upright and not sideways. 'I've got a lot of bottles in it,' he explained.

'Don't they have any liquor over here?' Gina asked.

'Oh, it's just aftershave and that kind of thing. But I don't want it to spill all over everything.'

They started off. The fat woman, behind Alan, spoke with approval of the wide, comfortable seats. 'They should build things like this nowadays,' she said.

'Nancy,' her husband told her, 'that's asking too much.'

'Trains, buses, the subway—everything nowadays is plastic. And skimpy.'

'It's the times we live in,' he said.

Beth and Alan turned their heads and said hello. They exchanged names. Nancy's husband was called Ed.

The coach entered the pinewoods. All at once the world was darker, quieter. It was like going from daylight into night. Beth looked at her watch. What it said meant nothing to her. There were time-differences between countries; that could mix you up to begin with. On top of that, you got tired. She asked, 'Does anybody know what time it is?'

Gina said, 'I always lose my sense of time when I'm on vacation.'

'You find another way of measuring it, that's all,' Alan said.

Nancy and Ed told a story about ordering breakfast in Mexico, but because they hadn't specified whether it was to be at a.m. or p.m., the waiter brought it up at eight-thirty in the evening, while they were still drinking their cocktails on the balcony. 'That was a different sense of time, all right,' Ed said.

Beth began to feel strange. She waited until it wouldn't seem that she was spoiling Ed's story, then she asked again if anyone knew what time it was. No one did. 'Relax,' Alan said to her.

The carriage rolled on. The landscape around them seemed without sound. They were the only noise passing through, their chatter foreign to the place, the steady rhythm of the horses' hoofs like the muffled pounding of a machine.

Beth said, 'Maybe this is that famous Scandinavian long night you read about.'

'But this is the wrong time of year for it,' Myrtle said over her shoulder. 'That's in the winters.'

'It feels like winter.'

'I didn't get any information at all on this part of the trip. It's all very mysterious. You know what would be fun? If it's one of those mystery games—know what I mean? They give you characters to play, and then there's a murder and you have to solve it. I had a couple of clients who wanted to go on one, but the price was too steep for them.'

Horace said, 'I heard about one of them they held in Venice. Somebody fell into the canal.'

'We're all tour operators, aren't we?' Alan asked.

From the back seat Ed spoke up. He said, 'What do you mean, Scandinavia? We were booked for Yugoslavia.'

'Austria,' Horace said. 'But it could be a lot of places. It sure looks foreign. That's about all you can say.'

'Well, where are we?'

'Ask the coachman,' Nancy suggested.

The coachman, sitting high up and beyond the barrier of his seat, was too far removed from them to be reached. They called out to him, but he didn't turn around.

They made conversation, stopped, started up again, and waited. At last the carriage came to a halt.

They all got down, although they could see that they hadn't arrived yet. They were at some kind of way-station. There was a small hut and a dim light in it. The passengers from the other carriage joined them.

They tried to get some information out of the two drivers, who didn't speak a language any of them could understand. By signs everyone was told that they were all to keep going.

They got back into their seats and started off again. This time, they felt, they were on the last lap; they'd be welcomed with light and warmth, a drink of something: their host would give them explanations, facts, plans.

They became talkative. As Alan and Beth's carriage moved through the forest, they called out stories to each other, leaning over the seats and saying, 'But this is the best part,' and, 'You aren't going to believe what he said then.' They talked about funny things that had happened in their businesses, swapped anecdotes about cities they'd been in, asked each other to describe the worst and best clients they'd ever had. And they all agreed that the brochure was a problem every year.

The coachmen pulled up again at a spot so like the first one that for a moment the passengers were bewildered. 'Isn't this the same place?' Myrtle asked. 'Do you think that man knows the way?'

'It isn't the same,' Sonny told her. 'I remember there was a log out of line up near the top there.' He raised his arm. 'It does look a lot like it, though.'

Nancy said, 'At the rate we've been traveling, they could have fixed the roof while we were gone.'

Myron, the man in the frontier costume, came over to where they were parked. He suggested that since it was turning out to be such a long drive, they might switch around: that way, they could all be acquainted by the time they got to their destination.

Alan was happy where he was. Somebody in the other carriage, he thought, must be a bore; but there was no polite way out of the invitation. 'Sure,' he said. Behind him, at the same time, Ed said uncertainly, 'Well, I guess so.'

On the third lap of the trip there was plenty of time to get to know Myron and his wife, Cora Bee. And after that, on the fourth stage, Sue and Greg, from Omaha. By the fifth and sixth times around, they all knew each other very well.

They traded family histories, got to know about the children, ex-partners and in-laws. They sang songs, played wordgames, wondered about the existence of God; and they asked themselves whether a unifying set of physical laws in the universe might do just as well as a divine being if you didn't want to take such things personally. They tried to remember lines from poems.

Alan began to lose heart. That was another trouble with traveling: everything was out of your hands. Someone else was behind the infor-mation counter and on the telephone and at the controls of the plane. You had to wait, patiently, as if you'd given up being human and had become just a package to be transported. If you were used to doing your own organizing, it was difficult to put up with that. He always felt more confident when he was the one in charge.

They ran out of things to say. Beth began to feel strange again. She whispered to Alan, 'I'm getting a funny feeling about this. It's weird.'

'Just relax, like I told you,' he said, 'and enjoy the scenery.'

She thought: *What scenery?* There was nothing but pine boughs, the darkness and silence, except for the creaking of the wheels and the sound of the horses' hoofs on the dirt track. There were patches of leaves on the ground, then sandy soil and pine needles, but no other variation in the landscape. She tried to think about getting to their destination; her mind went blank. But they had to stop. They had to get somewhere, otherwise nothing made sense. She made a great effort to hold within her mind some picture of the place they were meant to find. If she concentrated hard enough, they might get there.

They stopped again and changed around and started off once more. Alan looked up at the dark shapes of the trees that passed, in unceasing progression, above and around him. Everyone nowadays worried about conservation and the environment, yet it seemed that the forest they were in was limitlessly huge, its growth encompassing time as well as space—as if they were seeing all the trees that had ever been alive since the beginning of the world. It was—like the journey itself—unending. He changed his mind. He gave up.

The two carriages continued to roll forward. The hoofbeats sounded on the track. The wheels kept turning. Eventually the others began to feel that something was wrong.

'We're never going to get there,' Nancy stated. 'This is it.' Ed told her not to be silly: of course they were going to get there, in the end; it was just taking a long time. And if she started to complain, it was going to seem even longer.

'I think she's right,' Alan said. There was no other outcome he could imagine. They were going to keep traveling, forever. 'You'd be kidding yourself to think anything else.'

'Don't say that,' Beth told him. 'We'll get there pretty soon now. We've got to.' She was too frightened to allow for doubt. There could no longer be any question. She'd come to believe, like her friend, Ella, that all events were a matter of faith. And anyway, she'd decided that this holiday was going to make up for everything else. She'd been looking forward to it too long to let herself be disappointed.

She kept on believing. She never lost hope that if they continued to move ahead, somehow—all at once—they would reach the light. It would come upon them like a revelation of truth, a burst of sunlight. It would be amazing, overwhelming and out of this world—like the coming of spring, or like the sudden appearance of fire in the dream she and Alan had had, a long time ago, when they thought that they were dying in a plane crash.

Questions of Travel

There are too many waterfalls here; the crowded streams
hurry too rapidly down to the sea,
and the pressure of so many clouds on the mountaintops
makes them spill over the sides in soft slow-motion,
turning to waterfalls under our very eyes.
—For if those streaks, those mile-long, shiny, tearstains,
aren't waterfalls yet,
in a quick age or so, as ages go here,
they probably will be.
But if the streams and clouds keep travelling, travelling,
the mountains look like the hulls of capsized ships,
slime-hung and barnacled.

Think of the long trip home.
Should we have stayed at home and thought of here?
Where should we be today?
Is it right to be watching strangers in a play
in this strangest of theatres?
What childishness is it that while there's a breath of life
in our bodies, we are determined to rush
to see the sun the other way around?
The tiniest green hummingbird in the world?
To stare at some inexplicable old stonework,
inexplicable and impenetrable,
at any view,
instantly seen and always, always delightful?
Oh, must we dream our dreams
and have them, too?
And have we room
for one more folded sunset, still quite warm?

But surely it would have been a pity
not to have seen the trees along this road,
really exaggerated in their beauty,
not to have seen them gesturing
like noble pantomimists, robed in pink.
—Not to have had to stop for gas and heard
the sad, two-noted, wooden tune
of disparate wooden clogs
carelessly clacking over
a grease-stained filling-station floor.
(In another country the clogs would all be tested.
Each pair there would have identical pitch.)
—A pity not to have heard
the other, less primitive music of the fat brown bird
who sings above the broken gasoline pump
in a bamboo church of Jesuit baroque:
three towers, five silver crosses.
—Yes, a pity not to have pondered,
blurr'dly and inconclusively,
on what connection can exist for centuries
between the crudest wooden footwear
and, careful and finicky,
the whittled fantasies of wooden cages.
—Never to have studied history in
the weak calligraphy of songbirds' cages.
—And never to have had to listen to rain
so much like politicians' speeches:
two hours of unrelenting oratory
and then a sudden golden silence
in which the traveller takes a notebook, writes:

'Is it lack of imagination that makes us come
to imagined places, not just stay at home?
Or could Pascal have been not entirely right
about just sitting quietly in one's room?

Continent, city, country, society:
the choice is never wide and never free.
And here, or there . . . No. Should we have stayed at home,
wherever that may be?'

Biographical Notes

Alice Adams (1926–) Born Virginia and educated at Radcliffe. Novelist and short-story writer who lives in San Francisco, and among the most consistently praised of contemporary American authors.

Beryl Bainbridge (1934–) Born Liverpool. Author of some wonderfully eccentric novels and short stories, starting with *A Weekend with Claude* (1967), all chilling and comic and providing an unexpected angle on things.

Elizabeth Bishop (1911–79) Born in Massachusetts, grew up in Nova Scotia and spent a large part of her life in Brazil. One of America's most distinguished poets, and an inveterate traveller.

Elizabeth Bowen (1899–1973) Born in Dublin. Anglo-Irish novelist, and one of the most highly regarded short-story writers of the century. 'Human Habitation' was first published in the collection *Ann Lee's* (1926).

Raymond Carver (1938–88) Born Clatskanie, Oregon. Influential poet and short-story writer. Associated with Port Angeles, Washington, where he was living at the time of his death. Was married to the poet Tess Gallagher.

John Cheever (1912–81) Born Massachusetts. Celebrated author of six collections of stories and four novels, including *The Wapshot Chronicle*, all dealing ironically with an upper-middle-class suburban world. Awarded the Howells medal for fiction in 1965.

William Wilkie Collins (1824–89) Nineteenth-century novelist, best known for *The Woman in White* (1860) and *The Moonstone* (1868). Collaborated with Dickens to produce stories for *Household Words*.

Anita Desai (1937–) Born India, of a Bengali father and a German mother. Novelist, children's writer, and short-story writer, whose main theme is Indian bourgeois life since independence.

Charles Dickens (1812–70) Born Portsea. The most prominent English novelist of the nineteenth century sometimes took time off from his more protracted works to write a three-part story, of which 'The Holly-Tree' is a good example.

F. Scott Fitzgerald (1896–1940) Born St Paul, Minnesota. Outstanding novelist and short-story writer—one of those whose names are associated with an entire era and way of life which the title of his second novel—*The Beautiful and the Damned* (1922)—might be said to encapsulate.

Zelda Fitzgerald (1900–48) Wife of F. Scott Fitzgerald and author of a novel, *Save Me the Waltz*, as well as shorter works of fiction and non-fiction. Died in a fire.

Jane Gardam (1928–   ) Born in Coatham, Yorkshire. Began as a children's writer (*A Long Way from Verona* was published in 1971) before going on to produce some striking and original novels and short stories.

Elizabeth Hardwick (1916–   ) Distinguished critic and novelist, and advisory editor of the *New York Review of Books*. Was married to the poet Robert Lowell.

Rachel Ingalls (1941–   ) Grew up in Cambridge, Massachusetts, but has lived in London since 1965. Author of some highly praised novels and collections of short stories, including *Black Diamond* (1992).

Dan Jacobson (1929–   ) Born South Africa. Novelist, university professor, and short-story writer; began with *The Trap* (1955). Lives in London.

Diane Johnson (1934–   ) Born Illinois. Novelist, essayist, biographer, and short-story writer. Lives in San Francisco and is a frequent contributor to the *New York Review of Books*.

Jack Kerouac (1922–69) Born Massachusetts. Author and traveller, and prominent among the 'beat' generation. Best known for *On the Road* (1957).

Benedict Kiely (1919–   ) Born Co. Tyrone, Northern Ireland. Novelist, short-story writer, journalist, broadcaster, and university lecturer; now living in Dublin. *A Journey to the Seven Streams and other stories* was published in 1963.

Ring Lardner (1885–1933) Born Michigan. Began as a newspaper reporter and sports commentator, and went on to become famous as a humorist and short-story writer; stories were first published in the *Saturday Evening Post*. His best stories were collected in *The Love Nest* (1926) and *The Round Up* (1929).

Penelope Lively (1933–   ) Born Cairo. Like Jane Gardam, began as a children's writer, with a special interest in the connections between the past and the present. Went on to become a novelist and short-story writer; her novel *Moon Tiger* won the Booker Prize in 1987. Stories collected in *Pack of Cards* (1986).

David Malouf (1934–   ) Born Brisbane. Novelist, short-story writer, and author of six collections of poetry. Lived in Europe between 1959 and 1968; now lives in Australia.

Flannery O'Connor (1925–64) Born in Savannah, Georgia. Among the most powerful and original of American short-story writers, taking provincial southern life as her theme and presenting it in a variety of modes: comic, grotesque, disabused, idiosyncratic. Died young of an inherited disease.

William Plomer (1903–73) Born in Pietersberg, South Africa. Author of the novel *Turbott Wolfe* (1926) and of various short stories and satirical poems and ballads. His *Collected Poems* came out in 1973.

V. S. Pritchett (1900–   ) Born London. Best known as a masterly short-story writer, he has also received considerable acclaim for his reminiscences and criticism.

William Sansom (1912–76) Novelist and short-story writer who contributed to many periodicals, including *Horizon*, *New Writing*, and the *Cornhill*. Served as a fireman during the blitz on London; his first collection of stories—*Fireman Flower*—came out in 1944.

J. I. M. Stewart (1906–94) Novelist, short-story writer, Oxford don, and—under the name of Michael Innes—distinguished contributor to the detective genre. Highly regarded for his versatility and wit.

Paul Theroux (1941–   ) Born Massachusetts. Novelist, travel writer and short-story writer. His first novel, *Waldo*, was published in 1967, followed by many others. Lives in Cape Cod and London.

William Trevor (1928–   ) Born in Co. Cork. Novelist, short-story writer, and television and radio dramatist. Among the most subtle, ironic, and justly praised of contemporary authors.

Anthony Trollope (1815–82) Author of the *Chronicles of Barsetshire*, which established him as one of the key novelists of Victorian England. Managed to maintain a Civil Service career in the General Post Office while producing over sixty books. *Tales of Many Countries*, from which 'A Ride Across Palestine' is taken, was issued in two volumes, in 1861 and 1863.

Elizabeth von Arnim (1866–1941) Born in New Zealand. Novelist and autobiographer. Cousin of Katherine Mansfield, married first Count Henning August von Arnim-Schlagenthin, and on his death the brother of Bertrand Russell. Best known for *Elizabeth and her German Garden*, published anonymously in 1898; *Elizabeth's Adventures in Rugen* followed in 1904. Lived in Germany, England, and South Carolina.

Sylvia Townsend Warner (1893–1978) Born in Harrow, daughter of a schoolmaster. Author of poems, essays, a biography, seven idiosyncratic novels, and eight volumes of stories, all displaying her singular imaginative power and narrative gifts.

Evelyn Waugh (1903–66) Celebrated novelist and satirist who extended the range of English comic writing with such works as *Scoop*, *Put Out More Flags*, and *The Ordeal of Gilbert Pinfold*. The short story 'Cruise' was written in 1933.

Rebecca West (1892–1983) Pseudonym of Cicily Isabel Fairfield. Born London. Began as a journalist and feminist, and went on to become a distinguished novelist, critic, social commentator, and woman of letters. Created Dame Commander of the British Empire in 1959.

Edith Wharton (1862–1937) Born in New York. Author of more than fifty volumes of work, including fiction and non-fiction, and one of the most prominent and successful American writers of her day. Awarded the Pulitzer Prize for her novel *The Age of Innocence* in 1920.

Acknowledgements

The editor and publishers gratefully acknowledge permission to reprint copyright material in this book as follows:

Alice Adams, 'Greyhound People' from *To See You Again* (Alfred A. Knopf Inc., 1982). Copyright © 1981, 1982 by Alice Adams. Reprinted by permission of the publishers and International Creative Management Inc.

Beryl Bainbridge, 'The Man Who Blew Away' from *Mum and Mr Armitage* (Gerald Duckworth & Co. Ltd.). Reprinted by permission of the publishers.

Elizabeth Bishop, 'Questions of Travel' from *The Complete Poems 1927–1979*. Copyright © 1979, 1983 by Alice Helen Methfessel. Reprinted by permission of Farrar, Straus & Giroux Inc.

Elizabeth Bowen, 'Human Habitation' from *The Collected Stories of Elizabeth Bowen* (Jonathan Cape). Copyright by Curtis Brown Ltd., Literary Executors of the Estate of Elizabeth Bowen. Reprinted by permission of Random House UK Ltd. and Alfred A. Knopf Inc.

Raymond Carver, 'The Compartment' from *Cathedral* (Alred A. Knopf, 1983). Copyright © by Tess Gallagher. Reprinted by permission of Tess Gallagher.

John Cheever, 'Brimmer' from *The Stories of John Cheever* (Jonathan Cape, 1979). Copyright © 1978 by John Cheever. Reprinted by permission of Random House UK Ltd. and Alfred A. Knopf Inc.

Anita Desai, 'Scholar and Gypsy' from *Games At Twilight* (Heinemann, 1978). Reprinted by permission of Rogers, Coleridge & White Ltd.

F. Scott and Zelda Fitzgerald, 'Show Mr and Mrs F. To Number—' from *The Crack Up*, Copyright © 1934 by Esquire Publishing Co. Copyright renewed 1961 by Frances Scott Fitzgerald Lanahan. Reprinted by permission of New Directions Publishing Corp. and outside the US by permission of Harold Ober Associates Inc.

Jane Gardam, 'Chinese Funeral' from *Going Into A Dark House* (Sinclair-Stevenson). Reprinted by permission of David Higham Associates.

Elizabeth Hardwick, 'The Faithful' from *Best American Short Stories* (Houghton Mifflin, 1980). Reprinted by permission of the author.

Rachel Ingalls, 'Somewhere Else' from *Black Diamond* (Faber & Faber, 1992). Copyright © Rachel Ingalls 1992. Reprinted by permission of the publishers and Richard Scott Simon Ltd.

Dan Jacobson, 'Request Stop' from *A Long Way From London* (Weidenfeld & Nicholson, 1958). Copyright © Dan Jacobson. Reprinted by permission of A. M. Heath & Company Ltd.

Diane Johnson, 'Cuckoo Clock' from *Natural Opium, Travelling Tales* (Chatto & Windus, 1993). Reprinted by permission of Random House UK Ltd. and the Peters Fraser & Dunlop Group Ltd.

Jack Kerouac, 'Big Trip to Europe' from *Lonesome Traveller* (André Deutsch Ltd. 1962). Reprinted by permission of the publishers.

Benedict Kiely, 'A Journey to the Seven Streams' from *A Journey To The Seven Streams* (Victor Gollancz, 1963). Reprinted by permission of A. P. Watt Ltd. on behalf of the author.

Ring Lardner, 'Travelogue' from *The Best Short Stories of Ring Lardner*. Copyright 1926 and renewed 1954 Ellis A. Lardner. First appeared in Hearst's International Cosmopolitan, May 1926. Reprinted by permission of Scribner, a Division of Simon & Schuster Inc.

Penelope Lively, 'A Long Night at Abu Simbel' from *Pack of Cards* (Heinemann, 1986). Reprinted by permission of Murray Pollinger.

David Malouf, 'The Kyogle Line' from *12 Edmondstone St* (Chatto & Windus, 1985). Reprinted by permission of Random House UK Ltd. and Curtis Brown, Australia.

Flannery O'Connor, 'A Good Man is Hard to Find' from *A Good Man Is Hard To Find And Other Stories*, copyright 1953 by Flannery O'Connor and renewed 1981 by Regina O'Connor. Reprinted by permission of Harcourt Brace & Company.

William Plomer, 'Local Colour' from *Four Countries* (Jonathan Cape, 1949).

V. S. Pritchett, 'The Lady from Guatemala' from *The Camberwell Beauty* (Chatto & Windus, 1974). Reprinted by permission of the Peters Fraser & Dunlop Group Ltd.

William Sansom, 'Gliding Gulls and Going People' from *The Passionate North* (Hogarth Press, 1950). Reprinted by permission of Greene & Heaton Ltd.

J. I. M. Stewart, 'The Bridge At Arta' from *The Bridge At Arta* (Victor Gollancz, 1981). Reprinted by permission of A. P. Watt Ltd. on behalf of Michael Stewart.

Paul Theroux, 'Loser Wins' from *The Consul's File* (Hamish Hamilton, 1977). Copyright © Paul Theroux, 1977. Reprinted by permission of Hamish Hamilton Ltd. and Aitken Stone & Wylie Ltd.

Sylvia Townsend Warner, 'Siegfried on the Rhine' from *Scenes of Childhood and Other Stories* (Chatto & Windus, 1979). Reprinted by permission of Random House UK Ltd. and the estate of the author.

William Trevor, 'Death in Jerusalem' from *Lovers Of Their Time* (Bodley Head, 1978). Reprinted by permission of the Peters Fraser & Dunlop Group Ltd.

Evelyn Waugh, 'Cruise' from *Work Suspended and Other Stories* (Chapman & Hall, 1948). Reprinted by permission of the Peters Fraser & Dunlop Group Ltd.

Rebecca West, 'Deliverance' from *The Only Poet and Short Stories* (Virago, 1986). Reprinted by permission of the Peters Fraser & Dunlop Group Ltd.